W9-AMW-355

"Someone to watch."
—*West Coast Review of Books*

"A major talent."
—Charles Grant, *New York Times*
bestselling author

"Supertaut storytelling."
—*Kirkus Reviews* on *Lizard Wine*

"Unforgettable. Will make your skin crawl."
—John Saul on *Lizard Wine*

"Marvelous stuff; Lizzie and Emma came alive to me."
—Mercedes Lackey on *Lizzie Borden*

"*Lizzie Borden* is a real page-turner and white-knuckler. The tension mounts without letup."
—*The Maui News*

·Lizzie Borden

by Elizabeth Engstrom

A Tom Doherty Associates Book
New York

LIZZIE BORDEN

Copyright © 1991 by Elizabeth Engstrom

This book is printed on acid-free paper.

A Forge Book
Published by Tom Doherty Associates, Inc.
175 Fifth Avenue
New York, NY 10010

Forge® is a registered trademark of Tom Doherty Associates, Inc.

Library of Congress Cataloging-in-Publication Data

Engstrom, Elizabeth.
        Lizzie Borden / Elizabeth Engstrom
            p.   cm.
        A Tom Doherty Associates book.
        ISBN 0-312-86154-0
        1. Borden, Lizzie, 1860–1927—Fiction.   I. Title.
PS3555.N48L5 1991
813'.54—dc20   90-48777
                                                          CIP

First hardcover edition: January 1991
First trade paperback edition: August 1997

Printed in the United States of America

0   9   8   7   6   5   4   3   2   1

For Melissa Ann Singer and Anna Magee

FLOOR PLAN OF THE BORDEN HOUSE

First Floor

Second Floor

Adapted from: E. Porter, *Fall River Tragedy* (1893); V. Lincoln, *A Private Disgrace* (1967); And A. de Mille, *Lizzie Borden: A Dance of Death* (1968).

There is an astonishingly tiny universe of knowledge about Lizzie Borden, her friends and family. Most of what is known comes directly from trial transcripts and newspaper articles, both of which are filled with conflicting information.

This is a work of fiction, written within the framework of an actual incident. As such, personalities and character traits have been assigned to those who played a part in the great Borden mystery. Some of these are not flattering, and I apologize in advance to any descendants of those with whom I have taken liberties.

My purpose is not to offend; it is to justify.

Elizabeth Engstrom
Eugene, Oregon

Prologue, April 1865

ome over here, Lizzie. Sit beside me. That's my girl. Your worm still on the hook?"

Little Lizzie Borden, age five, sat down on the stream bank and lifted her fishing stick to show the pale worm to her father.

"Good girl. Put it back down there now, and we'll wait for a big trout to come and eat it."

Slowly, feeling sorry for the worm, Lizzie lowered her stick. Her papa had whittled the stick for her the day before up at the farmhouse. Tied onto the end of the stick was a length of black fishing line, and tied onto the end of the line was a hook. Stuck on the hook was a worm, a big one they'd dug out of the stream bank. But then it was happy, fat and red, and now it was kind of skinny, shriveled and white. Lizzie didn't think too much of fishing.

"Isn't this peaceful?"

She looked up at her father. Then she looked downstream for sight of Emma. Emma was squatting at the edge of the water, looking intently into its depths. She'd been like that for what seemed like hours. Lizzie was always amazed at the way Emma could be absolutely still for the longest time. Waiting was something Emma could do very well. Lizzie had no patience at all. But then Emma was fifteen. Emma knew everything, and Lizzie was sure that when she turned fifteen she would be able to wait, too.

The country was silent, or so it seemed at first, but then Lizzie heard the stream running, she heard the flutter of the

2

reed that was caught in the water, she heard birds clucking and chirping and a sudden flutter of wings, she heard the underlying hum of all the insects as they went about their business.

Maybe Emma wasn't waiting after all, she thought. Maybe she was listening.

It was odd to be away from home, out in the country, all the way out at the farm. It was odd to have Papa home all day long, but that's what they called a vacation. Lizzie loved the farm, though. She loved being out here with Emma and with Papa. Mother was back at the farmhouse baking wonderful pies. Lizzie had helped pick the bunches of rhubarb with their gigantic green leaves. She wiped the dirt off one of the stalks and took a bite. It tasted good, it was the right kind of sour, but it made her mouth wrinkle up and go dry. It would be better in a pie with lots of sugar. Then, Mother said, when they came back with their mess of fish to fry up she'd be cooling sweet rhubarb pies on the windowsill. Lizzie grabbed her fishing stick and was the first one ready to go. She wanted to get back home to those pies.

She looked down at her shoes. They were new, a pretty brownish red leather, but she was sure she'd get them dirty here, and vacation or not, Mother would be cranky about it. She lifted up her fishing stick again to look at the worm.

"You have to leave the worm in the water, Lizzie. The fish won't bite it if it keeps flying out of the water like that."

"He's cold."

"He's not cold. He's a worm. Put him back."

She let the worm go back down into the water. She leaned over and watched him disappear into the green.

"Isn't this is nice," he said, and leaned up against a rock. "The spring is my favorite time of year. The sun is hot and the air is cool. Everything's green and fresh. . . ." He put his arm around her. "And I've got my best girl right here by my side."

Lizzie leaned into his side, putting her head against his chest.

He stroked her hair. She closed her eyes.

"We have a nice mother, don't we?"

Lizzie nodded. Her eyes felt sleepy.

"Yes," he said, smoothing her fine blond hair from her forehead. "We have a nice mother now, and Emma is old enough to take care of herself as well as you, and things are back to being normal."

He reached down and took off his shoes, then his socks. His toes were white and hairy, and his toenails were long and cracked. Kind of yellow. He wiggled them.

"This is the kind of day that you should try to memorize, Lizzie," he said. "Look around you and see everything. Focus on everything. The way the water runs so shiny and fast in the middle of the stream, yet swirls slowly near the bank. The way the reeds grow in the shallows here. The color of the new leaves, the dampness of the earth. The clouds . . . This is the kind of day that you put in your heart and you remember during those times when life isn't quite so good, when life turns hard and mean, you pull out this streambed and you and me under the clouds . . ."

Lizzie looked around. Then she put her head back against him, hoping he'd start to talk again.

"I have wonderful dreams for you, Lizzie. Wonderful dreams. Do you want to hear?"

Lizzie nodded. She thought she saw a fish come up and take a gulp of air on the other side of the bank. But her eyelids were getting heavier and heavier in the warm sunshine. She'd mention it to him later.

"You'll be beautiful when you grow up. Your blond hair will be long and luxuriant. You will live in a big house on the hill with a nice view, and have many, many friends. Dozens of friends. Famous friends."

Lizzie could feel him talk more than she could hear him.

Her ear rested on the side of his chest and she felt the vibrations of his deep voice.

"I'm going to make us rich, Lizzie, very rich, very, very rich, and you will have your pick of thousands of eligible young men who would come courting. But you hold out for the very best. You'll have a substantial dowry, and you should have the very best husband. The very best."

Lizzie dreamed about the little rag doll that Emma had made for her.

"Lizzie, are you asleep?"

"Hmm?"

"Lizzie, I have to know. When you are so rich and popular, and I am such an old, old man, will you still love me?"

"Of course, Papa," she muttered, her voice thick.

"You will?"

Lizzie looked up at him and she couldn't tell if he was joking with her or not. He had a queer expression on his face, as if *he* didn't know if he was joking or not. She nodded, then settled her head against him to hear his vibrations some more.

"That's good, Lizzie," he said. "That's very, very good."

Lizzie wanted to look at her worm again, but as she brought the stick up, something grabbed it from down below and began to pull on it.

"Papa!" She was wide awake in an instant, holding onto the stick with both hands. "Papa!"

He laughed. "It's a fish, Lizzie! You've caught a fish! Hold on tight and bring him up. Have you got him? Do you need help?"

Lizzie put her bottom lip between her teeth and held onto that stick as tight as she could. She dug her heels into the soft mossy grass at the edge of the bank and pulled up on the stick. Something silver flashed in the water below her.

Then her father's hands were on her waist and he helped

her to stand up. "Okay now," he said. "Easy. Just bring your stick up and swing the fish right over here onto the bank."

When she was steady, he let her go and stepped back.

She swung the fish—a big one!—onto the bank and began to giggle as it flipped and flopped, its pink-striped speckled sides flashing and throwing off raindrops in the sun.

My fish, Lizzie thought. My beautiful fish.

"Look at my fish, Papa. I caught a fish, Papa. Emma, come look!" she said, but Emma was already standing there, tall and gangly, staring down at her fish.

"You certainly did, Lizzie. A beauty, too." Then he picked up a rock and slammed it down on the fish's head.

"Papa, no!"

"It doesn't hurt, Lizzie. It's just a fish. We have to kill it."

Again he smashed the rock onto the fish's head. Again. And again. He just kept doing it, over and over again, and when he finally stopped, beads of sweat stood out on his forehead, and where the fish's head had been was a red, pulpy mass.

"There." He stood up and threw the rock into the stream. "Good catch, Lizzie. Let's take this home and have Mother fry it up for supper."

The fish had lost its shine, the day had lost its magic and even Lizzie's new shoes weren't so nice anymore, she noticed as they walked back to the farmhouse. Her father carried the fish by the tail because she wouldn't touch it; it had been so beautiful and full of life just a moment before, he could have let it just die, it could have just *died,* or it could have flopped back into the water, that would have been all right, too, anything, *anything* but caving its head in with a sharp rock.

And Emma smiled.

Lizzie came to the dinner table that night, but she

wouldn't sit next to her father and she wouldn't look at the fish.

She held on to her little fishing stick, though, and vowed to remember this day just like her papa had told her to.

1892, January

izzie heard the front door open and close. A moment later, the draft of frigid air swept up the stairs and under her bedroom door. She gently refolded the letter from Beatrice and slipped it between the pages of the book she'd been trying to read.

Father is home.

She set the book down, smoothed her hair and skirt, then opened the bedroom door, closed it, locked it behind her and gently descended the stairs.

There was a package on the hall table. A book-sized package, wrapped in brown paper and string, with stickers and stamps and official-looking ink all over it, and Lizzie knew it was for her before she could see to whom it was addressed. It was the book Beatrice had promised to send from England. Heart pounding, she stepped down into the hallway in an orderly manner, ignored the package and went directly to the sitting room.

"Hello, Father."

"Lizzie. There's a package for you. I left it on the hall table."

"Thank you. Tea?"

"Please."

She left him to the reading of his mail, excitement gurgling in her stomach as she jangled down the ashes in the wood stove and put in a few more pieces of wood. Then she filled the kettle with cold water from the faucet and set it on the stove to boil.

10

Lizzie cut three of the little cakes Emma had made that morning, put two on a plate and ate the third while waiting for the kettle to heat. Then she poured two cups of tea and took the tray to the sitting room.

She set the tray on the coffee table and sat down next to Andrew Borden on the sofa. "Anything interesting?"

"No, not really," he said, and threw the open envelopes onto the tray next to the cakes.

Then he looked at her. "How about you?"

"Emma baked. I did some laundry."

Andrew Borden took a bite of cake and sipped his tea. "Not much taste to these, is there?"

"Wait until summer, Father, when there will be fresh fruit."

"Yes," he said. Then he sat back against the sofa and sighed. "I've got troubles at the mill," he said. "Employee troubles. Financial troubles. Bad troubles. And more problems at the bank."

"I'm sorry." Lizzie sipped her tea and thought about the book on the hall table. She'd heard this talk from her father before. Every day.

"Things are supposed to get easier as you get older, Lizzie, but they don't. They don't. They get much harder. Much harder. I work hard, and I try to be fair, but things just keep getting harder and harder."

"You're tired, Father. Here, let me take off your boots."

Lizzie untied his boots, slipped them off, rubbed his feet for a moment, then said, "Would you like me to read to you for a while? Maybe a little rest would do you good."

Andrew nodded. "You're a good girl, Lizzie. I don't know what I would ever do without you."

Lizzie knew the routine by heart. They did this same dance every day until she wanted to scream. *Where is his bloody wife? She is the one who should be comforting this* old man, she should be rubbing his feet and reading to him. "What shall we read today?"

"Anything. You choose."

She stood up and got the book they'd been reading daily for the last month. The bookmark was toward the end. "How about this one that we read yesterday?"

"Fine, fine."

"Remember where we were?" Is this what it's like to have a child? A brain-damaged child, perhaps, one that will never grow up?

"I think so."

Lizzie settled herself on the couch again, book in lap. She thought again of the brown-wrapped book on the table and resisted the urge to throw this tome at her father and go get her new book, hold it tightly to her breast and run up the stairs to rip it open in the privacy of her room.

"Let's see. . . . Here we are at chapter seventeen."

"Lizzie?"

"Hmm?"

"Don't ever leave me. I could never survive without you, you know."

"You have enough things to worry about, Father," Lizzie said. "Don't worry about that. It isn't likely that I'll leave you."

"When you were in Europe, you know, it was a terrible time for me. I thought you were never coming back."

This was new. He'd never mentioned her trip abroad, not once, not even when she wanted to tell him about it. She'd been gone only six weeks with some friends from church, but he hadn't wanted to hear a word about it. He was just frantically relieved that she was home. It made her want to kick that fat old cow of a stepmother. Did she do nothing for the man?

"But I did come back, didn't I, Father? And I'm here now. So don't worry. Try to relax."

Lizzie cleared her voice and began to read. Within moments, her father was asleep. When he began to snore quietly, she covered him with a lap robe and took the tea tray back into the kitchen. She wrapped the uneaten cakes in a napkin, got her book from the hall table and went quietly up the stairs.

She sat in her rocking chair, package in her lap, her mind still on her father, sleeping on the sitting-room sofa. Many times, once he had begun to snore and she had closed the book, she had studied his face, looked at the lines deepening in his brow, his cheeks, and wondered about her recollection of a younger, vibrant man who showed outward affection, who had time and energy to spend on his family, a man she had thought was as handsome as any god.

Time is cruel, she thought. Time and age have turned him into something else, something totally different from the way he used to be. He used to be such a . . . such a *father*. And now he was old, miserly, bitter. A wretch.

And whose fault was it?

Time. Cruel, cruel time.

Lizzie felt the familiar sadness when she thought of her aging father.

But those thoughts are for days when time lingers, she thought. Not for today. She looked around her room, at the dingy wallpaper that had been there since they moved into the house twenty-seven years earlier and had probably been there since the house was built. It had some little flowers on it, but she couldn't determine their color. She looked at the washstand, basin still filled with soapy gray water from her morning washing. There was one single bed with a chamber pot beneath, a small round rug in the center of the floor, a four-drawer dresser and the rocking chair she sat in. Two photographs hung on the walls, pictures of buildings Lizzie had never seen. The room was austere, just like all the other rooms in the house. Beatrice saved her from this room. A

13

letter from Beatrice made her forget everything else. For a while.

She looked again at the package she held in her lap. She studied the handwriting, almost as familiar as her own. She had met Beatrice in Europe, a brief meeting, but sometimes lasting friendships are forged in just that manner. Swiftly, surely, and forever. Their letters began tentatively and soon grew intimate. They discussed matters of life Lizzie could never discuss with another human being on earth. Lizzie told Beatrice all about her family: her hardened and embittered father; her fat slug of a stepmother, who was all but useless; and her jealous, suspicious sister Emma, who had nothing better to do than poke her nose into things that were not her concern.

Lizzie and Beatrice met on the ferry from Britain to France. Beatrice was fashionably dressed, all in peach from her hat to her shoes. Lizzie felt dowdy in her travelling blacks, and watched this lovely young woman take in the sights, have a cup of tea and be on an excursion by herself while totally self-possessed. Lizzie envied that quality.

And apparently, her envious stares did not go unnoticed. Lizzie sat at the end of a row of chairs with her travelling companions, their suitcases and packages littering the floor at their feet. Lizzie rubbed her temples, tired already of Sandra, Rebecca and Winnie. They moved and acted like consummate Americans, weird and ugly tourists to be taken for all their money and treated with no respect. They embarrassed Lizzie.

She hoped a headache wasn't coming on. She didn't want these three women to spoil her one and only opportunity for some real travel in her life.

And then she felt a presence at her side, a peachy presence, and Lizzie looked up into the world's deepest brown eyes, and the woman asked Lizzie to join her for a refreshment in the salon.

Lizzie had flushed a deep crimson, she still felt the blush when she remembered. The woman must have seen or sensed her staring. She looked at the litter at her feet as if it didn't belong to her and her group and accepted the invitation. Even as she did so, she wondered at herself. She felt so terribly inadequate and was quite puzzled that a woman such as this would spend a moment of her time with an American such as was travelling in that foursome.

"My name is Beatrice Windon," the woman said, pronouncing it Be-AT-tress.

"I'm Lizzie Borden," Lizzie managed to say, as they were settling themselves at a table.

"Oh. American."

"Yes."

"Travelling with that group of women?"

"Yes. We're a church group."

"Wonderful. You'll see many cathedrals and things on the Continent."

"I'm sure."

Lizzie ordered a cup of tea from the steward and Beatrice ordered a fruit juice; they waited in uncomfortable silence until the drinks were placed before them.

"British?" Lizzie finally asked, although it was a stupid question and she well knew the answer.

"Oh yes. I'm on my way to Paris to do some business for my father. He's fallen ill, and is unable to travel."

"I'm sorry."

"Yes. It happened quite suddenly, but he's now out of danger. So until he is able to resume, I shall run his little errands for him."

"So exciting, to just dash off to Paris."

"It was at first, but it becomes tedious, nonetheless." Beatrice sipped her tea. "Where in America are you from?"

"Fall River. In Massachusetts. It's a little tiny town, in quite a little state on the eastern coast."

"And what do you do there?"

"Do?"

"Yes. Are you married? Have you children? Do you teach, perhaps?"

"No, no, no." Lizzie's familiar discomfort rose to the surface. Lizzie didn't do anything. She was not educated and not equipped to do anything. Everybody else she knew did something, but Lizzie did nothing. Everybody thought she should be married. Everybody but she, Papa, of course, and Emma. "I live at home. I look after my father."

"Well, that's something we have in common, isn't it? Is he widowed?"

"He was . . . that is, my mother died when I was very young, but now he has another wife, quite a worthless one, I might add." Lizzie surprised herself. This was the type of gossip that came from other people's mouths, not from hers.

Beatrice leaned close. "I have a worthless stepmother as well. There's nothing more distressing, is there?"

"No. Do you live at home with them?"

"No, no, I have a flat in the city."

"London?" Lizzie's imagination fired up.

Beatrice smiled. "Yes, London. My parents live well out in the country." Beatrice had large, full lips and Lizzie found her eyes irresistibly drawn to them. Certain sounds were almost lisped, and it was so very becoming. . . . "Do you read?" Beatrice asked.

"Avidly. And you?"

"Yes. And I hunt."

"Do you? I fish."

"I love to fish. What will you see while you're in Europe?"

Lizzie rummaged in her bag for her itinerary and brochures, notes that she had taken. The papers came out looking like a terrible mess, a big wad of untidiness. She

16

looked up at Beatrice, with her peach smile and her peach dress, trussed up tightly at the bodice, and she felt foolish and inept.

"Oh," Lizzie said, "Just probably the usual . . ."

"Do let's see," Beatrice said. "You look like a true traveller."

Lizzie smiled. She'd love to be a true traveller. For the next hour, they went over all her notes and checked the itinerary, and Lizzie took more notes while Beatrice told her all the best places to eat, to visit, to see and to smell. "Europe is best seen, smelled, tasted and felt. Remember this, Lizzie. You must be yourself and make use of all your faculties on this trip. Let nothing escape. And that will continue when you return to America."

What an odd thing to say, Lizzie thought, yet this woman, undoubtedly in her middle to late thirties, had something Lizzie did not. Lizzie was happy to take advice— any advice—from a woman such as this.

Then Beatrice took her pen and wrote out an address in Surrey. "Send me postcards, Lizzie. I would so love to hear of your trip. You can only see Europe for the first time once, you know. Tell me everything."

And when the ferry landed, they hugged.

Lizzie sent her a postcard every day, and when she got home there was a letter waiting from Beatrice. Before she unpacked, she wrote back, telling of her return trip, and every day since then, Lizzie had written portions of a letter to Beatrice, her best and only friend in the world, so she could share every minute detail of her life with someone who cared. She considered it her living diary. She mailed her musings off to Beatrice once a week, but it often took more than a month to receive an answer to a question, as the mail service to Britain was so slow. Sometimes she worried about what Beatrice did with all her letters: Did she keep them, someday to be discovered and used against her, or did she destroy each one after it was answered?

She saved every letter from Beatrice, and when she read them, each word had the flush of those succulent peach-painted lips and that soft lisp with a British accent.

Beatrice was a godsend.

And now she'd sent a book. That book.

Lizzie had had a particularly bad time the previous summer. She was plagued with the sick headaches that were so severe they made her vomit. They came upon her suddenly, frequently, with no apparent cause, and no apparent remedy. It was a torturous time, and relief didn't come until fall, when the weather turned somewhat cooler.

Beatrice had written, "My dear Lizbeth, I am afraid for you. Three weeks have gone by without a letter (most unusual), and I am afraid something terrible has happened. Please . . ."

And Lizzie had written back a humble letter filled with graphic descriptions of the headaches, their history, their symptoms and things she'd tried, hoping to alleviate them. To her surprise, a letter came right back. Beatrice had a book, she said, a book that had changed her life. "Would you mind if I presumed to send you a copy? A gift, of course. Following the program outlined in this book has allowed me to make so many changes in my living habits, I am afraid I would be quite helpless and a sheepish person if I had never come across the principles . . ."

While Lizzie could never imagine Beatrice helpless or sheepish, she was excited about the idea that there might be yet another method to try that would rid her of the wretched headache curse.

And now the book had come. Lizzie held the book next to her. If only she could be rid of her headaches. If only she could wear peach. If only she could have a figure like

Beatrice's. If only she could be as self-assured and self-contained. If only she had good, wise advice to give to others. If only she could have a flat in the city. . . .

She untied the string.

Three brisk knocks sounded on her bedroom door. Emma opened it without a word from Lizzie. In her hand she held a white sheet of paper. Emma's mouth was a firm line and there were lines between her eyebrows.

"Have you seen this?"

"Seen what, Emma?"

"This letter from Father's attorney."

"No, of course not. Is it addressed to you?"

"No, it was on the tea tray. I was cleaning it up and wanted to throw out the trash, but I thought I ought to go through it first."

"Is Father still sleeping?"

"Yes." Emma stepped in and closed the bedroom door behind her. Emma, Lizzie's older sister, was forty-two years old. She stood tall and thin, and wore the same kind of dark, heavy clothes their father chose. She wore her brown hair pulled back so tightly it seemed to stretch her face, trying to tame the wiry graying hairs that always sprung loose. Emma had the deep brown eyes of their father; otherwise she was the very picture of their mother, with a long, thin face, a thin nose, eyes close together, shoulders sloped. Sarah Borden, Lizzie and Emma's mother, as Fall River remembered her, had been lively enough, and pleasant enough that people looked beyond her basic unattractiveness. Emma was not. And to compound matters, the years had not been kind to her.

"Father is deeding the farm in Swansea over to *her*."

"No, that can't be."

"Here." Emma thrust the sheet of paper at Lizzie. "Read for yourself."

Lizzie scanned the page. Emma was right. The new deed was being drawn up. "But that's our farm. That's *mother's* farm."

"So it is. *And* a large portion of our inheritance." Emma looked smug. Furious. Dangerous.

"What are we to do?" Lizzie was flabbergasted. For anyone but Emma and her to own that property was unthinkable. They had spent summers at that farm when they were children, and while it had now been rented to tenants for twenty years or more, it still evoked strong childhood memories. Lizzie frequently daydreamed of going back to the farm to live, where life was peaceful and rhubarb pies cooled on the windowsill.

"I don't know what *you* are going to do, my dear, but I won't stand for this. Not for a moment. That horrendous woman has the poor man so flummoxed he doesn't know which way is up. She and her poor relations. This is somebody's terrible idea and I intend to put a stop to it this instant."

"What will you do?"

"Think, girl, what will happen if I do nothing. That cow will have us as penniless as her kin when Father dies, and I won't stand for it." Emma snatched the letter from Lizzie's lap and twirled on her heel. She slammed the bedroom door so hard the walls shook.

Lizzie listened as Emma stomped down the stairs and began to argue with their father.

Lizzie held the package, still unopened, string dangling, to her breast, and rocked back and forth, listening to the sound of angry voices, her stomach knotted so tightly she was afraid to move. Within a few moments, a little wavy spot appeared in the center of her vision. She closed her eyes, but the spot remained. Lizzie sighed, and a tear escaped the corner of one eye. A headache approached. The spot enlarged

20

and became a ring as the center cleared. A ring of what looked like heat waves. The ring became larger and larger.

"No, no, please no," she said, and put her palms to her temples, but the ring remained. It got larger and larger, and soon was out beyond her vision.

And the headache began.

The sound of her father's footsteps up the back stairs as he went up to his room echoed in Lizzie's head. Somewhere, she realized that that meant he had had enough of Emma, which wasn't unusual, and that he was going upstairs to finish his nap. She heard his sigh in the next room. It was as loud as an elephant's trumpet. She heard his change jangle as he removed it from his pocket and placed it in a little bowl on his dresser. It sounded like tools clanging into a chest. Then the bedsprings creaked as he lay down, and Lizzie saw him in her mind's eye, a tired, worn-out old man who didn't know how to deal with life anymore.

She felt like running out and putting her head into the snow. She thought if she did, the snow would sizzle and melt in the heat of the headache.

She could understand Emma's feelings—after all, they had a right to that money, more right than their stepmother had, yet it was truly Father's money, wasn't it, and even though he'd promised it to them . . . it was his to do with as he pleased.

No, Emma had no call to argue with him the way she did. She found any excuse, any excuse at all to keep the emotional pot boiling in the house. She sometimes had no shame, that woman, and while Lizzie loved her with a fierce devotion, there were times when she not only did not understand Emma, she did not like her. Not at all.

This was one of those times.

Lizzie rocked back and forth in her chair. She heard Emma downstairs talking to Bridget, the maid, their voices thundering, echoing in her migraine, and then the kitchen door opened and closed. A chill ran up Lizzie's legs. The winter outside was a raw one.

Emma's cooking sounds began. Lizzie shivered.

Lizzie wanted to go into her father's room and comfort him, she wanted to yell at him, she wanted to ask him why, gently and tenderly, and hope for a rational, reasonable answer.

She wanted to go downstairs and throw something at Emma, she wanted to sit at the kitchen table and sympathize with her, plan retaliation toward their father for his actions.

She wanted to leave this house, move to a new town, where no one would know she was even remotely related to Emma and Andrew Borden, adopt a new identity and begin a new life. Teaching, perhaps. Wearing peach.

The lure of the freedom was delicious, but she had lived in this house for twenty-six of her thirty-one years and would grow old in it, probably. Her family was too important, and anyway, women did not just run off, leave their elderly parents and strike out on their own.

Besides, she had no money. And—so it would appear— if Abby Borden had her way, she would never have money. No money of her own, at least. She and Emma would forever be dependent upon the graces of their stepmother and her family.

Lizzie rocked, empathizing with Emma's fury, yet unable to fabricate fury of her own. There had been too many years of understanding, too many years of mediating, too many years of loving the man who held her hostage. It was easier to ignore. It was easier to have no opinion.

It was easier to be crippled by a headache.

In her mind's eye, she saw her father lying on his bed in the next room, hands folded over his stomach. She saw a horrible old man whose claws grasped money and held it to his soul as if it would be the saving of his species. She saw a pitiful old man whose meanness tried to mask his terror of growing old alone. She saw an embarrassment. She saw the patriarch of her family as a whining wretch, incapable of showing leadership and love to a family, yet oh-so-capable of running a financial empire. Lizzie could no longer be proud of the Borden family as headed by Andrew Borden.

Lizzie rocked, holding onto the book, which no longer felt exciting. She rocked and rocked, thinking about the house and how it had a hold on her.

She rocked and her head pounded until she was afraid she would fall onto the floor. And then she undressed, got into bed and held the book close.

The past receded, the family receded, wants, desires, inadequacies and all other thoughts were beaten down, pound after pound. Eventually, there was nothing but the pain, the awful, humiliating, all-encompassing, equalizing pain.

Lizzie delved into it, horrified by it, discouraged by it, yet freed because of it.

• • •

The next morning, feeling shaky and fragile, Lizzie avoided quick moves and bright lights. She lay awake in her bed for a long time before rising. She gently lowered herself onto the metal slops bucket and listened to voices in the kitchen. There were happy sounds, even a trill of laughter from Emma. Joyful sounds were such rare occurrences in the Borden household, Lizzie was intrigued. She cleaned herself, noticed with dismay that her menses had begun during the night and messed her nightgown, laid a cloth over the soiled pot and slid it back under the bed. She would empty the slops later. She donned robe and slippers and slowly, carefully, descended the stairs.

"Lizzie, you lazy thing. Aren't you ready yet?"

"Ready?"

"Our appointment at the dressmaker's. It's in a half hour."

"A half hour!" Lizzie jumped, then put a hand to her fragile head. "Why didn't you tell me?"

"I did tell you, I most certainly did. I told you when I made the appointment, and I reminded you last week. You've just had your head in the clouds, that's all. You need to learn to pay attention, child!"

Lizzie glared at Emma. She had not told Lizzie of the appointment. Going to pick out fabrics for spring dresses was one of the nicest things they did during the long winter. She would have remembered it. She would never have forgotten.

But Emma wanted to keep her off balance. Emma, Lizzie noticed, was dressed smartly, ready for a fitting with the best of the townswomen, while Lizzie . . . Her hair was dirty, she hadn't cleaned and pressed her town dress. . . . She felt her face go hot. "I'm not going," she said.

"Not going? Lizzie, dear, you *must*. Your spring wardrobe. Your summer dresses."

"I'm not fit. I need to bathe."

"Go, then, quickly, and bathe. We have time."

"My hair . . ." Lizzie had forgotten about being angry in a whirlwind of thinking how to be presentable enough to go for her fitting. Her mind was barely able to function after a night of racking pain, and she felt ill equipped to spar with Emma this morning. But that didn't change the fact that Mrs. Longworth wouldn't have another appointment available for months.

"Dash your hair. It's fine."

Lizzie looked at her older sister. It wasn't fine, and Emma knew it. Emma took every advantage to look, act and be superior.

"You never told me," Lizzie said as she took a bowl to the sink, filled it with cool water and warmed it with water from the kettle. "Remind me to ask for some fabric scraps while we're there."

Instead of taking it upstairs, where she normally bathed, Lizzie took it down cellar where she could bathe in privacy and then discard the water, which would be bloody with her menses, without embarrassing any other member of her family.

"I'm sure Mrs. Longworth saves them for you by now." Emma's voice followed her down the stairs. "You could buy yourself a yard or two of cotton at the store, you know."

Lizzie set the basin on the stand, then ran back up the stairs as fast as her brittle head would allow, through the kitchen and the sitting room, and up the stairs to her room, where she fetched clean underwear. She shook out her only presentable dress and brought them all downstairs and on into the cellar. Then she had to stop for a moment, hand on the clammy cellar wall, while the darkness cleared from her vision.

She undressed, throwing her soiled housedress into the corner, putting her menstrual rag into a bucket filled with a dozen others soaking in ice-crusted water under the sink. Then, dancing in the cold, Lizzie took a sponge, filled it with warm water from the bowl, soaped it and rubbed it all over her ample body. It was freezing cold in the cellar. The worn piece of wood that covered the dirt floor rumbled as she danced. Goose pimples rose all over her skin and her nipples shrank down to hard little nuts.

"Quickly, quickly," she breathed. She squeezed the soap out of the sponge and rinsed herself off, then briskly rubbed a scratchy towel around her skin. Then she donned a freshly laundered pad, pinned it to her own homemade belt—this one pink cotton with little red flowers, courtesy of Mrs. Longworth's scraps—got into her long underwear, her slip and petticoat, then pulled the dress over her head.

Then she squeezed out the sponge, rinsed the bowl,

turned it upside down and ran upstairs, barefoot, buttoning her dress.

"My goodness, Lizzie," Emma said.

"It's cold down there."

"You'll catch your death in your bare feet."

"Even in Europe we had bathrooms. Every floor had its own water closet and bath. Every floor."

"I know, I know," Emma said. "Every house in this neighborhood does, too. And gas! We're the only house not hooked up."

Lizzie noted the time. She still had ten minutes before they had to leave. She went upstairs, unpinning her hair, powdered a touch of cornstarch along her hairline and brushed out her long hair; it flew with static electricity. She twisted it, knotted it up, pinned it and checked the results in the mirror. Her glorious light-brown hair with its reddish highlights was not shiny and silky as it would be if she had just washed it; instead, it was cornstarch-dull, but at least it did not look oily.

She pinched her cheeks to bring up a little color, smoothed out her dress, donned stockings and her new button shoes, and she was ready. Not as ready as she would have liked to be, but ready nevertheless.

She walked down the stairs, opened the closet and took out the seal cape her father had given her on her thirtieth birthday, one of only two extravagances she'd ever known him to bestow, put the cape around her shoulders, picked up her bag and her gloves and walked back into the kitchen.

"I'm ready now, Emma."

Emma looked her up and down. Lizzie stood still for her appraisal, waiting for the deprecating word, but none came.

"Let's be gone, then," Emma said, and began to give orders to the maid.

They walked from the pinched little house on Second

26

Street to the dressmaker's, four blocks through the biting January winter. They walked in silence, Lizzie trying on different shades of peach in her mind, still miffed with Emma for taking most of the pleasure out of her semi-annual fitting. Next time, she thought, I'll make an appointment myself and go alone. It would be ever so much more fun. But they had always gone together, and no matter what Lizzie thought of Emma and her jealous ways, Emma did have superb taste. "How many dresses are we allowed?" Last year, Father put Emma in charge of the household budget, something that had only momentarily placated Emma's lust for control.

"We can each have three housedresses, one church dress and two town dresses."

"One church dress? That's hardly enough. I have enough ugly housedresses. I'll trade them in for another church dress."

"One church dress costs more than three housedresses, Lizzie, you must know that."

"So? I can't possibly go through the whole spring and summer with only one more church dress. The pastor's wife snickers over my wardrobe as it is."

"Lizzie!"

"Well, she does."

"All right. Two church dresses for you, then, if you must, but it will mean a month of decent meat."

"I don't care."

"See if you care when Father gets mutton instead of pork."

● ● ●

Mrs. Longworth had laid out the most fascinating array of colored fabrics in her salon. In every possible color and color combination, there were cottons, woolens, flannels, silks, linens, in solids, plaids, stripes and flowers. There were brocades and tapestries and beaded fabrics. There were laces and nets, eyelets and chintz. It was a feast for the eyes, and Lizzie wanted to gather them all up in her arms and whirl around the room.

"Good morning, Mrs. Longworth," Emma said.

"Emma. Lizzie. Excuse me for a moment while I tidy up. I've just fitted a bride and three bridesmaids."

Lizzie went to the pastels and began fingering some peach-colored calico. Emma, she noticed, went directly to the darker colors.

"Lizzie, come look at these fabrics. This green would accentuate your eyes."

"I think something pastel this spring, Emma," Lizzie said. "Like this peachy one, for example."

Emma curled her lip in distaste. "It clashes with your hair, with your eyes and with your complexion. It would make you look dead."

Lizzie picked up the bolt, unrolled a yard and held it in front of her face in the mirror. It did, she had to agree, make her look greenish. Lizzie's mousy brown hair and pale-green eyes needed the blues and greens, Emma was right. And the darker colors were more slimming. Beatrice had dark-brown hair, snapping brown eyes, and dark brows. She also wore makeup to accentuate her looks, whereas Father would allow no "paint" on any member of his household. No, peach was definitely a color for Beatrice, but not for Lizzie.

She put the bolt back and picked up a sunshiny yellow.

"No," Emma said, without even looking. "Come look at this blue. This cornflower color would look lovely."

Everything in Lizzie's closet was blue. She took the bolt from Emma and held it up. It was nice. It was very nice. But it was blue.

A familiar feeling began to come over Lizzie. She remembered now, about these fittings. It was the same every year, twice a year. She was bowled over by the shouts of the fabrics, but Emma chose the same colors, patterns and styles for her over and over and over again.

The feeling grew as Mrs. Longworth took her measurements and wrote them in her black ledger. Each number was larger than the one she had written down last year, and Mrs. Longworth mentioned that with each measurement. Emma clucked with every inch.

By the time they got to choosing the styles, there was no fun left for Lizzie. Emma chose all her fabrics and her styles, and they were just the same as she'd always had.

When they left the dressmaker, Lizzie was downcast.

"I don't know why you're such a brat," Emma said. "Those dresses will be very smart on you."

"Blue, green and lavender," Lizzie said. "No pinks, no yellows, nothing bright and cheerful."

"It's what you look best in," Emma said.

"Says you."

"Do you want to go back?"

For a moment, Lizzie considered it. But, just before they were finished, Mrs. Kelly and her daughters had come in for their fittings, and the shop would now be filled with emerald greens and bright yellows with eyelet and lace, and with feminine giggles. The redheads had all the luck when it came to wearing vibrant colors. Not so Lizzie Borden.

"No," she said.

"Then be grateful. You got two church dresses, you know."

"Both blue."

"Both expensive. They will last for years if you take care. And, of course, if you watch your weight."

Lizzie felt like a child. She felt as if she'd never break out of the icy igloo that having four parents had built around her. She was never allowed an opinion, she was never allowed her own taste, she was never allowed to express herself in any manner, if it were the least bit unconventional.

"I'm going to stop by the dry-goods store and buy some yellow and pink cottons," she said to Emma. "At least I can stitch myself a couple of dusters."

Emma nodded her approval.

She would sew them, Lizzie knew, but she had neither the patience nor the talent for needlework that Emma and their stepmother had. Abby Borden created masterpieces at the sewing machine, and Emma did intricate work by hand. Lizzie did adequate work, but it was rustic, and the result usually ill-fitting.

The sisters parted ways in town, Emma going to stop by the post office before heading back home, Lizzie going to the dry-goods store for her little calico symbol of rebellion.

That evening, when the two quiet knocks came at her door, Lizzie went down to take up her supper before Andrew and Abby were called to the table. Supper consisted of crusty bread spread with salted lard, and a bowl of stewed cabbage. Lizzie wondered if the household budget had really expired this early in the month or if Emma had made such a meager meal in order to spite Father. She ladled her bowlful and took it up to her room. She was glad she'd pilfered the cakes from yesterday's tea, because she had no appetite for the meal.

As always, she was glad to have slipped in and out of the kitchen without meeting anyone else; as far as she knew, Father was in his room, Bridget in hers, and Abby was out.

She dipped her spoon into the stew and blew across it to cool. It didn't taste bad, but Emma's culinary expertise had clearly fallen by the wayside for this meal.

Then her bedroom door opened and Emma came in, her eyes downcast.

"Emma. What is it?"

"I am at my wits' end with that old man, Lizzie."

"Emma, he's our father." She looked at the door that separated her bedroom from his. "And he might hear you."

30

Emma lowered her voice. "You may call him Father if you like. To me he's a miserly, mean old man. And I don't care at all if he hears me. He's heard it all before."

Lizzie set her bowl of stew aside.

"I'm going to leave."

"Emma, no."

"I cook for him, I clean for him, and he cannot even speak to me with a civil tone. The household budget makes allowance only for swill. We are ordered to wear a very few dresses, and those made of inexpensive fabric. We are never allowed to entertain. In fact, we have no friends, Lizzie."

"That's not true, Emma. . . ."

"It might as well be. I'm going to ask the wretched old man for my inheritance, and I will leave."

"Leave!" Lizzie was stunned. "Where will you go?"

"We have cousins. Mother has many relatives in Fairhaven. I can be in touch with them. Surely there are opportunities for a woman of my talents."

"Oh, I've no doubt about that, Emma, but whatever shall I do here without you?"

"You could come with me"—she took a deep breath—"if only you didn't have to be a nursemaid to him."

"Oh, no, no. I could never leave Father like that. I couldn't go . . . to another town, I don't think. Please don't make me choose between you, Emma."

"Why? That might force his lovely wife to start washing his underwear and drying his pots and pans. She might have to start *earning* her inheritance." Emma's face began to show that tight redness again. "That farm belonged to our mother, you know, Lizzie. He has no right to deed it to that woman."

Lizzie knew there would be no talking to her sister in this state. "You talked with him again, didn't you? Why didn't you just let it rest for a while, Emma?"

"I got nowhere."

"Let him think about what you've said for a couple of days. Maybe what you said will make him consider what he's about to do. Maybe he'll change his mind."

"Maybe."

They both heard the front door open and close. Emma sat on the edge of Lizzie's bed, looking at her hands in her lap, while Abby Borden's heavy footsteps stopped at the coat closet, continued through the dining room to the kitchen, stopped at the stove, then clomped up the back stairs to her bedroom. They both heard the door to their parents' bedroom open. Lizzie had pushed her dressing table up against the connecting door, but sounds were clearly audible.

"I can't stand to listen to the existence of that woman," Emma said, and walked through to her own room, leaving Lizzie to sit with her cold cabbage stew and sour stomach.

She set the food on the floor by her door, unlaced her shoes and took them off. Then she lay on her bed and brought a quilt up over her. She knew that her dress would wrinkle and that someone was sure to comment on it, but for the moment, she didn't care, she didn't care, she didn't care. She settled herself comfortably, unclenched her fists and tried to think of happy thoughts. She tried to think of some happy memories, but they somehow eluded her. She tried to remember her mother's face, but all she knew was one photograph of a young woman, a young Emma really, and a description of her personality from her father. She tried to remember games she and Emma used to play when they were little, but it seemed as though there never were games in this house; it seemed there never were children in this house.

So Lizzie went to the only place she knew that never let her down. She went to a place filled with warmth and beauty and solace.

In the midst of turmoil around her, Lizzie closed her mind, closed her eyes and went fishing.

E mma finished wiping down the kitchen counters and hung the soiled dishrag over the sink in the little washroom off the kitchen. Her stomach still burned from the confrontation with her father. Her unreasonable father. Her *elderly,* unreasonable father. Then she unlocked the kitchen door and threw the basin of dishwater into the snow. The dining-room clock chimed the half hour; Emma assumed it was eight-thirty. Her father and his wife had gone to bed an hour before, as had Bridget, the maid. Lizzie had never come down after dinner.

She fit a fresh candle into a candlestick, lit it and blew out the lanterns in the kitchen.

Why was it, she wondered, that she so cherished time alone in this house during the day, yet at night she longed for company? Emma walked through the empty dining room, places carefully set for breakfast by Bridget before she retired for the night. The candle she carried threw exaggerated shadows on the walls as she walked. They weren't satisfactory company at all.

She checked the front door to make sure it was tightly locked. For over two years—ever since the threats against Andrew Borden by his ill-treated employees began—security at the Borden house had been tight. Extra tight. Obnoxious. Every room in the house had its own key, and every personal room was always locked, whether it was occupied or not. The front door had three locks, the back door two, each of the bedrooms one.

What was there to steal, anyway? Abby Borden kept a few dollars and a few pieces of jewelry on hand, but there was nothing of value, nothing even of sentimental value, in this house.

Except, perhaps, the suspicion. The locking and unlocking of doors had created an air of suspicion about the house. Whenever Emma left her bedroom and locked it with a key, she always tried the knob one more time, to make sure it was locked. To make sure no one could get in. No one. And even though she *knew* that nothing was kept in any of the other rooms—to which she could have access if she wanted—just knowing that the other rooms were locked made her wonder what they were hiding. Emma had her secrets—oh yes, she had her secrets all right—but they were not in her room and they could not be found by prying eyes.

Even so, the thought of some stranger in her bedroom, next to her bed, looking around and having thoughts, or making comments, touching things or passing judgment on the state of affairs in her bedroom, made her sick to her stomach. It made her skin crawl.

The locking of doors had started with the threat from a former mill employee. Andrew Borden was not a kind man, and his manner of doing business was profit-motivated. As a result, those people who made his businesses actually run were frequently ground under the heel of his enterprising zeal.

And Andrew took the threat to heart. He would never let his family be left to the mercy of those inadequate souls who could not even cut the mustard at the mill.

Emma wandered into the sitting room. There should be storytelling going on in this room, she thought. A fire in the grate, gaslights in every corner and a spirited game of chess, or hearts, or some music or something. Something should be happening in this house at night, but there was nothing. There had been nothing since Mother died.

The gaiety died when Mother died, Emma thought. This house died, this family died when Mother died. And now the whole household goes to bed when the sun goes down, because there is no gaslight in this house and Father begrudges the expense for lamp oil and candles. "Go to sleep and save the candles," she had heard him say on more than one occasion.

Emma set the candle on the end table in the sitting room, then pulled the little drawer all the way out, trying to keep it from rattling, and set the drawer in her lap. She sat for a moment, listening. If anyone heard her rattling in the drawers, they would be down in a minute. If there was anything this family shared besides aloofness, that was its nosiness.

The photograph was still where she had first put it thirty years ago, in the little space behind the drawer. Emma reached in and pulled it out. A photograph of their mother. So young, so thin. The people of Fall River always said Emma took after her mama, and so it was, she saw again. She was her mother's daughter. They had the same cheekbones, the same fine nose, the same arched eyebrows and close-set eyes in a narrow face. They had the same medium-brown hair. But Sarah Borden had light-colored eyes—blue, her father said he thought he remembered them to be—while Emma shared his deep brown eyes.

Mama was so young. The photograph Emma held in her hand was the last one, taken just before she died. Mother would have been about thirty—about Lizzie's current age. . . .

Even though they told Emma that she was the one who had found her mother dead, Emma could not remember it, and she still could not remember the details of Sarah's death. Nor could she bring herself to ask Father.

Emma ran her finger over the photograph of her mother's face as if to feel the delicate skin. "I know there's a reason you died, Mother," she whispered. "It's taken me a long time to understand, but now I think I do." She gently kissed the photo and thought of taking it upstairs to her room, where she could keep it, either hidden or on display, and then decided to put it back behind the drawer again. It gave her pleasure to see Abby Borden sitting next to the end table, using it, with Mother secreted safely inside. Abby had destroyed everything in the house that remained of Sarah Borden, her predecessor in Andrew's bed. Everything except a locket that Lizzie had, and this photograph that would forever remain next to that wretched woman without her ever knowing it.

"I understand, Mother," Emma whispered again. "And I've raised Lizzie well. I know you'd agree. I know you'd be happy." She touched the paper face, touched the picture to her cheek, then tucked it back into the hole in the end table and reinserted the drawer.

Since Emma had changed bedrooms with Lizzie, the only way she could enter her own bedroom in this odd little house was to walk through Lizzie's. As a result, she always carried two keys in her pocket: a key to Lizzie's perennially locked door, and a key to her own. It was a nuisance, and she had the smaller room now, but at least her bedroom shared a wall with Abby Borden's dressing room rather than with the parents' bedroom. Lizzie now had that honor.

Emma carefully unlocked Lizzie's bedroom door, hoping not to wake her parents, not minding if Lizzie wanted to sit up and talk for a while.

She saw Lizzie lying on her bed, fully dressed, half covered with her quilt. Lizzie opened her eyes.

"Did I wake you?" Emma asked.

"I guess so," Lizzie said, rubbing her face. "I didn't intend to sleep."

"My goodness, child, you're fully dressed."

"I just lay down for a moment this afternoon after the

fitting, and then again after dinner. I imagine I needed the rest. What time is it?"

"About nine, I should think."

"The house is quiet."

Emma nodded, then sat in the rocking chair at Lizzie's bedside.

Lizzie plumped up her pillow and set it next to the wall, then hiked herself up the bed to a sitting position. Something crinkled in her bed.

"What's this?" She reached under the quilt and fumbled with her skirts. Then she pulled out a piece of string and a brown-paper-wrapped parcel. "Oh. The book. I forgot all about it."

"What book is that?"

"It's a book that Beatrice sent to me."

"Well, open it. Let's have a look."

"Maybe later."

"Why later? Aren't you curious? You rip open every letter you get from her the very moment the postman puts it in the box."

"I know, but . . ."

"Oh. It's *personal*." Emma couldn't help her sarcasm.

"Yes, in fact."

"Well. I never knew we had secrets."

"We don't have secrets, Emma. I just want to have a chance to look it over first, that's all."

"Hmm. Your relationship with that woman is odd and I daresay a little dangerous, perhaps sick, Lizzie. I should be very careful, if I were you."

Lizzie looked at her with wide-open eyes. "You know nothing about her. You have no idea. . . . You have *no* idea. . . ."

"Yes. Well. Nor am I interested. Mark my words, though, child." Emma rose. "Shall I light your lantern?"

"No. I'll do it."

"Suit yourself," Emma said, and unlocked her own bedroom door. Sometimes Lizzie could be so defensive. So confounding. Emma worried that she was so gullible. What on earth could this woman want from Lizzie, this woman from England? Something no good, that was for sure.

Emma undressed quickly, hanging up all her clothes, then donned her winter nightgown, leggings and cap, and knelt on the hard floor to say her evening prayer. She even included her father.

Duties done, she slipped between the cold sheets and blew out the candle, seeing the shaft of muted light under her door as it escaped from Lizzie's room.

The girl could do so much with her life, Emma thought. If only she'd try. She has so much potential. She has so many gifts. Her youth, her looks, her closeness to Father, her friends at church . . . it's all so *wasted* on her. Emma clenched her fists. Why *her*? What has *she* done to be the lucky one, while I wither, growing old in the house of my childhood, with a traitorous father and his . . . his . . .

A moan escaped her lips, and she clapped both hands over her mouth before she made more noise. Her face felt hot and her hands shook.

It was the same every night. Every night she went to bed and ranted and railed at the devastating blows life had given her, while her beautiful, clever younger sister got all the attention.

"I try to be selfless, Lord," she whispered, then knuckled her lower lip hard until she got herself under control.

Then she turned on her side, away from the long slice of light that said that Lizzie even had friends in England, and she curled her knees to her bony chest and eventually fell asleep.

●　　●　　●

In the morning, Emma woke to the sounds of roosters in the neighborhood. It was still dark outside, but she heard sounds in the kitchen and imagined that the cookstove was hot and its warmth had filled the whole kitchen. Emma's room was freezing. She arose, carefully used the chamber pot without touching it to her bottom, and dressed quickly in black leggings, long underwear and a maroon wool dress with a high collar. She made her bed and set the chamber pot next to the door. It would be bad for Maggie if she had to empty frozen slops. She brushed her hair, pinned it up, carried the covered pot out into Lizzie's room and locked her bedroom door behind her. She barely gave Lizzie a glance, knowing the girl would still be sound asleep. No one would know, save Lizzie herself, what time she turned out the lantern. She probably would not be ready for breakfast until noon, lazy brat.

She felt the warmth from the kitchen as soon as she reached the landing. Then she descended the stairs and turned into the dining room.

Bridget Sullivan, the little redheaded Irish maid, was lighting the lanterns in the dining room. She was disheveled, as if she hadn't quite put herself together yet. Emma could see her stepmother, Abby, thumping her two hundred pounds around the kitchen. Emma walked into the warm glow of the kitchen and set her pot of slops in the utility room.

"Good morning," Abby said.

"Why are you up so early?"

"Babies due this morning."

"How do you know that, did a message come?"

"No, but Mrs. Churchill said she thought Sophie Warren was in labor last night, so I'll make up a casserole now and take it over. She's supposed to have twins, you know. Runs in her family."

"So for that you got up before dawn?"

"It'll be a busy day. Is Lizzie awake?"

"No. Nor is she likely to be for a time yet. It's freezing cold upstairs."

"I know." Abby opened the oven and checked on the cakes.

"Didn't anybody make a fire in the furnace last night?"

Abby turned and looked directly into Emma's eyes. "Did you?"

"No." Emma hated it when the little pig woman looked at her like that.

"Well, I reckon nobody else did, either. Don't complain unless you do your share around here, Emma."

"I do my share, Abby. I do more than my share. I do more than my share *and* your share."

Emma poured a cup of coffee and stood in the middle of the kitchen, looking out the black window. Actually, what she saw was the reflection of her stepmother, concentration on her round, lined face, as she sliced vegetables and mixed them all together in a casserole dish. Abby had barely more gray hair than Emma did, a point that bothered Emma terribly. Abby's hair was long and brown, shot through with a silver that would look beautiful on a woman of smaller stature, and done up in a bun at the back of her neck. She had a wide nose and large, fleshy lips, two facial features totally foreign to Borden blood.

Abby turned abruptly and bumped into Emma. "Emma," she said in frustration. "Please. I'm busy in here."

Emma took her coffee and sat at the table in the dining room.

"Oatmeal, Miss Emma?" the maid asked.

"Thank you, no, Maggie."

"Bridget."

"What?"

"My name is Bridget, Miss Emma."

"Well, of course it is."

"You keep calling me Maggie. Maggie was your other maid. She left here two years ago, Miss Emma. My name is Bridget."

Emma looked at the girl's face. She was deeply freckled, with curly red hair and dark-green eyes. Typical Irish. And she had the temper and the brat attitude to go with it. She seemed impatient as well this morning. "Well, *Bridget,* then, no thank you. Toast, perhaps. And then be a good girl and make a fire in the furnace."

Bridget brought two slices of toast, the dish of butter and a jar of plum jam. Emma ate the toast dry.

Abby brought her breakfast in and set her place across from Emma. She had a bowl of oatmeal, two pieces of toast with butter and jam, and a plate of fatty fried bacon.

They ate in silence, avoiding each other's eyes.

Then Abby cleared her throat, looked at the tablecloth and said, "Your father has many pressures upon him."

"They are of his own making," Emma said, looking straight up at Abby, wishing she would raise her eyes.

"Be that as it may, he tries only to make a fine home for us."

"For you."

"You are an ungrateful girl."

"I am not a girl. I am a grown woman, and so is Lizzie. We have a right to say what goes on in this house and how the family finances are handled."

"You have no such right. The money is your father's to do with as he wishes."

"To do with as *you* wish."

"These conversations have cost him sleep."

"Oh. That's a terrible shame."

"Emma . . ." Emma put down her toast and regarded her stepmother. "I'm sixty-seven years old. Your father is sixty-nine. We won't live too much longer. I just wanted a little something to leave to my baby sister, Sarah. She's just married again and trying to make a go of things. You and Lizzie, you'll have everything."

"He's already given her a house in town."

"And he gave you and Lizzie just compensation. Besides, that house is much too small for Sarah and her family to live in."

Emma snorted. "Just compensation! He deeded us a pile of sticks filled with unruly tenants. If she doesn't like the house, she should sell it and buy a larger place."

"It isn't that easy, Emma."

"Then why doesn't he leave it to her in his will?"

"She needs a place to live now, Emma. He just thought this would be a better way—"

"Well, it's not." Emma felt her face flush again; she was in danger of losing control. "That property was our mother's. He can deed some other property to your stupid half sister. He can give her some bank shares. But that property, that *particular* property is the most valuable of them all, and it has the most sentimental value to Lizzie and me."

"I'll speak with him about it again."

Emma threw her toast onto her plate. "I'm sure you will." She threw her napkin on top of the toast, pushed away from the table and left the room.

She walked up the stairs quietly, the rage burning brightly within her. She unlocked Lizzie's bedroom door, hands pale and trembling in the pre-dawn light. She stumbled against Lizzie's chair and then dropped the key to her own bedroom on the floor. Tears began to blur her vision and she got down on her knees to find the key, furious at the prospect that she might cry, furious even more that she couldn't get into her bedroom to seethe in privacy.

She moved and heard the key slide across the wooden floor.

"Emma?" Lizzie's sleepy voice. "Emma?"

"Shut up," Emma said; then her fingers found the key

42

and she stood up, but she couldn't fit it into the lock. Her fingers trembled and it was dark and Lizzie was listening and her fury, her helplessness, her *impotence* were in a rage beyond thought.

"Emma?"

"Shut up, shut up, *shut up!*" Then the key fit into the lock and she turned it and opened the door. She took a deep breath. "I'm leaving here *today*, Lizzie," she said, and then entered her room, shut and locked the door behind her.

I'm leaving here today, she thought, as she clenched her fists and crossed her arms over her chest. I'm leaving here today. She paced back and forth from her bed to her closet. Her suitcase was in the closet, she had only to get it down and pack it full of her clothes, but she didn't trust herself at the moment. If she loosened her hands from their grips upon themselves, they might do something. So she paced, her face on fire, the muscles in her legs stiff and tense, her back straight, her jaw so tight it ached. I'm leaving here today, she thought.

A soft knock came to her door.

"What?"

"Emma," Lizzie said, "please let me in."

"Go away."

"I won't. Now open the door and talk to me."

Emma pressed her fingers to her eyes, pressed them hard until she saw yellow spots and it began to hurt. Then she opened the door.

Lizzie came in, her hair up in curling rags, nightgown wrinkled and smelling of sleep.

"What has happened?"

"Lizzie, there's nothing . . . I can't do . . ." She made a sweeping gesture toward their parents' bedroom. "He . . . oh God!" The tears threatened again. Her breaths came in sobs.

"Sit down and tell me."

43

Emma sat on the edge of her chair. The sobs began to abate. She took a deep breath, fetched a handkerchief from her pocket and ran it across her face and lips, then twisted it in her lap. "I'm going to New Bedford for a couple of days."

"No, Emma. Please don't. Please."

Emma felt better as soon as she said it. "I'll be all right, Lizzie. I'll stay with friends." Emma nodded. She would see friends, that was for sure.

"For how long?"

"A week." As long as it takes, she thought.

"Please don't. The last time you said one week, you stayed away three. And were half dead when you finally did return."

"Stop it. None of that is your concern. I hate it here. I'm going there for a breath of fresh air." Emma found she couldn't meet Lizzie's eyes. Lizzie knew who her "friends" were in New Bedford. Lizzie was the only one who knew, and Lizzie didn't approve.

"I'll come with you."

"You won't. Now leave me alone. I have to pack."

"I worry so, Emma."

"I'm a grown woman. There's a train at nine. Now good-bye."

"If I got down on my knees—"

"Leave me, Lizzie."

Lizzie stood looking at her for a long moment. Emma felt she should say something, do something, but she sat on the chair and avoided Lizzie's eyes. She felt alone, so alone. She wanted to say Yes, Lizzie, save me from having to go to New Bedford, but she didn't. She sat there, hands on her lap, eyes on her hands, and finally Lizzie left, closing Emma's door quietly behind her.

Emma lifted down the suitcase. Suddenly, the rage drained away, and in its place was anticipation. It had been a long time since she'd been to New Bedford. It was time, surely it was time. She took the money envelope from her bedstand drawer and counted it. Forty-three dollars was all she had managed to save from her weekly allowance of four dollars. Well, it would have to do.

She left with only a nod to Lizzie, who was still in her room, walked to the station in the early morning light and sat in the unheated waiting room. The train arrived at eight-fifty precisely; at nine o'clock it jerked and they were on their way to New Bedford.

The anticipation Emma felt in her freedom was sporadically deposed by the hatred that welled up inside her. The smell of a man's pipe touched it off. So did the cut of a matron's expensive wool coat. A fat woman jiggled down the aisle and Emma raged within again, trying in vain to calm herself. There were only two thoughts that had an effect on her rage. One was that she would never have to marry, and so she had this freedom, as meager and as simple as it was, to leave home, alone, for a week; and the other thought was of what lay at the end of this short train trip to New Bedford: peace.

In less than an hour, she arrived.

Emma hailed a cab; it took her to the Capitol Inn, a small hotel on Madison Street, one that she frequented whenever she came to New Bedford. She checked in under the name of Lucy Billings, with the cabby carrying her baggage, and she left the usual instructions with the clerk and made sure he wrote them down. She was under no circumstances to be disturbed until the night before she was to check out. There would be no maid service, there would be no messages relayed, there would be no giving out of her hotel room number to anyone for any reason. She sealed this promise with a most generous two-dollar tip. Then she went to her room.

The bellboy opened the draperies, but Emma hustled him out with ten cents in his palm. She was filled with excitement at the prospect of an entire week here in New Bedford, with no Abby Borden, no Andrew Borden, no Lizzie Borden, no church, no neighbors, no Maggie—or Bridget, or whatever the maid's name was—no pressures, no expectations of her or her behavior, no nothing.

She took off her travelling hat and sat on the bed. She checked her watch. Almost eleven o'clock. She left the room, pocketing her key, and searched the halls until she found a little Irish chambermaid. Emma gave the girl money and instructions, then went back to her room to unpack and to pace, awaiting the arrival of the week's cache of rum.

ff and on all day, Lizzie thought about Emma.

Emma had demons. There was just no other way to explain her behavior. The Borden household was not without its pressures, and its members certainly had their quirks, but Emma . . .

Emma went to New Bedford at least once a year, usually twice, and had done so ever since Lizzie could remember. She went without parental approval, without chaperone. She never asked permission and her parents never stopped her. She took all the money she'd saved from the allowance Father gave her, and went. There was never a letter from anyone in New Bedford, and Emma never spoke of anyone there, so Lizzie knew she had no friends there. Once, while nursing Emma after one of her trips, Lizzie came upon a receipt for a room at the Capitol Inn, so Lizzie knew where Emma stayed in New Bedford, and it wasn't with any friends. She never let Emma know she'd found the receipt. She just felt better knowing she could find Emma should the need ever arise.

There was no trouble guessing what Emma did when she was alone in the hotel room. Lizzie shivered to think of it. Her sister. Her flesh and blood. Her surrogate mother. Emma, the woman who raised her, the woman she had always looked to for guidance and inspiration. Emma.

Emma drank. She drank, and whenever she drank she also got into trouble.

Emma always came home from New Bedford sick, bruised, in pain and reeking of alcohol.

Lizzie marveled at her older sister. She couldn't imagine going off alone the way Emma did. She always tried to picture it in her mind. Where would she go to find liquor? True, it was a commonplace enough item, yet ladies didn't frequent saloons and taverns. Was it purchased in a regular store? And what did Emma do, once she had her bottle? Where would she go? Would she carry it around in a paper bag, to sit in her hotel room and guzzle? Did she use a glass, or did she swig straight from the bottle? Did she wake up in the morning, wash her face, brush her teeth and begin again, or did she moan and roll over, search blindly for the neck of her bottle and continue, never really beginning, never really ending? Was it her companions who bruised her so? What would happen if somebody got overly rough with Emma? What if someday she just didn't come home?

Lizzie had no idea what really went on in New Bedford, and it was the activities she conjured up in her imagination that worried her so much. Lizzie joined the Women's Christian Temperance Union when she realized what Emma was doing. She hoped legislation would be a way of averting her sister's seemingly inevitable downfall. Lizzie went to the meetings, Emma at the forefront of her mind, and she prayed for Emma's soul.

At dinner, Andrew Borden drew his white eyebrows together when Lizzie told him that Emma had gone to New Bedford to visit friends.

"Again?" he asked, his voice thunderous and disapproving.

Lizzie nodded, her eyes on her plate.

"Who does she know in New Bedford?"

"I don't know, Father."

"It seems that Emma gets upset about the least little thing and then goes running off to New Bedford to do whatever it is she does up there that lays her up at home for a week afterward. I don't like it, Lizzie, I don't like it one bit. One of these days she's going to do something to bring shame on the Borden name. And I won't stand for that. Do you hear me?"

"Yes, Father."

"Be sure you tell her that."

"Yes, Father."

"Drat the girl!" Andrew threw his napkin onto the table. "Does she think she has no responsibilities here at home? Does she think she can just up and leave us to assume her duties?"

Lizzie remained silent.

"Is she airing family laundry?"

"I don't think so, Father."

"Be sure you tell her, Lizzie."

"I will, Father."

There was a long silence at the table. Then, just as Lizzie finished and readied her dishes to take into the kitchen, Andrew Borden spoke again. "And what have you been doing all morning?"

Lizzie sat back in her chair. "Reading."

"Reading what?"

"I received a letter and a book from Beatrice. In England. Remember the package you brought from the post office?"

"Oh. A book. Is it worthwhile? Will it teach you anything practical?"

"I think very much so, Father, only I've just begun, so I can't tell too much about it yet."

"This is a good friend of yours, this Beatrice?"

"Be-AT-trice, Father. Yes, she's a wonderful friend. We carry on quite a lively correspondence."

"I should imagine. I can't think what you women do, day in and day out, to keep yourselves occupied. I should go mad without the challenges of the business world. And Lord knows, you don't do too much around this house, the lot of you. I can never find a cleanly pressed handkerchief to save my soul."

"I'm sorry, Father, I'll try to get some pressing done this afternoon."

When it was clear that her father had had his say about the state of the household, Lizzie cleared the table, did up the dishes in a hurry and ran back to her room. She could barely wait to get back to the book Beatrice had sent. Such a book! It was better than anything she could ever have imagined.

And Beatrice had inscribed it, just inside the cover.

"To my darling Lizbeth, so all your heartfelt desires may come true. Affectionately, Beatrice."

"Affectionately, Beatrice." How Lizzie wished to send something to someone signed "Affectionately, Lizbeth."

Lizbeth.

Beatrice knew that her name was Lizzie, that she'd been born Lizzie Andrew Borden, but in one of her first letters, she'd written, "My dear Lizbeth, I know that is not your true name, but it is ever so much more romantic, don't you think? Lizzie brings to mind a whole different style of woman than you, so if you don't mind, I shall keep you in my heart as Lizbeth, and it is on that ground that we shall meet via our letters."

Lizzie had fallen in love with the name immediately. Not "Elizabeth," a name so popular it was almost vulgar. Not "Lizzie," which, Beatrice was too kind to say, sounded like a barmaid, chambermaid or whore. No. "Lizbeth." Different. Daring. Wonderful. If only she could be a Lizbeth in true life, and not a Lizzie.

She sprawled on her bed, her room a rumpled mess. Lizzie always allowed herself the luxury of a messy room when Emma was in New Bedford. No one would enter her room for any reason, and so there was no reason to keep it neat. It was great freedom to throw clothes on the floor and pick them up not for the sake of neatness, but for practicality, and Lizzie would only pick them up when she wanted to. A small, distinct pleasure.

She unlaced her shoes, let them drop quietly onto the floor and picked up the book. Beatrice's letter fell out from under the front cover, to lie on Lizzie's chest. She ran her hand over the dark cloth cover of the book and set it aside. She picked up the letter and began to read:

My Dear Lizbeth:

There are many people in this world who are content to let life do with them as it will. There are few who set their sights on particular goals and never rest until the goals are accomplished. Those who do can be divided into two groups: 1. Those who strive for personal and selfish gain; and 2. Those who strive for the betterment of their fellows.

I send you this book, my darling, because I believe I know you well enough to know you have the interests of your family and your community at heart. You are a soft, sensitive, lovely woman, and with the proper training, there are no limits to the things you can accomplish.

The program outlined in this book is a simple one. If you follow the rules exactly, I guarantee that you will discover powers deep within yourself that you never knew existed. You will begin to take charge of the direction of your life and cease to be swept about by the winds of change blown by others. Let your winds do the sweeping.

But one word of caution. This is a serious work. Approach it with respect.

And may the moon and the stars be yours.
Affectionately, Beatrice.

● ● ●

Lizzie refolded the letter and laid it on her chest. Then she picked up the book again. She couldn't tell in the light whether it was maroon or black in color. It was a very slim volume, as slim as any volume of poetry ought to be. It felt nice to the touch. It was new. It smelled new.

On the title page was written *PATHWAYS*. There was no author, no date of publication, no publisher. The second page had two short paragraphs:

> You hold this book as the result of a friend's love and regard for you. It outlines a program of growth which demands rigorous self-discipline. It will take more than your passing interest to follow the exercises outlined, but if your desire is strong enough and your sincerity pure, you will succeed.
>
> Do not read ahead. Practice each lesson daily. Do not advance to the next lesson until you have mastered the first, by doing it daily, without exception, for an uninterrupted period of thirty days. Begin to master your life by practicing each lesson in the same place at the same time every day.

Lizzie read those paragraphs over and over again. She tried to squeeze another ounce of meaning out of them, but couldn't. She wanted to open the book and begin to read, to read it straight through, and she wondered why they advised against that.

They. Who were these Pathways people?

Would the program frighten her? Would it intimidate her? Would she think it a waste of time? Would she think it too easy? She puzzled over these questions, trying to glean some knowledge about the author or authors of the book without actually reading it. She studied the cover, the binding, the quality of the paper.

But with dinner over and a long span of time on her hands in which to do nothing but iron some handkerchiefs for her father and worry over Emma, Lizzie turned the page.

It was time to begin.

fter dinner, Abby Borden made sure that Maggie would be in charge of preparing supper; then she retired to her bedroom and picked up her hand sewing. The long afternoon loomed empty before her. Andrew was sure to come up in a moment, quizzing her about Emma's departure. She felt sick to her stomach, a familiar sickness, a regular sickness, considering her dealings with Emma and Lizzie.

If only the twins had been born this morning, she thought, there would have been a little brightness in this dreary January day. Abby loved a good birthing. Especially twins. When twins came, there was twice the joy. Birthings were terribly exciting, filled with midwives, parents, grandparents, neighborly ladies and other children, cousins and ruckus. And Abby always fed the whole lot. It made her feel good; it made her feel useful; it gave her a chance to do something constructive in the community.

And she had been looking forward to it so much. But no, Mrs. Churchill had been mistaken; Mrs. Warren was not in labor at all. Just a touch of indigestion. Dr. Harding thought it would be at least another two weeks. So Abby left a casserole that Mrs. Warren couldn't eat and took home a disappointment for company.

Abby slipped the needle in and out of the fabric; she was making Andrew a new silk shirt, and no sewing machine could detail the collar and cuffs the way she could.

Growing older makes life complicated, she thought. One

day you're saving for your old age and the next day you're dividing up everything you've saved among all the relatives biting and scratching for a piece of it.

She wished Andrew would retire. He no longer needed to work for the money—it was for mental stimulation that he continued to keep his irons in all the fires. Abby would have liked to do a little travelling, but that didn't interest Andrew at all. He was a homebody. At least he'd reduced his obligations at the office: Some days when he came home at noon for dinner he just stayed at home. Other times he came home, ate a bite and then went back until four or so.

Abby was grateful to have a husband in good health. She could live with a lot if she didn't have to nurse a sick husband for years.

She glanced at the clock, anticipating him. He'd gone out after dinner for a pipe, gone to stand on the landing of the back stairs in the cold, tamping his ashes out into a black pile that would continue to grow until spring.

She heard his heavy step on the back stairs.

Her muscles tensed.

He unlocked the bedroom door and came in, closing and locking it behind him.

"Have a little lie-down?"

"Yes," he said, "I think I will." He slipped off his shoes and suit coat and lay on the freshly made bed. Abby rose and covered him with the wedding-ring quilt she'd made for their wedding bed. "Did you speak with Emma this morning, Abby?"

"She came down to breakfast while I was making a casserole for Mrs. Warren."

"How was her mind?"

"She was agitated, I think, Mr. Borden. She spoke again of the property you've generously decided to give my Sarah."

"That damned property."

"I told her I'd speak to you about it. Perhaps . . ." Abby

suddenly felt on shaky ground. She looked down at her needle.

"Perhaps what, woman?"

"Perhaps another piece of property would be more palatable."

"But we decided on that property because of its location. Sarah needs more than a roof over her head."

"I know. I just hate . . ."

"*Finish* your sentences."

"I hate to see you persecuted because of your generosity."

Andrew Borden sighed and seemed to sink deeper into the mattress. "Perhaps she'll move to New Bedford."

Abby snickered, careful to make only the tiniest of sounds, sounds she could explain away if she were called upon to answer for them. Emma would never move out: She would fear that the Borden household could not run according to her way of doing things without her assistance. Without her direction. Without her meddling.

Abby kept stitching, her stomach easing up a bit, and soon Andrew was snoring.

If Emma knew all the facets of Andrew's will, she would have a fit. The thought of Andrew dying before her was abhorrent to Abby, but she would *love* to see the look on Emma's face as the attorney presented Andrew's last will and testament at a reading. Emma would discover that the bulk of his estate, of course, was divided between her and Lizzie; but a generous third—a *generous* third—was left to Abby for her old age. And Abby, of course, would leave her estate, including any assets obtained from Andrew's, to her heirs, namely Sarah, her half sister. And there were others—people significant in Andrew's success—to whom he meant to leave some money.

But Emma thought that everything Andrew had worked for all those years somehow belonged to her and her sister. As if they had ever done anything to deserve his generosity.

56

As Emma saw it, she and Lizzie should inherit everything should Andrew die before Abby, and Abby ought to be put out of the house instantly, penniless. After raising both girls. After putting up with them through their teenage years, through their young maidenhoods, through their coming of age, and even now, for Emma at least, through their middle ages. Even so, Emma would leave Abby without a cent. Oh yes, Abby knew Emma's mind. And it was not a pretty sight.

When she was finished with the shirt, she roused Andrew. He hrumphed himself awake, then dressed and left for the office. Abby followed him downstairs, stoked the fire and put the flats on the wood stove to heat; one good pressing and his new shirt would be fit to wear.

While she waited for the iron to heat up, she snacked on the cookies Emma had made the day before. She enjoyed the silence of the Borden house; well, she enjoyed the *empty* silence of the Borden house. Usually the house was filled with people and it was still silent, but that was more of a cold silence than an empty one. She didn't care for the cold silence. It made her edgy. It made her frantic, sometimes, to fill it, but she didn't know how.

"I wonder where that Maggie has got to," she said to the wood stove, and just then, the maid came around the corner, broom and dustpan in hand.

"Maggie?"

"Yes?" The Irish girl rolled her eyes at the insistent use of her predecessor's name. She was through trying to correct this odd family; if they hadn't gotten it in two years, they never would.

"What have you been up to?"

"I swept the stoop, ma'am, keeping the snow from turning to ice. I was going to warm up a bit in here and then get to dusting the sitting room."

"Oh. All right. Have you seen Lizzie?"

"She's in her room, the last I knew, ma'am. I freshened the sheets in the spare bedroom and heard her rocker."

"Fine." Abby spat on the irons. They sizzled. She set the ironing board up in the dining room and commenced to iron the silk shirt. It came about beautifully. Probably the finest silk shirt she'd ever made.

She ironed and thought about Lizzie. There had been a rift in the family several years ago—again over money—again over property—again over the girls' inheritance—and again over Abby's relatives and their share of it—and ever since that time Lizzie had called her Mrs. Borden. It was not so much that Emma did it; Emma had been fourteen when Abby married Andrew, and Emma had always called her Abby. But Lizzie had been just four years old when Abby entered the family, and had called her Mother. There was no other word like "Mother" to the ears of a spinster, and to have that so cruelly taken away in her latter years was a heartache Abby couldn't quite abide. And for that, she would never forgive Emma.

Abby met Andrew when she was thirty-seven years old and a spinster. She, had, of course, given up all manner of hope of raising a little girl, and then along came Andrew Borden, staid, staunch, rich (as rumor had it), and with two daughters, one still a baby. He took her walking after church one day, and the next Sunday he picked her up for church in his buggy, both girls dressed up in their Sunday best, and they rode to church like a family. Abby was thrilled. For once, hope that she would have a family blossomed in her heart. She would be able to raise a little girl—two, actually. That day, Andrew invited her to be his wife. He needed a mother for the girls, he said, and he would make a proper husband, and promised to be a good provider.

Abby was overwhelmed with the idea of having a family of her own, and she agreed before he was finished speaking.

58

They were wed the next day, and she came to live in the Borden house.

He made no false promises to her—he never lied—and if she had it all to do over again, she would probably jump at the opportunity, just the way she had. Only . . . only she might have looked a little bit closer at that fourteen-year-old Emma before she agreed to take her position by Andrew's side.

She thought of Lizzie up in her room, and wondered if there was something she could say to her. She could walk up the stairs, knock on Lizzie's bedroom door and say something, she could say something soft and gentle, or something clever—except that Abby was not a very clever person, not nearly as clever as Lizzie, and they both knew it—she could say something that would touch Lizzie's heart and leave it healed.

But there wasn't anything. There wasn't anything she could say.

She'd been over this and over this—a million times in the past few years, trying to reach back to the daughter she had raised. The daughter who thought her older sister had raised her. The daughter who mistakenly believed that blood was thicker than water.

Oh, Lizzie, Abby Borden thought. I want to come up to your room and play.

But she finished her ironing instead, and left the board up for Maggie to put away. She filled a plate with cookies and took them and the shirt up the back stairs to her room.

Abby pulled the shirt to and fro on a hanger, until it lay just right. Then she hung it on the closet door, ready for Andrew to wear in the morning. And tomorrow when he put it on, he'd never notice that it was new, or that it was handmade. Abby shook her head. Andrew was preoccupied, as always.

Then she straightened the bed.

Maybe Emma *will* move to New Bedford, Abby thought. It was a wonderful idea. Even more wonderful, it was Andrew's suggestion. She wondered if giving Emma money would really encourage her to go. The breath caught in her throat. Then the three of us can be a family again—it's not too late for Lizzie and me. We've shared too many memories for there to be an irreparable chasm between us.

Abby sat on the freshly tidied bed and felt tears coming on. I wish Emma would never come back, she thought, and began to nibble a cookie. I hope she stays at least a month this time, she thought, finishing that cookie and starting another. And when she comes back, perhaps she'll be sick to her death.

When the last cookie had been eaten and the crumbs brushed from her bosom, Abby went back down to the kitchen for more. She loaded up the plate again, leaving five behind. She looked at the plate and remembered happier times, when she and Lizzie might have shared a plate of cookies and a session with Lizzie's paper dolls. Oh, how Lizzie loved to play pretend with those dolls!

Maybe this is just the thing, Abby thought. She arranged the cookies nicely on the plate. She'd just knock on Lizzie's door and say, "Lizzie? I've brought you a cookie." Lizzie's enthusiasm for paper dolls had of course faded, but she loved her cookies just the same now as she did then. Perhaps the two of them could get in some good chatting, some girl talk over a plate of cookies.

I wonder. Should I bring a tray with tea as well?

No. Don't make it look too contrived. Make it look casual. Make it look like a spur-of-the-moment decision. This plate of cookies reminded me of you and paper dolls, Lizzie, and I wanted to bring it up to you.

Emma never played with paper dolls. Emma mooned

over her dead mother and spoke of death, destruction and hate. Always had, even to this day.

Carrying the plate, Abby went through the dining room to the front hall and looked up the stairs toward Lizzie's room. She would just go knock on Lizzie's door and offer her a cookie.

Slowly, she started up the stairs, but at the top she looked at the door so firmly closed; Abby knew it was locked. Lizzie would have to be interrupted from whatever she was doing —reading the book from her English friend, probably—and they would share a cookie and have nothing to say to each other. Or perhaps Lizzie wouldn't even open the door all the way. She would probably open it only four or five inches, just enough to see who it was and what was wanted. Then a hand would snake out of the open doorway, take a cookie, she would mutter a thank-you, *she would call me Mrs. Borden,* and she would close the door again. And lock it.

No, Abby thought, perhaps the time is past for that kind of gesture. Perhaps Lizzie will come back to me when she is a little older.

Abby passed by Lizzie's door and went directly into the guest bedroom, where Maggie had swept and dusted and freshened up.

A pattern for a new housedress was cut out and lying atop the sewing machine. Abby put the plate of cookies on the bed, took one off the top, and sat at the sewing machine.

She looked at the fabric, a heavy corded cotton; it would make a fine town dress. Too bad it would be as large as a tent. She ate another cookie and sighed. Then she opened the sewing machine, threaded it with the proper color of thread, ate another cookie and began to pin the pieces of the dress together.

If only Mrs. Warren had had those twins this morning, she thought.

• • •

When Andrew came home from work, his brow was furrowed and his temper short. Maggie fixed a nice supper of boiled meat and potatoes, then fixed herself a plate and retired to her room. Abby and Andrew ate in silence in the dining room.

"Seen Lizzie?"

Abby shook her head and helped herself to another portion of potatoes. They had just gotten a bowl of fresh sweet butter from the tenant at the farm, and it was wonderful on the boiled spuds. "I had hoped she'd come down for supper, but . . ."

"Did you call her?"

"No. Maggie did, I'm sure."

"She usually comes down when I come home from work."

"I know she does, Mr. Borden. Perhaps I should check on her. Perhaps she's ill."

Andrew nodded, then loaded his fork up again. Abby knew her potatoes would be cold by the time she returned. She smashed the butter down into them, then excused herself.

No one had set a fire in the sitting room, no one had even lighted the lamps. Abby got the matches from the mantel and lighted first the lamps, then a candle, which she carried up the dark stairs.

"Lizzie?" she called, halfway up.

There was no answer.

"Lizzie? Supper is on the table. Maggie has made one of your favorites."

Still no answer. Abby puffed the rest of the way up the stairs, then knocked on Lizzie's door.

"Lizzie, dear, do come down for some supper."

Then the door opened, and Lizzie stood there, looking slightly glassy-eyed in the light of the candle Abby held.

"Lizzie? Are you ill?"

Lizzie smiled warmly at Abby. "Not at all, Mother. Not at all." Then she looked around the hall. "Supper? Oh, I missed my afternoon with Father. I'm sorry. Tell him I'll be right down."

"You haven't been ill?"

"No, I'm fine. I've been, uh, reading." She rubbed her face and then brushed at the skirt of her dress. "Let me freshen up a bit and I'll be down."

"I'll keep a portion warm for you."

"Thank you." Lizzie pulled the bedroom door shut and Abby heard her lock it.

Abby turned around toward the stairs. She felt as if she'd been told some absolutely fantastic, unbelievable news. She felt like blinking and shaking her head in disbelief.

While Lizzie had always been a nice girl, a courteous girl, a conscientious and polite girl, there was a new dimension here that had been missing for quite some time. There was a warmth that hadn't been present—not since she was a child. There had been concern in her eyes. Lizzie had known she'd missed her afternoon "session" with her father, and had been apologetic. That was uncharacteristic in these latter days.

And she'd called Abby Mother. Mother. Again. At last. Mother.

Yes, Abby thought. We must do something to keep Emma away. When Emma is gone, everything is right.

Abby fairly floated down the stairs. "She'll be right down," she said to her husband, and touched his neck affectionately as she passed behind him. She pretended not to notice that he swiped at her hand as if the touch were from a troublesome fly.

Abby fixed a plate of food for Lizzie, then put it in the bun warmer on the cookstove. By the time she'd come back from the kitchen, Lizzie rounded the corner, smiling at her father.

"So," Andrew said. "Decided to finally come join the living, eh?"

"I'm sorry, Father. I was reading. I became quite engrossed."

"Oh? So engrossed you forget to eat? So engrossed you forget your family?"

"I'm sorry."

Abby fetched the warmed plate and set it before Lizzie. Lizzie whispered a thank-you and began to eat as if she hadn't eaten in days.

Abby's own plate had chilled. Half-melted butter had congealed on the potato, and it didn't look at all as it had before she left to coax the girl from her room. She added salt and ate it anyway.

Andrew cleared his throat and set his fork upon his plate, tines down, with a sound that commanded attention. Abby's potato stuck in her throat. She looked at him out of the corner of her eye, dread coursing through her. He was going to spoil whatever it was that had just begun to happen. Should she speak? Dare she?

"Lizzie, I've been thinking."

Dear God, Abby thought.

Lizzie looked up from her plate, chewing slowly, thoughtfully. She took a long drink from her water, then dabbed at the corners of her mouth and waited patiently for her father to collect his thoughts.

"I think I'll give Emma the money she wants so badly, and ask her to see if she can't live with her friends there in New Bedford."

The thrill that ran up Abby's spine at her husband's words stopped dead when she saw the expression on Lizzie's face.

Andrew cleared his throat. "Or. Well. She'd be a wealthy woman by any standards. She could buy her own house there, or here in town, for that matter."

64

The expression on Lizzie's face was unreadable. There was shock there, and disbelief, but something more, something Abby couldn't identify, and it seemed to disturb Andrew as much as or more than it did her.

Lizzie's fork, forgotten in her hand, slowly lowered itself to the plate with a light *ting*.

"She's become disruptive to the family, Lizzie," Andrew said.

Lizzie was silent, her eyes still on her father's face.

"She's a grown woman, Lizzie. She should have a life of her own, in a home of her own."

Lizzie set the fork down. Abby swallowed. Her eyes darted back and forth between her stepdaughter and her husband. She silently prayed, Dear God, not something new to rend this family, please, not something new.

"I would go with her," Lizzie said quietly.

Andrew let out a sigh. "Lizzie, don't say that. Don't lets make any firm decisions about this. It was an idea, a suggestion. I say we all sleep on it tonight and then discuss it again in the morning."

"Nothing will be different in the morning, Father," Lizzie spoke in full voice. "If Emma is to leave the house, then of course I must go with her. I, too, am a grown woman, and if you think she should be on her own, then I should also."

"But the three of us," Andrew pointed his fork at Abby, "get on so well together. And it would be *better* for us, given the chance."

"There are things you don't understand, Father," Lizzie said.

"Tell me." Abby heard a wistfulness in his voice, and she knew he had lost the battle. He would never, ever let Lizzie leave his side. Never. Ever.

"She's my sister."

"So?"

"She raised me, practically." Lizzie did not look up to see the knife twist in Abby's heart.

"You may think that, child, but—"

"I'm not a child, and I do think that. I also think . . ." Lizzie put her napkin to her face.

"Go on, Lizzie."

"I also think that Emma cannot get on by herself. I think she would die. And I owe her too much to let that happen."

"That's foolish talk, girl."

"You may think that," Lizzie retorted with a small smile.

Abby wanted so much to jump in and pour out her heart. She wanted to tell Lizzie how much she loved her, how she had always loved her wonderful green-eyed little girl, and how hard it had been for her all these years, deferring always to Emma and Emma's ways. Abby wanted to come around the table and clutch Lizzie to her and say, "Please, Lizzie, make an old man and an old woman happy in their last years. Please." But the words were not there. This was a discussion between Andrew and Lizzie, and while it affected her entire life, she was not to have a say.

Pictures came to Abby's mind. Pictures of Lizzie following Emma around like a puppy. Pictures of Lizzie copying everything Emma did. Pictures of a little girl idolizing her older sister, and an older sister who took advantage of that position. Emma had been jealous of the plump baby Lizzie since the day she was born, Abby was sure. Emma treated Lizzie poorly, always telling her she had no worth, and Lizzie believed every word. Abby would spend all day with Lizzie, talking to her, making her laugh, being friends and playmates, and as soon as the front door opened with Emma home from school, gaiety vanished in the household and Lizzie was once again Emma's.

Lizzie and her father were close, but there would be nothing to break the tie that held Lizzie to Emma.

"Just think about it overnight."

"As you wish, Father. Excuse me." Lizzie folded her napkin and arose. The icy exterior had returned. For some reason it had melted during the day, this frost that had covered Lizzie for the past few years, and now it was back, horrible and cold, yet . . . yet . . . Abby hated to admit it to herself, but the coldness was familiar. It was safe. It was comfortable.

She looked at her husband and the look on his face touched her soul. Such a good man. Such a good man. She hated to see his heart break over his daughters. Again. She touched Andrew's arm and he moved it away from her.

·March

ndrew Borden looked into the mirror and carefully combed what sparse white hair the Lord had seen fit to save for his declining years. He checked his shave with a hand that trembled and then straightened his bow tie. He didn't care much for mirrors; mirrors had a way of attracting one's scrutiny, and the more one gazed upon oneself, the more attention one paid to one's appearance. Vanity was employment for the foolish, he had always believed, and so there were only the necessary mirrors in his house; hand mirrors in each bedroom and a small one downstairs, on the wall in the foyer. Especially women, he thought. Give a houseful of women a houseful of mirrors, and there will be trouble. Serious trouble.

He finished his inspection, placed the mirror facedown upon Abby's dressing table and laid his towel over the bowl filled with cold soapy water and gray whisker-shavings. The warm smell of fresh biscuits baking wafted up from the kitchen. He knew there would be gravy left over from the evening meal to enjoy with them.

He patted down his pockets. He had the rent bills, his keys, his wallet, his money clip. He left the bedroom and locked the door behind him.

It was Saturday. Andrew liked Saturdays. They were a change of pace. They bore the fruit of his labors. On Saturdays, Andrew Borden collected his rents. It was usually one of his favorite tasks. Sometimes one of the tenants could not pay, and eviction made not such a pleasant day, but he hadn't had to evict a tenant for some time.

The thought of his pockets filled with money as he came home today brightened his outlook. Almost everyone paid in cash. He'd probably even come home with a treat or two from one or another of the farms. Some fresh butter—how Abby loved that freshly churned sweet butter—or maybe some milk or eggs. The very thought of his pockets full of money and his hands full of fresh food for his wife sparked his appetite. He went downstairs ready to enjoy a full meal.

He was right. Fresh biscuits were in the warming oven. He took two, cut them open and laid them on his plate, then ladled warm gravy from the pot over them. He took his plate to the dining room, where Abby and Emma were breakfasting. Abby poured him a cup of tea.

"Good morning."

"Morning, Father."

Andrew tucked his napkin into the neck of his shirt and spread it out over his front. He cut the biscuits into deliberate squares with his knife and fork, then sipped his tea and took a bite of biscuit and gravy. It was wonderful.

"Father?"

Andrew looked up at Emma. Her eyes were on her plate. Not a good sign.

"Do you think we could put in with some remodeling this year?"

"Remodeling? The house is comfortable. It has heat."

"I know. The wood furnace was a wise investment. No, I mean some other things that might make the house a little more comfortable. Like hot water in the kitchen. And perhaps a bath and W.C. upstairs."

Andrew felt his temperature rise. "We've been over this before, Emma."

"I know. How well I know. I thought I would ask you one more time." Emma set her fork down. "I thought that perhaps you had given it some consideration and come to a *sane* conclusion for once."

Andrew heard Abby gasp. He felt his face getting red and hot. "You may be excused."

Emma threw her napkin on the table and stomped from the room. Andrew pinched and pulled the skin on his forehead.

"I'm sorry, Mr. Borden," Abby said. "I don't know why she does that at your breakfast."

"I don't know either." Andrew took a deep breath and looked squarely at his wife. "Are you inconvenienced? Would hot water from a faucet and a bath upstairs be terribly different?"

"It would be nice, I grant you that, but . . ."

"But?"

"Well, I know how business is, Mr. Borden. Money is tight, as you say, and there are other things best done first."

"That's right, Abby. If I thought for a moment that it would make a difference, a substantial difference, or even a modest difference, I would have the plumbing installed today. But we have lived thus for twenty-seven years, and I am quite accustomed."

"Emma sees the neighbors . . ."

"Dash the neighbors! I know all about the neighbors. Emma and Lizzie care too much about appearances. They ought to concentrate instead on what goes on in their minds, not what happens in their bathrooms." He looked down at the gravy cooling on his plate. It had lost all its appeal. "I must go collect rents. My tenants expect me before noon. Good day."

He set his napkin beside his plate, donned his suit coat, his overcoat and his tall black hat, picked up his umbrella, although the day looked perfectly clear, and walked out into a perfect spring morning.

He turned and looked at his house. It was not the pretentious home that his daughters would prefer. It was not built in the prestigious neighborhood on the Hill. It was a small house, an unusually narrow house, no more than twenty or so feet wide as it fronted on Second Street. And it was indeed an odd shape, as he noticed again, what with the maid's bedroom he had added as a third story only on its very back. When he bought the house, it had been a two-family dwelling. They had put in a couple of doorways in order to connect some of the rooms and that had been the end of it. As a result, the layout was unusual, with the rooms strung along like beads; getting to one meant going through the others. His and Abby's room was only accessible from the back stairs off the kitchen, as was the maid's tiny cubicle, just above their room. The girls' rooms and the guest room were gotten to from the front stairs off the sitting room and parlor.

Yes, it was an odd little house, pinched a bit, he supposed, but it was serviceable, and he was in no mood to move to a new house at this stage in his life. Nor was he about to have the house torn up so pipes could be wandering about.

And so, dismissing his decision as being right, Andrew sniffed the air. He smelled the campfire scent of the cookstoves busy heating kitchens in the neighborhood. He smelled loamy earth awakening from the winter. He smelled the horses on the streets, their leathers freshly waxed and proud. The world seemed new, and Andrew felt like striding importantly down the street. All the dim unsettledness of the household was left behind, and it only came to mind when he caught a whiff of his overcoat, permeated as it was with the scent of the Borden home. And even then, the familial troubles seemed vague. Unreal.

At the corner in town, he stopped and pulled out his package of rent bills. He shuffled through them, knowing all the while which one was first. He always traveled the same route. He began his Saturday in town and finished it at the farm in Swansea. Whenever he added a new property to his portfolio, he would sit and plan the rerouting of his rent-collecting to include the new tenants. His method was efficient; he didn't want any unexpected inconveniences to mar the pleasure he got from his Saturdays.

He turned left down Main Street and passed the First Congregational Church. He'd be walking down this way again tomorrow morning, with his wife, if she felt up to it. Lately, Abby had taken to preferring to stay at home of a Sunday morning. But Andrew would be there with her or without her, and he would sit in the Borden pew with his two daughters. Lizzie taught Sunday school, and would have to be there an hour before the worship service, so she didn't join him on his Sunday walk to town. Perhaps Emma would. Perhaps Emma would take kindly to a Sunday stroll through town and perhaps the Lord would smile down on Emma and remove some of the bitterness that ruled her life.

Andrew collected all three rents due in town. Every tenant was home; every tenant expected his visit; every tenant had cash in the right amount ready and waiting for him. Feeling flush with the successes of his life, he walked around to the livery stable to borrow the carriage belonging to the bank so he could collect his money in the outlying areas.

The stable boy had the horse dressed and ready. Andrew climbed up into the seat and flicked the reins, turning the rig down the street and out of town.

Fall River was a small town, but even so, it had its ethnic sub-areas. There were areas filled with Poles, the Irish had their little town-within-a-town, the Italians had a neighborhood; Andrew rode through them all, keeping his eyes straight ahead, keeping his nostrils from breathing too deeply the odors of their nationalities. Andrew preferred town. He knew town. He owned some of town and was comfortable there. That was where he had raised his family, and where he would stay until the day he died.

The farm properties were very nice, and if Andrew ever gave a thought to retiring, he imagined being on the farm alongside the creek where he used to take the family for leisurely weekend vacations and where he took the girls fishing when they were younger. But Andrew and his family belonged in town.

Remembering those earlier times, those carefree times made him eager to drive out to the country. He snapped the reins and clucked the mare into a little more speed.

The buggy he was driving was not a particularly comfortable one; the springs squeaked and the leather seat was cracked and poorly patched in two places. But the bank was making money and as long as Andrew Borden had a say in its financial affairs—that is, its expenditures—the buggy was perfectly suitable as it was.

They trotted out of town onto a poorer road, one quite muddy with the spring thaw, and badly rutted. Andrew slowed the horse and found the change in countryside refreshing.

The fields were greening after being snow-covered for months. The air was fresh; there were even some newborn lambs curled up and sleeping as their mothers grazed beside them. The buggy carried Andrew over a clattering bridge that covered a swollen stream, muddied with runoff from the melt. He pulled his overcoat a little tighter around him. And he wished he'd brought Lizzie along for company.

Lizzie used to go with him when she was just a little thing. She used to sit jostling alongside him on this very same seat leather and talking a blue streak, asking questions about everything they saw, everyone they passed. A warm knot pressed against his breastbone as he thought of Lizzie. She was, without a doubt, the most precious thing that had ever happened in his life.

He worried about her, mostly about those dratted head-aches she got that made her so sick. They were the same headaches her mother used to get. Sarah, Lizzie's mother, had had headaches so bad she would fall unconscious to the floor. Andrew remembered Emma running to him the first time it happened; she must have been three or so, and she was shrieking and shrieking that her mama was dead, she was *dead,* she was DEAD! and Andrew found her lying uncon-scious on the kitchen floor. He carried her to their bedroom, and within a half hour she was awake, her headache gone. In its place, of course, was a large purple knot where she had hit her head as she fell. Dr. Bowen came right over when Andrew ran to fetch him, and he prescribed a sedative, which Sarah wouldn't take.

Dr. Bowen saw Sarah for many problems. Sarah had those headaches, and she had terrible tantrums, fits of rage so bizarre that Andrew used to take Emma and leave the house. He never knew if the house would still be there when they returned. He feared for the safety of his daughter when he was off at work all day, but nothing she did seemed to trigger her mother's spells. That always happened when he was around to rescue Emma and get her out of range. Sarah had a mighty throwing arm and she threw everything she could get her hands on. And her face screwed up into a mockery of humanity and turned purple-red. She would rage, using foul language and all, stomping and kicking, biting and scratch-ing when he got too close to her, and he would grab up Emma and run for a neighbor's house.

When the storm was over, Sarah would cry for hours, sometimes days, apologizing over and over. She didn't know what had gotten into her, she said, and her remorse was indeed pitiful. Her face would be swollen from crying, her eyes red, lost in the puffy tissue around them. Andrew couldn't bear to see her in such misery, but she would not be consoled.

When Emma was five years old, Sarah gave birth to Alice, who screamed from the moment she came into the world. Alice screamed so loudly and so long that the whole household was set on edge. She would not stop screaming in order to eat, and Sarah grew gaunt and hollow watching her baby daughter starving to death. On the third night, when Sarah had fallen unconscious from exhaustion, with Andrew by her side, the baby died.

Sarah's "spells" grew ever more vicious after that.

These spells put Andrew in a terrible frame of mind. He became frantic for a cure. Dr. Bowen could do nothing. He found no reason for the rages, and though he tried prescribing this and that, Andrew knew that Sarah took none of the medication.

Sarah had told him there would be no more children, but when she was well, she was so beautiful to his eyes, and playful, and . . .

Four years after the infant Alice Borden died, Sarah found herself again with child. Fear took over her life. For entire days at a time, she would sit, immobilized by the possibility that the life she felt moving within her would scream until its death. Andrew would walk Emma to her school, and Sarah would be sitting on the sofa when he left. When he returned, she would be sitting in the same place, and she would not even know that he had been gone. Emma learned to care for herself.

Fear for the baby's life almost consumed Sarah. He had to remind her to eat. Emma was entirely ignored. Andrew prayed for a healthy son, one he could name after himself, one who would grow up strong to be a man for his mother when Andrew grew older.

And a girl was born. Sarah snapped back to life when the

greedy little mouth suckled so efficiently, and she was lost in rapture, cooing to the fat, pink little creature.

This would be their last child. Andrew would not have his son. He named her Andrew anyway. Lizzie Andrew Borden.

For a while, Sarah's health improved. Ten-year-old Emma began to receive attention again, as her help was needed in the house. The baby Lizzie grew pudgy and healthy, and Sarah doted on her.

And then, about the time Baby Lizzie began to walk, the spells returned. Again, Andrew was snatching up the children and taking them out of harm's way.

Andrew's hopes for a normal, happy home life vanished, and he mourned those shattered dreams every day. But he loved Sarah more than he thought anybody could ever love another human being. So he lived with her rages. And her headaches. And the fainting spells that accompanied them and seemed to be more than just fainting spells. She would be fine one moment, a graceful hand to her temple, her eyes just a little bit off center from the headache pain, trying to manage her household just the same, and the next moment she would be slumped in her chair or lying on the floor, absolutely unconscious. Not in a swoon, but as if she were dead.

And then she did die. She'd fixed him a fine breakfast, seen him off to work and twelve-year-old Emma off to school, and was feeding baby Lizzie in her high chair when he left. When Emma came home from school, Lizzie was still in her high chair and Sarah was dead on the dining-room floor.

Emma calmly walked down the street to where Dr. Bowen lived and had his medical practice, brought him home with her and tended to the baby while Dr. Bowen attended Sarah. When Andrew, summoned, came home, Emma handed him the baby and then went to pieces.

Like her mother, Emma did what had to be done in a crisis. And like her mother, Emma raged. Andrew had long ago given up on changing Emma's behavior. A stronger will he had never seen in his life. He had even ceased to worry over her. She would go off, fueled by the fever of resentment, and be gone for weeks at a time. Then, when she returned, she would take to her bed for equally long, recovering from whatever damage her rages had done to her. Emma was a strong one, all right. She seemed able to handle herself. And if one day she ran off and never came back . . . well . . . that would be all right, too. It wasn't that Andrew didn't love Emma, for he did. But she had abraded that love until it was lusterless and shabby.

Emma never got over the death of her mother. It was during Emma's formative years that Sarah Borden put her through the worst tests of all, and then died when Emma was at the most sensitive age of twelve. No wonder the poor girl had grown to be a humorless woman. Emma blamed Andrew for Sarah's death. She made that very clear from the first moment. He didn't take good enough care of Sarah, or he made her work too hard, or he didn't hire a nanny for Lizzie though he knew that his wife was prone to those terrible headaches.

And Andrew wasn't so sure he didn't agree.

As a result, Andrew and Emma always appeared to be viewing the family—and life itself—from opposite angles. They seemed to be fighting even when there was nothing to fight about. They seemed opposed on every matter. Whether they were or not, Andrew always felt as if they were.

Emma blamed him and Andrew blamed himself. Upon that one issue they did agree. Upon that one issue and no other.

Sometimes it was very hard for Andrew to look at his family. Theirs was not a picture he cared to have on his desk. He did not brag about his wife and children the way other men did. He did not flaunt them about town. He used to, but those were younger, freer times. Life had taken Andrew's grief for a picture-perfect family and twisted it tightly around him.

Andrew pulled the buggy up in front of the first farmhouse, scattering a half dozen scraggly chickens. These tenants were not to Andrew's liking, being so private and personal about their affairs. Both husband and wife worked in the mill, and they left their children with Irish people during the day. He set the brake, found their rent bill in his pocket and got down from the buggy with weary legs.

They took care of the building and grounds, but the whole area smelled like the goats he heard in the back. The smell grew stronger as he walked toward the house.

The woman opened the door. "Mr. Borden," she said, smiling with bad teeth.

"I've come for the rent," he said, and handed the white bill toward her.

She shushed her children and slipped out the doorway to stand in the sunshine with him. She was disheveled and dumpy.

"Mr. Borden, my Howard took to his sick bed last Wednesday and didn't pick up his pay envelope on Friday. He's better now, and will be a-going to work on Monday. Can he drop the rent 'round your office then?"

Andrew thought of the husband that belonged to this woman standing in his bank office, smelling of goat and Lord knew what else.

"I collect the rents on Saturday, madam."

"Yes, I know, Mr. Borden, we been rentin' from you now for two years, and we always had the rent on your Saturdays. But this time, well, Howard just got so sick, and you know they wouldn't let *me* pick up his pay envelope . . ."

"I will confiscate his last paycheck, take the rent plus a

surcharge for my trouble, and he can pick up the balance of his pay."

"Surcharge?"

"Yes. It costs me time and money to come out here every Saturday. If you're not going to have the rent for me, then I must charge you for my time."

"How much, do you think? We barely make ends meet. . . ."

"One dollar."

The woman's hand fluttered to her throat. "A dollar? Mr. Borden, that would feed us for a week, what with raising our own goat milk and hogs and all."

"Then you should have your rent here on time."

The woman looked at the porch. Andrew felt ill at ease. It was these people who made him ill at ease. He didn't like their kind, not at all, and as soon as he could get them off his property, he would likely rent to a higher class of folk.

"Mr. Borden," the woman said, "would you please take some goat cheese to the missus?"

"If you fetch it in a hurry," he said.

She did, and he walked, itching, back to the buggy. He knew that she hoped the paltry gift of goat cheese would help ease the penalty. Well, maybe it would and maybe it wouldn't.

He climbed back into the seat, his ill-temper making the horse fidget. He took off the brake and snapped the reins. He knew the woman still stood on the porch, but he gave her no backward glance.

Now if Lizzie were here, he thought, she would say something gay, and the ride to the next farmhouse would be pleasant on this spring morning. Instead, he knew that he would grumble to himself the rest of the way, running through his mind things he should have said to his tenant, preparing what to say to the next tenants if they should try the same story with him.

He missed Lizzie on these rides, but he could understand her refusal to join him. Shame turned the spring day dark for Andrew as he thought about his sweet Lizzie and the terrible things he did to her on these trips.

It started years ago, when Andrew worked as an undertaker. He was frequently called to the outlying areas to confer with families, retrieve corpses and collect money. More often than not, these rides were less than joyous, so he would take Lizzie with him to elevate the atmosphere. It was his job to view the dead bodies of these people, and those who died from sickness or accident didn't bother him. It was the ones who died old who haunted all his moments. He feared for himself when age began to take its toll.

Lizzie would chatter all the way out and, little girl as she was, usually slept the whole way back, completely tuckered out from the fresh air and sunshine. She always brought along a blanket, and she would sleep curled on the seat next to him when she was little, with her head on his lap when she got a little older, and then in the backseat as she got too old to do that.

And when she was asleep, he began to talk to her. He told her things he would never tell another soul, never. He talked to her in a way that was quite surprising to himself; and every time he took off for the country, his angel of a little girl with him, he would promise himself not to talk to her in "that way" anymore.

But he seemed to have no control over the strange behavior that erupted during those moments.

They would jog along, the filly making a nice little trot over unused roads in the backcountry. Lizzie would be asleep next to him, her reddish-gold hair shining and blowing in the wind. He would reach down and put a work-hardened hand on her head and the very idea of her being his daughter would stun him.

82

He began to make promises to her. He promised her money, gold, health, happiness, a husband who would adore her, a house on the Hill, servants who knew how to serve, wealth and glory. He told her about the workings of business and the workings of life—as Andrew Borden saw them, not always a pretty picture. He told her of his life as a young man, of his family and the struggle he had to make a financial gain in Fall River.

And the more he talked, the more he realized that he struggled so hard for *her*. For her sake and for no other reason. He worked himself harder than he had any right to ask of an employee. He was amassing his fortune for her. Just for her. His purpose for being was to provide for his daughter, *this* daughter, and as the realization took place over several weeks, he realized also what would happen were he ever to make good on all his promises.

She would move away. She would move away and marry some man unworthy of her beauty, unworthy of her talents, unworthy of her affections and attentions. She would take everything he had given her—his *life*, for the love of God—and she would dismiss him just as the new generation dismissed the corpses of the old people he hauled.

From the time he understood the depth of deception that would take place were his unselfish, loving gifts received, Andrew Borden tried to hold his tongue and found that he could not.

And his running monologue toward his sleeping daughter grew more bizarre, even to his own ears.

Worse, he occasionally wondered if she was really asleep, or if she just pretended because she knew he would begin to bare his soul to her somnolent form as soon as he saw evidence she could no longer hear him.

He began innocently enough, talking of her future, and ended up talking of his future. He would describe to her, in lurid detail, every inch of his failing flesh. He would talk of incontinence and bedsores. He would ask her over and over again, the rawness of the question salt to his wound, if she would still love him, still care for him, still bring him tea and read to him when he was not fit for company other than that of the grave worms. He would imagine himself wrinkled beyond compare, old, old, a hundred years and more, drooling, blind, palsied, and he would describe the breakfast-table scene, for example, once Lizzie had carried him down to the table. He would go on and on about how she had to feed him and how irritable and mean he would be. He drew such scenes in great detail, always at the end wondering, agonizing, if she would continue to stand by him.

He wanted to know if there would be a line, further than which she would not go in her love for him. He had to know that boundary of Lizzie's affections, for he wished to die before crossing it.

But she was always asleep, and never answered those questions. As a result, they burned within him, brighter and brighter as each week went by.

And because he could never voice those terrible, detailed worries to her face, he resented the fact that he was so emotionally dependent upon her approval.

And he began to shame her in public.

This was the crux of the matter, as far as Lizzie was concerned. She would no longer accompany him on his Saturdays, because surely at one time or another, he would insult her or speak falsely about her to someone of Fall River or its environs, and Lizzie would never hear an apology.

He hated himself every time he did it; but how could he ever explain to her that she was the one who made him do it? She was the one. She was the entire reason for his existence. She drove him to conduct business that was sometimes unethical for collection of the dollar. She drove him to mutter to her sleeping form. She drove him to marry that Abby woman because he knew she needed a female besides poor, disturbed Emma to help bring her up. She was the one who made him tightfisted with the money, his money, *her* money, so she would never be able to fulfill all those disloyalties he was sure she harbored in her heart.

And, in fact, hadn't he proved it? He gave her money for a trip abroad, then begged her not to go. Did she listen to him? Not for a second. She made arrangements and was gone for six weeks. Six weeks during which he thought he would expire from worry and frustration. Six weeks without the light of his life plunged him into a dark depression so severe he wasn't sure he would ever come out to see the light of day again.

And then when she returned, his world righted itself and the family went on as a whole once more. It was as if nothing had changed. And nothing had, really, except that now Lizzie corresponded, a little too enthusiastically for his peace of mind, with a friend from Britain. That couldn't be too bad a thing, as long as he made sure she had no money to visit there.

His dependence on her shamed him. And for that, he shamed her among her peers.

And that made her angry. Angry enough to change churches! To change churches, after he bought the Borden pew at the First Congregational!

But Andrew couldn't blame her. She was angry at him, and with just cause. He hated to see her angry, but anger was all right. The girl had fire, and that was one of the wondrous things about her. She had fire in the midst of a houseful of ice.

Andrew sighed. There were many things in life that he could do nothing about. He snapped the reins. But his tenants and their rents were not among them.

He looked down at the package of goat cheese as it rode alongside him on the buggy seat. Those people made a fine cheese. I imagine that would fetch two bits at market today, he thought. I'll stop there on my way home. No sense in letting it go to waste.

I t didn't take Lizzie long to realize that if she were going to do the exercises in the book Beatrice had sent, she would need some privacy. She never knew when Emma would come barging through, and she needed to concentrate, particularly when she started on the second exercise in the book.

So, as soon as the weather turned warm, Lizzie packed up candles, candlesticks, book and a few other personalizations, and took them to the hayloft in the barn.

The barn was an old stable, but Andrew had gotten rid of the lone horse over two years ago. Since then it had been used for practically nothing—a little storage space, but nothing really. Lizzie enjoyed the barn. When she was young, she used to love to go upstairs into the loft and look down upon the horse, smelling his richness. Even after he was no longer there, she still liked to go up and lie in the dusty hay and read of a long summer afternoon.

And she needed a place of her own. A private place to be, to read, to study. It was central to the exercises in the book. The barn was perfect.

Emma had been in the kitchen getting started on the evening meal the day Lizzie began to move her study to the barn.

"Where are you going with those candles?"

"To the barn."

"The barn? What on earth for?"

"I like to go out there and read, you know, and sometimes I can't read when the sun goes behind the tree in the afternoon."

"You'll set the whole place on fire."

"No, I don't think so."

"Sounds like a stupid idea to me," Emma said. "Young women just don't read in the barn. They read in the sitting room."

Lizzie unlatched the screen door and walked out into the fresh spring air. It was a beautiful day. The pear trees were filled with blossoms. The neighbors were all out working in their yards. Lizzie took a deep breath and smiled.

The barn door swung open with its customary creak and Lizzie made a mental note to oil the hinges so she could come and go from her place without the entire neighborhood knowing it.

There was a small tack room on the left and a workbench area on the right. Father had sold all the tack, but the smell of oiled leather remained in the small room. The workshop area was filled to overflowing with piles of magazines, broken machines that her father fully intended to have mended someday—when he found someone who didn't want to charge him an arm and a leg to do it—a small pile of kindling that had lasted through the winter and boxes and crates of miscellaneous junk. Two empty horse stalls were next, their damp dirt floors smelling musty. They needed some fresh straw. The barn would smell hot and dusty as the summer wore on, but for now, Lizzie thought about putting some fresh straw in the stalls to freshen up the air and get rid of the moldy stench of a wet winter just passed.

She put the candles and candlesticks in a pocket of her duster, then climbed the ladder to the hayloft.

There were two piles of hay at the top, both brown and dusty. Lizzie had long thought about forking them down and using them as winter cover on the garden, but the garden was fairly overgrown anyway, sorely neglected, and the hay was where she lay to read. She thought of cleaning it all up, bringing table and chairs, maybe even a cot or sleeping mat of some sort.

She set the candlesticks on the windowsill, then flopped down into the hay. She'd have to buy a new mirror, and then hide it, for surely Emma would come up to investigate, to ascertain that Lizzie wasn't doing something Emma didn't approve of up in the loft.

The room needed a table of some sort, something to set the mirror and candles upon.

Lizzie jumped up, climbed down the ladder, emptied a produce crate of its load of mildewed magazines, tamped the dust out of it, then threw it up to the loft and climbed back up after it.

The box was perfect. Lizzie plumped the haystack up a bit to provide a backrest, set the box down and put the candles on top of it. She had an old silk scarf that would lend an air of elegance to the setting. Up she jumped again, and climbed down the ladder.

This reminded her of a "fort" she'd made as a little girl. It was out at the farm in Swansea. It was a secret place of her own. There was an old willow tree that had been storm-damaged and it leaned over all to one side. The curtains of willow leaves provided a wonderful green translucent screen, which let in plenty of light and no other eyes. Lizzie stole a scissors from the kitchen and very carefully cut the green trailing fingers out of the center, apologizing to the tree the whole way. Then she brought a pillow and her favorite picture book, a doll and some cookies. And whiled away a long summer day.

She heard Emma call her and it made her giggle behind her hand, even as her heart pounded, wondering if Emma would give her a spank for being naughty. She *was* being naughty, hiding from her sister, hiding from her mother, and she knew it, but that little green room in the middle of the

89

tree was just a treasure. She couldn't bear to leave it, she couldn't bear to have Emma find it, she knew it had to be hers, though probably hers only for just that day.

So she put her head on her pillow and played with the baby doll and ate cookies while she listened to Emma and her mother call and call and call.

That night she was sent to bed without supper, but Lizzie didn't mind. She didn't get a spank, she got a hug and a lecture from Mother instead. Emma told her that she had better things to do, so the next time Lizzie wanted to disappear for the day to just bloody well tell someone so Abby didn't make Emma run around hollering for her all day long.

Lizzie had forgotten all about that day. She wondered if the pillow and the doll were still in the midst of that tree. She wondered if another child had found that wonderful, peaceful paradise within that living, fragrant room. She'd ask Father if she could accompany him the next time he went out to the farm. She'd like to look for that old tree and see. She'd like to go out to the farm and spend some time in the quiet. Fishing. She'd like to go fishing.

She wondered if this was the way Beatrice felt the first day she rented her first flat in the city, and had a home of her own.

In her room, Lizzie got that silk scarf she'd envisioned, a needlepoint pillow and her hand mirror. She'd get another mirror the next time she went to town, but for now she was anxious to do her exercises again in her new space, to see if things were different.

Abby was busy with Maggie doing the spring cleaning, so nobody noticed, really, when Lizzie left by the back door. Even so, she stopped at the barn door to make sure she was going in unseen.

I'll have to get a latch for the door, she thought, so it can be locked from the inside. Then she climbed up the ladder, which always made her feel like a man, and began to rearrange.

When everything was in its place up at the hayloft, it looked like a shrine. Lizzie stepped back to the edge of the loft and surveyed her new room. It did look like a shrine. Like an altar, with *Pathways,* the Beatrice book, lying on the center of the overturned crate like a bible.

The book. The marvelous book. Even though it admonished her not to, Lizzie had read a few of the later exercises. All harmless. All, in fact, seemed a little bit ridiculous, just like the one she just performed with the candles and the mirror, but she had faith that Beatrice would not steer her wrong.

Each exercise was to be done for a full thirty days, so she was still only on the second exercise. Her letters to Beatrice were full of questions: Who wrote this book? Why? Who publishes it? How is it distributed? Can I buy copies? Why is it so mysterious? What will the end result be?

And Beatrice, cool, with her written British accent so clear in Lizzie's head, told her to mind her lessons and more understanding would eventually come. But cool as she might seem regarding Lizzie's strict adherence to the rules governing the lessons, she was overwhelmingly pleased that Lizzie was such an ardent student.

The first exercise was nothing more than two paragraphs to be read aloud three times a day for thirty days.

Within each individual reside many others. Your personality is made up of an infinite number of facets, continually turning and twinkling in the ever-present Light of Life. When we take control of our lives, we design the patterns of light. We line up the personality facets to accomplish that which we were born to do.

I now claim that which is divinely mine. I claim absolute control over each fragment of my personality, to be strengthened through purposeful, conscious unity. I now will that the Divine Power which motors the Universe now deed me the control over my own destiny. I now claim that I, and no other, am the architect of my future. I now command my rightful, unique place in the order of all material. So it is, so shall it be.

It was written with Lizzie in mind, she was sure. She'd never read anything like it before. It reminded her that she was responsible for her own emotions, attitudes and future. It mentioned God, and it seemed to suggest a spiritual way of life, both of which Lizzie approved. And when Lizzie read the passage aloud, especially the "I now claim" part, her heart pounded, and it felt to her as if it really *meant* something. She hoped it wasn't wishful thinking.

The second exercise was even stranger. She was to light two candles, and place one on either side of a mirror. Then she was to sit in the dark and view her face in the mirror for no less than one-half hour. Every day for thirty days.

At first, she could not do it. Her face turned gargoyle within three minutes, and her eyes, always pale, seemed to dissolve and fade away, leaving only empty sockets through which she could see unpleasant things floating about.

It was a week before she could spend fifteen full minutes at the task, and another week before a half hour passed and she could still view herself without nausea.

It could have been the setting—the darkness, the mystery surrounding the exercises in the book—it could have been the shadows the candlelight threw upon her face, or it could have been that she was fresh from the "within each individual reside many others" exercise, but the face that Lizzie saw in the mirror was not her own. It was close, it was very close, but it seemed to be just slightly foreign. It was almost her, but not quite.

92

Regardless, she started counting her thirty days from the day she first spent thirty minutes. Beatrice complimented Lizzie on her thoroughness. "Cheating on the exercises will not harm you, Lizbeth," she said, "but it could invalidate some of the work you're doing. Invest this time in yourself. Do it right and reap the full benefits." And in the meantime, to fill the other twenty-three and a half hours in every day, Beatrice suggested some books Lizzie could read, most of them on business. "Business is just busy-ness, Lizbeth," she said. "Life is about getting on with other people. And the more you practice, the better you get at it. But before you can practice successfully, you must have a fine image of yourself. The exercises will give you personal power. The books on business will tell you how to act with others. Be sure of yourself. Be bold. Be adventurous." And then she'd sign off with the inevitable "Affectionately, Beatrice."

Lizzie would hug those letters to herself, knowing that the next time she met Beatrice, she would not be a fumbling fool. She would be well practiced, bold, adventurous and self-assured.

Yes. Soon she would be ready to be a fit friend for Beatrice. But would she ever be ready for her father?

Lizzie lay back against the hay and thought about her father. He was becoming increasingly odd. A function of age, surely, Lizzie thought, as he'd always been quite eccentric; but of late he had become most abusive.

In church two Sundays ago, for example, he told the organist that Lizzie couldn't carry a tune even if it had two handles. Then he went on to explain that the laundry basket had two handles and she didn't seem to be able to carry it, either. Lizzie and old Mrs. Watkins listened in horrified silence as he expounded further on Lizzie's laziness. Lizzie finally turned and walked away.

Andrew caught up with her several paces down the church walk, catching up her arm in his hard little fingers.

Lizzie pulled away from him.

"Don't you dare walk away from me like that. You embarrassed me."

"*I* embarrassed *you*? Father, how could you say those things to Mrs. Watkins—especially since they weren't at all true. I can sing, you know I can sing. And your laundry doesn't go wanting, either." Lizzie felt herself near tears and that infuriated her.

Her father looked at her with astonishment. "It was said in jest, Lizzie."

"No, it wasn't, Father," she said, her breath coming in gulps. "It was said in meanness." Lizzie stalked away from him, fuming. She was conscious of him walking about two paces behind her, silent, all the way home.

She fumbled about while trying to unlock the front door, and when she couldn't fit the key in the lock because of the tears of rage and hurt that befuddled her, Andrew calmly took her keys, unlocked the front door, turned the knob and pushed it open. Angry though she was—angry too about her failure to control her emotion—when her father came and performed the simple task she seemed unable to do for herself, she felt small and cared-for. A surge of unbidden and unwelcome affection warmed her. But she took her keys from him without looking at him, and went upstairs to her room and locked the door behind her.

Emma was in her room, Lizzie could hear her rocking chair, and she hoped that Emma would stay there. She was in no mood to talk about family matters, or the sermon or Sunday School or anything else.

She flopped on her bed, fists clenched, wondering why he did such things—he always treated her poorly in public—and her gaze landed on the book from Beatrice.

She felt an immediate change in attitude. Instantly, the anger and frustration melted and she wondered how she could have handled the situation better. How could she have been more bold, more adventurous, more in control?

She could have laughed at his "jesting," and made light of it.

She could have turned to him calmly and gently, told him and Mrs. Watson both that those things were not true and asked him to explain himself.

Either one of those things would have been a far superior reaction than stomping off and crying. Either one of those things would have been far more adult. She would have been in control. She could have been self-assured.

The rocking stopped in Emma's room and Lizzie held her breath. Oh God, don't let her come in here.

But the key turned in the lock and Emma's door opened. "How was church?"

"Fine." Lizzie hoped if she kept to monosyllabic answers, Emma would take the hint and go away.

"I'm going down for a bite. Can I bring you something?"

"No."

"I think there's a piece of pie left."

"That would be nice, thank you."

"Is everything all right, Lizzie?"

"Yes," she said, but the anger returned in full force. Her fists clenched, and Emma noticed before she could relax them.

"You had a tiff with Father again?"

"He *insulted* me in front of Mrs. Watkins."

"Mrs. Watkins?"

"The organist at church."

"Oh, pooh."

"Yes, I know, it doesn't mean much in front of the organist, but why does he do that? He always does that. He *always* does that in front of other people."

Emma sat on the edge of Lizzie's bed, the last thing

Lizzie wanted. She wanted to puzzle this out in her own way—in Beatrice's way—in her own time. She wanted to be forgiving instead of complaining, but old habits died hard. She didn't want Emma to be interfering, confusing her with her twisted ideas of Father's behavior.

"If I were you," Emma said, "I would tell him that unless he can behave himself like a gentleman, he can bloody well find himself another escort. And then I would change churches."

Lizzie was speechless. She just stared at Emma. Emma patted her leg, got up and slipped out the door.

Change churches. Find a new start. A new pastor. A new Sunday school class.

All things new again. All things new. Beginning a new life, *starting down a new Pathway. I now command my unique and rightful place in the order of all things material.* It was a wonderful idea.

Lizzie had immediately changed churches. Last Sunday morning she had turned right when her father turned left, and had gone to the Central Congregational Church. To her delight, it was populated with people who lived on the Hill, exactly the new type of friends Lizzie was interested in making. And she immediately took a Sunday school class of Oriental children and joined the Christian Endeavor Society.

For the sad person Emma had turned out to be, now and then she had a good idea.

But there was nothing at all good about her ideas in New Bedford.

When Emma came limping home from her January trip, her face darkly veiled, she took to her bed for two weeks. Lizzie brought her meals up, but Emma would hide her face with the covers.

Only when the bruises began to pale and turn yellowish did Emma, starved for company, allow Lizzie to see her.

She had taken quite a beating. Her lip was split, her eye

was blackened, and there was a big bruise high on one cheekbone. She moved about in bed with severe discomfort, so Lizzie knew that the damage was not limited to her face. How could she? How *could* she?

And the worst thing, Lizzie knew, was that within another six to eight months, Emma would return to New Bedford for like treatment. It made Lizzie sick to her stomach.

But every time she tried to talk to Emma about it, Emma turned her head. It was something that was not to be discussed.

And in the two weeks during which Emma was bedridden, neither Andrew nor Abby had come to visit her in her room. Not once.

Not that Emma would have seen them; but not once did either of them make an effort, and Lizzie knew that Emma would have enjoyed refusing them admittance.

So Lizzie had changed churches, and knowing that her father had to explain the change to everyone in Fall River gave her a naughty little glee. It was a welcome respite from the guilt that always resided within her. She could never live up to the person he needed her to be.

Beatrice never had to live up to unreasonable expectations like that, did she? No. That was one of the most attractive things about Beatrice. She never strived for anyone else's approval. Lizzie felt boxed in most of the time, scrabbling for the approval of those who would never grant it.

She wanted her father to be proud of her, but clearly she had failed him in every way. He ridiculed her and humiliated her in front of others. He never missed an opportunity to shame her, especially in front of her friends and those people who counted in the community. But this was nothing new. Andrew had been saying terrible things about her, in front of her, since she was a little girl.

And she went out of her way to be a good daughter. She tried to keep peace in the family—not an easy task. She took off his boots every day when he came home for a rest. She rubbed his feet. She brought his tea. She read to him every day. She looked presentable and kept a good house.

And there were certain things that let her know, in spite of his actions, that he did love her, that he did approve of her. One was the trip he bought for her to go abroad with her church friends. That was an extravagant expense for him. He'd never done anything like that for Emma. Or Abby, for that matter.

Another reason she thought he really did love her was the way he fawned over her during their afternoon "visiting." He always mentioned something about growing old, and he always needed to extract her promise never to leave him. But that kind of need was different from approval for herself as a woman, as a person, as a contributing member of the family in particular and society in general. No, that he *needed* her, Lizzie had no doubt. But whether he *liked* her was another matter entirely.

And then there was the ring. If there was one single thread of proof that Andrew Borden loved his daughter, it was that he wore her high school ring on his pinky finger.

She had never been a scholar, and had not finished high school, but when all her classmates were buying their class rings, Lizzie saved her allowance and purchased hers along with the rest of them. She wore it proudly on the ring finger of her right hand. It was gold, with a yellow stone, and it had her initials on the inside.

Some months after Lizzie got the ring, a boy walked her home from school. That night, Emma told Lizzie that she would do better to be at home where an eye could be kept on things that were important, rather than frittering time away on silly social matters and the kind of schooling that taught people nothing but nonsense. Emma forbade Lizzie to see the boy again and withdrew her from school.

Lizzie didn't put up much of a fight about it—she wasn't very good at school, and it was true, much of the lessons were nonsense. She was not at all interested in the boy, but she found Emma's reaction to be quite amusing.

The next day, Lizzie was home when her father came home at noon. Lizzie, bored and missing her classmates on her first day of leisure, made him a fine meal and served him in the sitting room. She took off his boots and rubbed his feet. She waited on him and fluttered around him like a little bird.

When he finished eating, Andrew folded his napkin and set it on the tray next to his plate.

"That was very good."

Lizzie beamed.

"Come sit next to me, my dear." Lizzie snuggled up to him, and he put his long arm around her shoulder. "Have you decided against school, then?"

Lizzie nodded.

"It's just as well," he said. "There are better things. Education causes more trouble than it cures. You stay home here and let Emma and Abby teach you how to be a good woman, a good wife, good housekeeper. Those are skills that will do you more good in the long run."

Lizzie nodded against his chest.

"I love you, Lizzie. You are the most beautiful thing that has ever come into my life."

Overcome with affection for this man who so rarely spoke of love and beauty, Lizzie slipped the gold ring from her finger and put it on his. It only fit his pinky. But there she left it, and she never saw him without it again.

Surely he valued her, surely he approved of the woman she had become. Otherwise, he would put the ring in the drawer, or conveniently lose it, or something—wouldn't he? Of course he would.

But though he loved her, Andrew would never approve of Lizzie, because Lizzie was not a boy. Andrew wanted a son so badly he named her Lizzie Andrew Borden in disappointment, for he knew that she would be his last child. He would have no son to pass the family business to, he would have no son to teach the ropes of wealth accumulation. He would have no son, and he would have no grandson, and he was bitter and resentful.

Try as she might, Lizzie would never gain her father's approval. She was guilty of far too many infractions.

Emma had never approved of Lizzie, and never would. Emma had her ideas of how Lizzie should behave at all times. Emma had *standards,* and Lizzie would never rise to meet them. They were far beyond her. Emma had been charged by their dead mother with Lizzie's upbringing, and she had taken that task so totally to heart that it had left her mirthless, ruthless and disapproving at every turn. Emma didn't have a hard heart, but her heart had cooled over years of life's disappointments.

Lizzie had neither the taste, nor the good manners, nor the good breeding that Emma thought she ought to have, nor did Lizzie have the inclination to gain the same. Lizzie loved Emma, was devoted to her, but Emma wanted a small model of their mother in Lizzie, and Lizzie clearly had little in common with their mother. And even if she had, Emma had enlarged their mother's memory to goddess proportions, so Lizzie could never match her expectations. And Lizzie, in fact, had little enough in common with Emma.

Abby Borden would never see the family resemblance to a Durfee or a Gray in Lizzie's face. Lizzie knew how terrible it must be to have to raise another woman's children, never to be able to see one's likeness in the face of a child. Abby was thirty-seven years old when she met and married Andrew

Borden, a last-minute move that saved her from the curse of spinsterhood. She was too old to begin raising another woman's children at that age; she resented Lizzie. She tried only to have Andrew's attentions *and Andrew's money,* and other than that, she paid little attention to Emma and Lizzie. She was busier with her duties as midwife's assistant, and with her young half sister, who was more like a daughter to her than the Borden girls.

Sarah Whitehead, Abby's half sister, was a year younger than Lizzie, but had made some poor choices in life; and Abby seemed to take on Sarah's life as a puzzle that must be solved once and for all. For all the good that did. Sarah continued to get herself in the family way, something that Abby had never done, something that exasperated her no end. It secretly delighted Lizzie, and openly delighted Emma. Emma gloated over every little wrong turn in poor Sarah's life.

Abby had her own interests and they did not include Lizzie.

Lizzie had only herself to please. She would claim her rightful place in the order of the Universe. She need please no one else but herself and Beatrice, for Beatrice had no preconceived expectations.

Bold, adventurous, self-assured. From now on, Lizzie would do as she pleased and hang the lot of them.

Lizzie looked out the barn window. It was a beautiful spring day. Yes. The weather had turned, and while it was still cool enough to wear a coat in the barn, soon it would be summer, and she could while the entire day away in the loft.

She wet the wicks of the candles to be sure they were out. Emma would like nothing better than for Lizzie to set fire to the barn, so she could say "I told you so" about candles in the hayloft.

Lizzie took the candles, candlesticks, scarf and book, and hid them all under the corner of the haystack.

Father would be home soon from collecting his rents, and he would have picked up the mail in town. Perhaps he would bring home a letter from Beatrice.

And then the good idea came to her. The great idea.

Why not do the second exercise three times a day like the first? And why not keep doing the first along with the second, just adding the new lessons as she went, until she was finally performing all of the lessons three times a day?

It was a wonderful idea, she agreed—and besides, what else had she to do besides iron Father's handkerchiefs?—and she sat down, uncovered her ritual implements, lit the candles, and opened the book.

aggie? Where has that Lizzie got to?"

Bridget Sullivan stopped dusting the top of the china cabinet and looked down on Emma from the top of the ladder. She wiped her forehead with the back of her hand. "I don't know, Miss. Outside, I think."

"Don't give me that exasperated look, if you please. You have plenty of work to do, so I suggest you get on with it."

Emma spun on her heel and went back to the kitchen. She looked out the window at the barn. Yes, Lizzie was undoubtedly inside. Emma was overcome with curiosity about what Lizzie could possibly be doing in there, but she hadn't asked. A million times the question had poised itself on the end of her tongue and she'd always bitten it off. She wanted Lizzie to offer the information without being asked. She wanted Lizzie to confide in her. She wanted so badly for Lizzie to be her friend that she would rather die of curiosity than have to dig the information from her little sister. At least that *had* been her attitude.

But it had gone on long enough now. Things were missing from the house, and Emma knew that Lizzie had taken them out to the barn. Lizzie seemed to be slowly moving out of the house, piece by piece—only instead of moving to someplace respectable, she had taken up residence in the barn. At least she still slept in the house, but Emma had begun to wonder about Lizzie's mind.

As she stood there, hands on the counter, looking out at the barn, she heard her father's key in the lock and the front door opened. He was back from collecting rents. Emma closed her eyes and took a deep breath. Things had gone on long enough, she thought. Best apprise Father.

Emma walked into the sitting room, where her father was going through the mail.

"Hello, Emma. There's a letter here for Lizzie."

"Father." Emma took the letter. It was from that woman in Britain. "Father, have you noticed that Lizzie is acting rather peculiar lately?"

"Hmm? No. Why?"

"She spends all her time in the barn."

"Making herself a study, she told me."

"Oh?"

"Yes. Cleaning up the place, adding a few touches, said she needed a private place to read and study. I told her I thought it was fine idea."

"Oh." Emma had more to say on the subject, but she heard Lizzie come in the kitchen door. She appeared in the sitting room doorway, flush-faced and smiling.

"Hello, Father."

"Lizzie," he said, opening another letter. Emma handed Lizzie the letter from Beatrice and left the room. She had no stomach for what the two of them did together every afternoon. Lizzie rubbing the old man's smelly feet, then reading to him and listening to his moans and groans of old age. It was revolting. It was terrible. It was unnatural.

Emma went back to the kitchen, got down the big mixing bowl and a cake of yeast. Might as well bake some bread. She stoked the fire in the wood stove and went to work.

There was more to Lizzie's oddness of late than her propensity for spending days in the barn. She seemed always

104

to be smiling. She had stopped going to church with Father, had joined another church, which had scandalized the town, not to mention Father, and had begun teaching a Sunday school class for Chinese children, of all things. Chinese children! Where on earth did she get such an idea? Emma hadn't even known that the Chinese people could be Christians.

She heard the maid moving furniture and the ladder around in the dining room, and knew she was getting ready to clean the chandelier. That would take some time. She heard Lizzie's voice droning on in a cadence that could only mean she was reading.

Emma had time.

She untied the apron from her waist and slipped out the back door. She would see what Lizzie had been up to in the barn—something shameful, she supposed. Why else would Lizzie keep it so tightly to herself?

But the barn was locked. An old hasp and padlock that Emma remembered seeing in one of the old cartons of junk inside had been resurrected, reassembled and secured to the barn door. Emma gave the lock a shake, but it held fast. She would have given the door a kick, too, but she didn't take the time. She walked quickly back to the kitchen, where Lizzie held the screen door open for her.

At first, Emma was ashamed that she had tried to spy on Lizzie, but the smirk on her sister's face was too much to bear. "Why is the barn locked?" she demanded.

"It's no longer the barn," Lizzie said. "It's now my study. And I need my privacy."

"Privacy! Hmph." Emma shouldered her way past Lizzie and returned to her bread-baking.

"Why, what did you want out there?"

"Nothing. I just wanted to see what you'd been doing out there."

"Why didn't you ask?"

"Because you've been so obnoxiously secretive about the whole thing."

"So you waited until you thought you could spy and not get caught. Not very nice, Emma."

Emma slowly turned, willing the flush to leave her face. "I'd been hoping you'd tell me, Lizzie, but since you hadn't, I thought I ought to take a look for myself. A barn is not a proper place for a young lady to spend her days. You should be practicing your needlework. Or . . . or a thousand other chores that could be done around this house."

"Anything but keep secrets from you, right, Emma?"

"Don't get smart with me."

"You have *all* forgotten that I am an adult."

"Yes, Lizzie, I guess we have. You so rarely act like one."

"And your behavior qualifies you as a *lady?*" Lizzie's pale eyes, usually calm and peaceful, now smoked.

"I don't care to discuss it further," Emma said, her heart pounding. This was definitely new behavior for Lizzie, and Emma didn't like it. She didn't like it one bit. She turned from Lizzie and put her floured hands back into the dough.

"Well, *I* care to discuss it," Lizzie said, her arms crossed in front of her chest. She leaned up against the counter so Emma could not avoid her.

"All right, Lizzie," Emma sighed, giving up. "What is it?"

"You accuse me of secrecy, when all I want is privacy. I want to tell you that all I'm doing is fixing myself a place of my own where I can read and study undisturbed."

"What are you studying? That book from that woman?"

"Beatrice is her name. Yes. That's one of the things."

"Well, I'm sorry if my presence upsets you so. I had no idea that you needed to be so far away from me."

"It's not that," Lizzie said. "It's not *you,* although you *are* always in and out of my room."

Emma felt tears build up inside her. Nothing ever goes the way one wants it to, she thought. She shook her floured hands into the bowl, then pushed past Lizzie into the washroom, where she rinsed them in bone-achingly frigid well water. The blast of cold helped her get a firm grip on her emotions. She never wanted Lizzie to see her cry. Never. "Perhaps it would suit you if I moved." She turned and faced Lizzie again, in control.

Lizzie's face began to melt. "No, Emma, that's not what I mean, you're misunderstanding me. It's not at all what I want. You're fine. Coming in and out of my room is fine. I just want to have a place in the barn where I can go to read. Really. It's nothing about you. Nothing." Lizzie began to tremble and Emma heard the catch in her throat.

A close call, Emma thought.

"Well, all right, then, Lizzie, but I do wish you wouldn't keep it locked. Sometimes one needs to get in and out of the barn."

"Yes, Emma," Lizzie said and, head down, she walked through the dining room. Emma heard her walk quietly and slowly up the stairs to her room.

Emma found that she was trembling. Yes indeed, a change had come over Lizzie Borden. Never before would she have acted in such a manner. Imagine!

There's trouble brewing here, Emma thought. And the last thing I need in this life is trouble from Lizzie.

She went back to her bread. She could understand Lizzie's wish for privacy, a longing for a place of her own. It would be nice to have a place where she could do as she wished, without prying eyes or judgmental voices following her from room to room.

Perhaps the barn could be converted. Perhaps the old stalls could be torn down to make two studies, one upstairs for Lizzie, one downstairs for me. I could decorate it as I wished, even pounding nails into the walls to hang photographs. I could come and go as I pleased with no one knowing where I was at any particular time.

But that was the problem. Emma was needed at home, and the need in the house pulled her like taffy. She couldn't even go to the store without the tether that bound her to this house pulling tighter. This household needed her. Without her, any number of dreadful things might happen. Father would most assuredly give all his money to that Abby woman and she, knowing her financial future was set, would without doubt deed it all over to her worthless kin.

Father needed watching, too, so he did not bring scandal down upon the family. He, who was so worried about his good name being sullied about town, had the roving eye of a randy seaman. Many a time, Emma had escorted her father away from a situation he was only too eager to fall into. Why, one time, when at a church social, Andrew had been introduced to a nice-looking woman, a cousin or some other relation of one of the congregation. Andrew had stood talking with her for a short while, until the woman excused herself, and then he began to follow her around. The woman was clearly uncomfortable about it, and Emma had to step in and take Andrew's arm and escort him home before the woman began to shriek. Emma was sure it was innocent attraction on his part, but sometimes he had no common sense about him at all.

And Lizzie! If Emma wasn't there to keep close tabs on Lizzie, she might get married, or do some equally disastrous thing.

No, this house needed Emma to hold it all together. And what made her situation so miserable, was that none of them knew this, and none of them appreciated all the sacrifices she had made in their names.

Yes, Emma thought. A home of my own in the country where I could keep some laying hens and a milk goat would do me just fine. But it is not in my destiny. I must stay here and keep watch over the family.

For if I don't, who will?

I only wish Lizzie would understand. I only wish Lizzie *could* understand. But she can't. She won't. She couldn't possibly understand the kind of commitment a promise to one's dead mother means.

Emma turned the kneaded dough into a bowl liberally greased with bacon fat. She spread her towel over the top of it and set it on the shelf next to the woodstove. Then she washed her hands.

Father was still asleep on the sofa. Abby was somewhere . . . out with Sarah, her twit of a half sister, no doubt. Maggie was still working on the chandelier. Emma walked through the dining room and up the front stairs. For the first time, she thought she ought to knock before opening Lizzie's door. But that was silly, and it was a precedent she didn't care to set.

She took the key from her apron pocket and opened the bedroom door. Lizzie was in her rocking chair, letter in her lap, staring out into space.

"Lizzie," Emma said. "I almost forgot to tell you. Kathryn Peters has invited you over for supper tonight. Six o'clock. I told her that you would be there, and that if you could not make it you would send a message."

Lizzie still stared into space.

"Lizzie?"

Slowly, her eyes focused on Emma.

"Lizzie, did you hear me?"

Lizzie cleared her voice. "What?"

"You're expected at Kathryn Peters' for supper tonight. Six o'clock. Are you all right?"

Lizzie looked down at the letter in her lap. "Kathryn Peters?"

Emma walked over to her, touched her shoulder. Lizzie quickly folded the letter and slipped it back into the envelope. "Are you all right?"

"Yes, of course. I'm fine. Six o'clock at Kathryn's. Fine. Thank you." Lizzie stared off again.

Emma unlocked her bedroom door, went in and locked the door behind her again.

Lizzie was definitely not herself lately.

izzie stared at the envelope in her hands. Her mind had gone numb. She couldn't concentrate on the news, she couldn't begin to fathom the ramifications, she knew only that she had to *do* something, and she had no idea what.

Stop it, she told herself, and began to rock. The familiar noise her rockers made as they chewed over the same worn spot on the wooden floor settled her nerves. Then she heard Emma's rocker, and how fast Emma rocked, and a small smile came to her lips. Emma *worked* her rocking chair.

She stood up, stretched, threw the traitorous envelope on the bed and moved around the room, waving her arms. Motion. Movement. Something had to be done here, and the first thing to do was to move around, clear her mind, and begin to formulate a plan of action.

She couldn't imagine what kind of plan she could make. The news was so startling. She was dumbfounded. Thrilled. Terrified.

She flopped down on her bed, grimacing at the sound it made. Father and Emma both had admonished her for falling like a ton of bricks onto her bed. But she heard nothing from Emma's room about it, and Father was surely still asleep. She picked up the lavender envelope and smelled it. It smelled of Britain. She opened the flap and removed the letter.

My dearest Lizbeth,
I have the most wonderful news. Father has recov-

ered his health enough to resume his business in most of Europe. That is good news in itself, but the better news is that his affairs have travelled as far as America, and I shall be coming over to handle things for him, as he will not be able to undergo a journey of that magnitude, at least for a couple of years. Imagine! We shall be sitting together talking and resuming our friendship on a more personal note very soon now.

I have booked passage, and will tend to Father's business in New York City and Philadelphia. When that is finished, I shall come to your town, Fall River, and spend a few days, if that is agreeable to you. I'll post a letter to let you know exactly when I shall be arriving, but I imagine it will be sometime in late July.

I can hardly wait, I am so excited. I must close now, for there are many things to be done all at once, and I am behind in my preparations. I will write a longer letter soon, and continue our discussion of the varied topics we both seem to find fascinating.

Affectionately,
Beatrice

The wording hadn't changed at the second reading, or the third. Or the fourth. Beatrice was coming to Fall River. In July! That gave Lizzie as little as three months, perhaps four, to prepare.

Goodness!

In three months, Lizzie had to lose weight, fashion a new wardrobe, do *something* with the house, with the family, catch up on her studies, read all the business books Beatrice had suggested. . . . There were too many things to be done, too many things to be done. Too many! She wasn't ready. She couldn't possibly be ready.

Hold onto yourself a moment, she thought. Beatrice loved you two years ago. She will love you now. As you are.

Lizzie's heart calmed for a moment.

But *I* don't love me as I am. Not yet. And Beatrice cannot possibly respect me when I am as slothful as a garden slug. I must make progress. I must make appreciable headway prior to July, or Beatrice will not look kindly upon me anymore; her friendship is at stake here, and I cannot afford to fail.

Lizzie squeezed her eyes tight and rubbed her fists into the sockets. "Lord, please, help make me ready!"

She sat up suddenly and pulled all the pins out of her hair. She fluffed it out with her fingers, feeling the heavy silkiness of it.

"All right, Lizbeth Borden," she said, smiling to the ends of her auburn hair. "Here's the challenge: In every way, in every thought and every deed, be the person you want Beatrice to see. *Every* thought. *Every* deed. Beginning now. Bold. Adventurous. Self-assured. Claim control of your life and *live* it. *Be* it."

So saying, Lizzie found her heart calmed, the sweat dried on the palms of her hands.

I can be ready for her by July, she thought. I will just have to work harder than I thought I would. I shall be bold, adventurous and self-assured. And I shall begin now. Tonight. At Kathryn Peters'.

She slipped the letter back into its envelope and took it to the desk. The side drawer was filled with Beatrice's letters, tied up in bundles with peach-colored ribbons purchased at the dry-goods store. Lizzie added the newest letter on the top, then closed the drawer.

She smiled. I must be bold, adventurous and self-assured about Beatrice's arrival, she thought.

And she found that she looked forward to seeing Beatrice again.

She went to the closet and threw open the door. What shall I wear to Kathryn's tonight? she wondered. Something different. But it was all the same. The same clothes in the same closet. Lizzie closed her eyes against them.

But the dark-blue shirtwaist and black skirt always flattered her figure. They were silk, and well made. She would look nice, at least in her own mind, and it was only Lizzie now that Lizzie had to please, right? Right.

She grabbed her bathrobe, then flew down cellar to her bath.

Kathryn Peters, at thirty-one years old, was just a little younger than Lizzie. Kathryn had been a classmate and friend, but she had a more outgoing nature than Lizzie, had been far more popular, and had gone on to study nursing after school. She had traveled widely and was considered as much a pillar of the small Fall River community as a spinster lady could be.

Lizzie had always enjoyed Kathryn's company. They were both members of the WCTU and they had worked on various committees together. Lizzie thought of Kathryn's shining teeth and dainty hands as she soaped the musky smell from her body.

Kathryn stood about five feet tall and could not have weighed more than one hundred pounds, all told. She fancied laces and dainty handkerchiefs, tiny hats with delicate veils, shoes so small they would fit in Lizzie's hand; and she had a small trilling giggle that leapt up the scale and charmed everyone within earshot.

Everyone in Fall River, at one time or another, wondered why Kathryn had never married. Surely she was not without her suitors, but she never seemed to take any of them seriously, and had never kept steady company with a single one.

Kathryn's mother had died when Kathryn was small, another thing she had in common with Lizzie, but then her father had died while Kathryn was away at school. She came home to manage the affairs, which did not turn out to be a

114

substantial task, and just never returned to school. She traveled often, managed the affairs of her dead parents with admirable aggression and lived on the income her investments afforded her.

Lizzie liked Kathryn. They seemed to enjoy each other, yet there was ever present a slight tinge of wariness in their companionship, as though neither truly trusted the other.

Nevertheless, Kathryn was very good at games and, in addition, perhaps other guests had been invited. Lizzie was looking forward to the evening.

Bold, adventurous and self-assured, she thought, as she rinsed and toweled dry with the first sun-dried towel since last autumn. I wonder how Kathryn will like my new approach to life?

•   •   •

Kathryn answered the door dressed in a stunning wine-colored gown trimmed in black lace. A white cameo gleamed at her throat; her hair was done up with a twist and it shone in the gaslight. She even had a touch of lipstick on, Lizzie noticed, and some rouge.

Lizzie hugged her hostess, and the evening's first feeling of inadequacy came over her. If there was one thing about Kathryn that truly intimidated Lizzie, it was Kathryn's diminutive stature. Tiny, she was, almost like a fairy. Lizzie felt like a moose next to her.

Kathryn kissed her lightly on the lips, then chattered away gaily as she took Lizzie's cape and hat; the two women went into Kathryn's correctly appointed sitting room. Lizzie glanced into the dining room on her way past, and saw the table set for two. Wonderful. An intimate evening.

They shared a cup of tea and talked first about the good work the WCTU was accomplishing, then gossiped politely about some of the members. Lizzie became more and more relaxed. When Kathryn left the room to check on the

115

progress of dinner, Lizzie had the profound realization that Kathryn had invited her to her home for no other reason than that she enjoyed Lizzie's company. There was no committee work to be done, there was not a dinner party with an odd number of guests, there was no other reason. Kathryn had invited Lizzie because she wanted to share a dinner with her.

Lizzie blushed in spite of herself and sipped her tea.

Kathryn returned and they talked of art, a subject about which Lizzie was as ignorant as Kathryn was well-versed. They talked Fall River politics for a moment, then general Fall River news and personalities, and then it was time for dinner.

Kathryn had roasted two squabs and served them with an orange sauce, small freshly-dug carrots that she'd overwintered right in the ground, and a portion of goat cheese that she'd purchased last Saturday at the market. This spawned a discussion of cooking, another thing in which Kathryn was accomplished and Lizzie not.

But the holes in Lizzie's training did not confuse her this night with holes in her personality. Kathryn's life had taken different directions, and had led her down different paths. Lizzie did not feel more or less fortunate (except in looks and body) for once. She just felt different, and for the first time, instead of dwelling on her own insufficiencies, she reveled in Kathryn's accomplishments and queried enthusiastically about her life.

After dinner (Lizzie ate her entire bird down to the bones; Kathryn barely ate half a breast), Kathryn gave Lizzie a thorough tour of her kitchen, and then her artworks, which spread about the house. Lizzie had long admired the art that hung on Kathryn's walls, but as she'd only been at the house during a meeting, she'd never had opportunity to view each one in its glory. Each painting, sketch and drawing had a little story about where it came from, the artist, and how and where Kathryn had acquired it. Lizzie was totally charmed with this little, tiny, beautiful woman and her enthusiasm.

Eventually, the tour landed them back in the sitting room, where Kathryn sat on the settee next to Lizzie.

They talked about Europe and compared notes on what they had seen in common; and as Kathryn poured a fresh cup of tea, her hand touched Lizzie's, and it stayed there.

Lizzie was surprised at how warm it was, how soft and warm, and without thinking, she took Kathryn's tiny hand in both of hers. Emma's hands were harsh and bony, Abby's hands were fat and bloated, Father's hands were horny and hairy. This little perfectly manicured hand was warm and gentle. Tender. Lizzie turned it over to look at the palm, ran a finger down the center of it, and when she looked up, Kathryn had a most peculiar look in her eyes.

The expression on Kathryn's face reminded Lizzie of days long ago when she would sit in the window seat at the farm and look out the window, dreaming of things to be when she finally became an adult. She longed to be a housewife with a dozen children. She longed to have a protector, a provider, one she could kiss and hug, one she could sleep next to on a cold night. She longed to make her own decisions and not be driven instead by a ruthless older sister, she longed . . .

That was the expression in Kathryn's eyes. Longing.

Lizzie flushed and looked again at the tiny hand she held in her own.

"Lizzie?" Kathryn spoke so softly that even in the silent room, Lizzie was not sure that she had heard. She was suddenly shy, and almost afraid. Her heart pounded louder than Kathryn's tiny word. Eventually, she looked up into that beautiful face, and Kathryn's lips were gently parted, and she moved closer and closer, until Lizzie could smell her hair as well as see right through it, and she could smell the closeness of Kathryn, freshly bathed and powdered. She could smell Kathryn's breath, warm, scented with tea and cinnamon, and then Kathryn's lips were on her own, soft, so soft.

Then she was gone, and Lizzie found her eyes closed, so she opened them, and saw Kathryn, who was flushed and laughing, both of them embarrassed, and the small hand slid out from between Lizzie's and helped the other hand hold the trembling teacup.

But that wasn't right. It wasn't something to be laughed at. It was something to be explored. Once was not enough. Lizzie had to taste that again, she had to know that feeling, that sensation that had burst upon her senses and then fled before she really knew what had happened.

She moved closer to Kathryn on the settee, feeling like an elephant trying to capture a mink. But Kathryn was all too ready to be captured, and their kiss this time was lingering and sensitive.

Lizzie's mind reeled. She could feel her pulse in her panties. She wanted to get closer to Kathryn, closer and closer still, until they were of one body.

With a hand that seemed to have a mind of its own, she pulled the pins from Kathryn's hair and fluffed it as it fell around her face.

She broke off the kiss and stared into the other woman's eyes, eyes that held love and desire. Lizzie had never seen that before in anyone's eyes and it was hypnotic. It was intoxicating. She felt overheated. She felt foolish for wearing such cold-weather clothes on such a balmy spring evening.

"You are so beautiful," Kathryn breathed, and Lizzie was sure she had heard wrong.

Again she neared Kathryn, brushing her nose along Kathryn's cheek, taking in her perfume, but their positions were not right, they were both uncomfortable on the settee, and Kathryn kissed Lizzie lightly on the lips, then stood, holding her hand, and guided her through the house to the bedroom at the back.

And there, she proceeded to tenderly undress Lizzie, and then bed her, showing her the fascinating ways one woman can love another.

• • •

"Of course, discretion is all," Kathryn said quietly.

Lizzie, snuggled down in the soft, soft covers of Kathryn's bed, nodded. She couldn't take her eyes off the extraordinary profile. What Kathryn had just done to her, with her, for her, was the most amazing act of love Lizzie could ever even imagine. It was far beyond her imagination. In fact, she still couldn't believe it had happened.

The clock in the dining room chimed eleven.

"Eleven o'clock, Lizzie," Kathryn said, still staring straight ahead. Then she turned to look at her and their noses touched. "As much as I'd like you to stay, I think you'd best be going now."

Lizzie knew it was true, and reluctantly and shyly arose and dressed. She dared not meet Kathryn's eyes as she donned clothes that were wrinkled, inappropriate and too tight, knowing that Kathryn watched every move. Then she was dressed, and without knowing what to say, she just looked at Kathryn, and smiled.

Kathryn seemed old, somehow. She smiled back at Lizzie, but it was a wan smile, a tired smile. "'Bye," Lizzie said.

"'Bye."

Lizzie left by the front door and walked through the chill toward home. The night air felt fresh and wonderful. It tingled her skin with an icy touch.

A shocking wave of unreality stopped Lizzie in the middle of the road in front of the Anderson house. It couldn't have happened, she thought. It hadn't been real. It was something she had dreamed, some terrible sinful dream. It could never have happened that she and Kathryn Peters had just . . . No, never. She walked on. In the cold air of reality, what they had just experienced together seemed as foreign and as distant as her trip to Europe, or Beatrice coming. . . .

But Beatrice *is* coming, she thought, and anxiety began to pull on her.

Then she turned the corner onto Second Street, and the overwhelming brown feeling fell on her shoulders. Emma. Father. Abby. This house. This house.

She opened the front door with her key, locked all three locks once she was inside, blew out the lamp and took a candle with her up to her room.

Inside her room, her dingy, dark, boring little cell, Lizzie undressed, throwing her rumpled clothes in a pile on the floor.

She slipped under the covers and tried to believe that what had happened with Kathryn had truly happened.

It was unmistakable. Her scent was still in Lizzie's nostrils; neither the cold of the night nor the moldy stench of this house could mask that wonderful smell. The taste of her was still on Lizzie's tongue. The touch of her was still on Lizzie's skin. The memory of her rippling shudders at Lizzie's touch would never be forgotten.

Lizzie began to plan when she could see Kathryn again. Soon. Very soon. Lizzie could never bring her here, of course, but she had to see her again, soon. Very soon. Tuesday, in fact, Lizzie thought with a leap in her heart. There was a WCTU meeting on Tuesday.

• • •

The town hall was packed with Women's Christian Temperance Union members. Lizzie knew all the ladies

120

present, of course—she had been a member in good standing for several years—but she felt not at all like socializing. She kept looking about for the one person she came to see. She wandered incessantly, superficially greeting other members, not friends, just acquaintances, not stopping long enough to get involved in anyone's conversation.

And then, as soon as Mrs. Tuttle had struck the lectern with her president's gavel, Lizzie saw Kathryn come in the room, lit from within with the love of life, and she laughed and chatted and made her way to a seat in the back. She looked wonderful. Lizzie felt her face flush as she watched. She wanted to sit next to her, she wanted to touch her, she wanted to see that Kathryn still liked her, admired her, *loved* her, and she needed to see that look in Kathryn's eyes.

But she was stuck. She was already at a seat in the center of the hall, and it would be a bother, and a noticeable one, to return to Kathryn's section. She would have to wait for the break.

The Reverend Buck said the opening prayer, and Mrs. Tuttle called the meeting to order. Lizzie found it hard to concentrate. She felt Kathryn's presence behind her. She wanted to turn to look to see who Kathryn was sitting next to, who she was talking to. She wanted to know what they were saying, she wanted to know what Kathryn did after Lizzie left the night before, she wanted to know what Kathryn was planning to do tonight after the meeting.

Lizzie remembered the touch of Kathryn's small fingers as they smoothed the hair from the back of Lizzie's neck, and goose pimples rose up on her arms. She smoothed them down with a shiver.

Lizzie had waited anxiously since Saturday night for this meeting. She got nothing accomplished at home. She sat around and thought about Kathryn and thought about doing her Pathways exercises. She actually got them all done, but got little out of it. She hoped she was receiving the benefit of

121

them anyway. She could do little but think of Kathryn and her mysterious, wonderful touches in the dark. Lizzie could still taste her kiss. Lizzie could still smell her breasts.

She fidgeted through the meeting, wondering if it would ever end. Finally, she could bear it no more and stood up, made her way between the rows of benches and walked to the back of the hall. Kathryn smiled benignly at her, not giving her a second glance. Lizzie's face flushed a deep crimson, and she made her way quickly, head down, to the W.C.

She stayed in there until the break. She felt as if a knife had twisted in her stomach. Kathryn didn't even give her a personal smile. It was as if Kathryn didn't even know her. She heard the noises of voices approaching, so she patted at her hair and clothes and put on a brave face. She would seek Kathryn out one more time and see if there was perhaps a chance they could talk. Lizzie could not believe that Kathryn didn't want her. She could not imagine that Kathryn didn't feel exactly the same way she herself did. After the way they had loved each other. The way they had trusted each other.

Lizzie felt weak at the thought of it.

She pushed out through the approaching throng of women, and saw Kathryn in the hall foyer. Kathryn excused herself from talking with Margaret Reid and came over to Lizzie.

Lizzie felt immobilized by her presence. She felt her blasted face heat up again, felt her tongue tied as firmly as it had ever been.

"Lizzie!" Kathryn came and reached up for Lizzie's face, kissing her lightly on the cheek. "Nine o'clock," she whispered in Lizzie's ear. Then she stepped back and said, "How are you?"

Lizzie caught on quickly. "Fine. You look wonderful, Kathryn."

"Thank you." Then Kathryn saw someone else, and flitted away.

122

Lizzie had always envied that ability to flit at a social gathering, and her spirits soared at the thought that what she first assumed was a snub was in reality nothing more than mere discretion.

And discretion was all, just as Kathryn had said.

Nine o'clock! Lizzie tore her eyes away from her lover, reluctantly, and wondered how she would ever pass the time until she was able to hold Kathryn again.

She made small talk here and there among the crowd, then slipped out the door just before the meeting was reconvened. She walked around the town in the rapidly growing dusk, then finally went home, agitated and restless. She went directly to her room, where she freshened up, changed her clothes and paced.

At eight-thirty, the minute hand began to crawl ever more slowly. Finally it was eight-forty-five, and Lizzie left the house, walking briskly through town toward Kathryn's.

By the time she arrived, her breath was coming hard from the exertion and again she vowed to take a little more fresh air and exercise, so as to be a little more appealing to Kathryn and a little less fleshy.

She knocked on the door, and it opened almost immediately.

"Come in quickly," Kathryn said. "Did anyone see you come?"

"No," Lizzie said, and then Kathryn's mouth was upon hers, and her hands were inside her clothing. It was not gentle, it was not loving, but Lizzie felt the overwhelming need as much as Kathryn did. She returned the hard embrace, the brutal kisses, and her knees failed her. They tumbled to the ground together, groping, tasting, ripping, their passions too great to be withstood any longer.

Lizzie was quite overwhelmed. It was everything she had dreamed of, and more. They rolled along the floor, biting and pulling at each other's clothes until they were down to

123

their drawers. Kathryn jumped up and grabbed Lizzie by the hand; they ran to the bedroom, where a candle had been lit and the bed turned down, and climbed beneath the cool covers. The break in momentum seemed to settle them both down, although Lizzie's breath still came hard and fast. When Kathryn slipped into bed next to her, Lizzie saw the longing again on her face. She drank in that look. It was something she never wanted to forget.

Later, as they lay in Kathryn's spacious bed, in her large, well-appointed bedroom, Kathryn said, "I shall pretend not to know you well, you know."

Lizzie nodded, wondering at the feeling of this house. This house was really little larger than her own, and there was certainly no more furniture. But the air was spacious. There was tranquillity in this house; it could be felt in the wallpaper, in the carpeting, in the chandeliers.

The wallpaper, carpeting and chandeliers at the Borden house were dingy somehow, close and suffocating.

Kathryn's house was cool and gracious. Lizzie's house was stale and cramped.

Lizzie felt that she could even walk naked through Kathryn's house, but the thought of even *being* naked in her own home made her feel shame.

"If I were wealthy," Kathryn said, "I'd buy a sailing ship and go to Africa."

"But you *are* wealthy."

Kathryn laughed at the ceiling. "I am comfortable, Lizzie. I am not wealthy. No. I would sell this terrible house and sail for the Dark Continent and find a man to hunt elephants with. And I would drink rye whiskey and smoke cigars. Seduce native girls."

Lizzie turned in astonishment and looked at Kathryn's profile. It suddenly occurred to her that she didn't know Kathryn very well at all . . . there need be no pretending involved.

124

"What about you?"

"I'd buy a larger house, here in Fall River. On the Hill. I'd have dinner parties. I'd train to New York regularly to the theater. And I'd give a large share to the WCTU."

"The WCTU?"

"Yes, of course."

"You really believe liquor is evil?"

"I don't think liquor is evil; I think that people under the influence of liquor do evil things."

"I think liquor is lovely."

"But you're on the committee . . ."

"Oh, Lizzie. It's just a social organization."

Lizzie was stunned. "It's not!"

Kathryn still had not turned her head to look at Lizzie. She kept her eyes fixed firmly on the ceiling.

"Are you telling me that you don't believe in the work the WCTU is doing?"

"Oh, I suppose I must. I mean, the way liquor is available today, I'm sure I can't quite argue with the WCTU."

"But you've been a member for years."

"I know. That means nothing. Have you ever taken a drink, Lizzie?"

"Never."

"Would you like one?"

"No! And I'd like it if we never discussed it again."

"Well. I should think you would be in the mood to try some new and different things. I mean"—Kathryn turned and looked at Lizzie's breast, then touched her nipple. It instantly shrank—"you seemed to take to certain other things that were new and different." Kathryn looked up at Lizzie. "They *were* new and different, weren't they?"

"Oh yes," Lizzie breathed, her fire rekindling.

"Good. Then let us have a brandy."

"No," Lizzie said, and pulled the covers up to her chin.

"Why, Lizzie, what is it about a little drink?"

"It's no good, Kathryn. It makes people do things . . . terrible things."

"Suit yourself," Kathryn said, then climbed out of bed naked, picked a shirt from a hook in her closet, and walked out of the room.

Suddenly, Lizzie felt like a stranger. She didn't know if she'd offended Kathryn, she didn't know if Kathryn was coming back to bed, she didn't know if Kathryn would even like her after her comments on alcohol. It was clear that Kathryn found no harm in moderate imbibing; perhaps Lizzie was taking the WCTU issue too much to heart.

She slipped out of bed, took a robe that was far too small for her and walked into the living room.

Kathryn was looking at a magazine, a brandy in her hand.

"I'll have one too, if you don't mind," Lizzie said.

"Would you?" Kathryn raised an eyebrow.

"I think so."

"Well, good for you, Lizzie. The bottle is in the kitchen. Snifters are in the china cabinet."

Lizzie took a delicate glass from the china cabinet and poured a dollop of brandy into the bottom of it. Something had been lost with Kathryn during the course of this conversation, and she wasn't sure what, nor was she sure if she could fix it. She only knew that she was eager to fix it, desperately eager.

"Kathryn?"

"Hmm?"

"Will you care for me if this drinking goes badly?"

Kathryn laughed. "You have barely enough in that glass to wet your tongue, Lizzie. I have already had three times that much, and do I look like a raving lunatic to you?"

"No, of course not," Lizzie said, and smelled the liquor. It smelled rich and dark, sweet and bold. Bold. Bold, adventurous and self-assured. Lizzie wet her lip with it, then licked it off. It tasted just the way it smelled. She sipped a tiny bit, then saw that Kathryn was studying her with a critical look on her face. She took a larger swallow and felt the warmth slide down her throat and spread out in her stomach. "That's rather nice," she said.

Kathryn laughed. "Oh, Lizzie," she said. "We have much work to do on you."

ay

"Y̲ou should have seen her, Lizzie." Emma's insides were burning as she paced back and forth in Lizzie's tiny bedroom. "She was as phony as a two-dollar bill. 'Oooh, Oooh.'" Emma tried to mimic Abby in a high-pitched whine. "'All my money is missing. All my jew-ells.' I don't think I need to tell *you* who orchestrated that little robbery. *Or* who she's going to pin it on."

"Emma," Lizzie said, "you can't possibly think that Abby is going to blame you?"

Emma looked at Lizzie, sitting calmly in her rocking chair. Sometimes the girl could be so thickheaded. "That's exactly what I *do* think, Lizzie. They're trying to make life unbearable for me here. They think that sooner or later I'll leave, and then they'll be able to do as they damned well please around here with no thought to anybody's troubles but their own. Well," she said, growing ever more agitated by the moment, "they won't have it their way. They won't." Emma stopped pacing and stood quietly next to Lizzie's door. She could remember only Abby's eyes, filled with accusation when Emma went up the stairs to her bedroom to find out what had upset her so much. Accusing eyes. Accusing eyes.

Emma felt Lizzie's hand on her wrist. Lizzie pulled her hand away from her mouth and Emma saw blood on her knuckles.

"Your mouth is bleeding, Emma," Lizzie said. "You were

rubbing your lips again with your knuckles. Come. Sit over here. You've got to learn how to calm down."

"Calm down?" The concept was ludicrous. "Calm down? Lizzie, they're likely to have me arrested."

"It could as easily have been me, Emma, or Maggie. Lord knows she didn't have much worth stealing."

"That's the point." Emma blotted her bleeding lips with a cloth Lizzie handed her. Her knuckles were cut as well. "Who would want her ratty things? Not me. Not you. I'm sure Maggie has dusted her cheap jewelry every day for two years and has so far resisted temptation. Why would she suddenly take a shine to tarnished rhinestones?"

"How much money did she say was taken?"

"I think ten dollars."

"Ten dollars! That's quite a sum to be leaving about."

"Her emergency money, to hear her tell it. She says it was in her dresser drawer. Hidden. Said the thief had to have looked through her drawers to find it. But nothing looked ransacked to me. Everything looked normal. And only certain pieces of jewelry were missing, too. It's not like the thief took the entire jewelry box."

"I wonder . . ."

"Wonder! Wonder? I don't wonder, Lizzie, and I am *aston*ished that you would. Abby probably threw away that ugly old jewelry and gave the ten to her stupid half sister. And I am going to take all the blame." Emma felt like squeezing something. She squeezed and twisted that cloth that Lizzie gave her until it hurt her hands. She wanted to rip and tear, but she couldn't rip that cloth, and besides, squeezing, hurting, killing something living, something small and furry would be far more satisfying.

"Have you looked in your room?"

"My room?"

"Yes, Emma—if Abby is trying to blame you for the

burglary, then perhaps she put the missing items in your room."

Emma jumped up and went into her room. She looked in each drawer, under the bed, in the closet. There was no evidence that anyone had been in her room. She went back to Lizzie's. "You'd better search your room as well, Lizzie." Lizzie began to open her drawers and root about in them. "Although, you know, I don't believe either Abby or Father has a key to our rooms."

"Oh, I'm sure Father has. Leastways, Maggie does."

"Maggie. I believe we should talk to Maggie. I'll do it."

Emma went down the stairs and found Bridget stirring and seasoning the stew for supper.

"Maggie!"

"My name is Bridget, if you please, Miss Emma."

"Yes, of course. Did Mrs. Borden talk to you about her missing jewelry and money?"

"Yes, she did."

"Did she accuse you?"

Bridget's eyes grew large. "No, of course not, miss. Why . . . of course not."

"Did she let on who she suspected?"

"It were a robbery, miss. It were a burglary."

"So someone from the outside?"

"Must have been."

"The doors were locked. You and I were home."

"I . . ." Emma saw understanding cross the maid's face. "I dunno, miss." She turned back to her stirring.

"Have you seen Mr. Borden?"

"He isn't home yet."

"And Mrs. Borden?"

"She's out at present."

Emma turned on her heel and stomped through the dining room. She could hear the rockers on Lizzie's chair. She went up the stairs and into Lizzie's room. "Well," she

132

said. "She didn't accuse Maggie. And now she's gone out. I don't imagine she'll be back until after Father gets home. He'll come home and she'll come home right after him, take him aside, tell him all, accuse me and then sit in her corner sniveling to herself while he has the dirty work of proving his daughter innocent."

"I think you're taking this a bit too far, Emma," Lizzie said.

Emma fixed Lizzie with a stare. "Mark my words," she said, then walked into her bedroom and closed the door. And she began to pace. She would hear Father at the door. She would run down to talk to him before Abby had a chance.

No, that would be falling down to Abby's level of politics. No, let Father come to her with his accusation. She would meet him face to face. She would deny it all and there would be no proof, especially since Abby herself was the culprit.

Emma's lips began to hurt and she stopped pacing and looked at her hands. There was blood again on her knuckles. A bad habit, she thought. I must stop doing that.

Within the half hour, the front door opened. Emma jumped up from where she was sitting stonily in her chair. She opened the door to Lizzie's room and exchanged a glance with Lizzie. "Don't lie on your bed with your clothes on, Lizzie," she said automatically, then opened Lizzie's door and went out, without closing the door behind her. She descended the staircase and found Andrew Borden in the sitting room, shuffling through the mail.

"Father," Emma said.

"Hello, Emma."

"Father, have you spoken with Abby?"

"Not since this morning. Why?"

"It seems she's had a few things missing from her bedroom."

"Missing? Misplaced?"

"Stolen."

"Stolen? Stolen! Has she informed the police?"

"I think not, Father. I think she has a notion that I burgled the jewelry and some money."

"You? Well, that's nonsense. Surely she was upset at the time . . ."

Emma looked him straight in the eye.

"I'll speak with her. Is she home?"

They both heard the screen door in the kitchen slam. They heard Abby's voice as she spoke with the maid. Emma's face began a slow burn. She felt the flush come up from somewhere in her chest and burn its way up her throat to her cheeks. The tips of her ears felt on fire.

"Abby?" Andrew's voice was lower with concern.

Abby came into the room, taking off the sweater she had worn to town. "Hello."

"Abby, Emma tells me you've been missing some items."

"Yes, Mr. Borden. In fact, some pieces of jewelry were missing from my jewelry box this morning. And the ten dollars I keep on hand for emergency purposes."

"When was the last time you looked at that money?"

"Oh, mustn't have been but a week or so, I saw that it was in its place. And the jewelry, well, I wore the necklace yesterday."

"Have you a thought about it?"

"No sir, I haven't a clue. Emma and Bridget were home all day yesterday, and the bedroom door was kept locked as always."

"Have you spoken with Maggie and Lizzie?"

"With the maid, Bridget, yes sir. With Lizzie, no. She was not yet up when I left the house."

Andrew turned to Emma. "Is Lizzie here?"

"Here, Father." Lizzie rounded the corner. Emma knew she'd been standing on the stairs listening.

134

"Lizzie, do you know of some items missing from your mother's dresser drawer and jewelry case?"

"No, Father. Not except what Emma has told me."

"You were here all day yesterday? You didn't go out at all?"

"I was here."

"And you saw nothing, heard nothing that would lead you to believe that there was another person in the house?"

Lizzie shook her head, then looked at Emma. Emma looked away.

"And the maid was here all day? And Emma?"

"Emma was in and out, Father."

Andrew looked at his wife. "We should fetch the police, Abby. If there's been a robbery, then it ought to be reported. Perhaps the police . . . But how the deuce was it done? The bedroom door is always locked. The front door is triple locked, the kitchen screen is always latched. Could someone come in through the outside cellar door?"

"Padlocked," Lizzie said.

"Yes. Hmm." Andrew rubbed his chin, then fingered the pipe in his pocket. He was anxious for a smoke. "Perhaps after supper," he said, "perhaps we'll go for the police." And he went out and lit his pipe on the back porch.

Abby went up to her room.

"See, Emma? Nobody is accusing you."

"She is," Emma said. "She is."

Lizzie gave an exasperated sigh and flounced out of the room. A moment later, Emma heard the kitchen screen slam again as Lizzie either went to the barn, or went outside to sit with her father as he enjoyed his pipe. Either way, Emma was left alone to stew. She picked up the newspaper that her father had brought, and sat on the settee in the sitting room. Her eyes scanned the print, but she read nothing. She listened to the sounds about her.

Maggie was baking biscuits to accompany the evening

meal. Abby had retired to her bedroom to rest, probably, after her excursion to town.

A few minutes later, the screen slammed again, and Emma heard Andrew tell Maggie to fetch the police. She replied something that Emma could not hear, then the door slammed again. Emma jumped up and went to the kitchen.

"Here, Emma," Andrew said. "Maggie needs someone to watch the biscuits so they don't burn."

"You sent her for the police?"

"Of course. A robbery's been committed."

"They'll accuse me, Father."

"Why you?"

"Because *she*'ll tell them that I was the one who did it."

"Emma, I think you're going a little bit too far here."

"I know who did it, Father. She did. Abby did. She threw her old jewels away and gave the tenner to her stupid Sarah and now she wants to blame it on me."

"I think I've heard enough, Emma."

His loyalty to that fat woman infuriated Emma. Her hysteria reached a new pitch. "She wants me out of here, Father, can't you see that? Can't you see what she's doing to this family?"

Andrew frowned.

"Maybe I *should* move. Maybe that would just make everybody happy. Maybe I should just move out and leave you all to your own wicked devices. Nobody appreciates the things I do around this house anyway. Maybe I should just die."

"Maybe we should go sit down for a spell, Emma." Andrew took Emma's elbow. She ripped away from his touch.

"Don't touch me! You're on her side. You're *all* on her side!" Tears choked her and she hefted her skirts and ran for her bedroom.

Lizzie hadn't locked her bedroom door, and Emma's was still standing open. Emma ran through, slamming both doors behind her, and threw herself onto her bed. She could hear the springs creak beneath her as she heaved and sobbed. It was true, she thought. Father never once tried to correct her. Her thinking was perfectly accurate. The hurt seared like a hot poker.

Why doesn't anyone ever follow me, to try to console me? Nobody cares. Nobody cares.

Her wailing masked the sounds of her father's heavy footsteps on the front stairs. He walked through Lizzie's bedroom and laid a soft knock on Emma's door. "Emma?"

Emma jumped when she heard him. He rarely came to her bedroom; in fact, she couldn't remember the last time she had seen him in here. She swiped at the tears on her face and the moisture running from her nose.

"Emma, something has happened. Please come downstairs."

Something has happened? Emma remembered hearing the kitchen door slam twice. Once, she assumed, was Maggie, returning from her excursion to notify the police of the robbery. And the other . . . the policeman. Lizzie. Her head hurt.

She stood up, shook out her clothes, patted her hair, splashed her face in the basin of cool water, and went downstairs.

The family was in the dining room. Andrew sat at his place at the head of the table . . . in fact everyone was in their eating seat, even the maid, yet there was no food on the table. The stew smelled lovely, and so did the biscuits, but there was no food on the table.

In front of Lizzie was a dirty, rusted meat tin. And inside it were some dollar bills and Abby's missing jewelry.

Emma slipped into the room and sat at her seat.

Andrew cleared his throat.

"Now that we're all present, Lizzie, suppose you tell us about this."

"I found it in the barn," Lizzie said simply.

"Where in the barn?"

"In the storage area. Sitting on top of a box. Out in the open. I noticed it first thing as I walked in."

"And has the barn been locked?"

"No, sir, not since Emma asked me to leave it open."

Emma gasped. It was as if Lizzie had stabbed her.

"Do you know anything of this matter, Lizzie?"

Lizzie took a long time in answering. Emma saw a curious look cross her face. Her brow wrinkled and her eyes lost focus for a moment, an odd response to quite a straightforward question, Emma thought, but then it was quite an odd situation. "No, sir, I do not."

"Maggie?"

"No, sir. I know nothing."

"Emma?"

"I've already told you, Father."

"A simple yes or no will suffice, Emma."

"No, Father. I know nothing of the matter." She looked at Abby, who failed to meet her gaze. "Nothing," she spat at the woman's downcast eyes.

"Abby?"

"I can't imagine how they got to the barn, Mr. Borden. It's as if . . ."

"As if what? Finish your sentence."

"Well," she said, "if someone had wanted the money and the jewelry, they would have taken them away. This is . . . this is more like someone just took them for the . . ."

"Sport," Andrew finished.

Abby nodded, her eyes again on the hands in her lap.

Tension mounted. It was clearly Andrew's turn to speak, and yet he gave no sign of knowing what to say.

Then a knock came at the front door.

"Oh my," Abby said. "The police."

Everybody stood up and went to the front door. Andrew opened it and greeted the uniformed officer.

"Thank you for coming," he said, "but I'm afraid there's been a mistake. The money and jewelry have been recovered; it seems as though this was a simple case of misplacement."

"I see," said the officer, and took out his little notebook and began to write.

"So thank you anyway." Andrew seemed nervous. "I'm sorry you've had to make a trip out here for nothing."

"Nothing to worry about, Mr. Borden. Good day."

Andrew closed the door, but not before he saw Mrs. Churchill, the nosy next-door neighbor, looking over her fence. He turned and faced his family. He cleared his throat.

"An incident like this need never happen again," he said. "And we need never speak of this one, either. Understood?"

Everyone nodded.

"Dinner will be served in ten minutes," Bridget said, and everyone dispersed to their private corners of the house.

L izzie went back down for supper, out of curiosity more than anything else. She was so sick of Emma and the whole family drama, but this stealing of Abby's property was really strange. Even for Emma.

So she went back down for supper, in hopes of thinking of something besides the pain she felt as her heart was breaking. The pain over Kathryn's behavior toward her was so great when she was alone that at times she couldn't tell where the pain ended and she began.

The tin with Abby's found property had been removed from the table. Slowly, the family members gathered and had their meal together, an uncommon occurrence. Perhaps we are brought together at this time because we are such an odd family, Lizzie thought. Other families come together as a matter of course, and split apart over petty inconsistencies and discourtesies. Our family comes together only when one or another of us is under grave suspicion. Grave suspicion and heartache.

The meal progressed in silence. No one besides Lizzie had much of an appetite. Lizzie threw bread in her mouth as fast as she could swallow. She spread it heavily with salted butter and had extra portions of meat. Somehow she hoped that the hollow that Kathryn had opened in her stomach could be filled with food. She knew that all eyes were upon her. Abby began to eat a little after watching her, but Emma and her father ate almost nothing.

After supper, Lizzie lolled about a bit in the kitchen,

wanting nothing in particular. She didn't want to be in her room, she didn't want to talk with anyone, she didn't want to eat any more, she didn't want anything, except Kathryn. And Kathryn, it appeared, didn't want her anymore. Every time she thought it, she wanted to scream. Finally, when Emma shooed her out of the way for the third time, she went out to the barn. She opened the barn door and breathed deeply of its familiar smell. She looked at the piles of junk, looked at the box where the tin of booty had been found. Why on earth would someone do something so strange? It could only have been Emma. It could *only* have been Emma. Lizzie felt mildly guilty for thinking that, but Emma really was the only one who could be responsible for such a bizarre act.

Lizzie climbed the ladder to the loft. She crossed over and looked out the dusty window. From this vantage point she could see the side of the house and Second Street beyond. I'll have to bring a little box up here so I can sit and look out this window, she thought. It was a nice view, and a private one. Someone might see her looking wistfully out her bedroom window at the street below, but no one would catch her gazing out the window of the hayloft. Lizzie felt quite invisible.

She turned back to her study area, pulled *Pathways* from its hiding place under some hay, dusted it off and set it on the little table. Then she took her seat between the table and the haystack and contemplated the ritual she was about to undertake.

Lesson three was a meditation "to empower each of the individual selves which make up one's personality. We take them each in turn in order to know them, understand them, trust them, then enlist them in our endeavors. Only in this way can we align them purposefully toward our goals." And then there was a list of "selves." Lizzie was to take each in turn, spend as much time with each one as she felt she needed in order to convince it that it should not work at cross-purposes in her life. The list included the Angry Self, the Greedy Self, the Jealous Self, the Slothful Self, the Prideful Self, the Lustful Self, the Gluttonous Self, the Higher Self, the Healthful Self and the Whole Self.

She had tried to visualize the Angry Self, but hadn't had much luck. Sometimes she imagined she saw that face in the mirror, that distorted picture she saw when she did the exercise with the candles, the face with the vacant eyes. But it seemed to swim in and out of focus, and she could never enlist her Angry Self in conversation the way she supposed she was to do.

She opened the book to the first lesson, but the book was heavy and her heart heavier. She didn't have much enthusiasm for her studies. She felt leaden, cast aside.

But she tried. As always, she began by thinking about Beatrice and her impending arrival. The thought of it always made Lizzie's heart beat a little faster, there was so much to accomplish between now and then, and the days just kept flying by and Lizzie just could not see enough progress to feel good about herself. She felt squeezed, and that was what kept her coming to the hayloft three times a day to do her lessons and her reading and wonder why she kept eating like a hog when she *knew* she had to take some pounds off before Beatrice arrived. And oh God, how she had just eaten! She felt as tight as a tick.

Even Kathryn had made a comment. Lizzie had gotten used to Emma's snide remarks—Emma, who was always as thin as a rail, and looked hooked because of it, was always making remarks about Lizzie's heftiness—but then Kathryn said something of the same just two nights ago.

Lizzie had sat up in Kathryn's bed and asked her if she had something to eat in the house. Some sort of a snack. Their lovemaking always left Lizzie ravenous. Usually, she would go home and paw through the pantry, but this time she thought it might be fun to see what Kathryn, the gourmet cook, had on hand for snacks.

"I can tell you have quite a sweet tooth, Lizzie," Kathryn said. "No, we don't eat between meals here."

Lizzie had flushed deeply and felt quite odd for the rest of the evening. And had gone home and eaten far more than she ever had, and far more than she should. And she ate extra portions the next day as well, knowing all the while that she shouldn't, she really shouldn't. She *really* shouldn't.

And then it happened the very next night, last night. She wandered about the house listlessly, feeling blue and bored for no particular reason, and decided that what she needed was an evening with a good friend. She wanted to see Kathryn, not to bed Kathryn necessarily, but to spend some time with a good friend. She was sick to death of Emma and her whining.

So she went over to Kathryn's house and Kathryn answered the door in the same burgundy-colored dress she'd worn on Lizzie's first dinner there. "Not *tonight,* Lizzie," she said, and Lizzie heard the sound of company in Kathryn's front room. She looked at Kathryn's face, not understanding, and Kathryn rolled her eyes and said, "I have company, Lizzie," and then she shut the door.

Lizzie stood there, stunned. And then she had stepped over the flower bed that bordered the walk and looked in the front room window. Kathryn had returned to her guest, Cynthia Miller.

Cynthia Miller!

Lizzie could not believe her eyes, but Kathryn was definitely sitting too close to Cynthia for it to be a casual evening together.

Lizzie felt dirty. Used. Cheated. Abandoned.

She went home and ate everything she could find. Then she went down cellar and scrubbed every inch of her body. Then, upstairs, she took all the clothes she had ever worn to

Kathryn's and put them in the laundry. They were soiled. She was soiled, and no amount of scrubbing could wash away the sins of the flesh she had committed at the behest of that woman.

Lizzie lay back against the haystack. She should be starting her lessons, but her mind was on Kathryn now, and she couldn't quite let her go.

She should have seen it coming. Kathryn had gotten less tender and loving as the weeks went on. Could it possibly have been only two months ago, when they first began keeping such close company? Only two months since Kathryn had been so attentive? She had come to ignore Lizzie for long stretches of time, always keeping Lizzie off balance. Lizzie had never been in control of the relationship, not from the start, and Kathryn's power over her was a powerful distraction. A distraction during a time when she needed no distractions. She had work to do. She had lots of work to do on herself. Lizzie knew it, Emma knew it, Beatrice knew it, and Kathryn knew it. Kathryn, in fact, never let her forget it.

Kathryn had become quick to find Lizzie's faults. She had become snippy at times, and snubbed Lizzie when in public. Lizzie knew that Kathryn must keep up appearances, but there were times when a friendly, affectionate smile in public would not be construed as more than that, a friendly smile. But Kathryn seemed to use "discretion" as an excuse to ignore Lizzie, give her uppity looks, look at her and then giggle with the other women . . . and Lizzie hadn't cared for that at all.

There was a place within Lizzie that knew Kathryn wasn't a very nice person. That place inside Lizzie wished she had broken it off with Kathryn first. It would have been so much easier.

But the rest of Lizzie screamed in pain. Where on earth would she ever find another lover, someone who knew

Lizzie's secret places even better than Lizzie knew them? How could she *ever* find another lover?

She never would. She would never again feel the softness of lips on her own. She would never feel that shuddering urgency. She would never stroke another tender breast. She would never feel another's hands deeply tangled in her hair, or awake to find a leg thrown over her own.

Lizzie caught herself up, sat straight and rubbed her face. No, she thought. That will never happen again. I was misled. It was sinful. It will never happen again.

She opened the book to the first lesson and began to read aloud, but the picture that came to her mind was that of Kathryn Peters, someone who took advantage of her, someone who didn't return the affection Lizzie endowed, someone who was secretive and dishonest (a drinker!), someone who was just not . . . quite . . . right.

Lizzie sat back, the lesson forgotten. I'm acting like a lovesick teenager, she thought, with little patience. What exactly did I want from this affair? What did I expect? Respectability? Marriage?

Something in her heart turned over as she realized that now she would never marry. How could she, after being so intimate with another woman? She was a freak. She would never have children. She would never move out of this house, not until Andrew died, and probably not until Andrew and Abby both died. She would never move in with another woman, she would never have such an affair with another woman—she would never have a man suitor that she could take seriously, not after . . . not after Kathryn.

Kathryn made it very clear to her the kind of lovers men made. They were rough and insensitive—not so very unlike Kathryn herself at times—and selfish. Kathryn talked a lot about how men bedded women, which always put Lizzie off. It seemed as though Kathryn had had a lot of men in her travels. And while Lizzie had never been very interested in men, they had always seemed a last-resort means of getting out of the Borden house and out from under the oppressive eye of the family.

And now that could never be.

The loss of her dreams flattened Lizzie to the haystack. She gazed up at the cobwebs in the rafters and felt her heart beating, felt her pulse at the top of her head.

I'm no longer respectable in any sense of the word, she thought. Worse, I could be a terrible embarrassment to the family—and where would I be without them?

Her gaze settled on the blue sky out the window, then drifted down toward the little table and the *Pathways* book.

Beatrice made the world the way she wanted it to be. All I need to do is follow instructions. All I need to do is what I'm told to do. She picked up the book and hugged it to her, tears of frustration and heartsickness leaking out the corners of her eyes.

I don't think I'm capable, she thought. I don't think I *can* lose weight, become bolder, more adventurous, more self-assured. I am not bold. I am not adventurous, I am not self-assured. I am not in control of my life. Can this really turn me into something I long to be, but am not?

She opened the book at random and ran her finger down the broad lines of type. A little circle of heat waves blurred her vision right in the center.

Lizzie felt all the wind go out of her sails. A headache was coming on. She sat there, immobilized by her impotence. She knew she should get up and get down the ladder, into the house, and into the dark, cool bedroom before she was unable to do those things. She had perhaps ten minutes to prepare for the pain, because once the pain came, there was only the pain, the all-consuming pain. The pain and the vomiting and more pain.

Instead, she sat there, lying back into the haystack, feeling the crinkle of the dusty hay beneath her, feeling the little pieces of it poke her, feeling the soft cover of the book, watching the little swirly parts of the headache precursor.

And then she remembered taking the jewelry from Abby's dresser. And the money from the drawer.

She sat up, her breath caught in her chest. No, no, it was impossible, it was wrong, how could she . . . *why* would she . . .

She quickly hid the book under the corner of the haystack, pushed the table up against the wall underneath the window. She climbed as rapidly as she dared, her sight unsteady, down the ladder. Then she stepped gingerly across the junk-strewn floor to the barn door.

All the while she remembered. She could see herself, her hand as it took the bedroom key from the mantel, as she walked up the back stairs and opened the bedroom door. She saw herself pick up the jewelry and go directly to the drawer that held Abby's emergency fund. Lizzie had seen her take money from that envelope a thousand times when she was a little girl. It was no secret, that envelope. She took it all, tightly clenched in her fist, and she went to the barn.

Lizzie could remember it all, she could see it all, but as the circle of wavy lines receded past her vision, the pounding pain began to fade in. She stopped in the kitchen and put both hands up to her forehead. "Please stop," she whined. "Please."

But the migraine was relentless, and it increased a thousandfold in intensity. Weak-kneed, Lizzie made it to the stairs, then very gently, she climbed the stairs, her hands on both walls of the stairwell for balance.

She fumbled at the lock on her door, entered, pulled the blind and the curtains, slipped out of her clothes, put the chamber pot in a handy place in case she needed it quickly, brought the towel from the washbasin over, and slipped, wearing only her drawers, between the cool sheets.

The headache seemed to subside for a moment while she

moved with purpose. She got into bed, and had time for only one more thought. How strange that she could remember—barely remember—taking the jewelry and the money, but she could *not* remember why.

Sometimes Andrew Borden wished his whole damned family would just go away and leave him alone. This was one of those times. Usually, he prayed for peace under his roof—"the peace of the Lord," as he liked to put it. He prayed for the peace of the Lord to be within Emma, Abby and Lizzie. He would have liked nothing better than to come home from work, have Lizzie rub his feet and read to him, then sleep, awaken to a well-cooked and palatable meal, then relax with fine humor with his family. But his prayers hadn't been answered for some twenty-five years now, and the only prayer left to him was that they would just all go away and leave him alone. Sometimes he even included Lizzie in that prayer.

But this prayer was not likely to be answered, either. And in addition, there was no peace of the Lord in Andrew, either. Too many other matters pressed on his mind these days.

The mill had not been as profitable as it should have been in the past three quarters. Costs were up, income was barely holding, and it was up to Andrew to effect a management change. That was to be a time-consuming job, finding replacement personnel, especially if he had to handle the reins himself while he found the new managers.

Lizzie was acting queer again, spending all her days in the barn and all her nights out somewhere with God only knew who. When questioned, Lizzie professed quite convincing innocence. Kathryn Peters, she said, always volunteered her

149

home for WCTU committee work. That's where Lizzie could be found most nights, she said, and Andrew had no call to disbelieve her. But now she went out almost every night. Andrew didn't approve of outside interests that required someone's attention every night. There were family matters that needed attention. The home. The home came first.

But Andrew had learned that his daughters were headstrong and had almost outgrown caring about his dissatisfactions. He learned to save his criticism for important issues. They knew very well where he stood on family propriety, and he had to trust in their judgment, even though none of them had ever shown him very good judgment in any matter whatsoever.

Like Lizzie and this barn business. It was downright peculiar. He'd been out there to Lizzie's hayloft study, and seen nothing out of bounds, but just because the eye doesn't see something doesn't mean that there isn't trouble under the surface.

He was still trying to find the time of a Sunday morning to fake explanations to all the parishioners who asked about Lizzie's sudden change of churches. That was a slap in the face to all Bordens, but she didn't seem to give it a second thought. They all dressed in their Sunday clothes, left the house at the same time, but Lizzie turned right on Second Street, and Andrew and Emma and Abby (when she had a mind to go) turned left. It infuriated him every week, that she would go *down*town, to worship with the Polish and the Italians and those uppity Hill people, instead of *up*town, with the Anglos as was proper for a Borden. And to teach the Chinese! Heathens!

He just didn't have the time to think about it all. He didn't have time for the guilt, either. It was his badgering that made Lizzie change churches. He knew that as well as he knew his own name, but he didn't know what he could do about it. There didn't seem to be anything he *could* do. It made him more than furious. It hurt him. It gave him chest pains.

And then fancy Emma stealing Abby's jewelry and her ten dollars. That was just so strange as to set Andrew's head spinning. Being in business the way he was, he was used to personality conflicts among employees, used to backbiting, petty jealousies and even violent outbreaks. But this stealing of the jewelry and money and putting it into an old, rusty meat tin and leaving it in the barn was just too bloody strange. It verged on the incomprehensible.

Emma did it, of course Emma had done it, she protested too loudly not to have done it.

And Andrew was in the middle of it all again, for Abby had his ear on the pillow at night and she talked far into the night about the girls. He was beginning to believe that he was indeed too old to deal with such pettiness, and if Lizzie had to go with Emma in order to get Emma out of the house, then perhaps that would be the best idea of all.

But his heart clenched as he thought it.

And then, *and then* there was the Widow Crawford.

Every time he thought of her petite form, her tiny little nose, her reddish hair graying at the sides, her upturned face with the sparkle in the eye and the ready smile for him, all thoughts of his family fled, and he felt a stirring within. She was a delightful woman, very respectable, with two big strapping sons, both off to college. She worked for the law firm that handled the bank's work, and Andrew found that he frequented the law firm personally as a courier just to bask in her very special smile.

From the very beginning, he seethed with plans for a tryst, almost every waking moment. He thought of suggesting that they meet for lunch, and then his day would be confused, the daydreams of the two of them gazing into each other's eyes, of discreet electrifying touches of their fingertips at just the right moments, conflicting with the business decisions at hand.

But the daydream would only go so far. People would see them together in public, and as they had no common interest, other than each other, it would not be proper for a married man to be seen with a widow lady.

So then he thought of calling on her at her home one night, just knocking on the door. She would answer the door wearing a chaste, yet playful smile, and he would enter her chamber of pleasures and be kept a willing prisoner there for a week.

But he would never go to her home without an invitation, and she was far too proper to issue one.

He could invite her away. He could be inconvenienced, and ask that she meet him with important papers. They could meet for coffee in a public place, and as he looked over the papers in a law-firm folio, no one could possibly suspect anything but business was being carried out.

But his office was only blocks from hers, and both firms employed couriers.

Try as he might, Andrew Borden could find no way to approach this woman of his dreams, except by frequenting her place of employment, which he did at every opportunity.

And when he did show up, she brightened. He could see it.

And then the miracle happened.

Two days after the affair of Abby's missing property, Andrew stopped by the law office to sign some papers, and Mrs. Crawford halted his heart with a tiny, soft hand on his wrist.

"Mr. Borden?"

His mouth went dry. He looked into those sparkling eyes that appeared as if they had never taken anything seriously.

"Please excuse me for being so bold, but I am quite beside myself. I am truly at my wits' end."

"What is it?"

"My brother's family needs me to tend the children for the weekend—they live out south—and I haven't a way to get there. I wonder if I could press upon your kindness to see if you could loan me a rig and a driver. I should be very happy to pay."

Andrew's heart flew. "Of course," he said. "When would you be wanting to go?"

"Friday after work. It's only about an hour's drive. My sister-in-law has been ill, you see, and they need to travel to a doctor in New Bedford, and I'm the only kin . . ."

"What time shall I pick you up?"

"Oh, Mr. Borden, I couldn't possibly intrude on your generosity this way. Surely you must have a driver . . ."

"I would be honored, Mrs. Crawford. In fact, I have business out that way on Saturday. I'll just move it to Friday and be done with it."

"I would be ever so grateful," she said, and it looked to Andrew as if she meant it.

Andrew finished his business in the law office with a trembling hand. Then he said good-bye and left, chiding himself all the way back to the bank for acting like a foolish schoolboy.

And the buckboard had torn leather on the seat, too. Perhaps it could be fixed before Friday.

Suddenly, problems of the household vanished. Andrew lived for Friday. He only prayed that a runaway carriage would not strike him down, not when he was about to embark upon the hour-long excursion that would bring him true joy at last.

He had married Abby as a convenience for both of them, but neither one was very interested in nocturnal bedtime activities. At first, Andrew could not forget the soft feel of

153

Sarah's skin beneath him, and the glimpses he caught of fat Abby in her dressing gown put him right off. They had pretended a couple of times, Andrew always careful to spend his seed into the sheets and not his wife. He had no use for more children. But after those first halting tries, Andrew could tell that Abby was not impressed with the physical side of marriage, and he was not very interested in her as a partner, so they slept side by side every night and never again discussed it.

But never had he forgotten the feel of Sarah Borden, her smooth, cool white flesh under his fingers, her long lines, unintimidated, her abandon in their bedroom.

And now, for the first time, old sparks were rekindled when he looked into the joy-loving eyes of the Widow Crawford, and it was almost more than Andrew could hope for, but he did indeed hope that she would raise her skirts for him, at least once.

At least once. And perhaps on Friday.

On Friday, Andrew was up before dawn. He carefully bathed, shaved and donned fresh clothes. He viewed himself critically in the mirror, wondering if any woman anywhere could ever find him attractive. It was doubtful. He milled about in the kitchen until Abby got up, and then he was short with her and irritated by her behavior. He mentioned that he would be home late, perhaps very late, and then he left for the office.

But work came hard. Concentration was impossible. At ten o'clock, he went to the stable to inspect the new leather. The boy had done a fine job. The springs were freshly greased, the tack oiled, and he made sure the boy would shine up the horse in fine fashion before he came round to take the rig at five o'clock sharp.

Five o'clock! It seemed that five o'clock would never arrive.

154

But arrive it did, and Andrew helped the Widow Crawford up onto the seat next to him; he snapped the reins, feeling young and reckless, and they were on their way out of town.

At first, he was loath to say anything, feeling that perhaps his pleasure, his eagerness, would show through and put her off. But once out of town, she opened up and began chatting away. She pulled a shawl from her valise, and moved over a little closer to him when she resettled in her seat, and they talked of Fall River and common acquaintances.

Andrew found out she knew and liked Lizzie very much. Lizzie had just joined Mrs. Crawford's—Enid's—church, and was becoming a well-respected member of the congregation very rapidly.

Andrew made a mental note to visit that church someday.

As the conversation carried on, this way and that, Enid found reason to touch him, his arm, his knee, his wrist, and each time she did, a thrill ran up his spine and shuddered at the base of his skull. He could never get enough of this woman, he knew for certain.

And then she, bold as brass, suggested they pull off on a little side road so they could get out and stretch their legs.

Andrew pulled the horse up short and guided him into a small meadow. He jumped down, ran around and helped her down, and she lingered just a tad in his arms before looking down and moving away. Andrew secured the buckboard and uncoupled the horse's reins so he could eat while they walked.

They walked a ways, the shadows of spring falling long and cool over the emerald-green grass, little white and yellow wildflowers everywhere. And then Enid spread her shawl on the grass and sat upon it. "Sit with me for a while, won't you, Andrew?" Then she looked down, and said, "May I call you Andrew?"

Andrew almost fell on her, he sat down so quickly. She moved toward him, and put her hand on his cheek. Then she lifted his hand and placed it on her breast.

"You're a very compelling man, Andrew," she breathed.

"Miss Enid," he said, and then his voice failed him, for she was moving toward him in a different way, and there was no doubt at all about her purpose.

He took her, and almost without pause, took her again. He felt like a little stallion. Never, not even with Sarah, not even when he was young, had the experience been so wild for him. The smells of the meadow mixed with the scent of her perfume; the rustle of her skirts as they shifted beneath him (she wore no underwear at all!) the heat of his passion on his back, but the cool of the evening on his buttocks. And she moved beneath him like an untamed thing, quite out of control. He had never imagined someone could make sounds like that—so animal, so wonderful!

And when he was finished, and had rearranged himself, she sat up and smoothed her hair and said, "My, my."

He averted his eyes while she borrowed his hankie, then he helped her up and shook out her shawl. Then he helped her back into the buggy, suddenly shy and quite embarrassed about his—their—behavior.

They rode on for a little while, and then she spoke. "Mr. Borden?"

He noticed that "Andrew" had gone by the wayside.

"Yes, Mrs. Crawford?"

"My two boys are in college up in Boston, you know."

"Yes, so I understand."

"They're doing very well."

"You must be proud."

"I am, I am, but you know, Mr. Borden, college is terribly expensive."

Anger shot through Andrew and his face flushed. He wanted to dump her right here on the side of the road. But he looked over, and it was the same sweet face he had admired for so long, and their coupling had been so intense, so severe, so indescribably *sweet* . . . "Yes?"

"I thought perhaps you could loan me a little money for their tuition." She looked up at him and smiled. Bold as brass, that little woman.

"How much would you be wanting?"

"Oh, not much at all, Mr. Borden, not much at all. You see, I make a fair wage at the law firm, and there is still money left from their father, but . . . say one hundred dollars? Perhaps I could get it from you *next* Friday?"

And then Andrew understood. She would meet with him next Friday for one hundred dollars. And the next. And the next. But one *hundred* dollars! He maintained his entire household on half that much for a whole month! He looked over at her, sitting there, so attractive. *So* attractive. She could have chosen any man at all, yet she chose him. There was no harm in helping a nice widow lady put her sons through college. "I'd be delighted to help the boys, Mrs. Crawford. What are their names again?"

"Chester and Charles. Thank you ever so much, Mr. Borden," she said, and she laid a hand very lightly upon his knee.

Andrew felt himself stir again at her touch, and he looked across at her profile. She was smiling, the tiniest little smile. He could barely wait for next Friday.

And as regularly as clockwork, Andrew Borden took Mrs. Crawford for a ride on Friday afternoons. He discovered that little else mattered in his life. Mrs. Crawford, Lizzie and little else.

A bby awoke to hear only the pounding of her heart in her ears. Paralyzed with an unnamed fear, she opened her eyes barely a slit. She saw the outlines of the furniture in her room, vaguely illuminated by the small amount of moonlight that drifted through the lace curtains. She listened.

Hearing nothing but the silence of the sleeping house, she moved, gently at first, so that if an intruder were to see her, he would merely think she was turning in her sleep. She turned over, stretched, then opened her eyes once again. Nothing. There was nothing there.

Nothing but a feeling, a feeling of dread, of doom, of menace. Abby tried to calm herself. There was nothing.

Gradually, her heartbeat returned to normal, but sleep had flown. Abby looked at the clock on Andrew's nightstand. Two-forty.

She heard a horse clop down the street. The milkman.

The feeling of dread had been ever present in the past month or so. Andrew had a mistress, she could tell, and she seemed to have him quite bound up. She was afraid of losing him as a husband, she was afraid of losing him as provider, she was afraid that the good Borden name would be scandalized by he who professed to worry so much about the integrity of the same name.

He met her on Friday evenings, only on Fridays, and every Friday.

Andrew seemed oblivious of all the goings-on at the

house. He came and went, ate, slept, read, spoke as if he were in some sort of dream state. His most common phrase was "That's fine," and he said that automatically, without even hearing what the girls or she said to him.

It worried Abby mightily.

But it did more than worry Abby, it left her to run the household by herself, and her power as head of the household was nil as far as the girls went, and very little as far as the maid. It was a frustrating situation, all right, and the pantry and icebox were Abby's only solace.

Then a shadow moved across the wall. The room was dark, but there was a place that was darker than dark, and it moved.

Abby's heart hammered. There *is* someone in here. It's the someone who took my jewelry, come back to rob us again. He's here to kill us all, some business acquaintance of Andrew's, no doubt. She tried to be still, not to give away to the person or persons that she was awake and aware of his presence, but her heart beat so fast that she could not breathe. She opened her mouth and took in small breaths, trying desperately to look asleep.

But then there were no sounds, and surely she would be able to hear an intruder's step or breath, but there was nothing. Abby squinted her eyes up tight and rolled over onto her side, facing her husband. She pulled the covers up over her head. I'll just let them be, she decided. If they want to rob me, that's fine, they won't be the first. If they want to kill me as I lie in my bed, well then, that's fine, too. I just pray they make it quick.

But no hand came to touch her, and she heard the sound of no intruder. She said a little prayer, even though she only half believed, and then her mind wandered again to her husband's neglect of the fatherly chores in the house and her heart began to pump again, only this time in anger.

I'm too old to live in a house where everybody hates me,

she thought. Emma hates me, Lizzie sides with Emma, and Andrew has a lover. If he wants to take a lover, that's fine with me, but why should I have to put up with that *and* those girls as well?

Just then, Abby heard Lizzie's bedsprings creak, and the sound of the chamber pot scraping across the floor. She waited for the sounds of vomiting, but they didn't come.

Abby relaxed. Her heart went out to poor Lizzie with those blasted headaches. She had tried everything, but there was nothing to be done for them, nothing but a quiet, dark room and sometimes a cool cloth for the forehead. Poor Lizzie. She suffered so. Since her teens, she'd been plagued with those terrible headaches, headaches that made her vomit all day and half the night.

Abby could be angry at Lizzie, but she could never hate her, not the way she sometimes hated Emma for the foolish way Emma acted. And a grown woman at that! Emma was a fool, a greedy, money-hungry fool, whose penchant for rages made her highly undesirable as an acquaintance, never mind a stepdaughter!

But Lizzie, sweet Lizzie.

Abby listened as the bedpan was pushed under the bed again. It wasn't a headache for Lizzie tonight. Thank the gods for that. She'd had quite a group of them lately. Maybe four or five in the past two weeks. Every time, Abby had wanted to do something for Lizzie—she used to buy toys with the household money for Lizzie when she was sick. Even when she was a young woman, just beginning this terrible life with headaches, Abby always found a few pennies to spend on a treat for Lizzie.

But now, there was nothing to be done when the headaches struck, nothing but to tiptoe around the house, reminding Emma and Bridget, *always* reminding Bridget, to keep the noise level down so Lizzie could rest. And Abby

160

never brought a toy nor a treat. Abby's mothering instincts had begun to fade in the shadow of the abuse she'd been receiving from Emma. And Lizzie, by association.

Abby settled back into her bed, the fear of the dark shadows gone, the anger at Andrew gone, the worry over Lizzie having another headache gone. All that was left was that creeping feeling of doom.

It had been intensifying lately, that feeling. That terrible feeling that something was about to happen. The present status could not remain so for very much longer; everyone seemed to be strung just a little bit too tight. And when people are just a little too close, just a little too crowded, well, things begin to happen.

Like jewelry and money disappearing and reappearing in the barn.

A shiver ran through Abby. It was such a violation, that little robbery. It was such a slap in the face by some member of this household. On that day she almost gave the ultimatum to Andrew: We move or they move. But the tensions had eased some after that, and of course, there had been no repeat offense, nor had Abby any reason to think there would be. The point, whatever it was, had apparently been made.

And yet, the thought of the robbery was somehow inseparable from this feeling of dread that she had, this moving black shadow that was just a little darker than the dark, when nothing was there. The robbery was an omen, she thought, of terrible things to come, and if she were a real wife, and a real mother, she would *insist* that Andrew take her out of this house and save them all from themselves.

But she was not a real wife, and Andrew knew that, and she was not a real mother, and both Emma and Lizzie knew that.

So she would make do, as she always had, spending her time with Sarah and her many troubles, and the occasional birthing that came along in her little circle of acquaintances, and she would hope that when the end came, whatever it might be, it would be swift and sure, silent and without warning.

hen Lizzie woke up, Emma was already in trouble. Emma was headed for New Bedford.

The day began as normal, with Emma fighting life so hard it reduced her to stringy tendons and a cruel mouth. Emma fought with her clothes, her bureau drawers, her father, her stepmother, her breakfast, the maid.

Lizzie watched it all, listening, knowing that Emma was about to lose control. She knew the signs; after all these years, Lizzie knew the signs.

So when Emma threw her silverware on the floor, kicked at it until it skittled out of reach, and then ran upstairs—all this provoked by something innocuous that their father had said—Lizzie knew that New Bedford was not far away.

And sure enough, Emma appeared in the dining-room doorway in less than a half hour, wearing her traveling hat and carrying her valise.

Abby continued with her breakfast, Andrew read the morning paper. Neither one of them seemed to care that Emma was off to further her destruction at the hands of unknowns. Lizzie alone flew to Emma's side, her heart breaking in the midst of her pain over Kathryn. She felt as if she were drowning in emotional vapors.

But Emma would not be persuaded to stay. "I need some fresh air," she said, "some fresh scenery. I shan't be but a couple of weeks, Lizzie," and she shook off Lizzie's begging and went out the front door.

Lizzie's heart died. One of these days, Emma would be

unable to crawl back home to lick her wounds. One of these days, Emma would tangle with someone a little too rough, and be unable to crawl back home, ever.

The familiar box of worry closed around Lizzie, and she knew that it would not open until Emma came home. She knew that she was bound now to be thinking of Emma and praying for Emma day after day after day, leaving little room for study or housework or reading or preparing for Beatrice's visit or anything else. Where there had been mourning for Kathryn, there now was worry for Emma.

Lizzie watched Emma walk down the street, her back as straight as their father's, the little black plume on her hat bouncing with each step. Emma always timed it for that nine o'clock train to New Bedford.

Lizzie thought if she had any gumption at all, she'd run and pack herself a bag and follow Emma. Then she could find out where Emma went, and keep an eye on her so that she didn't get into too much trouble.

Next time, she thought with a pang of guilt. There is too much to do right now. I cannot afford to take two or three weeks baby-sitting Emma while she drinks herself half to death in New Bedford. After Beatrice's visit, when everything settles back down to normal, then I shall accompany Emma on one of her excursions and see that she takes care.

But Lizzie knew that that day would never come. She had to invent that lie, like thousands before it, to plug up the guilt before it flooded her.

She wandered back to the dining room and sat in her place. Her breakfast was cold, but she ate the soggy biscuits in cold gravy anyway.

"So Emma has gone to New Bedford again, has she?"

Lizzie looked at her father and nodded.

"Don't know what gets into that girl," he said. "Seems like she just looks for an excuse to go. Who does she visit there, again?"

"I don't know, Father."

"Well, I hope she doesn't come home sick this time. I was afraid she'd put the whole household in their beds the last time."

Lizzie chewed slowly, wondering how she could hate her father so much for his lack of feeling toward her sister, and for so many other things, yet love him so desperately and want to please him so thoroughly. She should tell him the truth about Emma, but that would accomplish nothing. Unfortunately, that would accomplish nothing. She kept on eating. Abby remained silent.

After breakfast, Lizzie went back upstairs to her room, undressed and slipped back into bed. She lay there, feeling slightly ashamed of her laziness, but the load of ironing, and the lessons, and the mending just weren't her cup of tea today. She fingered the worn lace on the edge of the pillowslips and idly wondered why Abby didn't have all the pillowslips in the house replaced with fresh ones. Surely there was enough money to sleep on decent linen!

Then she looked toward Emma's bedroom door. The days were long past when Lizzie used to go into Emma's bedroom and try on her clothes and get into her things, but for once, Lizzie was mildly curious about Emma's room. Were there things in there that Emma hid? Was there alcohol? Did Emma drink here at home? Lizzie turned over on her back. No, of course not. If Emma drank at home, they would smell it on her and she would have no need to go to New Bedford.

New Bedford. It was strange to Lizzie that Emma would have secrets from her much the way she had her Kathryn secret to hide from Emma. Emma would have a seizure if she knew the pleasures that Lizzie and Kathryn enjoyed in each other's arms. But then Emma enjoyed some pleasures of her own, didn't she? Some pleasures of some sort at the Capitol Hotel in New Bedford.

Pleasures Lizzie *used* to enjoy in Kathryn's arms. She flopped over onto her stomach and punched her fists up under the pillow. We should have a cat, she thought. It would be nice to have a cat to sleep on the bed, a cat to purr and cuddle with. . . . When I have my own home, I will have a cat.

And then the idea that came was so perfect, so logical, it startled her. *Why not now?* I could move into my own house, and it could be near enough that I could keep an eye on Emma. I don't have to have a house on the Hill—not yet anyway, there are some fine houses here in town, houses of which Father would approve, and he could either give me the money for one or invest in one on his own.

That would be so much different than if Father just gave Emma her inheritance money and told her to get out. Father had been wanting to do that for months now, perhaps years. If I had a house that was large enough for Emma and I, perhaps I could induce her to move in with me.

Lizzie jumped out of bed, her heart pounding in excitement for the first time in weeks. She had an idea, a wonderful idea, and Father was sure to go along.

She dressed carefully, did her hair up just right, smoothed down her eyebrows, made her bed—she wanted to be adult and serene around him, and didn't know if she could with her bed unmade—and then she sat for a moment, composing herself and quietly asking the God of all her selves to help her. Then she slowly descended the stairs.

Andrew was at the desk in the sitting room, going over some ledgers.

"Father?"

"Lizzie."

"Father, may we talk for a moment?"

"Certainly." Andrew finished jotting a note, then put his pen down and turned in his chair.

Lizzie sat on the edge of the sofa. It would be so much

166

easier if he were sitting next to me, she thought. "Do you remember some time ago—last winter—the last time Emma went to New Bedford, in fact—when you talked about giving Emma her money and having her move out?"

Andrew looked at his shoes. "Yes."

"Well, I have another idea."

Andrew's eyebrows went up.

"Come sit next to me." She patted the seat. He sat next to her. She took his hand in hers.

"If you gave me the money, I could buy a small house—"

"Never."

"Wait, you didn't let me finish."

Andrew withdrew his hand from hers. "Very well," he said. "Finish."

"I can barely speak when you have that attitude, Father."

"Don't you be talking about my attitude, Lizzie."

This was not going right. Lizzie took a deep breath. "Father? Let's start over again. I have an idea, and I'd like you to hear it." She placed her hand over his, but he didn't move a muscle. Be bold, be adventurous, but most of all, be self-assured, Lizzie, she thought. "I was thinking of another investment property for you. Another little house, here in town. A modest house. I could move in there and encourage Emma to join me. I could be close enough to keep an eye on her in case she decided to stay here, or I could even move back in here, for that matter. But, Father, I believe she would come. That would leave you and Mother here in peace, and I could watch out for Emma during her more trying times. We'd take care of each other."

Andrew was silent. Lizzie took that as a good sign.

"We could live very cheaply, Father. The house and a small allowance is all we would need . . ." She twisted her high school ring, which was still firmly on his little finger. Then she looked up into his face and saw his eyes were red and watery. Why was he crying? What made him cry? She

167

was struck quite speechless, and then tears came to her own eyes.

Whatever it was, they both let go of each other's hands in embarrassment, and they both rose at the same time, and Lizzie headed for the front stairs while Andrew went toward the rear stairs. Not another word was said.

In her room, Lizzie wondered why she'd bothered to make the bed. All she wanted to do was to get in it and cry herself to sleep. She flopped down on top of the bedspread, closed her eyes and was suddenly a little girl again, safe, with a dark-haired father and a lanky big sister, on the banks of a fresh stream, with her little fishing stick in the water.

It was midafternoon when she arose, hunger motivating her. She poured tepid water from the pitcher into the bowl and splashed her face. At least she hadn't bawled, that would have made her eyes intolerably puffy for a day and a half. She dried her face and checked her looks in the mirror. As she straightened the bed, a soft knock came at her bedroom door.

"Miss Lizzie?" It was the maid.

Lizzie walked to the door, unlocked it, then returned to the mirror. "Come in, Maggie."

Bridget entered and handed Lizzie a folded piece of white paper.

"What's this?"

"A note from a lady. She stopped by and I told her you were sleeping."

Heart leaping, Lizzie unfolded the note. "Lizzie—Dinner? Six. Kathryn." She felt a flush come to her face, felt the smile grow into a grin. Then she noticed the young maid was still standing before her.

"Not bad news, I take it, miss?"

"No, it's good—well, it's a dinner invitation," Lizzie said, trying to regain control of her composure. "Thank you."

168

"Quite all right, miss," Bridget said lightly, then turned on her heel, red curls bouncing behind her as she tripped delicately down the stairs.

The dread of family embarrassment again fell upon Lizzie. What if that wench, that flippant little Irish girl, knew, or even suspected Lizzie's involvement with Kathryn? That would give her power. That would give her terrible power.

Lizzie sat in her rocking chair and thought about that, her heart thumping, knowing she would see Kathryn again tonight. For dinner! That meant a positive, intimate experience. . . . Lizzie had avoided meetings and anywhere she thought she might run into Kathryn because she was afraid that Kathryn would spit upon her once and for all, and Lizzie could never live through that.

And now, dinner!

And that Maggie thing most likely knows too much. That insipid little housemaid could bring the wrath of Fall River down upon the Bordens. She could ruin Father's reputation, she could ruin Lizzie's standing in the community and in church. She could do much to throw the entire family into scandal—especially since she knew, or at least suspected, the nature of Emma's "illnesses" upon her return from New Bedford.

Lizzie would talk to Father about giving the girl a raise in pay. That might seal her fidelity.

Lizzie went down to the kitchen and began rooting around for something to eat. Her stomach was filled with jittery butterflies, thinking of dining with Kathryn. There were things between them that should be discussed.

She took a loaf of bread from the pantry and sliced off two thick slices.

What kind of things should be discussed?

She spread salted butter heavily on both slices, then covered that with Abby's plum preserves.

The things that upset you, Lizzie, she told herself, and the bread stuck in her throat.

She poured a large glass of fresh milk and washed down the bread.

Yes, she thought. Those things must be discussed.

She looked out the window at the barn. Her lessons awaited her, Beatrice's arrival demanded her attention, but there was no concentrating on them. This day would have to be devoted to two things: Approaching Andrew on a raise for Maggie, and talking things over with Kathryn.

Neither one provided much comfort, so Lizzie hunted around until she found the plate of cookies Abby had stashed in the tea tin, and set them before her.

• • •

Lizzie rubbed Andrew's feet as was her custom, and then she asked him to give Maggie a raise in pay. He started, and looked at her peculiarly, but he did not say no. Lizzie smiled at him while she made him comfortable, then read to him until he was asleep for his afternoon nap. Then she dashed upstairs to clean up and make ready for the coming evening.

• • •

Lizzie was so excited to see Kathryn that even though she noticed the fancy carriage outside Kathryn's house, it didn't register that Kathryn might have others for dinner besides her.

Kathryn answered the door wearing a beautiful pale-green chiffon. After the door was closed, she kissed Lizzie gently on the lips, and then danced out of the way as Lizzie leaned into the kiss, wanting it to last longer, more, taste deeper. Kathryn laughed and teased, and led Lizzie into the living room, where two men rose to meet her.

Lizzie flushed crimson and looked with questioning eyes

at Kathryn, but Kathryn only twinkled at her and introduced the gentlemen. From Boston. Scott Carrothers and Matthew Green. They were both wearing fine suits, and it was then that Lizzie upbraided herself for not noticing that the carriage was *directly* in front of Kathryn's house, exactly where it should be if the owners were inside.

She mumbled her greetings to them, then rushed to help Kathryn in the kitchen.

"Men?" was all that came out of her mouth.

"You'll love them, Lizzie," Kathryn said. "They're like us." And then she swept back into the living room, carrying a tray of small glasses filled with sherry.

The bearded man, Scott his name was, stood and held his glass aloft. "A toast," he said, and they all took their glasses. "To love and life and fine company."

"Hear, hear," the other man said, the small man, and the three of them drained half their glasses, but Lizzie barely put hers to her lips. She still was not certain if she approved of anyone drinking anything at all, much less members of the WCTU.

The evening progressed, Lizzie on the sidelines. She was caught up in the love of life that drove her three companions for the evening, and yet she wondered if any of the neighbors would see that two unmarried ladies were accompanied by two unmarried men, unchaperoned. That would bring a terrible scandal upon the Borden name. She also wondered what Kathryn meant when she said that the men were "just like us." No matter how she put herself and Kathryn side by side with these two jocular and entertaining men, she could see no similarities.

They tried with unmuffled earnestness to include Lizzie in their gaiety, yet they were careful to tread lightly enough not to embarrass her or put her off. She was impressed with their sensitivity. Kathryn seemed to be bold, almost brazen, in her laughter with these men, and it seemed to Lizzie that they must be old friends indeed. In fact much of their humor revolved around old times together.

Kathryn served wine in the parlor and then a fabulous feast that seemed to require less than little time in the kitchen and in serving it. Lizzie, beginning to be dazzled by the intelligent rapport between the men and Kathryn, was astonished at how easily Kathryn tossed off this little dinner party. There was no tension; her absences from the room to tend to culinary matters were rarely excused and almost entirely unnoticed. And she served a fine pheasant, with roasted potatoes and early lima beans swimming in butter.

The Borden household had never, ever seen such a table.

And there was brandy afterward. Lizzie had sipped wine throughout the meal, but had not attributed her warm and growing affection for her dinner companions to the wine. After Kathryn had swept through the dining room and cleared the dishes, the men invited Lizzie back to the sitting room for a brandy. And she accepted.

"Have you ever been to Boston, Lizzie?"

"Infrequently," she said, taking a sip and loving the deep flavor.

"You must come up for the weekend. You and Kathryn. We would show you such a wonderful time. Have you been to the theater?"

"No."

"Well, my dear, we have theaters—granted, they're not like New York, but still they're professional and very, very good—and sometimes we are even invited to attend the cast parties afterwards, aren't we, Scott?"

"Yes, indeed, Lizzie," Scott said, relaxing against the back of the sofa. "In fact, you and Kathryn should come to Boston and we'll go to New York, the four of us, and see some real theater!"

Lizzie flushed. What an exciting idea, to spend a weekend

172

with Kathryn in New York City! But then wouldn't Father be scandalized, especially if word should ever get back to him that they were accompanied—unchaperoned—by a pair of gentlemen.

"Ooh, Scott," Matthew said, "we could stay at the Carlton. Remember the first time we stayed at the Carlton?"

"Indeed," Scott said, and a look passed between them that mystified Lizzie. And then Scott put his hand on Matthew's knee and squeezed it, and Lizzie understood *exactly* what Kathryn meant, and she thought for a moment she would lose her dinner right here in the sitting room.

Her face flushed, she stood, and unsteadily set her glass of brandy on the side table. Then she hurried to the kitchen, where Kathryn was stacking up the soiled dishes.

"Kathryn," Lizzie breathed. "Those men are . . ."

"Are what, darling?"

Good breeding failed Lizzie. She knew of no names for what she wanted to say.

"In love with each other? Yes, they are. Scott and Matthew have been lovers for over five years now. They met and fell in love in college."

Five years. Lizzie thought of herself in another five years. She would be thirty-seven years old, and still chasing after rainbows. She would never be any closer to having the kind of money or independence she so desperately wanted. The walls of the kitchen began to close in on her.

And then the other thought occurred to her. What do men do to each other when they're lovers? Whatever it was, it sounded terribly distasteful, especially if they were as rough and as selfish as Kathryn had always maintained. But just enough sherry, wine and brandy made Lizzie a little giddy, and she didn't know if she would laugh at her thought or perhaps be sick because of it.

But Kathryn hustled her back into the sitting room, and there they sat and talked, Lizzie mostly silent, watching the two men, the thought of their hands on each other's naked bodies quite sickening. And soon they rose, said their thank-yous, kissed both Kathryn and Lizzie lightly on the cheek, and then they were gone.

Kathryn collapsed on the sofa. "Pour me a sherry, will you, Lizzie? That's a good girl."

Lizzie poured one for each of them, then sat next to Kathryn. They both sipped their wine.

"Aren't they rocking good sports?"

"I guess so."

Kathryn sat up and looked Lizzie in the face. "You guess so—didn't you enjoy their company?"

"I did," Lizzie said, "but they made me a bit uncomfortable, I guess."

"Uncomfortable how?"

"Well, we were unchaperoned—"

Kathryn let out a hoot. "A lady could never be safer than with those two, Lizzie."

Lizzie's face burned. "And that, too, made me a feel a little strange."

"Why? They're like us."

Lizzie didn't care for the comparison at all. People like that were a certain way, and Kathryn wasn't that way, and neither was she. But she couldn't quite put her finger on what way that was, so she didn't mention it.

Kathryn turned Lizzie's head with a gentle finger and kissed her lightly on the lips. "The night is yet early. . . ."

And Lizzie rose and pulled Kathryn along with her. Then they ran for the bedroom, disrobing and giggling like a couple of high school girls until they were again in each other's hot and passionate embrace, and Lizzie felt as if she'd come home. Home at last.

Later, Lizzie told Kathryn what the men had said about their going to join them in Boston or in New York, and

174

Kathryn had screamed in laughter. "What a fabulous idea," she said. "Being out on the town with those two men would be a terrible lot of fun. We certainly *must* do that sometime, Lizzie. Perhaps after the heat of the summer has passed."

Lizzie agreed. After the heat of the summer, she would go to the theater with these three odd people. Sometime after Beatrice had come and gone, after she had lost enough weight so that her gowns would fit her again, after her father had lost his mind and let her go to New York unchaperoned with Kathryn and two men.

And she lay entwined with Kathryn, thinking it was time she got home, and she wondered if Scott and Matthew were at that very moment making their strange brand of love, or lying abed with their legs entwined, talking about Lizzie and Kathryn.

"Lizzie?"

"Hmmm?"

"I had a dream about you."

"Oh?"

"I dreamed you had split into two people. In my dream, you were here with me, but somehow you were pacing back and forth in your house. It occurred to me that when you are here, you are either wishing you were home or worried that you ought to be home, that our activities here will be found out about your family."

"I feel sometimes—"

"Let me finish. And also in this dream, while you were with me here, like this, and you were also at home, you were in two places at your house, as well. You were in your bedroom upstairs, sleeping, but you were also pacing the floor, walking into the others' rooms and pacing back and forth by their beds."

"I've been worried about Emma."

Kathryn was silent.

"And Cynthia Miller," Lizzie added.

Kathryn said nothing, just reached over and squeezed Lizzie's hand.

It was clear that there would be no comfort or reassurance forthcoming from Kathryn.

And it was not until Lizzie was at home, in bed, reliving the events of the evening, that she remembered, ever so vaguely, that at times she *was* at home in bed . . . *and* pacing the floor at the foot of her father's bed at the same time.

June

mma lay in bed, her head pounding, her body aching. She slowly, painfully turned on her side and saw the breakfast tray that Lizzie had brought, still on the bedstand. The thought of food nauseated her, yet she knew she should eat. She needed the strength. She needed lots of strength just to heal.

With a thin, trembling hand, Emma grasped the side of the mattress and pulled herself into something like a sitting position. Then she reached out and took a cold piece of toast that had been spread with jam. It looked awful. She took a bite, then another. It tasted as sour as her breath. She put the toast back, swallowed with difficulty, then slid back beneath the covers.

Her arms looked stringy and pale, and a large, round bruise puffed on one shoulder.

She was afraid to look into a mirror.

She'd been home from New Bedford for a week, and still she was hardly able to move. Since undressing with Lizzie's help and getting into bed, she hadn't been up yet, except to urinate some dark, foul-smelling stuff into the slops pail. Her hair felt greasy and her scalp itched. Her teeth were furred and the bleached and sun-dried sheets rasped her sensitive skin.

"I'll never go back there," she said softly to herself. "This was the worst. This time I mean it. I'll never go back." And yet, deep in her heart, she knew that she was as likely to stop herself, once she was riding high on the fury that was her mother's legacy, as she was likely to stop a slow-moving freight train. The lunacy was beyond her control.

She always went to New Bedford with agitated anticipation. She began to drink alone in her room and then she would suddenly "wake up" and find herself in some tavern or other, some loud, boisterous woman's voice coming from her lips. Sometimes she would "come awake" back in her hotel room, and sometimes she would awaken again in someone else's hotel room or house, and sometimes she would awaken and there would be many people around her. And each time she would have no knowledge of where she was, nor memory of how she got there. But a little more liquor seemed to soothe the stomach-clenching fear of being out of control. And it wouldn't be long before she awakened again somewhere else, in some further state of disrepair.

But somehow, it always came back to the same thing. Somehow, she always found someone to beat her. Always.

Maybe a trip to New Bedford wasn't really a trip to New Bedford without being beaten silly, she thought with a wry grin that hurt her head. Or, more likely, the trip wasn't over until she could barely walk, what with being sick half to death from a two- or three-week binge, not to mention the physical damage done to her by person or persons unknown.

This time was the worst by far. She'd awakened in her hotel room, dried blood smeared on her sheets and pillowcases. She'd dressed somehow, covering her face with her darkest veil. She called down to the front desk and the bellman had helped her down and into a cab. Then the cabbie had helped her onto the train, where she was afraid she would fall senseless and miss her stop. Another cabbie brought her home and half carried her up the walk, until Lizzie could help her up the stairs and into bed. She hated all that help, but there was no way she could have made it on her own. She would have fallen. She would have died.

At least this time she wasn't bleeding, except from a few

scrapes on her face, knees and hip. There had been times when she had bled, not her monthly bleeding, but from the same place. One time in particular it had gone on and on and on, for more than a month. She knew without being told that permanent damage had happened inside.

Perhaps that's why she never ended up in trouble, because surely during those times, men had . . .

She knew they had. At first she had been able to pretend that it hadn't happened, but as time went on, the evidence was all around her that men, faceless men, had taken advantage of her in her inebriated state. And yet, she could not remember it. She could not remember a single instance. Apparently, it only happened when she was "gone away from herself," as she referred to those vacant periods, those lapses in her memory during her drinking.

At first, her face burned with the thought of her behavior during times she could not be aware of, those times when she had no control over herself. But as time went on and lack of control over the trips to New Bedford increased, the fact that she was continually sexually molested by blurry-faced men in dark rooms was lost in the overflow of the horror of it all.

And occasionally, when she was at home afterward, secure if not welcome, safe if not protected, and warm if not loved, she would try to remember those times, and now and then a face would ripple up from the dark, or a gesture, a word, a sensation, a thrust against her hips, and she would almost remember, and she would almost smile.

The first two days at home all she did was sleep and drink the juice Lizzie brought to her. The next two or three days she lay there, staring at the stains on the ceiling, at the uneven application of wallpaper, and felt the bedsores ripen on her elbows and heels. She begged Lizzie to ask Maggie not to bleach and starch the sheets so heavily, but Lizzie was absent-minded about things, and when Maggie came and changed the sheets, their rawness scraped Emma's sores anew.

Emma tried to ignore the sores, so she thought about her life. And then she began to think about the family.

Something odd was happening in the family.

After so many years in the same home with the same people, one became so finely tuned to a place that any breath of newness reverberated soundly.

And there was newness all around.

None of it good.

Emma wished she were well enough to be up and about, sniffing out changes, seeing what affected her and how much, but the most she could do from her bed was to talk to Lizzie when she brought a meal tray, emptied slops or just sat by her bedside for a while.

She could discern little from Lizzie, although Emma had a feeling that Lizzie was the epicenter of it all.

Days and nights blurred for Emma; she slept so often during the day and was awake so often during the night that the two were completely interchangeable in her mind. During the day, the stiff blinds and heavy curtains were drawn against the sun that hurt her eyes and her head; during the night she lit a stub of a candle that flickered and waved against the walls, creating monstrous shadows, and she would lie there and think strange thoughts.

And sometimes there was another presence pacing in her room. She couldn't see it, but she could feel it. Something paced in her room at night. Something troubled. At times it seemed as if she could almost see it, just a shadow upon a shadow. Sometimes it seemed to pass right through the wall into Abby's dressing room. Emma could feel its absence. And then she could feel its presence, again, when it returned.

She didn't mention it to Lizzie, because in the daytime, it seemed like a ludicrous notion, and when she thought about it, which was not often, she more likely feared that it was the work of a brain damaged by excesses.

But at night, when it began again, there was no doubting its existence, and Emma longed to call out, to touch it, to give it peace and rest.

But she had no peace and had never rested herself, so what made her think she could offer solace to another troubled soul?

So at night the shadow paced the floor and Emma's mind paced in place.

•   •   •

Reentry into the family was always a considerable chore for Emma. She felt like a stranger. She felt almost as if, during the six weeks she was absent from the household—three in New Bedford, three in bed—her opening in the family had healed closed.

She felt reluctant to approach her father; she felt unworthy. She found she could not meet his gaze. She kept her eyes lowered, not because she was ashamed, necessarily, although she would be if her father knew where she'd been and what she'd been doing, but rather because she felt like an outsider again, and had no voice in the family affairs. She felt she had to first gain reentry to the family and then reclaim her station.

She could not speak to Abby for a long time after each trip to New Bedford. Abby did make her feel shame. As difficult as Abby was, as bewildering and dangerous as she was to Emma and Lizzie's welfare, Abby did many of the things that Emma secretly longed to do. She longed to be the mistress of a well-run house. She longed to hold her head up as a matronly pillar of the community, having reared her share of the world's next generation, and be on to one's own interests. Next to Abby, Emma felt such burning, torturous shame that she could not look her in the face for a long time after returning from one of her sojourns.

Emma had few interests outside the family. There were some cousins in Fairhaven whom she had always got on with, but Lizzie was the social butterfly in the family, not Emma. Emma had no patience for small talk and insignificant nonsense.

Lizzie made Emma believe that Emma's presence in the household meant nothing. Lizzie acted as if Emma had never been gone, and while she oohed and aahed and squeezed her hand and spoke words of sympathy to Emma while she was healing, life went on at the Borden household with nary a ripple of discomfort or neglect because Emma had been absent for six weeks.

The first family supper together was always uncomfortable as well. Emma always felt as though she ought to make application to come down. And then, once seated, Emma was always anticipating the question. The question that would have her face her father and choose to either tell him the terrible truth about herself or else look him squarely in the deep brown eyes and lie. Every time it was the same; Emma pushed food around her plate until the meal was over, the question almost visible in everyone's minds, but never spoken.

If it wasn't spoken at the first supper together, it wouldn't ever be spoken—at least not until the next time. And there would never be a next time, Emma had vowed.

●   ●   ●

Friday morning, Emma ferretted out the first "newness" in the house. She had come down for breakfast and found Abby with her nose in her plate, shoveling food in as fast as she could, and her father dressed slick and preening. It was as clear as the dawn. Andrew had a lover. That explained why his mind had been absent from the house.

183

A lover. For a moment, Emma's world rocked. What if he ran off with her? What if he took his assets and left? What if *she* took him for substantially more than he carried in his wallet?

Emma closed her eyes. There was the Borden name, she thought. He will not sully the Borden name. She breathed a little easier, and regarded Abby. It was clear that Abby knew; she was putting on weight as fast as she possibly could. Her mind was on the icebox, of that there was no doubt at all. Abby's world was crumbling, and she was finding solace in the bread box.

And while Andrew's mind was on his snippet, he would pay no attention whatsoever to the family. He would still have his afternoon sessions with Lizzie, and his naps, but besides that, he would either be at work or else lost in some sort of daydream. Emma looked at her father and felt empathy for him, which surprised her. It's a shame that the man never really found true love, she thought, at least not one that lasted. He may have loved their mother, but he had murdered her as sure as he was now murdering Abby with his wenching and his faithlessness.

So the household was without parental constraints.

That left Lizzie and Maggie.

Maggie, that simple-minded Irish twit, most likely used her unsupervised time to chat over the fence with the neighbor's maid, another Irish. She always was a lazy brat, and for sure, Emma noticed, the windows hadn't been washed in a month of Sundays. Well, that nonsense would end, and it would end right now! Someone had to take the reins of this family, and the way Lizzie had been these past few weeks, it was surely not to be her.

Lizzie.

Lizzie rarely showed her face at the breakfast table, being prone to bedding late and rising around noon. In fact, more often than not, Emma had heard Lizzie coming in the house very late every evening, and of course no one else had noticed, because they were all so busy, buried deeply within their own activities.

Well, midnight was way too late for a young woman to be coming home. Unescorted, yet.

The breath caught in Emma's throat. It could be that she's been going out with a *man*. Oh Lord, that would never do. No, that would never do. All this time Emma had assumed that Lizzie was out for some church reason or WCTU meetings or committee work of some sort—that had always been something Lizzie was prone to, poor dear, but to be coming home so consistently late . . .

Emma laid her fork on her plate and folded her hands in her lap. Her heart beat so hard she thought for sure her parents could hear it—if only they paid attention to something other than themselves.

Andrew kept smoothing his hair down—what a fool! And Abby helped herself to a huge third portion of fried potatoes and gravy.

I will sit here quietly until Lizzie comes down, she thought. And then I will get to the bottom of this.

But the more she thought about it, the more she could not sit still.

She excused herself from the table, took her plate into the kitchen. Bridget had just come down from her room, her face still puffy with sleep. She poured herself a cup of coffee and took a muffin from the warming oven.

"The windows must be washed today, Maggie," Emma said. "I'd like all the windows washed on the first floor today. You can do the second floor tomorrow."

The maid's eyes opened wide. The house was small, but there were many windows. To do all of the windows on the ground floor in one day was unthinkable. But Emma's mouth held its firm line and the maid dropped her eyes. "Yes, Miss Emma," she said, then took her breakfast into the dining room to eat.

Emma paced back and forth in the kitchen. She must stop Lizzie from seeing this man. She must stop it. She must *stop* it.

Her fists balled into knots, Emma looked toward the ceiling. "I swear, Mother, she will not marry. She will not end up like you and that poor wretched Abby. No man will do that to Lizzie. Or to me. I promise. I promise upon your grave. I promise upon your memory—"

Andrew walked through the door, and stopped, looking queerly at Emma.

"Emma."

"Father."

"Were you speaking?"

"No. Well, no. I was wondering about Lizzie. Hasn't she been coming in awfully late these past few nights?"

"Don't know, Emma. I know she's gone most every evening, but I hear there's committee meetings over at Kathryn Peters'. I don't know what time she comes in."

"Is today a special day of some kind, Father?" Emma could not help herself.

"No, no, why do you ask?"

"Well, you're all dandied up, is all. Looks like you'll be stepping out."

Fury flashed into Andrew's eyes. "Hush yourself, girl. Don't be letting your mother hear you talk like that. Shame on you. No. Be off with you. Do some laundry today." And he made little sweeping motions at her with his hands, and then went up the back stairs to his bedroom.

Confirmed. Andrew had a lover. Emma let him brush her off like that because she had a mind full of things other than Andrew.

Lizzie was the item to be dealt with this day.

Emma walked back through the dining room, head held high, pretending not to notice the scowl that crossed Bridget's face. We must certainly look for a new maid, she thought. Abby, she noticed, was still eating, although she had slowed down some. The flesh of her jowls jiggled as she chewed.

Emma walked up the front stairs and opened Lizzie's bedroom door. The curtains were drawn. Emma whipped them wide open.

Lizzie blinked and squinted in the light. "Emma! I'm sleeping."

"No, Lizzie, we need to have a talk."

"Later."

"Now."

"Emmm-ma," Lizzie whined.

"Sit up here, girl, and let me have a look at you." Emma sat in Lizzie's rocker and leaned over into Lizzie's face.

"Get away, Emma," Lizzie pushed at her sister, then sat up in bed and rubbed her face.

"You're gaining weight again,"

"Shut up, Emma."

"And you're all puffy. Are you seeing a man, Lizzie?"

Lizzie's eyes opened wide, but Emma could see that the element of surprise had served her well. Lizzie was innocent. She was seeing no man. "No, Emma, I'm not seeing a man. Is that what this is about?"

"You're keeping mighty funny hours for a lady, especially a Borden lady, Lizzie. I need to make sure that you're not doing something to disgrace the name." Emma said the words, but in her heart she hoped Lizzie would not be the one to point out the fact that she, Emma, had just arisen from bed where she had lain in disgrace for the past three weeks.

"I do not disgrace the Borden name, Emma. I study. I work. I go to meetings. I teach Sunday School. I'm busy,

Emma, doing the things I always do, plus some. Now can I go back to sleep, please?"

"Absolutely not. It's time for you to be up. This house has gone to rack and ruin since I've been gone and it's time somebody put it right again. There's a houseful of laundry and mending and ironing. Maggie will begin with the windows on the first floor this morning, and there is just a whole spring cleaning that was never quite accomplished. Up, lazy thing. Get up."

Lizzie groaned and pulled the covers over her head, but Emma knew that she would be up presently. Emma went into her own room and closed the door. The stress of the morning had been quite a strain on her health. She was not up to her usual energy level yet; it would take a while. She took off her shoes and lay gently on the bed. Just a quick rest, and then she would be up and about, cracking the whip on the lazy waifs who lived in this house. It was time someone gave a little direction around here.

izzie lay in bed on her thirty-second birthday until noon, with nothing to look forward to except a Christian Endeavor Society meeting at seven o'clock. Other people had birthday parties—some quite elaborate, some modest and meaningful—but nobody in the Borden family had ever celebrated the anniversary of Lizzie's birth.

When she finally went downstairs, dressed in clothes that smelled like yesterday and the day before, she found that Abby had made a cake with fresh goat milk and duck eggs that Andrew had brought back from the farm. No mention was made of a birthday.

The cake must have been meant for her, because as soon as Lizzie admired it, Abby cut it and began to eat a large slice. Lizzie had no appetite for it, so she just watched Abby waddling about in the kitchen, eating the cake and stuffing bits of this and that into her mouth. Lizzie suddenly saw herself in another thirty years.

Thirty-two years old. A spinster lady. What a terrible label! Useless in the eyes of the public, wretched and evil in the eyes of God, having relations with another woman. And there was shame, too, a shame that Kathryn had given her.

But Lizzie tried not to think about that. It burned too brightly, it stung too harshly.

The worst sin in Lizzie's life was that she was so weak. Not bold, not adventurous, not self-assured. Not slim, not pretty. Not independent. Not all those things she dreamed for, worked so hard for, and which eluded her so completely.

Yes, *Pathways* was right. She had myriad selves, all of them inadequate to the simple task of life.

Lizzie came down the stairs late on her thirty-second birthday because she had not slept well. She hadn't slept well for months. She'd been restless. She dreamed that her Angry Self paced all night, then she'd wake and be exhausted, as if she had actually *been* pacing all night.

And along with the sleeplessness, Lizzie's attention was continually drawn away from the barn. Even when she was in her loft, ready to do her exercises, her concentration seemed to have permanently fled. She did them anyway, hoping that somehow she would continue to grow in spite of her lack of concentration. But she got little from them, and couldn't wait to be finished. As soon as she was, she put her things away and then lay back in the hay and dreamed of owning her own home in town. She dreamed of inviting Kathryn over for the evening. She dreamed of doing as she pleased, when she pleased, with whom she pleased. She dreamed of decorating the house to her own taste, and not to dreary old Emma's taste. She dreamed of wearing peach, even if it was not her best color. She dreamed of posting a letter to Beatrice and inviting her to come stay for as long as she wished. She dreamed of eventually returning to Britain to stay for an extended visit with Beatrice in her flat.

She longed to share these dreams with Kathryn, but Kathryn again had become increasingly distant, snippy, almost rude.

But Lizzie finally broached the subject anyway.

Kathryn's response shocked her. "Oh, Lizzie, your father will never allow that."

"He will," Lizzie said. "He will, eventually."

"You've lost your mind, girl. He has you firmly under his thumb, and you do exactly what he wills. You will never be free of him, Lizzie, not until he and that silly wife of his are dead."

190

"You're wrong, Kathryn."

Kathryn turned to Lizzie and fixed her with a fishy stare. "Am I?"

"Listen, Kathryn, you don't know about my relationship with—"

"It's late."

That was Kathryn's dismissal. Lizzie was to dress and go home so Kathryn could have a nightcap alone and then go to sleep. The ritual had always irked Lizzie, had always made her feel like an underling, like a servant, brought to this house to satisfy only one certain need, and then cast aside until the next time the mistress beckoned. "I think you ought to know something about Father and me before you make such rash statements—"

"You bore me, Lizzie, you and your uppity Borden sentiments. It's time you went home."

Lizzie was struck dumb. Slowly, she slid to the edge of the bed and sat up. She began to dress, knowing she should say something, *anything,* but words were out of her grasp.

"I shan't be home for the next two weeks, Lizzie," Kathryn said casually.

"Oh?" Lizzie choked out. One more word and she would begin to cry.

"Scott and Matthew have invited us to Boston."

Lizzie's hopes rose. "Us?"

"Well," Kathryn said, "Cynthia Miller and I."

Cynthia Miller! The tears surged back where they came from, chased by a bolt of anger. "And you'll be there for two weeks?"

"Perhaps longer. Listen, Lizzie, I believe this little affair between us has run its course, don't you agree? I feel like traveling a bit, so when we come back from Boston, I might just go abroad for a time. Perhaps I'll call when I return."

"Fine," Lizzie said, the anger giving her a dangerous

calm. She finished dressing and left the house without another word.

Now the shame burned. Now the shame burned so brightly Lizzie felt brazenly illuminated in the soft summer evening.

She felt as if her shame, her sins, her shortcomings were highly visible to everyone in Fall River. Surely the newspapers would be filled with the news in the morning.

She had failed the Borden name, that was a sure thing, and even if there was no public outcry—Kathryn was, after all, most discreet—Lizzie would smolder with shame and the stench of it would be with her soul forever.

She went directly home, her feet somehow carrying her one step at a time toward the goal of her darkened bedroom. She carried herself poorly, hunched over, head down, shoes occasionally scraping the pavement.

She should have seen it coming. *She should have seen it coming!* This was the second time Kathryn just tossed her off to one side. The first time hurt so badly, hurt *so badly,* why did Lizzie imagine that the second time would hurt less?

She unlocked the front door, slipped in, locked it behind her. It was early, and there were lamps in the sitting room and in the kitchen; she didn't want to talk to anyone. She made her way up the stairs with leaden feet, unlocked the bedroom door and fell upon the bed without even removing her sweater.

She was beyond tears. She wanted to release the awful pain, but there were no tears. There were no racking sobs, those terrible-wonderful things that washed the world and made it fresh. There was no forgiveness here, not from her emotions, not from her body. There would never be forgiveness.

She thought about *Pathways* in the barn. She was unworthy of it. She was too stupid.

Automatically, she began to whisper the first lesson into

her pillow. "Within each individual reside many others." The words choked her. They were beautiful words. They were filled with hope and loveliness and power. And Lizzie had none of those things. She *was* none of those things. And not even her other selves could save her.

She thought about taking her own life, but then she knew who would find her; the one person for whom she needed to live: Emma. Instead, she just gripped her balled-up sheets in her hands and squeezed them until the cords stood out on her arms, in her neck, until perspiration beaded up on her forehead and dripped down into her hair.

Eventually, she slept. And paced.

● ● ●

Lizzie watched Abby wolf down cake until she couldn't take it anymore.

She slammed out the screen door and made for the barn.

She locked the big door behind her. She breathed deeply of the friendly smell and climbed quickly to the loft, uncovered *Pathways* and lay back in the familiar hay. This was a place where she could sit and think and not be disturbed by anything.

Except her thoughts. And this day her thoughts were most disturbing.

She went through her first lesson, reading the paragraph aloud. Then she lit the candles and set up the mirror and watched her face change.

And then she called forth her Angry Self.

It surged forward like a tidal wave, enveloping Lizzie, suffocating her. Her anger roared toward Emma, skinny, mean Emma. Emma, who had held her hostage all these years, Emma who held in the palm of her hawklike hand the key to Lizzie's self-consuming guilt. Emma, cursed Emma, who always looked down her nose at Lizzie, who always wanted more than Lizzie could give. Blasted Emma who

193

stood in the way of Lizzie's future, who barred Lizzie from ever having any happiness. Damn Emma! Damn Emma!

The tide flowed and then ebbed, changed directions, and the wave washed over the head of Abby. Abby, the damned. Abby, the one who always looked at Lizzie as if Lizzie owed her something. Abby, who always wanted more from Lizzie than Lizzie was able to give. Abby, who wanted Lizzie to be her child, when Lizzie couldn't, she *couldn't,* she belonged to a tyrannical older sister and a dead mother and it wasn't her fault, but Abby just could never forgive her for that. Abby, who held her father's ear at night and filled him with traitorous ideas about Emma and Lizzie, Abby, who paired Emma with Lizzie and never saw them as two individuals, Abby who resented her husband's daughters from the moment she came into the family, Abby who never had children of her own, who tortured the household, who ate until she was a monster, whose unhappiness filled the house to overflowing.

When the wave washed back, nothing was left of Abby but pitiful bones and gelatinous mounds of lard.

And then it struck down Andrew. Andrew. Andrew, who ignored Lizzie beyond endurance, and only paid attention when it suited him to refuse her most heartfelt desires. Andrew, who didn't care at all for Emma—a man who hated his daughter!—and in so doing, chained his other daughter to her woeful older sister forever. Andrew, who cared not for his current wife, who felt nothing, *nothing* for the dead wife who bore him three children, one dead in infancy. Andrew, who worked from early until late and squeezed a nickel until it chirped. Andrew, who would never let the Borden girls claim their rightful social place by allowing any fresh air or fresh faces into the still, musky house. Andrew, who would never part with a dollar unless his life depended upon it, who made the girls bathe with a cloth and a bucket in the cellar, whose only toilet was a hole, hidden, dirty, in the cellar, who would never allow decent plumbing or a hookup to the gas line. Andrew, who would probably die of poisoned mutton that had been on the table six days in a row rather than buy enough fresh meat to feed his family. Andrew, damn you, damn you, damn you, Father!

Sweat poured off Lizzie's face and stray whisps of hair stuck to her. The tidal wave was over, wasn't it?

No, not quite. The power and fury were gone for the moment, but in their wake floated pieces of corpses. There was Mother, her thin face so like Emma's, yet with a softness that made her so beautiful. She floated with some of the others, her grave having been disturbed by the storm. I hate you, Mother, Lizzie's mind screamed. You could have made the difference in my life, but you left. You left me all alone with Emma and Abby and Father, and for that I will *never* forgive you.

Kathryn floated there as well, but Lizzie just gave her dead face a shove with her mental foot and she floated out beyond the horizon. There were classmates in there, a couple of boys, and Lizzie looked at them all with wrath and scorn.

And then the anger began to well again, and it took on more specific forms. She could see herself hitting Emma, smashing her in the face, she could see herself coming up behind Abby and cracking her hard on the head. She could see her father, lying on the sofa so coolly asleep and she could see herself pouncing upon him and ripping his eyes out.

And Lizzie's hand was up under her skirt and her fingers were rubbing and pulling hard at herself, not soft and tender the way that Kathryn had done, not at all.

She groaned and rolled over on her side.

Then she jumped up, shook out her dress and stood at the edge of the loft. I shall dive off, she thought clearly, and then did it.

Time slowed. She saw the dust motes in the slanting ray of light that came in through the dirty window. She saw the piles of trash by the door. She saw the empty stalls, she saw where she would land, headfirst, and break her neck on the newly raked dirt. She smelled that dirt as she approached it, her last thought—

Lizzie gasped and sat up. She was still in the hayloft. Had that been a dream? No, there was no way she could have dreamed that. She inched over to the side of the loft to see if her body was down there, dead on the floor. No. Nothing.

Perspiration trickled down where tears had just been.

My God, she thought, my God.

She wiped the perspiration from her head. She felt the soreness where she had pounded herself so roughly, and shame brought a flush to her cheeks.

And then another flush of shame rose to her cheeks as she thought of stealing Abby's jewelry and money. It was the same kind of thing. She could have sworn she was in the barn at the time, and yet the evidence showed . . .

And this sneaking into Abby and Andrew's bedroom at night. And Emma's. Lizzie dreamed of pacing back and forth, back and forth, and somehow, the dreams were so real, so accurate. . . . In normal dreams, things always happened, there were people who talked and acted, there were different, strange places, there were triple levels of meanings and innuendos that only meant something for a moment or two upon awakening, but not this, no, not this, this was just endless pacing, back and forth, back and forth, worried pacing, the weight of the world upon her shoulders.

And when she awoke, she was exhausted, and even the muscles in her legs were cramped as if she actually *had* been pacing, but she knew *she* hadn't really been, it had been something else.

Something else.

Something else stole Abby's jewelry. Something else paced at night as Lizzie slept. Something else just dove

196

headfirst off the loft. Something else, something else, something else.

What?

Something in me? Something of me? Me? Another self?

What if I could tame that other thing, make it work for me. What if I could have that "something else" all the time?

Wouldn't that be tricky?

And wouldn't Beatrice be impressed?

ndrew Borden found a quiet moment at home, when everyone else was busy, to sit at his desk in the sitting room and contemplate a major decision. He looked again at the paper in his hands.

If he were to change his will at this time . . . He set the paper back on the desktop, facedown, and folded his hands on top of it. If he were to change his will at this time . . . Well, there was no other way but to keep all knowledge of it strictly away from Abby, Emma and Lizzie. If any of them were to find out, there would be hell to pay, and that was no exaggeration.

And yet, there was this burning desire to make some strong move, to do something lasting, something reasonably permanent for the Widow Crawford and her sons.

She was using him, that had been clear from the beginning. He was no fool. But she did save every Friday afternoon for him. She did it for her sons, for her boys, for her family, and, Andrew had begun to believe, she also did it for Andrew. And for herself.

Their Friday afternoons had become something extraordinary. Their trysts had become so special, so looked forward to, that even he was moved by their intensity. And intensity of that nature cannot be had by one person alone. It must be shared. There was intensity of lust, there was intensity of secrecy, there was that naughtiness that accompanied the forbidden.

And she made him laugh. She made him laugh with

abandon, something that hadn't happened to him since he was young and first in love with Sarah.

Life had made an old man out of Andrew Borden, and Mrs. Crawford was reversing that. He was young again in her presence, and for that he was eternally grateful. He was grateful to the tune of something substantial in his will.

He unfolded his hands and took up the paper of instructions to his attorney. There were several problems with this. The first problem was that his attorney was Mrs. Crawford's employer, and eyebrows would be raised. Andrew couldn't be sure of confidentiality if he used the same Fall River lawyer who had drafted his original will. And confidentiality was mandatory. That was a solvable problem, but it was not the only problem.

There was also Abby, Lizzie and Emma. Didn't the money belong to them?

Not necessarily. If the money belonged to anyone, it belonged to Lizzie, who loved him and cared for him. Abby deserved something for her faithful service through the years, but all he felt for her was the fondness one would have for a loyal servant of thirty years. And Emma! Well, Emma deserved little more than her current four dollars a week, just enough to keep her mean every month for the rest of her life. Emma was a cantankerous sort, and Andrew owed her little.

But what would they say if they found out about the will before he died? Would they make life hell for him? And what on earth would they do to Mrs. Crawford?

What would they do to Mrs. Crawford even if they didn't find out until after he died? Would they contest the will and make a public spectacle of his affair?

And then again, there was no reason to assume that Mrs. Crawford would continue their liaison until Andrew died. It could just be that when the boys graduated, she would put him off with a wave of her dainty hand and that would be the end of it.

He couldn't bear to think of the end of it. No, he thought, she enjoyed his company too much. She would not do that.

What were his alternatives? He could deed an asset to Mrs. Crawford without her knowing it, and merely put the deed in an envelope addressed to her. Any attorney would post it upon his death.

Another would be to rewrite the will, as he felt so strongly moved to do, and damn the results. Let the women have a catfight over the stupid money; he would have no further use for it.

Another would be to make a generous gift to Mrs. Crawford now, while he was alive and they both could enjoy the moment.

This was a good idea. He drummed his fingers on the desk for a moment, then unlocked the side drawer and drew out a copy of his most recent financial statement. He checked over his real estate holdings to see if there was a property suitable for her—one on which she could collect rents to help with the college payments of her sons, and that she could sell when they were finished with their educations.

But a rental property is such a bother. She would have to collect the rent from the pikers, and sometimes they were difficult enough for him to deal with, never mind having a woman try to make them pay up.

Mrs. Crawford's feisty face came up before his memory, and he had no doubt that she could handle a recalcitrant tenant. But perhaps that was not the best way. One more burden—and a tenantless property was indeed a burden, especially at tax time—was not what the fine woman needed. No.

Andrew folded up the new instructions, put them into the envelope with his old will, refiled them and locked the desk drawer. He would go round to the attorney's office tomorrow and get the original. Mr. Pratt wouldn't like that very much, but he could send his will and the changes over to another attorney in Fairhaven, where nobody knew Mrs. Crawford, and that might be the best way all around. At least it would give him more time to think on it. And perhaps he could even confide in this new attorney, and receive some good legal advice. For free, of course.

But there was another issue that Andrew would not be able to dodge much longer. Lizzie wanted her own house. She had mentioned it once, and she would mention it again soon.

His first thought was to absolutely forbid it; unmarried women just did not live by themselves, not when they had family. And Lizzie's idea of "modest" would probably not stay that way, once she began to decorate and furnish this little nest of her own. Andrew could see his investment dollars winging away on the breeze.

But not having Emma underfoot was an idea that merited further consideration. And Abby would enjoy the peace. Abby would be able to be the mistress of this house at last, and Andrew felt as if he owed her that. It would be good for Abby to have the household to herself. She could instruct the maid—perhaps without the girls, there would be no need for a maid!—she could take care of the menus and the meals herself; there would be far less laundry to do, and the house would be free of the godawful tension that reverberated through its rafters.

Yet it is probably the tension that keeps this house standing, Andrew thought.

But on the down side, the girls and their involvement in family affairs that were really none of their business, provided a diversion for Abby, so that she probably noticed not at all about his Fridays. And those Fridays were so precious to him. . . . If she were mistress of the house, surely she would ask after his whereabouts of a Friday evening, and he would have to lie to her. That would not be good.

A decision must be made on this issue, he thought. Lizzie will be wanting an answer.

Friday nights were so precious. . . .

The only answer he could give her now would be no. He needed Lizzie around. He needed Emma. So until something happened to change his priorities, for now they would continue to live under his roof. Emma would have to go visit her friends from time to time, and Lizzie would just have to wait.

He sighed. Telling Lizzie this would not be easy.

He saw her moving about in the kitchen. Might as well get it over with.

He stood from his hardbacked chair at the desk and slowly straightened up. His seventy-four years were just beginning to catch up to him. Sometimes this fact made him very cranky, and sometimes it just made him sad. He took a couple of faltering steps, then walked into the kitchen.

"Lizzie?" There was no answer. "Lizzie?" He opened the screen door and stepped out onto the porch, automatically reaching for the pipe in his pocket. He leaned against the post and lit the pipe. "Lizzie, are you there?" Still no answer. He stepped down off the porch and looked around the house. There was no one there. He sat on the steps. It was going to be a hot summer, he thought, yes indeed, it was going to be a hot summer.

Just then, the barn door opened and Lizzie stepped out. "Did you call me, Father?"

"Come sit with me a spell, Lizzie."

Lizzie walked toward him, but stopped and examined a branch of the pear tree. "I've never seen so many baby pears, have you?"

Andrew regarded the tree. "Never," he said. "We'll have a fine harvest in a couple of months."

Lizzie sat next to him on the step. Andrew puffed on his pipe.

"Been thinking about fishing, Lizzie," Andrew said.

"Me too."

"Been thinking we ought to go one of these days. It's been a long time."

"A long time."

"Too long."

They sat in silence for a while, Andrew puffing great clouds that were borne away on the early summer breeze.

"I'm going to tell you no on buying the house, Lizzie." He found he could not look her in the eyes.

Lizzie slumped.

"Let me tell you why."

"It doesn't matter." Lizzie stood up.

"It *does* matter. Sit down."

"I've got things to do, Father."

"Lizzie, please. It isn't right for two unmarried ladies to be living by themselves, not when they have family. It isn't right. It wouldn't look right for the Borden name."

"I'm miserable, Father, Emma's miserable, Abby's miserable, you're miserable. But the Borden name is right. The Borden name has always got to be right."

"Yes, it does. Misery passes, Lizzie, but scandal never does."

"Plenty of women live alone."

"Not when they have family."

"Yes, they do."

"Bordens don't. You'll have plenty of life, both of you, when Abby and I are dead. Then you can do as you please."

Lizzie just walked back to the barn without a backward glance.

Andrew's Fridays were secure for the time being, but at what price? He felt as if he had lost something else, something perhaps even more precious. He tapped the ashes out onto the step and put the pipe back into his pocket. It was time for his nap.

hen the sun slanted in the barn loft window, Lizzie knew she had to leave and make ready for the church meeting. She was probably already late.

She hated to leave the barn, but she had to. The church's Christian Endeavor Society, a fancy name for the church council, met at seven o'clock, and she had to make her report. Her committee was "Bringing the Message to the Orientals," and since she was the only one doing anything about it by teaching a Sunday school class to the little brats, she had to attend.

She'd much rather stay in the barn.

She was still overwhelmed by the experience of having dived off the loft. Having dived off the loft and yet not. And then after the little talk with Andrew, it had happened again.

She carefully hid all the things she'd taken to the loft, then climbed down the ladder. She shook the hay from her clothes, patted down her hair, and then opened the door into the yard.

It was indeed late. She quickly crossed over the yard and knocked on the screen door. Maggie let her in.

Lizzie grabbed two muffins from the steaming stack that had been laid out for supper and trotted through the sitting room and up the stairs.

Andrew had turned down her request for a life of independence. It infuriated her that he used that same worn-out old excuse of maiden ladies living alone. And the

204

Borden name! Bah! The real reason he didn't want Emma and her to leave had more to do with Abby. He didn't seem to care much for that hippopotamus, and no wonder. If she and Emma left, well, then, that would leave the two of them and the Borden name. Scant comfort for an old man's seventies.

When he'd told her that, her first reaction was resignation. She'd known he would respond that way; she hoped against hope that it would be otherwise, but she knew that his ultimate answer would be no. Kathryn knew it, too. And this was what made Lizzie the unhappiest. Kathryn knew it, too.

After their talk, she'd gone back to the barn, where her anger again began to burn. She started kicking hay and kicking at the wall, and suddenly she could see herself walking in town, with long, purposeful strides. She stared at the loft corner, unpainted planks nailed together and covered with dust and cobwebs, but while she could see them, she could also see herself walking in town. She wore the same clothes: the white shirtwaist with the blue patterned silk skirt, her hair was done up the same, but this was no daydream, this was something else, for she could see out this Lizzie's eyes.

And other people could see her! People on the street nodded as she strode past.

The barn wall looked flat and dull, as if she were seeing it through a thin dark film. The street in town seemed extraordinarily bright, as if suffused with a little of the sparkling heatwaves she saw when a headache approached. She walked down Main Street, then turned onto Third, where she stopped. She looked quickly around her, noticed that no one was looking, and then all of her was back in the hayloft, staring at that same corner. The vision was over. The *something else* had come back.

As before, a cold sweat covered her brow, her breathing

was heavy and rapid, and she sat down and leaned against the haystack.

Lizzie was absolutely dumbfounded. She didn't know what to make of it at all. She could not control it. And she wondered: Could it speak? Could it move things around? Was it just an apparition? Did other people really see it as well, or was it a hallucination? Did this happen to anyone else? Why had she never heard of anything like this before?

Lizzie ate a muffin on her way up the stairs. The day felt so strange, as if she had just been living through a very vivid dream. She could hardly believe that those things had really happened. She rinsed her face in the washbowl in her room, tidied her hair a bit and changed her clothes. She didn't want to go to a church meeting at all, *at all,* she wanted to stay home and ponder what on earth could have caused her to be so odd, *so* odd.

But she was duty bound to go. She locked her bedroom door behind her, flew down the stairs. "Going to church," she said to nobody as she unlocked the three front-door locks and stepped into the warm evening.

It was still daylight as Lizzie strode toward the church. If Emma had been with her, she would have said, "Take more care, Lizzie, you're beginning to walk like a cowboy." And then Lizzie would have given her a look and Emma would have said, "It isn't ladylike."

Ladylike. Bah. Sometimes one just had to walk hard. Loosely. Feel the muscles. Something Emma never did. There were a lot of things Emma never did.

Lizzie strode hard and looked forward to the meeting, because as soon as it was over, she could leave again. She only joined this Christian Endeavor Society because changing churches created such a scandal that she thought Andrew ought to have something to say in explanation. So she joined the council and offered to work on a committee to reach out to all the newly transplanted Orientals—Chinese, mostly—

206

who had come to Fall River to work in the mills and in the laundries.

And then she got saddled with the stupid Sunday school class. But it was all right. The children were strange, but they also had their good points.

Lizzie slipped in the side door of the big church and went right to the meeting room, just off the side of the main chapel. The meeting was already in session. Good. She came late; she could leave early. There was only one vacant seat at the long table; she sat down as unobtrusively as possible.

The pastor was in the middle of a discussion on the summer activities for the church youth group. Good, Lizzie thought. My report can't be far behind.

She looked around the table. In every organization, there was a central core of people who did all the work. Lizzie looked at each face. Give or take a couple of people, she would bet that ten years ago, this table had the same people around it and still would ten years hence. There was a certain appeal to that sort of commitment. But Lizzie didn't have it. Not to this church, anyway. Perhaps that was something that came with time. She was only thirty-two. Most of the faces around this table were in their late fifties and early sixties. Some, though, were her age. She avoided those. They might want to get chummy, and she had no time for chums.

The pastor called on the woman sitting next to her. She stood, then addressed the council in a clear voice. She gave the names of all those who had agreed to grace the altar with flowers for the next six weeks. She also reported the roster of which men had agreed to take care of the churchyard and cemetery for the coming month.

Lizzie listened to her. She was calm, self-assured and clear. She was prepared. That was something that Lizzie never was. In fact, she was never any of those things. The woman sat down, turned and smiled at Lizzie.

She was beautiful. She was petite, like Kathryn. She had a

large, soft mouth and twinkling blue eyes. The skin at the corners of her eyes wrinkled up beautifully when she smiled, and her skin was lightly bronzed from the sun. Such a refreshing change from all those who kept their bonnets on for fear of freckles. Freckles abounded on this woman's face, and her teeth were even and white.

Gray shot through the reddish-brown hair, which was cut short and brushed back from her face. She was absolutely breathtaking. And unconventional in many ways. Lizzie liked that. Lizzie was intrigued.

She heard the pastor call her name, and the woman next to her reached over and gave her hand a little squeeze. Lizzie's heart pounded in her chest. Her mouth went dry. She stood, and felt her knees tremble and her breath come hard, as if she had been running. She wasn't sure she could make her voice speak clearly at all.

But she did. She made her report, and didn't leave anything out. She told that plans were already under way for a celebration of Chinese New Year next year, and that more Oriental social events were coming forth in the fall. She reported on the progress of teaching about Jesus to the youngsters, and the help the mill was giving her in encouraging the Orientals to come to church on Sunday. She didn't mention that she'd had to beg her father to make a bulletin and have it translated. He thought all Chinese were heathens, and godless to boot. He thought her ministry was a colossal waste of time and had no problem expressing himself to her. But he did it anyway, and the turnout was getting better all the time.

There were now Bible-study groups for them, and once they were *in* the church, then they could become integrated into the church community.

It was an adequate report. She sat down again, breathless. The woman next to her turned again and smiled, then gave her attention across Lizzie to the man on the other side of her, who then stood and began to speak. But Lizzie could not take her eyes off the woman.

There was no wedding ring on her finger. She looked to be in her early forties—perhaps Emma's age, but what a difference! This woman was vibrant. This woman was healthy. And she had kindness written in each of those tanned wrinkles.

Nothing at all like Kathryn . . . yet . . . yet she exuded *something* akin to Kathryn. There was that same sensuousness in her touch, there was that smile.

Could she possibly be like me? Like Kathryn? Would there be the slightest possibility that this woman could know the same kind of loneliness?

Lizzie knew she was staring, but she could not stop herself. She could not take her eyes off the possibility of another woman in her life, a source of tenderness, of joy, of togetherness. Someone to share her life with.

The woman shifted her gaze and looked directly into Lizzie's eyes.

Immediately, Lizzie flushed and looked away. But not before she thought she perhaps had an answer. The woman did not look offended at Lizzie's steady gaze, she merely met her eyes.

Lizzie put both hands in her lap and struggled to take even breaths and to remove the color from her face. By the time she had done so, the man had finished speaking and another woman was talking about the Fourth of July picnic. Lizzie took one deep breath and then brought her eyes up to rest on the person who was speaking. She fought to keep from sliding around to look at the wonderful lady in the seat next to her.

She remembered her plan of escaping the meeting early, but now that seemed impossible. She couldn't draw more attention to herself. Besides that, she might have the opportunity to meet this sparkling woman, she might have the opportunity to be touched again, by accident, perchance. She might find that the woman was interested in a friendly chat over a cup of tea—if not tonight, well, then, sometime.

If she didn't walk away from Lizzie with a backhanded comment about someone uncouth enough to stare.

Lizzie's mind turned back to the woman's appearance. Was her hair really short? No respectable woman wore short hair. Those who did were either white trash, ill kempt or loose. Yet this woman carried it off. Without meaning to, Lizzie turned and looked at her again. Yes, her hair was short. Wavy and brushed away from her face. She was beautiful. And suddenly her face was very familiar. As if Lizzie'd seen her hundreds of times. As if they were old friends, but Lizzie just could not remember her name.

Lizzie called upon her Self of Fear. Help me through this, she prayed. I must be bold, adventurous and self-assured. I must speak with her after the meeting.

The meeting ground on, with Lizzie's stomach in such an uproar she knew she would have to take some cod-liver oil when she went home, to soothe the agitation. She waited, her mind filled with the scent—real or imagined—of the vision next to her. She was constantly out of breath, trying to imagine her first line of introduction when the meeting ended. There was no way she was going to leave this hall without at least discovering this woman's name. Oh, how her stomach hurt, and oh how strange life suddenly turned out to be.

Then the committee reports were finished, there was no new business to be discussed, the minister said a blessing and the meeting was adjourned.

Lizzie suddenly froze in her seat, distracted and panicky.

Then there was a touch on her shoulder. She whipped around to see the woman next to her standing, with one finger on Lizzie's shoulder. She smiled down at Lizzie, tapped her once on the shoulder, and then walked away.

Lizzie almost turned her chair over in her hurry to catch up with her, but by the time she collected herself, the woman was walking slowly with the minister, deep in conversation. Lizzie went over to Alice Russell, who was picking up the leftover cookies.

"Alice."

"Hello, Lizzie. Say, you're doing such wonderful work with the Orientals. We've needed someone to do that type of ministry for a long time. Bless your heart for taking it on. It must be terribly time-consuming. I know just the secretarial dut—"

"Alice, who was the woman sitting next to me?"

"Next to you? Hmmm." Alice tapped at her head. "I can't seem to recall—"

"Short hair. Graying. Her face had been in the sun."

"Oh, Enid Crawford. You must mean Enid Crawford."

"Enid Crawford," Lizzie whispered.

"She's very active in the church. Has been since long before her marriage. She was a Fall River girl, you know, parents died just after she married Charles—"

"She's married?" Lizzie struggled to keep her voice even. She took cups and swept cookie crumbs to act casual.

"Oh, her husband died a few years back. Has two sons in college up in Boston. Wonderful woman, Enid. Quite an inspiration, the way she works so hard to put those boys through school. They're both going to be lawyers, she says."

Enid Crawford. Lizzie was sure she'd never heard that name before. But she would never forget it.

She looked around. Enid was gone. Alice was still prattling on about how expensive it is to rear children, never mind college, and Lizzie just let her continue talking and wandered off. She shook hands with the minister and then went out into the soft summer night.

Enid Crawford. Enid Crawford. Enid Crawford.

I must have her, Lizzie thought.

· July

"I swear this is the hottest I've ever been," Sarah White-head said as she poured a glass of cool tea for Abby Borden. "Can you imagine how hot it is, Abby?"

Abby mopped her forehead with her handkerchief—freshly ironed this morning and now damp and gray from the sweltering humidity and her own perspiration. Abby picked up the tea and drank it right down. "Pour me a little more, child."

Sarah dutifully refilled the glass. Abby sipped at it, then wiped her face again. She didn't tolerate the heat well at all. Never had. Sometimes it felt as if her heart were swelling in all this heat, and she worried—walking on around town the way she did—that one of these hot days it would just up and burst and she would fall dead on the walk.

"Yes, indeed, if you think it's hot now, Abby, you just wait until August! You know it's always hotter in August, and it's just been getting hotter and hotter all month long."

Just the talk of it brought more perspiration out on Abby's face.

"Sebastian calls these dog days, isn't that funny? I mean what could that possibly mean? Dogs don't like this heat any better'n the rest of us, now, do they? He also says that this is the weather where people go crazy. He's a policeman, you know, or at least he used to be, and so he would know. He says that when the heat gets bad, it turns the world into a steam cooker and people start popping their seams. Isn't that a funny thing to say?"

214

Abby felt a little dizzy. She set her tea on the coffee table and tried to catch her breath. She mopped at her face again.

"You look a little peaked, Abby. Let me get you a little something."

Sarah left the room and Abby leaned back against the sofa. Her breaths were coming in short—like panting, she thought. Maybe that's why these hot days are called dog days. They make people pant. But the humor was lost in the discomfort. She would have liked to share that with Sarah, it was the kind of thing that would make her little sister laugh and laugh, and her light little laughs were joyful and the sole reason Abby visited her so often. There was so little laughter at the Borden house. Sarah had her manifold troubles, and still she laughed.

Sarah returned from the kitchen with a generous slice of lemon meringue pie on a plate. "It's cold, Abby, I kept it in the icebox. Sebastian ate almost the whole thing last night, but I kept a slice out for you, because I know it's one of your favorites."

"You're a dear," Abby said, but made no move to take the pie. She needed to lie back on the sofa and rest for a while.

Sarah set the pie on the table, then sat down and picked up her knitting.

"Sebastian can't understand how I can knit in this heat. He's always looking at me and telling me I'm crazy for holding this heavy afghan on my lap, but it don't seem to bother me much. Sometimes about midday it gets a little warm, but toward the evening, it doesn't hurt. I should knit some sweaters and smaller things during the summer, I guess, and leave the coverlets for winter when I really do need something over my knees."

Abby eyed that slice of pie. Its cool yellow shimmered. And Sarah made such a fine crust. Abby had given her a goodly amount of lard that Andrew had brought home from the farm one Saturday, and Sarah made some good lye soap with half of it and saved the rest for pie crusts. And she knew how to make crusts.

With an *oompf,* Abby raised herself up to a sitting position, and took the plate. She cut a bite with a shaky fork and slipped it into her mouth. She looked over at Sarah, who was watching for her reaction.

"Um-mmm," she said, and rolled her eyes.

Satisfied, Sarah went back to her knitting, and talking, prattling on about nothing in particular, punctuating her monologue with trills of laughter—at her two older children, both from her previous husband; at Sebastian, her current husband; at their year-old baby; and at the baby that just began to show as a mound on Sarah's stomach.

Usually, a visit with Sarah lifted Abby's spirits. She was Abby's only living kin, so Abby worked hard to maintain a bond between the two, even though they were on such opposite ends of society.

Sarah was thirty-one years old, the daughter of Abby's father and his second wife. She had poor taste in men, raised her children without habits of cleanliness, and would forever be poor. She had bright eyes and a sunny disposition, but she had a habit of wearing men's clothes, and they hung like rags on her thin frame. Abby was sixty-seven, grossly overweight, genteel—or so she liked to think; she dressed in as rich a wardrobe as she dared to purchase with Andrew's money, and worked hard to keep up her end of the Borden household.

Two sisters, two worlds.

Before Sarah met Sebastian, she and her babies were without a place to stay. Andrew generously gave her this nice little house, although it was probably as much a bribe to keep them out from under his roof as it was a gift of generosity.

Abby looked around. The house *had* been nice. She clucked to herself. The damage children can do, she thought. The damage children can do.

But in this heat, Abby would not be comfortable anywhere, and watching Sarah work on that wool blanket made her skin itch. She felt heat rashes spring up all along where her underwear chafed, and the thought of walking home with damp drawers rubbing against rashes made her heart pound even harder.

She wrapped her handkerchief around the sweating glass of tea and cooled it, then mopped her face one more time.

"I'd better be off," she said, and struggled to be free of the sofa.

"So soon? The children are playing over at the neighbor's. And the baby's asleep. Isn't it pleasant? I had hoped you would stay a little longer."

"Another time. Perhaps when it isn't so hot. Thank you for the tea. And the pie."

Sarah put away her knitting and stood to hug Abby. "Come back again soon, dear."

Abby nodded, her breath already being sucked away by the heat.

Sarah stood in the doorway of the house as Abby made her way toward the street. "Um, Abby?"

Abby turned, a trickle of perspiration leaking its saltiness into one eye.

"Did Andrew . . . you know . . ." She looked around furtively. "The *will*?" she whispered.

"Not yet, Sarah. But don't worry, he will."

"I know. I just wish . . ." She gestured at the squalid house she lived in with her family.

"Don't worry. See you soon." Abby didn't have the strength to reassure her further, or even to wave good-bye. She just turned her bulk toward home and began walking.

• • •

At six o'clock, Sebastian walked through the door. Sarah could smell him even before she could see him. He hung his sweat-soaked hat on the peg by the door and began to undress in the kitchen.

"Go down cellar for a bath," she said, "and I'll have some nice sandwiches for you when you get up."

"Sandwiches again? What kind?"

"Cheese. Now go. You smell."

"I need some meat."

"We ain't got meat. Now go bathe."

"What happens to all the money?"

Sarah turned and looked him full in the face. She knew he didn't like it when she did that. "Sebastian," she said, "are we going to go through this again? I pay our bills. We don't have any creditors knocking on our door, now do we? And we don't even have a mortgage, thanks to Abby, do we? Sometimes we have a little extra, and I buy some meat with it. I know you need meat. So do the children. But sometimes we just don't have enough money. And, as it happens, this cheese was a gift, so we got to just thank God about it and be done. Now go."

She hated talking to him like a child, but sometimes that's what he needed. And the expression on his face as he went down cellar was just exactly like that of her boy when he'd been chastised and sent to his room.

Sebastian! Men! They were all little boys.

She arranged the cheese on the bread so as to make the sandwiches seem a little fuller, then cut extra slices for Sebastian's sandwiches. He really did need meat. She'd have to cut a corner somewhere else next month.

When he came back up, wearing a towel around his waist, she yelled for the children to come in.

The boy, eight, and the girl, six, pounded up the back steps, and fell to the sandwiches without even sitting down.

"Sit," Sebastian said.

The children, chewing enthusiastically, sat.

218

"You ought to have washed your hands," Sarah said, spooning oatmeal into the baby. She shrugged and looked at Sebastian, who glared at her.

Sebastian sat at the table and wolfed down his sandwiches, then drank a big glass of milk. Sarah oughtn't have given him a full glass like that, but she felt so bad about the meat. Now the children would be hard pressed for milk on their oatmeal in the morning.

The children finished eating, then got up and slammed back out the kitchen door. Their friends had been waiting outside, and summer evenings were long and magical. Sarah smiled as she picked up their plates.

"There's a piece of pie left, Sarah," Sebastian said.

"No, Abby stopped by and lemon meringue is her favorite."

"It's my favorite, too."

"I know, Sebastian," she said, exasperated. "But you ate nearly the whole thing last night."

Sebastian lowered his eyes and laid his hands flat on the table. This was a sign. He was composing himself. Soon he would gently speak to her about all the things she was doing wrong in the house.

She wished it was cooler, she could have a cup of coffee. But it was way too hot to start a fire in the stove. She sat down, moved her plate away, and waited for Sebastian to get on with his lecture. Soon it would be over and she could get on with her evening.

"I know Abby does nice things for us, Sarah," Sebastian started out, "but I am the breadwinner in this family, and there are certain things I want to have in my house. One of those is meat for a meal at least two or three times a week. I don't think that's too much to ask for, since I work in that sweltering mill every bloody day of my life!" He took a moment, his fingers spread wide on the table, to recompose himself. "And when you don't let me have meat, when your priorities run in different directions, like *wool* for a blanket in the dead heat of July"—he put a palm up against her defense, and she closed her mouth—"then a piece of lemon meringue pie seems to help smooth things over. Do you know what I mean?"

Sarah nodded. Sebastian was a good man. He was pretty mad right now, but at least he didn't beat her, not the way that Jonathan had. And he was *so* good to her children. . . .

"Besides," Sebastian continued in his slow-paced voice, "think about poor Abby's weight. She can't afford pie, Sarah. She's likely to die in this heat anyway. And if she dies . . ." Sebastian's eyes lost their focus. He paused for a long moment. Sarah waited. Then his blue eyes drilled right into her. *"If she dies,"* he said, "then Andrew would inherit all her property and those old-maid daughters of his will inherit *everything* when he dies."

Sarah sat stunned. She felt as if she had been pinned to her chair with a spear.

"Jesus Christ, that's right," Sebastian said, his hands going to his face. "If old man Borden doesn't die first, then we've got . . . nothing. Just this shack."

"But if it's in his will . . ."

"Don't be an ass, Sarah. If Abby's dead, those daughters of his will convince him that he doesn't owe her kin anything at all."

Sarah knew he was right.

"No," Sebastian said. "Andrew Borden will have to die first."

Sarah stood up and began doing the dishes. She didn't like Sebastian's tone of voice, not at all, not at all. It made her weak in the knees.

Sebastian continued to sit at the table, his big square hands still on the tabletop. He didn't move when the

220

children barged through the kitchen door, running and giggling, and he didn't say anything when they slammed back out again.

Sarah cleaned up the kitchen and went to the living room, where she picked up her knitting and prayed that Sebastian would stop all that thinking.

But he didn't. He was silent all evening, the newspaper opened and forgotten in his lap. And when they went to bed, Sarah cuddled up close and he put his arm around her shoulders, but he continued to stare into the darkness of the ceiling until she fell asleep and dreamed of wolves snatching bites of flesh from her children. She chased the wolves with her butter knife and yelled, "They ain't had any meat. Let 'em alone!" But the wolves continued to chase, snapping and howling, and Sebastian was nowhere to be seen.

●   ●   ●

The next day dawned stifling hot. Abby's nightclothes were wound around her and stuck in the creases of her flesh so tightly she waited until Andrew was up and dressed and out of the bedroom before she endeavored to untangle herself, flopping about on the bed, awkward and jiggling. The effort left her hot and perspiring.

Most mornings she would arise and go quickly through the house, closing the windows and pulling the shades, hoping to preserve some of the coolth that the night had brought. But this morning it was already too late. The morning sun, rising so early in late July, had stolen what tiny respite the night had offered. The day was hot and she would swelter until her rashes began to bleed.

She smoothed the sheet over her and adjusted her nightcap in case Andrew returned to the bedroom for something, and then relaxed. She should be up and closing the windows anyway, to keep out the heat—would Bridget or one of the girls think to do that? Of course not. But the thought of dressing in those clothes undoubtedly still damp from yesterday and perpetually too tight, made her cringe. She looked up at the ceiling and prayed that she would get through the heat of the summer. Especially August, when the heat made people rabid, as Sebastian said. Dog days indeed.

Then came a loud pounding on the front door. Abby sat up in bed like a shot, and gathered her bedclothes to her chest. It was so early, who on earth could be—

And then before Andrew could possibly pass from the kitchen to the front door, the pounding began again; this time there was yelling, too. Abby hurried out of bed, donned her dressing gown and slippers, drew the cap off her head, ran a brush through her hair and began her way down the back stairs.

She had gotten barely halfway when the front door opened and she could hear Andrew's voice, speaking in his normal tone. A man with a terribly thick accent began shouting. Andrew was admirable, she thought, in keeping himself under control when the other man was so irate.

Abby continued down the stairs, went through the kitchen, exchanged glances with Emma, who seemed as surprised and as mystified as she, and then entered the sitting room, where she kept her distance, yet could see the little man, Italian she thought, shake his fist at Andrew and turn red in the face.

She couldn't hear what Andrew was saying to the man, but finally the little man slumped, as if he were defeated in the final battle. He turned and walked down toward the street.

Abby approached Andrew, who kept the door open. "I told you from the very beginning," Andrew called out after him.

The little man turned and looked at Andrew with hate

deeply carved into his face. He spat on the walkway. "Thas what I think of your beginning," he said. "You rich bastads all alike. You keepa whatcha got and don *ever* let another one in. Choke on it! I hope you choke on it! And *die!*" He spat again, then trudged down the street.

Andrew closed the door. Abby was aghast to see that his face was red, almost purple.

"Come, Mr. Borden," she said, taking his arm. "Sit for a moment."

Andrew shook her off. "My breakfast is cooling," he said, and walked into the dining room. Emma had not moved. Andrew sat at his normal place, and Abby wandered back and forth a little bit, wanting to ask, but not knowing quite how to approach the subject. She went into the kitchen and brought out a plate of muffins and poured coffee all around.

Lizzie showed up at the door, disheveled from sleep. "Who was that, Father? What was that all about?"

"An Italian man, Lizzie, nothing to worry about."

"Nothing to worry about? He shows up at your home before the household is up and proceeds to curse you and wake the entire neighborhood!"

"He was upset. Those people tend toward tempers, you know."

"What had you done to make him so upset?"

"Lizzie!" Abby stopped cold, jam knife filled and spilling. "Your father has done absolutely nothing to bring on that type of display."

"That's right, Lizzie," Andrew said. "The man signed a lease for a shop space in town. The lease says no liquor sales, and when I went by there, he had a whole wall of wines for sale. So I had his store locked up. He can pick up his wares and peddle them elsewhere. But not in my storefront."

"He looked dangerous," Emma said.

"He'll cool."

Then Bridget Sullivan, looking equally disheveled from interrupted sleep, entered through the kitchen. "Did I hear yelling?" she asked.

"Oh, Maggie," Lizzie said, and took her arm and led her into the kitchen, where Abby heard her explaining the events to the maid.

Abby turned to Andrew. "You are not concerned about this then, Mr. Borden?"

"No," he said, and cut open another muffin. "Not at all."

L izzie rocked slowly in her bedroom, her outward calmness belying her inward anxiety. She was to have dinner at Enid Crawford's house.

It had been three Sundays since she saw Enid Crawford for the first time in the council meeting. Since then, Lizzie had sought out her company, and they had sat together, holding hands, at church every Sunday. They had walked and talked of insignificiant, trivial things after church, and each week Lizzie had fallen more and more deeply in love with her.

Here was a woman who stood solidly outside of convention. She had opinions, and not always popular ones. She dressed plainly, yet with a certain elegance. She lived alone, she held a job, she was the sole support of her sons in college. She had buried a daughter and a husband, was widely read and highly intelligent. She wore her hair short for convenience: it was reddish brown, gray at the temples. Her eyes were crystal blue. Lizzie had never seen such clear blue eyes. Sparkling eyes. Shiny eyes. Enid boldly went out of the house and worked in her garden of a weekend with no hat, so her face and hands were lightly tanned, freckled and generously sprinkled with tender wrinkles. Her hair was reddened by the sun. She had a real laugh, a teasing, provocative laugh, and she had a wide grin, showing her teeth instead of hiding her mirth behind the shield of a hanky or the palm of her hand.

Lizzie would go home from their walks and talks after

225

church, floating on air, feet barely touching the ground, and she would ensconce herself in the loft and go over every detail of their time together. Enid didn't sing well, so her voice barely whispered the songs, but Lizzie felt Enid's emotion at the words of praise and adoration for the Lord.

Once or twice when the children of the congregation performed, Enid clapped with glee, completely forgetting herself and the impropriety of clapping in church.

And by the time the long week between Sundays came to an end, Lizzie had dreamed of this giant of a woman, larger than life, with attributes mostly associated with deity, and then they would meet, again on Sunday, and Lizzie would be floored again at how tiny Enid was.

Lizzie rocked, anxiety gnawing at her empty stomach. It was Wednesday night. She had been invited to Enid's house for supper. Lizzie tried not to think of the night she had been invited for supper at Kathryn Peters' house, tried not to think of the burgundy gown Kathryn had worn, tried not to think of that first intoxicating kiss she had received, and how mystifying, intriguing and exciting it all had been. She tried not to think that she would behave in that way toward Enid. She didn't want anything of Kathryn Peters to be in their evening; Kathryn was so coarse and callous, and Enid so refreshing and simple. If something magical happened between them, Lizzie wanted it to be spontaneous. Something *of* them, not something that Lizzie orchestrated.

Lizzie rocked. She knew what she would wear, she knew how she would attend her hair, she knew the route she would take to Enid's house . . . and the butterflies flew through her stomach and fluttered under her heart.

But there was a dark spot amid Lizzie's eager anticipation and newfound joy of life. It was a soft spot, a spoiled section of her life, and if she could have nicked it out with the point of a paring knife like the bruise on a pear, she would have.

226

This spot seemed small at the moment, amid the current ocean of happiness, but it embraced every aspect of her life.

All the nasty things in Lizzie's life had been relegated to this area, this small, smelly cesspool at the back of her mind. Even as she rocked, she knew she should clean it out, bring fresh air and light to it, but later, always later, and that pool had not only begun to smell, it had become poisonous. Dangerous.

Andrew's will was in there, and Emma's drinking. Abby's pressure to make Lizzie her baby swam in there, and so did dozens of high school friends who were now married and had lots of children. Kathryn, dear Kathryn, was there, and each and every one of Lizzie's failures, shortcomings and broken promises. Dozens of cookies and cakes. And lately, of course, though Lizzie hated to admit it, Beatrice, her book and her visit.

Lizzie's chest constricted and her breathing came a bit hard whenever she thought of Beatrice's visit. She wasn't at all prepared for it, and it was looming on the near horizon. The end of July, Beatrice had said, and it was nearly that. Lizzie didn't know what she would do when Beatrice arrived. Surely she would find Lizzie unkempt, unprepared, with one or more pimples, probably unbathed and during her monthly, with Emma raging and Abby stuffing herself with food and irate Italians pounding on the door to curse Andrew.

Lizzie had no idea how long Beatrice would stay, or even where she would stay. Would she stay here in the guest room? It seemed the most appropriate for a visiting friend, and yet Lizzie was loath to have anyone see the household in its reality. Beatrice under this roof! There was an inn in town, but could one put a visiting friend up in an inn?

And what on earth would they talk about?

Well, Lizzie could tell her of those weird, weird experiences she had of walking down the street and talking to people while she was still in the barn.

The barn! Oh, what would Beatrice think of the dusty old hayloft as Lizzie's place to study and practice?

Beatrice's visit was inconceivable. Lizzie would not be ready for Beatrice to visit her, Beatrice of the peach, Beatrice the perfect. Lizzie would not be ready, not until she was on her own, rich, elegant, and firmly ensconced in her own element.

And the Borden house was definitely not her element. It was no one's element.

So Lizzie pushed Beatrice and the endless reminders of her failure at life back to the edge of the slime pit and began rocking again, working hard to regain the excitement of dinner at Enid's.

The last letter Lizzie had received before Beatrice set sail for America held a saving grace for her: "You will find at times during your life that your lessons mean nothing. You will want to discount them, or worse, disregard them. Please do not. Please do the lessons as instructed, even when you cannot put your entirety to them. It appears as though your attitude or willingness is less important to their effectiveness than the actual act of performing them."

Lizzie was fairly frantic without letters arriving from Beatrice on a regular basis, but Beatrice was en route. Lizzie did her lessons, she continued with them, daily, but she got nowhere. They were automatic, done by rote, and touching each of her selves was a dismal failure. She'd been successful—too successful—in contacting her Angry Self. When she tried to contact her Prideful Self, she had a vision that scared her. It was as if she cracked open the door on a closet so stuffed full of junk that were she to open it more than the slightest bit, the whole lot would come crashing down on her head. Lizzie slammed the door shut and thought she ought to try a different self. She knew she'd have to come back to that one, but another time. Another time.

Right now, she thought as she rocked, she ought to be talking with her Lustful Self.

"What are you sitting here looking so smug about?"

Emma had walked through the door and Lizzie hadn't even noticed.

"Nothing." Emma always put Lizzie on the defensive.

"I swear, that man will have us all murdered in our sleep one day."

"What man?"

"Your father."

"Emma." Lizzie turned away.

"You didn't hear that man, that Eye-talian man. I tell you, Lizzie, we haven't heard the last of that. Something difficult, something violent will befall us because of your father's ridiculous business practices. Mark my words." Emma began pacing in Lizzie's room. Lizzie hated it when Emma paced in her room. She wanted to tell her to go pace in her own room if she had to pace. But Emma had started to rub her knuckles across her upper lip again, and Lizzie knew that she was lost to all logic and reason.

Fear rose in Lizzie as Emma burbled up from the sludge pool in the back of her mind. Emma was about to enter a rage, and the only ending of it was that she went to New Bedford and came home half dead. This would make three times this year and the year was not yet two-thirds over.

". . . he drives us to consider murdering him, doesn't he?"

"Emma!"

"He does, Lizzie, he does, you know it." Lizzie flushed, because she *did* know it. "We are all thinking of murdering him, he's such a terrible, terrible man, and if his actions can do that to members of his family, imagine what some of his tenants think. And those poor people who have to work for him! No, Lizzie, something terrible has begun here, and it's not going to stop until something really ugly happens." Emma's lip had begun to bleed, and two little dabs of pink froth appeared at the corners of her mouth. "And I can't be here when it happens. I can't. Someone will come in here and murder us all as we sleep, Lizzie, can't you see that? I can't stand by and let everything just be put down like that, do you understand? Oh God, I wish I could just smack him in the head with a hammer. Just once and end it all. Just put an end to his whole miserable life. How happy we would all be if he were only dead!"

Lizzie was dumbfounded.

Suddenly, Emma fell to her knees and grabbed Lizzie's hands in her own. Lizzie felt Emma's hard, cold, bony hands grip hers so tightly it hurt. "Lizzie, we've got to get out of here. We've got to get away. Far, far away. And we've got to do it now. Soon. Fast. Something is going to happen, I feel it in my bones, and we'll be powerless to stop it. Please."

And then Emma stopped raving and her face was twisted with fear and anxiety. But she wasn't mad, not yet. There was sanity in her eyes.

"All right, Emma. We'll leave. You go lie down now for a while and I'll see if I can make some arrangements."

A wild look of hope transformed Emma's face. She looked like a child about to be rewarded for doing something particularly difficult. It was such a new experience, it caught Lizzie totally by surprise. For once she was the older sister, the parent-sister, taking care of Emma. That had never happened before. For once, Emma sought her help and depended on her to see the project through.

"All right? You *will* go lie down for a while?"

Emma looked at her with distrust, and Lizzie could see that what sanity Emma still had fluttered like a distant and indistinct flag.

230

"No one will come this afternoon, Emma. We're safe for the time being. Now you go to your room and lock your window and your door. I'm going out tonight, and I'll make all the arrangements."

"All right." Emma released her hold on Lizzie's hands, then pulled herself up off her knees. She stood shakily, uncertainly. Then, as if trying to regain a drop of dignity, she walked, back straight, to her bedroom door, unlocked it, opened it, entered and shut it behind her without a backward glance.

Perspiration ran down Lizzie's face.

She felt in danger of sliding backwards into the pit. She could almost feel the slime oozing up over the rockers of her chair. She sat stock-still, staring straight ahead, her mind empty. She didn't know what to do, she didn't know what to think. Soon her mind began to grapple with words to describe the experience, and her fists began to clench. And suddenly, the struggle was full force. She desperately clutched for meaning as her thoughts merged and swirled with images from the pool faces and slices of conversation, embarrassments, taunts.

And then, suddenly, she was in the backyard. The light was sizzling bright. Everything seemed highly polished. Lizzie sat in her rocking chair in the upstairs bedroom, her hands in her lap, and she was also in the backyard, running her hand along the weather-splintered boards of the fence. She looked into the neighbor's yard, saw their young son sitting on the step eating something with his hands. She walked over to the barn, slowly, gently, as if she had all the time in the world, as if leisure were her only virtue. Her fingers trailed from the fence to the tops of the weeds, some flowering, some about to flower. She trailed her fingers across the front of the barn, not minding the dirtiness of it, whereas usually Lizzie needed to keep her hands very clean indeed. She moistened a dirty finger in her mouth and made a long mark across the dirty barn window, then continued on.

And all the while, Lizzie could see her dresser, her bed, her washbowl, dimly lit, as if a background set on a stage.

The outside Lizzie stopped and leaned her back against the barn, put one foot up on its side as she looked down at her hands. And then the maid, hair plastered to her scalp with perspiration, opened the kitchen door with a pot of dirty dishwater, looked at her and nodded.

The outside Lizzie spoke. "Is there a dessert, Maggie?"

"Miss Emma made blackberry tarts," Bridget answered, then threw the dishwater onto the lawn and disappeared back into the kitchen, the door slamming shut behind her.

Just as suddenly, Lizzie was wholly in her room. The other Lizzie was gone. She looked at her hands. They were clean. They were damp. They ached from being wrung.

She jumped up and ran downstairs, through the dining room, through the monstrously hot kitchen, out the back door.

There was a long mark on the dusty barn window. Fresh.

Lizzie slowly walked back up to the house.

"Just where had you got to, Miss Lizzie?" Bridget asked.

Lizzie didn't answer her. She suddenly had no words. She took a tart from the cooling tray and went back up to her room, locking her bedroom door. She put the tart on her bedside table and then lay down on the bed. She had no words, she had no ideas, she had no feelings. She only yearned for the days that used to be.

She tried to relax her hands, her neck, her shoulders. She floated Emma away, and Kathryn, and Andrew, and everybody, and everything, and surrounded herself with the cool green of a spring morning on the bank of a deep, swiftly moving stream.

● ● ●

232

She woke up one half hour before she was to be at Enid's for supper. She flew from the bed, took her towel and ran down the stairs, through the dining room and kitchen, then pounded heavily down cellar. She went to the toilet, then let cold water into the tub, undressed, stood in the tub and soaped herself down and rinsed, all with the frigid well water. She had no time to deal with her hair.

She dried off quickly, feeling the soap still on her skin, knowing it would give her a rash before she bathed again, then slipped hurriedly into her bathrobe, threw her soiled clothes into a pile on the dirt floor and ran back up to the kitchen. The cellar had a summer smell, an unpleasant sour odor, that went away in the winter as the wood furnace dried everything out down there. But in the summer it smelled of rot, not to mention the stench of the privy, and the flies that hovered above it. How on *earth* could Beatrice bathe down here?

The Borden house irritated Lizzie more and more each day, but she couldn't think of it now. Now she had an appointment, and she musn't be late.

Back in her room, she ate the tart as she dressed. She chose a light blue summer-weight skirt, as it was broiling hot outside, and a soft white silk blouse. She carefully donned her dress shields, or the blouse would be ruined in less than the ten minutes it would take to walk to Enid's.

She brushed out her hair, parted it down the middle, then wrapped it up in a long coil and pinned it down. Not the best job, but not bad.

She popped the last of the tart in her mouth, and as she did, a glob of berries fell out, ran down her blouse and came to rest on the lap of her skirt.

Lizzie closed her eyes and clenched her fists. Slowly, she picked up the offending fruit and then took her clothes off, wadding them up, knowing they would be ruined forever if she didn't take the time to care for the stain. She shoved the wad under the bed. She opened the closet. Nothing else was presentable. Nothing else was ironed.

She pulled out another white blouse, this one cotton and a little bit too tight, and put it on. She found another skirt, this one darker and heavier, but still light enough for a scalding July evening. She smoothed herself out, looked in on the sleeping Emma, then took her housekeys in her pocket and left. Late.

The heat outside hit her like a blast furnace. She briefly wondered why the "outside Lizzie" hadn't seemed to feel the heat. It was definitely too hot to hurry, she would really spoil her clothes, but at least her wrinkled appearance would not seem out of the ordinary.

She walked as quickly as she dared, without bringing down streams of perspiration, trying to remember Enid's directions to her little house, which was on the Hill, tucked in behind another, larger house. She cursed her faulty memory and wished that she'd just written the instructions down instead of being so vain as to impress Enid by claiming that she could remember everything.

But there it was, a little tiny house shaded by huge maple trees, tucked away in the backyard of a large house, a house that Lizzie had somehow never noticed before, even though it looked as though it belonged somewhere in Atlanta.

She stood for a moment in the shade of the big house, patting her hair and her clothes, and then walked up to Enid's door and knocked.

Enid wore men's pants. And a man's shirt, with buttons up the front, tucked into her pants and showing off her tiny waist. Her short hair was brushed back and she looked like a man, almost, a little tiny man with a big grin.

"Lizzie! Come in." And she opened the door wide.

It was cool inside. It was very, very cool inside. Cool and filled to the rafters with books, newspapers and magazines.

"Here," Enid said, and she picked up a pile of magazines from the end of the sofa and dropped them onto the floor. "Sit down. Or maybe you'd rather freshen up? I know it's a scorcher out there. The bath is down the hall."

Lizzie couldn't believe that Enid had not cleaned house in preparation for her visit. Lizzie could not believe that Enid lived like this. "Bath? Yes, I think I . . ." She followed Enid's gesture down the hall.

It was a bathroom. It had a bathtub. Lizzie turned the faucet and water came out, right into the tub. And there was a flush toilet. And a sink. And a large mirror framed in wood. She looked at herself. She looked monstrous, huge, red-faced. She ran cold water into the sink and splashed her face. The bathroom was spotless.

"There," Enid said. "You look a little better. Sorry about the house. It's always this way. I find the older I get the more interested I am in everything. I read all the time."

Suddenly, Enid was the delightful person Lizzie had come to love and covet, not a stranger who lived in a mess.

"I've just made us a salad for dinner. I hope you weren't expecting anything hearty."

Salad? Lizzie thought. There had never been a salad served in the Borden house. Meat, potatoes and gravy. Every night. Enid handed her a cool glass of lemonade.

"Sit. Relax. Tell me about yourself."

Lizzie settled back into the sofa, setting her drink on top of yet another stack of books on the coffee table. Enid sat at a little desk chair turned around, and she crossed her legs.

"Tell me about your family," she said.

Just as Lizzie was about to open her mouth, she noticed that Enid had gone just a little bit out of focus. She blinked, then blinked again, but the center of her vision was furred, and that meant only one thing. She closed her eyes and the sparkly fuzz was still there. Disappointment, despair, anger thrummed at her. She covered her face with her hands.

"Lizzie? Lizzie, dear, what is it?"

The stack of newspapers next to her slid onto the floor and then Enid was next to her, stroking her arm. "It's the heat, it's the damned heat," she said.

Lizzie had never heard a woman swear before, but her amazement was overshadowed by the fact that within ten minutes she would be lost in the depths of a soul-tormenting headache.

She put down her hands and lifted her face. The whole center of Enid's face was distorted. Soon the spot would grow and then hollow out, becoming an ever-widening ring. When the ring reached just past the outer edges of her vision, the pain would begin.

"Headache coming on," she said. "I get these terrible, terrible sick headaches, and now one is coming on." Tears of frustration leaked through, and Lizzie clamped down hard on them. She didn't want Enid to see her crying on top of everything else.

"I'm sorry," Enid said. "Can I get you something?"

"No, there's nothing, but I could never manage to reach home, and they sometimes last for . . . hours."

"Are they . . ."

"Dreadful."

"Should you eat?"

"I'd vomit it back up, I'm afraid."

"Well, then. You're my guest and we'll just have to make the best of it."

"I'm sorry, Enid. I'm terribly sorry. I feel like an invalid."

"We'll put you down in my bed, and I'll go to your house . . ."

The sparkling ring had hollowed out and Lizzie saw something peculiar on Enid's face. She put her hand on Enid's.

"I'll go to your house and tell your family that you won't

be home tonight. You'll sleep here and in the morning I'll fix you a breakfast instead of supper and you'll be on your way, good as new."

The thunder of the headache loomed on the horizon.

"I need dark. And quiet. I'm so glad it's cool here."

"Come. Let us make you comfortable. I even have a nightshirt that will fit you."

Lizzie pulled the pins out of her hair as she followed Enid into her bedroom. She somehow wasn't surprised to see piles of books on both sides of the bed, by the nightstands. Enid pulled a big cotton nightshirt out of a dresser drawer as the pain began to sound. Lizzie sat on the edge of the bed, her eyes half closing.

Enid drew down the shades and pulled the draperies closed.

"Come, Lizzie, let me get you out of those clothes."

Lizzie fumbled at her clothes, and Enid helped. She wished she could enjoy the act of being undressed by Enid, but now she felt limp, drained, and wanted only to be in the nightshirt, in the bed, with a soft pillow under her, so she could rest, just she and her pain, while they became reacquainted.

Sometimes it felt as if her headache pain was her only friend, her only consistent, loyal confidant. She could tell her pain anything, and if she didn't tell, then it wrenched the information from her. It visited her when she needed it the most and took everything she had to offer. Everything and more.

Lizzie felt her bare feet sliding between cool sheets, and lay her head on a fresh pillowslip. The pain moved in and moved Enid out. Lizzie never heard the door close.

hen the quiet knock came at the door, Andrew Borden was sitting at his desk, totaling his accounts. At first, he wasn't sure that he had heard a knock at all.

His first thought was of that bloody Italian man again, but he had pounded on the door, that stupid little greasy man had, and unless this was his wife— No, those wop bastards had greasy wives who would probably pound just as loud.

Then it came again, a soft little rapping, as if made by a child's hand.

He rose and went to the door.

He undid all three locks and opened the door.

There stood the Widow Crawford. Her hair was askew, her clothes hastily prepared. She wore a shawl to cover the fact that her dress was not properly pressed. In spite of himself, he whipped his head around to see if Abby approached.

"Good evening, Mr. Borden," she spoke with a clear, loud voice.

"Ma'am," he said.

"My name is Enid Crawford. I am a member of the Central Congregational Church, where I attend services with your daughter Lizzie."

"Oh?" Andrew had no idea what was going on, but he found his face flushing a deep crimson, something he always found becoming on Lizzie, but which he detested on himself.

238

"I invited Lizzie to dinner tonight—"

Anger flooded Andrew.

"—and just before we were to eat, she succumbed to a terrible headache." The anger fled. Lizzie had another headache. His heart went out to her. "I have put her to bed, and came to tell you that she wouldn't be home until morning."

He stood, staring at her.

"So you and your wife wouldn't worry, Mr. Borden."

"Of course, of course," he said. He still didn't know what to do or how to act.

"Mr. Borden?" Abby called from the kitchen. In a moment, she was at his side, pulling the door wide open, and the two women regarded each other for a long moment. Andrew was deeply ashamed at his wife's size. "What is it?"

"Lizzie went to Mrs. Crawford's home for dinner and was seized with a headache—" he began.

"Oh, my dear, please come in, come in, let me get you a coffee." As Abby turned, Enid gave Andrew a small smile, a knowing smile, a sly smile, a naughty smile, and she stepped over the threshold and began to look around.

"Well, perhaps Mrs. Crawford needs to attend . . ."

"Lizzie is asleep, or at least resting," Enid said, "and I'd love a cup of coffee. Cold, please, Mrs. Borden. No sugar."

Abby bustled her bulk ahead. "Come in, have a seat. I have coffee all ready."

"You shouldn't have come," Andrew whispered. He didn't know what else to say, what else to do.

"And just let you worry about Lizzie? She won't be home tonight. I had no choice. Besides . . ." She stepped in front of him and made herself comfortable on the sofa in the sitting room.

"What was Lizzie doing at your house anyway?"

"We've managed a friendship, Andrew," Enid spoke loud enough to make Andrew's heart race, but soft enough to keep her words for his ears only.

"Oh, Enid," he said, surprised at the way it sounded, it sounded like a moan, like the moans she elicited from him under highly different circumstances, it sounded intimate and personal, it sounded as if they were friends, lovers, when in actuality, they were rather business partners. But even business partners begin to realize a touch of affection for one another over a period of time, don't they? And perhaps, Andrew thought, as he realized how his "oh, Enid" sounded, he had fallen in love with her a little bit and liked the idea of being able to say such a thing to her.

"It's a harmless thing," Enid whispered, then straightened as Abby's heavy step sounded in the hall. "Lizzie and I were going over some church business. She's very involved with the Orientals, you know."

"Yes, isn't it wonderful?" Abby said, bringing in the glasses of coffee. Andrew regarded her with disdain. She was acting as if this were a social call, instead of a notification that their daughter was holed up in this woman's house sick and unable to leave. "I don't know much about Orientals at all, and Lizzie's changing churches just like that for no apparent reason was quite a shock to us all, as well you can imagine, but God does his mysterious works, doesn't he?"

"He does, Mrs. Borden," Enid said. "We all feel very fortunate to have Lizzie active in the Christian Endeavor Society. She is a wonderful person. An asset."

"What does your husband do?"

"My Charlie passed away years ago, Mrs. Borden. I work at the law offices to keep my boys in college up in Boston."

"Well . . ." Abby said, breathlessly, and had no more to say.

"Lovely home," Enid said, and the platitude fell quietly to the floor. Everyone looked at their feet. Andrew felt completely ill at ease. Bile burned at the top of his stomach and a cold dislike for Enid began to creep in around the gills. He brought his eyes up and met hers squarely. They looked at each other, Andrew felt his face an expressionless mask, and a queer look—almost fear, almost regret—crossed Enid's. Then they both looked at Abby, and her eyes were busily looking back and forth between them.

She knew. He knew she knew. He looked again at Enid, and saw that she had also seen the light in Abby's eyes. Andrew felt frosty toward the woman.

Enid set her untouched coffee on the table and stood up. "I'd better go back and check on Lizzie," she said. "I'm terribly sorry to have disrupted your evening."

"Oh, no trouble at all," Abby said, and Andrew wanted to slap her and tell her to shut her silly yap. "Give Lizzie our love. Sometime in the night her headache will pass, and in the morning she'll be better. Believe me. We've lived through many of Lizzie's headaches, haven't we?"

Andrew nodded. "She's like as not to vomit," he said.

Enid nodded. "Well, good-bye, then. I hope to see you again."

Andrew opened the door, Enid stepped out, and he closed it again, without another word. He turned all three locks, as if Enid had taken all his odd feelings with her and he never wanted them to return. Abby turned on her heel without so much as a glance toward him, took up Enid's glass from the table and disappeared into the kitchen.

Andrew went back to his ledgers, but his mind was not on numbers.

The house fell silent about him. He wished Lizzie were home, he wished Abby were not so overwhelmingly fat. He wished Enid had never come to the house. He wished Emma loved him still, he wished life were just a little bit easier for a man in his elder years, he wished for those youthful times, those good times, when he was a daddy, a hero to his little girls, and he used to take them . . .

Fishing! He and Lizzie had talked about fishing a while ago. Wouldn't it be good to take her—take both the girls, if

Emma had a mind to. Some nice fresh brook trout would be excellent, and the fresh air and sunshine—

—reminded him of rutting on the damp ground, Enid moving urgently beneath him, and his body stirred.

What in the *hell* was Lizzie doing at Enid's house? More important, what was Enid doing with Lizzie?

The stirring stopped. The inflation deflated. The moment of warm, pleasurable thought was replaced by another thought, one that put a cold stone in his lower belly. There was a hard edge to a woman who wore her hair short. There was a ruthlessness about a woman who wore no underwear and shamelessly seduced an older man for money. Blackmail was in Enid Crawford's soul, and Andrew saw how foolish he had been to allow their little business affair to carry on for so long.

And he had been going to put her in his will!

Surely she was after even more money, and would try to milk it, using Lizzie in some way.

He leaned his elbows on the desk and put his face in his hands. His hands were cold. He took off his specs and rubbed his face. It felt good, the cold, hard hands on his face, and when he looked up, and his vision cleared, Abby was standing in the doorway, wiping her hands on her apron.

"Are you ill, Mr. Borden?"

"No, no, just . . . worried about Lizzie, I think. She hasn't been away from home for a night before."

"When she was abroad . . ."

"Yes, I know, but she was not ill. I feel as though I should go and check on her."

That was the wrong thing to say. As soon as he said it, he knew how it sounded. It sounded as though his Fridays with Enid Crawford were not enough, and now he wanted to add a Wednesday to them as well. He knew she kept her gaze steady on him, but he could not meet it. "I don't think I shall, though. I don't even know where Mrs. Crawford lives."

"Doesn't the bank do business with that law firm of hers?"

"I believe so, yes."

"Hmm." She turned and went back to the kitchen.

Andrew was stunned with anxiety. His life was disintegrating. First Emma. Then Lizzie became too independent and decided she wanted to live in her own house. And now, he was fool enough for Enid Crawford, and Abby was feeling it personally. And what on *earth* might Enid do to Lizzie?

He would take it up with Enid on Friday.

He went into the kitchen and took a tart into the dining room, sat down, hoping Abby would join him. She didn't. He ate it, then went upstairs to bed.

hen Lizzie awakened, her whole being was awake in an instant. She smelled the difference in the room, felt the different sheets, the larger size of the room. Disoriented in the darkness, heart pounding, she recalled the headache, and before the headache, readying for dinner at Enid Crawford's.

A low moan escaped her before she could stop it. How could she have a headache at Enid Crawford's? What a terrible thing to impose.

"Lizzie?"

The word was whispered so close to her ear, at first Lizzie thought she was still dreaming. She turned her head, and there was Enid, tucked into bed next to her. A tiny hand found hers under the covers, and a smooth foot slid over and nestled next to hers. "How are you feeling?"

"Better." Lizzie turned her head away. This was what she had wanted, this was what she had dreamed of for weeks: to get Enid Crawford into bed. And here they were, Lizzie not clever, not adept, not bold or adventurous, but pitiable, weak, small, injured, stupid. Enid was in bed with her all right, but it was not to love her; no, it was to comfort her, as a parent might sleep with a sickly child.

Lizzie wanted nothing more than to get out of bed, dress and fly home as fast as her feet could possibly take her.

"I was terribly worried about you." The whisper was still close to Lizzie's face, intimate, quiet. A tear leaked out of the corner of Lizzie's eye. "I went to see your parents to tell them that you wouldn't be home." A sob escaped Lizzie and two more tears fell. Enid squeezed her hand tighter, then moved closer. Her arms came around Lizzie, and soon Lizzie's head was on Enid's shoulder, and she was sobbing, crying as hard as she had ever cried. Enid smoothed her hair and kissed her forehead and rocked her gently back and forth, saying "Shhh, Lizzie, it's all right. Everything's going to be just fine."

Eventually, the emotion was spent, and Lizzie lay quietly within Enid's calm. Her life was a mess, and that left a gaping hole in the pit of her stomach. She didn't seem to be able to do anything right, any of those pitiful little attempts she made at doing anything at all. Everything turned bad in one way or another. Life, it seemed, was a terrible joke, a practical joke played by God, in his infinite torturous ways, upon all his timid, unfortunate subjects.

"Your father said you might vomit," Enid said.

Lizzie was horrified. "He *did*?"

Enid chuckled.

"Oh God." Then Lizzie found the humor in it, found the humor in everything, suddenly, and she began to laugh. "Aren't they a pair?"

Enid began to laugh harder, and the bed shook with the two of them holding onto each other, unable to speak, racked with laughter. Eventually, Enid said, "Your mother didn't like me."

"She's afraid of small people, like an eleph—" Lizzie laughed until she cried. "Elephant of a mouse."

Enid wiped her cheeks with both hands, bouncing Lizzie's head around. Lizzie reached around Enid, and brought her tiny body close. She felt a lot like Kathryn, but more tender, gentler, softer.

They held each other close for a long time, now and then a chuckle escaping in remembrance.

Lizzie felt that she held within her arms the first good

thing that had happened to her in her whole life. Somehow, she wanted Enid to know it.

"I love you," she said, before she thought twice.

Enid hugged her closely. "And I am falling in love with you."

They entwined their legs, and Lizzie watched Enid's profile as she stared at the ceiling, until sleep overcame her and she slept.

When next Lizzie awoke, sunshine streamed in the gauze-curtained window and her heart soared. Enid was up, and the smell of bacon and eggs and fresh coffee permeated the room. The house was cool; at this time of day the Borden house was already sweltering, but the big shade trees kept Enid's house cool enough so she could light the wood stove and cook breakfast. Including a fresh pot of coffee. Lizzie floated out of bed and into the bathroom.

Sometimes this happened after a headache, this feeling of lightness, feeling of rightness. Lizzie felt as if the world were her gleaming possession this morning, as if she could do, be or have anything she wanted. She wanted to laugh in the face of all her troubles, laugh at everyone's troubles. She wanted to sing and make light of the woes of the world.

She flushed the toilet and watched the yellowed water swirl down. She wanted one for her bedroom. Well, she would have one, too, in her new house. A beautiful bathroom. Just like this one, only better.

She washed her face, then brushed out her hair. She knotted it back up on top of her head quickly, and went into the kitchen, still wearing the nightshirt that Enid had loaned her the night before. Somehow it felt more personal, more intimate, more appropriate than the clothes she had worn to supper the night before.

"Good morning!" Enid looked as happy as Lizzie felt. Lizzie hugged her.

"I don't normally eat bacon and eggs for breakfast, but

246

since you had no supper, I thought you'd be hungry this morning."

"You were right."

"Well, sit down, then, and I'll fix your plate."

Lizzie cleared a stack of newspapers from the end of the sofa and sat down. Enid brought her a steaming cup of coffee. "It's so nice and cool here."

"This is a nice house. It's always been the coolest during the hot summer months. I swelter in the office all day long, and then just come home and take off my clothes. Sometimes I soak in the bathtub filled with cold water."

That sounded like the strangest idea in the world to Lizzie. "Bathtub filled with cold water? I never heard of such a thing. Hot, soapy water, I always thought."

"You should try it sometime."

Shame tried to poke a hole in Lizzie's good mood. She dared not reveal that their house didn't even have a flush toilet, never mind a bathtub. And her baths were almost *always* cold water. Frigid water. Well water, straight from the tap. "I shall," she said, and blew across her coffee.

Enid dressed and left for work, leaving Lizzie a light kiss on the lips to remember, and an invitation to stay as long as she liked. First, she poked through Enid's things, and found all her cabinets to be as filled as the open flat spaces. The Borden cabinets were filled too—with china, with useless things that were always "too good" to be used for every day; yet the special occasions were so rare as to hardly warrant cleaning them when the time came. Enid's cabinets were filled with tools, books, magazines, newspapers and gadgets, piled in profusion and disarray. Everything looked useful, although Lizzie couldn't identify half of the items. It was a joyous, crowded house.

Lizzie fingered the clothes in Enid's closet. They were of good quality, but less expensive than the clothes Lizzie wore. Most were cottons; there were a few silks. One bedroom had

247

two beds, and the clothes closet in there was filled with men's clothes. Lizzie closed the door quickly on that one; she didn't know if the clothes belonged to Enid's deceased husband or to her two sons. It didn't matter. She was comfortable fingering Enid's belongings, but the men in her life were a mystery to Lizzie, and they were best kept mysterious.

When she had snooped to her heart's content, she heated enough water to both wash the dishes and take a bath.

Soaking in the tub was a thrilling luxury. Enid had perfumed soap crystals—they looked like a gift from someone—and it didn't appear as though Enid partook. Lizzie knew that Enid wouldn't mind if she did. She generously sprinkled the salts into the water, swirled them into oblivion with her foot, then lay back and relaxed as the scented steam rose about her.

"I now claim that which is divinely mine," Lizzie said to the wallpapered ceiling. "Enid. Enid is divinely mine. I claim absolute control over each fragment of my personality, to be strengthened through purposeful, conscious unity." She knew the words by heart, but this time she wanted only to have Enid Crawford for her own, and if that was the purpose toward which each fragment of her personality had to strive . . . so be it. It made good use of these stupid lessons, she thought. "I now will that the divine power which motors the universe now deed me the control over my own destiny with Enid. I now claim that I, and no other, am the architect of my future with Enid. I now command my rightful, unique place in the order of all material. In Enid's tub. So it is, so shall it be."

She soaked until her fingers puckered and the water chilled. Getting out of a chilled tub was even better, for the day had turned warm, even in Enid's cool house. She dried, dressed and, reluctantly, went home.

I must have my own home, she thought as she made her

way quickly through the heat. Perspiration soaked right through her dress shields, and trickled down her breasts. She wanted to be home quickly before her enthusiasm dampened, before anyone noticed her evening wear on this hottest of mornings. She wanted to get home and get a lighter cotton duster on before she perished in the heat. The heat was awful.

But her own house would be in the shade of the trees, just like Enid's. And she would have a clawfoot tub as well. And a large bathroom, with a flush toilet, and a private yard with lots of fruit trees. Particularly the pears. Perhaps she could have someone grow a piece of the Borden house pear tree, and she could put it in her backyard. That tree yielded the tastiest pears ever. It was the only good thing about that terrible, stupid house.

The Borden house had once been divided into two apartments. When Andrew and Sarah Borden bought that house, they did no remodeling at all. Therefore, the layout was bizarre, the rooms small, unconventional, cramped and inconvenient. Lizzie longed for a house that made sense, a regular house with nice large rooms. It would be absolutely divine if her house could be on the Hill, near Enid, where she could enjoy a view of Fall River, the church, the river, the farms. But all she really needed was a home of her own, even if Emma had to live there with her. She could invite Enid over for dinner with Emma there. She could have Beatrice for the weekend with Emma there. She could do neither of those things while living in the Borden house. That terrible, terrible house.

Lizzie turned the corner and looked at that tiny, narrow, ugly litte house on Second Street. It was shameful to live in that squalid little building. Lizzie stopped dead in her tracks and looked at it, as if for the first time, and she could smell the interior. It smelled of old, musty dust. It smelled of mildewed, sour cellar. It smelled like Emma and Andrew and

Abby and all that was wrong with the world, and Lizzie didn't want to go inside.

She looked around her. She had nowhere else to go.

She would speak with Andrew that day *that day* and she would not relent until she had his agreement that she should have her own home. She would *not* relent.

She walked around the side of the house, along the narrow path between their house and the neighbor's, knocked on the screen door to the kitchen, and when Maggie opened the door, Lizzie filled her lungs with the stench of food that had been left out in the heat too long, food that had been breakfast again and would be dinner *again,* the stench of the Borden home.

ugust

Monday, August 1

"h, Lizzie?"

"Yes, Mrs. Churchill?"

"Have you a new horse?"

"No, Mrs. Churchill." Lizzie turned to see the next-door neighbor leaning out her kitchen window.

"You're spending so much time in the barn."

"I know," Lizzie said, and then continued on. Mrs. Churchill kept her finger on—or her nose in—every tiny bit of information on the whole neighborhood. She kept Abby apprised of the birthings in the area, and sometimes she had some valuable information. Lizzie bore Mrs. Churchill no ill will. She hoped someday Mrs. Churchill would be the first on the scene with some really big news, and so become deified within her gossip group.

It was so hot in the hayloft that Lizzie could barely breathe. She unearthed her book, took a deep breath and began to read her first lesson. She unbuttoned the top of her blouse, and let her skirt ride up her thighs. She let the perspiration run freely off her face and arms, and watched the dark stains appear on her clothing. She read the paragraph, and when she finished, she automatically began setting up the candles and the mirror, and idly wondered if that initial lesson had any meaning left for her, or if it had all been squeezed out like the rind of a lemon. Or perhaps it had just

252

become rote, like some of the things in church, or like furniture that is taken for granted and no longer even noticed. Perhaps she should spend some time again with that first lesson.

But she was too tired.

She moved a piece of board over the window to darken the room, lit the candles, looked at her watch, and then regarded her reflection in the mirror.

This, too, had become boring. What was the purpose of it? She watched as the edges of the mirror became indistinct, and then her face changed shape, all of it swirling a bit around the two eyes. Her eyes locked onto those of her reflection, and the many faces of Lizzie Andrew Borden faded in and out around them.

Within ten minutes, she had had enough. She blew out the candles, took the board down, shoved the box from her and picked up the book again. Lesson three. God, she was sick of lesson three.

She had tried talking to her Angry Self, but nobody ever answered. She thought that perhaps it was the Angry Self that went walking, but if it was, it wasn't talking to her. She tried talking to her Greedy Self, too, and her Jealous Self. She had been on this lesson for months, *months*, and had gotten nowhere, except to believe that those selves did indeed exist within her. Yet she didn't feel as if she could go on, not until she'd gotten to the bottom of the list, not until she'd gotten to talk with her Higher Self, and her Healthful Self, and her Whole Self. That seemed to be of paramount importance in this program of Beatrice's. Besides, she wanted to talk to her Whole Self.

She took a deep breath, relaxed and began again. "Angry Self?" she whispered, and then waited to listen for a reply. Nothing. "Greedy Self?" She waited. Nothing.

Lizzie threw the Beatrice Book against the wall. She began to pace. She wanted to leave Fall River *right this minute* and never return. She never wanted to hear the next chapter in the life of Andrew Borden. Or Abby. Or Emma. Or the church or the Orientals or Beatrice, or . . . or . . .

Life was out of control. Lizzie seemed to be at the end of a long chain of people, running as fast as possible, and they were whipping her about, hoping she'd fall off, hoping they'd shake her loose and be rid of her. Well, they were close. Lizzie had had about enough.

But if she left, there would be an end to her friendship with Enid, a most uncommon friendship, something intimate and quite beyond words. Enid was the best friend Lizzie never had, she was the big sister Lizzie never had, she was the mother Lizzie never had. Enid had opened a need so deep within Lizzie that Lizzie was afraid to look down the hole. She was afraid that it went on forever, unfillable, she was afraid of what was crawling around down there in the dark and the muck of her nether selves.

But by opening that door, Enid was also allowing fresh air and sunshine into that place, that dark place of longing, that place Lizzie hoped Beatrice and her book of lessons could fill. Beatrice and her book could never hope to mend a rent of that proportion. But perhaps Enid could.

Lizzie knew that such thinking was dangerous. Her life was already in the hands of too many others—and here she was again, placing her most precious asset of all—her trust—in the hands of a woman she hardly knew, yet whom she felt as if she knew through and through.

It was hard. It was agonizing. She wanted to leap into Enid's lap and nurse at her breast. She wanted to run from Enid as well as the rest of them and never hear the name again.

And so she flopped down in the hay, where the heat was filled with dust motes and her skin gleamed slick and she couldn't keep her hands away from that center part of her that was her only solace in times like this.

254

Lizzie slowly fingered herself and thought about Enid. At church, Enid had looked like a queen. Her short hair was newly cut, and its thick waves, brushed back from her tanned face, made her seem exotic. Lizzie thrilled every time she looked at her. They sat next to each other and held hands, Lizzie's skin itching to be out of her gloves and touching Enid's skin.

That she had been such an inconvenience for Enid, what with her stupid headache and all, and to have Enid still care enough about her . . . Only family do that for one another, don't they?

But family do it whether they want to or not, because they *have* to. They're *expected* to. But when Emma was in such dire need, did either Andrew or Abby visit her? No.

Life should be clean and simple, Lizzie thought. Everyone should have someone to love them and take care of them. Everyone should have purpose in life, and something to look forward to.

Lizzie had none of that. The only thing she had to look forward to was church next Sunday, and sitting next to Enid. But any moment, Enid might turn the way Kathryn did, and that would be the end of that.

Lizzie threw her skirts down over her knees, stood up and began to walk back and forth. It was at least ten degrees hotter at her head than at her feet. Sweat poured anew.

What if Beatrice should show up this very moment? She said the end of July or the first of August. This was the first of August. She said she'd write, but what if the letter were lost, or delayed, or . . . What if she just showed up and knocked at the door? Perfect in peach, cool and collected, rich beyond anyone's imagination, calm, in control. Lizzie would just waltz out of the barn, bedraggled and soaked through with her own juices. She would shake hands with her and they would sit on the back porch in the shade and eat pears right off the tree.

Lizzie wondered if she wasn't becoming a bit hysterical.

She looked around and saw *Pathways* on the floor in the corner. She retrieved it, opened it to the first page and began to read aloud, standing in front of the loft window, as if the whole of Fall River were her audience. Halfway through the first paragraph, she paused.

If Beatrice came right now, she thought, I would send my other self to greet her. First, I would send my other self to the cellar to bathe, then to the bedroom to change clothes. Then she and Beatrice could have a fine discussion, and whatever was decided between them could be between *them*. It wouldn't have to have anything to do with me at all.

Lizzie dropped the book, scattering up a ruffle of dust. Then she sat on the edge of the loft, letting her legs dangle over the edge. A knot caught in her throat. Life is hard sometimes, she thought. Life is really hard.

She allowed one tear to leak out and mix with the sweat on her face, then she swung down the ladder and out of the barn, locking the door securely behind her. Anything to make Emma angry.

In her bedroom, she dared a look at herself in the mirror. She was a mess. Hair unkempt and frazzled from the relentless heat and perspiration, Lizzie gathered new clothes and made ready for the bath. As she came down the stairs, a knock came at the door. Fear flooded Lizzie. What if it was Beatrice? What if it was? She listened, but she heard no one else home. There was no one else to answer the door.

Heart pounding, she walked to the door and said, "Who is it?"

"Sarah Whitehead," was the answer. Lizzie breathed a sigh. She unlocked the front door and let Sarah in. Weird little Sarah. Lizzie never got over the fact that Abby's half sister should have the same name as Lizzie and Emma's mother. It was not right, somehow.

"Hello, Sarah."

"Lizzie." Sarah had put on a dress for the occasion. Lizzie was impressed. "Is Abby here?"

"I don't think so."

"Would you check, please? It's ever so important."

"All right. Wait here." But Sarah followed her into the sitting room and sat on the sofa. Lizzie went through the kitchen and called to Abby up the back stairs. She answered, and in a moment, her bulk came jostling down the stairs.

"Sarah is waiting for you in the sitting room," Lizzie said, then went down cellar to bathe.

The cellar was nice and cool, and if it hadn't smelled so bloody rotten, Lizzie could easily see spending her August days amid the cool. She opened the faucet and let cold water into the bucket. She poured several bucketsful into the bathing tub, fetched a mildewed towel from the nail, and stripped off her clothes. She stepped into the tub and poured a bucket of cold water over her head. It was shockingly cold, but it felt wonderful.

She sat down, as well as she could fit, inside the washtub, and washed herself and her hair with the rough lye soap that Emma made every autumn when Andrew brought home lard from the farm. Then, with a clear bucket, she rinsed herself, feeling her hair fan out over her skin. Then she sat up, playing with the soap bubbles, her knees up to her chest, the cold settling in deep. Soon, she was shivering.

Oh, wasn't it a luxury to be cold. But why had it to be either hot or cold? Couldn't cool do? Couldn't there be a cool, pleasant place in all of Fall River this August? Lizzie shivered and thought how odd it would be to ask Abby to send down her cape. Her seal cape. Her fancy seal cape, made from "seals from the Prussian Sea."

Andrew had given her that cape, in a rare, odd moment. It was expensive, of that there was no doubt, and Andrew was not prone to moments of extravagance. Lizzie doubted that there was a Prussian Sea, or that the seals in her cape came from it, but if that's what it took to sell the cape to Andrew, then she would allow him that bit of romanticism. But it was the finest cape in all of Fall River, Lizzie was certain, and she wished she had it now.

Then she began to giggle again. The thought of it. Sitting naked in the little washtub, knees to her chin, surrounded by that luxurious cape. What a sight! Oh, but she would get soap all over it, and that would never . . . oh. The cape had a smear of lampblack on it, and Lizzie had never taken it in to be cleaned. Well, she would have to do that before the cold weather hit. . . . And her spirits lightened again at the thought of cold weather hitting, it seemed so unlikely in the midst of this terrible heat wave.

She splashed more fresh, cold water over herself and watched the goose pimples rise, watched her nipples shrink. She would be cramped when she tried to stand up.

Perhaps I'll just send one of my other selves out with the cape, she thought, mirth clearly on her mind.

And then the day was unusually bright and she was walking down the street. It was blazing hot, it was so hot that nobody was out in the streets, nobody was in the sun. Shop doors were open, windows were open, women wore their housedresses in public, because they would barely survive with corsets and stays. Lizzie walked jauntily down the street, and she felt a smile on her face, a giggle just on the tip of her tongue. She was wearing the clothes she ruined this morning, and then she noticed that she hadn't ruined them; the skirt had some paint splattered on it from the time she helped repaint the barn. So she hadn't ruined the clothes after all. . . . They were the right ones to wear to the barn. But they were not the right ones to wear to town.

She continued down the street, smiling, with an "I don't care" attitude, and she turned right into the drugstore.

The weasel-faced man she'd seen in there before stood behind the counter. "Good day," he said.

She nodded at him, looking around at this and that. Then, finally, with much self-control, she walked to the counter and said, "I'd like to buy some . . . prussic acid."

"Prussic acid! Whatever for?"

Lizzie had to turn away for a moment to keep the smile from breaking out on her face. She touched her fingertips to her mouth until she was sure she could do this without laughing. "I want to clean a sealskin cape," she said, and she was sure she said it without a hint of mirth.

"I'm sorry, miss, but the druggist isn't in, and he would have to be the one to dispense prussic acid.'"

"I only need a small amount," Lizzie said. "It isn't a very big spot." She wanted to go on about prussic acid being the only thing that could clean skins from Prussia, but it just became too much.

"I'm sorry," he said, as she fled the store.

Outside in the sun, in the heat, it suddenly didn't seem so funny anymore.

Lizzie splashed in the cold water, and felt her muscles tighten. She wanted this other self—which one was it, anyway?—to disappear, she wanted to be totally back in the cellar, where she could be back in control. She wanted to dry off and get out of the tub.

But the other self had other ideas, as well, and the downtown Lizzie did not turn toward home, but instead strolled down the street toward Andrew Borden's bank.

No, Lizzie in the tub thought. Not Father's bank.

But the other Lizzie didn't go in, just walked past, smiling at everyone, past the mill, taunting, it seemed, the Lizzie in the tub.

And then she saw Emma.

Emma, dressed in black, dressed *shabbily* in black, striding toward her. Emma, pinched face hatchet sharp, stray hairs escaping the tight bun, Emma, all knees and elbows, rushing far too fast in this heat, headed straight for her. "Lizzie! Lizzie! I say!" and Town Lizzie stood there and waited, small smile on her lips, as Emma approached.

"Lizzie, get yourself home this minute and put on some decent clothes. Where are your gloves? I swear you have suffered a seizure in this heat. Get home right now, and wait for me. I have news. Oh dear me, I have news." And Emma strode on, down Main Street, and Lizzie watched as she entered into the law office.

Town Lizzie did start down the street toward home, and then disappeared.

And Lizzie shivered with cold and fright from head to foot in the tiny tub down cellar.

With great aching effort, she stood up and dried her wrinkled skin with the smelly towel. Then she dressed in a simple wrapper and went upstairs.

The sitting room was empty. Sarah Whitehead had gone. She went to her room. Her door and Emma's door were both unlocked and open, the only time Lizzie had ever seen them so.

Lizzie sat down in her rocker and rocked, sure of bad news as soon as Emma returned. She was sure that bad news marched toward them from several directions. She rocked slowly, and waited.

uch, Emma! Emma, you're hurting me!"

"Sit down, Abby. Sit down right now and listen to me." Emma released her grip on Abby's wrist when she seemed willing to leave the plate of cakes on the kitchen table and come with her into the dining room. They sat across from each other like adversaries.

Emma looked at her stepmother across the table, and she hardly seemed familiar. Abby's face was puffy and bloated. She looked terrified. Well, she had a few more surprises coming. "I overheard your conversation with Sarah Whitehead this morning."

"That was private."

"And, I went to the law offices to look at Father's will."

Abby drew in a sharp breath. "You have no right."

"I did, and so do you. But that's beside the point, because Father's will is no longer there."

Emma sat back and watched with satisfaction the range of emotions that crossed Abby's face, from puzzlement to disbelief, to amazement, to anger. "But then, where?"

"Good question. That's what you must find out from him tonight. If Sebastian Whitehead means to do Father some harm Abby, then we need to know just exactly what is in his will."

"Emma, I can't—"

"If you don't, I will. And believe me, Abby, I *will* get answers from the old man."

Abby began to cry. "You're a hateful person."

261

"Perhaps. Your cakes are waiting." Emma left the room quickly. The sight of the pitiful woman made her sick to her stomach.

She went up the stairs and unlocked Lizzie's door.

Lizzie sat there, in her rocker.

"Lizzie! You're home."

"Yes."

"And bathed? How could that be?" Emma had seen Lizzie not fifteen minutes before, in the middle of town, and Lizzie always made such an event out of bathing that the whole house knew of it.

"What is it, Emma? What is so important?"

"Sarah Whitehead was here this morning, talking to Abby. I happened to overhear their conversation."

"Just *happened* to?"

Emma ignored the implication. "It seems as if Abby has been unsuccessful in getting our father to change his will in Sarah's favor, and so now Sebastian, that little twit's husband, has taken it upon himself to do harm to our father so that Abby, as wife, will inherit everything. Then Abby can do as she wishes with her inheritance, even give it all to her sister and leave us right out of it."

"What are you saying, that Sebastian is going to kill Father?"

"That's what Sarah said, not me."

"I can't believe that, Emma."

"Well, then listen to this. When I saw you in town, I was headed straight for the law offices. I demanded to see a copy of Father's will, but he took the original out some weeks ago and has not brought it back. The will is missing, Lizzie. And if it is not to be found, then for sure Abby will inherit everything."

"Wait, Emma. This doesn't make sense. Why would Father's will be anywhere other than at the law office? Father would just write instructions and have them sent over, they would write a new will and be done with it. Just because they told you they didn't have it, doesn't mean that they don't have it. It's not your will, after all, and perhaps they have a responsibility to their clients to keep their affairs confidential." Even as she said this, Lizzie realized she could imagine no little law clerk being a match for Emma when Emma was like this.

"They looked for it, Lizzie. I asked them to make sure his will was in order, and they went into the vault and came back with a note that said that Mr. Borden had removed the original copy of his will sometime in July."

"Have you looked in his desk?"

"No. I just got home and told Abby to find out from him what is going on, and to find it out today."

"Don't you think someone should tell the police that Sebastian is threatening Father's life?"

"I think that's up to Abby. She'll have to tell Father, of course, and that won't bode well for Sarah being included in his will either, will it? And if they both decide that the threat is real, well, I suppose they will tell the police." Emma stopped her pacing and looked at Lizzie, sitting so calmly in her rocking chair. Her fingers were idly picking at her skirt. "I just don't understand you, Lizzie. I don't understand how you can remain so calm throughout all of this. It's not right. It's not quite human."

"Calm? I guess I am, although I don't quite feel calm. I feel quite odd, actually, as if none of this is really happening."

"Oh, it's happening, all right," Emma said, "and as soon as Father gets home, even more is going to happen, I assure you." Emma turned to go into her room, and then said to Lizzie, "If you hear Father coming in the door, be sure to call me."

Lizzie nodded, and Emma wasn't entirely sure she heard, but didn't feel like repeating herself. She closed the door of her room and stood there, arms crossed, fists clenched. She felt the familiar taste come to her mouth, the taste of hate. She felt the rage build from a burning in her throat to a furnace in her gut. She felt her face redden, and with a will of their own her knuckles began to rub against her lip, and she began to pace.

Occasionally, a coherent thought or phrase would run through her mind, and be snagged and repeated until the sounds lost all form or meaning. Most of the time, there was no coherence. There was only depth. Vast injustice. And sometimes Emma recognized fear. This time she knew exhaustion as well. She was tired of this, tired of it all. She was sick and tired of being sick and tired, and the old man was the cause of it all.

She couldn't wait for him to come in the door. She would see to it that he would finally, *finally* understand his family obligations and not leave all his money to that Sarah thing, or to his slut.

But then she had told him all that before, hadn't she? And had it made a difference?

The rage burned hotter. The thought fled through her mind, *I've got to get out of here*, but Emma pushed it away. Not yet, not yet.

She didn't want to go back to the Capitol Hotel, although a little drink would be welcome to help calm her nerves.

Out of the question. It would dull her senses. It would also cast her into the other helplessness, that place where she would stay, submerged, for weeks at a time, surfacing only to crawl home. She could never do that in Fall River. Never.

Fairhaven! The Fairhaven relatives. She had always got on with her mother's kin in Fairhaven. She could go talk to them, stay with them, stay away from New Bedford, and if they agreed with her reasoning, she could bring them back with her to Fall River to speak with Father. They would never want their mother's offspring to be destitute while the second wife's half sister, or a tart, for God's sake, inherited the lot.

That's good. That's good. That's very good.

She took a long breath. She pulled her knuckles away from her lip. She slowly took control of the madness that she had always allowed. Her upper lip, she noticed, was already beginning to swell. She took herself to the bed and got down on her knees.

"Mother," she said, "I will take care of Lizzie, as I have always promised you. I won't let that man fritter away all that you and I worked for. I promise you that. I promise you that. Even if that Abby woman has to die first." Emma gasped at that thought. She was astonished that such a thing would come from her lips in a prayer to her mother. She put her forehead on the bed and covered her face with her hands in an attitude of shame, thinking that killing Abby and then killing Andrew was not such a bad idea after all.

Think of the problems it would solve.

Perhaps she should have a talk with Sebastian Whitehead.

hen Lizzie heard her father's key in the front door, she quickly and quietly slipped out of her bedroom and locked it behind her. She didn't want Emma to know he was home. She tiptoed down the stairs and met him in the entrance to the sitting room.

"Hello, Father."

"Lizzie."

"Any mail?"

"Yes, in fact, a letter from your British friend."

"Oh?" Lizzie took the letter. It was postmarked Washington, D.C. She slipped it into the pocket on her duster.

"There are a couple of cookies left, Father. Would you like some cold milk?"

Andrew looked at her over his glasses. He smiled. "Yes, that would be nice."

Lizzie helped him to sit down, took off his boots and then went to the ktichen to fix him a plate.

Abby stood in the kitchen.

"Not now, Abby. Let me have a few moments with him first, please."

Abby turned without saying a word, and made her way up the back stairs to her bedroom. Andrew would be joining her up there for his afternoon nap, most likely, unless he slept on the sofa in the sitting room. Regardless, there would be no confrontation until Lizzie said so.

She took the plate of cookies and glass of milk in to him, where he was reading his mail. "Anything interesting?"

"No." He set the mail aside and took a cookie.

"Will we read today?"

"Of course, Father," Lizzie said. "What would you like to read?"

"Anything you choose, Lizzie."

"All right." Lizzie got up and fetched the book they had been reading together. It was almost finished. She sat back down next to him, made him comfortable with a pillow and then opened the book.

Emotion clogged her voice, though, and she had to pause for a long moment. Andrew drank his milk and went for another cookie, so the interruption was not necessarily noticed. She was overcome with love for this strange, strange man. The thought that Sebastian Whitehead might want to murder him for his money made her . . . made her . . . not mad, just sad. Terribly, terribly sad. He was just a man after all.

She got control of herself and began to read.

Within minutes, Lizzie recognized the even breathing of her father sleeping. She picked some cookie crumbs from his vest front, touched her gold high school ring on his little finger, closed the book and set it on her lap. She watched him sleep for a long time. All the harshness of his face was gone. But the lines seemed to deepen, as if his worries intensified in his dreams.

Lizzie carefully reached into the pocket of her wrapper and pulled out the letter from Beatrice.

My Dearest Lizbeth:
What an exciting country America is! I'm accomplishing much amid my wide-eyed wonder at the newness of it all. I can't wait to sit with you and tell you of all my adventures. By current reckoning, I should be in

Fall River the evening of August third, or the morning of the fourth.

Kisses.

Affectionately,

Bertrice

Wednesday night!

Lizzie's breath caught in her throat. She wasn't ready for Beatrice. She needed to be something else before Beatrice could arrive with her tales of independence and excitement. Lizzie sat, outwardly calm, the paper in her hands not even trembling, while her heart raced and pressure built up behind her eyes. There was a peculiar taste in her mouth—

And just then, Lizzie realized the signs. If she didn't get up and do something, some other self would pop out and embarrass her or complicate things. Careful not to waken Andrew, she rose from the sofa, pocketed the letter, and went upstairs.

She knocked on Emma's door.

Emma turned the key as if she'd been standing right next to the door when Lizzie knocked.

"Father is downstairs," Lizzie said. "He's sleeping. Let him rest before you attack him with your accusations."

"*Attack* him, why—"

"Yes, attack him, Emma. You know exactly what I mean."

"There's no call for you—"

Lizzie shut Emma's door in her face. Emma slammed her fist into the other side, but did not open the door. Lizzie slipped off her wrapper and donned a light cotton town dress. She let her hair down, brushed it about a half dozen strokes and twisted it up again, fastening it loosely with a couple of pins. Then she fixed her stockings, stepped into shoes, locked her bedroom door and tiptoed down the stairs.

God, the heat.

It had been hot in the house, especially upstairs, but

268

outside, where there was no shade . . . Lizzie felt her dresss wilt and dampen instantly. She walked slowly and carefully toward town, hoping that Enid was home from work.

Lizzie didn't know exactly what she wanted from Enid, or why it was so important to get to Enid's house. A terrible feeling of dread, of impending doom, surrounded her. For the moment, she knew that Enid's company would provide some relief for her soul, and her cool house would provide some relief from the heat.

Anger at the father she so dearly loved squeezed tears out of her eyes. Anger at her sister, who had been so much a mother to her, yet who was so clearly crazy, squeezed more tears. Anger at her real mother for leaving her while such a youngster, anger at Abby for never really bucking Emma to take over the motherly role . . . Lizzie walked the route without every really seeing where she was going.

And then she was there. The little house, set back amid the trees. She suddenly felt shy.

She wiped the tears and the perspiration away together, and walked up to the front door. She knocked twice.

Enid opened the door. "Lizzie! Come in."

The house was as much a mess as usual. Lizzie loved it. And it was cool.

"How about a glass of coffee? It's cold."

Lizzie nodded, her voice failing her. Suddenly, she began to tremble. She picked up a stack of magazines and put them on the floor, then sat down and put a hand over her face. She didn't feel like crying, exactly, she just felt worn out. Fragile. For the first time in her life, Lizzie felt capable of breaking.

"Lizzie, dear, what is it?" Enid put a cool hand to Lizzie's forehead.

"Everytime I come over here—" The tears showed up. Lizzie tried to overcome them, but the sobs won.

"Shhh. Shh. That doesn't matter. That makes me feel good. That makes me feel as if you like me. And that you trust me. And that's true. That's right. That's good. You can come over here and cry to me anytime you want." Enid slid down the arm of the sofa and squeezed in next to Lizzie. She cradled her head and rocked her back and forth.

It felt so strange to be held like that; it felt so good. As the sobs waned, Lizzie felt an overwhelming surge of affection for this woman. She hiccupped a few times, then drank the cool, sweetened coffee. Enid got her a damp cloth and Lizzie wiped her face and hands. And suddenly, she could smile again. She giggled, eyes shyly downcast.

Enid began to talk about her sons, which gave Lizzie time to compose herself. Lizzie had arrived unannounced, unexpected, and found understanding, compassion, caring. Lizzie never wanted to leave. She never wanted to go back to that house. Ever.

Enid chatted on, and soon Lizzie was laughing with her, through stories of her boys, the family, the job. Such a family! Such a close family, where they talked about things, shared feelings, traveled together and laughed together. Such a feeling of life, of joyousness, Lizzie had never known. And it was sad for everybody when Charles died, but the boys had a strong mother to look to for strength. And look at Enid now! Not a mourning widow, but a woman still filled with life! Lizzie envied those sons who were off at college in Boston. She wished she were their younger sister, but of course . . . she was far too old. The boys were nineteen and twenty, and Lizzie was thirty-two already. Old enough to have teenage sons of her own!

Enid made them both salads with fresh vegetables from her garden and refreshed the cold coffee; they ate in the sitting room with the salads on their laps and the drinks on stacks of periodicals. Enid continued to talk.

"There came a time," she said, "not too long after Charles died, when I went through all his financial affairs and came to the realization that he left us in the exact condition I

270

would expect. The house was paid for, there was enough for us to live until the boys left home, and then there was enough for me to survive—barely, I'm sure—the rest of my life.

"But that wasn't enough for me. The boys wanted to go on with their studies. Charles didn't allow for that, but I had to. I could never deny my boys something so important for their future. So I got a job with the law firm. And I work hard. And even that isn't enough . . ." Enid looked off into the ether. Then she shook her head, smiled at Lizzie and came back to the moment. "So I do what I have to do to keep my boys in school. And I will do whatever it takes to see them through. Charles Junior is almost finished. And he already has employment opportunities."

There was a long silence. Lizzie had nothing to say, except to voice her admiration, but that was somehow inappropriate.

"I guess the point is, Lizzie, that I've done some things I'm not necessarily proud of, in the ruthlessness of providing for my sons. I have been ruthless. And cunning, I think. And not entirely aboveboard, if you know what I mean. But I would do it all again, and more. And more.

"And yet . . . I see Charles Junior's education coming to an end, and I wonder if those things I did that weren't very nice . . . were they really necessary? I mean, if I had refused to do those things, would other means of finding the money for him have come along?"

Lizzie picked at her cuticles, suddenly embarrassed by this revelation.

"Well!" Enid stood up, took Lizzie's dinnerware and disappeared into the kitchen. "How about a piece of pie?"

Seizing the lighter moment, Lizzie said, "You baked a pie? In this heat?"

"No. I bought it. Apple. Want some?"

"Oh, yes, please."

Enid brought in two generous slices of pie. "I don't

generally indulge myself, but now and then, one must . . . don't you think so?"

"Now and then," Lizzie said seriously, "one must." And then they attacked their dessert.

They lingered, then, filled with good food and comfortable in the silence between them.

"Spend the night," Enid said. "Whatever was making you so miserable at home will still be there in the morning. Stay here and put it off for a night."

Lizzie thought about what was going on at home. Bridget was hiding in her room; she did that every time there was a disturbance with Emma. Emma was pacing or foaming at the mouth or raging at Father. Father was being confronted, probably by Abby, who was to tell him that some one of her kin was trying to kill him. Oh, she had no desire to go back there. None.

"All right," she said. "That would be nice."

"A nice, cool tub?"

Lizzie laughed. "Yes. Yes."

Enid drew a tub for Lizzie, and poured a generous amount of salts in it for her. Lizzie disrobed, throwing her smelly, sweaty clothes into a pile in the corner. She stepped into the tub, one foot at a time, and the cool water surrounded her deliciously. This was heaven.

She heard Enid moving about in the kitchen and sitting room, and knew that she could take as long as she liked in this tub. It smelled so good, it felt so good. Lizzie wanted nothing more than just to stay in this house tonight and then forever. Enid could go to work every day and Lizzie would clean house and cook and do the laundry for her, making sure everything was just right . . .

But it was a short-lived fantasy. Lizzie knew that Enid could barely support herself and her sons, never mind a hanger-on.

She could get a job.

Ha.

Lizzie splashed sweet water on her face and resolved not to think about it anymore. She was chained to her father for the rest of his life. Just as Kathryn Peters had said.

And yet Enid had been ruthless, too. Enid had done things she wasn't proud of, Enid had done whatever it took to get money for her sons.

Enid had the courage to do what she had to do; Beatrice had the courage to do what she had to do. . . . Buying a small house of her own in town was not nearly the monumental task the other two women faced. Surely Lizzie could accomplish that little detail with her life.

She splashed her face again and resolved not to think of it anymore. Instead, she looked around the bathroom and saw Enid's little pieces of jewelry, cosmetics, creams, lotions, perfumes. And the stack of magazines next to the tub. Lizzie picked one up. *Harper's*. She opened it and lay comfortably back in the cool tub. This was good. This was very good. This was the way life was meant to be.

•   •   •

Dried, fully refreshed, smelling of feminine perfumes and lotions and wearing Enid's cotton robe, Lizzie again sat in the living room. Life at the Bordon house could easily have been on the other side of the world. Lizzie was caught up in Enid's completely unorganized way of living, and she loved it. She carried the magazine with her from the bathroom and set it upon one stack of magaines in the living room, where it stayed. Later, when they talked about sleeping, Lizzie picked up another from a different stack and carried it to the bedroom. She could easily see how the piles could grow, disorganized and wanton.

Lizzie again donned the nightshirt she'd worn to bed with the headache the week before. Enid wore her nightie, and a sleeping cap. Lizzie just let her hair down loose.

"Your parents won't be worried about you?"

"I don't think so."

They slipped between the covers, and Enid turned down the lamp. "This reminds me of when I was a little girl," she said. "I used to sleep over with my cousins. Three of us in one bed, and we'd tickle each other's backs and tell romance stories about the men of our dreams."

"I have cousins," Lizzie said, "but we never did anything like that."

"No? Poor girl. Here. Lie on your stomach. Pull your nightshirt up, that's a girl. Now I'm going to write a message on your back, one letter at a time, and you try to guess what it is."

Enid's fingers sent thrills across Lizzie's naked skin. Goose bumps rose and fell in waves, and she felt her face flush in the dark.

"What's that letter, Lizzie?"

But Lizzie couldn't speak.

"C'mon." Enid's fingers traced the same pattern again.

"L."

"Good. And this one?"

"O. V. E."

"That was our favorite word. And then we had to erase the word like this." And Enid's fingers gently caressed Lizzie's skin, softer and softer, until finally the fingertips just barely floated over her back and all Lizzie could feel was the heat from Enid's hand.

Then Enid bounced on the bed, rolling over and pulling up her nightie. "Your turn."

Pale moonlight shone through the bedroom window. They were to sleep with only a sheet over them, but the sheet was down around Enid's thighs and her firm bottom showed smooth and round in the moonlight. The skin on her back was lightly dotted with moles. Lizzie's mouth went dry. She poised her hand over Enid's back, but could not think of a single word to spell. She put her palm down on the center of Enid's back and rubbed lightly.

"Umm. That feels wonderful."

Lizzie sat up so as to use both hands, and soon she was rubbing Enid's back, sides, neck, shoulders. The nightie came off. Lizzie worked Enid's feet, her lower legs, her thighs, her beautiful, beautiful round butt, and then she couldn't help herself, she just had to, just had to . . . and she kissed it. "You're so beautiful," she said.

Enid turned and brought Lizzie to her in a warm embrace, and their bodies fit together as if they were molded for each other. Lizzie kissed Enid with raw passion, Enid finessed Lizzie's coarser moves with a practiced hand.

But this was not like Kathryn Peters. No. Kathryn Peters was selfish and greedy. Enid was giving and gentle. Understanding. Lizzie had never felt so wanted, so desirable. So loved.

After a time, they slept, entwined. And when she woke up, Enid was looking at her, their faces close, and Lizzie closed her eyes and kissed Enid's lips, and soon they were dancing again, pleasing each other, learning about each other, and it was a glorious time, a glorious time.

Tuesday, August 2

When Lizzie opened her eyes, summer shone through the window, and Enid sat in front of it, wrapped in nightie and robe, chin on her fist, elbow on a stack of books. Lizzie stretched and yawned, feeling smiley and cozy, but when Enid didn't even look around, she worried.

"Good morning," she said.

Enid looked over at her, but her face was eclipsed by the bright light behind her. Lizzie could see no expression. "Hi," Enid said, her voice soft. She stood up and stretched. "Well, I better get going."

Something was definitely wrong. Guilt surged through Lizzie and she jumped out of bed and blocked Enid's way. Enid would not meet her eyes.

"What is it?" Panic began to rise. "God, what is it?"

"Nothing, Lizzie."

"Please don't do that, Enid," Lizzie pleaded. "Please don't say 'nothing, Lizzie.'"

Enid's small hand touched Lizzie's cheek and her eyes flooded. "You're so sweet," she said. "You're so wonderful. No, Lizzie, it isn't you. It's me. There's something the matter with me, and it's not you. You're wonderful." Then her eyes dropped again, and one tear fell down her cheek and she tried to get around Lizzie.

"Please tell me." Lizzie wouldn't let her pass.

276

"I've done some terrible things in my life, Lizzie," Enid said, looking at the floor. "Somehow, when Charles died and the boys left home, I thought my life was pretty much over, except for church and the garden. So I never thought it mattered much what I did. And now I see that it does. That's all."

Reluctantly, Lizzie let her pass. Enid went into the bathroom and closed the door. Lizzie went into the kitchen and poured two glasses of tea. It was already too hot to make a fire in the stove. She found a coffee cake and cut two pieces, and then quartered a pear. Her stomach burned. Why was there always something? There was *always* something! If not at home, then at Kathryn's. If not at Kathryn's, then at home. If not at Kathryn's, or at home, then at Enid's. God! And now, and *now,* there was something going on at home *and* at Enid's, *and* at Kathryn's, and more coming via Washington, D.C., tomorrow night!

Lizzie wanted to hide.

But the toilet flushed and the bathroom door opened and Enid came out, looking sheepish and apologetic. Her eyes were red-rimmed; she'd been crying in the bathroom.

"Come have breakfast."

Enid sat down, smiling a small smile. She cut a forkful of coffee cake and washed it down with tea. "I'm sorry, Lizzie, I'm really not very hungry." She put her fork down. "But I want you to understand something." She took both of Lizzie's hands in her own. "Last night was more than I had ever dreamed would happen to me again. I'm not an old woman, Lizzie, I'm only forty years old. But life has a way of excluding you from things, especially in Fall River. The skeletons in my closet have nothing to do with you. I think you are the sweetest, most precious thing that has come into my life in a long, long time. And I'm just afraid that my past actions will hurt you."

"There's nothing you could do to hurt me, Enid," Lizzie said.

Enid smiled sadly and sipped her tea. "I'd better be getting ready for work."

Lizzie hated the thought of going home. She followed Enid into the bedroom, where the heat of the new day was already burning. Enid pulled the shades and let the draperies fall over them. Then they both dressed.

They kissed at the door. Then Enid opened it and they put on faces for the world, false faces, faces of happiness and composure, when both of them felt their insides being gnawed away by forces beyond their control.

● ● ●

Lizzie opened the door and Emma ran to greet her, a dangerous light in her eyes. "They *are* going to kill Father," she said eagerly.

Lizzie was so tired of this. She was so blasted sick and tired of Emma and Father and Abby and their stupid little dramas. "No, Emma. Nobody is trying to kill Father."

"They are, they *are*, Lizzie, listen, you don't know what happened yesterday."

The thought briefly flew through Lizzie's mind that Emma didn't even notice that she hadn't come home all night. Or if she had noticed, it was unimportant compared to her latest news of Andrew's impending murder.

"Emma. I'm not in the mood."

That stopped her. "Not in the mood? Our father is about to be slaughtered in broad daylight and you're not in the mood to hear about it?"

"All right. Come up to my room and tell me. Where is everybody?"

"Maggie is doing laundry. Abby is out with someone birthing, I think. Father is at work."

Lizzie walked up the creaky stairs in the tiny cramped

house that was already hot and close. The house smelled like the cellar floor, like steamed dirt. Now that Lizzie was used to Enid's gay profusion of books, magazines and other paraphernalia, the singular lack of reading material and personal possessions made the Borden house seem uncommonly austere. And hot. And stuffy. And staid.

Bridget was stripping the bed in the guest room. "Maggie, what are you doing?"

"Mr. Morse is arriving, miss."

Lizzie's uncle John Morse, her mother's brother, was an infrequent visitor. He and Andrew had begun investing their money together many years ago; occasionally he would come to visit, and he would stay far too long, talking business and investigating new investment opportunities. Usually his presence meant nothing. But this was Tuesday and Beatrice was due to arrive Wednesday night or Thursday morning. "When is he coming?"

"I'm not sure." Bridget looked to Emma. Emma shrugged.

So there would not even be a bed in the house for Beatrice. Lizzie's shoulders slumped. She unlocked her bedroom door, and Emma followed on her heels.

Lizzie untied her shoes and took them off. The air upstairs was even denser. She pulled the draperies, raised the blinds and opened the window. No relief. She loosened her corset and lay upon the bed, daring Emma to say something. Emma was silent.

When Lizzie was settled, she pointed at the rocking chair. Emma sat down. Why, all of a sudden, was Lizzie in control? "All right, Emma. What happened?"

"They were in the sitting room. I listened from the stairs. Abby wanted to know, once and for all, if Sarah was mentioned in his will. He wanted to know why, and she said because Sebastian was beginning to get kind of pushy.

"'What kind of pushy?'

279

" 'I don't know, Mr. Borden.' " Emma imitated Abby's voice. " 'Sarah came to see me in tears, yesterday, afraid. I had promised her, you see, and Sebastian is frustrated at his wages and not being able to provide better for her. He's afraid that I will predecease you, and that you will then forget all about Sarah.' There was a long pause. 'It would be much easier, Mr. Borden, if you would just give her that property now. Then they can be enjoying it now, while they need it. Or you could sell it to them.'

" 'I'll consider it. The will is in transition. I'm making some changes to it.'

" 'Changes?'

" 'For the better.'

" 'Well, then, that's fine, whatever you want. Only what shall I say to Sarah?'

" 'Tell her to find herself a husband who can support her and her children in a proper manner and to stop hounding me about what I will or will not do with my assets.'

" 'Sarah was in such a state, Mr. Borden, that she fears for your life.'

" 'My life?' "

" 'She said that Sebastian has reached such a point that he has talked of murder.'

" 'In order to inherit what may or may not be written in my will? Preposterous. He's a madman!'

" 'Nevertheless, I think some sort of statement ought to be made.'

" 'Tell them that I am rearranging my affairs, and that I may very well remember them. And that then again, if they cannot show the proper respect, I may ignore them. Tell them that, Abby.'

"Well, I don't need to tell you," Emma went on, "that I wasn't about to sit there on the stairs and let him get away with those veiled threats about the will. So I walked into the room and demanded that he spell out the changes."

280

Lizzie gasped. "You didn't!"

"I did."

"What did he say?"

"He said he wouldn't. He said we'd all find out when he was dead. He said that some people did things for him and some people did things against him and we would have only our consciences to thank when it was all over.

"I told him that wasn't good enough. I've lived here all my life, doing his cooking, his laundry, raising his second daughter, and I was not about to be cut off without a cent because he took a disliking to me in his dotage."

Lizzie brought her hands up to her face. She could imagine Emma saying such things, but they embarrassed her just the same. The horror of it all made her smile.

"He made me sit down. He made the cow sit down as well. 'This is how it is worked out,' he said. 'Certain people who have granted me special favors over the years will receive a bequest. Abby will be taken care of for the rest of her life. After that, you, Emma, and Lizzie will inherit everything. Is that clear enough for you?'

" 'You mean we'll have to live here with *her* until she dies?' "

" 'Don't push me, Emma.' "

" 'Just who are these *'special people'*?' "

" 'People who have shown niceties.' "

" 'Your whore?' "

Lizzie shrieked and then clapped her hands over her mouth. "Oh, Emma, you *didn't!*"

"I did."

"And?"

"And his face got red, and he said, 'This interview is over.' That's what he's doing, Lizzie. That whore of his has turned his head so far that he's going to cut her in on his will."

"He wouldn't."

"He would. Just to spite us."

Lizzie expected that with this kind of drama in the Borden house, Emma would be pacing and bruising her lip between knuckles and teeth and frothing at the mouth and then ready to go to New Bedford. But she was doing none of that. "Why are you so calm about this whole thing, Emma?"

"Calm? I don't know that I'm calm."

"Calmer than I would expect, under the circumstances."

"Well, look at you, lying on your bed fully clothed, lounging as if you had the world at your fingertips."

"I'm sick of it all, Emma," Lizzie said. "Don't you get tired of all this?"

"Tired of it? Lizzie, it is our life. *It is our life!*"

It may be your life, Lizzie thought, but it is not mine.

"Besides," Emma said. "I have a plan."

282

Andrew Borden was at his office in the mill when the sickness hit. He felt as if he had been hit in the stomach with a stick. He ran from his office, holding his stomach, and made it to the street before vomiting his breakfast in a gush.

His first thought was of Emma's cooking; she paid poor attention to that which needed it the most. His next thought, as spasms shuddered through him, was of poison, and that Sebastian Whitehead should be damned to eternal hellfire.

After the initial sickness subsided, Andrew rose from his knees, brushed off his pants and his hands, and made his way toward home. He left everything as it was on his desk, and while that made him vaguely uneasy, it made him more uneasy to think that the worst was yet to come of this sickness, and he did not want to be taken home or to Dr. Bowen's by way of some stranger's charity. At least he hadn't left his will on his desk, for the prying eyes of Fall River. It was with him, with the new instructions, ready to post. He felt the mailing tube in his jacket pocket. He would leave it in the box, if he could.

He made his way unsteadily, feeling increasingly shaky, sweating profusely in the heat. He heaved twice more before arriving, but there was nothing to vomit, and the heaves did not drive him to his knees. He wanted to get into bed. His head ached. His fingers felt tight. His face felt swollen.

He fumbled with his keys at the front door, then finally, through shear will and prayer, he got the door open. Andrew

283

closed and locked it behind him. He went through the sitting room, took the key to his bedroom from the mantel, and went through the kitchen, up the back stairs to his bedroom.

Abby was in bed. Stale vomit reeked from her chamber pot. She barely moved when he got into bed beside her. Even in the heat, even with someone next to his sensitive skin, bed felt wonderful.

He'd never been so sick.

He reached down and pulled his chamber pot into a convenient location and put his head on the pillow.

Faintly, he heard the sounds of Bridget vomiting and coughing up in her little room above theirs.

Blood pounded in his eyes. He felt every heartbeat in every vein.

He closed his eyes and waited to die.

Enid Crawford typed a letter for her employer, but her mind was not on it. At the third typing error, Enid turned from the typewriter and rested her face in her hands. The burning in her stomach was more than she could bear. She was never good with guilt.

She tried to satisfy it by giving it promises. "Lizzie will come over tonight," she tried, "and I will tell her everything."

It was not good enough. She didn't know that Lizzie would be over, and besides, it was not up to Lizzie to see that Enid's feelings of guilt were assuaged.

Before thinking, she opened her desk drawer, took out her purse and turned to Mrs. Watkins, the bookkeeper. "I'm not feeling well, Cecilia. I'm going to go out for a walk and I'll be back in an hour or so."

"In this heat?"

But Enid didn't answer her. She just went out the door and walked directly to the Borden house and knocked sharply on the door.

She knocked again. And again. Disappointment rose in her. She was all ready to confess her multitude of ugly sins to Lizzie, and now she would have to hold onto them, keep them longer, live with Lizzie's innocence and her guilt on her mind for another while longer.

Just as she was turning away, she heard locks turn in the front door. And it was opened by a tall, thin, angular, humorless woman.

"Is Lizzie at home?"

"She's resting."

"It's quite important, if you don't mind."

"Wait." And the woman closed the door and locked it, leaving Enid to stand in the heat. In the sun.

In a moment, the locks were snapped back and Lizzie threw the door open. Her face lit up with a delight that made Enid's heart sore. "Enid! Come in, come in."

"I'd rather you came out, Lizzie. Can we walk down to the river?"

Lizzie looked at her queerly. "Of course. Give me a moment to get ready. Come in, won't you?"

Enid stepped into the hall and walked into the sitting room, where she had been just a week before, with Andrew and his fat wife. That had been a terrible time, and this was a terrible time, and she hoped never to set foot inside the Borden house again.

When Lizzie was ready, they went out the front door and turned right, away from town. They walked in silence, emotions raging inside Enid, and suddenly she wondered why she felt so compelled to confess all to Lizzie. What difference did it make? Would it make a difference to Enid? Would it make a difference to Lizzie? Yes, both would be altered by her confession. Enid felt that a change had come over her life in the past weeks. Lizzie had brought that change, that wonderful refreshing revelation that life went on. Yet confessing to Lizzie would hurt the very thing that had unlocked Enid's cage. Could she, in good conscience, do that? *Should* she?

Somehow, with Lizzie by her side, all the bad feelings wanted to fly away. She felt so good with Lizzie, she wanted to just smile and be rid of all the unpleasantness. There was so *much* unpleasantness in life—couldn't there be one small refuge from that? And couldn't that refuge be Lizzie?

"I wanted to see you, Lizzie," Enid started, "because I

feel so good—because you make me feel so good—that I need to confess some of the terrible things I've done."

"To me?"

"Well . . ."

"Why not talk to the pastor?"

"Well, because they affect you." Enid wanted to bite the end of her tongue off. She hadn't meant to say that, and she hadn't meant, necessarily, to confess to Lizzie anything specific.

"Oh?"

Enid stopped, put a hand on Lizzie's arm. "I've been entertaining men for money," she said.

Lizzie's face remained unreadable. "What does that have to do with me?"

"I needed you to know that."

"Why?"

Enid's insides squirmed. "Because."

"What is it, Enid? What are you trying to say?"

"I need money to put the boys through school. Charles Junior is almost finished, so it shouldn't be too much longer."

"You mean you still . . . entertain men for money? And you plan to continue to do so?"

Enid thought for a moment. She would like to stop, she really would. But the financial hardships of tuition and all that on her miserly salary . . . And she was so afraid, so *afraid* of being poor, poor and alone. . . . Then again, there was something quite self-satisfying about raising her skirts to the tune of a hundred dollars a week for men who found her desirable. She had always maintained two "boyfriends," as she referred to them, since Charles died. A Friday boyfriend and a Saturday boyfriend. And now . . . Lizzie. "I don't know, Lizzie. I don't feel quite right about it, and yet I'm quite reluctant to give up the money. And the satisfaction." This was not going at all as Enid had planned.

"Satisfaction?"

"Well, yes. There is satisfaction knowing that men will pay me a weekly allowance for my favors. There is satisfaction in a swelling bank account that will see me through any hardship in my elder years."

"They pay you a weekly allowance?" Lizzie was clearly flabbergasted by Enid's revelations, and Enid couldn't help but be a little bit proud.

"I see two men, Lizzie. And each one gives me an allowance for my boys' schooling."

"I can get money, Enid. You don't have to do that."

"What is the difference?"

Lizzie's eyes grew dark. "This would be one friend helping another, Enid. I can get money from my father."

"No, Lizzie."

"Why not?"

"I don't know. I don't know anymore." Enid felt like crying.

"Then why tell me this?"

Enid shrugged, knowing full well that she intended to tell Lizzie more.

"You don't want me to come over on the days you have your friends over?"

"Oh, Lizzie, no."

"Then what? Why did you tell me this?"

Enid looked up. Lizzie's eyes had gone pale. She was agitated, and Enid had only herself to blame. Lizzie was so joyous, so carefree when they were at the Borden house just moments before, and now . . . now she'd ruined everything.

"Lizzie, I'm sorry."

Lizzie turned and began walking back home. Enid ran a couple of steps to keep up. She caught at Lizzie's sleeve. Lizzie was crying. "I loved you," Lizzie said.

Enid touched Lizzie's cheek and they hugged, Lizzie clinging to her fiercely. "And I love you. Think about it, please think about it, dear Lizzie." Lizzie's hair smelled of the bath and of their lovemaking the night before. "Just two evenings a week, and my boys . . . Lizzie, you don't have children, you don't know. Charles didn't leave enough money for them, and . . . and I'm putting money away for my old age, too. Lizzie, it's such a little thing, for a couple of hours a week. I'm not going to be able to do it much longer, you know. I thought I wanted to stop it, I came here to tell you that I would, but I can't, Lizzie, not until the boys are out of school . . . I really can't."

"Well then, you've made your choice." Lizzie sniffed, released Enid and wiped her face on her sleeve.

"I guess I have." Enid's heart was breaking. There were no words, just a terrible tearing of her greedy soul.

"How much do you get?"

"A hundred dollars a week. Each."

Lizzie turned, astonished, a little smile at the corners of her mouth. Enid couldn't help but be a little bit smug. "Two hundred dollars a week! I could own my own house and live on my own in town on one hundred dollars a month!"

They both laughed, but there was no humor in it, and Lizzie went into her house and Enid went on to her office, and neither one of them felt very good about life.

he woman who came to call for Lizzie didn't look at all like the type of person Lizzie should be friends with, according to Emma's way of thinking. Her hair was short, and she wore no hat, even in the sun. A face that was burned brown from the sun was as attractive as an old shoe, and showed about as much sense. It was against Emma's better judgment that she fetched Lizzie upon this woman's command, and by the time Lizzie left with her, Emma was ready for some breakfast.

The mutton roast they'd all eaten the night before was still sitting on the kitchen table. Emma filled a pan with water, and put the meat in it; she'd have soup for them for dinner, if she could bear to make a fire in the stove. Then she poured herself a glass of chilled milk and took a pastry from the shelf. She sat at the kitchen table, listening to the heat. It was almost noon, and the house was creaking with the weight of the oppressive heat. Emma's thighs were sticky, and strands of her hair hung like noodles from her normally tidy, tight bun. Even the milk tasted odd. But the cake was all right, so she ate it and went back upstairs to think about presenting her idea to Lizzie.

But before Lizzie came home, sickness welled up and out of Emma almost before she had time to aim toward her slops pail. It took her so suddenly and surprisingly that she had no time to prepare. Immediately after vomiting, she felt better, but in a moment, perspiration beaded up on her face and she felt as if she might faint.

290

Quickly, she removed her housedress and lay on her bed in her underdrawers. She felt dizzy.

It's the milk, she thought. The milk has been poisoned. She was glad she had only had a sip or two. That Sebastian Whitehead. Damn his eyes.

And then she slept.

Wednesday, August 3

The long, hot night slowly turned into day. There had been no respite from the dogged heat all night long, and daybreak brought with it the promise of even more heat. Lizzie had lain awake most of the night, drifting in and out of unconsciousness rather than really sleeping. As the rooster crowed, she heard rustlings in the kitchen, which must mean that members of the household were up and about. The house had been furnace hot and eerily still the day before, with everybody sick. It was pleasant, in a way, to walk through the house, grateful that she never drank milk, knowing that no one would speak to her, or even see her. And yet it was eerie, for she could *feel* all those people sick in their beds. Maggie was in her little loft, the hottest of the hot on the third floor. And Emma. Hot. Sick. And her parents, she could imagine them in bed, hot, sick, sticking to the sheets and barely able to bear their own feverishness, let alone the others'.

There was something terrible about this sickness. It seemed they were all more than sick, sick almost to their death. Poisoned. But that was Sebastian's plan, wasn't it?

Or was it Emma's plan? Emma surely was not as ill as the others. No, Emma would never poison the family. Take after them with an ax, perhaps, but she would never intentionally poison them all.

Well, somebody was downstairs, and Lizzie felt as though she ought to go see who was there.

Besides, Beatrice was due to arrive this evening or the next morning, and Lizzie felt she ought to bathe and make herself presentable. The household was in disrepair and everyone lay dying around her, but at least Lizzie could be clean.

Lizzie was surprised to find Emma in the kitchen. Emma generally made a great amount of noise when going from her room through Lizzie's, but this morning Lizzie must have been soundly asleep.

"What are you doing?"

"Making breakfast."

"You've made a fire?"

"I felt like a coffee."

"You're better, then?"

"Much."

"What about the others?"

"I've not heard."

"Shouldn't someone check on them?"

"You mean in case they're all dead?"

Emma had such a compassionate nature. "Well, yes."

"Go do it, then. I'm busy."

Lizzie walked up the narrow stairs toward her parents' room. She hadn't been up these stairs in years. Twenty years, probably, not since she was a young girl. Well, except for that time with the jewelry and the money. The stairs were the same. They smelled the same. The wood was a little more worn, otherwise it was all the same, the walls unadorned with wallpaper, pictures or anything else. Black marks where little hands had trailed along the wall in the dark.

She got to the parents' door and knocked.

"What is it?" Andrew answered.

"It's Lizzie," she said, suddenly shy. "I just wanted to see if you were all right."

There was some mumbling, but Lizzie couldn't make it out.

"We're better. We'll be down."

"Good." She continued up the stairs to Bridget's room. She knocked.

"Yes?"

"Maggie, are you all right?"

"I think so, miss."

"Will you be down for breakfast?"

"I think not. Perhaps later."

"All right, then." Lizzie went back downstairs, feeling fortunate indeed that the sickness hadn't touched her.

"Is everyone alive?"

Emma's tone touched Lizzie as a bit whimsical, considering. They were all very ill, and Emma had no right to make light of such a thing. It was perhaps an attempt on their father's life! "They'll be down," was all she said.

"Well, good. I have a thing or two for that father of ours. He will not escape this breakfast table without explaining himself."

"Emma."

"Emma nothing. It's the only way. With all of us present. It's the only way, Lizzie." Emma dried her hands on her apron and left the room.

Lizzie selected a pear from the bowl on the table and sliced it into pieces. She took the plate and cup of coffee out of the fiery hot kitchen, into the dining room and sat down. Emma had brought in the morning paper and Lizzie picked it up and began to read.

In less than a minute, Emma appeared in the doorway, pale, clutching something in her talons.

"Lizzie, I've found it."

"What, Emma?"

"The will. The old man's will."

"Where?"

"It was in his suit-coat pocket."

"Emma." Lizzie wanted to chastise Emma for snooping again, but curiosity got the better of her. "Why?"

"I don't know."

"He's sick, that's why."

"That's of no matter. This must be it. It's in a mailing tube, and it's ready to go to a lawyer in Fairhaven. It *must* be the will!" Emma sat down on the edge of a chair. Lizzie couldn't remember when she'd ever seen Emma's eyes so bright. "If we open this now, Lizzie, we'll have accurate information when he comes down for breakfast. We can speak to him about his affairs with knowledge, and we can plan our strategy."

Lizzie was intrigued. As long as Emma did the actual deed, she was actually innocent. And she was all for seeing what he had up his sleeve. "Well?"

Emma took a paring knife from the table and slit open the package. She unwrapped the paper and opened the end of the tube. It was a will, all right, bound in blue paper. She pulled it out and read the cover letter in a whisper: " 'Dear Mr. Stockworth: I'm making a few revisions to my will. I am taking this out of the hands of my present attorney as I wish these changes to remain confidential until my death. Please redraft the document and send to me for my signature. I have enclosed a cheque in the amount of twenty dollars, which I assume will cover all your fees. Very sincerely yours, Andrew Borden.' "

Emma laid that sheet of paper on the table and looked at the will. "Look! He's cut Sarah Whitehead out. She was in. She *was* in, and now he's taken her out. Good." She flipped through another page, eyes scanning the lines.

Lizzie's pears had turned sour in her mouth.

"Oh!" Emma's hand flew to her mouth. "I was right!" She smiled with glee. "I was right, oh, Lizzie, he is, he is going to leave a property to his whore."

"No."

"Yes! Yes! See? Right here. 'For niceties rendered,' he said. I'm sure! Some tart named Enid Crawford."

Understanding struck Lizzie dumb.

She felt the blood flow from her face. Her hands were suddenly cold and trembling. She wanted to go to her room, but she couldn't trust her feet to take her there, so she just sat, feeling sicker than she ever had, listening to Emma prattle on and on about her discovery.

And then there was a pause. A deathly pause. A pause so dramatic that it even shook Lizzie from her humiliation, her anger, her despair.

Emma said, "He's leaving everything to her."

"To whom?"

"Abby."

"Emma, no."

"Yes." Lizzie saw the fury begin to burn in Emma. She stood up, crumpling the will. Lizzie made a half-hearted grab for it, but it was too late. Father would know that someone had been at his will. "He decided to leave Sarah stupid Whitehead out of the will and leave everything to Abby, to let her decide how to divide it. And you know what *she'll* do, don't you, Lizzie? She'll leave it all to that stupid midwives' organization or the church or something, and we'll have to beg for our livings."

"Emma . . ."

But Emma was beyond hearing. She was gone. She paced back and forth and rolled up the will, then fit it back inside the mailing tube. She took the whole thing to the kitchen and threw it into the fire.

"Emma!"

"Now, Lizzie, now I hope he dies. If he dies without a will, everything will go to her anyway, but nothing will go to the whore. Maybe he'll die and she'll die, too, and that will take care of everything. In fact, maybe they'll both die of

296

Sebastian Whitehead's poisoning and then we won't have *anything* to worry about. Ever again!"

"Emma, hush!"

"Maybe he'll die before he can get a new will together. Maybe I ought to set fire to him while he sleeps. Maybe I'll take an ax to both their ugly faces before tomorrow morning. Right in their beds. Right when they sleep. He's always said he wants to die in his sleep. Ha!"

Lizzie had heard Emma rant and rave before, but never like this. This time it was evil, it was almost . . . believable. She paced back and forth by the dining-room table, her hands flying out in wild gestures, banging against the walls, and she didn't even feel it. Soon she would be rubbing her knuckles on her lips and the little spots of froth at the corners of her mouth would turn pink.

Lizzie sat, immobilized by the enormity of it all. Uncle John was arriving today, and then Beatrice. Emma was a wreck, in fact she would probably leave for New Bedford to be beaten—perhaps until she was dead—Father, Abby and Maggie had all been poisoned, Enid was Father's whore, *Enid was Father's whore,* and all Lizzie could do was to just sit and watch her sister pace and rave.

And then she remembered that during times of emotional stress, that other thing was likely to happen to her. When the "other Lizzie" came out and walked around town doing God-knows-what.

Lizzie jumped up from her chair, upsetting the coffee. She pushed past Emma and ran up the stairs. She had to do something. She had to do *something.* She paced back and forth in her room for a moment, then took her towel and a clean housedress down cellar. To bathe, she took down the pot of dishwashing water keeping hot on the stove. But this time she must not let her guard down. She must soap up, rinse off and remain consciously in the cellar the whole time.

Though it was so blistering hot upstairs, the cellar was

cool and damp. Lizzie shivered as she took off her clothes and got into the tub. She mixed the cold water from the faucet with the hot from the kettle and stood in the tub, washing her body with a rag. Then she washed her hair with the same yellow lye soap, rinsed it all off and rubbed her body dry with the towel.

Maybe I could go to the church, she thought, but nothing happened at the church on a Wednesday. Maybe there's a WCTU meeting. But there wasn't. Solitude struck her like a hollow bell. Without Enid, she had no friends. She had acquaintances—the women at WCTU, some of the people at church—but there was no one, *no one* with whom she could talk about this problem. No one! She hadn't a single friend in all of . . . in all of creation.

I'll clean the house, she thought. I'll clean the barn. I'll do the ironing! Nobody ever wanted to iron, especially in this heat, and the mound of clothes had been mounting. But the thought of it made her feel faint. Well, at least I'll sprinkle the clothes, wrap them up and see.

But the day loomed long.

Emma was in her room when Lizzie returned, toweling her hair. She knocked on Emma's door. "Emma? Emma, open the door."

The door opened. Emma looked terrible. Lizzie wondered if this was the edge for her. If things hadn't gotten just a little too much for a fragile person like Emma. She just stood there, not moving, not even really seeing Lizzie. She just stood there, a vacancy in her eyes, slackness in her expression. Lizzie wondered if anybody else ever thought of Emma as fragile.

"Emma, are you leaving for New Bedford?" It suddenly occurred to Lizzie that things would be much easier if Emma left again, as much as she hated to think that. And Emma could be hurt very badly this time, too . . . In fact, she might never come back, and if she stayed in New Bedford under an assumed name, they might never know her fate—a frightening yet somehow unburdening idea.

Emma's eyes focused at the question. "No, of course not. No. No. No, of course not. No, Lizzie, I'm going to Fairhaven to see our cousins. We have attorneys, do we not? One of them is bound to know this Mr. Stockworth and I'll find Father's connection to him. It's time we got some legal advice of our own, Lizzie."

Lizzie was quite astonished to hear such lucid words come out of Emma at such a time. And yet, it was probably the most constructive thing that could be done at the time.

"Besides," Emma went on, "I ought to leave here before I see his face, or I'll strangle him, I swear to God I will murder the man before . . ." Her fists were clenched and the cords stood out in her neck.

"Pack, then, Emma," Lizzie said. "Hurry up and go." Emma came back to the present moment. She went to the closet like an automaton and brought out her traveling valise. Lizzie retreated to her room and sat in her rocker.

Emma was gone within the hour.

bby Borden, wearing only her thin cotton dressing
gown, descended the stairs carefully, one step at a
time, afraid she would faint and fall clear to the
bottom. The only respite from the damnable heat was
the cool kitchen floor on her bare feet.

She stood in the kitchen, looking around. The stove had
been heated, but that would have been Emma making
breakfast coffee. She looked at the clock. It was half past two.
She felt dizzy and disoriented. She didn't know where to
begin. Then she saw Lizzie, sprinkling clothes. Good Lord,
the girl wasn't thinking about *ironing!* Why, she'd have to fire
the stove all over again to heat the flats.

"Lizzie, are you all right?"

"Yes, I'm fine, Abby," Lizzie said. "The sickness didn't
touch me."

"You're fortunate. My God, I don't know what I'm
doing up. Your father insists on going to the office this
afternoon, and I have to fix him something to eat. I can't
imagine eating. Where's Emma?"

"Emma's gone to Fairhaven."

"Oh? Well . . ."

"Abby, do you suppose Sebastian . . ."

Abby whirled around, then held her swirling head. "No!
No, of course not, Lizzie, how could you even think such a
thing? No, it's the flu, that's all. Something serious going
around. That's all . . . Now, where was I?"

Abby's concentration had fled. Lizzie had given voice to

the refrain that had played in her head all the day before as she lay hot and sick enough to die. But Sebastian would gain nothing by killing her. No, it couldn't have been Sebastian. Just some illness they had caught, that was all.

Her hands shook as she opened the heavy corner on the stove. She let it drop with a clang.

"Lizzie, would you help me, please?"

"There are cakes in the cupboard, Abby," Lizzie said. "And cold mutton gravy on the sideboard."

Abby spread gravy on the cakes and put them out with a cold cup of coffee for her husband. It was all she could manage. The sickness had left her feeling as if there was lead in her veins.

"Have a cookie," Lizzie said. "Emma said they helped settle her stomach."

Abby opened the cabinet and took a cookie. She took a small bite. "Emma wasn't so ill, then?"

"She was yesterday."

Andrew came down the stairs and into the kitchen.

"Lizzie," he said.

"Mr. Borden, I really don't think you should be going to the office this afternoon."

"There are things that need to be done."

"But you're so pale." He looked pale and thin, drawn and old. Very, very old. His mortality stared at Abby and made her shiver.

"As needs be. Is this my food?"

"The best I could do."

"Hardly looks worth eating, does it?"

"Lizzie said that a cookie helped settle Emma."

Andrew took a cookie and bit. "Where is Emma?"

"Gone to Fairhaven."

"Oh? Just as well. I'm off." He put the cookie down and went into the sitting room. Abby looked at Lizzie and saw her tense. Her nose was in the air like a fox's. They listened, but heard only the whine of the heat.

Then the sounds of Andrew unlocking his desk. Then the drawers opening and closing. Then the key again, and he reappeared in the kitchen.

"Lizzie, have you seen a package? A tube? I was to mail it."

Lizzie shook her head.

"Hmm." He hung his head for a moment, thinking, but he looked old. Very old. "Well," he said, looking very old, very ill, "I'm off." And he turned and left.

Abby looked at Lizzie. Lizzie took a cookie. Abby took the cookie that Andrew had abandoned and they nibbled in silence.

izzie was in her room lying fully clothed upon her bed when Andrew came home and began opening and closing all the drawers in the house. Her conscience bothered her only a tiny bit; after all, it was Emma that stole the will, read it and burned it. It was quite out of Lizzie's hands. But should she tell him? Should she tell him that his will had been burned in the fury of his eldest daughter? Should she tell him that she had been a witness, had stood by and done nothing while Emma did it all? Should she tell him that she knew all about him and Enid?

Oh, Enid. The wound opened anew and bled.

No. She would tell the old man nothing. He was to leave her out of his will. He would rather leave property to a woman who regularly prostituted herself than to his own flesh and blood. Well, good. Fine. It would be well if he had a heart seizure while looking for the blasted will. He would never find it.

Enid! God. They had walked down by the river yesterday and Enid had something to say, yet didn't say it. Instead, she told Lizzie that she intended to keep sleeping with her men friends, indeed, bleeding her father dry at a rate of one hundred dollars a week! Oh, Enid. There were no tears in Lizzie, but her heart ached just the same.

When Andrew knocked at Lizzie's bedroom door, she was not surprised, just startled. She unlocked it and opened it, then stepped back. The look on her father's face was even more startling. He looked ill, very ill. Greenish. And old.

"Lizzie, I'm missing that mailing tube, and I just can't find it anywhere. Please think, now, and see if you can remember seeing it."

"I've seen nothing like it, Father."

Andrew stared at her and Lizzie knew that he saw the lie.

"Emma's room, then. Have you a key?"

"No." Another lie.

"I'll get one or I'll break the blasted door down." He turned on his heel and stomped down the stairs.

In a moment, he was back. Lizzie followed him, not quite knowing how to act or what to do. She'd never seen her father like this before. Ever. He unlocked Emma's door and banged it open. He stomped in and looked around, and it occurred to Lizzie that perhaps he hadn't been in Emma's bedroom since they had moved into this house twenty-seven years ago.

Then he began pulling drawers out of her dresser, fumbling through them and throwing them on the ground. The first one split when it landed, and Lizzie cringed. He went through the room like a madman, flinging dresses from their hangers, going through each shoe, each shoebox, each hatbox, searching, searching.

Lizzie was appalled.

Finally, he finished. He sat down on Emma's bed, perspiration flowing down his face. He took his handkerchief and mopped. "It's not here, Lizzie," he said, then slumped in the chair. Lizzie thought for a moment he had fainted from the sickness and the heat. "It's not here," he whispered.

She went to him and sat at his feet. "It's not that important, Father," she said, and then remembered that she wasn't supposed to know that it was his will. "Perhaps you should go downstairs for a little nap. Shall we read, maybe?" She felt as if she was coddling one of her six-year-old Sunday school students.

"Yes," he breathed, "maybe we ought." But he made no move.

Lizzie put her cheek against his knee. Despite the fact that she sometimes hated him, the affection she felt when she realized how old and frail he was overcame her. He was her father, after all, and didn't that count for something? Of course it did. Blood was thick, especially Borden blood, and Lizzie felt a tremendous amount of loyalty to her father. To her father and to her sister.

She wondered what Emma was doing in Fairhaven, and as if he read her thoughts, she felt his hand upon her head.

"I'm such a foolish old man, Lizzie," he said. "I've no right to a daughter as wonderful as you are, and it makes me so very afraid that you will leave me in my old age."

"I won't," she said with a sigh. "I would like to have a little house of my own here in town, Father, but I will never really leave you."

"Never?"

"Of course not."

"Your sister Emma is leaving me. All I've done for her and she's leaving me, she's leaving me as sure as we're sitting here."

"She's visiting cousins in Fairhaven, Father."

"That's what you think. That might even be what she thinks, Lizzie, but Emma left me long ago. Took her affections and locked them up in this room." He leaned forward and kissed the top of her head. "Please don't you ever leave me. I can't bear the thought of growing older without knowing that I will always be able to count on you to nurse me if I should fall ill. And that's why you can never move out, Lizzie, because it would be so hard for you to give up your little house to come home if I needed you."

A hollowness opened up in Lizzie. The hollow center of conflicting emotions swirled deep in her gut. This man was everything to her. Everything she loved, everything she hated. He was her potential freedom; at the same time, he was her prison. She sat there, her head resting on the side of his knee, his hand on the top of her head, and she listened to the things he said that were not the normal things a man should say to his daughter. They were sick. He was sick. He was sick and old and it was time for him to die.

Why don't they all just die and leave me alone?

Lizzie stood, held out her hand for him to grasp, and helped him up. She thought perhaps tears had mingled with the perspiration on his face, but she was not sure. "Come, Father, let's finish that book."

He let her lead him down the stairs, down to the first floor where the heat was only oppressive, not overwhelming.

Abby was not in the kitchen; Lizzie supposed she had gone back to bed. Maggie had yet to make an appearance at all. The whole family sick and Uncle John arriving at any time!

Andrew sat on the sofa; Lizzie removed his boots. Then he fell sideways, and she put a pillow under his head. He rearranged himself somewhat and she fetched the book, sat next to him and began to read.

She hadn't read three pages when she knew he was asleep. She closed the book and sat there, hurting, hurting from Enid, hurting from her father, hurting from the restlessness that was steeped in the house, when she felt that familiar sensation, saw that eerie brightness and was once again looking out the eyes of another Lizzie, a Lizzie who was in the kitchen.

The other Lizzie selected a knife from the drawer and an onion from the hamper. Without peeling it, she began to chop it with hard, brutal strokes.

Lizzie sat in the sitting room, hearing the chopping going on in the kitchen as she watched herself hack away at the onion until there was nothing left but mush and milky juice.

Then, knife still in hand, the other Lizzie—the Angry Lizzie—opened the icebox and took out the milk. She smelled it and then laughed. She *laughed,* and suddenly Lizzie was very uncertain about what had made the family sick. It wasn't like . . . it wasn't like when she stole Abby's money and jewelry, was it? It wasn't, was it?

Suddenly, the air in the room was too rare for her. Suddenly, she had to gasp to breathe. The Lizzie in the kitchen opened the screen door and walked out into the backyard, knife in hand. She picked a pear from the tree and ground it to pulp beneath her heel. Then she went to the barn and went inside. The air was choked with hot dust. She climbed the ladder, knife still held awkwardly in one hand, and stood tall in the loft, a dizzying height in this heat. She kicked at the hay and uncovered the book, then picked it up and opened it to the very first chapter, the chapter of the beautiful words, the paragraph she was to repeat every day. Lizzie knew it by heart, but the Barn Lizzie read it out loud, and in her voice it was something horrible, something awful, it was something devilish, something demonic.

Lizzie had always thought of that particular passage as being of love, and life, and health, but perhaps the existence of this other Lizzie, this hellish thing that had motives of her own, was a direct result of that book. Could that be?

The Barn Lizzie put the book on the floor and sent the knife right through it.

Then she was gone.

Lizzie gasped for air, perspiration running freely down her face, darkening stains everywhere on her dress. She threw the book she'd been reading to the floor and escaped the house.

Out on the street, she looked both ways. Where could she go? She had nowhere. She had no one. She needed someone who could understand. . . .

But there was no one who could ever understand. Except, perhaps, Kathryn Peters.

• • •

Kathryn answered the door with a surprised smile when she saw Lizzie. It appeared to Lizzie to be a genuine smile, but for the moment, Lizzie didn't much care. She needed a refuge, and Kathryn would provide it, willingly or not.

"Lizzie! How nice to see you."

"Kathryn, can I come in?"

"What is it, dear? My, my, you do look a sight. Please come in. I'll fix you something cool to drink."

"Please." Kathryn's house was almost as hot as Lizzie's, but it was neat, clean, and dust-free, even in this heat. Lizzie sat on the edge of a chair, her insides agitated and churning.

"We had a marvelous time in New York, Lizzie," Kathryn said as she brought a tray of drinks into the sitting room. "You simply *must* go with us next time."

Lizzie took the cool tea and gulped it down.

"Really, my dear, you are in quite a state. Tell me. What is all this about?"

"I'm so afraid, Kathryn," Lizzie said, rather surprised that of all the things there were to say about the situation, that fear was the one she gave voice to.

"Oh?"

"I fear someone has poisoned the milk." What a stupid thing to say.

"The milk?"

Lizzie nodded.

"Have you contacted the police?"

"No, it's far too complicated. There's a book. And she's to arrive tonight or tomorrow. And then there's Emma, who's gone to Fairhaven, but she's so furious at Father, that . . . well, she had to leave, don't you see?"

"Whoa, girl, settle down. Here. Put your feet up on the

stool. That's right. Now put your head back and close your eyes. I'm going to rub your forehead for you while you just concentrate on relaxing. That's right."

Lizzie felt the tension slide right away from her as Kathryn's fingers rubbed her forehead.

"You're even more beautiful now than the last time I saw you, Lizzie," Kathryn said. "We must spend a little time together now and then, don't you think?"

Lizzie felt Kathryn's hand on her breast. She sat up and looked Kathryn right in the eye. "I'm in trouble, Kathryn. Our whole family is in trouble. I came here because I thought perhaps you were a friend who would care."

"I am, Lizzie. I do care. I'll fix us something to eat here in a short while. Would you like to take a cool bath?"

Lizzie took a long look at Kathryn. She looked like a shark. Lizzie realized with a thud that she had hoped for loving understanding from this woman, the way she would have received it from Enid. Just because they had touched each other in *that* way didn't mean that they loved each other, she thought, and the sadness welled up. "No, Kathryn, I think I better go."

"Go? But you just arrived."

"I'm sorry," Lizzie said, and ducked her head so that Kathryn wouldn't see the tears. She left the front door open, and didn't look back.

Oh God, where to now?

She couldn't go home. She couldn't wander the streets: She had no hanky and her nose was running. Beatrice was due to arrive at any moment, and her eyes would be swollen like a frog's from crying.

Stop crying! Lizzie stiffened her lip and sniffed. But the "nobody loves me" refrain was difficult to suppress.

There's a W.C. at the church, Lizzie thought. There will be a tissue there.

Lizzie slipped in the side door of the church and made

directly for the ladies' room. She blew her nose and splashed cold water on her face. That was better. She was leaning against the wall, letting her face dry, when the door opened and Alice Russell walked in.

"Lizzie!"

"Hello, Alice."

"Is there a meeting?"

"No, I was just caught outside and needed . . . you know."

"I do," Alice said, and washed her hands. "Lizzie, is everything all right?"

"Oh, Alice, no, I don't think so—" And the tears began to run again. Lizzie's throat felt raw from trying to hold them back.

"My dear!" Alice patted Lizzie's back. "Why don't we go over to my house, I'll fix you something nice to drink, or eat, or whatever you want, and we'll have a long talk."

Lizzie nodded.

"I'll go tell Reverend Buck that I'm leaving. You'll be all right here for a moment?"

Lizzie nodded.

In a moment Alice was back. Lizzie took her last sniff and they left the church, silently walking the three blocks to Alice's house.

Alice and her husband lived in a modest little house with a lovely garden. They were both in their late fifties, and childless. Lizzie had been to two church-committee meetings at Alice's house; in fact, it was during a meeting at Alice's house that she volunteered to teach the Oriental Sunday school class.

Alice settled Lizzie in her homey, lived-in front room and went to fix a glass of lemonade.

What am I doing here, Lizzie wondered. How on earth could I tell this fine, innocent, churchgoing woman about what's been happening? How can I?

Alice returned with a glass of lemonade and a smile. She sat on the edge of the sofa and sipped.

"Now, Lizzie," she said. "Share your burden with a friend."

"I'm not sure. I don't know. I want to be safe. I need to be safe, but there doesn't seem to be anyplace . . ."

"What is it? Exactly."

"I'm so afraid something dreadful is going to happen. I feel it in my bones. One of Father's tenants threatened him a little while back, and then Abby's jewelry was stolen. And now someone has poisoned the milk and made everyone sick, and I'm just so certain that something terrible, something awful is about to happen, and I don't know what I should do . . . or if I *can* do anything to prevent it."

"All right. All right. Let me fix you something to eat. You go into the bathroom and freshen up. A little nourishment and a little cleanliness go a long way toward clarity of mind."

"Yes. Yes." Lizzie got up and went into the bathroom. Another house with full plumbing. Alice's bathroom was basic, but it looked like her. And her husband's toiletries were out in plain sight. Lizzie smelled his shaving soap. It had a nice perfume to it.

Lizzie unbuttoned her shirt and took it off. She washed her face, hands, arms and chest. The cold water felt wonderful. She toweled off with a soft towel that smelled sweet. The Oriental laundry. Oh, what she wouldn't give to have a few of the material pleasures—a few material *basics* that everybody else in town enjoyed, but that her father was too cheap, too mean to provide for his own family.

Refreshed, she returned to the kitchen, where Alice had laid out strips of cold chicken on brown bread with crunchy mustard and cranberry sauce. It was a wonderful meal, and Lizzie ate it gratefully. As her stomach was filled with the first good food she'd eaten all day, that terrible anxiety slipped away. She could almost relax.

311

"Where's your husband?"

"He'll be home in a while."

"He's missing a fine meal." Lizzie felt grateful. She wondered if she had other friends that she didn't know about. She didn't really want to stay at Alice's house, and she certainly didn't want to spend the night, but she didn't want to go home, either. Home. Just the thought of it gave her shivers.

Alice began to talk, and the more she talked, the easier Lizzie felt. Eventually, they talked about every mutual acquaintance, all the history of the gossip at church, and finally they ran out of conversation. Lizzie dragged herself to her feet.

"Well, I'd better go. I'm sorry I barged in on you like this, Alice, but thank you for taking me in and providing a delicious dinner."

"Lizzie, won't you stay?" There was a pleading in Alice's eyes, and Lizzie thought that this woman could become a friend, a good friend, someday.

"No, I think I'd better go. Thank you." And she left.

The evening stretched long, as August evenings will, and the twilight settled slowly over Fall River. Lizzie's dread began to grow again; she was afraid to go back home; she was afraid of what might happen when she got there.

She wondered if Beatrice was there, and knew she could not possibly face her friend looking the way she did. In fact, she should never be out in public looking like this.

She walked up the Hill, turned down Enid's street and walked past her house, but refused to turn her head to look. The fury had dulled to an ache in her heart, and her throat caught every time she thought of it. There was treachery there, and perhaps an underlying motive for Enid's involvement with her, but Lizzie couldn't help but feel that Enid had cared for her, had cared for her deeply, and was selling her only marketable commodity for her sons.

312

Lizzie wanted to believe that. And she did. *Somewhat.* But did she have to sell to Lizzie's *father?*

The evening deepened and Lizzie found herself out by the river. Decent folk were not out after nightfall, particularly womenfolk, particularly women alone, but even though Lizzie could hear her father's admonitions in the back of her mind, she discounted them as the ramblings of a foolish old man. He had never been credible, why should he be credible now?

The air cooled perceptibly by the river, and Lizzie listened to its rushing, and the frogs and crickets as they came out for some cool air after the stifling heat. She pulled her skirts tightly around her and sat down in the long grass up the bank. She should have her fishing pole. She could probably sneak home, go into the barn for it, and come back here and fish all night with nobody ever knowing. No one would ever miss her.

But if she went home, she would want a shawl, so she'd have to go into the house, and she would see that same old mutton broth on the dining-room table and that would make her sick. And she would smell the heat of the sick people in the house and that would make her sicker. And she would look at her father and the anger would come up again, and the worry over Emma, and the anxiety over Beatrice, and . . .

She pulled the sleeves of her shirt closer and wrapped her arms around herself. She would have to go home eventually, she knew, particularly since the cool of the river was becoming a chill and the sky was definitely darkening.

The evening star shone brightly above the glowing horizon to the west. In the east, the sky was a deep blue, stars beginning to twinkle.

Eventually, she stood up, shook out the cramps in her legs and walked slowly toward home. A coach passed her, and she hid so no one would see her. She tried to concentrate on happier thoughts, but there was nothing in her future but more of the same. More of the same, godawful life she had always known. More of the same.

And while she was walking, she saw the telltale brightening, not much more than a heightening of light and shadow, and she felt as though there were two of her, as if her other were walking side by side in step with her, seeing the same things, their visions so closely coordinated that there was little difference, except a feeling, a very odd feeling that she was not quite right with herself.

She walked through the yard of their neighbor to the rear, and climbed over the fence into the Borden yard.

She took a pear from the ground, and stood there eating it, wondering if she should really go into the house or if she should sleep in the barn.

The house was silent and dark. She chose the house. She went through the front door and directly up the stairs to her room.

The door to the guest room was closed, so Uncle John must have arrived.

Her slops had been emptied and her washbowl freshened, so Maggie had been up and around.

Lizzie locked her bedroom door behind her, took the key to Emma's bedroom from her dresser and looked in on it. It had been put right again after Andrew's search.

She took off her clothes, dropped them onto the floor and got into bed.

She didn't sleep. She listened to the house and waited for something terrible to happen.

Thursday, August 4

he neighbors had a rooster that woke Abby up at inconvenient hours of the morning, and most days she had nothing but unkind remarks about it. But on this particular morning, she waited to hear it, and when she finally did, it signaled to her that morning had come, and though it was still dark, she got out of bed.

Lizzie had come in late again, and Abby worried about the girl. Besides, John Morse had arrived, and his presence in her house still made her nervous, even after almost thirty years of his visits. She never seemed able to forget that she was not Andrew's first wife, not his first choice, and his life was still filled with that other woman. She could never forget that.

So while the presence of another person in the house changed the atmosphere, Emma's absence changed it again, and then Lizzie's actions changed it yet again, and Abby had lain awake listening to the walls. She wondered at the sickness that had scared her half to death, scared them all more than any would admit, scared her more than any idle threats could have. Abby lay awake almost all night long, listening and wondering. Worrying.

But with the crow of the rooster, she slipped out of bed, lit a candle, dressed quietly so as to not wake her mate, and went down to the kitchen to make a nice breakfast for her family. Somehow it was important, it was *very* important that John Morse know that her family was a good family, a normal family, and that she was a good wife.

John Morse was Sarah Borden's brother. Sarah Borden, wife of Andrew, mother of Lizzie and Emma. John had business in Fall River and was not an infrequent visitor, but his visits always seemed to last too long. He was a fine guest, a creative conversationalist, and he and Andrew had business dealings that they never seemed to tire of analyzing. Abby liked to have Andrew thus entertained; there were no other friends in Andrew's life, not really, and it pleased her for him to have company. Except that John Morse always reminded her that she was Andrew's second choice in a wife, and not the mother of his children.

She couldn't bear to start a fire in the wood stove. It was just too hot. The night air had not cooled the house at all. To start a fire in the stove would mean the heat in the kitchen would remain in there all day long. But she would have to, if she were to make fresh coffee.

She took the lid off the stove and looked down inside. There was a half-burned mailing tube inside. A few things clicked into place. Emma. Emma had burned that thing that Andrew had looked for, and then she had left town.

Abby pulled the charred remains from the stove and looked at them. The label, written in Andrew's hand, said Fairhaven.

Abby brought the candle closer and looked down inside the tube. Something thick had burned in there, some papers. But they were mostly ash. Abby thought it best not to mention this incident to Andrew, at least until after John Morse had gone. She wanted no scene, she wanted everything to appear normal.

She gathered up some bits of newspaper and kindling, put the mailing tube back into the stove and lit it. Just enough for coffee, she thought. She filled the enameled pot

316

with water, added a handful of coffee grounds and a pinch of salt, and put it on to boil. She looked in the cupboard and found a whole plate of store-bought cookies.

She took one and nibbled it while she thought what else she would feed John Morse for breakfast.

She took the leftover mutton gravy from the table, put it on the stove to warm and began to mix up some biscuits. There would be pears to go with all this.

Morning light peered through the windows as Abby finished mixing the biscuit dough. She blew out the candle and adjusted the coffee pot on the stove.

Then she listened, again, to the house. It seemed to have a presence of its own these days, something different, something new.

She wondered what Emma was doing in Fairhaven, she wondered what Lizzie was doing outside at all hours, she wondered about the new feeling in the house, and she wondered why on earth she couldn't just *ask* the girls those questions.

She took a moment for a small prayer, asking God to keep everything normal in the house, at least until John Morse was gone, so he would speak kindly of the Borden family to his friends and neighbors. She prayed that no irate tenants would be knocking at the door threatening Andrew, she prayed that nobody would be stealing anybody's jewelry, she prayed that no fits of rage would be on display, she prayed that Sebastian wouldn't be lurking about, she prayed that the milk would be good.

It seems as though there is a lot of evil about just now, she thought, listening to the presence in the walls.

Hoping that John Morse wouldn't notice, she began to roll out the biscuits.

bby puts on a fine feed for John Morse, that's a fact, Andrew thought as he wiped his lips on his napkin and set it next to his plate. "I'd best be off," he said, then stood, shaking hands with his brother-in-law. "Will you be back for supper?"

"I will," John Morse said. "I've business in the country this morning." He checked his pocket watch. "And I had better be on my way. I'll be back by supper."

"Fine. We'll talk over the property then."

"Good."

Andrew donned his hat and black coat, even though it was already high in the eighties at eight o'clock in the morning. He left the house and took a deep breath of the thick, humid air.

He walked toward the bank with slow steps, trying to concentrate on too many things at once.

First on his mind was the date. It was Thursday, which meant he had only this day and part of the next to live through until he could again see the Widow Crawford. For all her wily ways, her disturbing relationship with Lizzie, and that disastrous visit to the house, Fridays with the Widow Crawford continued to be a high point of his week. He had given consideration to breaking off with her—but that had lasted the briefest of moments. There was no reason to break off with her. She was discreet, and that visit to his home was motivated by concern for Lizzie. Oh yes, the Widow Crawford. Enid Crawford. Friday.

Next on his mind was John Morse and the peculiar investment proposal he had brought with him to Fall River. John Morse and Andrew had invested together before, sometimes on the basis of John's ideas and research, sometimes at the behest of Andrew. But this time, this affair, was entirely unconventional, and while it had not been Andrew's experience that John suggested investments lightly, Andrew would have to give this serious consideration. All of their joint endeavors had made money, and they still owned property together, another profitable venture. But he would wait and see about this property. If they were to build an inn according to John Morse's plans, the project would require much capital, much supervision and a close eye on hired management. Andrew wasn't sure he had that much left to devote to an investment project. There were other things in life. Like Fridays. There was more to be discussed. Andrew didn't have all the information from John yet. That would come in the evening, after supper.

Next on his mind was his will. And Emma. She had taken it and gone to Fairhaven, as sure as he was walking to work. What on earth could be on that girl's mind? He would have to have a new will drawn up, and that would be both time-consuming and expensive, damn her eyes. And with John Morse in town, he couldn't do it until next week. Damned inconvenience.

And then there was Lizzie. Andrew had felt a change coming over Lizzie in the past weeks. There was something very strange about the girl, but he couldn't quite put his finger on it. It was just that . . . when he went home, and Lizzie was there, the house didn't feel as it used to, or as it normally did. There was just something a little odd about the place. As if someone else was there, too. As if Lizzie had a friend over, and you didn't really know, but the house felt a little different—perhaps there were too many footsteps for one person, or there was one extra set of noises. Something added.

And then there was that blasted maid washing windows. It seemed that was all she did this whole summer. Someone was always having her wash some windows or other. It was positively unnerving to be resting, or working quietly, then to turn around and see the maid staring in from outside with a washrag in her hand.

He wished she would quit it.

izzie lay in bed listening to the sounds of the house. Abby was baking. *Baking!* In this heat! But then Uncle John was here, and she would want to go overboard to impress him, the way she always did.

Sometimes Lizzie felt sorry for Abby, always having to run harder to catch up with life, it seemed, and now she was old, and fat, and her hair was turning white, and she was still running, even though she was old enough to know by now that she would never catch up.

Lizzie heard Uncle John get up, use the slops pail, dress and go down for breakfast. She could hear the murmur of conversation at the breakfast table, and heard the front door close behind her father, her uncle's climb up the stairs to his room next to hers; then he, too, went out the front door.

Lizzie stretched. There was no real need for her to get up, was there?

There was a knock at the front door.

Lizzie's heart froze. Beatrice. Oh God.

She heard Abby's heavy footsteps in the hallway. Beatrice would be standing there, glorious, waiting to embrace her friend who had gotten fat and had done nothing, *nothing* to deserve her friendship.

The front door opened. Abby did not call out to Lizzie, so it must be someone else.

Maybe it was someone coming to harm Father. Maybe it was someone coming to blackmail him with tales of unnatural acts that Lizzie had committed with both Enid and

Kathryn. Enid was certainly not above taking money for something that would thwart a friend, and Kathryn had no morals at all. Either one of them could turn a fast dollar with a discreet word that Andrew Borden's daugther was a freak, and Andrew, in his desperate attempt to keep from airing family laundry, would pay. He would pay, and he would pay dearly.

And Lizzie would pay for that.

She jumped out of bed, her insides agitated. She made her bed up tightly, and chose a blue wrapper. She knotted up her hair and went downstairs. Abby was in the sitting room talking with a woman whom Lizzie had never seen before. She went straight through the dining room into the kitchen.

Biscuits. She took three, cut them open and ladled the hot gravy over them. Bridget was sitting in the dining room, her head in her hands, a cup of coffee before her.

"Maggie, are you all right?"

"Not so well, miss," she said, and even her brogue sounded ill.

"Eat something, then."

"God, no, miss, I couldn't stand the sight or the smell of that mutton again. Not one more day."

"It tastes all right."

Bridget groaned and put her face down into the crook of her arm.

"Who is that with Abby?"

Bridget shrugged.

Lizzie ate her breakfast, which sat heavy and greasy in her stomach. Soon the front door opened and closed and Abby came into the dining room, wiping her hands on her apron, as if she had gotten something on them by talking to that woman.

"There's a birthing, and it could be trouble. I'll have to go," she said.

"You don't look as if you want to go," Lizzie said.

322

"Well. Mr. Borden doesn't like me to be going to that side of town. It would probably be best if I didn't, but . . . well, we'll see." She turned her attention to the maid, who looked pale and fragile. "Bridget, I need those windows finished today. John Morse is already here, and still the windows aren't done."

"Yes, ma'am."

"Lizzie, are you going to iron that pile of clothes you dampened yesterday, or are you going to leave them to molder?"

Lizzie scowled. Abby took her plate into the kitchen and in a moment they heard her climb the stairs to her room.

Lizzie took the spoon from the congealed gravy and let the glop of gravy slide from it into the pot with a plop.

Bridget saw that. Her eyes got large, and with both hands held over her mouth she ran for the backyard and threw up.

Lizzie smiled. She piled the dishes for the poor girl to do up before she got started on the windows, then set the ironing flats on the stove to heat. She pulled a magazine from the kindling box and sat down to thumb through it while they heated.

It was a *Harper's*. She remembered looking at a *Harper's* at Enid's.

Enid.

She closed the magazine and threw it back into the kindling box.

The maid came back in, took a drink of water and spat out the back door. Then she clanged the bucket and got her cloths and things and went about getting ready to clean the windows.

Lizzie checked the flats. They were barely warm. The fire must have gone out in the stove. And it was definitely too hot to rekindle it.

"Oooh, miss. You should see the carriage out here."

Beatrice! Lizzie's heart stuck in her throat.

Lizzie jumped up and went to the little maid, who was looking out the parlor window. Lizzie grabbed her arm. "Maggie, if someone should come to the door looking for me, tell her that I am not home and am not expected."

There was a blank look on the poor girl's face. Lizzie squeezed her arm until she chirped. "Do you hear?"

"Yes, yes, yes."

Lizzie lifted the side of the curtain and looked out. It was a fine carriage, all right. Pure black. Black and fine, with liveried attendants. It looked like a carriage Beatrice would travel in.

Lizzie looked down at herself in her plain blue wrapper. She turned again to the maid. "I'm not home, remember?"

"Yes, miss."

Lizzie ran through the dining room, through the kitchen, banged out the back door and ran across the small yard to the barn. She unlocked the door, then stood there, out of sight, and listened. She heard nothing. She went back under the pear tree and picked up several nice pears that had dropped.

Then she heard the knock at the front door and scurried inside the barn. She climbed the ladder to the loft and looked out the loft window, but she couldn't see the carriage from this vantage.

She paced.

Surely that was Beatrice, and here she was, after inviting her to visit, hiding like a coward in the barn. Anxiety gripped her chest in its talons.

Why should she be doing this? Why should she be the coward? What on earth had driven her to cowering in the barn loft?

The Fearful Self, she thought. The fear of inadequacy, the fear of Emma's fate, the fear of being an old maid, the fear of dying old, alone and poor, the fear of being found out as an unnatural thing, the fear of the future, the fear of future pain, the fear of life, the fear of *everything* slowly began to turn to anger. The cold tips of fear she felt burrowing under her skin began to glow white-hot, and an unfamiliar fury began to take hold.

"It's *her* fault," she said, picturing Abby Borden in her mind. Somewhere that sounded vaguely familiar, as if those were words she had once heard Emma utter in one of her rages, but the familiarity was fleeting.

"It *is*. It's all her fault." Lizzie began to pace. "It's her fault that Emma is the way she is. Without *her*, Emma would be fine, there would be no problem with a will, there would be no one poisoning our milk, there would be nothing to worry about, there would be *nothing to* WORRY ABOUT!"

Lizzie sat down, leaned against the hay, and as if her fingers had memories of their own, they unbuttoned her sweat-soaked clothes and found their way under her drawers, to that wonderful secret place. Lizzie groaned when the hate met the pleasure, creating a tornado in her soul.

She rubbed harder and harder, and then she saw Abby. Abby was changing the pillowslips in Uncle John Morse's bedroom. She was humming to herself, the bag.

Lizzie crept up behind her.

Abby whirled around, but there was no one there. She could have sworn that she heard someone behind her.

She shook the pillow down into the case, plumped it up right—not the way that silly Bridget did it—and laid it nicely on the bed.

She smoothed it down, stood up and listened.

Bridget had answered the knock at the door, and Abby had waited for the call. She was expecting to be called a second time to the birthing, but had decided not to go. Mr. Borden would definitely not approve.

She went back to the task at hand, smoothing the pillow.

She whirled. There it was again, a presence. This time, though, she almost heard breathing. But there was nothing there. Nothing.

The hair prickled at the back of her neck and stood up along her arms. She rubbed it down, and walked around the foot of the bed.

izzie knew what the Other Lizzie was about to do. The idea of it excited her beyond anything Kathryn had ever done for her. She closed her eyes, arching her back, the pleasure she was giving herself fierce.

The Other Lizzie raised the little kindling hatchet.

Lizzie brought her knees up to her chest and whispered, "Do it!"

The hatchet whispered through the air and glanced off Abby's skull.

T he first blow struck so hard and so silently that Abby saw the swatch of her scalp land on the freshly made bed before she actually felt it.

She wheeled around, but there was nobody there. There was *nobody* there.

Wait. Was it Lizzie? She almost recognized—

She had a split second to notice that even though she couldn't see it, she could hear it, and then the unseen hatchet buried itself in the right side of her brain and the lights of the world were lost.

izzie pounded herself as she imagined pounding Abby, the thrusts to herself more and more brutal. She loved it, she hated it, she wanted to hurt, bite, squeeze, kill. She rolled, curled over, in the hay, muscles twitching and throbbing as the hatchet continued to lay blow after blow on her stupid stepmother's head. The orgasm shuddered to a violent conclusion.

When it was over, she cried.

A ndrew Borden felt uneasy all morning at the office. Around noon he received such a jarring pain in his head that he thought it had split in two. He closed his eyes and waited for the ensuing headache, but the pain was brief and it left no lingering aftereffects. It had to do with the illness, he thought. There was still some of the illness left in him.

Well, he would try very hard not to succumb to it. He could possibly leave early today, go home, have Lizzie rub his feet and read to him and have a little lie-down on the sofa, and he would be as good as new. He must take care not to have a relapse. Tomorrow was his time with the Widow Crawford.

But the uneasiness Andrew felt had little to do with the sickness, or the pain in his head, even though those were a part of it. The uneasiness had more to do with the feeling that the reins of control were slipping from his hands.

In business, he was relinquishing control a little bit, taking a lesser role in management and a greater role in profits. Let the younger men do all the hard work. But at home . . . at home, Emma was certainly out of control, Lizzie was . . . well, Lizzie was quite devoted to her sister. Abby was sweet Abby, as always, but there was something about the character of his homelife that was slipping away from him. It might have started when Lizzie changed churches. Their relationship hadn't been the same since.

And Emma. Poor Emma.

Andrew made a note to himself to visit the law office in person on Monday and have a new will drawn up. He would include and exclude whom he wished and let the tongues wag.

He rubbed his hands over his sweating face and looked out the window. It was wide open, but not a breath of air stirred. Flies buzzed lazily. It was too hot even for the flies. Underneath his black wool coat, Andrew sweltered. He looked at the clock.

Perhaps I'll go home soon, he thought, and see what Lizzie's been up to.

izzie came in from the barn, feeling weak, dizzy and profoundly guilty. She went down cellar and discovered blood in her drawers. For a moment, she thought she had injured herself, and then she realized it was just time again for her monthly. She rigged up a pad, then splashed cold water on her face and rubbed it on her arms. It was mildly refreshing, but she couldn't quite shake the guilt. Such terrible excitement, imagining Abby's death.

Lizzie feared that there was something seriously wrong with her. She went upstairs, hoping to run into Abby, hoping to make things right with her, somehow. Maggie was washing windows in the dining room.

"Didn't you just wash those windows, Maggie?"

"Yes, miss, but Mrs. Borden can't seem to have them clean enough."

"How are you feeling?"

"Not so well, miss. Not well at all."

Lizzie wandered around the kitchen, looking for something to eat. Except for the biscuits left over from Abby's baking this morning, nothing had been baked for weeks. The cupboard, which Emma was in charge of, held only a plate of store-bought cookies. And that would be a fine meal to feed Uncle John for dinner. Oh well. That was Abby's problem, wasn't it?

"Your friend came."

Lizzie stopped, her blood cold. "Beatrice?"

"The Brit."

"What did she say?"

"I just told her like you told me. That you weren't home and weren't expected."

"What was she wearing?"

"Pardon?"

"What was she wearing?"

"Kind of a dark green dress."

"Silk?"

"I don't know, miss."

"Did she look cool?"

"No, miss, she looked as hot as the rest of us."

"Will she be back?"

"No, miss, she said she had to leave for New Bedford to catch a boat back to England. She had a lovely carriage."

"Yes . . ." Lizzie slumped down into a chair. There was nothing to worry about with Beatrice. She was hot like everybody else, and she couldn't stay overnight anyway. It would have been fun to see her. Lizzie hadn't had to hide in the corner of the hayloft to avoid her, and now she would never write again and all that friendship would be lost.

Well, it was not the only friendship lost in the past few weeks. Lizzie gritted her teeth.

It's that book, she thought. That book is heartache. She got up from her chair and let the screen door slam behind her. She went into the barn, choked in its stillness, went up the ladder and found the book under the edge of the haystack, where she kept it hidden.

She looked at it, rubbed her fingers over the cover. She had loved this book. It had meant so much to her at first. But now she thought that perhaps it was not good. It taught the wrong things. It taught independence and self-reliance, everything that the family and church was against. It let loose the beasts—the demons—of Anger and Lust. Fury and Hate.

I never touched myself *like that* before this book. I never touched another woman before this book. I never, *ever* would have thought of doing anything *like that* to Abby before this book.

I'll burn it.

She took it down the ladder and back into the house, through the dining room. Bridget was taking a break at the dining table, her head down on her arms. Lizzie hid the book, but Bridget didn't look up. Lizzie took it up into her bedroom, where she wrapped it in that old paint-stained dress that Emma had been after her to burn. The next time there's a fire in the stove, she thought, this goes in.

• • •

When she heard her father's key in the front-door lock, Lizzie leaped up from her rocking chair. She needed some company. Scant comfort though she might be, Emma did provide plenty of company for Lizzie, and Lizzie sorely missed her when she was gone. She missed her and she worried about her.

Lizzie unpinned her hair and brushed it quickly, then knotted it back up. When she was finished, her father was knocking on the front door. He couldn't manage to open it. She hoped he wasn't sick.

She looked down from the landing, but Maggie had beaten her to the front door; the maid looked greatly inconvenienced. Lizzie laughed in spite of herself, and the maid turned and gave her a look that said she didn't appreciate her or her father.

Andrew walked in the door looking at the key in his hand. He didn't look particularly ill, but he didn't look very well, either.

"Hello, Father."

"Lizzie."

"Any mail for me?"

"Not today."

"Come in and sit down. Are you well? Would you like to read?"

"Some cold water, Lizzie."

Lizzie got him a glass of water and put two cookies on a plate. By the time she returned from the kitchen, he was already lying down on the sofa. She handed him the water; he sat up and took a couple of swallows, then she took the glass away from him. She unlaced and removed his boots. The more she looked at him, the sicker he looked.

"Are you all right, Father?"

"Just tired, Lizzie. Read to me."

She got the book and began to read. Within minutes, he was snoring softly, but she continued to read. There were only two pages left to go in the book and then they could begin another, so she kept reading, her voice lowered, reading aloud only to herself.

Andrew stirred, and Lizzie interrupted herself to look over at him. His eyes were slitted, but they were open, looking straight at her.

"You're all I've got," he said quietly. "You're the only one who will take care of me in my old age." Then he closed his eyes again.

Lizzie looked at the pages of the book, but the words were blurred. She closed it, patted his knee and got up.

She went to the kitchen, but the burning sadness was too much for idle wandering, so again she went to the barn. She picked up some fallen pears on the way and closed the heavy door behind her.

I am all he's got, she thought. I'll end up washing his bedpans for the rest of my life. I'll never have time to go fishing.

Fishing.

That was exactly what Lizzie needed. She needed to go fishing. She needed fresh air. She needed a diversion. She needed to sit in the quiet, with only the birds and the fish and the insects to entertain her. She needed her little green room cut out of the center of a willow tree. She needed some privacy, some quiet, she needed everybody to leave her alone, just leave her alone for a little while. She stopped pacing, set the pears down on a box of junk on the floor and began hunting through the junk for iron to use as sinkers. The last time she went fishing, she didn't have any sinkers, and the bait floated downstream and caught on the weeds. If she had a nice piece of iron to tie onto her line, then the worm would wait at the bottom of the stream and she would be able to catch a nice trout.

Trout for dinner. That would feed Uncle John.

She began to paw through the boxes of useless junk, but there wasn't anything suitable. Everything was either too small or too large. She should go to the hardware store and buy herself some right sinkers.

She picked up the pears and sat on an overturned bucket. She rubbed them one at a time on her skirt.

If she lived alone, she could go fishing whenever she pleased. If she lived alone, she wouldn't have to deal with Father, or Abby or Emma. She would only have to instruct the maid as to cleanliness, guests expected and menus. She could be a woman living alone; she wouldn't have to be a *spinster*. She wouldn't have to deal with Emma's rages, or Father's insults or his lifelong dream of enslaving her to his bedridden incontinence.

Old people are such a bother, she thought. If he were dead, she wouldn't have to deal with any of the problems he brought her. She would be free, and rich, and happy. If he were dead, she wouldn't have to feel guilty about having such thoughts. If he were dead, she would never have another problem. She could come and go as she pleased.

If he were dead . . . if he were dead.

If *only* he were dead!

336

Sadness welled up and filled her eyes. She rested her chin on her fist and rubbed a pear up and down her leg.

"I don't want to be all you've got, Father," she said softly, and then she was in the room with him, much brighter than the barn, and she looked down upon him from what seemed to be a great height.

She could see the graying of his skin, thin, wrinkled with a thousand creases. His hair was thin, too, long and white. His eyes were closed, but behind the lids were brown eyes, brown like Emma's, only they had turned blue around the edges of the irises, and they seemed to float instead of holding solid. She loved the face. She hated the face.

She thought if she had a little hatchet, a little kindling hatchet, she could split it right down the center.

She crunched a big bite of the pear.

She would split one of those loose eyes right down the middle like a grape.

She crunched another bite, and the juice ran down her chin.

Again and again she would hit him, just hit him and hit him, feeling the bones crunch

    like a green pear

    watching the blood spurt

    like sweet juice

    pieces of brains would fall

    a chunk of pear landed on her lap

and she would never, never, *never,* NEVER have to deal with the old man again. Never. Ever.

She stood up and screamed. "Never!" And threw the pear against the barn wall. It splattered.

She looked around herself. Oh God, not again. Shame burned her face. Twice in one day, she'd thought about killing her parents. Thought about it in detail.

I love you, Papa, she thought. I'm sorry.

Pear juice covered her hands, and rivulets had run down her forearms. Dust from the barn stuck to it, leaving dark trails.

I think there's something wrong with me, she thought. Surely other people didn't think about their parents in the same way.

She stood, and was surprised to notice that her knees shook. She gathered up the uneaten pears and took them outside, threw them back underneath the tree. She'd have to go to the hardware store for some sinkers.

She left the barn, washed her hands in the utility room and looked once again in the kitchen cupboards.

Maggie was just finishing up the windows in the kitchen.

Lizzie walked into the sitting room.

Andrew's face was covered with blood. One half-eyeball hung from where his cheek used to be.

Disbelief stunned Lizzie. She looked for a long moment. Blood still oozed from the massive wound and puddled on the floor. Her gold high school ring glinted on his little finger.

She began to feel light-headed. She turned around and, feeling her way toward the door, went out the kitchen door and leaned against the casing.

I didn't do it, she thought. It was not my fault.

As the truth of that sank in, she felt immense relief.

And Emma will be so pleased.

And then she remembered Abby. Abby and her feelings earlier. Abby. What of Abby? Something dropped heavily into her stomach. Again, her knees felt a bit weak.

"Lizzie?"

It was Mrs. Churchill next door, looking out her window.

"Lizzie, what is the matter?"

"It's hot," Lizzie said.

"Isn't it?"

Lizzie sat down on the step. She put her face in her hands.

"Lizzie?"

Lizzie smiled. Mrs. Churchill's day in the sun at last. Lizzie lifted her head and looked straight into Mrs. Churchill's eyes. "Oh, Mrs. Churchill," she said. "Do come over. Someone has killed Father."

· Epilogue

The bodies of Abby and Andrew Borden lay on the dining-room table in the sweltering August heat for three days while the police examined them. Then, finally, their heads and stomachs were removed and the remains buried.

On August 11, Lizzie was arrested for the murder of Andrew and Abby Borden. No murder weapon was ever found. No blood was found on Lizzie or her clothes immediately after the killing. The most damning testimony came from Alice Russell, who had seen Lizzie burn the paint-stained dress. The prosecution considered that destruction of evidence.

After a grueling trial, Lizzie was acquitted on June 20, 1893. The jury deliberated little more than an hour.

She and Emma bought a stylish fourteen-room house on the prestigious "Hill" of Fall River, and there they lived together until 1905, when Emma, unable to tolerate Lizzie's life-style any longer, moved to Fairhaven.

Lizzie changed her name to Lizbeth, traveled and entertained quite lavishly, and carried on a flamboyant affair with actress Nance O'Neil.

But though the courts had acquitted her, Fall River had not. She lived in solitude, except for her servants, pets and out-of-town friends. She was an oddity, an embarrassment to the community, and her every move was dutifully noted in the local newspaper.

In 1927, she died as the result of complications from gallbladder surgery. She was sixty-eight.

Praise for Mark Maske's *War Without Death*

"There is no tougher world to get inside than the secret society that is the NFL. In *War Without Death*, Mark Maske does just that. If you enjoy pro football and wonderful reporting and writing, this is a book you have to read."
—John Feinstein

"Mark Maske has taken the cold, gray steel of the NFC East and spun it into gold. This book reveals pro football in layers you never imagined."
—Tony Kornheiser, *Washington Post* columnist, cohost of ESPN's *Pardon the Interruption,* and *Monday Night Football* commentator

"Mark Maske is not the gold standard for NFL journalism; he's the platinum standard. It is almost a given among people who follow the NFL that his work represents the most knowledgeable, comprehensive, and in-depth look at the world's most successful league. Sports historians will be plowing through Mark Maske's works well into the twenty-second century."
—James Carville, political commentator and strategist and satellite radio sports talk host

"Covering the NFL for the last twenty-three years, I've seen how hard it's become to get to the heartbeat of why the biggest football decisions are made, how big-ego people can work both together and divisively and why teams win and lose. Mark Maske gets to the core of all of those in *War Without Death,* a page-turner you won't be able to put down. Want to know what makes the most powerful people in football, like Dan Snyder and Jerry Jones, tick? Read this book." —Peter King, *Sports Illustrated,* HBO, NBC Sports

"*War Without Death* is propelled by the unrelenting directness of the competing franchises. . . . What makes this book compelling is Maske's focus on the personalities that shape a team's policies and performance."
—*The Washington Post Book World*

"Maske . . . brings the Moneyball approach to coverage of the NFL. . . . The scenes that will jump out from this taut tour of a year in the life of one of pro sports' toughest divisions are the intimate views of Redskins owner Dan Snyder, whose endless battle against the independent media that dare to cover his franchise without his approval leads him to cut off most access to daily reporters. Maske pierces the veil." —*The Washington Post*

"Terrific . . . Captures the behind-the-scenes action very insightfully."
—Playboy.com

"Maske spotlights Johnes, Snyder, Philadelphia Eagles owner Jeffrey Lurie, and New York Giants owner John Mara in this comprehensive look into business games that are played among the movers and shakers of the megabusiness that is the NFL." —*The Arizona Daily Star*

"There is much to delight any fan of NFL football in *War Without Death*. But NFL fans who are also businesspersons will find it a particularly enriching read." —*The Ledger* (Florida)

"The four teams in the NFC East have won ten Super Bowls, and Maske, a sports columnist for the *Washington Post,* offers an up-close look at these storied franchises throughout 2006. . . . The book excels." —*Publishers Weekly*

"A good read with a fine overview of the teams and the divisions." —The Associated Press

"Captivating." —McClatchy-Tribune Information Services

"Mr. Maske is a good writer and just as importantly, he's a writer who knows his subject well. Mr. Maske has spent years watching, studying, and reporting on the Dallas Cowboys, New York Giants, Philadelphia Eagles, and Washington Redskins—and it shows. But more than that, Mr. Maske has worked to understand how the league works. Although *War Without Death* provides an in-depth look at the four teams of the NFC East, fans of any football team should find this book invaluable. . . . True to his current job as a reporter covering the entire NFL, that one division seems too small for Mr. Maske at times. He wants to understand the entire NFL." —hailRedskins.com

"*War Without Death* delivers the goods, especially when Maske delves into the public and private personas of some prominent NFL owners, such as Jerry Jones and Daniel Snyder. Maske also shines a light on the inner workings of the players' association and how the owners and the union maintained labor peace during a time of great uncertainty as a new contract was hammered out. And as luck would have it, Maske is there for the last season of commissioner Paul Tagliabue's tenure and includes the process of finding a successor. A well-written, multifaceted look at the business, egos, and passion that make up the nation's most popular sport." —*The Hartford Courant*

"A good read with a fine overview of the teams and the division." —*Canoe—Jam!* (Canada)

PENGUIN BOOKS

WAR WITHOUT DEATH

Mark Maske is a *Washington Post* staff writer and sports columnist. He also writes the *Washington Post*'s NFL Insider blog, and is a frequent guest on ESPN, ESPN radio, and other sports media. He lives with his family in Silver Spring, Maryland.

WAR
WITHOUT
DEATH

A YEAR OF EXTREME COMPETITION
IN PRO FOOTBALL

MARK MASKE

PENGUIN BOOKS

PENGUIN BOOKS
Published by the Penguin Group
Penguin Group (USA) Inc., 375 Hudson Street, New York, New York 10014, U.S.A.
Penguin Group (Canada), 90 Eglinton Avenue East, Suite 700, Toronto,
Ontario, Canada M4P 2Y3 (a division of Pearson Penguin Canada Inc.)
Penguin Books Ltd, 80 Strand, London WC2R 0RL, England
Penguin Ireland, 25 St Stephen's Green, Dublin 2, Ireland (a division of Penguin Books Ltd)
Penguin Group (Australia), 250 Camberwell Road, Camberwell,
Victoria 3124, Australia (a division of Pearson Australia Group Pty Ltd)
Penguin Books India Pvt Ltd, 11 Community Centre, Panchsheel Park, New Delhi – 110 017, India
Penguin Group (NZ), 67 Apollo Drive, Rosedale, North Shore 0632,
New Zealand (a division of Pearson New Zealand Ltd)
Penguin Books (South Africa) (Pty) Ltd, 24 Sturdee Avenue,
Rosebank, Johannesburg 2196, South Africa

Penguin Books Ltd, Registered Offices:
80 Strand, London WC2R 0RL, England

First published in the United States of America by The Penguin Press,
a member of Penguin Group (USA) Inc. 2007
Published in Penguin Books 2008

1 3 5 7 9 10 8 6 4 2

Photo Insert Credits
p. 1, top: © Chip Somodevilla/Getty Images; bottom: © David Drapkin/Getty Images;
p. 2, top: © David Drapkin/Getty Images; bottom: © Jamie Squire/Getty Images; p. 3:
© Diamond Images/Getty Images; p. 4: © Drew Hallowell/Getty Images; p. 5, top: © Drew
Hallowell/Getty Images; bottom: © Doug Benc/Getty Images; p. 6: © Stephen Dunn/Getty
Images; p. 7: © Scott Boehm/Getty Images; p. 8, top: © Greg Fiume/Getty Images; bottom:
© Chris Graythen/Getty Images

THE LIBRARY OF CONGRESS HAS CATALOGED THE HARDCOVER EDITION AS FOLLOWS:
Maske, Mark.
War without death : a year of extreme competition in pro football's NFC East / Mark Maske.
p. cm.
Includes index.
ISBN 978-1-59420-141-7 (hc.)
ISBN 978-0-14-311396-6 (pbk.)
1. National Football League. 2. Football—United States. I. Title.
GV955.5.N35M37 2007
796.332'640973—dc22
2007014217

Printed in the United States of America
DESIGNED BY AMANDA DEWEY

TO ANGELIKA, CLAIRE, AND JAKE

My best friends

CONTENTS

AUTHOR'S NOTE

When the New York Giants beat the previously undefeated New England Patriots, 17–14, on February 3, 2008 in Super Bowl XLII before a record-setting television audience, it was the culmination of a dramatic playoff run engineered by their coach, Tom Coughlin, and their quarterback, Eli Manning. But it was much more than that. It also was the product of years of planning and a series of difficult decisions made by John Mara, the owner who kept the much-maligned Coughlin as his coach, and Ernie Accorsi, the former general manager who'd made the once-seemingly ill-fated trade for Manning on draft day 2004. Only a few weeks before, few fans would have praised the choices made by the two men. But all of that changed in an instant. That is the bottom-line nature of the business for those who run the NFL and its teams, and to really understand what happened on the field at the University of Phoenix Stadium in Glendale, Arizona, on that magical evening in which Manning and Coughlin became champions, you must understand what led up to it. This is a look at how the NFL works, and how de-sions are made at both the league and team levels, as viewed th gh the lens of the 2006 season in th

WAR
WITHOUT
DEATH

PROLOGUE

January 13, 2007 . . . New Orleans

Jeffrey Lurie stood with his hands in the pockets of his gray suit, not quite knowing for a moment where to go or what to say. He did know that the most important thing was simply for him to be there, so he stood quietly on the light-brown carpeting and surveyed the scene. He was surrounded by Philadelphia Eagles players, *his* Philadelphia Eagles players, glumly tossing their football gear into bags and dressing in front of bright red metal locker stalls. It was quiet in the locker room except for the low murmur of players talking in hushed tones to one another and to reporters, and the muffled roar, heard through the walls, of New Orleans Saints fans hollering and celebrating on their way out of the Louisiana Superdome.

It was 10:40 p.m., and the Eagles had just lost to the Saints in an NFC divisional playoff game. The story had played out as most of America had wanted, with the Saints moving on to the first NFC championship game in their history in their season of rebirth. They were a symbol of revival in New Orleans seventeen months after the city had been devastated by Hurricane Katrina, and this triumph came in the building that had housed so much human suffering in the days after the massive storm and the floods that followed it.

But that didn't ease the sting of defeat for the Eagles or Lurie, their owner. Their view at the moment wasn't so global. They'd had a storybook season unfolding, too. They'd won their previous six games after their season had looked to be in ruins. They'd overcome the loss of their seemingly irreplaceable quarterback, Donovan McNabb, to a season-ending knee injury to secure their fifth NFC East title in six years. They'd been riding the wondrously rejuvenated play of quarterback Jeff Garcia and had beaten their division rival, the New York Giants, on a last-second field goal in the first round of the playoffs. They'd been playing better, it had seemed, than anyone else in the NFC, and the Super Bowl had appeared within their reach. Now, that suddenly, their season was over. So, too, was the NFC East's season. Lurie's ownership counterparts within the division—the Giants' John Mara, the Washington Redskins' Daniel Snyder, and the Dallas Cowboys' Jerry Jones—already had experienced the empty, helpless, season-ending feeling that Lurie now felt.

It would go down as a pretty good 2006 season for the NFC East. After months of diligent planning and hard bargaining with agents to sign players and carefully craft rosters, the time for pay had, in the parlance of NFL players, given way to the time for play. The battle plans mostly had held up as three of the division's four teams reached the playoffs. The one that didn't, the Redskins, at least managed to be intriguing while losing, though Snyder had spent big money yet again to try to recapture the franchise's glorious past. But more had been expected. The division was thought to have been a powerhouse, and it wasn't. The NFC East teams managed only one playoff victory between them, the Cowboys losing in Seattle in excruciating fashion in the first round of the postseason in what would be Coach Bill Parcells's sendoff and the Eagles falling in New Orleans after beating the Giants.

The division had dominated the sport in the 1980s and '90s. In a span of fourteen years between the 1982 and 1995 seasons the Redskins,

Giants, and Cowboys combined to win eight Super Bowl titles. Between the 1990 and '93 seasons those three teams won four straight Super Bowls. It wasn't at that level now. Joe Gibbs, the Hall of Fame coach brought out of retirement by Snyder, had suffered through his second losing season in three years in his second go-around with the Redskins. His lavish spending of Snyder's money on assistant coaches and free agent players had produced a 5-11 record, a bitterly disappointing follow-up to reaching the second round of the playoffs the previous season. Jones's high-profile coach, Parcells, had done better. He'd managed to keep his emotions in check while dealing with exasperating wide receiver Terrell Owens. He'd unveiled a promising new starting quarterback in Tony Romo and had reached the playoffs for the second time in four seasons with the Cowboys. Still, what had begun as a Super Bowl–or-bust season had gone bust at the end. The three Super Bowl championships that Jones won with former coaches Jimmy Johnson and Barry Switzer were a fading memory, and Parcells was about to walk away from the Cowboys and perhaps from coaching, announcing sixteen days after the bitter playoff defeat in Seattle that he was retiring. And Giants owner Mara was saying his good-byes to his retiring general manager, Ernie Accorsi, who was heading to Florida to relax and watch spring training baseball games without knowing if the franchise-altering trade that he'd made for quarterback Eli Manning nearly three years before would be remembered as the crowning achievement or the defining mistake of his long front-office career.

The area in which all four owners were big winners was finances. The Redskins, Cowboys, and Eagles had been estimated to have franchise values of greater than $1 billion each in the latest *Forbes* magazine survey, and the Giants soon might surpass them all with the opening of the $1.4 billion (and the costs were rising all the time) stadium they were planning to build in New Jersey with the New York Jets. The Giants had been something akin to a mom-and-pop operation under Mara's late father Wellington, who had run the team for decades. They were such a conservative outfit that they didn't even have cheerleaders. Now, as Mara tried to figure out those ways in which he needed to emulate his legendary father and those in which he needed to change with the times and be his own man, he was about to start swimming in the waters occupied by Snyder, Jones, and the league's other money-making sharks.

The NFL had been through a year of upheaval. It not only lost its longtime commissioner, Paul Tagliabue, to retirement, but the owners also had bitter battles among themselves and with the players' union about how to divide the sport's annual revenues of around $6 billion. Tagliabue and his right-hand man and eventual successor, Roger Goodell, had worked with their usually close ally, union chief Gene Upshaw, to achieve a temporary cessation of hostilities with a labor and revenue-sharing settlement that the owners reluctantly approved to avoid a confrontation with the players. But many owners thought that Upshaw had outmaneuvered Tagliabue and Goodell this time around to craft a deal overly favorable to the players, and the tussles were sure to resume in the future. It was the one ominous black cloud in otherwise sunny skies for the country's most popular and prosperous sport. The NFL was a thriving league with new national television contracts worth nearly $4 billion per year. It was setting single-season attendance records on an annual basis. Stadiums were filled to 90 percent of capacity; only 7 of the 256 regular season games in 2006 were blacked out on TV in the local market of the home team for failing to sell out the required seventy-two hours in advance.

Tagliabue liked to downplay the sport's violent nature. He liked to say the game is so popular because it's about what he called "contrived adversity": Obstacles are put in front of teams, players, and coaches and they have to attempt to overcome them. It is, to Tagliabue, like an athletic soap opera in which no episode can be missed. But to ignore the attractiveness of the violence is to be in denial. Violence sells. Football's natural breaks in play make it the perfect sport for TV, true, but it is engrossing as an athletic metaphor for war. It's about ground acquisition and aerial attack. It's about covert intelligence. It is, as the saying goes, war without death. Most people cringe, and rightfully so, when players liken themselves in locker room interviews to soldiers heading off to war. It is insensitive and self-important. But really they are on to something.

That is only part of the NFL's successful formula, though. The people running the league have also implemented a brilliant business model. For decades, they've made certain that the teams are on relatively even economic footing, so everyone starts every season with a realistic chance to be the Super Bowl champion. The saying about how one team could beat another on "any given Sunday" actually is true. The entire sport has been set up to be a regression to the mean. Every team is dragged back toward average:

- By the draft, in which the worst teams pick before the better ones.
- By the scheduling formula, in which bad teams in one season play some of their out-of-division games the following season against other bad teams and good teams play other good ones.
- By free agency and the salary cap, which rip apart the rosters of the best clubs every offseason.

Maybe that makes for a diminished quality of play, but that is a difficult thing for the average fan to ascertain. That fan only knows that his or her favorite team is competitive with everyone else in the league and that is enough. The more teams that remain competitive and in playoff contention later in a season, the better it is for the league as a whole. It keeps fan interest high in more places all season. Free agency has given football the sort of offseason "hot stove" league, with players scurrying from team to team, that once had been baseball's exclusive domain. Fans now follow pro football feverishly year round. Even the practices for the Senior Bowl college all-star game and the scouting combine workouts have become TV events. The NFL has launched its own cable TV channel and put regular season games on it for the first time in the second half of the 2006 season.

But for the owners, it isn't enough to thrive economically en masse. Jerry Jones likes to say that no one got into NFL ownership for the money, and there are a thousand other ways for wealthy people to get better returns on such hefty investments. The owners had, in fact, made piles of money under Tagliabue, but Jones was at least partially right. Wealth wasn't enough. The owners also wanted the extra boost that came from winning football games. They were competitive people accustomed to success, and each of them wanted to have a toy shinier than the next guy's toy. They competed with their minds and wallets every bit as hard as their players competed with helmets and shoulder pads. Paul Allen cofounded Microsoft and was ranked by *Forbes* as the seventh-richest person in the world, with an estimated net worth of $21 billion, when the team that he owned, the Seattle Seahawks, qualified for the first Super Bowl in franchise history by beating the Carolina Panthers in the NFC title game in January 2006. But Allen sounded giddy and wide-eyed as a bug that day as he spoke while standing in the middle of the home locker room at Qwest Field. "I seem like a pretty mild-mannered guy," he said, "but inside I get like, 'Let's win this game. Let's *please* win this game.'

"Come on," he gushed, "we're talking about the Super Bowl here."

That was the euphoric feeling that Lurie, Mara, Jones, and Snyder wanted to have. If they hadn't felt it before, they wanted to feel it. If they had, they wanted to feel it again. Lurie's life was in most ways a spectacular success, but he still didn't know what it was like to stand in the winning locker room at the end of the final postseason game. Now as he looked around the somber, losing locker room in New Orleans he knew he would have to wait at least another year to find out.

A large section on one side of the room was for Eagles offensive players, and a smaller segment on the other side was assigned to the defense. The trainer's room was in between, where players hurt during the game were receiving treatment from the team's medical staff. The floor was littered with the large black travel bags assigned to the players on road trips, along with uniforms and the discarded white towels the players had been wearing after coming out of the showers. There were open trunks with notebooks and other supplies spilling out of them. Eagles linebacker Shawn Barber, who'd hurt his ankle during the game, stood on crutches, his foot in a walking boot.

Lurie gave guard Scott Young, who'd been forced to fill in for injured starter Shawn Andrews and had been called for a key penalty late in the game, a pat on the back. He shook a few hands and made his way toward the front of the locker room and an office with a sign on the door with an Eagles logo next to the green letters ANDY REID and the red letters ABSOLUTELY NO ADMITTANCE. Lurie asked Butch Buchanico, the Eagles security chief, who was standing outside the door, if Reid had made his way back from his postgame press conference. Buchanico nodded his head. Lurie ducked inside and sat on a chair commiserating with his head coach for fifteen minutes.

Joe Banner, the team president who'd been Lurie's friend since both were teenagers and had helped him build the division's smoothest-running organization, walked silently and swiftly through the locker room wearing gray slacks and a gray and red sweater. Offensive coordinator Marty Mornhinweg, already dressed and wearing a gray overcoat with a bag slung over his shoulder, passed Banner and spotted Garcia at his locker. Garcia was finishing putting on a blue pinstripe suit. He and Mornhinweg slapped hands and told each other it had been a good season despite the disappointing ending. Garcia walked away and hugged Buchanico on his way out the door. Lurie emerged from Reid's office and stopped momentarily in the middle of the locker room.

"I can't be more proud of this team," he said. "We came a couple plays away from the championship game. Great heart. Great character. It was a hard fight. Two very good teams played out there and one won by three points to get to the championship game. Two very good teams. This team was defined by its ability to play well when it had to in the last six games. That should serve us well in the future. We're pretty young. Our veterans are still terrific. It was a very gritty, courageous, tough team that was three points away from reaching the championship game for the fifth time in six years."

Lurie shrugged his shoulders. There wasn't much more to be said at the moment. He headed slowly out the door. A long and draining season was over.

PART 1

THE

PLANNING

JANUARY

CHAPTER

- 1 -

January 1, 2006 . . . Oakland

John Mara stood by the door to the locker room, wishing his father were there.

Since he wasn't, the Mara now running the New York Giants did what his father would have done: He greeted the Giants' players and coaches appreciatively after a big game. They were spilling into the dank, cramped visitors' locker room at McAfee Coliseum in Oakland. New Year's Eve was giving way to New Year's Day back home on the East Coast and the Giants had just beaten the Raiders to punctuate their 2005 season with an NFC East title. The room was barely big enough to hold all the people in the Giants' traveling party and it was impossible to move around without bumping into someone. The players were coming down from the emotional high of the competition and congratulating one another for the win. It hadn't been an easy season. The players had often been at odds with their taskmaster coach, Tom Coughlin. There had been ups and downs with their prized young quarterback, Eli Manning, in his first full season as a starter in the NFL. But now it felt like a successful season. The franchise last had been the division champion in the 2000 season and, like everyone else in the NFC East, had spent four seasons since then chasing the Philadelphia Eagles. For now at least the Giants had caught and surpassed the Eagles. They would be headed to the playoffs along with the Washington Redskins, while the Eagles and Dallas Cowboys were about to begin picking up the pieces.

Before the players dressed and packed hurriedly for their overnight trip home, Coughlin stood amid them and delivered his postgame speech. There was nothing to berate them for on this night. Coughlin told them they'd found a fitting way to honor the memories of Wellington Mara and Bob Tisch, the team's two co-owners who had died during the season.

John Mara found himself near tears as he listened. He had taken the helm of the franchise along with Tisch's son Steve and was shepherding the Giants toward a promising future. Plans for a new stadium in East Rutherford, New Jersey, were in the works and the Giants would become one of the league's wealthiest teams when it was built, as a club operating in the shadow of New York City rightfully should be. The jury was still out on whether Manning would become the player that general manager Ernie Accorsi had envisioned when he had mortgaged the team's future to trade for the youngest member of quarterbacking's first family on draft day in 2004, but at least Manning's season was looking like it would end up having more good than bad in it. Coughlin, the coach Mara had hired with his father's approval and Accorsi's help, created a contentious and stressful locker room environment and generated negative publicity, but at least he was winning. Coughlin and Accorsi didn't always agree, but Mara remembered what his father had told him: If his head coach and general manager always agreed, he wouldn't need both of them. Accorsi had postponed his planned retirement for another year. It should have been a night of pure triumph for Mara.

But it was also, inevitably, a bittersweet moment.

His father had died of cancer on October 25, 2005, at age eighty-nine. Wellington Mara was one of the most significant figures in the his-

tory of the NFL. At the annual league meeting in March, five months
after Mara's death, the NFL would rename its official game football
"The Duke," Mara's nickname. The same day, the U.S. House of
Representatives would pass House Resolution 517 recognizing the life
of Wellington Timothy Mara and "his outstanding contributions to the
New York Giants football club, the National Football League and the
United States." Wellington Mara had been associated with the Giants
since 1925, when he was a nine-year-old ball boy for the team owned
by his father, Timothy, who'd purchased the franchise that year for $500.
Joe Carr, the NFL's president, had wanted a showcase franchise in New
York and had offered it to fight promoter Billy Gibson. Gibson declined but introduced Carr to his friend Tim Mara, a successful promoter,
businessman, and bookmaker, a legal undertaking at the time. In 1930,
Tim Mara turned over the franchise to Wellington, then fourteen, and
Wellington's older brother Jack. Wellington Mara talked his father out
of making him go to law school after he graduated from Fordham
University and ended up being involved in the team's operations for
close to eighty years, the only interruption coming when he served in
the navy during World War II.

Most of the stories about Wellington Mara were about what a kind,
decent man he was. Many were told by John in a moving eulogy at his
father's funeral at St. Patrick's Cathedral. He told of the painful but
touching final days of his father's life. He told his parents' love story, saying he couldn't recall them ever raising their voices to one another.
"When my parents celebrated their fiftieth wedding anniversary about
a year and a half ago right here in St. Patrick's," he said, "my mother
asked him if they could renew their vows. He was very reluctant at first.
'The original ones haven't expired yet, have they?' he said. Of course,
he went along with it. But when Cardinal Egan asked him during the
ceremony, 'Will you accept children lovingly from God?' the look on his
face seemed to say, 'Your Eminence, I think that ship sailed a long
time ago.' "

He considered employees like family members and he'd look up former players and coaches while on road trips with the team. If a fan

wrote him a letter, he'd answer. Once, John was watching a game with his father. He became exasperated with a player and yelled out, "What is he doing out there?"

"What he's doing," his father said, "is the best that he can."

He served on just about every important NFL committee and was instrumental in determining how the league conducted its business. In the early sixties he and Jack agreed to share the league's television revenues equally with the other franchises even though a team in New York obviously had TV rights more valuable than those of a team in Pittsburgh or Green Bay. The greater good mattered to the Maras. Jack Mara died in 1965, and his son Tim became the team's co-owner. Wellington and Tim didn't coexist peacefully and the Giants, after losing the NFL championship game in 1963, didn't make the playoffs again until 1981. But the Maras, on the recommendation of then–NFL commissioner Pete Rozelle, hired George Young as their general manager in 1979 and the club thrived again, winning Super Bowls in the 1986 and 1990 seasons with Bill Parcells as its coach.

Two days before Wellington Mara died, the Giants overcame a 13-point fourth-quarter deficit to beat the Denver Broncos by a point at Giants Stadium. Manning threw the winning touchdown pass to wide receiver Amani Toomer with five seconds left. In the locker room after the game, one of Wellington Mara's grandsons, Conor, told Manning that his grandfather, watching the game from bed in Rye, New York, woke up and saw the Giants win, then went back to sleep with a smile on his face. The players chanted, "Duke! Duke! Duke!" in the locker room.

Mara had eleven children and, at the time of his death, forty grandchildren. In the days before his death he told family members that he didn't want to be a burden and they should go home and take care of their own children. The day before he went home, hardly able to talk and knowing his doctors could no longer help him, he held John's hand and told him that he knew he was headed to a better place. "I'll be there when you get there," he said to his son.

Mara's funeral was like a state funeral for the NFL. There was an overflow crowd. Giants players, coaches, and staff members arrived on seven chartered buses with a police escort. Jerry Jones, the owner of the Cowboys, was there along with his coach, Parcells. So were fellow NFL head coaches John Fox and Romeo Crennel, both former Giants assistants.

Five days after he died, the team that Wellington Mara had loved so much trounced the Redskins, 36–0, in Giants Stadium. Tailback Tiki Barber had two long runs during the game but didn't reach the end zone on either one. On the sideline, one of Mara's grandsons, Tim McDonnell, said to him, "Are you going to score a touchdown or are you going to keep teasing me?"

Barber had his career-best rushing day to that point and scored a touchdown later in the game with the Giants comfortably ahead. He held on to the ball and delivered it to McDonnell.

"Timmy," Barber told him, "this is for you, your grandfather, and your family. Thank you for everything you've done for me. I love you."

Scenes like that one ran through John Mara's mind in the locker room in Oakland as he walked around and shook hands. Finally he stopped in the middle of the room and said, "I'd rather have had my father standing here because he would have really enjoyed it. This was never his favorite franchise that we played today so I think he would have enjoyed this win."

What he didn't know was that the Giants had experienced their final victory of the season. Eight days later, they were overwhelmed by the Carolina Panthers in the first round of the NFC playoffs. Manning threw three interceptions and the Giants were shut out at home in a postseason game for the first time since 1943. The frustrations boiled over afterward. Barber told reporters that the Giants had been out-coached. Wide receiver Plaxico Burress skipped the team meeting the day after the game.

Barber met with Coughlin the day after the loss to discuss the postgame comments that he'd made. His tone was conciliatory.

"Tom, can you say we don't have the same thoughts, the same goals, the same ideals?" Barber said.

"No," Coughlin said.

"Whatever gets expressed outside this room doesn't really mean anything," Barber said.

Barber had felt a personal connection to Coughlin since one time during Coughlin's first season with the Giants in 2004 when Barber's son A.J. was sick. A.J. had a fever and was suffering from seizures, just as Tiki and his twin brother Ronde had as young children before growing out of it. Coughlin told Barber to put his family before football.

"If you need to go," Coughlin had told Barber, "go. If you need me to send people over there, I will."

Barber had known then that Coughlin the man was quite different from Coughlin the unyielding coach. But that didn't mean that coexisting professionally would be easy.

Barber would end up thinking that the 2005 Giants were the best team on which he'd played, better even than the version that reached the Super Bowl in the 2000 season before being crushed by the Baltimore Ravens. If only the injuries hadn't depleted the defense for the playoffs, Barber thought, these Giants could have gone far. They had begun the season not knowing if Manning would develop rapidly enough in his second pro season to transform the team into a contender and not knowing if Coughlin could get along with his players. They ended as division champs but, thanks to the bitter disappointment of the final game, still not knowing what the next step for Manning would be or whether Coughlin and the players could find a way to avoid being at each other's throats. It would be an intriguing offseason indeed. Mara's style was to stand to the side and let Accorsi shape the roster with help from Coughlin. Mara would offer input and sign the checks but basically stay out of the way. That made him far more like Eagles owner Jeffrey Lurie than like Jones or Redskins owner Daniel Snyder.

He would be a highly interested bystander in an offseason that would prove to reshape not only his team but the entire league.

CHAPTER

-2-

January 2 ... Philadelphia

Andy Reid walked down a hallway at the NovaCare Complex, the Eagles' lavish training facility in South Philadelphia just down Pattison Avenue, on the opposite side of Broad Street, from Lincoln Financial Field. The burly coach was headed toward the office of Brad Childress, his offensive coordinator. It was a Monday morning, the day after the Eagles' season had ended with a loss to the Redskins at the Linc that sent Joe Gibbs's team to the playoffs. The Eagles were accustomed to readying for the postseason at this time of year, but this year it wasn't happening. Their season had been undone by a string of controversies involving wide receiver Terrell Owens and a sports hernia that plagued, then sidelined, quarterback Donovan McNabb. Their 6-10 record was their worst in a season since they'd gone 5-11 in 1999, Reid's first year as their coach. Childress and Reid's other assistants were conducting the exit interviews with players that were part of each NFL coach's postseason routine.

Reid was going to deliver news that, for Childress, was good: The

Minnesota Vikings had called to request permission to interview him for their head coaching job. It was a formality. Under league rules, the Eagles couldn't block an assistant coach from interviewing for or accepting a head coaching position with another team. But it was part of the protocol for the Vikings to ask and for Reid to tell Childress he'd be hearing from the Vikings soon. For Reid, the development was a mixed bag. The Green Bay Packers and other teams were also interested in Childress as a head coaching candidate, and Reid knew that Childress almost certainly would get a job somewhere. His time had come. Other teams were looking to tap into the magic that Reid and his staff had worked while transforming the Eagles from a doormat into an almost annual Super Bowl contender. In previous years, timing had kept Childress off the head coaching market. The league's tampering rules kept an assistant coach on a team still participating in the playoffs from accepting a head coaching job with another franchise, and all the head coaching jobs generally had been filled by the time the Eagles were finished playing. They'd participated in four straight NFC championship games and one Super Bowl. This year, that wasn't an issue.

Reid was happy to see his protégé move up. Reid had prepared for the inevitability of losing him by having Marty Mornhinweg, the former head coach of the Detroit Lions who had worked with Reid in the college ranks as a graduate assistant and then again in Green Bay, on the staff as a replacement-in-waiting. But there would be a sense of loss both personally and professionally for Reid. Childress had been on Reid's original coaching staff in Philadelphia back when Reid and his assistants inherited a 3-13 team and worked in offices in the basement of the old Veterans Stadium, joking that the rats they encountered there were bigger than the cats living on the premises. Reid trusted Childress completely, having turned over the offensive play-calling duties to him for much of the second half of the 2005 season. The Eagles, more than any other team in the division, were an organization in which each of the decision-makers had a role and did what was expected and all the parts fit together nicely. It worked because the ruling triumvirate of owner Jeff Lurie, team president Joe Banner, and Reid made it work.

Lurie and Banner had a long history together. They grew up about a mile and a half from each other in Brookline, Massachusetts, and met as teenagers through a mutual friend who'd attended a summer camp in Maine with Banner and had been on a trip to Europe with Lurie. The friend invited Banner to watch a football game at Lurie's house. Lurie saw in Banner someone who shared his passion for sports, and they would talk about the things the Boston teams were doing. Lurie always would be amazed at how the Red Sox in those days routinely would pursue the big-name player and end up with a collection of stars that didn't fit together and didn't win while Red Auerbach would make moves for the Celtics that the fans didn't like but that worked and produced cohesive, winning teams. Lurie in particular remembered Auerbach being lambasted for trading down in the 1980 NBA draft, bypassing center Joe Barry Carroll to select a slow, white power forward while getting a seemingly useless center in the deal. The slow, white power forward was Kevin McHale and the seemingly useless center was Robert Parish. That taught Lurie something about paying too much attention to what the fans thought or what generated the splashiest headlines. Lurie always dreamed of owning and running a pro sports team. He had attended the first game in Patriots history on the day after his ninth birthday, watching them lose to Denver on September 9, 1960. His uncle played tennis regularly with Robert Kraft, who would end up owning the Patriots. Lurie's grandfather, Philip Smith, owned the General Cinema movie theater chain, and the family greatly increased its fortune with wildly successful investments in Harcourt General and the Neiman Marcus Group.

Lurie and Banner went their separate ways to college, Banner to Denison University in Granville, Ohio, and Lurie to get a bachelor's degree from Clark University, a master's in psychology from Boston University, and a Ph.D. in social policy from Brandeis. Lurie taught at Boston University before heading to Hollywood to produce movies, forming Chestnut Hill Productions in 1985 and churning out a string of forgettable films that included *Sweet Hearts Dance* in 1988 and *I Love You to Death* in 1990. Banner worked in Philadelphia as a sports producer and reporter for an AM radio station, WCAU. He went back to Boston and ran a retail clothing business with stores there and in Chicago. He worked for City Year, a national service organization.

He stayed in touch with Lurie and the two would meet up on vacation occasionally and play golf together for a couple days. They weren't best friends, but they were friends. Lurie still maintained his dream of buying a sports team. Banner knew about that but never had been given any indication by Lurie that he was part of that dream. Lurie tried to buy the Patriots, an effort that would end in failure when his old family friend, Kraft, won the bidding and purchased the franchise from James Orthwein in January 1994. By then, Lurie would be looking at more than one possibility. During the bidding on the Patriots, Lurie inquired about the Los Angeles Rams because he was living there at the time. He found out the Rams were interested in moving but not selling. During his talks with the Rams, team president John Shaw called him one day.

"You know, this team back east that's a really potentially good franchise, a good fan base, is going to be available," Shaw told Lurie. "Would you be interested?"

Eagles owner Norman Braman was interested in selling. Lurie indeed was interested. He began making calls. One of them was to his old pal Joe Banner. Banner got home from a vacation and had a message from Lurie.

"I have decided to really get serious and try to buy a professional sports team," Lurie said in the message. "I'd love to have you help me with it. Give me a call when you get back."

Banner called and said he was in. He didn't even bother to ask what he'd be doing or how much he'd be paid. Lurie told him about a few possibilities, including the Eagles. He knew Banner had worked in Philadelphia.

"Well, what do you think of that?" Lurie said.

"The good news, I think, as an owner or somebody who was helping to run a team, you won't be spending any time stirring up interest," Banner said. "It's really passionate. It's intense. It would be really exciting. But just realize it cuts both ways."

"I think this is one we should look into further," Lurie said.

So they did. Lurie and Banner spent plenty of time in New York living out of suitcases and hotel rooms while Lurie and his lawyers worked on both the Patriots and Eagles deals. By the time the Patriots deal fell through, Lurie was well into his negotiations with Braman for the Eagles. They reached an agreement in principle in April 1994 for Lurie to buy the team for about $195 million. Lurie was forty-two. Banner was forty-one. They had no idea what they were getting into.

Banner ran the day-to-day operations of the Eagles from the moment the other NFL owners approved Lurie's purchase in May 1994. He would get the title of team president in August 2001. Lurie and Banner hired Ray Rhodes as their coach in 1995 but fired him after a three-win season in '98. As they prepared to launch their next coaching search they decided to put their analytical abilities to use. They studied all the coaches in the history of the NFL who had led their teams to at least two Super Bowls. They pored over statistics and they called people who knew the coaches.

"Tell me what he's like," they'd say. "How does he manage? How does he think? How does he work? Who does he surround himself with?"

What they found, to their surprise, was that X's and O's were no predictor of great coaching success. Coaches had reached that level with all different ways of playing the game. It didn't matter if you hired an offensive-oriented coach or a defensive-oriented coach, a coach who ran the ball or threw the ball, a coach who blitzed on defense or played it safe. There was no commonality among the great coaches in those areas; it was all over the board. But when it came to the descriptions of the person, that was an entirely different story. It was as if everyone they'd contacted had been talking about the same person: He was a phenomenal leader. He was obsessed with detail to the point of being anal-retentive, so much so that he drove everyone around him crazy. He was open to input but had certain convictions that he wouldn't abandon even in the face of heavy criticism. He placed incredible importance on having the right people around him on his coaching staff. Lurie and Banner were running their coaching search like they were FBI profilers. They had their list of personality traits. Now all they had to do was find someone who possessed them, something that perhaps would be easier said than done. They weren't looking for the hot offensive or defensive coordinator. They were looking for the right leader.

They started making calls about coaches. One person on their list was Andy Reid, a little-known quarterbacks coach from the Packers whom the Eagles had considered as an offensive coordinator candidate when Jon Gruden had left Rhodes's staff following the '97 season. The people they asked about Reid said that he'd be a great head coach someday but it was a couple years too soon to hire him. Wait a second, Lurie and Banner said to one another. First of all, how did everyone really know exactly when the guy would start being a good head coach? And even if it did take Reid a couple years to reach that point, so what? The Eagles probably wouldn't be ready to be a good team until then anyway.

They brought in Reid for an interview. He was a lumpy former offensive lineman at Brigham Young University who had once dreamed of being a sportswriter, a decidedly modest goal, but he made quite an impression. He walked in with a binder full of lists and notes that he'd compiled over the years about how he'd run a team as a head coach, how he'd win a championship. The notes covered everything from travel plans to marketing ideas. Reid's binder was a blueprint for getting to a Super Bowl, something he had experienced twice as a Packers assistant coach under Mike Holmgren. Talk about anal-retentive. Reid had lists of the top ten coaches, in his view, at each position. Talk about valuing his staff. Lurie wanted a coach who would be able to work with everyone in the organization, from the football staff to the marketing staff. He wanted someone who would work hard and be upbeat. He also wanted someone who was tough-minded.

"A coach has to make a lot of hard decisions and a lot of unpopular ones," Lurie told Reid during the seven or so hours they and Banner spent together during the interview process. "You're going to replace popular players."

Reid said he was willing to make the tough choices and Lurie and Banner believed him. They had their man. Reid's own team, the Packers, didn't consider him head coaching material at that point, but Lurie and Banner were sure of it. It just fit too perfectly, and Reid was a classy guy on top of it all. They picked Reid over more celebrated candidates like Jim Haslett and Dom Capers.

"I have never been this sure of something," Banner told his friends, "and ended up being wrong."

Looking back eight years later, Banner would marvel at how on-target Reid's coaching lists had been. No one had ever heard at the time of Ron Rivera, who would go on to be the highly successful defensive coordinator of the Chicago Bears, but he was on one of Reid's lists. Reid didn't hire Rivera, but he did hire Jim Johnson as his defensive coordinator and Childress as his quarterbacks coach, later promoting him to offensive coordinator. "What Andy interviewed to be and what attracted us to him and what we were looking for in this profile," Banner said, "is exactly who he's been every minute of every day."

There was no way for Lurie and Banner to sell their selection to Eagles fans. They didn't even try. They were accused of hiring Reid because he was inexpensive. Reid would have to sell himself eventually by winning. Lurie had hoped his new coach, whichever coach he chose, would want to use the second overall pick in the 1999 draft possessed by the Eagles on a quarterback. Lurie thought you couldn't pass up an opportunity to draft a prospective franchise quarterback. So he was pleased when Reid decided to select McNabb, a quarterback from Syracuse, even though Eagles fans who wanted the team to go with Texas tailback Ricky Williams booed the choice. The Eagles went 5-11 under Reid in 1999 but went 11-5 and reached the playoffs in 2000 and won the first of their four straight division titles in 2001.

Lurie and Banner didn't only want to have a winning football team. They wanted to have the most creative marketing approach in the league. They wanted to have the best team Web site. They wanted to have the best stadium. They tried to be innovative. They were the first team to have "NFL Experience" props and games for fans at their training camp. They were the first to sell the naming rights to their training facility, the first to create a foundation that not only gave out grants but ran nonprofit programs. They wanted to create an environment in which employees felt empowered to make decisions and take some risks—smart, calculated risks—without fear of being second-guessed, unduly criticized, or fired. Lurie preached stability and Banner was among the very best executives in the league. He looked far more like a banker than a football guy, but he had a hand in virtually everything the Eagles did from business operations to player acquisitions. He oversaw the team's moves into its $37 million training facility and its $512 million stadium. He was the keeper of the salary cap. He planned for the draft with Reid and Reid's right-hand man in the front office, Tom Heckert. He loved trying to fit the pieces together properly to form a successful NFL team.

Reid had the final say over player-related decisions but was fully in sync with those in his front office. Decisions were made by consensus and Reid rarely if ever invoked his final-say authority. The Eagles developed a strategy of building through the draft, focusing especially on the offensive and defensive lines, and re-signing their own young players long before they reached free agency. Banner spoke of having a good batting average. You didn't need to be right all the time about players. There were no set numbers. But you had to be right more often than your competitors were and you had to be right more often when you were handing out a $10 million signing bonus than when you were handing out a $3 million signing bonus. Free agent signings were for supplementing the building being done with draft picks. Lurie wanted his football people to make sure they were finding ascending players, not descending players with bigger names and higher profiles. The Eagles became known as conservative in their salary cap management, but Banner bristled at the notion that they didn't take risks. They once signed cornerback Troy Vincent when he was coming off major knee surgery for a torn anterior cruciate ligament. They once signed right tackle Jon Runyan and made him the second-highest-paid offensive tackle in all of football and by far the highest-paid right tackle. They once traded for defensive end Hugh Douglas when people in the New York Jets organization were bad-mouthing him. They once drafted middle linebacker Jeremiah Trotter when about two dozen other NFL teams had flunked him on their physicals because of his creaky knees. They hired Reid. "We think of ourselves as risk-takers—educated," Banner said. "We're not wild, crazy, uninformed risk-takers. But we're not afraid."

And, of course, they traded for Owens before the 2004 season. "We will pass, I would say, one hundred percent of the time if we think there are some issues around a player," Lurie said. "The one exception was Owens. We didn't think they were disciplinary problems. We just thought, you know, he was a little crazy at the time. But we soon learned that it was more complicated than that."

The Owens move had come after the Eagles had lost their first three appearances in the NFC title game under Reid. Each defeat had been more agonizing than the one before it. The final two had come at home, but Lurie remained supportive. After the Eagles lost the title game to the Carolina Panthers to end their 2003 season in demoralizing fashion, Lurie addressed first his players and then his coaches and told Reid and the other members of the staff that they'd done the best coaching job he'd seen as the owner of the team. Still, it was time for the Eagles to stop doing business as usual. Before the 2004 season they made two un-characteristically high-profile and risky acquisitions, signing brittle de-fensive end Jevon Kearse as a free agent and trading for Owens. The 2004 Eagles lapped the field in the NFC East, winning 13 of their first 14 games and finishing 13-3 while the Redskins, Giants, and Cowboys each went 6-10. They cruised through the playoffs even with Owens sidelined by a high ankle sprain that required surgery. They met the Atlanta Falcons in the NFC title game at Lincoln Financial Field on a blustery day after a snowstorm with temperatures in the teens and 35-mph wind gusts. The players felt they'd been tight before the title game defeat to the Panthers the previous year and didn't want a repeat, so Douglas staged a dance party in the trainer's room about forty-five min-utes before game time. One of the participants was Lurie. The Eagles beat the Falcons easily, and the players who had been around the longest seemed to feel even better for Reid than they did for themselves.

That had been one of the last happy moments for the Eagles as a group. Owens returned early from his injury and gave a splendid performance in the Super Bowl, but McNabb was erratic and the Eagles lost to the Patriots by three points. There was no reason to think in the immediate aftermath of the game that the Eagles wouldn't be back in another Super Bowl in a year. But Owens soon began taking verbal shots at the organization and at McNabb, and tried unsuccessfully to get the team to rework his seven-year, nearly $49 million contract after one season. His antics eventually led the Eagles to suspend him for four games without pay seven games into the 2005 season, then deactivate him for the final five games of the season. McNabb's season was cut short when surgery was required for his sports hernia. When Brian Westbrook suffered a season-ending foot injury, the Eagles were left with Mike McMahon instead of McNabb at quarterback, rookie Ryan Moats instead of Westbrook at tailback, and rookie Reggie Brown playing for Owens at wide receiver. The defense stayed healthier but didn't play well either.

Yet the Eagles weren't panicking now as the offseason began. It was time, they thought, to get back to their guiding principles. So to Reid, losing a cog in such a generally smooth-running machine wasn't pleasant. He popped his head into Childress's office and delivered the news about the Vikings' interest. Vikings owner Zygi Wilf had told his coach, Mike Tice, the previous day that Tice's contract wouldn't be renewed. By Tuesday, two days after the regular season, there would be seven other teams looking for head coaches. In all, ten NFL clubs would end up opening the 2006 season with new head coaches.

Childress's phone rang just as he was finishing his final exit interview. He answered and found himself on a conference call with Zygi Wilf and Wilf's brother Mark. After introductions and pleasantries, the Wilfs told Childress that they wanted to interview him for the Vikings' head coaching job. Childress said that would be wonderful; he just had to tie up a few loose ends in Philadelphia and he'd be there as soon as possible.

"How about Wednesday?" he said.

"We were thinking dinner tonight," came the reply.

"Tonight?" Childress said. He was ready for head coaching interviews but not specifically one with the Vikings. He wondered if the Wilfs merely wanted to see how he held his fork. He'd have little more to offer them at this point.

"We just want to get to know you," the Wilfs said.

Childress wasn't going to argue with his prospective new bosses. He headed to his house, shaved, put some things into a bag, and got a ride to the airport. He had dinner with the Wilfs that night. He met former Vikings coaching great Bud Grant, who told the Wilfs that Childress was their man. The Wilfs put on the full-court press. Childress canceled an interview with the Packers that was to come Wednesday and by Thursday his agent, Bob LaMonte, had negotiated a five-year contract for him to be Tice's successor.

The Vikings also were looking for a front office chief and seemed interested in hiring Heckert to work with Childress. But the Eagles moved quickly to make sure that wouldn't happen by promoting Heckert from vice president of player personnel to general manager. Heckert was staying put. Reid carried out his plan and made Mornhinweg Childress's successor as offensive coordinator.

The coaching carousel was spinning, just as it did after every NFL season. Dan Snyder went to work spending money on coaches even before the Redskins' season ended with a playoff loss in Seattle in an NFC semifinal. The NFL has a salary cap for players but none for coaches, and Snyder took full advantage. He'd learned since becoming the Redskins' owner in 1999, through the school of hard knocks, that it didn't matter how much money he spent on players if he didn't have the right coaches. Gibbs was among the league's highest-paid coaches at $5.7 million per season. Gibbs's top defensive assistant, Gregg Williams, was on the verge of becoming a popular head coaching candidate around the league, but Snyder kept him off the market by signing him to a three-year, $7.8 million contract. The deal gave Williams the use of a luxury suite at FedEx Field and included a $1 million bonus that Williams would receive if he didn't end up succeeding Gibbs as the head coach. That way Williams would eventually cash in, either by becoming the Redskins' next head coach or by depositing another Snyder check into his bank account. Other owners wouldn't be happy with Snyder for shattering the league's salary structure for coaches yet again. Williams would end up earning more than about one-third of the head coaches in the league in 2006. But what did Snyder care? Williams had nearly complete autonomy to run a defense that had been the key component in the team's run to the playoffs. Snyder had the money to spend. The salary made sense within the parameters of the Redskins' finances, and Snyder certainly didn't want to go back to losing games and being disliked by his own team's followers, in addition to being mocked by the national media and loathed by fans in other cities.

Williams knew he was taking himself off the market in a year in which he likely would have landed a head coaching job. Representatives of five teams had called Williams's former boss with the Buffalo Bills, Tom Donahoe, to ask about him as a head coaching candidate. Williams wanted to prove at some point that he could be a better head coach than he'd been in Buffalo, where he'd compiled a 17-31 record in three seasons before rehabilitating his reputation with the Redskins under Gibbs. But what was the rush? Snyder's offer was so overwhelming, Williams couldn't say no. Making offers that couldn't be refused was Snyder's negotiating modus operandi. When he signed wide receiver Laveranues Coles as a restricted free agent from the Jets in the spring of 2003, Snyder offered Coles a contract with a signing bonus of $13 million. That was $3 million more than Coles and his agent, Roosevelt Barnes, had been seeking in their negotiations with the Jets. When Barnes called Coles to tell him about Snyder's offer, Coles screamed into the phone, "Call him back before he changes his mind!"

Snyder had raised the salary bar to get his last two head coaches, Steve Spurrier and Gibbs. He'd raised it to get $1-million-a-year defensive coordinator Marvin Lewis for Spurrier and now to keep Williams for Gibbs. But he wasn't done. The Redskins made another big move to bolster Gibbs's coaching staff soon after losing to the Seahawks. The team's offense had sputtered badly in its two playoff games, particularly in a first-round victory in Tampa over the Buccaneers. Gibbs went out and got Al Saunders to be the Redskins' offensive boss and used Snyder's checkbook to sign him to a three-year deal worth $6 million. Saunders had interviewed for Oakland's head coaching job but his deliberations with the Raiders hadn't gotten very far, so he, like Williams, took himself off the head coaching market and signed up for Daniel M. Snyder's assistant coaching multimillionaires' club. Each of the Redskins' coordinators would make far more during the 2006 season than the NFL's reigning coach of the year, the Bears' Lovie Smith, whose $1.35 million salary was the lowest among the league's head coaches. The Saunders move was significant not only because of the amount of money that Snyder was spending but also because Gibbs was giving up control of the offense—*his* offense—to another coach. Gibbs traditionally had turned over responsibility for the defense to an assistant. Years ago it had been Richie Petitbon and now it was Williams. But the offense had always been his. This was a major step for him. Gibbs had gone to Saunders's home in Leawood, Kansas, and had told Saunders that he needed help. The offense's failure in Tampa during the playoffs had demonstrated that, Gibbs told Saunders. The get-together went late into the night and the deal for Saunders to join Gibbs's staff was struck around 1 a.m.

The Cowboys lost their top offensive assistant when Sean Payton was hired as the head coach of the New Orleans Saints. Payton took Cowboys linebackers coach Gary Gibbs with him as his defensive coordinator. But the Cowboys wouldn't be losing Bill Parcells. Parcells was three seasons into the four-year, $18 million contract that he'd signed when Jerry Jones had lured him out of retirement in 2003. He'd just had a trying season in which he'd lost his younger brother Don to brain cancer and had watched the Cowboys miss the playoffs for a second straight year with a record of 9-7. The annual rumors about Parcells's retiring were flying around the league. Those who thought Parcells might exit were focusing on the fact that he'd had a disappointing, draining season. But what they ignored was that Parcells truly liked the players on this team and thought they were a diligent, hardworking bunch. They also ignored the fact that Parcells had been left with little in his life but football. He enjoyed spending time with his grandchildren, but his marriage had broken up before he'd taken the Cowboys job—he and his wife Judy divorced in 2002 after forty years of marriage—and now his brother was gone. Some of his close associates thought he was clinging to football tighter than ever.

Parcells agreed with Jones to extend his contract by a year, through the 2007 season. Under the new deal Parcells's salary would jump to $5 million in 2006 and $6 million in 2007. Parcells evaluated his health and energy level after every season. He had enough money and he'd promised himself that he wouldn't fool himself when the time came to walk away from coaching again. But he felt he'd been treated fairly in Dallas. He still felt energized and challenged. He thought the Cowboys could have been a 12-win team if they'd kicked a few more field goals at the right times. He wanted to keep going. He signed the extension because he didn't want to be viewed, especially by players thinking of signing with the Cowboys, as a lame-duck coach entering his last season. That wasn't good for business.

The Giants thought they might lose their defensive coordinator, Tim Lewis, to a head coaching job. He interviewed with the Jets, Packers, Lions, and St. Louis Rams. Lewis was qualified. That hadn't been enough for much of the NFL's history for an assistant coach who was black, like Lewis, to earn a promotion. But the league had been pushing for three years to improve its minority hiring record. In late 2002, attorneys Johnnie Cochran and Cyrus Mehri had issued a scathing report about the NFL's dismal hiring record with minority head coaches and had threatened to sue the league if it didn't take action. Commissioner Paul Tagliabue and the owners responded by enacting a rule requiring each team with a head coaching vacancy to interview at least one minority candidate. The league had formed a workplace diversity committee headed by Pittsburgh Steelers owner Dan Rooney; the interviewing rule became widely known as the Rooney Rule. The efforts of Cochran and Mehri had led to the formation of a group called the Fritz Pollard Alliance, named for the first black head coach in NFL history in the 1920s, to promote diversity within the league.

The league had an all-time-high six African-American head coaches in the 2005 season, up from two in the season before the Rooney Rule went into effect. John Wooten, the chairman of the Fritz Pollard Alliance, figured that the Rams job would come down to Lewis and Ron Rivera and the Lions job would come down to Lewis and Steelers offensive line coach Russ Grimm. He was wrong. The Rams hired Miami Dolphins offensive coordinator Scott Linehan and the Lions hired Buccaneers defensive line coach Rod Marinelli. Only two of the ten head coaches hired league-wide in the hiring cycle were black, increasing the number of minority head coaches in the league to seven. Wooten thought the interviewing rule was being followed and working as it should, but he was troubled because league officials told him that the owners had not been as involved in hiring their teams' coaches this time around as they'd been in the past. That, Wooten was promised, would change. In the meantime, the Giants still had their defensive coordinator, and teams around the league could stop worrying about reshuffling coaches and start focusing on the potential comings and goings of players.

But first some bigger problems had to be solved.

CHAPTER

-3-

January 9 ... New York

Gene Upshaw felt the clock ticking.

The executive director of the NFL Players Association, once a guard for the Oakland Raiders whose playing exploits had landed him in the Hall of Fame, always had been able to work smoothly with Commissioner Paul Tagliabue to craft the sport's next collective bargaining agreement long before any hint of labor strife was on the horizon. Labor peace had become a major ingredient in the NFL's winning formula.

But this time, Upshaw knew, things were different. The issues were tougher. The money was bigger. More was at stake.

It was a Monday and Upshaw had traveled to New York for a bargaining session. He'd been hopeful of some progress since this meeting had come on the heels of a break in negotiations. But there had been no breakthroughs. Not even close. Both sides seemed to be getting entrenched in their bargaining positions.

"They would tell you they made a significant move with their offer,"

Upshaw said. "In our view they didn't move at all. To us, we're just re-arranging the deck chairs on the *Titanic*."

The NFL was riding higher than any sports league in history. Its king-of-the-hill status had just been reinforced by a new set of national television contracts with Fox, CBS, NBC, ESPN, and DirecTV. The NBC and ESPN deals had been completed in April 2005, about five months after the Fox, CBS, and DirecTV contracts had been hammered out. The deals brought the NFL a substantial increase over the rights fees it had been earning from its previous set of TV contracts. The league would earn an average of more than $3.7 billion per season from the new contracts, or roughly $117 million per team annually, up from about $2.8 billion in the 2005 season under the old deals.

When the league launched this round of TV negotiations, industry analysts had maintained that the networks couldn't afford another sub-stantial increase in rights fees. But this was the NFL. It found a way not only to make the network executives believe they could afford it but also to convince them that they simply *had* to have the product the league was offering. Fox increased its annual rights fee for NFC games on Sunday afternoons from $550 million to $712.5 million. CBS upped its rights fee for Sunday afternoon AFC games from $500 million to $622.5 million per year. Those six-year contract extensions would run from the 2006 through the 2011 season. DirecTV extended its contract for its Sunday Ticket satellite package for five years through the 2010 season and agreed to increase its annual rights fee from $400 million to $700 million. ESPN took over Monday night games from ABC beginning in 2006. ESPN agreed to pay $1.1 billion per season in the eight-year contract, double the $550 million ABC had been paying. NBC got the Sunday night package formerly possessed by ESPN, and in a six-year contract beginning in 2006 agreed to pay the same $600 million per sea-son ESPN had been paying.

In early 2006, the league decided it would, for the first time, show regular season games on the TV channel it owned, the NFL Network, beginning that fall. The two-year-old channel had carried only presea-son games to that point. The league had been shopping an eight-game

package of prime-time games on Thursday and Saturday nights to other
networks. But in the end Tagliabue and the owners decided to keep the
games for themselves. They decided they had enough money from TV
rights fees; what they really needed was an asset. This way Tagliabue and
the owners hoped they could get the NFL Network into far more U.S.
households than the approximately 35 million it was in at the time and
perhaps make cable and satellite companies pay more for the channel.

Even so, there remained that storm cloud on the NFL's horizon.
There were two fights about to take place, one pitting owners against
owners and the other pitting owners against players. The twin tussles
promised to be far nastier and more problematic than any that the sport
had seen for quite some time.

That's what had Upshaw worried.

For decades, the owners had operated on the premise that keeping
the teams on a relatively even financial footing was good for the competitive balance of the league, which in turn was good for the overall
product that the owners were selling to the public. The all-for-one, one-
for-all business model was held sacrosanct by the league's old-guard
owners. If the Green Bay Packers could compete evenly with the New
York Giants, the reasoning went, more fans in more cities would watch
and become hooked on the sport and every team would have a chance
to be successful both on the field and on the accounting ledger. The owners didn't want football to disintegrate like baseball into a sport of
"have" and "have-not" franchises in which the New York Yankees and
Boston Red Sox far outearned and outspent everyone else and only a
handful of teams began each year with realistic hopes of being the final
club left celebrating at the end of the season. When the 2006 Major
League Baseball season began, the Yankees had a player payroll of $195
million and the Florida Marlins had one of $15 million. That didn't
mean that the Yankees would win the World Series, but it certainly gave
them a greater margin for error to outspend their player evaluation mistakes. The NFL didn't want any of its teams to have such a buffer.

In the NFL the teams shared revenues from national TV and radio
contracts and national sponsorships equally. They pooled and evenly

split the visiting club's one-third portion of the gate receipts from each game. Each team received an equal portion of a 12 percent royalty on every NFL-branded piece of merchandise sold. After that, the clubs were pretty much on their own. When owners like Jerry Jones and Dan Snyder came into the sport, they found ways to exploit revenue streams they didn't have to share with the other teams. Snyder was particularly adept at maximizing locally generated revenues from sources such as stadium naming rights, luxury suites, local sponsorships, and local TV and radio deals. Under Snyder, the Redskins' annual revenues roughly tripled between 1999 and 2005. In September 2005, *Forbes* magazine estimated the Redskins' worth at $1.264 billion. *Forbes* listed the Cowboys next at $1.063 billion, the New England Patriots third at $1.04 billion, and the Eagles fourth at $952 million. The Giants, at $806 million, came in seventeenth, but that was sure to change with the opening of their new stadium. Jones also had a new stadium on the way for the Cowboys. *Forbes* listed the Redskins' annual revenues at a league-leading $287 million, with an operating income (defined as earnings before interest, taxes, and depreciation) of $53.8 million. The Cowboys actually were listed as having a higher income, $54.3 million, on revenues of $231 million. The Eagles were said to have revenues of $216 million and an income of $24.5 million, and the Giants to have revenues of $175 million and income of $26.7 million. The league averages were $188 million in revenues and income of $32.4 million. The average franchise value was $819 million. The Arizona Cardinals were estimated to have the lowest revenues at $153 million.

The revenue disparities, to that point, had not resulted in competitive disparities between teams on the field, but some owners were worried about the eventual result if the revenue gap continued to widen. The Redskins had nearly doubled what the teams on the low end of the revenue-generating spectrum were making. The salary cap kept Snyder's spending on players somewhat in check, but the cap was a flexible spending limit that could be exceeded, and Snyder usually could fix his cap problems by throwing even more cash at them via reworking players' contracts. There was no restraint on his spending on coaches. When

Snyder started throwing money at coaches to assemble Joe Gibbs's all-star staff, to some owners it was as if he was rubbing it in. They wanted a revised revenue-sharing system to transfer more money to lower-revenue franchises. The system had to change with the times, they contended. Snyder, Jones, and the owners of other high-revenue teams felt they shouldn't have to subsidize clubs that might be poorly managed and failing to take advantage of their revenue opportunities.

Jones liked to point out that owners like Snyder and the Houston Texans' Robert McNair had paid huge prices for their franchises and had immense debt service payments to make. They'd spent money to make money and they shouldn't be penalized for that. Jones warned the union to be wary of seeking drastic changes to a system under which the players had flourished financially. Having a system in which the teams that were the best money-makers had to give away too much of those funds would be a disincentive for owners to find new and creative ways to bring revenues into the league. Upshaw responded by telling the owners of high-revenue teams that if they believed some franchises were being mismanaged, they and the league should fix the problem by eliminating the nonperformers.

"You should do what you do to the players and cut them," Upshaw told Jones at an owners' meeting in Detroit in October 2004.

The collective bargaining agreement between the owners and players was due to expire after the draft in the spring of 2008. It would keep the sport's existing salary cap system in place through the 2006 season, then there would be a season without a salary cap in 2007 before the labor deal expired. The owners and players had extended the deal seamlessly in every set of negotiations since the existing system of free agency and the salary cap had first been put in place in 1993. Tagliabue and Upshaw saw eye to eye on most issues and worked closely to fortify the sport together. Tagliabue kept Upshaw in the loop on all big decisions, and many in the league regarded Upshaw as a virtual co-commissioner. Upshaw was derided in some circles for his cozy relationship with Tagliabue. Marvin Miller, the former head of the Major League Baseball Players Association who had built that organization into one of the most powerful and combative unions in America, liked to dismiss Upshaw as a pro-management unionist.

But whereas Miller was an idealist, Upshaw was a realist. Upshaw's view was that if he and Tagliabue could work together to make the league as successful as possible and he could guarantee his players a fair piece of the revenue pie, he was doing right by his constituents. He and Tagliabue had worked together to put the NFL on top of the nation's sports heap. They'd made a lot of people involved in the game a lot of money. The average NFL player's salary reached just under $1.4 million in 2005; for starting players the average salary was $2.259 million. The minimum player's salary in 2005 was $230,000 for a rookie all the way up to $765,000 for a ten-year veteran. Some observers decried the lack of guaranteed contracts in football. If a baseball player suffered a career-ending injury one season into a ten-year contract, his team owed him his salaries for the nine seasons left on the deal. That wasn't the case in football. A player was bound by his contract and couldn't leave for another team in the middle of it, but he could be released by his team without the team's having to pay him his prescribed salaries for future seasons. Union officials, though, had calculated that guaranteed income, mostly in the form of signing bonuses, had increased to the point where it represented about half of total player compensation in the league, and Tagliabue made the argument that more guaranteed income would be bad for the players as a whole. Guaranteed contracts, he maintained, gave money to players who weren't deserving of it at the expense of players who did deserve it. Tagliabue thought the NFL's way better rewarded players for their performances.

The relationship between the league and its players hadn't always been so good. The NFL Players Association was formed in 1956, and a series of lockouts and strikes followed. The acrimony between labor and management intensified in the early 1980s. An eight-week strike in 1982 produced a five-year labor agreement, but there was a twenty-four-day strike in '87. One week of games was lost and the owners played three weeks of games with replacement players. The players sued the league over free agency restrictions. The litigation, bearing the name of

Eagles defensive end Reggie White, was settled in 1993 with a labor deal that put the existing system of free agency and the salary cap in place. The deal was extended in 1998 and 2002. Upshaw believed the sport's labor strife in the past had resulted from the owners and players never talking to one another until they absolutely had to do so, when a dispute was already brewing. He and Tagliabue took the opposite approach. They talked constantly. Once a labor deal was completed they started immediately on the next one. Negotiations didn't really begin and end. They were going on all the time.

Upshaw respected that Tagliabue didn't talk down to the players. A former college basketball player at Georgetown who'd become a labor attorney, Tagliabue had joined the NFL in 1969. He'd experienced the league's labor strife in the seventies and eighties. There had not been a single work stoppage since he'd succeeded Pete Rozelle as commissioner in 1989, and Tagliabue listed that as being among his greatest accomplishments. He'd learned not only from Rozelle but also from the owners who'd made sacrifices as the league grew. He'd heard the stories about the early days of the New York Jets (first called the New York Titans) when the crowds were so sparse that it would have been easier to introduce the fans to the players than the players to the fans. He'd been told stories by Buffalo Bills owner Ralph Wilson about having to loan money to the Raiders in the early 1960s to keep them in business. He likened it to having parents who'd lived through the Great Depression and survived to see better days. The lesson, he thought, was: Enjoy but don't forget.

The owners' new revenue streams weren't something the union's leaders had just noticed. They'd seen years earlier that the most resourceful owners were finding new ways to make money. Upshaw and his top lieutenant, union general counsel Richard Berthelsen, took a wait-and-see approach at first, not wanting to ask the owners to surrender too much of that new money too soon. They wanted the Joneses and Snyders of the world to have time and incentive to fully develop those revenue streams for their own gain. To Upshaw there was one constant about the economics of the NFL: The owners would always find new ways to make money. It was up to him to make certain that the union kept up in getting the players their share.

The players already were getting 40 to 45 percent of the new revenues under a "spillover" provision in the collective bargaining agreement. The players thus were doing better than the owners of the lower-revenue teams who weren't sharing at all in the new revenues. But as this labor negotiation officially got started, Upshaw decided it was time to go after the new revenues and get the players their full share of them under the salary cap system. It wouldn't be business as usual. At the opening bargaining session, Upshaw introduced the concept of "total football revenues" to the owners and said that the players wanted at least 60 percent of the expanded revenue pool. Under the existing salary cap system, the players were receiving 65.5 percent of a smaller revenue pool, called "defined gross revenues," in the 2005 season. They were to receive 64.5 percent of that revenue pool in 2006. How much money was at stake? In 2006 dollars, it was about $350 million. Under the existing system, the thirty-two teams were slated to devote $113 million apiece to players' salaries and benefits in 2006 (the salary cap was to be set at $92 million to $95 million, and the rest would be in benefits). Under the setup Upshaw was seeking, that number would be $124 million.

As the negotiations progressed, Upshaw would come to wonder if the owners thought that his demand was merely an opening bargaining position from which he eventually would retreat significantly. He didn't. He didn't drop his demand below 60 percent of total football revenues until the final hours of negotiations, and even then he would compromise only to 59.5 percent. The owners quickly agreed to the concept that players should share in all the revenues. Their initial bargaining approach was to allow the salary cap to be based on total football revenues but to lower the percentage of the new revenue pool enough for total player compensation to remain about the same. Upshaw was having none of that. What bothered him most of all was that about half of the high-revenue teams weren't devoting what Upshaw regarded as a fair share of their revenues to paying their players. Snyder certainly didn't fall into that category. His Redskins spent plenty on players. But Jones was, in the union's view, among the worst offenders. In the data of "cash over cap" spending (the amount of money that teams spent on players above the flexible salary cap), it didn't seem to matter what time frame you picked; the Cowboys always seemed to rank next-to-last ahead of only the Cincinnati Bengals. Yet Jones would tell Upshaw and Berthelsen, "I'm good for you. Look at all the revenues I bring in. Don't call for a change in the system that hurts me."

It wasn't only Jones who griped to Upshaw. The union boss heard the same objection from every owner of a high-revenue team. They all thought the low-revenue franchises merely wanted handouts.

"All they want," the high-revenue owners told Upshaw repeatedly, "is for me to write a check."

Upshaw and Berthelsen always knew the labor and revenue-sharing deals were inextricably connected and would have to come simultaneously. Otherwise, the low-revenue teams couldn't afford the increased salary cap obligations to the players and wouldn't vote for the labor agreement. Tagliabue knew it, too. A labor deal would need twenty-four votes among the thirty-two owners to be approved. But Jones and other owners kept insisting they could do a labor deal first and worry about the revenue-sharing issue later. When the union brought up revenue-sharing concerns during the labor negotiations, the league's standard response was that revenue-sharing was an internal matter for the owners. That would remain the owners' stance until the final stages of negotiations.

For now Upshaw knew only that it was the new year and he was getting restless. He and Tagliabue were going to make a push to wrap everything up by March, but time was running short.

"I can't believe we're sitting here and it's already January," he said, "and it's still not done."

January 24 ... Mobile, Alabama

Ladd-Peebles Stadium's artificial turf field was tucked away in a quaint neighborhood amid tree-lined streets, surrounded by hedges and a chain-link fence. It was a sunny, pleasantly breezy Tuesday afternoon on the Gulf coast of Alabama with temperatures in the 60s, and Tom Coughlin sat alone and pensive in a corner of the stands behind one end zone. He wore a blue Giants cap and blue Giants pullover with tan khaki pants and white tennis shoes. No one was within three rows of him as he sat in the metal bleachers and propped his feet on the row ahead of him.

The season had ended for Coughlin's team only sixteen days before, but this trip was not about winding down or getting away from it all. It was time to get back to work. That was programmed into Coughlin, just as it was programmed into every other NFL coach and every front office executive. Football is the most passionate and emotional of games, but the feelings have to be put aside quickly once a game or a season ends. During the season some coaches call it a "midnight" rule: You savor a win or agonize over a loss for the rest of the day, then find somewhere to tuck away the emotions when the clock strikes midnight and you have to set your mind to getting back to work. Now Coughlin had to set aside the wildly conflicting emotions of a 2005 season in which the Giants rose rapidly to prominence and won the NFC East title but then exited quickly and meekly from the playoffs. "It's part of the cycle," he said. "It's part of the way you're raised, at whatever level of football you're at. You get through the season and then you move on with your evaluation and recognizing what your needs are. You just move into the next cycle."

It was two days after the Pittsburgh Steelers and Seattle Seahawks had won the two conference championship games to advance to Super Bowl XL in Detroit. For those two teams, it was still *this* season. But for the other thirty teams in the league, it had already become *next* season, and the Senior Bowl in Mobile was the unofficial launching point of the process. Scouts, coaches, general managers, and other executives spent the week watching some of the best college players who would be eligible for the NFL draft in April practicing for the Senior Bowl, an all-star game that would be held that Saturday at Ladd-Peebles. By Friday most of the NFL people would be gone. They didn't care about the game. They could watch that on television or later on tape. They wanted to see the practices, to get firsthand looks at how the players moved and competed.

Coughlin was keeping a particularly close eye on University of Miami wide receiver Sinorice Moss. He was tiny, at 5 feet 8 and 185 pounds, but his brother Santana was a standout for the Redskins and he, too, possessed rare speed and elusiveness. The Giants lacked those elements in their offense. Coughlin watched intently as Moss darted around the field during drills. "You see the players live in practice, being right there with them," Coughlin said. "You get more than tape. You get to know who the opposition is, see how they're lined up, see them competitively. You watch the one-on-one drills. You see all those kinds of things."

Simply being here while the Steelers and Seahawks were making Super Bowl preparations was a reminder for these coaches that things had not gone precisely as they'd envisioned the last time they were in Mobile. New England Patriots coach Bill Belichick was making what was for him a rare appearance in Mobile, and he looked grim about it. He was accustomed to being preoccupied at this time of year, having won three of the last four Super Bowls. But the Patriots had lost in the second round of the playoffs and he and his front office chief, Scott Pioli, plopped down in the middle of the bleachers along one sideline dressed in matching blue jeans and gray sweatshirts. If it was odd to see just about every important and recognizable decision-maker on the thirty-two NFL teams gathered in one spot in Mobile, it had been even stranger in the days when at least one of the two practices each day had been held at a nearby high school field. Cars had been left on dirt parking lots and every NFL coach and general manager had stood right there on the field only a few feet from where the drills were being conducted. Now the coaches and executives were relegated to the stands at Ladd-Peebles twice per day. The practices, as with everything else in the NFL, had become a big deal. Portions of them were televised by ESPN and the NFL Network. The event qualified as big news locally. Hotel rooms in Mobile had been sold out for weeks. A man who arrived at the Enterprise Rent-A-Car counter at the airport that morning because, he'd just been informed, their company was the only one with any cars left, was told to his dismay that they'd just rented their last available car too. "The Senior Bowl's in town, you know," one of the workers said.

A local news station did live broadcasts every evening from the Riverview Plaza Hotel, the game's headquarters. Even a strip club tried to get into the act, running an ad in a local newspaper that read: "NFL coaches, come check out *this* talent."

For the players it was their first exposure to NFL coaching. The teams were coached by the staffs from two NFL clubs. This year it was the coaching staffs of the Tennessee Titans and San Francisco 49ers, and the players were being pushed hard. "The first day a lot of guys were about to swallow their tongues," University of Memphis running back DeAngelo Williams said. "I was one of them."

The end of each practice brought a free-for-all on the field as media members and team officials competed for chances to interview players. After the Tuesday afternoon practice, a Miami Dolphins representative walked up to Alabama quarterback Brodie Croyle and told him the team's coach, Nick Saban, wanted to meet with him at 7:15 that night.

"But I already have a meeting with you guys scheduled for tomorrow night," Croyle said.

"Well," the Dolphins representative replied, not wanting to make any snap decision that might end up upsetting Saban, "just show up tonight and then we'll see about that one tomorrow night."

The job fair also was being conducted in the stands. Out-of-work coaches showed up looking for jobs. With ten NFL teams having just fired their head coaches and most of their assistants along with them, there were plenty of assistant coaching jobs still to be had. The agents were in Mobile in force as well. The college players who were on the field already had signed with agents and the free agent market for veteran NFL players wasn't scheduled to open for more than a month. But with so many decision-makers for the teams gathered in one place, the agents couldn't stay away. One of them, Drew Rosenhaus, wore two cell phones as he sat in the stands to watch a practice. He had his hair slicked back and was wearing jeans and a black sweater. He was trying to keep a low public profile in the wake of his recent Terrell Owens debacle, but there was still business to be conducted. He had a conversation with New York Jets general manager Terry Bradway as he left the stadium, promising Bradway to do all he could to help with a couple players.

"I wouldn't steer you wrong," Rosenhaus told him.

He wouldn't have the chance. Bradway would be nudged aside as the Jets' general manager little more than two weeks later, agreeing to take a diminished role while assistant GM Mike Tannenbaum moved into the general manager's chair.

Agent Jimmy Sexton also made the rounds in the stands. It was a busy day for Sexton. Two of his clients who had just been fired as head coaches, Jim Haslett and Dom Capers, were completing deals to take new jobs. Haslett, the former New Orleans Saints head coach, was becoming the St. Louis Rams' defensive coordinator. Capers, the ousted head coach of the Houston Texans, was finishing negotiations to work for Saban in Miami. But Sexton was focused for now on finding Vinny Cerrato, the vice president of football operations for the Redskins, and wanted to talk about a quarterback he represented, Patrick Ramsey. Sexton thought he and Ramsey had secured a promise from Joe Gibbs to trade Ramsey this offseason. Ramsey had lost the starting job to Mark Brunell and the Redskins were grooming young quarterback Jason Campbell as Brunell's eventual replacement. But Sexton was afraid the Redskins were going to renege on their promise now that they regarded themselves as solid Super Bowl contenders in 2006, not wanting to leave themselves with one too-old quarterback and another too-young one in a season with so much riding on it. Sexton found Cerrato and sat next to him in the stands, making his pitch to get Ramsey out of D.C.

The practice ended. The postpractice mingling on the field gradually dissipated and a mad dash to get out of the crowded parking lot commenced. As Coughlin walked to his car he pondered what was ahead. "You've got to get over the disappointment of the last game first," he said, "and then you can balance the achievements that you did have as a team, winning eleven games and winning the division, versus losing the playoff game and not playing well, not having your team represent itself very well. You've got to balance that out. But I think you move a little bit down the road and you start to look at things a little bit more objectively. From there you start making plans for the future and your excitement, your energy level, comes right back up and you look forward to what you're going to try to accomplish in the offseason."

Above all, that meant signing players. There was much, much work to be done.

FEBRUARY

CHAPTER

- 4 -

February 3 ... Detroit

As usual, Dan Snyder threw a lavish party during Super Bowl week. This one was in an office building in downtown Detroit on the Friday night before the game and took up much of the fifteenth floor. A dessert table filled an entire conference room, and a balcony overlooked the outdoor festivities set up by the NFL and local officials to try to get visitors to enjoy the chilly weather instead of gripe about it—a skating rink, and a sledding run made with manufactured snow. When Snyder had run into Paul Tagliabue on Thursday, he'd made sure to point out to the NFL commissioner that it was close to 60 degrees in Washington that day; it was a small sally in Snyder's ongoing campaign to secure a Super Bowl at the Redskins' home stadium, FedEx Field.

The party crowd was more CEO than celebrity. Some Redskins players, including tailback Clinton Portis and wide receiver Santana Moss, mingled with the business executives. Snyder was drinking and laughing it up with Mark Shapiro. Snyder had taken control of Six Flags, Inc., and in December had installed his business partner Shapiro, whom he'd

lured from ESPN, as its chief executive officer. Shapiro and Snyder
walked around greeting guests. They shook hands and traded jokes.

Snyder saw a reporter from *The Washington Post* and said to Shapiro,
"Hey, look, it's the enemy."

This was Snyder in his element. He quickly became bored with
downtime and usually surrounded himself with groups of business associates or friends. He was a ball of energy who slept little, preferring
to conduct business by phone late into the night. There usually was more
than one TV going in his corner office at Redskins Park and his focus
darted from subject to subject during a conversation. He could be over-
bearing, and his management style early in his Redskins tenure had
been to make employees fearful for their jobs, believing that increased
productivity. But he wasn't all ogre all the time. He was charitable with
his money and he was a doting father whenever his three children were
around. He and his wife Tanya had their son by a surrogate in 2002 after
Tanya's first two pregnancies had serious complications. When Brian
Schottenheimer, the son of former Redskins coach Marty Schottenheimer
and an assistant coach during his father's season in D.C., was diagnosed
with thyroid cancer, Snyder got the Schottenheimers in to see his doctor. Snyder underwent successful surgery for thyroid cancer in 2001.

He enjoyed his excesses. He bought a $10 million estate on fourteen
acres by the Potomac River, once owned by King Hussein of Jordan,
then rebuilt it. He liked to smoke cigars and devour steak dinners at
Morton's. He had a public image as a spoiled, rich bully and he had trouble projecting a softer persona because he was fidgety when speaking on
camera or in front of large crowds, but he had his moments. When he
attended a previously scheduled luncheon during Marty Schottenheimer's
0-5 start in 2001, fans bombarded him with complaints about the state
of the team and his operation of the franchise. One man stood up during the question-and-answer session and complained that he had seats
in the stadium where the sun was routinely in his eyes.

"Note to self: Move the sun," Snyder said, drawing laughter from the
crowd and illustrating the point that keeping all his constituents happy
was going to be next to impossible no matter how much money he spent.

His bout with cancer hadn't changed him much, but he had been deeply affected when his father, Gerald, had died in 2003. It took months for him to regain his usual verve. He could barely get the words out when he spoke at his father's funeral, hiding his tearful eyes behind sunglasses as he said, "My father was my best friend." One of the parking spots closest to Redskins Park has a sign that reads, RESERVED: MR. SNYDER. The unoccupied spot next to it still bears the sign RESERVED: GERALD S. SNYDER.

Gerald Snyder had been a journalist who once worked for United Press International and wrote books and freelance magazine pieces for publications that included *National Geographic.* He and his wife Arlette lived modestly for most of their lives and were everything their son wasn't—quiet, gentle, unassuming, and unfailingly polite. They lived in New York when Dan's older sister Michele and Dan were born, then moved to the Maryland suburbs of Washington, D.C., where Dan Snyder grew up in apartments in Silver Spring and Rockville. He would become the young, wealthy, wildly aggressive sports owner that fans in most NFL cities loved to loathe, but he hadn't led the life of privilege many of his detractors supposed. Gerald kept the family moving, living in England and back in New York. He took his children to historic sites. He had them follow the path of Lewis and Clark with him while he did research for his writing. Schoolwork didn't really interest Dan as a kid. He wanted to find a way to make money and worked at a bookstore while he was in high school. He did stints at Montgomery College and the University of Maryland without graduating. Gerald and Arlette didn't scold their son. They saw his passion for business and told him to do what invigorated him.

Snyder's parents and sister were his earliest business partners, but not all the ventures were successful. As a high schooler, Snyder got his father to help him try to sell travel packages for fans of the Washington Capitals hockey franchise to take the bus to see the team play the Flyers in Philadelphia. It proved a tough sell. Snyder was undeterred. A few years later he began selling spring break travel packages to college students and built that into a $1 million venture. That led to an idea for a magazine geared toward college students, and Snyder enlisted the help of his father and sister. He also pestered Fred Drasner, who was running *U.S. News & World Report* and later would oversee the New York *Daily News,* to convince his business associate, publishing and real estate mogul Mort Zuckerman, that they should invest $3 million. The magazine failed, but Snyder impressed Drasner and Zuckerman with his ambition and nonstop work. He established Snyder Communications, Inc., with his family helping him do the work and pay the bills. Snyder worked and pushed and willed his way to the top of the advertising and marketing world. He bought his first private jet in 1991 at age twenty-six. He had *Fortune* 500 companies as clients and he became the youngest CEO of a company listed on the New York Stock Exchange when he took Snyder Communications public in 1996. He sold his company in 2000 for more than $2.3 billion.

He also had another passion in life: the Redskins. He saw his first Redskins game on television when he was two. His father took him to a game at RFK Stadium when he was seven. He wore a Redskins belt buckle as a kid. For games he'd put on his belt and his Sonny Jurgensen jersey and eat a bowl of his mother's "Redskins chili" while sitting on a blanket next to his father in front of the family's black-and-white TV set—when the family had a TV set, that is. There were times when he and his father had to walk to a nearby store to find a set to watch the Redskins.

Snyder's twin passions for business and Washington's football team merged after Redskins owner Jack Kent Cooke died in 1997. Instead of leaving the franchise to his son John, Cooke arranged for it to be sold by his estate. The sale was overseen by Dick Cass, a D.C.-based attorney who had worked closely with Jerry Jones and would go on to become the president of the Baltimore Ravens. John Kent Cooke tried to buy the Redskins from his father's estate but couldn't muster enough money. Snyder originally was recruited as an investor for the prospective ownership group headed by New York financier Howard Milstein, then put together a bid of his own after Milstein was convinced by the league to withdraw an offer considered too debt-laden by NFL officials.

Snyder managed to structure the bid to the league's satisfaction and won the right in 1999 to pay a whopping $800 million for the Redskins, their stadium and their Ashburn, Virginia, training facility. His investors included his family members and his two longtime business backers, Zuckerman and Drasner. The Snyder family originally owned about 70 percent of the franchise, with Zuckerman and Drasner splitting about 30 percent. Zuckerman never took an active role in the team, and his shares were bought by the other partners relatively quickly. Drasner was a close adviser to Snyder at first, then faded out of the picture and sold his stake. Snyder would sell 35 percent of the team for approximately $460 million to a trio of new investors—Federal Express founder Fred Smith, Virginia homebuilding magnate Dwight Schar, and Tampa insurance executive Robert Rothman—in 2003, using the money to pay down the Redskins' debt.

At age thirty-four Snyder owned the team he'd adored as a child. His favorite player as a kid, Jurgensen, became a friend and a football confidant. Snyder had the Redskins logo painted on his jet, which he named *Redskin One.* But the Redskins inherited by Snyder weren't the Redskins who'd won three Super Bowls for Jack Kent Cooke with Joe Gibbs as the coach. These Redskins had left behind storied RFK and played in a huge but aura-deficient stadium in Landover, Maryland. They had a coach, Norv Turner, and a general manager, Charley Casserly, who blamed each other for the franchise-altering mistakes they'd made in the draft by selecting quarterback Heath Shuler and wide receiver Michael Westbrook. They were coming off a 1998 season in which they'd begun 0-7. They'd missed the playoffs for a fifth straight season under Turner, and Casserly had failed to sign quarterback Trent Green to a contract extension because the Cooke estate wouldn't authorize him to make a lucrative multiyear offer while the franchise was in the process of being sold.

Snyder immediately ordered big changes. He assured employees they wouldn't be fired, then fired many of them anyway. He brought in new employees and then dismissed many of them, too, or watched them leave. He saw that Casserly and Turner couldn't coexist. He'd pledged publicly to keep both but he quickly came to believe he'd made a mistake. It was too late in the year to find a new coach—the other NFL owners approved Snyder's purchase in May and he officially took over in July—so he reached a financial settlement by which Casserly resigned as general manager.

"You fired the wrong guy," Casserly told Snyder.

"If you're right," Snyder said, "you'll be the first to know."

Snyder later would end up calling Casserly to tell him that he'd been right.

Snyder brought in Vinny Cerrato, a former San Francisco 49ers executive who'd served as a consultant to the Milstein-Snyder group, to run the front office. Some of Casserly's best moves had been made in his final days as general manager. He'd traded for quarterback Brad Johnson when Green, deeming the Redskins' contract offer to be too little and too late, signed with the St. Louis Rams as a free agent. Casserly had selected cornerback Champ Bailey and offensive tackle Jon Jansen in the first two rounds of the 1999 draft and had left the Redskins well stocked with salary cap space and draft choices. In Snyder's first season as owner, the Redskins won their first NFC East title since 1991, but even that ride was a bumpy one. They squandered a three-touchdown lead in the fourth quarter to lose to the Cowboys in overtime in Snyder's first game and the defense was terrible early in the season. Defensive coordinator Mike Nolan found cartons of vanilla ice cream stacked outside his office door to reinforce Snyder's message that he didn't want the defensive play-calling to be so "vanilla." Snyder had Turner bring in veteran coach Bill Arnsparger as a defensive consultant. He verbally assailed Turner in a tiny equipment room just inside the front door of the visitors' locker room at Texas Stadium minutes after an October defeat to the Cowboys. The two men screamed at each other while Turner's stunned players sat silently and listened to every angry word. But the team regrouped and Snyder and his family members celebrated with a late-night toast at a San Francisco restaurant after the Redskins beat the 49ers on a touchdown catch in overtime by fullback Larry Centers to clinch the division. The team won a first-round NFC playoff game at home against the

Detroit Lions, then lost at Tampa when a bad snap foiled a would-be game-winning field goal attempt in the closing moments.

Snyder kept Turner as his coach for a second season but wasn't satisfied to try to build gradually on the successes of season one. He orchestrated the most aggressive free-agent spending spree in NFL history, signing defensive end Bruce Smith, safety Mark Carrier, cornerback Deion Sanders, and quarterback Jeff George. Turner didn't want George on the roster. Johnson was so angry about the signing and the lack of progress in his own contract negotiations that he immediately resolved that he would depart as a free agent after the season. Casserly had left the team with three first-round draft picks that year, and Snyder and Cerrato traded to end up with one fewer first-rounder but with the draft's second and third overall selections. The Redskins chose Penn State linebacker LaVar Arrington and Alabama left tackle Chris Samuels. The 2000 Redskins were celebrated as the first NFL team ever to have a $100 million player payroll, although the final figure would fall just short of that under the computation method used by the Players Association. The so-called $100 million team began well, overcoming season-ending knee injuries to Westbrook and guard Tre Johnson to win six of its first eight games. Then came a wild loss at home to the Tennessee Titans on a Monday night and a calamitous defeat in Arizona to the woeful Cardinals just before a bye week. Snyder, prodded by master instigator Drasner, began to sour on Turner.

The *Post* reported a few days after the Arizona game that Turner would be fired after the season if the Redskins didn't make the playoffs. It wasn't news to Turner, but he suspected that the story had come from Snyder. A few days later at Redskins Park he saw the reporter who'd written the story and said, "I see you talked to him. He didn't have the guts to talk to me."

Turner was cursing. His voice was rising and he wasn't hiding his growing disdain for his bosses. He was standing in the main hallway at the Redskins' training facility right at the top of a stairwell leading down to the locker room. He went on and on. Employees were walking by, shooting glances Turner's way. Not surprisingly, word got back to

the Redskins' owners about Turner's outburst and it reinforced the notion held by Snyder, and especially by Drasner, that their coach was
cracking under the pressure. The boiling point was reached a few weeks
later when the Redskins lost at home to the Giants to drop their record
to 7-6. Turner dispatched venerable kicker Eddie Murray to try a long
field goal that would have won the game even after his players implored
him on the sideline to leave the offense on the field because the kick was
too far for Murray. Murray's kick fell predictably short. The Redskins
lost. In the owner's box, Drasner fumed that Turner had sent Murray into
the game knowing the kick would be missed as a screw-you gesture to
his bosses. It wasn't true—Turner had simply made a highly question-
able tactical decision in the heat of the moment—but it illustrated how
things had deteriorated. Snyder didn't share Drasner's suspicion, but he
was plenty angry about the team's downward spiral. The owners decided
later that night to fire Turner with three games left in the season.

They briefly toyed with the idea of giving the job to Pepper Rodgers,
a former college coach who was in the team's front office after working
for Federal Express and trying with Fred Smith to get an NFL franchise
for Memphis. Defensive coordinator Ray Rhodes wouldn't take the job
out of loyalty to Turner. Snyder and Drasner finally settled on fiery wide
receivers coach Terry Robiskie. He gave a spirited locker room speech
before his first game in Dallas, yelling that he was going to go out and
kick the Cowboys' asses and asking, "Who's going to join me?!"

The team's jaded veteran players hid their faces to avoid being seen
chuckling. Apparently no one joined him. The Redskins lost, 32–13,
and afterward Sanders referred to his new coach as "Coach Robinskie."
The Redskins also lost the next week before closing with a meaningless
victory. Snyder was in the market for a new coach. He couldn't get the
coach he truly coveted, Steve Spurrier, to leave the University of Florida.
Neither Gibbs nor Dick Vermeil was interested in coaching at the time.
Vermeil pointed Snyder and Rodgers toward Marty Schottenheimer,
the former Cleveland Browns and Kansas City Chiefs coach who'd said
on the air in his role as an ESPN analyst that he could never work for
Snyder. A couple of face-to-face conversations and a four-year, $10 mil-

lion contract changed Schottenheimer's mind. It was a mismatch from the start. The dictatorial Schottenheimer made Snyder promise to keep out of the team's football operations. Snyder kept his word and stayed out of the mix when Schottenheimer fired Cerrato and cut Centers after the fullback told the coach that Schottenheimer didn't know how to coach star players. Sanders refused to play for Schottenheimer and announced he was retiring. How meticulous was Schottenheimer? He once summoned a Redskins employee to his office at Redskins Park and had a lengthy conversation about whether a comma should have been used in the sentence that Schottenheimer had just read.

At his one training camp with the Redskins at Dickinson College in Carlisle, Pennsylvania, he had alarms installed on the front doors of the dorms to catch players returning after curfew. He fined players for tossing the ball to the wrong person after a play on the practice field. He gave backpedaling lessons to legendary graybeard cornerback Darrell Green, and he ran a punishing camp that immediately alienated veterans like Green and Bruce Smith. The team's players were in near revolt by the time the regular season started and it showed, as the Redskins ineptly lost their first five games. The fifth loss was to the Cowboys at Texas Stadium and Drasner, a rough-and-tumble businessman who once had been a New York City cab driver, found himself contemplating Schottenheimer's coaching demise as he watched the game from a suite. "Marty Schottenheimer," Drasner declared, "is the only coach in the NFL who could commit suicide by leaping from his ego to his IQ!"

Snyder remained calmer, not wanting to repeat the mistake he'd made by firing Turner during a season. Schottenheimer won 8 of his last 11 games and Snyder was willing to keep him as coach. But he wasn't willing to allow Schottenheimer to retain total control over football decisions, and Schottenheimer wasn't willing to live with a reduction in responsibilities, so he was gone after only one season. This time Spurrier was willing to leave Florida, and Snyder hired him for a five-year, $25 million deal. Cerrato returned to the front office.

Spurrier never fit in. The preacher's son from Johnson City, Tennessee, was a genuinely decent man. He was just different. He thought differently and acted differently than most coaches did, and tact and proper protocol weren't part of his formula. He went to a meeting with high-level editors of the *Post* soon after being hired and gave them a rah-rah speech more suitable for the college town booster club about everyone needing to pull together to help make the team successful. The editors looked at him like he was from another planet. He forgot the names of his defensive players and Redskins staff members or never managed to learn them in the first place. He called Michelle Tessier, the team's public relations director, "Melissa." The identities of most opposing players were a mystery to him. When defensive tackle Michael Myers came to Redskins Park for a free agent visit between Spurrier's first and second NFL seasons, he introduced himself to Spurrier. Spurrier said hello and added, "Who did you play for last season?" Myers had played for the Cowboys, who had faced the Redskins twice in Spurrier's first season.

The highlight of Spurrier's two-year Redskins reign came in his first preseason game when he beat the 49ers in an American Bowl in Osaka, Japan. For one day at least he could crow that his "Fun 'n' Gun" offense worked just fine in the NFL. But it didn't work for long, and he went 12-20 in his two seasons. He got his feelings hurt when Snyder and Cerrato outvoted him and made him cut his Heisman Trophy–winning Florida quarterback, Danny Wuerffel, at the beginning of his second season. He talked about ignoring the ridicule being heaped on him but he couldn't. He'd take a copy of a critical newspaper article and send it back to the writer with notes handwritten in the margins. Midway through his second season, with rumors circulating that he might resign, Spurrier looked around the room during a team meeting. He picked out highly paid players like Samuels and Arrington and asked them if they liked their contracts. They said yes.

"Well, I like my contract, too," Spurrier said, "and I'm not going anywhere."

He'd broken a cardinal rule for NFL coaches: Never, ever make it about the money during the season. The season is supposed to be the time for play, not the time for pay.

Spurrier's wife, Jerri, grew increasingly miserable in Washington, and Spurrier had a coaching staff full of longtime associates he didn't want to fire. He probably could have turned things around by hiring assistants with more NFL seasoning, but he couldn't bring himself to overhaul his staff so he hired Memphis-based agent Jimmy Sexton to negotiate his divorce from Snyder and the Redskins. Spurrier was on a golf course in Florida when Sexton worked out the final details. Spurrier didn't even know things were official when a reporter reached him by cell phone between holes. First he said he hadn't quit, then a few holes later he acknowledged he had. It was a bizarre ending to a bizarre NFL fling for a coach who never should have left the college ranks. He sat out a season, then took a college job at South Carolina.

Joe Gibbs was having lunch with Atlanta Falcons owner Arthur Blank in Charlotte when Spurrier quit. Gibbs had known Blank, the founder of Home Depot, for years. They were NASCAR business associates and Gibbs had a small ownership stake in the Falcons. When Blank called Gibbs, just as he was calling other investors in the team, late in the 2003 season to say that he was firing Dan Reeves as his coach, Gibbs piqued Blank's interest by saying he was contemplating a return to coaching. Jerry Jones once had tried and failed to lure Gibbs back to football to take the Cowboys job. Snyder had asked before. But Gibbs was happy owning an auto racing operation and had given serious thought to returning to coaching only once previously during his time away, when the expansion Carolina Panthers had come calling in 1994. He wasn't ready to get back into the game then, but by the winter of 2003 he was. One of his sons, Coy, wanted to become a coach, and what better way was there to get Coy into the profession than going back himself and teaching his son the job? Gibbs was sixty-three but he felt healthier than he'd been when he'd left coaching in 1993. He had diabetes but had been able to manage the disease. He wanted his grandchildren to know he'd been successful in that "other" sport, too. He broke the news to his wife, Pat, got her approval, and then began exploring his options.

Blank flew to Charlotte, where Gibbs's NASCAR operation was

based, two days after the season. In the middle of their meal, Blank's cell phone rang and he got the news that Spurrier had resigned. Gibbs's phone rang at about the same time and Blank knew immediately that he had no chance to hire Gibbs. The next day Dwight Schar called Gibbs around noon to ask if he was interested in coaching the Redskins. Schar knew Gibbs through Youth for Tomorrow, Gibbs's home in Virginia for at-risk teens, to which Schar was a contributor. Gibbs said he needed time to think about it. Schar wasn't accepting that for an answer, and by 3 p.m. Snyder and Schar had flown on Snyder's jet to Concord, North Carolina, outside Charlotte, to meet with Gibbs at the airport. Gibbs didn't say yes but he didn't say no. Snyder and Schar flew back to Dulles Airport around six. Snyder picked up Cerrato and left that night for San Francisco, where the two were scheduled to interview former Giants coach Jim Fassel and former Minnesota Vikings coach Dennis Green.

The next day was New Year's Day 2004. Schar stayed in the D.C. area and continued his pursuit of Gibbs by phone while Snyder and Cerrato interviewed Fassel on the West Coast. Snyder and Cerrato interviewed Fassel and Green for about twelve hours each over a three-day span, then returned to Washington. On January 4, Snyder and Schar went back to Charlotte and spent much of the following day meeting with Gibbs at a hotel. The meeting stretched into the night—it went for nine hours in all. At one point Gibbs asked Schar on the side if he'd be able to work for Snyder; Schar reassured him that he could. Snyder and Schar left believing they had a deal. Snyder and Gibbs agreed to the financial parameters of the deal in a matter of seconds. Gibbs took Snyder's plane that night to Buffalo to get Gregg Williams on board as his defensive coordinator. He got back to Charlotte around 5 a.m. on January 7 and signed his five-year, $28.5 million contract later that day. Snyder was giving Gibbs the title of team president as well as head coach. The blaring headline across the top of the *Post*'s sports section on January 8, 2004, read: THE RETURN OF THE KING.

Gibbs knew his comeback wouldn't be easy. When he first told his wife, Pat, he was considering a return to coaching, she wagged her finger at him and said, "You're going to ruin your good name." After Gibbs looked lost and out of touch and the Redskins went 6-10 in 2004, his first season back, he told her, "We're halfway there."

But the run to the NFC semifinals in the 2005 season gave everyone in the organization, including Gibbs, renewed confidence. Maybe, just maybe Snyder could have it all in football. The money side of the sport had come easily to him. Even when Snyder's Redskins were failing on the field, they were succeeding wildly as a business venture. Snyder thought the Redskins had become a lazy, dysfunctional business under John Kent Cooke and he threw all his considerable energy and marketing expertise into turning the team into a smooth-running financial machine. He took Jack Kent Cooke's name off the stadium and sold the naming rights to Federal Express for $205 million over twenty-seven years. He cut a huge deal for the team's radio broadcasting rights. He poured money into stadium improvements and added seats to FedEx Field wherever he could find room. He added luxury suites. He sold sponsorships. He lapped the money-making field.

But at Snyder's Super Bowl bash in Detroit the partygoers were talking about football, not business. Virtually everyone at the event had the same thing in mind, from Bernard Shaw, the former CNN anchorman and a regular in Snyder's box at games over the years, to Redskins radio announcer Larry Michael: Next year in Miami, the Redskins would be playing in the big game.

Now it was up to Snyder, Gibbs, and Cerrato to assemble a team to make it happen.

CHAPTER

-5-

February 5 . . . Detroit

Even as celebrated agent Leigh Steinberg and his marketing associate, Ryan Tollner, sat in Ford Field and watched their client, Pittsburgh Steelers quarterback Ben Roethlisberger, play in Super Bowl XL, they were at work on Roethlisberger's post–Super Bowl endorsements. Roethlisberger had begun growing a shaggy beard during a regular season losing streak and had been too superstitious to shave it off when the Steelers had begun to win. It wasn't a fashion statement; his plan was for the beard to be gone as soon as the Steelers' season ended. "It was mondo Grizzly Adams," Steinberg said. "He was dying to shave it but he felt he'd better not."

A sports marketing executive had approached Steinberg and Tollner about setting up a deal with Gillette if the Steelers beat the Seattle Seahawks in the Super Bowl to have the company's new Fusion razor used to shave Roethlisberger's beard on the *Late Show with David Letterman.* It would be reminiscent of a famous $10,000 deal New York Jets quarterback Joe Namath made with Schick in 1968 to have his Fu

Manchu mustache shaved off. As Steinberg and Tollner watched the game they communicated with a Gillette executive via text messages on Tollner's cell phone. Steinberg turned to Tollner at one point and said, "Write this: 'People, forty years later, are still talking about Joe Namath shaving his mustache. If you do this deal you will go down in the pantheon of great advertising deals. Do the deal.' "

The high-five-figures deal got done before the final whistle, contingent on the Steelers winning.

The Steelers won.

Roethlisberger didn't play well, but it didn't matter. He'd become, at twenty-three, the youngest quarterback to win a Super Bowl and his already considerable popularity was on its way to becoming enormous. Roethlisberger made his appearance on the Letterman show the following night. Steinberg figured Roethlisberger was looking at $15 million to $20 million in endorsement income over the next couple years, depending on how much time and effort the young quarterback wanted to put into pitching products. So while Eli Manning was winding down from the extreme highs and lows of his second NFL season, the quarterback drafted ten spots beneath him in April 2004 was enjoying the spoils of being a Super Bowl winner and celebrating his burgeoning celebrity by introducing Kelly Clarkson at the Grammys. Manning's accomplishments would always be measured against those of the two quarterbacks the Giants had valued less than him in 2004, Roethlisberger and Philip Rivers.

It had all worked out for Roethlisberger, but none of it had been what he'd had in mind on draft day 2004. That day he gladly would have traded places with Manning or Rivers.

Many scouts had the three quarterbacks rated virtually even as the draft approached, but Giants general manager Ernie Accorsi had become convinced that Manning was a once-in-a-generation prospect. When Accorsi was the general manager of the Baltimore Colts, he had been ordered to trade John Elway to the Denver Broncos when the future Hall of Fame quarterback balked at playing in Baltimore. Accorsi never got over it. He looked at the possibility of obtaining Manning as his redemption, even if he wouldn't always admit it. Manning had grown up as football royalty, the son of former New Orleans Saints quarterback Archie Manning and the younger brother of Peyton, and he'd handled it well. He was more easygoing than Peyton, who was so exacting that if there were two clocks in the Indianapolis Colts' locker room a minute apart, he couldn't handle it; one had to be reset so they were in unison. Eli was different. He'd once called home before an important high school game on a Thursday night to remind his father and his mother, Olivia, to tape *Seinfeld* for him. Eli, unlike Peyton, followed his father to the University of Mississippi. Once there, he became a star in his own right. When Accorsi went to scout the youngest Manning in person, it was love at first sight.

The problem was, the Giants had only the fourth pick in the draft. The San Diego Chargers had the top choice and wanted a quarterback. Chargers general manager A. J. Smith had become enamored with Rivers, a less gifted but more polished quarterback out of North Carolina State, at the Senior Bowl but he probably couldn't sell the idea of taking Rivers over Manning to his team's fans. The idea of a trade between the two teams looked like a natural, particularly when the Manning family informed the Chargers through agent Tom Condon that Eli wouldn't play in San Diego. The Mannings weren't in charge, and their threat to have Eli sit out the season if the Chargers drafted him carried little weight. But the whole affair gave Smith the excuse he needed to be able to trade Manning to the Giants and end up with Rivers.

Smith and Accorsi initially couldn't agree on the trade parameters. The Chargers wanted the package to include pass-rushing prospect Osi Umenyiora, a defensive end who'd been a second-round pick in the previous draft. Accorsi said no and told the Chargers the demand was a potential deal breaker. The Giants were leaving open the possibility of staying put and using the fourth selection on Roethlisberger. There were questions about the level of competition Roethlisberger had faced while playing at Miami University in Oxford, Ohio, but his physical skills were obvious and he didn't lack confidence. On the day before the draft in New York, Roethlisberger attended a media luncheon at Chelsea Piers. He was asked if all the attention Manning was receiving for the refusal to play in San Diego bothered him. Roethlisberger said no, it didn't bother him, because he was confident all the attention would shift to him once both got into the NFL.

Steinberg was based in southern California, in Newport Beach, and knew how rabid Chargers fans were for the club to draft Manning. He knew Smith liked Rivers and he knew Accorsi coveted Manning. He followed the acrimony growing between the Manning family and the Chargers and he guessed a draft-day trade between the Chargers and Giants was the most likely outcome. His feelings were confirmed when draft week came and went without any calls from the Chargers or Giants indicating Roethlisberger was their man. On the Friday before the two-day draft's opening Saturday, Steinberg told Roethlisberger to be prepared for a plummet through the draft order. After the Giants and the fourth pick the next team looking for a quarterback was the Steelers at eleven. "He was not overjoyed," Steinberg said, "but he understood it."

Roethlisberger understood, that is, until later Friday afternoon when his college coach at Miami, Terry Hoeppner, told him that he'd just heard from Tom Coughlin.

Coughlin had told Hoeppner that if the Chargers took Manning first, the Oakland Raiders took Iowa left tackle Robert Gallery second, and the Arizona Cardinals took University of Pittsburgh wide receiver Larry Fitzgerald third, be prepared for the Giants to grab Roethlisberger fourth. Roethlisberger's hopes soared. On Saturday morning as Steinberg rode with Roethlisberger to Madison Square Garden for the draft, he tried to keep his young client's expectations low. He told Roethlisberger any trade between the Chargers and Giants was likely to happen after the draft began.

"Please remember," Steinberg told Roethlisberger, "San Diego has been locked on to Rivers since the Senior Bowl and Ernie Accorsi has been locked on to Eli Manning forever. I've had the first pick in the draft eight times and the second pick in the draft seven times. I've been here before and nothing happens until the end. Prepare yourself that this very likely is going to happen on the clock and you're very likely going to go to Pittsburgh."

But it was no use. When Steinberg and Roethlisberger walked into the building the backstage buzz was that the trade wasn't going to happen and the Giants were going to take Roethlisberger. The draft began and the Chargers selected Manning, forcing him to stand uncomfortably on stage in front of the TV cameras as the pick of the team he'd shunned. The Raiders chose Gallery. The Cardinals picked Fitzgerald. The Giants were up next. Backstage Steinberg reminded Roethlisberger he'd get a phone call before seeing his name called on television. But Roethlisberger's phone wasn't ringing. The minutes felt like decades. As the Giants' fifteen-minute time limit neared its end, Steinberg noticed that there was movement near where the Manning camp was seated.

"That," Steinberg thought to himself, "is not great."

Accorsi and Smith had made the trade. The Giants drafted Rivers and traded him and a package of draft picks to the Chargers for Manning. When the deal was announced, Hoeppner slammed his fist on the table and the shoulders of those in the Roethlisberger entourage slumped. They would have to wait for the Steelers' pick to come and, as Steinberg said, "Draft time is not real time. It's excruciating, agonizing, Chinese-water-torture time."

But Roethlisberger composed himself by the time the Steelers took him. Steinberg completed a contract with the Steelers that summer to get Roethlisberger to training camp virtually on time, just as Condon got Manning to camp on time with the Giants. Rivers wasn't as lucky. Jimmy Sexton had a protracted set of contract negotiations with Smith that cost Rivers much of training camp and any shot he had of opening his rookie season as the Chargers' starter. The Chargers stuck with the quarterback they'd wanted to dump, Drew Brees, and he ended up having a spectacular season and leading the club to the playoffs. The Chargers used their franchise player tag to keep Brees off the unrestricted free agent market after the 2004 season and he had another good season in 2005 to keep Rivers relegated to backup status. The first-round pick in the 2005 draft the Chargers got from the Giants in the Manning deal was used on University of Maryland linebacker Shawne Merriman, who became the NFL's defensive rookie of the year. The Chargers got a productive kicker, Nate Kaeding, with another of the picks they got from the Giants and traded yet another to the Tampa Bay Buccaneers for offensive tackle Roman Oben. The Giants, in effect, had missed out on Merriman and two other useful players as well as Roethlisberger or Rivers to get Manning.

"I'd always thought A. J. Smith was either extremely fortunate or extremely shrewd," Steinberg said as he reflected twenty-two months later on that draft day. "With Manning he was like a person being pushed into an arranged marriage. But he ends up getting a person he doesn't want to marry to reject him and he gets a huge dowry to marry the person he really did want to marry."

The Giants could only hope their pairing with Manning would turn out to be equally blissful someday. Manning had begun his rookie season backing up Kurt Warner, the former two-time league most valuable player for the St. Louis Rams. Nine games into the season, with the Giants on a two-game losing streak but still in the thick of the playoff race with a record of 5-4, Coughlin benched Warner and went to his prized rookie. It wasn't exactly a happily-ever-after ending from there. The Giants lost Manning's first six NFL starts. Roethlisberger was in the process of helping the Steelers to a 15-1 regular season record as a rookie. He had a far better team around him than Manning did, but it still left room to wonder whether Accorsi had chosen the right quarterback.

After a particularly feeble start in Baltimore, Manning sat by Giants quarterbacks coach Kevin Gilbride during the team's train ride home and asked for help.

"We need to run some plays I'm comfortable with," Manning told Gilbride.

Gilbride told Manning it was time for him to become a leader, time for him to go to Coughlin and say what he wanted. So Manning met with Coughlin, and Coughlin agreed to streamline the offensive game plans to develop a core of plays Manning was comfortable running.

Things got better from there. Manning's rookie season ended on a positive note when the Giants beat the Cowboys at home on a last-second touchdown run by Tiki Barber. Manning successfully lobbied the coaching staff on the sideline to trust him to take two plays into the huddle and make the proper audible call at the line of scrimmage. He did, switching from a passing play to a running play after looking over the Dallas defense.

He spent the offseason after his rookie year studying tapes of his college games to get back to his old throwing motion, more over-the-top than sidearm. He took his girlfriend on the Mannings' first family vacation in six years. He went with his parents and his brothers and their families to Destin, Florida. He and Peyton lifted weights together and competed against one another running sprints. The two brothers didn't get a chance to compete very often anymore. Archie had taken down the hoop at his home in New Orleans, not wanting the two to get hurt playing basketball against each other. Peyton was too good at golf for Eli to have a realistic chance of beating his older brother. But Eli showed up at the Giants' training camp in Albany, New York, in the summer of 2005 happy to be able to brag about who'd prevailed in the sprint on the beach. "I won't tell you who won," he said with a grin one day while sitting outside the Giants' dining hall, "just because I don't want to embarrass him."

He was the unquestioned starter for a greatly improved offense and he was more at ease off the field as well as on it. He lived in Hoboken, New Jersey, because it had a small-town feel that reminded him of Oxford, Mississippi. He got the Giants to the playoffs but ended the season with a clunker of a performance. He still had those games in which he looked lost and overwhelmed. But all in all he'd had a pretty good season, and he and the Giants could envision his improvement continuing.

Wherever Accorsi and the Giants hoped Manning could go, however, Roethlisberger had already gotten there. A few hours after the Super Bowl win in Detroit, he and Steinberg rode together on a bus back to the Steelers' hotel. Steinberg had been allowed by Roethlisberger to watch the Super Bowl in person after the quarterback had banned the agent from attending the AFC championship game in Denver two weeks earlier. Steinberg had attended the Steelers' loss at home to the New England Patriots in the AFC title game in Roethlisberger's rookie season, and Roethlisberger had held him accountable. When Steinberg had called the week of the Broncos game to ask about his tickets, he'd been told his presence was not desired.

"I guess this means I'm cleared for future Super Bowls," Steinberg said during the bus ride.

"Yeah," Roethlisberger said, "but not conference championship games."

February 16 . . . New York

It was the Thursday before the NFL scouting combine was to be held in Indianapolis and nothing had improved on the labor front. This day's bargaining session had produced nothing, and Gene Upshaw was headed to California for a few days. Upshaw and Paul Tagliabue had skipped the Pro Bowl in Hawaii the weekend after the Super Bowl to return to the East Coast and resume negotiations but there had been no progress, and now Upshaw was ready for a showdown with the owners.

"They don't seem to believe we're willing to take it all the way," he said. "I guess that's because eighteen of them weren't there in '93. But we are."

Negotiating sessions were scheduled for the following Tuesday and Wednesday in Indianapolis, and Upshaw was to address groups of agents Wednesday and Friday. He hadn't addressed the agents en masse in years, but they were gearing up to get their clients who were free agents signed to contracts in this time of great uncertainty and Upshaw didn't want any screwups. He was planning to tell the agents that there would be no labor deal and the sport was headed toward a season without a salary cap in 2007, so they shouldn't agree to any stupid contracts keeping their clients unnecessarily bound to teams beyond the 2006 season.

There was rampant speculation that the opening of the free agent market might be pushed back from March 3 to April 1 if there was enough progress in the labor talks to warrant such a delay, but Upshaw planned to tell the agents there would be no such change. If the sport was going to have a season without a salary cap, he figured, bring it on. Upshaw had turned up the rhetoric a few notches during Super Bowl week by saying that if there wasn't a deal by March 3, the beginning of the new year on the NFL calendar, he'd recommend when the players' executive board met on March 9 in Hawaii that the players should vote to put in motion the process to decertify the union. That tactic had been used previously by the union between 1989 and 1993. It was a step toward a labor confrontation, not a labor negotiation.

In a normal negotiation, the leverage is the threat of a strike by the union and the threat of a lockout by management. If the NFL players decertified their union they would be taking away their ability to strike, but they would also be making it virtually impossible for the owners to lock them out; it was unlikely a court would allow the owners to lock out the players if the union was decertified. The players had planned ahead: The existing labor deal contained a provision that if the players opted to decertify the union again, the owners would not legally contest the move. Richard Berthelsen, the union's general counsel, regarded the provision as perhaps the best thing the players' side had negotiated into the deal. The players could keep playing games and keep getting paid while the details of the sport's new economic system were being determined. Decertifying the union would allow the owners to impose whatever set of work rules on the players they wanted, but with a significant caveat: The players, if they didn't like the system implemented by the owners, would have the option of filing an antitrust lawsuit, an option they wouldn't have with the union in operation. The owners wouldn't want that.

The players viewed a 2007 season without a salary cap as a financial windfall. Teams would be able to spend whatever they wanted, with no ceiling. The owners' competitiveness, the players figured, would kick in. If a team like the Redskins wanted to spend $150 million or more on players' salaries in pursuit of a Super Bowl title, it could. If the salary cap was allowed to go away, Upshaw vowed he would never allow it to return. But many people on the management side thought the players might be overestimating the salary bonanza they expected minus the salary cap. Some rules would change in an uncapped year. Players would need six seasons of NFL experience instead of four to be eligible for unrestricted free agency. Each team would have an extra "transition player" tag to use on a player in addition to its "franchise player" tag, allowing each club to limit the free agent mobility of two of its players instead of one. There no longer would be a minimum player payroll for teams, meaning a low-revenue club could significantly reduce its spending if it wanted.

Upshaw set the Friday of combine week—February 24—as the deadline for a deal to be struck. The management side viewed the deadline as artificial: Would Upshaw really reject a proposal giving him everything he wanted if it was delivered on February 25? But the deadline made sense to the union boss. It was flexible, yes. There was wiggle room to move it back. But Upshaw wouldn't agree for that to go on indefinitely. The way he looked at it, the only way he could affect the economics of the 2006 season was to get a deal and a new system in place before the free agent market opened. The rules couldn't be changed midway through the signing season. If the market opened without a new deal and Upshaw no longer was able to affect the economics of the 2006 season, why should he bother to keep negotiating?

If there was going to be a labor war, Upshaw was going to fight hard. The players would stop participating in the league's G-3 stadium loan program without new labor and revenue-sharing deals. Stadium construction had been a major ingredient in Tagliabue's formula for success. When the owners' search committee had interviewed him in the fall of 1989 for the commissioner's job, he'd told the owners the league had to be more robust and proactive in helping teams build stadiums. Soon after becoming commissioner he'd met with groups of civic leaders and told them the league wanted to be their partner in building stadiums. The league's stadium loan program, called G-3, was established in 1999 and was run in cooperation with the union. Since the program's incep-

tion, ten teams had received $773 million from the fund to build or ren-
ovate stadiums. The money given to a team was called a loan but in truth
it was more of a grant; it was repaid in a way that wasn't felt by the team
repaying it. The bulk of the money was repaid from the visiting teams'
share of club seat receipts from games played in the new stadium. The
teams collectively contributed $100 million per year to the G-3 program
to fund the stadium grants. The union's pulling out of the program, in
Upshaw's view, would affect funding for proposed stadium projects for
the Cowboys in Arlington, Texas; for the Giants in East Rutherford,
New Jersey; and for projects in Indianapolis and Los Angeles. The owners could keep building stadiums if they wished, but as far as Upshaw
was concerned they'd have to do so on their own dime. People on the
teams involved didn't even seem to know their stadium projects were
potentially affected. They knew the owners had approved their funding,
but not that Upshaw hadn't signed off on it.

On February 17, the Friday before the combine, union attorney
James Quinn sent an e-mail to Tagliabue and Harold Henderson, the
league's chief labor executive. It read:

> As you both know, we are rapidly approaching the next League Year
> and our ability to get a deal done in this short time frame seems
> doubtful. Gene, Jeff [Kessler, another union attorney] and I are par-
> ticularly concerned that so little progress has been made on the core
> economic issues that we have been discussing for nearly two years.
> Since I may not be able to participate in the discussions in
> Indianapolis next week, I wanted to be sure that your side fully un-
> derstands the exact nature of these concerns.
>
> We have long articulated three bedrock issues which it has now
> become clear are fundamentally connected and must be ad-
> dressed together:
>
> 1. In order for us to continue any form of salary cap, the players
>   must obtain a significant increase (both in dollars and percent-
>   age) in our overall share of total league revenues. We recognized
>   from the start that achieving that goal is inextricably intertwined

with numbers 2 and 3 below. You have our very specific October 14, 2005 proposal on the numbers which we believe is both fair and economically do-able given the billions of TV dollars being injected into the league over the next few years. We have also indicated our willingness to agree to some upside protection for the clubs as discussed in detail in our recent meetings.

2. We have said from the outset that in order for you[r] side to meet these financial demands, some form of cost or revenue sharing among the clubs would be required. In that regard, we have repeatedly made clear that we will not agree to any form of salary cap that does not deal with the "free-rider effect" which unfairly benefits a handful of high-revenue clubs. When we agreed to a salary cap in the early 1990s it was never intended to allow certain clubs to pay a significantly lower percentage of their revenues for their player costs. Such a system is both unfair to other clubs and inequitable to the players. We believe that each club should be required to spend at least some minimum percent of [its] total club revenues on player costs. At the very least, the cost of collectively bargained benefits should be paid in proportion to each club[']s revenue. As you know, we have suggested a variety of ways that this can be accomplished but so far nothing has happened. It is not our intent that non-performing teams be "subsidized." As Gene told many of the owners in our meeting last year in Detroit, it is our view that you should "cut" non-performing owners like you do non-performing players. We will leave that for you to figure out how to deal with that issue.

3. We have also made clear from the beginning that the players are prepared to continue the "G-3 Program" in a form that makes sense to both sides. However, our approval of projects will not only focus on the amounts expended but also on dollars actually generated by these investments. In this regard, we are willing [to] consider some form of deduction for the cost of stadium construction in connection with whatever revenue/cost-sharing program is ultimately agreed upon as discussed in number 2 above.

I apologize for the length of this e-mail, but I thought it was important to get these thoughts down on paper clearly before the meetings next week.

However bleak matters looked in the labor negotiations, though,
they didn't compare to the unpleasantness brewing among the owners
over the revenue-sharing issue. The things Upshaw heard from the owners' side as he readied for the trip to Indianapolis were ever more ominous. The latest was that the owners of the nine wealthiest teams had
banded together and were threatening to sue if they had a plan for bolstered revenue-sharing shoved down their throats. That faction of owners could block the approval of any revenue-sharing plan as long as it
had nine votes. League rules required a three-quarters vote to implement
such a measure, or twenty-four votes among the thirty-two clubs. But
if the group lost even a single member, litigation might be the only re-
course for the remaining owners in the bloc.

A confrontation was looming.

CHAPTER

- 6 -

February 23 . . . Indianapolis

Ernie Accorsi and Tom Coughlin hunkered down in a hotel suite to listen to one draft prospect after another tell his story. It was combine week and, like every other team, the Giants were prodding players mentally and emotionally as well as physically.

The entire league had reassembled in Indianapolis for the NFL scouting combine. More than three hundred draft-eligible players were on hand along with virtually every coach, front office executive, and scout in the league. They stayed in the downtown hotels clustered around the RCA Dome and adjacent convention center. The NFL had the dome to itself but had to share the convention center. In most years there was a huge cheerleading competition taking place there at the same time as the combine, which meant having hundreds of shrieking ten-year-old girls running around with their parents. This year it was Indiana's Midwest Builders Convention.

As with any other event that drew the decision-makers from every team to one place, the agents also showed up to do business. Gene

Upshaw met every year at the combine with the members of the league's competition committee, stressing player safety while discussing possible rule changes. This year Upshaw would meet with Paul Tagliabue and the owners on the bargaining committee. The union was in charge of certifying and regulating agents, and it conducted an annual seminar for them during combine week.

The prospects walked around in dark gray sweatshirts with yellow and white letters and numbers identifying them by their last names, their positions, and the numbers assigned to them for the combine. A day at the combine was a long day for a player, sometimes beginning at 5 a.m. and ending after midnight. The players were measured and weighed. They underwent physicals. They were drug-tested. They took the Wonderlic intelligence test. There was always a tug-of-war between general managers and agents over whether the players in attendance would perform the workout tasks administered on the field inside the dome—the forty-yard dashes, shuttle runs, high and long jumps, bench presses of a 225-pound weight bar, and position-specific drills, like throwing sessions for the quarterbacks. The GMs told the players they had a captive audience at their disposal, and a bad performance wouldn't work against them. But the players, thanks to their agents, knew better. They knew a poor showing at the combine would hurt their draft status plenty. The agents often advised the top players to show up to be weighed and measured, do the meet-and-greet routine with the teams and the media, and then get out of town and wait for their upcoming predraft campus workouts, when they would be in a familiar environment doing things on their own terms.

For the interview, the players went one at a time to talk to a team's general manager and head coach. A few assistant coaches and scouts were also likely to be in the room for the sessions, which lasted fifteen minutes. That wasn't enough time to delve too deeply into issues. Mostly, the coaches and general managers just wanted to emerge with a feel for the player's personality and get him to explain any legal or disciplinary incidents in his past. Players now were prepped in every way for what they underwent at the combine. Even the players' answers in the interviews had become very scripted. Bill Parcells, who used to bring along a former FBI agent to help interview players with troubled pasts when he was with the New York Jets, would say he sometimes felt like he was talking to the person who'd prepared the player for the interview, not the player himself. But that wasn't always the case, and every once in a while an exceptional player with an exceptional story to tell came along.

At this combine that was Penn State defensive end Tamba Hali. Accorsi and Coughlin listened intently to his story.

As a boy, Hali had lived in Liberia, an African nation being ravaged by a bloody civil war. His childhood was filled with the sounds of gunfire and the sights of dead bodies stacked by roadsides and young boys carrying rifles. Rebel attacks were frequent. Hali's stepdad would pack the family into a car and drive to a distant village to go into hiding for six months at a time. The family fled to the Ivory Coast and managed to get in touch with Hali's father, Henry, who had relocated to the United States nine years before and was teaching chemistry and physics in New Jersey at Teaneck High School and Fairleigh Dickinson University. His father filed for Tamba and his siblings to join him in the United States, but Henry had remarried and couldn't file for Tamba's mother, Rachel Keita, to come along. So Hali left his mother behind. He had last seen her in 1994, and there had been long stretches of his life in the United States when he hadn't been able to even get in touch with her. At one point she was shot in the knee while walking with a few friends in Monrovia, Liberia's capital city, and was fortunate not to be killed.

Hali tried playing basketball but had a rugged playing style that led to too many offensive fouls. He found a sport, football, where you could hit people without being penalized and grew to enjoy it. When he was first offered a scholarship to play the game at Boston College he didn't know what to say. He hadn't known you could get a college scholarship to play football. He signed on at Penn State because he liked Joe Paterno, not because Paterno was a legendary coach but because he seemed like a good guy. Hali had come to talk to his mother more regularly, once or twice a week, and was in the process of attempting to become a U.S. citizen so he could file for her to join him. Once she got to the United States she would go from living in a hut to living in the nice house her son planned to buy for her, courtesy of the wealth soon coming his way for playing an American game his mother didn't understand.

Accorsi and Coughlin were entranced. When Hali finished, the room was silent. Accorsi had grown up in Hershey, Pennsylvania, and had once worked in the Penn State athletic department. His daughter had graduated from Penn State. Coughlin was a Syracuse alum and the two men liked to spar over the schools.

Accorsi turned to Coughlin.

"Why," Accorsi said to his coach, "do you keep getting surprised by Penn State people?"

Accorsi wasn't one to ask a player, as some teams did during interviews, what he would go back into his home to retrieve if it was on fire and he only had time to get one item. He kept the process simpler and more straightforward. He believed people reverted, for the most part: A person's past was the best indicator of future behavior. He was old school in every way: He believed what he saw on game tapes instead of what he could try to project from forty-yard-dash times, strength tests, and psychological profiles. Even in this day of endless TV coverage and mammoth scouting budgets, he still believed there were diamonds out there to be unearthed. The starting tailback for the just-crowned Super Bowl champions, after all, had gone undrafted. Willie Parker had barely played in college at North Carolina, but the Pittsburgh Steelers had signed him as an undrafted rookie because one of their scouts—Dan Rooney, the son of the team's owner—had once been a high school coach in North Carolina, where Parker was a speedy prep star. A find like that was, to Accorsi, the great joy of the business.

He was the only true general manager in the NFC East. No one had the title with the Redskins. Jerry Jones had it in Dallas. Tom Heckert had just gotten it in Philadelphia but Andy Reid was his boss. Accorsi's plan had been to be retired by now and John Mara had learned from his father always to have a short list of prospective general managers and coaches handy. But Mara hadn't wanted to have to replace Accorsi just yet, and Accorsi hadn't wanted to create any more tumult for the organization on the heels of the deaths of Wellington Mara and Bob Tisch. He hadn't wanted to retire with the Giants perhaps on the cusp of accomplishing great things. If they were going to win a Super Bowl in the 2006 season, he wanted to be around for it.

He had just about seen it all and done it all in sports. He once had been a sportswriter. He'd been the general manager of the Baltimore Colts and Cleveland Browns. He'd worked in the league office under Pete Rozelle. He'd been an executive for baseball's Baltimore Orioles and had worked in college athletic departments at St. Joseph's and Penn State. When he was with the Colts in the early eighties he helped the producers of the movie *Diner* as they prepared the famous scene in which one character gave his bride-to-be a quiz about the Colts she had to pass for the wedding to go on as scheduled. They had Accorsi look over the questions. He determined they were too easy and rewrote them.

Accorsi greatly preferred dealing with agents over the old days, when he'd negotiated contracts directly with players. One March when he was with the Browns, wide receiver Brian Brennan came to Accorsi and wanted to negotiate his contract. Accorsi didn't want to be bothered. In the days before free agency, March was a downtime for NFL executives.

"Brian, you're going to ruin my March," Accorsi told Brennan. "Get an agent and come back in April."

"No, I don't need an agent," Brennan said. "I want to do it now."

Brennan came to Accorsi's office and handed him a piece of paper with a proposed salary for the following season written on it. Accorsi looked at it and said, "I'll get back to you."

Brennan was indignant. "What do you mean you'll get back to me?" he fumed. "You mean you're not going to give it to me?"

"This is a negotiation, not a surrender," Accorsi said.

Brennan stormed out of the office and Accorsi didn't hear from him for months. Accorsi called an agent, Vern Sharbaugh, and asked him to intercede and represent Brennan. Sharbaugh tried, but Brennan refused the agent's offer to get involved. Training camp arrived and Accorsi still hadn't heard from Brennan. As the Browns players were checking in for camp, Accorsi got a call from the kid checking the players into their rooms, who informed Accorsi that Brennan had shown up and was demanding a key.

Accorsi had the phone handed to Brennan and told him, "Brian, you can't have a key. You can't participate in training camp. You don't have a contract."

Brennan was enraged. "What, you're locking me out?" he screamed into the phone. "Just give me a contract and I'll sign it."

So Accorsi got a contract and Brennan signed it.

"A million times out of a million," Accorsi said, "I'd rather deal with an agent. They're professional negotiators. Players take everything personally. Players want to do contracts the way they play: They want to knock your block off."

Accorsi had been a busy negotiator in the late stages of 2005, signing key players like Jeremy Shockey and Osi Umenyiora to rich contract extensions. Center Shaun O'Hara was the only starter on the team whose deal was due to expire after the 2006 season. Now it was almost time for Accorsi to begin fine-tuning the roster. He needed to bolster the linebacking corps and he needed to shore up the defensive backfield. Those were the priorities. Like everyone else in the league, he needed players. He was in the right place.

February 24 . . . Indianapolis

The union reserved two meeting rooms at the Indianapolis convention center, Sagamore 1 and 2, for its seminar for the agents. One room served as a registration area. The agents, about five hundred of them, were seated in rows of chairs in the other room. As Gene Upshaw prepared to walk into the crowded meeting room on the Friday morning of the combine he saw a group of reporters standing outside the door. He invited them inside to listen to him speak.

"Come on," he said. "I've got nothing to hide."

The labor negotiations had resumed in Indianapolis three days earlier. There had been no movement during that Tuesday bargaining ses-

sion. The two sides broke and planned to reconvene Wednesday at
3 p.m. with a slightly different dynamic. Jerry Jones and St. Louis
Rams president John Shaw were going to join the owners' contingent.
But Upshaw left the Wednesday meeting at the Westin Hotel frustrated that, even with Jones and Shaw in the room, nothing had
changed. Neither side had budged and the session ended when it became
clear the parties were talking in circles.

Upshaw had spoken earlier Wednesday to a group of agents that included Drew Rosenhaus, Jim Steiner, Mark Bartelstein, Fletcher Smith,
Vann McElroy, Michael Sullivan, Ralph Cindrich, Tony Agnone, Ian
Greengross, Paul Sheehy, and Angelo Wright. The agents had been chosen to be a cross-section of their industry. Some were big-timers; others
weren't. Some had supported the union's efforts; others had been dis-
senters. Upshaw told the agents the outlook for a labor deal didn't look
promising; he would hold out for a fair settlement and, despite the
Friday deadline he'd set publicly, he would leave open the possibility of
a last-minute compromise with the league as late as the following
Thursday, the day before the free agent market was to open.

Upshaw and Paul Tagliabue saw each other Thursday at a meeting
of the competition committee but didn't negotiate. Now, on Friday,
Upshaw was ready to deliver what amounted to a state-of-the-players-
union address to the agents.

"March third will be the beginning of a new league year," he told
the agents, "and we are just not there yet. I'm taking the position now
that it won't get done."

Upshaw told the agents that each percentage point of the "total
football revenues" pool over which he and the league were haggling was
worth $2 million per team on the salary cap early in a labor deal, $2.5
million per team in the middle of an agreement, and $2.9 million per
team near the end. He wasn't going to do a deal just to preserve the
peace. He would agree only to a fair deal.

"We want to have a higher percentage," Upshaw told the agents.
"We want more dollars to come into the system."

When Upshaw was finished speaking, he exited through a back door
and headed straight out of town. First he told the agents one final thing.

"I'm leaving," he said. "We're running out of time. You might as well prepare as if we are heading for an uncapped year."

The first of Gene Upshaw's deadlines had come and gone.

February 24 . . . Indianapolis

Bill Parcells and Drew Rosenhaus had lunch together on Friday at the combine. It might not have seemed like a good match, the no-nonsense football coach from Jersey and the slicked-back agent from Miami Beach, but Parcells and Rosenhaus got along well. Parcells thought Rosenhaus was a self-made guy and respected what he had accomplished. Rosenhaus had the most clients of any agent in the league. He worked out of an office with two other people in it and when the phone rang he answered it. They'd had differences of opinion, but Parcells trusted Rosenhaus to tell him the truth.

The Eagles were trying to trade Terrell Owens and had given Owens and Rosenhaus permission to speak to other teams. But it was clear the Eagles weren't going to be able to get anything in return for Owens in a trade and were going to end up releasing him in March. Everyone in the league knew that. The Cowboys and everyone else were going to have to decide if they would be interested in Owens in free agency. Jerry Jones already had decided he was interested. He thought Owens was talented enough to be worth all the baggage he brought with him. Parcells didn't feel any particular need or desire to have Owens on his team but since Jones wanted him, Parcells had to decide if he objected strenuously enough to make a serious issue out of it.

Parcells famously said during his time with the New England Patriots that if he was expected to cook the meal, he should be allowed to shop for the groceries. He wanted say over which players were brought into the organization. But that was a different time and a different place. Nowadays in Dallas he seemed content sharing decision-making responsibilities with Jones; Jones's son Stephen, an executive with the team; and Jeff Ireland, the Cowboys' vice president of college and pro scouting. In New England, Parcells felt he was in a situation in which no one else knew what to do. He didn't feel that way about the Cowboys.

He particularly liked working with Ireland, the thirty-six-year-old grandson of former NFL player and executive Jim Parmer and the stepson of E. J. Holub, a center and linebacker for the Kansas City Chiefs in the 1960s. Ireland was a former kicker at Baylor who'd tried coaching, then had worked his way into scouting. The Cowboys had promoted him from being their national scout to scouting director before the 2005 draft.

Parcells would tell Ireland, "Look, if I can just leave you with one thing when I leave here, it's my eyes. What do my eyes see?" He wanted to teach Ireland to see the game as he saw it, to see the things in players he saw. Ireland was a willing and eager student. But in some ways he was also the teacher. Because Ireland had all his time to devote to scouting while Parcells had so many other things to worry about, Parcells would trust what Ireland had to say about players. Ireland regularly would bring up a player and say to Parcells, "Hey, Bill, have you seen enough on this guy?" If Parcells would say no, Ireland would say, "Well, come look," and Parcells would be off to watch more tapes of the player.

With Ireland's help, Parcells felt he knew the 120 or so players on his draft board better than he'd known any previous group during his Cowboys tenure. It made him excited for the draft and reinforced his confidence in Ireland. Parcells had worked with Ireland to overhaul the way the members of the team's scouting department evaluated players. Parcells didn't want the scouts merely to find him good players. He wanted the scouts to find him players who would be good playing *for him.* That meant tough-minded players, for one thing. It also meant knowing the positions at which Parcells wanted his teams to be jumbo-sized. Parcells felt he'd had to reset the "prototypes," as he put it, for the sorts and sizes of players he wanted at each position after he'd gotten to Dallas. Finally, everyone was thinking alike.

Jerry Jones portrayed his role as being the tiebreaker when the coaching and scouting staffs disagreed about a player. But because Parcells and Ireland were coming to think so much alike, the need was unlikely to arise. Still, Parcells knew he could be outvoted. He knew in some instances Jones's vote could be the only one that mattered because the owner had the power of the checkbook. After every season the members of the Cowboys' brain trust would sit down and outline what they thought the team's needs were. Some needs were put into the highest-priority "musts" category. Parcells would say what he thought the team needed to do, and then the economics of potential moves and the effect they'd have on other players already on the roster would be debated. Parcells thought he could defend the logic of every move the Cowboys had made during his tenure. But that didn't mean some of them hadn't turned out to be the wrong decisions. In fact, too many of them had turned out to be the wrong decisions, given that the Cowboys were coming off consecutive nonplayoff seasons.

Parcells would end up thinking the situation he'd inherited with the Cowboys was more problematic than those he'd faced with other teams because the club had invested money in two quarterbacks, Quincy Carter and Chad Hutchinson, before he'd arrived and neither had worked. Parcells had considered signing Jake Delhomme or Jake Plummer as a free agent before his first season with the Cowboys, but had decided against spending money on a third quarterback. The Cowboys had been lucky, in Parcells's view, to win the division title with Carter in 2003, in Parcells's first season. Parcells briefly thought to himself maybe Carter was the answer. He wasn't. The Cowboys were still looking for the answer at quarterback.

Parcells had come to believe player acquisition was about a fifty-fifty proposition and you were fooling yourself if you thought you could improve your success rate much beyond that. Parcells liked to draw horse-racing analogies: When the Kentucky Derby neared that May, he said, he would be asked which horse he liked. His answer would have less to do with which horse he thought was going to win than with how he would manage his money at the betting window to come up with combinations to try to maximize his income: You bet a little to make a lot, he said. You don't bet a lot to make a little.

In the case of Owens, the Cowboys would have to bet a lot to make a lot. Parcells had to make sure he'd be comfortable placing the wager.

Rosenhaus told Parcells that Owens was upset about what had happened in Philadelphia and wanted to put all that behind him and get his football career going again. Parcells trusted Rosenhaus, but his homework on Owens didn't end there. He talked to Eagles wide receivers coach David Culley, whom Parcells had successfully recruited to Vanderbilt when he coached there in 1973 and '74 and Culley was a quarterback out of Sparta, Tennessee. Culley told Parcells what people with the San Francisco 49ers had once told the Eagles about Owens: Yes, he had problems, but practicing hard and playing hard weren't among them. Parcells got along well with Andy Reid and the two spoke at the combine, but they didn't talk about Owens. They talked about which one of them could lose more weight in the offseason. Parcells did talk to players who knew Owens and had one important question for them: "Does he respond to competition?"

You could say what you wanted about Owens as a person, but you couldn't say he wasn't a competitor on a football field. That was the answer Parcells got from everyone he asked. He felt better. He'd been warned about players before—players like volatile linebacker Bryan Cox, whom he'd coached with the New York Jets in 1998 and '99—only to end up adoring them. Parcells didn't worry so much about what Owens had done in San Francisco and Philadelphia. He was more concerned about what Owens would do in Dallas, what Owens would do playing for him. Parcells ended up concluding that while he certainly could live without Owens, he wouldn't object strongly enough to keep the deal from happening.

The Parcells-Rosenhaus meeting at the combine created the impression around the league that the Cowboys were the favorite to land Owens, but Rosenhaus still had to try to stir up interest elsewhere if he could. He regarded the Chiefs as a potential suitor. He walked past their new coach, Herman Edwards, at one point during the combine, wearing his usual assortment of phones.

"We need to talk," Rosenhaus told Edwards.

"Okay," Edwards said, "when you stop talking on those phones, we'll talk."

Bill Parcells, for one, had heard enough on the subject of Terrell Owens.

CHAPTER

- 7 -

February 24 . . . Indianapolis

Dan Snyder, Joe Gibbs, and Vinny Cerrato gathered in the lobby of the Marriott, across the street from the RCA Dome and convention center, on the Friday night of the combine. They were joined by Robert Rothman, a minority owner of the Redskins. They checked out the Champions bar at one end of the lobby, but it was too loud so they settled into comfortable chairs around a table in the quiet lobby lounge. Gibbs spoke politely to a couple of fans who wandered by, but otherwise the group got left alone. Snyder, who had arrived in town earlier in the day, was wearing a black leather Redskins jacket. It was an alcohol-free gathering. Snyder and Gibbs sipped on sodas.

They talked about things rich guys talk about—commiserating, for instance, about how hard it was to land a private plane at certain small airports. Gibbs told the others about a tiny airstrip in North Carolina. An adjacent farm had a crane at the edge of its property and a pilot had to bring a plane in over the crane and dip suddenly to land. Gibbs trusted his pilot but his stomach was in knots every time.

Snyder had Cerrato tell a story about how the two of them recently had been sitting around bored when Snyder, while going through his mail, came across a letter from a real estate agent in Aspen. The agent had a wealthy client who wanted to purchase the summer home Snyder owned there. Snyder had Cerrato call the real estate agent and say he was Daniel Snyder's personal real estate broker. The agent made Cerrato an offer of $18 million for the mansion on Buttermilk Mountain.

"Eighteen?!" Cerrato had barked into the phone as Snyder laughed. "I can't even call him unless the number starts with a two."

Without hesitating the agent upped the offer to $20 million. In a span of thirty seconds Snyder had made another $2 million. But he wasn't interested. He liked the house and had no way to easily replace it.

Cerrato was derided by some in the league as being nothing more than Snyder's racquetball buddy, but Snyder thought he was a capable football executive. Cerrato was a former college player, a quarterback and wide receiver at Iowa State, who'd served as Lou Holtz's recruiting coordinator at Notre Dame, then jumped to the NFL in 1991 as the director of college scouting for the San Francisco 49ers. He became director of player personnel four years later and demonstrated a knack for uncovering players. Getting Terrell Owens in the third round of the 1996 draft was among his successes. But he never lived down selecting a bust of a quarterback, Jim Druckenmiller, in the first round in '97 and he got on the bad side of the franchise's higher-ups. He was nudged out of a job and word spread around the league he was a bad guy. The best work he could get was as a consultant for Howard Milstein's group when it was attempting to purchase the Redskins. That put him in contact with Snyder. Cerrato became the enabler of Snyder's early free agent excesses. He was fired by Marty Schottenheimer and spent a year working for ESPN but returned when Steve Spurrier became the coach.

When Gibbs was hired and got the title of team president as well as coach, many people around the league figured Gibbs would fire Cerrato, but he didn't. He opted to give Cerrato a chance and see how things would work. Any doubts Gibbs might have had about the wisdom of building a team through free agent signings were erased soon after the Redskins added defensive tackle Cornelius Griffin, linebacker Marcus Washington, and cornerback Shawn Springs in the first offseason. Gibbs would come to regard that free agent class as the heart and soul of the team. The early successes in free agency convinced Gibbs that the Redskins' setup was workable. Cerrato evaluated the players. Gibbs picked them. Snyder made sure they got signed. The Redskins, in stark contrast to the Eagles, figured free agency was the safest avenue for adding players because the players you were adding already were in the NFL. You didn't have to try to figure out how successfully they'd make the jump from college to the pros.

In the days before the salary cap, Gibbs and Bobby Beathard had been able to make any move they'd wanted as long as they could get late Redskins owner Jack Kent Cooke to sign off on the expense. If they wanted to keep a ten-year veteran as a backup, all they had to do was convince Cooke to pay for it instead of shipping out the older player and bringing in a cheaper rookie. Cooke usually consented. The days of keeping around expensive veteran players as backups were long gone, but Gibbs still saw a lot of Cooke in Snyder. Both wanted to win desperately and were willing to sign big checks to do it. The difference was that Snyder was much more involved in the deliberating process than Cooke had ever been.

Now the Redskins were hoping they would be back in the market soon. They had an offseason shopping list that included a wide receiver or two, a pass-rushing defensive lineman, a safety, and a cornerback. But Gibbs and Snyder knew the team's salary cap situation would be dire if there was no extension of the labor deal. The salary cap for the upcoming season was projected to be somewhere between $92 million and $95 million per team without a new labor deal. It would climb above $100 million per club with a labor agreement. No owner was being tugged in different directions in the labor and revenue-sharing debates more than Snyder. He needed a labor deal to ease the Redskins' salary cap crunch, but no owner would have to write a bigger check to subsidize other teams if there was a revised revenue-sharing system. Others around the league figured Snyder's will to spend money in pursuit of winning would ultimately prevail over his objections to the revenue-sharing proposals.

They were right.

Sitting in the lobby of the Marriott, Snyder and Gibbs joked about jumping out of their hotel windows if the labor extension didn't get done.

"What floor are you on?" Snyder asked.

"The eleventh," Gibbs said.

"Good," Snyder said. "I'm on the fourteenth. I'll land on you and you'll cushion my fall."

Someone else at the table suggested that plenty of people from other NFL teams would have similar plans if the labor deal didn't get done.

"It'll be like 1929," Gibbs said.

They figured they'd know by midway through the following week which way the labor negotiations were going to go. Snyder would be in Palm Beach, Florida, staying at the lavish home owned by another of the team's minority owners, Dwight Schar. Snyder invited Gibbs to join him but Gibbs said he had to go back to Washington after the combine.

Eric Schaffer, the Redskins' salary cap expert and contract negotiator, walked across the lobby, sat down at the table, and joined the conversation. Before working for the Redskins he'd worked for superagent Tom Condon and he still moved easily in those circles. He told the group he'd been hanging out with some agents and many of them remained convinced the labor deal would get done. He had a card Drew Rosenhaus had given him listing Rosenhaus's clients who were about to be free agents or had been given permission by their teams to seek trades. Snyder took the card and looked over the list of names on it, then handed it to Gibbs.

"It's like a menu," Snyder said to his coach. "Pick one. Pick two if you want."

In less than a week, they hoped, they would know if the salary cap rules would allow them to pick as many as they wanted.

February 25 . . . Indianapolis

Jerry Jones was a busy man at the combine. He participated in the labor talks. He scurried from room to room at the Westin Hotel heading from one meeting to another. He huddled in hallways with other key participants in the revenue-sharing deliberations. He even found time to sit in the stands at the RCA Dome and watch players work out. He seemed omnipresent. His bus, painted in Cowboys colors and adorned with the team's logos, was parked outside the Westin each day.

Jones ran into Norv Turner, the Cowboys' offensive coordinator during their glory days before going on to become a less-than-successful head coach with the Redskins and Oakland Raiders. Now he was the offensive coordinator of the San Francisco 49ers. Turner said he'd seen the bus parked on the street.

"Have you seen the inside of the bus?" Jones asked Turner.

"No," Turner said.

"You have to come see it," Jones said. "We've got artwork up in there. We've got screens with Cowboys DVDs playing. You know, the guy who drives that bus signs more Cowboys autographs than anyone. He'll drive all over the country and he'll stop somewhere for gas and he'll have to sign all these autographs. It's gotten so bad that I've bought nine buses. They just drive all over the country and the drivers stop and talk about the Cowboys and sign autographs for people."

"You really have nine buses driving all over the country?" Turner said in amazement.

"No," Jones said, breaking into a grin. "We don't have nine buses." Jones loved to talk but you couldn't make the mistake of believing everything he said.

Jerral Wayne Jones was a born salesman. He'd gotten the gift from his father, Pat, who owned a supermarket in North Little Rock, Arkansas. Pat Jones had grown up in Arkansas but he and his wife, Arminta, were living in Los Angeles when Jerry was born in 1942. The family moved back to Arkansas when Jerry was young and Pat Jones opened a fruit stand that grew into a market. The young Jerry would greet customers at the front entrance. Jerry was drawn to football as well as business. He played fullback in high school and was a 190-pound guard in college at the University of Arkansas, where he was coached by the legendary Frank Broyles and was a senior on an unbeaten team recognized as the 1964 national champion. Jones was coached on his freshman team by Barry Switzer, and one of his fellow team captains as a senior was his road roommate, Jimmy Johnson.

He married Gene Chambers, a banker's daughter and beauty queen, during college and the couple had the first of their three children, Stephen, in the summer before Jerry's senior season. Charlotte and Jerry Junior were born by the fall of 1969. All three would end up being Cowboys executives working for their father. During and after college Jerry Jones worked for his father in Pat's latest business venture, an insurance company in Springfield, Missouri. Jerry Jones tried a little of everything, investing in real estate, pizza parlors, and chicken farming. Some of his investments went bad and left him nearly broke. But that didn't stop him from thinking about trying to scrape together money to buy an 85 percent stake in the American Football League's San Diego Chargers for $5.8 million. His father talked him out of it. Jerry regretted that when the Chargers were sold soon thereafter for more than $11 million.

He went into the oil business in the early 1970s and struck it rich. He also was successful when he decided to try drilling for natural gas in the early eighties. A heavily scrutinized drilling deal with Arkansas-Louisiana Gas (Arkla), a public utility, greatly increased Jones's fortune. Jones and partner Mike McCoy formed the Arkoma Production Co. and paid Arkla $15 million for a half interest in a nearly 29,000-acre plot in Arkansas. Arkoma agreed to spend $30 million over three years to develop the field and reserve most of the gas it found for Arkla, which in turn agreed to buy three quarters of Arkoma's production at a premium price whether it needed it or not. Gas prices dropped sharply, but Arkla was locked into paying top dollar for Arkoma's production, and in 1986 Arkla paid Jones and McCoy $175 million for Arkoma. Jones was cleared of wrongdoing in an investigation by a state agency, but Governor Bill Clinton took advantage of the controversy while defeating Republican challenger Sheffield Nelson, who'd been the president of Arkla, in the 1990 Arkansas gubernatorial election.

By late 1988 Jones had enough personal wealth to begin negotiating to purchase the Cowboys from their financially troubled owner, H. R. (Bum) Bright. The Cowboys weren't exactly an economic jewel at the time. The team was completing its third straight losing season. Attendance was down. The NFL lacked labor peace and Pete Rozelle was retiring as commissioner. There were forecasts that the next round of television negotiations could bring a reduction in the league's rights fees. The Cowboys had lost close to $10 million in Bright's final year as owner. Previous potential buyers—including Bob Tisch, the chairman of the Loews Corporation, who would become Wellington Mara's ownership partner with the Giants—had backed out and Jones's financial advisers warned him he might end up losing $25 million per season.

Jones had rarely seen a risk in business he didn't want to take, however, and he badly wanted to own a football team. He'd stayed in touch with his college friend Jimmy Johnson when Johnson was coaching at Oklahoma State and Jones was drilling oil wells in Oklahoma. He lined up Johnson, by then at the University of Miami, to be his coach as he negotiated with Bright. In early 1989 Jones became the forty-six-year-old owner of "America's Team" by agreeing to pay Bright approximately $140 million for the Cowboys and their lease at Texas Stadium. Jones used all his life's earnings to swing the deal, putting up $90 million in cash and borrowing the rest against personal assets. Between the interest he was paying and the interest he was no longer receiving, Jones figured the deal was costing him around $40,000 per day.

What he bought himself initially was ridicule. He immediately fired Tom Landry, the only coach the Cowboys had ever had. Landry had once posted twenty straight winning seasons but he had just gone 3-13, and Jones wanted Johnson. Jones traveled to Landry's vacation home near Austin to dismiss him. Tex Schramm, the Cowboys' president and general manager and one of the most powerful men in the league, resigned when the sale to Jones officially was approved. Jones cleaned house and thumbed his nose at tradition. In a routine that would be repeated by Dan Snyder a decade later in Washington, he changed virtually everything about the way his team did business. He ceased the extravagant spending once authorized by Schramm. He was derided by the team's fans as being a hick from Arkansas who was out of his league, but he knew if he could make the franchise a winner again and run the business in a sensible manner the Cowboys had enough cachet to make plenty of money. He and Johnson worked side by side to gut the team's roster. The NFL was known as a no-trade league, but Jones and Johnson made trades by the dozen. The best was the move to send running back Herschel Walker to the Minnesota Vikings for five players and seven draft picks. It was the sport's all-time fleecing. The Cowboys traded two of the players they got from the Vikings to get two more draft choices.

The two J.J.s dove into the NFL's Plan B free agency, which allowed each team to protect thirty-seven players on its forty-five-man roster but left the others free to sign elsewhere, to get players like tight end Jay Novacek and safety James Washington. They drafted very well. They used the top overall selection in the 1989 draft on UCLA quarterback Troy Aikman, who had begun his college career playing for Switzer at the University of Oklahoma before transferring. They traded up to get Florida tailback Emmitt Smith in the first round of the 1990 draft. In the '91 draft they got defensive tackle Russell Maryland, wide receiver Alvin Harper, linebacker Dixon Edwards, offensive tackle Erik Williams, defensive tackle Leon Lett, and cornerback Larry Brown. They'd inherited wide receiver Michael Irvin, a first-round draft pick in 1988 out of Miami, from Schramm and Landry. The Cowboys went 1-15 in 1989 under their new bosses, but they won seven games in year two of the Jones-Johnson regime and reached the playoffs in the 1991 season. The next season they won the first of two straight Super Bowl titles.

That proved Jones knew how to win football games, at least with Johnson at his side. Jones also was demonstrating he could make money in the sport. When Jones bought the team, only six of the more than one hundred new luxury suites at Texas Stadium installed by Bright had been sold. As soon as the Cowboys started winning again Jones got all of them sold. He built more suites. He sold sponsorships. In four years, Jones more than doubled the franchise's annual revenues. He cut marketing deals for the Cowboys outside the framework of the league's marketing deals. He regularly butted heads with the league and the old-guard owners who remembered that the NFL had been founded, had survived, and had flourished on its all-for-one, one-for-all mentality. Jones bolstered his sales staff while cutting back on spending elsewhere. When the Cowboys won their first Super Bowl under Jones in the 1992 season, they ranked twenty-fourth among the twenty-eight NFL teams in player payroll; Jones turned a $20.5 million profit that season.

All should have been right with Jones in March 1994. The Cowboys had just beaten the Buffalo Bills, 30–13, for their second straight Super Bowl championship, and Jones had helped to negotiate the league's new $1.6 billion television contract with Fox. But all was not well between Jones and Johnson, even with their team's success. They were getting on each other's nerves. Both craved attention and credit. Neither was willing to share those commodities equally. Johnson wanted Jones to leave him alone and let him coach. Jones wanted Johnson to respect him as the boss. They sniped at one another publicly and privately.

The league meetings that year were at the Hyatt Regency Grand Cypress in Orlando, and Jones and Johnson had an awkward encounter when they came across each other at a party one night. Jones retreated to the lobby bar at the Hyatt and drank late into the night. He told a few reporters there were five hundred coaches who could have coached the Cowboys to the Super Bowl and he just might fire Johnson. Word spread quickly and a week later, after a reconciliation attempt failed, Johnson was out. He agreed to a $2 million settlement with Jones, who then hired Switzer. Switzer had been out of coaching for five years since being forced to retire from his successful but scandal-ridden program at Oklahoma, and he had never coached in the NFL. He didn't know the names of players on opposing teams. He let his own players do basically as they wished. But he, unlike Steve Spurrier, had players like Aikman, Smith, and Irvin. The Cowboys lost the NFC title game to the 49ers in Switzer's first season but won the Super Bowl in his second. Jones had proved he could win a Super Bowl without Johnson.

Jones's third Super Bowl triumph was followed by a string of less satisfying seasons under Switzer and his successor, Chan Gailey. Then, the Cowboys hit rock bottom under coach Dave Campo, suffering three straight 5-11 seasons after Jones promoted the longtime assistant to head coach. Jones thought something dramatic needed to be done. The 2002 season wasn't over yet when Campo learned via a television report that Jones was courting Bill Parcells to come out of retirement and coach the Cowboys. Yes, Campo was a failure as a head coach. But he'd been a loyal employee for fourteen years and deserved a more gracefully orchestrated exit.

Parcells's coaching magic seemed as potent as ever when the Cowboys went 10-6 and reached the playoffs in his first season. But Jones and Parcells cut their starting quarterback, Quincy Carter, in training camp the following summer amid reports that Carter had failed a drug test. Parcells went with one of his old standbys, Vinny Testaverde, at quarterback but the Cowboys went 6-10. Jones opened his checkbook in 2005 to try to ensure that there wouldn't be a repeat of such misery. The Cowboys signed another former Parcells quarterback, Drew Bledsoe, who had been released by the Buffalo Bills, even before the unrestricted free agent market opened. In the first two days of free agency Jones handed out $29 million in bonus money and $66.5 million in total contracts to sign defensive tackle Jason Ferguson, cornerback Anthony Henry, and guard Marco Rivera. The Cowboys had two first-round draft picks that spring, thanks to a trade with the Bills the previous year that had allowed Buffalo to draft quarterback J. P. Losman out of Tulane, and used them on outside linebacker DeMarcus Ware and defensive end Marcus Spears. The Cowboys were better, going 9-7, but missed the playoffs again.

Jones was desperate to get back into the postseason, so desperate he was willing to sign Terrell Owens.

February 27 . . . Washington, D.C.

Gene Upshaw was back in the union offices in Washington. It was a
Monday afternoon, three days after his address to the agents, and he was
about to board a train headed to New York for a Tuesday bargaining
session.

Paul Tagliabue had told a group of general managers before leaving
Indianapolis that a labor deal could be completed as late as 4 p.m.
Wednesday. Many people on the management side remained confident
that a deal would be done. An owners' meeting was scheduled for the
following Monday and Tuesday in Dallas, and executives from many
teams were convinced that Tagliabue and Upshaw were about to finish
a deal that Tagliabue could take to the Dallas meeting for the owners'
approval. The start of free agency would be pushed back by a week and
all would be well with the world.

At least that's what everyone hoped. Teams had been doing their best
to prepare for free agency without knowing what the salary cap would
be. Each of them had one plan for what it would do with a labor deal
and one for what it would do without a labor deal. Many, like the
Redskins, were facing severe salary cap crunches if there wasn't a settlement. The Eagles were different because they had their salary cap in
order, so labor chaos would benefit them in the short term; they'd be
able to gobble up the players released by the cap-strapped teams. In their
quiet, selfish moments, some in the Eagles organization allowed themselves to root just a little bit for the labor deal to fall through.

Most of the agents had been expecting the labor deal to get done and
had been a bit unnerved by Upshaw's pessimism in Indianapolis. They
weren't all fans of the current system. Leigh Steinberg, for one, thought
the salary cap eroded the depth of teams and hurt the overall quality of
play in the league by forcing veteran players to leave teams prematurely
and youngsters to play before they were ready. But he had an apprecia-
tion of what the salary cap system had done for the league, ushering in
an era of unprecedented prosperity in large part because fans could be

certain the games would be played uninterrupted by a strike or lockout. If the genie was let out of the bottle and the salary cap went away, Steinberg thought, it might never come back and the sport might be facing a decade or so of labor unrest without a collective bargaining agreement. Maybe people around the league believed there would be a settlement because the alternative was so unthinkable.

While Upshaw rode toward New York on his train, rumors were flying that a labor deal was either imminent or already in place, pending a revenue-sharing agreement among the owners. Tagliabue had sent a memo to the teams telling them officially what he'd told the GMs in Indianapolis—they'd know by 4 p.m. Wednesday whether there would be a labor extension. Tagliabue also told the teams in the memo they'd be informed Wednesday exactly what the salary cap figure would be. In Upshaw's view, the rumors of an imminent deal had sprouted from Tagliabue's memo. It was wishful thinking. He remained skeptical that he and Tagliabue could complete a deal. He was right.

The next day, Upshaw walked out of the bargaining session without an agreement. The negotiations broke off with the league offering the players 56.2 percent of the expanded revenue pool and Upshaw still seeking at least 60 percent. He considered the talks deadlocked and headed home to D.C. Tagliabue canceled the owners' meeting in Dallas and summoned the owners to New York for an emergency meeting that Thursday morning at 8:30 at the Grand Hyatt. The league issued a written statement saying the owners would be told at the meeting how the union was "overreaching" in the negotiations and there would be no discussion of "internal" revenue-sharing issues. Football had reached the precipice of labor strife.

MARCH

CHAPTER

-8-

March 2 . . . Ashburn, Virginia

This was supposed to be the best day of the year at Redskins Park, the Redskins' version of Christmas Eve.

The final preparations for the opening of the free agent market should have been getting made on this Thursday. The private jets should have been getting gassed up and positioned on airport runways to whisk Redskins assistant coaches all over the country to pick up players and accompany them back to this northern Virginia suburb of the nation's capital near Dulles Airport. Joe Gibbs, Vinny Cerrato, and Dan Snyder should have been checking and rechecking their free agent list and readying their speed dials so that at the stroke of 12:01 a.m. Friday they could get going. Gibbs would call players to tell them how beautifully they would fit in with the Redskins while Cerrato, with help from salary cap expert Eric Schaffer, would start lining up the deals with agents.

All of that could still happen at a moment's notice. The planes were on standby. The Redskins had done all their prep work.

But Christmas was a moving target this year, if it came at all.

Snyder was in New York for Paul Tagliabue's emergency owners' meeting to find out.

Cerrato, here at Redskins Park, kept his phone in hand and anxiously awaited news. The Redskins didn't know whether to feel their usual giddy anticipation for free agency or dread. It all depended on the outcome of the labor talks—deal or no deal, salary cap wiggle room or salary cap calamity. Schaffer had to prepare for the worst. He'd been working the phones frantically to make sure the team could get under the cap as painlessly as possible if there was no labor extension. He haggled with agents and lined up reworkings of players' contracts.

He offered to restructure linebacker LaVar Arrington's contract, but Arrington would end up going in another direction. The team's onetime golden child had spent two injury-filled and frustrating seasons under Gibbs and Gregg Williams, who wanted defensive players who did exactly as instructed instead of following their instincts on the field. Arrington didn't get along with linebackers coach Dale Lindsey, and his relationship with Snyder had soured after he'd accused the team of shortchanging him by $6.5 million in a contract extension. Arrington sensed the coaches didn't want him to stay. Releasing Arrington immediately gave the team no salary cap relief, but the leverage the Redskins had was that Arrington's contract called for him to receive a $6.5 million roster bonus in mid-July. The team could wait until just before that money was due and then release him to avoid paying the bonus. Arrington would be left without a job at a time of the year when other clubs would have little or no cash and salary cap space left to sign him to a significant contract. So Arrington decided he wanted out sooner rather than later. He and the team negotiated a deal by which he would be left without not only the $6.5 million roster bonus and the future salaries in his contract, but also $4.4 million in deferred bonus payments owed to him by the Redskins. He would waive those payments in exchange for being released now. The Redskins would cut him and get salary cap credit for the $4.4 million. Arrington would be on the market at a time when there were still good contracts to be had.

But the Redskins wanted to be adding at this time of the year, not subtracting. Cerrato and the organization's scouts spent much of the year getting ready for free agency. They evaluated every player on every NFL team. For each player in the league the Redskins had a file on a computer with the player's height, weight, and speed, plus summaries of his strengths and weaknesses and his potential value. The Redskins assigned each player a letter grade. A grade of A— or better signified a good player worth pursuing if he was available; a B was a backup. As the opening of the free agent market neared each year, Cerrato put up a big board in his office with the names of the available players. The color of the border around a player's name corresponded to the letter grade he'd been assigned. Once the Redskins' season ended the team's pro scouts met with Cerrato and went over all the players league-wide who were eligible for free agency that spring, both unrestricted and restricted, plus players with voidable contracts who could become free and players who might be cut or traded.

Under NFL rules, a player became a restricted free agent after three seasons in the league if his contract had expired. His team could, by making him a "tender" offer at one of three predetermined salary levels, maintain the right to retain him by matching any contract offer sheet he might sign with another club. That also gave his team the right to receive a draft pick from the player's new club as compensation if it allowed the player to leave. The round of the pick depended on the tender offer the player had been given. The lowest tender gave the team the right to receive a pick in the same round in which the player originally had been drafted; the middle tender meant a first-round pick; the highest tender meant first- and third-round picks.

After four seasons a player with an expired contract became an unrestricted free agent, free to sign with any team he chose. The only string that could be attached was if his team used its "franchise" or "transition" tag on him. Both enabled the team to retain the player by matching any offer from another team. The franchise tag also entitled the team to two first-round draft picks from the player's new club as compensation if the player was allowed to depart (or in some cases it could take the player off the market altogether). Using the transition tag required a team to give the player a one-year contract with a salary equal to the average of the ten highest-paid players in the league at that position; the franchise tag required a salary equal to the average of the five highest-paid players at the position. A team could use only one franchise or transition tag per offseason.

Cerrato and the Redskins' scouts compiled a position-by-position list of the players they thought could improve their team. They removed the names of any players with significant character issues. Once the team's coaches got back from the short vacations they took after the season, Cerrato gave each assistant coach a list of the available players at the position he oversaw. He gave the coach only names, bios, and game tapes, not the scouts' assessments of the players. He wanted an independent opinion. The coach had two weeks to grade and rank the players he'd been assigned.

Before the NFL scouting combine, Cerrato and Gibbs would oversee three to four days of meetings about the offensive players who would be available and three to four days of meetings about the defensive players who would be available. The Redskins would deal only with their positions of need. This year that meant they spent time on wide receivers, tight ends, offensive linemen, defensive ends, defensive tackles, linebackers, cornerbacks, and safeties. They also evaluated the Kansas City Chiefs' two reserve quarterbacks, Todd Collins and Damon Huard, figuring they'd want to add one backup already familiar with Al Saunders's system.

When the receivers were up, for instance, Cerrato and Gibbs would meet with Saunders, top holdover offensive assistants Don Breaux and Jack Burns, wide receivers coach Stan Hixon, and the pro scouts. Any other offensive coach who wanted to be there was welcome. Cerrato would read the first name on the list and the scout to which that player had been assigned would read his report. Hixon would read his report next. Then the group would watch tapes of the player. For a receiver, they would watch a cut-up of all the plays from the previous season in which the receiver had touched the ball or the ball had been thrown in his direction. The lights would come back on and Cerrato would ask each scout—Louis Riddick, Don Warren, Terry Ray—what he thought. He'd ask Hixon what he thought, then Saunders. Gibbs would assess how the player might fit in. When the group got through the list Cerrato would have the coaches and scouts add the players already on the Redskins' roster to the rankings. If there was no available player better than what the team already had on hand, it didn't make sense to do any shopping. If there were a half-dozen players out there better than anyone the team had at the position, it was an area where the Redskins really could improve.

Cerrato would emerge from those meetings and compile a free agent wish list. On one side of a sheet of paper he'd have a list of the offensive players the Redskins might pursue, with each player's height, weight, speed, grade, agent, and agent's phone numbers. On the other side of the paper the defensive players were listed in the same fashion. The Redskins called it their "hit list." Cerrato would take the hit list to Snyder and say, "This is who we want."

More often than not, Snyder would work right from the top of the list. When the Redskins added Santana Moss and David Patten at wide receiver in 2005, they were among only three wideouts on the hit list. "What the fuck?" Snyder would say to Cerrato, teasingly wondering why his scouting lieutenant would bother to grade dozens of players at a position when his boss almost invariably would spend enough money to get the best player available. "Why do you make it so difficult?"

While the Redskins' hit list was being compiled, financial considerations didn't factor into the equation. The scouts and coaches simply listed the best players, in their estimation, at each position. Finances became a consideration later. Snyder certainly wasn't against spending big money, but he wanted to try to get the most out of his expenditures. When Jevon Kearse had been available as a free agent in 2004, Snyder and Cerrato had carefully weighed whether to spend a $16 million signing bonus to get Kearse, or to get linebacker Marcus Washington and defensive tackle Cornelius Griffin for a combined $15.3 million in signing bonuses. They'd gone with Washington and Griffin and ended up being happy they had.

This time around the Redskins ranked fifteen wide receivers and put Antwaan Randle El, an unrestricted free agent from the Pittsburgh Steelers, and Brandon Lloyd, a restricted free agent from the San Francisco 49ers, at the top of their list. St. Louis Rams unrestricted free agent Adam Archuleta was their top-rated safety. Andre Carter of the 49ers, an unrestricted free agent, was their top-rated defensive end ahead of New York Jets pass-rush specialist John Abraham. The Redskins figured Carter, unlike Abraham, could also play effectively against the run.

A labor deal, combined with the giveback by Arrington, would give the Redskins plenty of salary cap room to maneuver. No labor deal was an entirely different story. "We were hosed," Cerrato said later. "We were cutting guys."

The Redskins had ten contract restructurings lined up with players to reduce their salary cap overage if there was no labor deal. They would have had to release some backup players. They couldn't have re-signed their own free agents and they couldn't have been spenders on other teams' free agents. They could have traded for Lloyd, and he would have had to play a season for the tender offer he'd received from the 49ers in restricted free agency before getting a new contract. That would have been it. But there would have been one significant consolation: The Redskins would have been a year away from readying for a season without a salary cap, when they could get their revenge on every other team in the league by far, far outspending them. "It was going to be a tough year," Cerrato said. "But then the next year it would be like, 'Hey, fuck you guys.'"

The Redskins at some point were going to fuel up the jets, wine and dine some free agent recruits, and spend the money. There was only one question.

When?

March 2 ... New York

Lamar Hunt, the seventy-three-year-old founder and owner of the Kansas City Chiefs, traveled to New York and got to bed at the Grand

Hyatt in Manhattan at 3 a.m. The emergency owners' meeting called by Paul Tagliabue was to start five and a half hours later. The old-guard owners had seen plenty of labor strife and weren't panicking. "I don't think it's a dire situation," Ralph Wilson, the eighty-seven-year-old owner of the Buffalo Bills, said just before he entered the meeting room. "We've got a great game. It's going to go on. We'll work something out along the way. These things always get worked out eventually, maybe not this morning but eventually."

Snow was falling outside as the owners settled into leather seats in the hotel's Manhattan Ballroom. Jerry Jones walked into the room talking with Carolina Panthers owner Jerry Richardson. Dan Snyder walked in grim-faced. Joe Banner gobbled down breakfast at a table outside the room. At 8:44, Tagliabue closed the heavy doors. Owners drifted in and out of the room as Tagliabue spoke inside. Tagliabue was giving an overview of what had happened in negotiations. Jones, as a member of the bargaining committee, knew the history. In fact, he'd helped Tagliabue write the speech the commissioner was delivering. He sat outside the room for much of the meeting. "All I can say is when they ain't coming, there's no stopping 'em," he said.

What in the world did that mean?

Jones explained that if you host an event and people don't want to come, there's nothing you can do to make them come. If the union didn't want to play ball in the negotiations, the owners couldn't do anything about it. At 9:14, Snyder joined Jones sitting at a table outside the meeting room. They sat and talked for fourteen minutes. Indianapolis Colts owner Jim Irsay wandered outside the room. He'd been a vocal proponent of increased revenue-sharing. The owners' chorus on this day was that this wasn't about revenue-sharing; it was about the players' unreasonable demands. But Irsay couldn't quite bring himself to fall completely in line. "Obviously both go hand in hand and we'll see what happens," he said. "We need to keep what's built this league and that's the strength of revenue-sharing."

Inside the room, the owners unanimously approved their bargaining committee's recommendation to reject the players' 60 percent proposal and resolved that the players' proposal did not serve as a basis for further negotiations. The meeting broke up at 9:41. The owners had met for only fifty-seven minutes. They hadn't discussed revenue-sharing at all. Hunt had gotten to bed at three in the morning for this? Tagliabue met with the members of the bargaining committee for ten minutes, then headed up three floors to a conference room to address reporters. He stood behind a podium and assailed the union's demands as excessive and unrealistic. It was a show-of-solidarity, bash-the-union exercise. Tagliabue called the situation "about as dire as dire can be" and said the next step wasn't about him talking to Upshaw but about the players "fundamentally changing the character of their proposal and the character of their demands." When he finished saying what he'd wanted to say he cut off the questioning and exited.

Down in the lobby Hunt was readying to leave town. He'd already had a long day and it wasn't even noon. "It's one of these things that has to run its course," he said.

But Hunt, like Irsay, couldn't pretend it was all about owners versus players. A new revenue-sharing plan had to be part of the solution. "I think overall the membership understands we do have to have a league where all thirty-two teams have a chance to be successful," he said.

The owners and players were standing at the edge of the cliff together, peering over into the canyon below.

But they weren't ready to jump quite yet.

Upshaw and Tagliabue spoke later that day. Both understood the owners' actions that morning had been more show than substance. They agreed to push back the start of free agency seventy-two hours. They'd give themselves three more days to try to work everything out. They thought they owed that to the people they represented. Teams would have until 6 p.m. Sunday to cut players to get under the salary cap, which by then had been set at $94.5 million per club. They would actually have to be under the cap by midnight, and free agency would begin at 12:01 a.m. Monday. Two owners, Dan Rooney of the Pittsburgh Steelers and Richardson, stayed in New York to participate in the next round of bargaining, and Tagliabue instructed the owners to leave Tuesday open on their schedules. They'd meet that day in Dallas if there was a deal to ratify.

Face-to-face negotiations resumed Friday and continued Saturday. Upshaw spoke by phone Saturday morning to Troy Vincent, the veteran defensive back for the Bills who was the president of the union.

"Hang in there," Vincent told him, "and try to hammer it out."

The owners, in Upshaw's view, had believed throughout the negotiations that the players' will for a labor confrontation would crumble when things got hot and heavy. Vincent indeed was telling Upshaw the players wanted a deal. But he was also telling Upshaw a bad deal was worse than no deal. "I'm pushing him," Vincent said later that day. "We need a deal. But we can't just sign any deal. If it's the wrong deal, long term it could be a disaster."

The wave of players already being released by some teams hadn't frightened Vincent into surrendering at the bargaining table. "A lot of those players were going to be released anyway," he said.

Upshaw returned to the bargaining table and for the first time dropped his insistence that the players get at least 60 percent of total football revenues. He was at 59.5 percent, just down from 60.2 percent. The owners went from 56.2 percent to 56.5 to 56.6. But the two sides got no closer than that.

There was no way Tagliabue was going to be able to complete a revenue-sharing agreement in the seventy-two-hour window he and Upshaw had allowed for a labor settlement. So if there was going to be a compromise, the two sides might have to come up with a different way to, in the short term, address the concerns of the low-revenue teams about the big-revenue clubs being able to consistently outspend them for players. The conversation turned to "cash over cap" expenditures by the teams. In the twelve seasons the salary cap had been in place, the teams collectively had outspent the cap by an average of about 4 percent per season. The owners argued that such expenditures should be figured into what they were offering. That way, they maintained, the difference between the 56.6 percent of the total football revenues pie they were offering the players and the 59.5 percent the union was seeking really was no difference at all. The problem with that reasoning was that cash over cap expenditures had decreased to zero over the previous five seasons. So, the union shot back, how can we figure in an extra 2 or 3 or 4 percent when it might be zero? Was it right to look at the twelve-year trend or the five-year trend?

When that couldn't be resolved, the talk turned to the prospect of crafting a mechanism to limit cash over cap so high-revenue teams couldn't consistently outspend the cap to gain a competitive advantage. Upshaw made an offer: If the teams as a whole outspent the cap in a season, the cap automatically would be reduced the next season and the clubs responsible for the overage would be penalized individually on their salary caps. If the teams' collective spending didn't reach the cap in a season, the cap automatically would be increased the next season. That way, whichever side got the short end of the spending stick in a particular season would have things adjusted in its favor. But that proposal produced no immediate progress, and by Saturday afternoon the talks again were going nowhere. Upshaw was told the owners needed to have a conference call and his presence wasn't required. He exited and soon thereafter left a message for Roger Goodell, the NFL's chief operating officer, that he was leaving town. Whenever Upshaw needed to get a message to Tagliabue throughout the negotiations, he knew he could send an e-mail to Goodell's BlackBerry and Goodell more often than not would be in close proximity to Tagliabue. Upshaw and Richard Berthelsen hopped into a cab and began heading back to Washington.

"The owners are not capable of compromise," Upshaw said during the taxi ride.

Upshaw's pessimism was short-lived. After he got back to Washington on Saturday night, he began trading e-mails with people on the owners' side. By midnight he finally thought the two sides could agree to a percentage of the revenues to be given to the players. For the first time he believed a deal was about to be struck. Negotiations would resume Sunday. Upshaw dashed off a late-night e-mail to one acquaintance that read: "We are now in the area where we will get a deal. I think it may be there. It comes down to a few final points."

He joked that if a deal indeed was struck Sunday it would be the first labor agreement in the history of the sport negotiated via BlackBerry. Plans were made for the negotiators to reconvene in New York at the offices of Dewey Ballantine, the law firm where union attorney Jeffrey Kessler worked. Upshaw and Berthelsen caught an 8 a.m. flight and were in the city shortly after 9:00. The owners' negotiators arrived about 9:20. The bargaining session officially began around 11:15. At noon the union's negotiators thought a deal might be imminent. Word of the progress in the negotiations made its way around the league. Dan Snyder wondered if he was about to have a revenue-sharing plan shoved down his throat but he knew the Redskins' salary cap situation would benefit from a labor agreement. The talks disintegrated throughout the afternoon, though, and Upshaw cut off the bargaining around 6:30 in the evening. The union's negotiators gathered in a room.

"We should have stopped at noon," Kessler said.

Upshaw declared the labor negotiations over and said free agency would begin at midnight. Bring on the uncapped year, he said. He stayed in New York and took the members of his negotiating team, including Berthelsen and Kessler, to dinner at a restaurant on the street level of the office building where the talks had been conducted. The first round of drinks arrived at the table.

"Let's toast an uncapped year," Upshaw said.

"To an uncapped year," the others said to the clinking of glasses.

Vinny Cerrato, Joe Gibbs, and Snyder were searching frantically for information back at Redskins Park.

"What's going on?!" Snyder barked into the phone.

The deadline for teams to release players to get under the cap had already been pushed back from 6 p.m. to 10. Now it was being pushed back again until 11:30. That was odd. If the negotiations really were over, why push back the deadline? Cerrato wondered if it was merely to give the teams sufficient time to complete their paperwork.

Or maybe it was because the labor deliberations really weren't dead.

All day the league's contingent of negotiators had been going from the Dewey Ballantine offices on Avenue of the Americas back to the NFL's offices on Park Avenue to conduct conference calls with the owners' bargaining committee. The owners were beginning to realize a settlement could happen only with a revenue-sharing deal coming at the same time as a labor agreement.

"I've been telling you for eighteen months you have to do it all at once," Tagliabue lectured the owners on a conference call that night.

The owners had been unable to reach Upshaw while he was at dinner. Kessler had told his associates their cell phones and BlackBerrys wouldn't receive signals inside that restaurant, especially with the group seated toward the back. When the union's negotiators got up to leave and reached the front of the restaurant around 9 p.m., Upshaw's BlackBerry began beeping. He had a message from Goodell that read: "Where are you? The CEC is on hold. Can you call Paul?" (The owners' bargaining committee was technically the Management Council Executive Committee, or CEC for short.)

The talks were back on.

By night's end, Upshaw and Tagliabue agreed to push back free agency another three days, the second seventy-two-hour delay of the market's opening. They also agreed that Tagliabue would present the union's final proposal to the entire ownership group. Tagliabue put the Dallas meeting back on the schedule. The owners would convene Tuesday, two days later, at the Grand Hyatt at the Dallas–Fort Worth airport. The meeting would begin at 2 p.m. Dallas time and likely would spill over into Wednesday. That was the day Upshaw would travel to Hawaii for the players' executive board meeting, the one at which discussions of decertifying the union for a labor confrontation were to commence.

Tagliabue had his work cut out for him trying to get the twenty-four votes among the owners needed for approval of a union proposal not all that different from the one the owners had just rejected during their rah-rah meeting in New York. Upshaw still viewed the owners' inability to agree on revenue-sharing as the major obstacle. But there nevertheless were reasons for the union's leaders to hope. They figured their proposal had a better chance with the owners as a whole than it had with the harder-line owners' bargaining committee and they were convinced that Tagliabue would do everything he could to shepherd the proposal through the meeting in Dallas toward ratification.

There were media reports Monday morning portraying the agreement between Upshaw and Tagliabue as a tentative labor settlement. The NFL acted quickly to get out a different spin on the story. League officials told reporters that Tagliabue would merely present the union's proposal without making any recommendations to the owners about whether they should ratify it. The union's leaders were told of Tagliabue's objection to the notion that he was on board with the proposal and they understood. If the proposal got rejected by the owners, Tagliabue would be in a tough spot if it was perceived publicly to have been *his* proposal, too, and not merely Upshaw's. The union leaders still believed that Tagliabue would work for a settlement, and many people on the management side of the dispute were convinced of the same thing. But the semantics mattered in this case, at least to the league. The negotiators met Monday in New York to put the proposed settlement on paper. The two sides resolved that there would be no further negotiations. If the owners rejected the deal, teams would have until 9 p.m. Wednesday to make cuts to get under the salary cap. They'd have to be under the cap by midnight and free agency would begin at 12:01 a.m. Thursday. If the owners approved the settlement, everything would be pushed back by twenty-four hours.

Tagliabue had long been telling Harold Henderson, the NFL's chief labor executive, that the deal would get done at the eleventh hour and fifty-ninth minute.

"Eleventh hour and fifty-ninth minute before what?" Henderson would say in recurring exchanges, often over working dinners.

"I don't know," Tagliabue would reply. "It's just going to be the eleventh hour and fifty-ninth minute."

The two men had looked at the clock Sunday night when Tagliabue was done making his arrangements with Upshaw.

"Now I know what you mean when you talk about the eleventh hour and fifty-ninth minute," Henderson said. "We're now at the eleventh hour and twenty-fourth minute."

"Wait until we get to Dallas," Tagliabue said. "If we have more than sixty seconds to spare, it will be a miracle."

It would be Tagliabue's final miracle as NFL commissioner.

CHAPTER

- 9 -

March 6 . . . Chicago

Antwaan Randle El and his wife, Jaune, were following the labor negotiations closely. Randle El was a wide receiver who'd spent his first
four NFL seasons with the Pittsburgh Steelers. He'd been a hero of their
Super Bowl triumph, throwing a fourth-quarter touchdown pass to fellow wideout Hines Ward on a trick play to seal the victory. Now his future was at stake. He was about to be an unrestricted free agent. He
needed to know when the market would open and which teams could
afford to be bidders. There had been rumors that the Redskins and
Chicago Bears would pursue him intently. That was fine with him and
his wife. Both were from Chicago. The couple had three kids. If Randle
El signed with the Bears, Jaune would have a mother and a mother-in-
law nearby year-round to help with the children. Going to Washington
would be a big change, but Randle El recalled a Bible verse instructing
him to be open to change. Jaune researched the school systems in northern Virginia.

It was an anxious time, and the second postponement of the opening of the free agent market was almost more than Randle El and his wife could take. They stopped paying attention to the sports news. They refused to allow *SportsCenter* to be on their TV.

Their phone would ring, they knew, when free agency began.

Randle El had grown up five blocks from the Chicago city limits in Riverdale, Illinois. His father, Curtis, was a dockworker. His mother, Jacqueline, ran a day care business for children, first out of the family's home on West 136th Street and later at a center. She didn't charge parents who couldn't afford it. Antwaan and his brothers Curtis and Marcus occasionally were awoken at 6 a.m. by the knock on the door of a neighborhood parent dropping off a child. Theirs was a deeply religious household and a strict household. The three boys had to be on the front porch when the streetlights came on in the evening. All three excelled in sports and went on to play college football. Antwaan was a three-sport standout at Thornton High in Harvey, Illinois, starring in basketball and baseball as well as football. His true love was baseball, and he was thrilled when the Chicago Cubs selected him in the fourteenth round of the 1997 draft. He had a chance to make about $500,000 and play professional baseball in the summers in their minor league system while retaining his collegiate eligibility in other sports. He was eager to sign but his parents vetoed it, saying his education came first. He refused to speak to them for a month.

Virtually every big-time football-playing school in the country wanted him, but there was a catch: They wanted him as a running back, wide receiver, or cornerback. He wanted to play quarterback and was about to go to Ohio University when there was a coaching change at Indiana. New coach Cam Cameron didn't make Randle El any promises but told him he'd get a fair shot. That was enough for Randle El to accept a football scholarship to Indiana. He became a record-setting quarterback there and also played baseball briefly, and two and a half years of basketball. Randle El went to the NFL scouting combine and was timed at 4.4 seconds in the 40-yard dash, after which all but a few teams projected him as a wide receiver. The Steelers drafted him in the second round and he became an effective complementary player on a Super Bowl champion.

Now he and his wife didn't know where they'd be going, but they did know it wouldn't be back to Pittsburgh. The Steelers had negotiated with Randle El and his Skokie, Illinois–based agent, Fletcher Smith, before the season and again after the Super Bowl. They'd offered Randle El a five-year contract worth about $15 million to keep him. Randle El hadn't expected an offer comparable to the four-year, $25.83 million deal that Ward had signed in September but he'd expected better than that. He wasn't bitter. It was just business, he knew. He was a unique player who could throw the ball and run with it effectively as well as catch it but he'd never had more than forty-seven receptions in a season, in an era in which the most productive wideouts topped one hundred catches in a season. Randle El told the Steelers he would give them the chance to keep him by matching any offer he got in free agency, but he knew his stay in Pittsburgh was over.

Adam Archuleta wasn't married and didn't have to worry about schools for the kids, but the safety was still anxious to find out what his next NFL stop would be. It had become clear to him that he wouldn't be staying in St. Louis. The Rams' season had been so miserable and unsettled that the team didn't even have a wrap-up meeting. The season simply ended and the players went on their way. The Rams had gone 6-10 and had been terrible on defense. Coach Mike Martz was fired and the club hired Miami Dolphins offensive coordinator Scott Linehan to replace him. Linehan brought aboard just-fired New Orleans Saints coach Jim Haslett as his defensive coordinator. The Rams' front office wanted the new coaching staff to come in and evaluate which players to keep and which to let go. Archuleta figured he'd be testing the free agent market.

Little had been handed to him in football or in life. He'd been born in the tiny town of Green River, Wyoming, and had lived there until he was six. His father worked for one of the big mines in the town. Adam's mother wanted to find a place with more opportunity for her children and followed the advice of her brother, who lived in Arizona. She moved there and worked for the growing city of Chandler, where one of her tasks was to help name streets. She occasionally would sneak in a name, like Adams Avenue, for one of her kids. Archuleta played linebacker and safety in high school, and when he wasn't recruited by colleges, he decided to walk on at Arizona State. Archuleta quickly demonstrated to the coaches there that he could play. They showed him game tapes of the team's undersized linebacker, Pat Tillman.

"Can you do this?" the coaches asked.

"Yeah," Archuleta said, "I can do it."

Tillman would become an American hero when he walked away from his pro football career as a safety with the Arizona Cardinals to join the U.S. Army Rangers and was killed in a friendly fire incident in Afghanistan in April 2004. Back then he was Archuleta's football role model. The two were friendly but didn't spend much time together off the field. Archuleta earned his scholarship and became a standout player. He'd been working since he'd been in high school with Mesa, Arizona–based trainer Jay Schroeder, whose methods helped Archuleta become a scouting combine marvel. He was drafted in the first round by the Rams in 2001, twentieth overall, and became a starter as a rookie on a team that went 14-2. He'd had back problems in 2004 but had come back to play well in 2005.

He hadn't gotten along with the Rams' previous coaching staff and felt he could become a better player if he was coached better. He had no idea where he stood with the Rams until Haslett called him about three weeks before free agency and said he'd like to have him back. But Archuleta and his agent, Gary Wichard, wouldn't receive a contract proposal from the Rams until the day before the market opened. It was too little, far too late. Archuleta wanted to see what else might be out there for him. His phone would soon be ringing.

March 7 . . . Grapevine, Texas

The barons of pro football gathered on a Tuesday at the Grand Hyatt at the Dallas–Fort Worth airport to determine the sport's future.

The hotel was in Terminal D, and the meeting rooms were one floor down from the terminal level. One problem quickly became apparent: The meeting rooms were at one end of the lower lobby and the bath-

Harold Henderson (*left*), Paul Tagliabue (*middle*) and Gene Upshaw at a congressional hearing on Capitol Hill. The close relationship between Tagliabue, the NFL's commissioner since 1989, and Upshaw, the longtime executive director of the players' union, had produced unprecedented labor peace and prosperity for the league, but all of that was put to the test early in 2006 as Upshaw sought a bigger piece of the revenue pie for the players in negotiations on a new collective bargaining agreement with Tagliabue and Henderson, the league's chief labor executive. By March 2007, only Upshaw remained in his job and many owners of NFL teams thought the union had negotiated too good of a deal for itself, one that disrupted the economic formula under which everyone had been thriving.

Saints Coach Sean Payton (*left*) and Roger Goodell talk before the NFC title game in Chicago. One of the problems that Goodell inherited from Paul Tagliabue when he succeeded Tagliabue as NFL commissioner was what to do about the Saints, who had returned to New Orleans a year after being displaced from the city by Hurricane Katrina. But mostly, Goodell inherited a smooth-running league and he had to figure out how to keep it that way.

John Mara signs autographs before the October 8 game against the Redskins. Mara represented the next generation of Giants' ownership. He had to spend the year figuring out the ways he should emulate his legendary father, Wellington Mara, who'd died the previous fall, and the ways he should be his own man. Meanwhile, he had to figure out how to get a new stadium with a price tag inching ever closer to $2 billion built, and how to manage an organization with a retiring general manager who might have picked the wrong quarterback, and a coach who couldn't seem to coexist peacefully with his players.

Katie Holmes (*left*), Tom Cruise (*middle*) and Dan Snyder watch from the first row of the owner's box as the Redskins lose their season opener to the Minnesota Vikings. It was a year of exciting new business possibilities for Snyder, the owner of the Redskins. He struck a deal with Cruise to fund the movie megastar's production company and bought the diner chain Johnny Rockets. He spent big money on his football team, too, but the return on that investment was minimal.

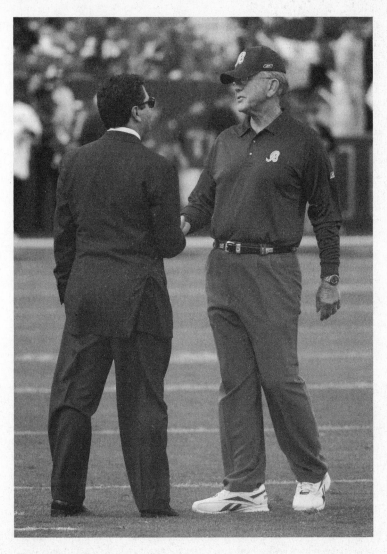

Dan Snyder (*left*) and Joe Gibbs consult on the field before the October 1 game against the Jacksonville Jaguars. The Redskins by this point were well on their way to falling apart after reaching the playoffs the previous season. Gibbs, their Hall of Fame coach, seemed to have lost his Midas touch after surrendering control of his team's offense to newly hired assistant coach Al Saunders. Gibbs felt he was letting down his free-spending boss, but Snyder continued to believe in Gibbs, who'd coached the franchise to Super Bowl victories when Snyder was growing up worshipping the team.

Jeff Lurie (*left*) and Jerry Jones on the field at Texas Stadium before the Christmas Day game between the Eagles and Cowboys. This game was for first place, and Lurie, the owner of the Eagles, was being rewarded for continuing to trust his team and his coach when everything had appeared to be unraveling at midseason. Jones, the Cowboys' publicity-loving owner, was trying to help hold things together after being the catalyst behind his team's off-season addition of difficult-to-manage wide receiver Terrell Owens.

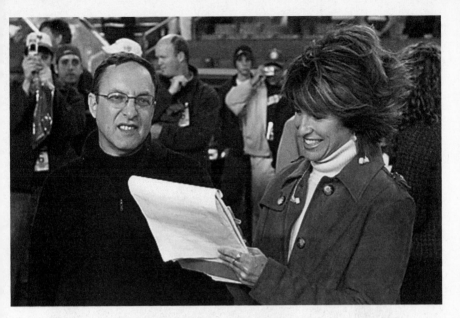

Joe Banner (*left*) talks to ESPN's Suzy Kolber on the sideline at FedEx Field in 2005. Banner looks more like a banker than a football guy, but the Eagles' president has a hand in virtually everything they do and plays a big role in making them one of the best-run organizations in the league.

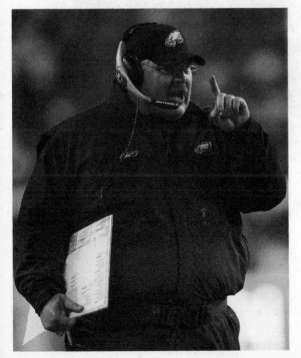

Andy Reid makes a point during the rainy playoff win over the Giants. The Eagles' coach had gotten his team to the playoffs again because he hadn't panicked when quarterback Donovan McNabb had been hurt and the season looked lost. He didn't turn on his players. He told them that everyone, including the coaches, needed to bear down and perform better, and his players appreciated being treated like grown men instead of berated like misbehaving children.

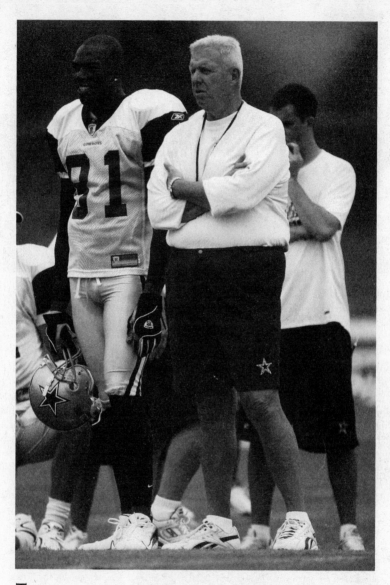

Terrell Owens (*left*) and Bill Parcells watch a training camp drill. No one in the league thought that the combustible combination of the strong-willed receiver and the demanding coach would work. It didn't, ultimately. But it wasn't because of any lack of trying by Parcells, who did everything that he could to attempt to understand Owens and make him another in the long line of players who gave Parcells headaches during the week but performed admirably for him on Sundays.

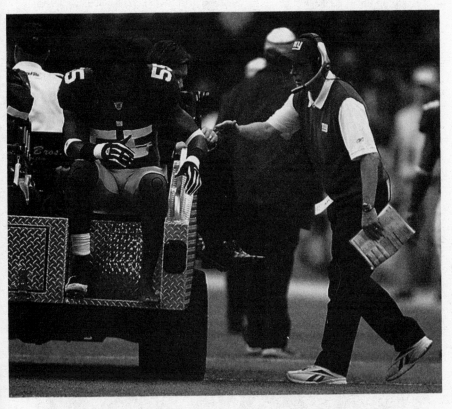

LaVar Arrington is carted off the field at Texas Stadium after suffering his season-ending injury as Tom Coughlin offers words of solace. Arrington thought he'd found a perfect landing spot following his bitter departure from the Redskins. Signing with the Giants kept him in the NFC East, close to his hometown, Pittsburgh, and his adopted hometown, Washington. He knew Giants defensive coordinator Tim Lewis. But his body was betraying him, and just when things started to come together for him, his season was ended by a torn Achilles tendon.

Adam Archuleta during his lost season with the Redskins. Archuleta wanted to get out of his comfort zone when he decided to sign with the Redskins instead of the Chicago Bears in free agency. The Bears ran a familiar defensive system and were coached by his former defensive coordinator in St. Louis, Lovie Smith. But Archuleta opted for the big money and the opportunity to try to succeed in a different system. It took only until the end of training camp for both Archuleta and the Redskins to begin to realize they'd made a huge mistake.

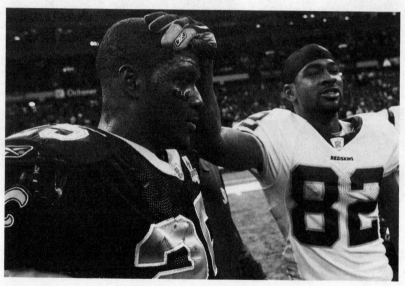

Saints rookie Reggie Bush (*left*) and Antwaan Randle El leave the field at the Superdome following the Redskins' surprising December victory. Randle El was a Super Bowl hero when he left the Pittsburgh Steelers for the Redskins as a free agent. The Redskins were offering more money than the Bears, Randle El's other top pursuer and his hometown team, and he thought he'd be an integral part of an offense that would throw the ball often. As it turned out, the ball wasn't in his hands nearly as much as he had hoped. But things got better as the season progressed, and he ended the season believing he hadn't been wrong to pick the Redskins.

rooms were at the other end; in order to get to the bathroom, owners had to walk through the roped-off area where the league's security staff had put media members. That was no problem for Jerry Jones: He staged four impromptu press conferences on the first day alone, the first before the owners huddled at 2 p.m. He had finally abandoned his stance that the labor deal could be done first without revenue-sharing, he declared.

There would be no recommendation made by the bargaining committee to the other owners about whether to ratify the proposed settlement. Normally there would be a committee recommendation on a matter of such importance, but Paul Tagliabue was taking no chances that the bargaining committee would recommend rejection.

Tagliabue did almost all the talking for the meeting's first three hours. He told the owners to expect to meet for about eight hours, then break for the night and reconvene early Wednesday morning for a full day of talks before taking a vote late in the day. Tagliabue had promised to give Gene Upshaw an answer by 8 p.m. Eastern, 7 p.m. Dallas time.

Tagliabue had tried his best throughout the negotiations to be optimistic, but he'd suspected in recent weeks that he might have been viewing things through rose-colored glasses. By the time he'd gotten to Dallas, he'd become skeptical of his ability to push something through. But then he ran into Oakland Raiders owner Al Davis.

When Tagliabue first became commissioner in 1989, Davis had called and spoken to him several times to urge him to make the league's relationship with the union less confrontational. Davis had advised the new commissioner to be firm with the players but also to respect them. The players could be tough, Davis had told Tagliabue back then, but they understood their place in the game and what was important. If Tagliabue understood the same things, Davis had advised, he could build a healthy relationship. The relationship between Davis and the league had devolved into a combative one itself, but Davis arrived at this meeting ready to support the commissioner. He thought the future of the league might be at stake.

"You've got the votes," he told Tagliabue when they saw one another.

"I do?"

"Yeah," Davis said. "Now you just have to figure out what they're voting on."

"That's not too easy," Tagliabue said.

About four hours into the meeting, Tagliabue began to sense that Davis was right. Perhaps he could push something through. But he still had to figure out exactly what that something was. He'd outlined the union's proposal to the owners. Now, in response to a question posed to him from the floor, he launched into what many people in the room would consider the best, most impassioned speech they ever heard him deliver. Tagliabue started by talking about being a young attorney in his first year working for the NFL and going with Pete Rozelle to a federal courthouse in New York to testify in the landmark Curt Flood case that brought free agency to baseball. That, Tagliabue told the owners, gave him his first view of how destructive a poor relationship between management and a players' union could be.

"If you fight with someone who should be your partner," Tagliabue told the owners, "you are going to waste a lot of energy. If you can build a relationship and then spend your energy on promoting the game—working with youth football, building great stadiums for the fans, expanding the league, moving into new communities, into the Hispanic community and into communities that might feel disenfranchised when it comes to football—those are the things that really can build. You can't do that if you're just spending all of your time fighting with the players."

Tagliabue said over his thirty-seven years of involvement in the sport he'd seen wonderful periods in which the energies of those in the league had been channeled properly. But he'd also seen terrific opportunities lost because of conflicts over issues that nearly were resolved but weren't, leading the parties to spend five years directing their energies toward putting the broken pieces back together. He told the owners many of them hadn't been around to experience the league's past labor strife firsthand and they didn't want to experience that now. This was the best offer they were going to get from the union and they owed it to themselves, the fans, and the game to find a way to resolve the differences they had among themselves and with the players so they all could work together for the good of the sport.

So much for just presenting the proposal and letting the owners decide. Tagliabue, as he'd promised Upshaw, was doing everything he could to shepherd the settlement through.

The tone Tagliabue had sought was that of a general rallying his troops, telling them to pull together and fight for the right thing. In truth perhaps it came across more like a parent lecturing misbehaving children. Either way it was effective.

When Tagliabue was done something happened that stunned practically everyone in the room. Davis spoke up in his support.

The commissioner had done a lot of good, Davis said, and his advice should be heeded. He said he'd been around ten years longer than Tagliabue and he seconded what the commissioner was saying.

This was coming from a man who'd made fighting the league and Tagliabue in court a virtual hobby, an owner who reveled in his renegade status. When Rozelle once had to hand the Super Bowl trophy to Davis, an underling had advised the commissioner to clutch the trophy with two hands so he wouldn't have to offer a handshake that Davis might refuse in front of all the cameras. At this meeting, Davis needed a walker to get around. He looked weary and weak. But his mind was still strong, and so was his passion for the sport. "I love our country," Davis said later that day. "It's got its faults. But it's the best in the world. I love our league. It has its faults. But it's the best in sports."

Tagliabue let the owners have a few bathroom breaks and a dinner break. During one break Jones gathered a media crowd and allowed Dan Snyder to slip by the reporters unnoticed. Snyder grinned and gave an exaggerated chuckle under his breath: "Heh, heh, heh." The meeting broke up around 10:15 that night. As Davis headed to his room he said, "There were a lot of very friendly people in there who are willing to give away money. The problem is, the money that they're willing to give away is someone else's, not theirs."

Tagliabue stayed at it until after 1 a.m., talking to members of the

league staff and a few owners, then slept for a few hours and got back
to work Wednesday morning at seven. The owners reconvened at eight.
This would be the day they got into the nitty-gritty of revenue-sharing.
Spreadsheets were passed around the room. Numbers were crunched.
The owners had begun the meeting the previous day discussing three
revenue-sharing proposals. Now they were down to two—one formu-
lated by New York Jets owner Woody Johnson and Bob Kraft's son
Jonathan, the Patriots' president, and another proposed by Baltimore
Ravens president Dick Cass and Steelers owner Dan Rooney's son Art,
Pittsburgh's team president. Around 10 a.m., Jim Irsay made his way
to a bank of elevators and said, "We need the ghost of Saint Wellington
to appear soon with some of the forefathers."

This indeed was a time when Wellington Mara would have stood up
in the meeting room and convinced his fellow owners to do what was
right for the entire league, not only for their individual franchises. But
in his absence Tagliabue was plowing ahead. He made his way upstairs
to his suite at lunchtime and met with John Mara, Denver Broncos
owner Pat Bowlen, and Jerry Richardson. Tagliabue put those three
owners in charge of melding the two revenue-sharing proposals into one.

There would be a Mara involved in the solution, after all. John Mara
had been torn during the revenue-sharing debate. He was the son of the
ultimate league-first man, but now he was in charge of a franchise about
to become the financial heavyweight that it perhaps should have been
years earlier. During a previous owners' meeting, Mara had asked his
peers, "What is the objective we're trying to reach here?"

The debate had raged for months and months without a clear consensus among the owners as to what the answer to that question was.
Was the purpose of revenue-sharing to make sure each team had enough
money to meet its salary cap obligations to its players? Or was it to overhaul the economics of the sport and redistribute the wealth far more
equally among the franchises? Mara thought the answer was somewhere
in between: Each team should be able to compete and still turn a reasonable profit, but not every franchise should be guaranteed being as
wealthy as the Redskins, Cowboys, Eagles, Patriots, or Texans.

Mara, Bowlen, and Richardson did as instructed and blended the two revenue-sharing proposals. Jerry Jones and Atlanta Falcons owner Arthur Blank tweaked the new proposal and all nine teams that had worked on it sponsored it. For about three hours in the afternoon, the owners' talks began to unravel. The tone inside the meeting room veered toward, "If this is how it's going to be, I can live without a deal." But Tagliabue and Roger Goodell knew just when to call for a break and let all the owners simmer down. At 3 p.m. the NFL was forced to share the space outside the owners' meeting rooms with another function booked in an adjacent area, and the league lost one of its two press rooms because of a dinner. Such compromises with other people's reality were not at all usual; perhaps they helped. Whatever the case, momentum was moving toward a settlement, and the mood lightened. Jones and Davis mugged for the TV cameras during a break.

"I'm going to give Al a Super Bowl ring for all the good players he gave me," Jones said. "He deserves half a Super Bowl ring."

"He just wants to get on TV," Davis said.

Were truer words ever spoken?

The new revenue-sharing plan would transfer $895 million from high-revenue teams to low-revenue franchises over six years, beginning with $100 million in 2006 and rising to $200 million in 2011. The existing revenue-sharing system would have transferred $240 million over the same span. The top fifteen revenue-generating clubs would be the payers. The top five teams would be hit the hardest. That, of course, meant the Redskins. But Snyder knew he needed the labor settlement to ease his team's salary cap burden. He swallowed hard and voted for ratification. The resolution was approved by a vote of 30–2, with only Ralph Wilson and the Cincinnati Bengals' Mike Brown voting against it. Brown didn't think it was a good deal for the lower-revenue teams. Wilson objected to the fact that the complicated revenue-sharing plan had been presented in only forty-five minutes. "It's a very complex proposal and I didn't really understand," Wilson said just after the meeting. "I didn't think I was a dropout but maybe I am."

The owners ultimately had figured out revenue-sharing by working backward. They resolved that every team should be able to spend competitively on players, which they defined as being able to spend 2 percent above the salary cap, and no team should have to exhaust more than 65 percent of its own revenues to do so. From there the owners calculated how much money would have to be transferred to the low-revenue teams for each of them to be able to spend 2 percent above the salary cap without using more than 65 percent of its own revenues.

What eased the sting for the owners of the high-revenue teams was that the bulk of the funding would come from the future diversion of revenues generated from digital media sources. That eliminated the argument by the high-revenue owners that they needed all the money they were generating to offset the debt they'd incurred purchasing their franchises and building new stadiums. They were mostly giving away money they didn't have yet and hadn't budgeted to get. The revenue rankings of the teams would be refigured annually to determine which fifteen clubs would be payers; approximately thirteen franchises would be receivers. Other details still were not firm. Tagliabue was going to appoint a committee of owners to help determine which teams would qualify to receive revenue-sharing funds, but the commissioner ultimately would be responsible for setting the criteria.

The owners' vote was completed at 7:35 p.m. Dallas time, thirty-five minutes after the deadline Tagliabue had set to give Upshaw a verdict. No matter. Deadlines had meant little in recent weeks. Joe Browne, the league's top public relations man, told reporters maybe the deadline had been eight o'clock Dallas time. He could barely contain a smile when he said it. Upshaw and Richard Berthelsen were on a plane to Hawaii when the vote was taken. Upshaw sat on one side of the aisle and Berthelsen and his wife sat on the other. As the plane landed Upshaw turned on his BlackBerry earlier than he was supposed to do so and got the news first. He saw a message from Harold Henderson that said, "We've got a deal. Congratulations."

The NFL, once more, had labor peace.

The salary cap was set at $102 million per team for the 2006 season and $109 million per club in 2007. The $16.5 million jump in the cap, up from $85.5 million the previous season, was the largest ever from one season to the next. By Tagliabue's calculations player payrolls would grow to close to $170 million per team during the life of the new labor agreement. The owners, in the union's view, could afford it. The union estimated that the league's total revenues over the six seasons would be $48 billion.

The salary cap would work like this: The percentages of the league's expanded revenue pool that the players would receive as compensation were set at 57 percent in the 2006 and 2007 seasons, 57.5 percent in 2008 and 2009, and 58 percent in 2010 and 2011. The deal assumed that the teams collectively would outspend the cap by 2 percent per season. That set the "trigger points" at 59 percent of revenues in 2006 and 2007, 59.5 percent in 2008 and 2009, and 60 percent in 2010 and 2011. The deal thus assumed that the players would receive an average of 59.5 percent of total football revenues over the duration of the agreement. The cap automatically would adjust from year to year based on whether the teams' collective spending on player compensation reached the trigger point. If the entire league's spending on players exceeded the trigger point in a season, the teams responsible for the overspending would be penalized for the remainder of the labor agreement. If, for example, there were four years left on the labor deal following a season in which the league as a whole outspent the trigger point and the Redskins were $2 million over the trigger point that season, their individual salary cap would be reduced by $500,000 for each of the following four seasons. If the league's total spending on players failed to reach the trigger point in a season, the cap would be adjusted upward the following season for all the teams. There was one ominous note: The deal contained a provision by which either side could opt out of the agreement after four or five years. Either side could notify the other by November 8, 2008, that it intended to reopen the deal and make 2009 the final season of the agreement with a salary cap. Or either side could inform the other by November 8, 2009, that it intended to reopen the deal and make 2010 the final season with a salary cap.

Tagliabue was relieved. He was also worn out. He couldn't even remember what day it was. He was led to a cramped press conference room by Browne and Browne's top PR lieutenant, Greg Aiello, and spent a little while answering questions before turning over the podium to Jones. Tagliabue started to make his exit, but before he could leave the room Jones addressed him directly. "Paul, I know that all the owners appreciate what you're about right here," Jones said, "and more important than anything, I'm so thrilled, thrilled for your individual accomplishment."

There was no doubt in Jones's mind that Tagliabue was almost singlehandedly responsible for getting the deal approved. The financial stretch the teams were making made Jones uncomfortable and he knew the deal couldn't be judged until five or six years down the road. But at least a labor fight had been averted. The conspiracy theorists would contend that Upshaw and Tagliabue had been in cahoots all along, that they'd had a handshake deal in place for a while and simply put on a public show to drag out the process long enough to pressure the owners into approving the settlement. Even some owners told Upshaw they believed that. He told them it wasn't true. He told them he truly had thought the negotiations were unraveling in the final days of bargaining.

The owners of the lower-revenue franchises later would grumble that the players and the high-revenue teams had won. Upshaw had gotten what he'd wanted, and the Snyders and Joneses of the world had not been hit as hard as they might have been. But Upshaw wasn't thinking about the deal as a triumph for himself or the union. He thought it was a triumph for the entire sport to preserve the peace. During the Hawaii meeting, the player representatives voted unanimously to ratify the settlement and elected Troy Vincent to another two-year term as union president. The deal eventually would be put to a vote of all the players and was approved by 1,690 of the 1,695 who voted. After the union meetings, Upshaw stayed in Hawaii to vacation for a couple weeks.

For others, it was back to work immediately. Just after the owners' vote in Dallas, Snyder got on his jet and headed home. He arrived around midnight. He was tired and he'd just lost millions of dollars in revenue-sharing, but now he could do some free agent shopping. The salary cap shackles were off. He'd been scheduled to take a trip to Orlando but now he intended to cancel it. There was work to be done.

CHAPTER

- 10 -

March 11 . . . Ashburn, Virginia

Joe Gibbs called Antwaan Randle El at 12:05 a.m. The NFL's free agent market had been open for four minutes. Randle El figured that meant that he was first on the Redskins' list. It showed him something. Gibbs spoke to him in a familiar tone, as if the two had known one another for years.

"Hey, we want you," Gibbs told him. "We want you here."

Randle El hung up the phone.

"This might be the team," he thought.

He was antsy. He and his wife stayed up late talking about the decision they soon would have to make. Chicago Bears coach Lovie Smith called less than an hour after Gibbs did. The Redskins and Bears, as Randle El had suspected, would be the two main competitors.

Adam Archuleta also got a call from the Redskins that night. The jet would be on its way in a few hours.

The spending season was under way. Dan Snyder had been getting revved up for it from the moment his plane had landed back in the

Washington area late Wednesday night from the trip to Dallas. His jet had barely touched the ground when he said to an acquaintance, "What do you think of Adam Archuleta?"

Before they could begin adding, the Redskins had to subtract. They released center Cory Raymer, safety Matt Bowen, punter Tom Tupa, cornerback Walt Harris, and defensive tackle Brandon Noble to clear about $7.5 million in salary cap space. They got their $4.4 million salary cap credit for cutting LaVar Arrington. Gibbs's calls were made once the free agent market officially opened and Snyder's jet was dispatched to pick up another coveted player, the 49ers' Andre Carter, and his wife in San Jose, California, then Archuleta in Arizona. Randle El and his agent, Fletcher Smith, came aboard in Chicago. Redskins minority owner Dwight Schar's plane was sent from West Palm Beach, Florida, to get Todd Collins, a reserve quarterback from the Kansas City Chiefs who was on vacation in the Bahamas. Escorting the players back to Washington was a task that fell to the assistant coaches. Al Saunders went to the Bahamas to get Collins. Defensive line coach Greg Blache, safeties coach Steve Jackson, and wide receivers coach Stan Hixon were on the flight with Carter, Archuleta, and Randle El.

The planes landed and Randle El, Archuleta, Carter, and Collins were brought to Redskins Park. Snyder greeted the players: "We want you guys here. From an athletic standpoint and personality-wise, you guys will fit this team. We need guys like you."

At 6:30 p.m., four limousines lined up out front and the players were off to a dinner of steaks and seafood at Morton's and a Washington Wizards–Detroit Pistons basketball game at the Verizon Center downtown with Snyder, Gibbs, Vinny Cerrato, Gregg Williams, offensive assistant coach Don Breaux, and tight end Chris Cooley. Archuleta and Cooley had the same agent, Gary Wichard. At the basketball game Snyder had both a suite and courtside seats. Cerrato took Carter and Carter's wife down to sit there for a quarter. Cerrato was friendly with Pistons coach Flip Saunders—the two had been young assistant coaches at the same time at the University of Minnesota—and Saunders provided postgame passes to the Pistons' locker room. When the players got back

to Lansdowne, the resort and conference center a few miles from
Redskins Park where the team was putting them up, they had fruit
baskets and Redskins jerseys with their names stitched on the backs
waiting in their rooms.

The Redskins' plan was to strike fast and sign the players before they
left town. They'd identified these players as the ones they wanted the
most. They didn't want to give any other teams a chance. The Redskins
knew they might have to pay a premium price to get the players to sign
immediately, but they accepted that as the cost of doing business. This
set of negotiations wouldn't be easy. The Denver Broncos wanted Carter.
The Bears were after Archuleta as well as Randle El. Archuleta had
played for Lovie Smith in St. Louis when Smith was the Rams' defensive coordinator. Smith and Bears general manager Jerry Angelo kept
calling Wichard.

"He's like my son," Smith told Archuleta's agent.

The Redskins launched serious contract negotiations Sunday. "We
aren't getting any of them," Snyder told Cerrato late that afternoon.

But the Redskins pressed ahead with Fletcher Smith, Randle El's
agent, who was on hand for face-to-face negotiations. The Redskins'
one constraint was that they'd resolved not to pay Randle El more than
Santana Moss, their Pro Bowl wide receiver, who'd signed a contract the
previous year worth $31 million over six seasons, including $11 million
in bonuses. The sixth season in Moss's deal could be voided to make the
contract worth $26.55 million over five years.

The money was an important consideration for Randle El in his first
foray into free agency, but it wasn't the only consideration. The biggest
nonfinancial hurdle for the Redskins was to convince Randle El that he'd
be an integral part of the offense. He'd had to settle for a bit part with
the Steelers, who were a run-first team on offense and then looked initially to Hines Ward when they wanted to throw the ball. Randle El was
wary that if he signed with the Bears he'd be in a similar situation. The
Bears had been one of the NFC's best teams the previous season, and
Randle El thought the Chicago offense would be better if quarterback
Rex Grossman could stay healthy. But the Bears' approach reminded

him too much of the Steelers' approach and they already had a go-to receiver in Muhsin Muhammad. The Redskins had their opening.

Al Saunders made his first significant contribution to the organization. Gibbs had told Randle El that even with Moss already on the roster, things would be different for him with the Redskins. It was up to
Saunders to convince Randle El of that. Saunders managed to do it by
sitting Randle El in front of a grease board and diagramming plays to
demonstrate the ways he'd be used in Saunders's offense. Randle El believed he could tell when someone was blowing smoke and he didn't
think that was what Saunders was doing. He was convinced he'd be a
significant part of a varied offense on a championship-contending team.

Randle El had picked up his wife at the airport earlier that day.
She'd been concerned about living somewhere she'd never been. But
after looking around she liked the area. Fletcher Smith was negotiating
with the Redskins in person and with the Bears by phone. The Redskins
were winning the money part of the tug-of-war as well. The Bears were
offering a five-year contract worth $18 million. Their offer included an
$8 million signing bonus and a total of $10 million over the first three
years of the contract. The three-year barometer was used by many agents
and players to judge the true value of a contract, the sense being that
most good players would stay with a team for at least three seasons after
signing a big contract, but things got increasingly uncertain from there.
The Redskins were offering more than $9 million in bonuses. Smith
went back into Snyder's office to negotiate some more. Randle El spent
some time in Snyder's office, some time sitting outside of it, and some
time on the other side of the building with the coaches. Snyder upped
the Redskins' offer to $10 million in bonuses and a total of $13 million
over the initial three years of the deal, then upped it again. Randle El
had been planning to go back to Chicago for a face-to-face meeting
with Lovie Smith, but he reconsidered.

"I'm going to be a part of the offense," he said to himself. "My wife
likes the place. Let's do it."

He called Lovie Smith. He didn't get through but left a message. He
told Smith what the Redskins had offered and how he would fit into
Saunders's offense. He said he was going to sign with the Redskins.

Randle El agreed to a seven-year contract worth $31.25 million, including $11.5 million in bonuses. There was a $5 million signing bonus and a $5 million option bonus. The seventh season of the deal could be voided, making the contract really worth $26.25 million over six years. Randle El had Fletcher Smith call the Steelers to give them the last chance they'd been promised. He knew it was a formality with the money the Redskins were offering, but he wanted to keep his word. The Steelers declined to match the offer. The Redskins had Randle El on board.

The Archuleta deal came next. It got done with Wichard over the phone late that night while Archuleta was sleeping in his room at Lansdowne. Archuleta had enjoyed the ride on Snyder's plane but was telling himself not to get carried away with the razzle-dazzle aspects of the Redskins' recruiting effort. He had good conversations with Williams and hunkered down to watch tapes of the Redskins' defense. He became convinced he could fit in, and Williams thought the same thing. Archuleta watched nine hours of game tapes over a two-day span. Redskins officials joked that Archuleta had studied more tapes in two days than LaVar Arrington had in six years. Archuleta thought Williams could make him a better player.

"Is this a place where you want to be?" Williams asked him.

"Yeah," Archuleta said. "It seems like a good fit."

Archuleta called Wichard.

"What do you think?" the agent asked.

"Let's get it going and see what they're talking about numbers-wise," Archuleta said.

Wichard got the contract negotiations with the Redskins going in earnest. Archuleta didn't feel the need to make a visit to Chicago because he knew what Lovie Smith was all about from their time together in St. Louis. He considered the Bears a known commodity. Playing for Smith would be within his comfort zone, but that didn't turn out to be a positive in Archuleta's deliberations. He thought you had to challenge yourself and leave your comfort zone sometimes. If the money was right, Archuleta decided, he would sign with the Redskins.

Under those circumstances Snyder was never going to come up short.

Archuleta was in his room at Lansdowne when he called Wichard around 12:30 a.m.

"Look, dude, I'm going to sleep," Archuleta told his agent. "I'm not staying up. I'm tired. Leave me a message. I'll wake up in the morning and let you know."

The deal was struck around 3:30. Archuleta woke up Monday morning and had a message from Wichard about the tentative contract terms. He called Wichard.

"Okay," he said. "Let's do it."

Archuleta's contract was worth, not counting the voidable seventh year, $30.18 million over six seasons and included $10.585 million in guaranteed money. It was the richest free agent contract ever signed by an NFL safety. There was a $5 million signing bonus and a $5 million option bonus due in March 2007. If the Redskins didn't pick up the option the salaries would become fully guaranteed for the next three seasons at $595,000 in 2007, $1 million in 2008, and $3.405 million in 2009.

The Redskins were two for two. When they successfully signed defensive end Andre Carter for $32.5 million over seven seasons, they were three for three. They also traded wide receiver Brandon Lloyd, a restricted free agent from the 49ers, during the weekend.

Fans and even some executives from other teams wondered how the Redskins could keep spending and spending and fit it all beneath the salary cap. The answer was simple: They took full advantage of how the cap worked and Snyder was always willing to throw the necessary cash at any problems. The Redskins were among the teams that annually stretched the salary cap to its limits, but there were others, including the Falcons, Dolphins, and Raiders. The NFL's salary cap was not an airtight spending limit. It was flexible. In any given season many teams had player payrolls that, in actual cash, far exceeded the cap.

To understand how the salary cap works, it's necessary to understand that a player's salary cap figure—how much he counts against his team's salary cap in a season—is different from his salary. Take the example of a player who signs a five-year, $10 million contract that includes a $5 million signing bonus and annual salaries of $1 million per season. The team pays the player $6 million in the first year of the contract, the signing bonus plus the salary for the first season. But the player counts only $2 million that season against the team's salary cap because the salary cap figure is derived by dividing the signing bonus by the length of the contract ($5 million over five seasons, or a cap charge of $1 million per season) and adding the player's salary for the season ($1 million).

The complications come if the player is cut or if the contract is reworked. Say the player in this example is released by the team after two seasons. The player doesn't get the $3 million in annual salaries due to him for the remainder of the contract and that money doesn't count against the team's cap. But he already has received $3 million in signing bonus money that hasn't been counted yet against the cap. That money "accelerates" and counts against the team's cap in the season after he is released. Salary cap space eaten up by charges for players no longer on the team is known as "dead money." (If this player is cut after June 1 only $1 million of the acceleration would count in the following season and the remaining $2 million would count in the season after that. The new labor deal allowed a team to treat up to two player cuts per year as if they'd come after June 1 even if they hadn't.) Executives often cited the salary cap as the reason when a player was released. In truth, it hardly ever was purely for the salary cap. It almost always was how the team felt about the player's abilities in relation to his salary cap charge.

Now say the team, instead of cutting the player after two seasons, wants to renegotiate his contract after two seasons to lower his salary cap charge. The team and player could agree to reduce the player's $1 million salary for the season to the league minimum. If that minimum was $400,000 the team could pay the player the other $600,000 as, in effect, a new signing bonus. The $600,000 would be prorated over the three seasons left on the contract and count $200,000 per season. The player's new salary cap figure for the third season of the contract would be $1.6 million (the $1 million charge from his original signing bonus, his new $400,000 salary, and the $200,000 charge for the new signing bonus). The player receives the same amount of money, yet the team reduces his impact against the salary cap that season from $2 million to $1.6 million. The problems for the team are that the player gets $600,000 of guaranteed money in his pocket and the player's salary cap figures in the fourth and fifth seasons of the contract increase by $200,000 each year.

There was a saying in the NFL that "cash solves cap." The Redskins lived by it. Reworking contracts meant paying guaranteed money to players, but it fixed salary cap problems. Executives on other teams annually predicted that the Redskins' mortgaging-the-future approach would catch up to them. But it hadn't happened yet. Snyder and Cerrato thought they could keep it from ever happening if they avoided carrying too much dead money on their salary cap and Snyder remained able and willing to continue solving cap problems with cash expenditures.

Once more, the Redskins were wheeling and dealing and stretching the salary cap as far as it would go. They were the champions of March yet again.

Unfortunately for them, no one was handing out rings for that.

CHAPTER

- 11 -

March 13 . . . Potomac, Maryland

Dan Snyder sat in his house and stared at his television as Dave Feldman, the sports anchor of the Fox affiliate in Washington, talked about the moves the Redskins had made. Snyder aimed his remote at the TV and turned down the sound once Feldman was finished talking.

"People are pumped up?" he said. "Why? We just got two receivers, a safety, and a pass rusher. What's the big deal?"

He was kidding. It was a big deal to him, a big deal to the team, and, he knew, a big deal to the Redskins-mad city. None of the Redskins' additions was a sure thing. Antwaan Randle El had never put up big numbers. Another pickup, Brandon Lloyd, had a reputation as a troublemaker. Andre Carter's NFL career had been mostly disappointing. Adam Archuleta was coming off what others in the league had regarded as a subpar season and often struggled in pass coverage. But in each case, the Redskins had gotten the man they'd wanted. They needed the newcomers to be contributors, not stars. Snyder had learned from his 2000 spending spree that older wasn't the way to go in free agency, so now he looked for players entering the prime of their careers. He was adding players at positions of specific need. He was adding to an already successful team with an accomplished coaching staff.

Now as it neared eleven o'clock on Monday night, the Redskins' free agent rush was over.

"I'm tired," Snyder said. "I need a vacation."

The market had been open for only three days, but Snyder knew that much of the big spending was done. That was what free agency had become in the NFL: There was a mad scramble for three or four days when the market opened, and then teams ran out of cash and salary cap space and players were left scurrying for jobs and more modest contracts. In a few weeks, most of the still-available players would have little choice but to sign minimum-salary contracts.

Snyder was about to head to New York for three days, then he would spend four days with his family in Orlando. But he didn't sound weary and in need of a vacation. He sounded energized. Snyder had dispatched the jet Sunday to pick up Christian Fauria, a tight end who'd been on two Super Bowl–winning teams with the New England Patriots. Fauria had been signed by day's end to replace Robert Royal, who'd signed Saturday with the Buffalo Bills. The Redskins weren't having as much luck re-signing their own free agents as they were signing everyone else's. Safety Ryan Clark was about to sign with the Pittsburgh Steelers. Todd Collins had returned to the Bahamas earlier Monday, but the Redskins would complete a two-year, $2.5 million contract with him Tuesday that included a $450,000 signing bonus. That deal would enable them to trade Patrick Ramsey to the New York Jets for a sixth-round draft choice.

Snyder liked to dream about winning Super Bowls, not just one but several. As he sat in his house late on this Monday night, though, he wasn't getting carried away.

"I have to start," he said, "by winning one."

He was fretting about Terrell Owens. The wide receiver was about to be cut by the Eagles and become a free agent. Snyder was worried about the rumblings that the Cowboys might sign him. He called an acquaintance who told him the Cowboys looked like the favorite but a handful of other teams could be in the running. Snyder's next call was to Drew Rosenhaus. It was after eleven but he knew Rosenhaus would be awake and working. Rosenhaus, like Snyder, never stopped working. Snyder got right through.

"Is T.O. about to sign with Dallas?" Snyder asked.

"Where did you hear that?" Rosenhaus said.

"Someone in the league told me," Snyder said. "Someone who doesn't know anything. If you stick him in Dallas, we're coming to see you. I don't want him to go there. I worry about that. Tell him if he goes there, I'm going to buy Sean Taylor a car if he knocks his ass out."

Rosenhaus knew Snyder was just messing around. The two had a smooth working relationship and had done many deals with one another. Taylor, the Redskins' hard-hitting safety, was a Rosenhaus client. But Rosenhaus wasn't going to tell Snyder where Owens was headed. Snyder sensed that and said good-bye.

"Be cool, man," he said. "Hey, get me a corner and a backup lineman."

Snyder hung up, but the notion of Owens signing with the Cowboys continued to nag at him. He knew his free agent activity was catching Jerry Jones's attention. It had to be. Snyder, after all, knew how he'd feel if he were in Jones's place.

"After what we just did," Snyder said, "I'd be very worried."

Jones's response was in the works.

March 18 . . . Irving, Texas

Terrell Owens and Drew Rosenhaus were flying with Jerry Jones from Atlanta, where Owens lived, to Dallas on Jones's jet. The Cowboys were announcing Saturday at their Valley Ranch headquarters that they'd signed Owens. The worst-kept secret in the league officially would be out. But first Jones had to make sure of one thing.

"Is there a problem with the money?" he asked Owens.

"No, sir," Owens said.

"Is there gonna be a problem with the money?" Jones asked.

"No, sir," Owens repeated.

That was the key point to Jones. Everything that had gone so wrong for Owens in Philadelphia had resulted from the fact that he'd felt his contract was insufficient. If he didn't feel his contract with the Cowboys was insufficient, Jones reasoned, everything should be okay. He sensed Owens equated money with respect. So he was going to give Owens plenty of respect. He was, in effect, buying Owens's loyalty. Stephen Jones had done the negotiating legwork with Rosenhaus and the Cowboys were signing Owens to a three-year contract worth $25,005,280. The deal would pay Owens a $5 million signing bonus and a $5 million salary for the 2006 season. The team then would be able to make annual decisions about whether to retain him. There was a $3 million bonus due if Owens was on the club's roster June 3, 2007. He would have a $5 million salary for the 2007 season. There was another $3 million roster bonus due June 3, 2008, if the Cowboys kept him that long and a $4 million salary for the 2008 season. By making the roster bonuses due in June instead of March, when most roster bonuses written into NFL players' contracts were due, Jerry Jones was giving himself almost the entire offseason to monitor Owens's behavior before having to decide whether to keep him for the following season.

The Eagles had released Owens with little ceremony earlier in the week to avoid paying him a $5 million roster bonus due on the fifth day of the league year. The Eagles announced the move with a brief written statement; the ugliest, loudest divorce in recent sports history thus was finalized with an anticlimactic hush.

The melodrama between Owens and the Eagles had begun after the 2003 season with a gaffe by David Joseph, then Owens's agent. Owens had a clause in his contract with the San Francisco 49ers enabling him to void the remainder of the deal and make himself an unrestricted free agent. But the deadline for filing the paperwork voiding the rest of the contract had been changed by rules agreed to a few years earlier by the league and the Players Association. Joseph missed the revised deadline. Union officials said they notified agents of the revised deadline; Joseph said he never received such notification. The 49ers consulted with the NFL Management Council, the labor arm of the league office headed by Harold Henderson, and were told that Owens remained under contract to them. They wanted no part of him any longer, but the ruling enabled them to trade Owens to the Baltimore Ravens and get something in return for him. The Ravens were delighted to have the sort of game-changing wide receiver they thought they needed to be a Super Bowl contender. But their delight quickly dissipated when Owens informed the team he didn't want to play in Baltimore and wouldn't report. Owens had taken one look at the Ravens' erratic young quarterback, Kyle Boller, and had decided he would be better off just about anywhere else.

The union bailed out Owens and Joseph. It brought a case before Stephen Burbank, a University of Pennsylvania law professor who served as the league's "special master" charged with resolving disputes between management and the union arising from the collective bargaining agreement. The union contended that the trade to the Ravens should be voided and Owens declared a free agent. Attorneys for the union argued that the revised deadline affecting Owens had never been intended to prevent a player in Owens's situation from becoming a free agent and had never been locked in by a formal agreement. The league's lawyers countered by saying the new deadline should be enforced because both the league and the union had recognized it and abided by it for several years. The league's arguments weren't convincing to Burbank. At the end of the hearing, he said to the league's attorneys, "Is that all you have?"

His message was clear: He was prepared to rule in favor of the union and Owens. That led to a hastily arranged set of settlement talks. The league wanted to avoid the precedent of having Owens declared a free agent by Burbank. The trade to the Ravens would be undone and the 49ers would trade Owens to the team of his choosing, the Eagles. Owens would get the new contract he wanted from the Eagles and he would play with a highly regarded quarterback, Donovan McNabb. Gene Upshaw, aware that the union and Owens suddenly had all the leverage,

asked Owens if that was what he wanted. Owens said yes. The contract
Joseph negotiated with the Eagles was worth $48.97 million over seven
seasons. It contained a $2.3 million signing bonus and a $6.2 million
first-year option bonus, plus a $5 million roster bonus and a $2.5 million option bonus in 2006. In all that was $16 million in bonuses.
Owens perhaps could have gotten more on the open market but he certainly wasn't going to go hungry. Even so, union officials took a look at
the contract and advised Owens not to sign it. They didn't like the language in it calling for Owens to refund portions of his bonus money if
he misbehaved. Owens ignored the warnings and signed the deal.

The Eagles got to the Super Bowl in the 2004 season, but Owens
began making noises about his dissatisfaction with his contract early in
the offseason. He verbally assailed the organization all spring and summer. He aimed public barbs at McNabb, feeling the quarterback wasn't
being supportive of him in his contract stare-down with Eagles management. He said the Eagles had gotten him to sign a waiver before the
Super Bowl absolving the team of liability if he reinjured himself in the
game. He fired Joseph and hired Rosenhaus to get him a new contract.
Rosenhaus argued that Owens had outperformed his contract and deserved a new one. The agent maintained that NFL contracts weren't
worth the paper they were written on, since a player's annual salaries
generally weren't guaranteed and a team could release him without having to pay the salaries still owed to the player for future seasons. The
Eagles remained adamant that they weren't going to renegotiate a seven-
year contract after one season. Owens skipped a mandatory offseason
minicamp, technically putting him in violation of his contract and giving the Eagles the right to demand the repayment of a portion of his
signing bonus—$1.725 million. The contract language to which the
union's leaders had objected all along was coming into play. The Eagles
made no move to actually collect the money, but Rosenhaus and Owens
didn't want to tempt the club any further and decided to have Owens
report to training camp on time rather than hold out.

They made it clear that if Owens did show up, though, he'd be unhappy. That prompted Andy Reid to send Owens a letter dated July 26,

2005, less than a week before Owens was scheduled to report to training camp. In it, he warned Owens not to disrupt the team. Owens reported to training camp in Bethlehem, Pennsylvania, as scheduled August 1 with Rosenhaus in tow. Rosenhaus suggested a clear-the-air meeting involving himself, Owens, Reid, and Joe Banner. But when Owens showed up for the meeting he refused to shake Reid's hand and let Rosenhaus do his talking. Owens wasn't speaking to McNabb, Reid, or offensive coordinator Brad Childress. Childress kept saying hello to Owens on a daily basis for about a week. Finally Owens snapped at him, "Why do you talk to me? I don't talk to you."

Owens was limping on an injured groin muscle in practices. He refused to participate in autograph sessions for fans deemed mandatory by the team. Reid confronted him. The two got into a heated exchange that continued in Reid's office. Each told the other to shut up and Reid sent Owens home for a week. It was a banishment more than a suspension, since NFL players weren't paid their salaries during training camp. Reid sent Owens another letter dated August 10, 2005, again with a shape-up-or-else tone. Owens headed to his home in Moorestown, New Jersey, and conducted a round of television interviews in which he was unapologetic. Reid sent yet another letter two days later after Rosenhaus had contacted the team to inquire about the grounds for the coach's actions. Reid wrote:

Dear Terrell:

When I sent you home on August 10, it was my hope that you could cool off and return with a renewed attitude and focus. I attempted, in a non-provocative way, to give you a chance to start from scratch. Since that time, you have made a spectacle of this situation, continued to criticize teammate and coaches, and made false statements to the media. I am trying hard to work with you and give you the benefit of the doubt; you are making that almost impossible.

In my initial letter dated July 26, 2005 I notified you that your threats to me during a telephone conversation that "when (you) report to training camp (you) plan to be disruptive and act in a deviant manner"

*{were} an unacceptable stance and would be dealt with accordingly. By
your own admission, last night in front of a national television audience, you have ignored me and others and been insubordinate to me and
confirmed that you told our offensive coordinator "only speak to me when
I speak to you." You also said that you "don't think so{"} when asked
if you can succeed with our QB. Most concerning is your statement that
you will not change your behavior when you report back to camp on
August 17, 2005. Clearly you have followed through with your threat
from our phone conversation and your actions have been totally inappropriate and detrimental to the team. I am now putting you on notice a
third time that this is a violation of Club rules which allows the Club
to impose fines against you in accordance with Article VIII of the NFL
Collective Bargaining Agreement and the Club's 2005 Maximum
Discipline Schedule. Continuing violations of Club rules will constitute
Conduct Detrimental to the Club, which will subject you to a fine of an
amount equal to one week's salary and/or suspension for a period not to
exceed four weeks. You cannot expect me to continue to warn you and not
take significant action if this continues.*

*In addition, we put you on notice on at least two previous occasions,
specifically on July 26, 2005 and August 10, 2005, that paragraph
2 of your NFL Player contract states: "(Player) agrees to give his best
effort and loyalty to the Club, and to conduct himself on and off the field
with appropriate recognition of the fact that the success of professional
football depends largely on public respect for and approval of those associated with the game." Failing to appear at two mandatory autograph
signing sessions is a violation of paragraph 2 and a clear breach of your
contract. Your actions will not be tolerated any longer and we will deal
with any further violation by using all and any avenue available to us.*

*Lying about signing a non-existent waiver is certainly not construc-
tive in terms of our relationship, and does not further anyone's goals.
Especially since the reality is that we bent over backwards to make you
aware that we were more than willing to share the risk with you.*

*We also want to make you aware of at least three instances in which
you violated team rules. On August 4, 2005, you did not bring your
playbook to a team meeting. At a separate meeting, you also refused to*

open your playbook. On August 5, 2005 you slept through a team meet-
ing. This result{ed} in the coaching staff having to correct you during
practice to make sure you {were} in the proper position. Finally, on
August 5, 2005 you were late to a mandatory treatment session with
our trainers. Although collectively these are violations of the team rules,
we are not going to fine you for these violations at this time, but you are
on notice that further violations of squad rules may result in doubling
and tripling of fine amounts for repeat violations, and continued viola-
tions thereafter may result in fines and/or suspension for Conduct
Detrimental to the Club.

We expect you to treat our coaches and your teammates with respect
and to communicate with the people who attempt to communicate with
you. In addition, if there is any mandatory team activity you are re-
quired to appear on time, participate in it and behave professionally. If
you do not comply with the directives I have outlined above, you will be
in violation of the terms of your contract and/or subject to fines and/or
suspension.

Let me stress again that we are putting you on notice for the third
time that your actions are inappropriate. If you continue to act this way
we will deem this to be conduct detrimental to the club which will sub-
ject you to a fine of an amount equal to one week's salary and/or sus-
pension for a period not to exceed four weeks. It is my hope that contrary
to your public and privately stated positions, your behavior will change
when you return. I have been very clear in what we deem to be appro-
priate and inappropriate behavior on at least three occasions now, and I
advise you to take my words to heart.

    Sincerely,
    Andy Reid
    Executive VP Football Operations/Head Coach
    cc: NFLPA
        NFL Management Council

On August 17, Owens rejoined the team at the NovaCare Complex
amid a carnival atmosphere, with fans lined up outside the gates and TV
satellite trucks parked along the street. Owens met with Reid and re-

sumed practicing, and his teammates appeared perfectly willing to welcome him back. Things improved for a while. Owens continued to defy Reid by violating the coach's dress code and parking his vehicle in coaches' spaces or handicapped spots at the practice facility. But he was being as productive as always during games, and the team was playing reasonably well in the early stages of the regular season. The Eagles' biggest problem became the sports hernia with which McNabb was trying to play, not Owens's antics. Owens and McNabb were far from friendly but they were coexisting. Both were showing up when Eagles players gathered on Monday nights to socialize and watch football together.

It all fell apart in early November. Owens got into a trainer's-room scuffle with former Eagles defensive end Hugh Douglas, by then a front-office employee of the team. Far more significant, he assailed the team and McNabb again in an ESPN interview. Owens's representatives had set up a seemingly harmless interview with a Syracuse University freshman named Graham Bensinger who was an ESPN contributor. But Bensinger was no pushover. He asked real questions and Owens, to his detriment, answered with his true feelings. He said the Eagles lacked class because they hadn't properly acknowledged his one hundredth career touchdown catch.

"Your friend Michael Irvin recently said that if Brett Favre was the starting quarterback for the Philadelphia Eagles, they'd be undefeated right now," Bensinger said at one point during the hour-long interview. "What do you think of that comment?"

"I mean, that's a good assessment," Owens said. "I would agree with that."

Eagles officials were furious. Reid told Owens that he would be suspended unless he apologized to the organization publicly, worked things out privately with McNabb, and addressed his teammates. Owens performed the first task, walking into a meeting room at the facility where reporters were gathered and reading a terse public apology to the Eagles, but refused to do the rest. The Eagles informed him he'd be suspended from that Sunday's game against the Redskins at FedEx Field. Owens's replacement, rookie Reggie Brown, had a touchdown catch in the game but McNabb threw a costly late interception and the Eagles lost. Reid announced the following day that Owens would be suspended for three more games for conduct detrimental to the team and then deactivated for the final five games of the season. The Eagles were suspending Owens for four games without pay in all, and were willing to pay him for another five games not to play for them.

A day later Owens and Rosenhaus conducted a press conference on the front lawn of Owens's home. Owens read a written statement in which he apologized to McNabb, his other teammates, Reid, Banner, Jeff Lurie, and Eagles fans. Then Rosenhaus took center stage and things deteriorated. He launched into an increasingly angry and combative monologue in which he defended Owens, called for him to be reinstated immediately, and attacked Owens's critics in the media. Reporters shouted questions at Rosenhaus and he repeatedly refused to answer by saying, "Next question." At one point, a media member asked what Rosenhaus had done for Owens other than get him kicked off the team. It ended as the spectacle of all spectacles, and the Eagles didn't change their minds. The next day in the locker room, Eagles players who had watched the proceedings on TV chuckled about Rosenhaus's performance. Cornerback Sheldon Brown said he'd liked Owens's apology and thought it was sincere but the whole thing was ruined for him when Rosenhaus took over. Many in the room agreed.

Jeremiah Trotter led a movement by some players to try to get Owens reinstated, but to no avail. Civil rights leader Jesse Jackson took up Owens's cause, calling the punishment excessive. The union attempted to bail out Owens again, taking the case before arbitrator Richard Bloch. The union argued that the four-game suspension was too harsh, given that the collective bargaining agreement called for players to be subject to escalating punishment and the Eagles had not officially sanctioned Owens at all prior to the suspension. The union argued that the five-game deactivation violated the labor deal, which set a four-game suspension without pay as the maximum punishment for conduct detrimental to the team.

The day before the hearing, Rosenhaus called Banner.

"Is there any way we can resolve this?" Rosenhaus asked.

"I don't think so," Banner said.

"Neither do I," Rosenhaus said.

Rosenhaus, Owens, Reid, and other Eagles officials attended an all-day hearing before Bloch at a Philadelphia airport hotel. The hearing went late into the night and union officials were confident they'd put on a winning case argued by Richard Berthelsen and Jeffrey Kessler. Many people in the league expected Bloch to reduce Owens's punishment. The Eagles were prepared to release him before the end of the season if Bloch ruled their deactivation of him was improper. But when Bloch's ruling came, it was a complete victory for the Eagles and the league. Bloch ruled that the four-game suspension was justified and Reid had the right to deactivate Owens if he chose. Bloch bought the Eagles' contention that Rosenhaus and Owens had engaged in a campaign to disrupt the team in an attempt to get the Eagles to trade or release Owens if they weren't going to give him a new contract. In a thirty-eight-page ruling, Bloch called Owens's behavior "unparalleled detrimental conduct" and wrote, "The Coach could properly conclude that, however excellent Owens' performance was on the field, his off-field conduct and demeanor were seriously devitalizing the organization."

Bloch's ruling might have felt like the right thing to do, but it ignored the applicable provision in the collective bargaining agreement establishing what a team could do to a misbehaving player. It would have been one thing to rule that Reid had the right to bench Owens; Bloch took it a step further and allowed the Eagles to send Owens home. Upshaw reacted angrily, exercising the union's veto power over Bloch's continued use by the league as an arbitrator. Days after Bloch's decision, Berthelsen was driving to a Redskins game with his son listening to WTEM, a Washington sports talk radio station. A host wondered who had represented Owens and how that person could have lost the case. Former Redskins running back John Riggins was on the show and said, "I know who represented him. It was Richard Berthelsen."

Berthelsen couldn't escape, and the sting of the defeat didn't go away quickly. He simply couldn't believe that Bloch had ruled the way he'd ruled. Kessler had asked Reid during his cross-examination of the coach why he'd deactivated Owens and Reid had said that it was because of Owens's detrimental conduct. That, essentially, made the union's case—that Reid had imposed a punishment not allowed by the labor agreement. Yet Bloch ruled that Reid was exercising his prerogative as a coach.

Owens met with the Denver Broncos after the season when the Eagles granted him and Rosenhaus permission to talk to other teams. The Broncos found Owens to be unrepentant and unchanged. But Jerry Jones looked at the possibility of signing Owens as a rare chance to acquire a tarnished but still-valuable commodity, much as Jones had done when he'd purchased the Cowboys. Jones remembered that Michael Irvin, the Cowboys' former receiving great, had been far from saintly and yet the team had won Super Bowls with him in the lineup. When Bill Parcells raised no strenuous objections, Jones made his move. Parcells stayed out of contract negotiations except to suggest occasionally that a player with a weight problem should have a weight clause inserted. The structure of Owens's contract was Jones's area, not Parcells's. If Owens had remained with the Eagles he could have made $20.27 million during the 2006 through 2008 seasons. Instead he would be making $25 million with the Cowboys. He would have made $8.52 million in 2006 in Philadelphia. He'd be making $10 million in Dallas. He might have lost in front of Bloch and in the court of public opinion but he'd won where it mattered to him. Owens taunted the Eagles with a lengthy rap song posted on his Web site. It went, in part:

> *When it comes to this game I'm the best in the field*
> *Some said I was gonna sign just a one-year deal*
> *But I got what I wanted up front, 10 mil*
> *Changed the rules of the game so now how you feel?*

Parcells was at his vacation home in Jupiter, Florida, and didn't show up at the press conference announcing Owens's signing. But he never showed up at press conferences announcing the signings of players. Jones announced Owens's signing and did better than Reid had done when he'd begun Owens's stay in Philadelphia by mispronouncing Owens's first name—saying "Ter-RELL" instead of "TER-rell"—at his introductory press conference with the Eagles. Jones got it right.

The Cowboys sold 1,500 Owens jerseys online in the first forty-eight hours after signing him. The phones at the team headquarters were ringing off the hook with fans calling simply to offer opinions about what they thought of the signing. Two days after the signing, publisher Simon & Schuster announced that a book by Owens about his two seasons in Philadelphia would be released in the summer. That was the first the Cowboys had heard about it.

Parcells usually required a player to participate in forty offseason workouts at Valley Ranch, four per week over a ten-week period. But Rosenhaus told Parcells that Owens had some outside business needing to be taken care of and Owens would prefer to do it before he showed up in Dallas. Parcells said okay. He wasn't concerned about Owens's conditioning. He'd been told by all his sources that wouldn't be a problem with Owens, a fitness fanatic. But Parcells was concerned about Owens learning the offense. Owens had spent his entire career playing in the West Coast offensive system, first in San Francisco and then in Philadelphia. Playing in Parcells's offensive system would be a big adjustment.

"Hey, this is not going to be like rolling in and getting used to running with what you know," Parcells told Owens when the two had their first in-person meeting.

Owens agreed to spend ten days meeting with the coaching staff before the Cowboys' minicamp in early June.

Parcells also told Owens there was no way Owens would have one hundred catches in a season in this offense.

"You have to be ready for that," Parcells told him.

Owens nodded in acknowledgment but thought to himself that this would be subject to change. He was, after all, a playmaker, and he thought Parcells would come to realize that the ball should be in his hands as often as possible.

Owens had twenty-five million reasons to be in perfect harmony with Jones, but Parcells wasn't signing the checks and hadn't done anything to buy Owens's loyalty. Making that relationship work would be far tougher, but Parcells planned at least to try.

CHAPTER

- 12 -

March 21 . . . East Rutherford, New Jersey

Keyshawn Johnson and Jerome Stanley climbed into a white limousine parked outside Giants Stadium and sped away toward the New Jersey Turnpike.

Johnson was a wide receiver without a team. He would remain that way for at least another day. The Cowboys had cut him and the Giants, despite their best efforts, wouldn't be signing him.

Johnson and Stanley, his agent turned unofficial adviser, had arrived in the New York area the night before and had dinner with Giants officials. They'd stayed in town overnight and Johnson underwent a physical on this Tuesday morning. If the money was right, Johnson was ready to sign a contract with the Giants on the spot. He officially was representing himself in negotiations, because Stanley was serving a one-year suspension imposed by the NFL Players Association for his representation of Cleveland Browns wide receiver Dennis Northcutt. In the same offseason that David Joseph had missed the revised deadline to file Terrell Owens's paperwork, Stanley had missed the deadline to file paperwork on Northcutt's behalf to make him a free agent. But in Northcutt's case, unlike Owens's, the new deadline actually had been later than the one written into Northcutt's contract, and Stanley had still missed it. The agent admitted his mistake and was suspended.

The Cowboys had just released Johnson to pave the way for Owens's arrival. They'd avoided having to pay Johnson a $1 million roster bonus due on the fifth day of the league year. Johnson had 141 catches in two seasons with the Cowboys, but was turning thirty-four in July. By releasing him the Cowboys saved about $2.5 million in salary cap space. Getting rid of Johnson was difficult for Bill Parcells, who liked Johnson as a player and as a person. But the economics of the game dictated that the move had to be made. Johnson put the Giants and Eagles on his shopping list along with the Carolina Panthers, Seattle Seahawks, Kansas City Chiefs, and Miami Dolphins. He thought he was worth more than the $2.5 million he would have made with the Cowboys in 2006—the $1 million roster bonus plus a $1.5 million salary. The Giants were seeking a receiver to complement holdover starters Plaxico Burress and Amani Toomer. They put on a hard sell to try to sign Johnson on the spot and offered him a deal worth about $3 million per season. But Johnson refused to accept the offer and he and Stanley got into their limo and drove away. The Giants asked Johnson to stay in touch but told him their offer wouldn't be increased.

Their chance to sign Johnson ended when he drove off.

He headed next to Charlotte to meet with the Panthers and signed a four-year, $14 million deal with them that included a $5 million signing bonus. The ways of the current free agent market had been underscored. Players once had taken their time touring teams' training facilities, talking to coaches, figuring out exactly how they might fit in and pondering competing offers. That was passé. Now it was a mad dash for teams to sign players before all the good ones were gone, and for players to get contracts before clubs ran out of money and salary cap space. If you really wanted a player, you didn't let him leave your building without signing a contract. Vinny Cerrato and Dan Snyder were right about that much.

John Mara didn't participate in the meetings with Johnson and Stanley. He spoke to Ernie Accorsi every day and had every contract run past him before it was signed. Mara knew which players would be pursued as free agents, and he would offer a suggestion from time to time. But Mara hadn't even met Eli Manning before the Giants traded for him. The Manning pedigree and Accorsi's convictions had been good enough for him. He wasn't one to veto big signing bonuses, but he admired the salary cap discipline of the Eagles and wanted the Giants to be similarly shrewd. He didn't set an annual payroll budget but knew Accorsi would be reasonable, and he always made sure to remind Accorsi to leave enough salary cap room to make emergency player moves during the season if necessary.

Mara would go to some of the draft planning meetings with the football staff, but wouldn't stay in the room around the clock as his father had done. He limited his practice field appearances to once or twice per week, but he knew the importance of what his father had done when it came to seeing and being seen by the coaches and the players.

Yet Mara, even while missing his father dearly, didn't make all his decisions simply by asking himself, "What would Dad have done?" In some ways, he knew, he had to be different. The one thing that had struck him when he first joined the Giants in 1991 after working for a big law firm was that the team was still being run like a small-time operation. The club didn't even have a marketing department. Some of the biggest tussles between father and son over the years had come when John wanted to raise ticket prices. For years the Giants had ticket prices ranked near the bottom of the league, and John would urge his father to increase them. His father usually resisted, particularly if the Giants were coming off a less-than-stellar season.

"How can we charge people more money," he'd say to his son, "for a lousy product?"

The team's business approach had begun to change, and it would have to change even more dramatically. The financial stakes were about to be raised by the new stadium. John Mara and Steve Tisch, a movie producer in Los Angeles, had pushed for the project over their fathers' reservations. Bob Tisch had favored renovating Giants Stadium and looked at John Mara like he was insane the first time the two discussed the idea of a new stadium. When John took his father to an early planning meeting, Wellington Mara walked out midway through the session muttering under his breath, "I was happy at the Polo Grounds."

Even with a new stadium, John Mara would never be a Jerry Jones or a Dan Snyder. He didn't have their ferocity about business. He didn't want to. He was too grounded, too normal for that. He was kind of boring, really, but that was how he liked it. "Nice" wasn't a derogatory term to him. He'd coached his kids' CYO teams in baseball, softball, and basketball. His own children had outgrown that, but a couple years before he'd been convinced to coach his niece's basketball team and he'd ended up loving it. It was easier to coach without one of your own kids on the team, and the squad had just reached the county championship game before losing.

The security guard at the front gate outside the Giants' offices referred to him as John, not Mr. Mara. One sunny day that spring Mara walked to the lobby himself to greet a visitor and then walked back to his modest office with a view of the parking lot. There was a larger office waiting for him to move in. It was his father's old office. His mother had urged him to make the move, and he'd thought about it. "I just, emotionally, have not been able to do it," he said.

He finally would move into the office about a week and a half before the 2006 season. He once had been told that you never really feel like a grown-up until your father passes away. Now, at age fifty-one, he'd come to believe it. He'd been close to his father his entire life and there never had been much doubt he'd take over the family business. The family joke was that he was the crown prince. In John's eighth-grade yearbook there were projections about what each of the students would be doing in twenty or twenty-five years. John's said he would be the president of the Giants. He spent every summer as a kid at the Giants' training camp, back when training camp lasted six weeks. He would work as a ball boy or help out in the locker room. Later he worked in the press room. During the season he would attend all the home games and most of the road games. But it wasn't always easy being Wellington Mara's son. All his classmates knew who he was and the Giants mostly had pitiable teams while he was growing up.

John didn't beg to be allowed to work for the team as soon as he left law school. He wanted to do something else first, and he spent almost a dozen years practicing law with two different firms in New York City. He was a labor attorney and did a lot of work for the city's hotel and restaurant unions and building-service employees. He didn't have much to do with the Giants during those years, although he would talk regularly to his father and occasionally to George Young. Still, he never wavered in the belief that eventually he would go to work in the family business. He stayed away during his father's dispute with Tim Mara, but once that was settled and Bob Tisch bought Tim's share of the franchise, the timing was right.

"Now, I think, would be a good time," his father told him. "I'm getting older. You've been practicing law long enough." John agreed.

He didn't know much about how the team operated but caught on quickly. He gradually took over the responsibilities of Ray Walsh, the team's longtime business manager who'd been his father's classmate at Fordham and was easing into retirement. Then he gradually took over his father's responsibilities. The process generally went smoothly, but there were a few bumps in the road. He'd been on the job only a few months and was at his first training camp as a Giants executive when he was speaking to his father on the field during a practice. He'd made some arrangements with the team plane and had forgotten to tell his father until after the fact. His father scolded him.

"Do I have to run every single decision I make past you?" John said, getting a bit irritated.

His father looked at him calmly.

"You'll make fewer mistakes that way," he said.

Now John Mara was left to make the decisions without his father's guidance. He was busy planning for the new stadium while Accorsi went to work on the roster. The Giants, like most other teams, had begun the offseason with some subtractions. They'd released linebacker Barrett Green two seasons into a five-year, $13.75 million contract.

He'd clashed with Tom Coughlin and had gotten hurt regularly. Coughlin had a great disdain for players getting hurt and an even greater disdain for players who didn't go along with his program. In Coughlin's first season with the team, Green had been one of three Giants players on whose behalf the union filed grievances after Coughlin fined them $500 apiece for being merely on time to a team meeting instead of the Coughlin-mandated five minutes early. The players wanted to avoid drawing even more of Coughlin's ire and didn't want to file grievances, but union officials felt they had to take a stand against Coughlin's bullying tactics. The union was forced to drop the case, however, when the players refused to attend the scheduled arbitration hearing.

The Giants also released guard Jason Whittle and announced that safety Brent Alexander would retire. Accorsi actually jumped the gun on the Alexander announcement. Alexander hadn't made a final decision about retiring. Either way, his days with the Giants were over. Whittle had once been a favorite of Wellington Mara. The previous summer the team's coaches and front office members had their season-opening roster all but set and were down to choosing between Whittle and two other players for the fifty-third and final roster spot. Accorsi called Mara, who was by then too ill to attend the final roster meeting as he traditionally had done. Mara wouldn't meddle in a roster decision, but he clearly didn't want to see Whittle get cut.

"Well, do what you want," he told Accorsi, "but I'm not going to be very happy."

Whittle made the team. Accorsi told him the story after Mara died. When the Giants released him, Accorsi guessed Whittle probably figured the Giants were getting rid of him because Mara was no longer around to protect him. That wasn't really the case. Whittle was to have a salary of $1.5 million for the 2006 season, and the salary cap generally didn't afford a team the luxury of keeping around such an experienced, relatively costly player as a backup. A club could get a younger, cheaper player to fill that role and use its cash and salary cap space to retain as many of its frontline players as possible. Whittle's talent level and role on the team didn't justify his salary.

Accorsi moved quickly in free agency to remake the Giants' secondary. He signed cornerback Sam Madison to a four-year, $7.4 million contract on the day before the unrestricted free agent market opened; the Giants didn't have to wait because Madison had been released by the Dolphins. Drew Rosenhaus negotiated the deal on Madison's behalf. He had a good relationship with Accorsi and was able to get things done with the Giants, having negotiated contracts with the team for free agents Burress and Antonio Pierce, the starting middle linebacker, the previous year.

Free agent cornerback Will Allen left the Giants by agreeing to a four-year, $12.1 million contract with the Dolphins that included $5 million in guaranteed money. The Giants and Dolphins essentially had swapped Madison and Allen. The Giants signed R. W. McQuarters, a cornerback most recently with the Detroit Lions who was represented by Tom Condon, to a three-year, $6 million contract that included a $2 million signing bonus. They signed Will Demps, a free agent safety from the Baltimore Ravens, to a five-year, $12 million deal that included a $3 million signing bonus. Demps was coming off a knee injury. He'd suffered a torn anterior cruciate ligament the previous November but planned to be ready to participate in a June minicamp. The Giants lost a player they'd wanted to keep, defensive tackle Kendrick Clancy, when he signed a four-year, $8.1 million deal with the Arizona Cardinals on the day the market opened. But they managed to re-sign backup quarterback Tim Hasselbeck and kick returner Chad Morton. Accorsi re-signed veteran offensive tackle Bob Whitfield to serve as a backup and added center Grey Ruegamer, who'd been with the Green Bay Packers, to back up Shaun O'Hara. The Giants whiffed on signing Johnson but did better re-signing their own free agent wide receivers. They re-signed Tim Carter to a two-year, $2 million deal that included a $500,000 signing bonus. Carter had been ineffective as the team's number three receiver. He was fast and could get open, but actually catching the ball was another matter entirely. Losing Johnson, though, had limited the Giants' options. The club re-signed David Tyree, a Pro Bowl selection on special teams, to a five-year, $7.5 million contract that included a $1.5 million signing bonus. Tyree had been a restricted free agent and there were rumblings that the Ravens

might sign him to an offer sheet, so Accorsi moved quickly and signed
him to the sort of long-term contract not usually given to a player who
didn't contribute much on offense or defense. Accorsi felt he'd never had
a better special teams performer on one of his clubs.

The Giants gave themselves a little bit of depth at linebacker by
signing veteran Brandon Short to a minimum salary contract, and they
kept their punter by talking Jeff Feagles out of retirement. Feagles had
told the Giants at the conclusion of the season that he was retiring; he'd
decided that eighteen seasons and a league-record 288 consecutive games
were enough. He and his wife and four sons had moved to Phoenix. He'd
received a rocking chair from his teammates as a gift. But the Giants
needed a punter, and Coughlin was willing to make some rare conces-
sions to convince Feagles to play another season. He would allow Feagles
to train on his own for the remainder of the offseason, and if the punter's
family didn't move back to New Jersey during the season, he would
allow Feagles to leave the team at times after a Sunday game to go to
Arizona and not return until Wednesday's practice. Accorsi joked that
he couldn't allow the forty-year-old Feagles to retire before he did and
tweaked a contract that was to pay Feagles an $810,000 salary. Feagles
agreed to play a fourth season with the Giants.

The Giants had to be patient to make their splashiest free agent
move. LaVar Arrington made visits to the Dolphins and Giants to start
his free agent tour. He wanted to take things slowly and carefully. He
wanted to pick the right team and not put himself into another situation in which he'd end up feeling betrayed. Agent Kevin Poston initially
was dealing with about ten teams.

Pierce lobbied the Giants to sign his former Redskins teammate. He
didn't make it to Accorsi's office but he made sure to tell Coughlin and
Tim Lewis not to believe the negative things they might be hearing.

"He's not a bad guy," Pierce told the coaches, "and he's sure not a
bad player."

Arrington's decision would come down to the Giants and Packers.
The Packers were offering a little bit more money, and quarterback
Brett Favre took part in the recruiting. He called Arrington.

"Me and you are going to ride together," Favre told him.

Arrington made a second visit to the Giants in April and underwent a physical. On his first visit, he and Poston merely provided the results of a previous physical. Poston regarded undergoing a physical for the Giants without what he considered a suitable contract offer a sign of good faith. The Giants regarded it as a necessity before any serious negotiations would begin, given that Arrington had undergone two knee surgeries within a twenty-month span in 2004 and 2005. The results of the physical satisfied the Giants that Arrington's creaky right knee was sound enough for them to sign him. Accorsi scolded media members during his annual predraft press conference not to get carried away with the Giants' chances of signing Arrington, but negotiations between Poston and Kevin Abrams, the Giants' assistant GM, intensified later that day. Within twenty-four hours, the deal was virtually completed. Arrington signed the day after that, one week before the draft. Arrington's camp portrayed the deal publicly as a seven-year contract worth as much as $49 million. That was technically true, but Arrington would have to cash in on every incentive clause for the deal to be that lucrative. Really, he'd settled for far less. The deal contained a relatively modest signing bonus of $5.25 million. It would be worth $3.7 million per season without the incentives and $5 million per year if he hit the reasonable incentives. At least he'd managed to recoup the money he'd refunded to the Redskins, remain in the NFC East, and stay close to both Pittsburgh, his hometown, and Washington, his adopted hometown.

The Giants, as the defending division champs, were the team to chase and the Redskins had set the early free agent pace, but the Cowboys were making waves as well. Jones had emerged from the labor settlement believing every team in the league would have to do some belt tightening and operate differently, but he didn't mind that. He liked to tell a story from just after he'd bought the Cowboys, when he would drive to his private jet in a well-worn Ford Bronco.

"You're driving a five-year-old Bronco up to a jet plane?" someone who was with him asked. "Something doesn't ring right."

"Well, it's perfectly logical," Jones said. "The way you get to fly a jet plane is to drive a five-year-old Bronco. You can't have it all."

Even so, Jones was planning to be aggressive in free agency for a second year in a row. The Cowboys had released defensive tackle La'Roi Glover, who had once been a Pro Bowl player but had become an afterthought. He was going to play only about a dozen snaps per game and the Cowboys didn't really need him. They addressed a key area of need on the day the market opened by signing offensive lineman Kyle Kosier to a five-year, $15 million contract that included a $5 million signing bonus. In an NFL career that had begun with the San Francisco 49ers, Kosier had started games at four different positions before he'd settled in at left guard for the Lions the previous season. He'd signed with the Lions as a restricted free agent but had agreed to only a one-year contract to enable himself to be an unrestricted free agent this spring. Kosier was signed after Brian Gaine, the Cowboys' assistant director of pro scouting, took up the cause.

"We need to look at this guy right here," Gaine said.

Parcells and the rest of the team's brain trust took a close look at the tapes. Parcells thought Kosier was a developing player who would end up being a pretty good value, especially when compared to what it would cost to retain veteran left guard Larry Allen. The ten-time Pro Bowler was thirty-four and he'd had a rocky relationship with Parcells. The previous summer he'd failed Parcells's conditioning run and had been forced to sit out four days of training camp. The Cowboys would owe Allen a $2 million roster bonus April 1 if they kept him that long. He was to count $7.5 million against the 2006 salary cap if he stayed, and the Cowboys could save $3 million in cap room by releasing him. The signing of Kosier and the re-signing of Andre Gurode, who could play center or guard, sealed Allen's departure.

The Cowboys signed free agent offensive tackle Jason Fabini to a three-year, $4.5 million contract. The deal contained a $1.75 million signing bonus. Fabini had been the New York Jets' starting left tackle but had been released. The Cowboys, hoping left tackle Flozell Adams would return successfully from a knee injury, penciled in Fabini to play right tackle. The offensive line had been a major problem area for the Cowboys the previous season even with the addition of Marco Rivera at guard. Rookie Rob Petitti had been the starter by necessity at right tackle and Adams's injury had forced Torrin Tucker to fill in at left tackle. That duo had been exploited badly in some games. The Cowboys lost one linebacker when Scott Fujita signed with the New Orleans Saints but added another on the third day of free agency, signing former Jacksonville Jaguars starter Akin Ayodele to a five-year, $17 million contract that included a $5 million signing bonus.

There was one more big move to come. The Cowboys' kicking job had been a revolving door under Parcells. The team had been through three kickers the previous season and the results had been predictably ugly. The Cowboys decided to throw some money at the problem and signed free agent Mike Vanderjagt to a three-year contract worth $5.4 million, including a $2.5 million signing bonus. Vanderjagt had lost his job in Indianapolis two days earlier when the Colts signed the New England Patriots' two-time Super Bowl hero Adam Vinatieri to a five-year, $12.5 million contract that included a $3.5 million signing bonus. Kicker signings usually didn't amount to big offseason news, but Vinatieri and Vanderjagt were the exceptions. Vinatieri was the best clutch kicker in league history. Vanderjagt had connected on 87.5 percent of his career field goal tries, making him the most accurate kicker ever in the NFL. That was a bit misleading, since he'd gotten to play his home games indoors while Vinatieri and others were more often kicking cold, rock-hard footballs on muddy fields in wet, windy conditions. But it was indisputable that Vanderjagt was good—so good, in fact, that he felt he could violate the code that kickers didn't qualify as real football players and thus should be seen and not heard. He was outspoken, even ripping quarterback Peyton Manning and coach Tony Dungy one year after one of the Colts' postseason failures. That drew a swift rebuke from Manning, who referred to Vanderjagt as an "idiot kicker" during a televised interview. Vanderjagt also clashed with the team when the Colts, unhappy with his short kickoffs, brought in other kickers to serve as kickoff specialists.

The Colts felt they had to live with the headaches caused by Vanderjagt as long as he was making field goal after field goal. But things had changed in the just-completed playoffs when Vanderjagt badly missed a 46-yard field goal attempt in the closing seconds of the Colts' heart-stopping defeat to the Pittsburgh Steelers in an AFC semi-final. A season in which the Colts had once seemed poised to go un-beaten ended agonizingly short of the Super Bowl. Yet Vanderjagt didn't exactly sulk over the miss. He went on the David Letterman show after Dungy had rejected an invitation to appear. It was clear to everyone, in-cluding Vanderjagt, that the kicker's days in Indianapolis were over. He, like Vinatieri, was eligible for unrestricted free agency.

Colts president Bill Polian had noticed that Vinatieri was a free agent but hadn't even bothered to call the Beachwood, Ohio, office of Vinatieri's agent, Neil Cornrich. Polian figured Vinatieri would re-sign with the Patriots. Cornrich was close to Patriots coach Bill Belichick and had a reputation, deserved or not, for liking to send players Belichick's way. The Patriots let Vinatieri hit the open market, not wanting to make him their franchise player in February because that would have cost them a one-year contract worth $2.96 million. Vinatieri scheduled a free agent visit with the Packers, but Polian still assumed Vinatieri would re-sign with the Patriots. He didn't want to make an offer that would merely be used by Vinatieri and his representatives to get the Patriots to match it.

Everything changed when Vinatieri fired Cornrich's firm following the Green Bay visit and hired Henderson, Nevada–based agent Gary Uberstine. Vinatieri told Uberstine to make him the game's highest-paid kicker even if it meant leaving New England. The Colts jumped into the fray and Polian's negotiations with Uberstine lasted less than an hour. Vinatieri never even visited Indianapolis or talked to Dungy be-fore agreeing to the contract. The kicker wars were on. Vanderjagt was a candidate in New England and Miami, but after he visited Dallas he had agent Gil Scott complete the deal with the Cowboys. Vanderjagt had begun his career in the Canadian Football League and Scott, his agent, worked out of Ontario. The kicker who had been considered a locker-room problem in Indianapolis would barely be a blip on the radar screen at Valley Ranch with Owens there.

In the spend-off between Dan Snyder and Jerry Jones, Jones had upped the stakes by signing an idiot kicker as well as a team-wrecking receiver.

Parcells became annoyed when his former assistant, Sean Payton, and the Saints signed safety Keith Davis to an offer sheet. Davis was a Cowboys restricted free agent; his flirtation with the Saints would cost the Cowboys money if they wanted to keep him. They did.

The Cowboys retained Davis by matching the Saints' offer and gave themselves an alternative at the position by signing veteran Marcus Coleman. The Cowboys had addressed every need in free agency they'd set out to address when the offseason began. That was a good feeling with the draft nearing. They could take the player ranked the highest on their draft board regardless of the position whenever their selection came around. The focus adjusted accordingly.

CHAPTER

- 13 -

March 26 . . . Orlando, Florida

It was the opening Sunday of the annual league meetings at the Hyatt Regency Grand Cypress resort, and Paul Tagliabue was uncommonly relaxed. Six days earlier, Tagliabue had announced his retirement as commissioner. He'd told Gene Upshaw during the labor negotiations this would be it for him. He wasn't going to let anyone talk him out of leaving. He was sixty-five and he was done. He now had the labor and revenue-sharing deals as well as the TV contracts completed. The league had no team in Los Angeles, but the process of returning a franchise to the nation's second-largest market was under way. The sport had avoided a steroid scandal approaching the scale of the one baseball was facing with Barry Bonds. Just about all the league's ducks were in a row and Tagliabue had secured a virtually untainted legacy. He wanted to get out at a time when the league had its major issues settled and when it could deal with a commissioner search that wouldn't be as divisive as others had been in the past, including the one that yielded him in 1989.

This wasn't his first attempt to leave. In the spring of 2004 he'd figured he had a year left in him and he planned then to retire in May 2005, but Dan Rooney, Jerry Richardson, Pat Bowlen, and Bob Kraft had spoken to him and convinced him to stay at least through the spring of 2006. Tagliabue's contract was restructured so he could go down either of two paths—stay as commissioner through the expiration of the deal in May 2008 or retire as commissioner in 2006 and become a senior adviser for the remainder of the contract. After the labor and revenue-sharing deals got wrapped up, he didn't give the owners another chance to talk him out of retiring. The only owner he talked to about the issue was Rooney. About a week after the labor deal was ratified, Tagliabue called and told him the plan. He said his only question was whether they should announce his retirement before the league meeting or wait until sometime between that meeting and the next owners' meeting in late May. He himself thought it was best to announce it sooner rather than later and eliminate the uncertainty. Rooney said he would leave it up to Tagliabue and accept whatever judgment he made.

On the morning of March 20, a Monday, Tagliabue called Rooney back and said he was ready for the announcement to be made immediately. Their biggest enemy would be uncertainty and speculation, while their greatest friend would be candor and continuity. Rooney sent an e-mail to the other thirty-one teams at noon, and the league made a public announcement about an hour later. It was typical of how the ultra-image-conscious Tagliabue operated the league office, doing all he could to control what was written, said, and reported about the NFL. Tagliabue spoke to Saints owner Tom Benson that morning and reassured him that the franchise's attempt to make a successful return to New Orleans after Hurricane Katrina would remain a top priority for the league. He addressed his senior staff members late in the afternoon and told them it was a time of great opportunity, full of possibilities related to digital media, the Internet, games being played in foreign countries, and new stadium construction.

Upshaw, still in Hawaii, was surprised only by the timing of the announcement. When Upshaw spoke to Tagliabue the previous week, Tagliabue had told him he was headed to his vacation home in Maine and might buy a boat to use in retirement if his wife Chan would allow it. After hearing that Tagliabue's decision was final, Upshaw sent an e-mail to the commissioner that read: "I didn't expect I'd start my Monday morning this way. I guess you bought the boat."

Tagliabue hadn't, but he certainly could have afforded it. He'd earned more than $9 million in his final year as commissioner. He'd been worth every penny to the owners. During his reign, the league's television revenues had grown from $468 million in 1989 to $3.7 billion in 2006. The average rating of an NFL broadcast had gone from beating the average rating of a prime-time network TV show by 13 percent in 1990 to 60 percent in 2005. Total league revenues had gone from $970 million to nearly $6 billion annually. The values of franchises had increased by a factor of ten. The league had grown from twenty-eight teams to thirty-two and reshuffled from six divisions into eight. The salary cap had provided competitive balance. In Tagliabue's seventeen seasons as commissioner, eleven different teams had won Super Bowls. He hoped to retire by July 31 but agreed to stay beyond then if his successor was not in place. He spoke to Rooney and league attorney Jeff Pash, who helped manage the diversity committee, about ensuring that minority candidates would be considered. He also wanted to make certain there would be candidates from outside the sport.

As Bob Kraft watched Tagliabue still scurrying around on a sunny Sunday in Florida, he reflected that Tagliabue had set things up to avoid the sort of chaos that had followed Pete Rozelle's retirement. Some owners had resented the fact that Rozelle had stacked the search committee with old-guard owners. Kraft hoped it would be different this time. He thought the owners had given away too much in the labor negotiations, but he still believed in the product the league was offering. He'd paid a then-record $172 million for the Patriots in 1994 when he'd outmaneuvered Jeff Lurie to get the team, but a dozen years later the franchise's estimated value was more than $1 billion. He gave Tagliabue much of the credit and believed that Tagliabue should be remembered not only as one of the nation's greatest sports commissioners, but as one of its greatest corporate CEOs.

"It's been like other great executives, like Sandy Weill at Citigroup or Jack Welch at General Electric," Kraft said. "What he's done here is pretty special. I know anyone who bought into the league when we did appreciates it."

Early the next morning, Tagliabue gave his meeting-opening address to about three hundred owners, team executives, and head coaches. When he rose at the front of the room to speak, the audience stood and gave him a standing ovation.

"Thank you," Tagliabue said with a smile. "Please sit down and let's go."

He spoke for about half an hour. The game was healthier than ever, he said: Stadiums had been filled to 90 percent of capacity in the preceding season, the league was coming off a Super Bowl that, with nearly 91 million viewers, had been the third-most-watched TV program in history, and the Harris Poll in December showed pro football's lead as the nation's most popular sport continuing to widen.

"The critical elements of success are in place," Tagliabue said. "This should enable us to accomplish twin goals. The first is to present great football to the fans in 2006 while maintaining the momentum we have created on all business fronts both domestically and internationally. The second goal is to manage the search for a new commissioner in a well-organized, inclusive way that will strengthen the league and underscore that the NFL is indeed the world's preeminent sports organization."

There was little doubt about the NFL's preeminence in the minds of the people who filed out of the meeting room after listening to Tagliabue talk. For his next and final trick, Tagliabue would just have to get them to agree on a new leader.

March 28 . . . Orlando

As Jeff Lurie stood in a hallway during a break in the meetings, he reflected that the Eagles' belief that the draft in April, not free agency in March, was the key to building and sustaining a winning team was being tested as never before. They were coming off a miserable season, and their demanding fans were howling as they watched the team do little while the Redskins and Cowboys made big moves. Still, the Eagles stuck to their convictions.

Lurie wanted to compete for wins, not headlines. He thought the Eagles had drafted well the previous year when they'd gotten defensive tackle Mike Patterson, wide receiver Reggie Brown, tailback Ryan Moats, safety Sean Considine, offensive lineman Todd Herremans, and defensive end Trent Cole. A repeat performance in four and a half weeks in the draft was crucial. The Eagles would be highly competitive in the division again, he thought, if Donovan McNabb remained healthy and in the lineup.

"As long as we have the best quarterback in our division," Lurie said, "we're looking forward to the season."

The Eagles didn't want a repeat of the Mike McMahon fiasco if McNabb got hurt again, so they'd given themselves an insurance policy in free agency by signing veteran Jeff Garcia to a one-year, $1.3 million contract to be their backup quarterback. He and McNabb would have plenty to talk about. Garcia had been the target of Terrell Owens's barbs when the two were together in San Francisco. Owens criticized Garcia's play and later suggested publicly that Garcia might be homosexual, a supposition supported by no apparent evidence, and bemusedly denied by Garcia.

Garcia had once been a Pro Bowl quarterback in San Francisco. Marty Mornhinweg was the offensive coordinator of the 49ers for part of Garcia's tenure there, so the Eagles figured a reunion might do Garcia some good. Garcia's career had sagged with disappointing stints with the Cleveland Browns and Detroit Lions the previous two seasons, but the Eagles thought Garcia had actually played relatively well in Cleveland with a bad team around him. They'd faced the Browns during that 2004 season and needed a 50-yard field goal by kicker David Akers in overtime to win. The Eagles figured things were such a mess for Garcia in Detroit, they'd just throw that out. Garcia had some possibilities with other teams in which he probably would have had a better chance of competing for the job than he'd have in Philadelphia, but after what he'd been through in Cleveland and Detroit he was merely looking to be in a stable organization. He was ready, for the first time in his career, to accept being a backup. The Eagles released McMahon after adding Garcia.

The club made what Andy Reid had regarded as a significant free agent addition, even if the fans didn't, when it had signed defensive end Darren Howard to a six-year, $30.5 million deal. The contract included a $9.5 million signing bonus and a $1 million roster bonus, and gave the Eagles an effective pass rusher to play opposite Jevon Kearse. Howard could be moved to defensive tackle in some obvious passing situations so the Eagles could have him, Kearse, and Cole on the field together. The New Orleans Saints had named Howard their franchise player in each of the previous two offseasons, preventing him from leaving as a free agent. The second time they'd done it only so they could trade Howard and get something for him. But a proposed deal to Dallas had unraveled when the Cowboys refused to part with linebacker Dat Nguyen, and Howard had spent an unhappy final season with the Saints. It was the season the franchise spent as nomads after being displaced from New Orleans by Hurricane Katrina. The team was based in San Antonio, and housing there was so tight that some Saints players had to purchase $500,000 homes because they couldn't find anything decent to rent.

The Eagles put aside their differences with Drew Rosenhaus long enough to sign one of his clients, free agent wide receiver Jabar Gaffney, to a one-year deal. Gaffney was a former University of Florida standout who had never fulfilled his considerable promise in four seasons with the Texans, but he would give McNabb another option in his Owens-less receiving corps alongside Brown and Greg Lewis. Gaffney, a cousin of Eagles cornerback Lito Sheppard, wasn't a great player, but Reid didn't think he needed great players at wide receiver. He only needed good ones. Before Owens arrived, Reid's offense had been predicated on an even distribution of passes to many different receivers, and he planned to get back to that now that Owens was gone. Still, the Eagles kept looking for receiving help on the trade market. Tom Heckert talked to the

Saints about Donté Stallworth. The Saints were asking for a second-round draft pick, but the Eagles thought they might be able to get Stallworth for a third-rounder or something of equivalent value. They filed that away for future reference. Green Bay's Javon Walker, Buffalo's Eric Moulds, and Denver's Ashley Lelie were also available or were about to become available. The Eagles wanted Walker, but thought the receivers they already had would give them as much production as Moulds or Lelie.

Right tackle Jon Runyan was re-signed after he tested the free agent market. Runyan visited the New York Jets, and the Baltimore Ravens called. He made his decision while traveling home from his visit to the Jets. The Jets were offering more money, but he'd already made a lot of money in his career and he liked living where he lived. He would stay with the Eagles. He had agent Ben Dogra complete a three-year contract worth just less than $12.5 million. In June the Eagles would take care of the other member of the right side of their offensive line by signing guard Shawn Andrews to a seven-year contract extension potentially worth as much as $40 million. The six-year, $12.26 million deal that Andrews had signed as a rookie ran through the 2008 season. This extension kept him under contract through the 2015 season and contained about $10.5 million in bonuses. It was nothing new for the Eagles to sign a talented young player to an extension well before he was eligible for free agency, but Joe Banner and Andrews's agent, Rich Moran, had to wrestle with the issue of whether Andrews, long-term, was a guard or a tackle. Tackles usually made more money. Andrews was playing right guard but had played right tackle in college and was slated to eventually take over for Runyan at the spot. The issue might have been even more troublesome except that two contracts signed earlier in the offseason—guard Steve Hutchinson's seven-year, $49 million deal with the Minnesota Vikings and center LeCharles Bentley's six-year, $36 million pact with the Browns—set a precedent that the top interior offensive linemen indeed could earn tackle-like money. That made it easier for Banner to give Andrews a contract he felt would be justified whether Andrews played guard or tackle, as long as he played well.

The Eagles' version of Christmas morning came on the opening day of the draft. They'd spent all year getting ready. Heckert and Reid worked side by side. After the season, Reid had taken a week off and then began watching tapes of college players. Heckert watched college players year-round. He already knew the players well by the time Reid got around to seeing them, but it was important to the two men that they agreed a player was worth drafting. If they disagreed, they put the player's name on the discard pile. When Reid sat down to watch tapes of college players, Heckert sat alongside him. All their deliberating— and, if necessary, their debating—was done then. They reached a consensus then so there would be no dissent later in the process, especially on draft day. Heckert thought Reid worked harder on the draft than other coaches did—harder even than Jimmy Johnson, the master talent evaluator for whom Heckert had once worked in Miami. Of course, Heckert had never been able to be quite sure just how many hours Johnson put into draft preparation, because Johnson didn't allow anyone to watch game tapes with him.

Scouting football players was far more art than science. This wasn't like baseball where you might be able to plug stats into a formula you'd devised and outmaneuver foes to emerge with a winning team on a shoestring budget. You had to study a player and figure out if he could do those things he'd be needed to do for your coach in your offensive or defensive system. You had to make sure he was big enough, fast enough, smart enough, and willing enough to play at this level and succeed on your team, doing the things your team did. If he had raw athletic ability but you couldn't tell on the game tapes whether he actually could play or not, you had to figure out if your coaches could turn him into a player. It was all about nose-to-the-grindstone work and gut instincts and trained eyes and, often, guesswork. Those teams that did it well were the ones that thrived.

Along with Jason Licht, the Eagles' vice president of player personnel, and the team's scouts, Heckert would set up the club's initial draft board before the scouting combine. Once Reid became involved, the names on the board would be moved around. Heckert thought the

Eagles were successful in large part because they eliminated more players from their draft board than other teams did, tossing aside a player's
name if they had any questions at all about his character or intelligence.
The Eagles' offensive and defensive schemes were complicated, and they
didn't want to draft a player who wouldn't catch on. They didn't want
a player in their organization who might upset the team chemistry that
Reid valued. Until bringing aboard Owens, this Eagles brain trust had
not taken a major gamble on a player, rookie or veteran, it thought
could possibly be a troublemaker. For Heckert it was another way in
which working with Reid differed from working for Johnson, who had
been far more willing to roll the dice on a player who was borderline on
character or intelligence issues.

Banner had emerged from the Owens episode believing it was okay
to take a gamble on a player but not okay if that gamble threatened the
core values of the organization. Smaller-scale risks were acceptable. The
Eagles certainly weren't being overly cautious when it came to Winston
Justice, a gifted offensive tackle from the University of Southern
California. Justice had spent much of the predraft evaluation process explaining to NFL teams why he'd been suspended by the school for two
semesters in 2004, missing the entire football season, following an incident in which he pulled a replica pistol on another student. The gun
was only a pellet gun, but the damage to Justice's reputation was real.
He told teams that he and some friends had been playing a game and
thought they knew the person who was pulling up in a car before they
pulled the toy gun. They didn't. Justice entered a no-contest plea to a
misdemeanor charge and was given probation in which he had to wear
an electronic monitoring bracelet for two months and could leave his
parents' Long Beach, California, home only for workouts, counseling sessions, and meetings with the USC office of student affairs. In 2003,
Justice had also been given probation after being charged with solicit-
ing a prostitute.

Justice had made his first collegiate start in 2002 on his eighteenth
birthday, becoming the first Trojans offensive lineman in six years to
start a game as a true freshman. He was part of USC's national champi-

onship team in 2003, then watched the Trojans repeat as champions in 2004 while he was suspended. During his suspension Justice was taken by a friend to the Wild Card boxing gym in Hollywood to work with trainer Freddie Roach, who'd trained Mike Tyson and a string of other world champions. Boxing, Justice found, helped his football. He emerged with better footwork and quicker hands. It also gave him something to do other than feel sorry for himself. His next decision was whether to return to a team that had just won a national championship without him. That hadn't exactly made him feel needed. He wrestled with the decision a bit, but returned to USC and ended up being happy he did. He then passed up his senior season to enter the draft.

The Eagles decided they would leave Justice on their draft board. They considered the pellet gun incident an immature prank more than a menacing episode that might be a warning sign of future troubles. Reid had talked to Justice about the solicitation arrest and could understand why it had happened. Justice came from a deeply religious family of Jehovah's Witnesses. He was nineteen years old when it occurred. Reid, a Mormon, considered it a forgivable show of rebelliousness by a kid who'd had a strict upbringing and then had gotten out on his own for the first time and received a little coaxing from his friends.

Even with left tackle Tra Thomas returning from back surgery and Runyan again in the fold, Reid was intrigued by the possibility of using the Eagles' first-round pick on Justice. He'd played right tackle at USC to protect the blind side of the Trojans' left-handed quarterback, Matt Leinart, but could be shifted to left tackle in the NFL. He was regarded as the second-best offensive tackle available in the draft after Virginia's D'Brickashaw Ferguson, a top-five selection who would be long gone by the time the Eagles picked. Reid liked to use early draft choices on linemen. Yes, the Eagles had Thomas and Runyan, but they were on the downsides of their careers. The Eagles' draft philosophy was to avoid the temptation to bypass the best player available simply to address a need that seemed more pressing; your needs could change in a matter of a few seasons or even a few months. One of the Eagles' best drafts had come in 2002 when their first four picks had been Sheppard, safety Michael

Lewis, cornerback Sheldon Brown, and tailback Brian Westbrook. All became starters and solid contributors but Lurie still had a vivid memory of the team's being heavily criticized for the Sheppard and Brown picks because the Eagles had veteran cornerbacks Troy Vincent and Bobby Taylor at the time.

By the time the Eagles made a decision on a player in the draft they had at least five reports on him from Heckert, Licht, and the scouts. The scouting reports would include a player's height, weight, speed, and grade, the number assigned to the player to reflect the round in which the Eagles thought he should be selected. A 1.00 represented the best possible grade. A grade of 2.00 meant the player was a second-rounder, a 3.00 was a third-rounder, and so on. Heckert compiled all the grades and put a final grade on the player. The sixth set of eyeballs to see the player belonged to Reid, who watched all the players the Eagles projected as fourth-round choices or better plus selected players graded to go in later rounds.

The Eagles were toying with the possibility of using a late-round selection on wide receiver and kick returner Jeremy Bloom, who had made it to Indianapolis for the combine only three days after returning from the Winter Olympics in Turin following his sixth-place finish there in freestyle moguls. Bloom was a two-time Olympic skier, having finished ninth in the 2002 Games in Salt Lake City. He was planning to retire from that sport to return to football, which he'd played at the University of Colorado before losing an eligibility dispute with the NCAA.

Bloom's father, Larry, had grown up in the Philadelphia area—in Villanova, Pennsylvania—and lived there until he was eighteen. He'd wrestled at Lower Merion High School. He was a huge sports fan who would end up coaching Jeremy in football between the fifth and eighth grades. Jeremy Bloom grew up in Colorado while John Elway was playing for the Broncos and his passion for football ran deep. He'd competed in both skiing and football while in high school and college and his coaches in both sports always had been accommodating and encouraging. He had some eye-catching moments during his two-year college football career in 2002 and 2003. The first time he touched the ball he scored on a 75-yard punt return against Colorado State. He had a 94-yard touchdown catch and, in all, had five plays of 75 yards or longer. He was a pretty good wide receiver and a really good kick returner. He'd needed money to fund his skiing career and he'd begun cashing in on his cover-boy good looks and appealing personality in 2004 by doing endorsements. The NCAA had allowed other athletes to turn professional in one sport while retaining their amateur status in another, but it ruled that Bloom's case was different because his income was coming from endorsements. Bloom exhausted the appeals process before finally walking away from football, disgusted with the NCAA but not disillusioned with the sport. Now he was ready to come back to football and try to do it in the NFL. He'd been clocked at 4.49 seconds in the 40-yard dash at the combine, not a show of blazing speed but more than acceptable under the circumstances. Even so, Bloom thought he'd probably go undrafted. The Eagles had other notions.

In most years the Eagles assigned twenty or twenty-one first-round grades in a draft class. This year they'd assigned only fourteen, but having the fourteenth overall pick meant they would end up with one of those players. They thought it would be either Justice or Brodrick Bunkley, a defensive tackle from Florida State. During the two weeks leading up to the draft, Reid and Heckert would meet each day for two hours with Lurie, Banner, and Licht. They would go over draft day scenarios. It was no-holds-barred conversation. Input from organizational higher-ups like Lurie and Banner was welcomed, not resented. The group wanted to make sure it explored every alternative.

During those meetings it was decided that if both Bunkley and Justice were available for the Eagles' pick, the team would take Bunkley.

The success of the Eagles' entire offseason would hinge on what happened on a single weekend in late April. That was the choice these men had made. They would be ready.

APRIL

CHAPTER

- 14 -

April 18 . . . Washington, D.C.

Gene Upshaw and Richard Berthelsen sat in Berthelsen's seventh-floor office at the union's headquarters on L Street in downtown Washington. It was about an hour before they had to leave for a union-sponsored charity function, and Paul Tagliabue wasn't the only top NFL leader with retirement on his mind in the aftermath of the labor talks.

"He had agreed to come back to get through this," Upshaw said as he leaned back in a chair on one side of the room while Berthelsen sat behind his desk on the other side. "He made it clear that this was his last one and I made it clear this would be the last one I would negotiate. I'm sixty. We have an age limit here. It's sixty-five."

Berthelsen chuckled. He told Upshaw to remember who had installed that age limit.

"I put it in," Upshaw said.

Berthelsen's message was clear: Upshaw could stay longer if he wanted.

That would become evident in the fall when Upshaw agreed to a contract extension running through the 2010 season. Troy Vincent would approve the new deal in late November and it would be announced at the Super Bowl.

But for now Upshaw was insisting he wouldn't be around that long.

His main concern as the owners' search for a new commissioner got under way was that Tagliabue's successor wouldn't respect the players the way Tagliabue did. The odds of such a switch in outlook would increase greatly if the owners hired from outside the league, but Upshaw thought Roger Goodell, the NFL's chief operating officer, was well positioned to become the next commissioner. It made sense for the owners to promote from within during such a highly prosperous time. The search committee had held one meeting and was planning to hold another before the next full owners' meeting in late May in Denver. Upshaw would turn sixty-one in August and didn't plan to be a candidate, not for a job that required building a three-quarters consensus among such a disparate group of owners to get anything done.

"The only way I'd do it," he said, "is if they change their voting procedure."

April 29 ... New York

As University of Texas quarterback Vince Young sat in the players' waiting area backstage at Radio City Music Hall on draft morning, he and his representatives were hearing rumors that the Cowboys were trying to trade up to pick him.

Young soon learned that you couldn't believe much of what you heard on draft day.

The Detroit Lions called to say they were attempting to trade up to get him. That never materialized either.

With the Tennessee Titans on the clock for the third overall choice, Titans general manager Floyd Reese called to say his team was taking Young. Finally some accurate information: Paul Tagliabue called Young's name moments later as the Titans' pick.

The league had moved the draft to Radio City Music Hall, its third different New York City site in three years. It was an opulent venue, but that didn't really matter to the key decision-makers for the individual teams, who were back in their home cities at their clubs' headquarters, connected by phone to the desks on the draft floor.

At the Eagles' complex, things were frenzied. Javon Walker had visited the night before the draft and had left that morning. He wanted to play for the Eagles. The Eagles wanted him. They were a little bit concerned that Walker was coming off a knee injury but were willing to live with the risk. The problem was that the Denver Broncos were offering the fifth pick of the second round to Walker's team, the Green Bay Packers. The Eagles would have to trade their first-rounder to beat that.

They knew they could trade for Donté Stallworth later if they wanted.

They reluctantly decided to pass on Walker and draft Brodrick Bunkley or Winston Justice with the fourteenth pick.

The Packers traded Walker to the Broncos.

Andy Reid, Tom Heckert, and Joe Banner were still resolved to select Bunkley, the Florida State defensive tackle, ahead of Justice, the USC offensive tackle, but now the Eagles didn't think Bunkley would be around for their pick. They thought Bunkley would go somewhere between eighth and twelfth. They talked to everyone—including the Buffalo Bills, who had the eighth pick—about trading up but teams were asking for too much. The Eagles decided to wait for either Bunkley or, more likely, Justice to fall to them.

The surprise of the draft came the night before it started, when the Houston Texans, who had the top overall choice, signed N.C. State defensive end Mario Williams, not USC tailback Reggie Bush. Still, that did nothing to change the Eagles' plans. Once the draft began, Bush went to the New Orleans Saints with the second choice. Things were unfolding the way the Eagles expected—not necessarily pick for pick, but the players they thought would come off the board early were coming off the board. There were no surprises among the first seven players drafted.

Then the Bills' turn came up.

The Eagles figured the Bills would choose Bunkley or perhaps another defensive tackle, Haloti Ngata of Oregon. Wrong. The Bills took Ohio State safety Donte Whitner, projected by most teams as a mid-first-rounder. Bunkley remained available. In the Eagles' war room at the NovaCare Complex there was surprise but not outward glee. Everyone remained calm. They still figured that Bunkley would be gone by number twelve, a pick belonging to the Cleveland Browns, and they'd be getting Justice. The Eagles tried to trade up for the twelfth choice but couldn't. Instead the Browns and Baltimore Ravens, who had the thirteenth pick, swapped places via a trade.

The Ravens took Ngata twelfth.

The Browns took Florida State linebacker Kamerion Wimbley thirteenth.

The Eagles, thankful for their good fortune, chose Bunkley.

Then a funny thing happened as the rest of the first round unfolded: No one took Justice.

The Eagles didn't think he'd slip past the San Diego Chargers, who had the nineteenth pick. But the Chargers took Antonio Cromartie, a cornerback from Florida State who hadn't played at all the previous season because of a knee injury. Clearly other teams were more concerned about Justice's arrests than the Eagles were. The Eagles tried to trade back up into the first round to get him. They nearly had a deal with the Chicago Bears, who had the twenty-sixth pick. But the Bears instead traded the choice to the Bills, who took N.C. State defensive tackle John McCargo. Justice continued to drop and the Eagles continued to try to trade up. Veteran defensive tackle Hollis Thomas had told the Eagles he wanted to be traded and the Saints were interested. The Eagles knew they could get a pick later in the draft for Thomas, but they decided to first try to use him to move up to get Justice. They offered him to the Saints, who had the second pick of the second round. The Saints instead traded the pick to the Browns. The Browns used the choice on University of Maryland linebacker D'Qwell Jackson.

Finally the Eagles found a taker in the Titans. They traded a fourth-round selection to the Titans to move up six spots in the second-round order, from forty-fifth to thirty-ninth, to get Justice. The Eagles had targeted two players for their first-round choice and had ended up getting both of them. But there was more work to be done.

The Eagles had projected Chris Gocong, a defensive end from Cal Poly they would use at outside linebacker, as a second-round pick. They watched as he slipped by three or four teams they thought would take him and resolved to trade up again. They moved up five spots in the third round, sending a seventh-rounder to the New York Jets, to get Gocong. As Saturday ended, the Eagles were weary but thrilled.

"And then," as Heckert said later, "we saw Jean-Gilles sitting there."

Max Jean-Gilles, a massive guard from Georgia the Eagles had projected to go late in the second round or sometime in the third, was still available. Reid decided he wasn't done rebuilding his offensive line. It was back to work. This time the Eagles had overnight to swing the deal. The Saints were ready to make the Hollis Thomas trade. The Eagles sent Thomas to the Saints to move up nine spots in Sunday's fourth round and got Jean-Gilles with the second selection of the draft's second day. With Jean-Gilles in the fold, the Eagles could part with left guard Artis Hicks. They had a pick later in the fourth round, number 127 overall, and sent it and Hicks to their old friend Brad Childress and the Minnesota Vikings for a choice twelve spots higher in the fourth round plus a sixth-rounder. The Eagles immediately sent those two picks to the Packers for the 109th overall choice and used it on University of Michigan wide receiver Jason Avant.

Evaluating players might have been more art than science, but there was a mathematical precision to trading draft picks for draft picks. Every team in the league had a "value chart" assigning a numerical value to each pick in the draft. There were variations from chart to chart, but all were similar. The chart used by one team, for instance, assigned 3,000 points to the top pick in the first round, then 2,600 points to the second pick, 2,200 to the third pick, 1,800 to the fourth pick, and 1,700 to the fifth pick. The gaps between the values got smaller from there. The thirty-first pick in the first round was worth 600 points and the thirty-second was worth 590 points. When two teams talked about trading draft choices each consulted its value chart and matched up points.

When the Eagles got the 39th pick from the Titans to select Justice they were by this chart receiving a choice worth 510 points. They surrendered 512 points in return, 450 for the 45th pick and 62 for the draft's 116th selection. That was about as close to even as it got. Teams didn't always have the picks available to make the points even out so exactly. When the Eagles got the 71st pick from the Jets to choose Gocong they received a selection valued at 235 points. They gave up 213.4 points-worth of picks, 210 for the 76th choice and 3.4 for the 220th. The 109th pick the Eagles got from the Packers to use on Avant was worth 76 points, and they had to trade away 81.4 points-worth of selections to obtain it, 64 for the 115th choice and 17.4 for the 185th.

Jeremy Bloom and his family watched the draft on television in their living room. The Broncos had three picks in the fourth round.

"If they don't pick him now," Bloom's father Larry said to himself, "they're not picking him."

The Broncos passed. During the fifth round, Larry Bloom saw the Eagles' pick coming up. He thought how interesting it would be if the hometown team from his boyhood drafted his son. He kept his thoughts to himself; his parenting style once his children had become adults was to give his opinion only when asked. Jeremy's cell phone rang. He didn't recognize the area code on the caller ID, but Larry Bloom did. The call was coming from Philadelphia. It was Heckert, informing Jeremy that the Eagles were choosing him.

It was a far quieter draft weekend at Redskins Park. Joe Gibbs wanted a linebacker. The Redskins didn't have a pick until number fifty-three and knew they'd have to trade up to get one of the three linebackers Vinny Cerrato liked: Miami's Rocky McIntosh, Alabama's DeMeco Ryans, and Texas–El Paso's Thomas Howard. The Redskins began trying to trade up beginning with the top pick of the second round. The Texans kept that selection and took Ryans (who would be the NFL's defensive rookie of the year). The Redskins thought they'd had a deal with Denver for the fifth pick of the second round, but it unraveled when the Broncos instead traded the choice to the Packers for Javon Walker. The Redskins turned to the Jets, who had the third pick of the second round. It cost the Redskins their original second-round choice, a sixth-rounder Sunday, and a second-rounder in 2007, but they managed to move up and take McIntosh. The rest of the Redskins' draft was predictably underwhelming, full of players who were long-term projects or destined to play bit parts.

An early run on safeties in the first round kept the Cowboys from addressing that need. When their first-round pick, the eighteenth overall, came around, they took what they thought was the best player left regardless of position and chose Ohio State linebacker Bobby Carpenter. He fit one of Bill Parcells's prototypes because he was an outside linebacker who was big, at 255 pounds, as well as athletic. Parcells also knew Carpenter would be sufficiently tough-minded because his father, Rob, had been a fullback for Parcells's Giants teams. Parcells put Rob Carpenter in the same sentence with Phil Simms and Lawrence Taylor when talking about the players who had established his foundation for early coaching success. In the second round, the Cowboys traded down four spots and selected Notre Dame tight end Anthony Fasano. They did get a safety in the fifth round, trading up a dozen spots to choose Florida State's Pat Watkins.

Ernie Accorsi wanted to get a pass rusher, a cornerback, or a wide receiver first for the Giants. The wideout he wanted was Sinorice Moss. Tom Coughlin had spent that day in Mobile tracking Moss and had liked what he'd seen. Accorsi had once missed out on drafting Moss's older brother Santana and he didn't want to miss out on Sinorice. He'd said as much to Moss's parents when he'd been introduced to them by Drew Rosenhaus at Miami's pro day. Tamba Hali, whose interview had been so captivating to Accorsi and Coughlin at the scouting combine, was gone by the time the Giants' pick came around at number twenty-five. He'd gone twentieth to the Kansas City Chiefs. The Giants liked Boston College defensive end Mathias Kiwanuka and Miami cornerback Kelly Jennings, both still on the board. Accorsi thought he could safely trade down seven spots in a deal with the Pittsburgh Steelers and still get Moss, Kiwanuka, or Jennings. The Seattle Seahawks took Jennings with the thirty-first selection, leaving Accorsi to choose between Kiwanuka and Moss. He took Kiwanuka, but still made good on his pledge to Moss's parents by trading up in the second round to get Moss forty-fourth. When the draft was over, Accorsi thought the Giants had done okay. They wouldn't be atop anyone's draft report card, but they'd plugged a hole at wide receiver and they'd planned for the future at defensive end beyond Michael Strahan's retirement, whenever that came. It could have been worse.

PART 2

THE
BUILDUP

MAY

CHAPTER

- 15 -

May 13 ... Philadelphia

There was rain all around the area but it was bright and beautiful at the NovaCare Complex when the Eagles took the field to open a three-day minicamp.

That was a good sign. Maybe the sun would shine on the Eagles this year.

There would be a downpour by lunchtime, but only after Donovan McNabb had a chance to stand hernia-less in a Terrell Owens–less huddle, and after the Eagles' brain trust had a chance to get its first on-the-field look at its draft class. Jeff Lurie wore shorts, a blue T-shirt, and tennis shoes and stood with his arms folded to watch the offensive line drills as Winston Justice and Max Jean-Gilles got their first exposure to NFL coaching. Joe Banner, wearing jeans to go with a green Eagles pullover and a green Eagles cap, walked over to stand next to Lurie.

The Eagles planned to use Justice at left tackle, and lined him up with the second string behind veteran starter Tra Thomas. For now the Eagles had a starting offensive line of Thomas at left tackle, Todd

Herremans at left guard, Hank Fraley at center, Shawn Andrews at right guard, and Jon Runyan at right tackle. Jean-Gilles began his pro career as the third-string left guard.

"Watch Tra!" offensive line coach Juan Castillo barked at Justice when he couldn't master the proper technique during one drill.

Jean-Gilles paired up with Andrews for another drill teaching the blocker to stay low and balanced. Justice was left to work with undrafted rookie tackle DeJuan Skinner while Thomas paired up with Runyan. This time it was Jean-Gilles drawing Castillo's attention.

"Stay down, Max!" he yelled. "You're a big leaner!"

In the locker room after practice, Jeremy Bloom had a crowd of reporters around him. Bloom wasn't asking for the media attention but it was coming his way anyway. A member of the Eagles' public relations staff finally cut off the questions and the crowd of reporters dispersed. "It's kind of a double-edged sword," Bloom said. "I appreciate the attention because it means people are interested in what I'm doing and in my career, and I appreciate any support I can get. But I don't want to step on any toes here."

Agent Gary Wichard felt like he was representing a rock star, not a fifth-round draft pick. Reporters who called from Philadelphia wanted to talk to Wichard about Bloom and not about the Wichard client the Eagles had drafted in the first round, Brodrick Bunkley. Bloom would be taking a pay cut to go from skiing to football. He'd had a seven-figure income from skiing with a wide array of endorsement deals. Now he was looking at a rookie contract with a signing bonus of around $170,000 and a league minimum salary. Bloom knew a rookie, especially a fifth-round draft pick, wasn't allowed to act like a star in an NFL locker room. He'd spent a good deal of his practice field time being tutored by John Harbaugh, the Eagles' special teams coach, on catching punts. That skill was coming back to him quickly, but he wanted to make an impression on the offensive coaches as well with his play at wide receiver.

It was the time of the year when every player could dream about playing well and every team could regard itself as a contender.

May 15 ... East Rutherford, New Jersey

The Giants finished a minicamp for their rookies with an afternoon practice inside their practice bubble next to Giants Stadium. Tom Coughlin didn't like to hold practice inside, but the rain outside had left him with little choice. Inside the bubble was a 65-yard field with artificial turf; a yellow goalpost hung from the white ceiling above the sole end zone. Coughlin presided over the practice quietly, mostly standing at midfield and simply observing the proceedings while wearing tan slacks and tennis shoes with a blue Giants pullover and a blue Giants cap. John Mara, wearing a red tie with a blue shirt and carrying a gray raincoat, stood along the sideline. It never hurt to be seen. Mara chatted with a group of front-office members that included his brother Chris, the team's vice president of player evaluation, and Ernie Accorsi.

The offensive linemen began practice doing drills in a corner of the end zone not far from where a rolled-up tarp and three plastic trash bins were lined up along the wall. The players wore no pads, just jerseys and shorts. The practice was conducted mostly at half- to three-quarter speed. The purpose of the minicamp was for the players to start learning how things worked, not for the coaches to make any firm evaluations.

Antonio Pierce and LaVar Arrington showed up to check out the indoor practice. They watched the rookies intently. They saw Sinorice Moss show off his speed and they kept a close eye on Mathias Kiwanuka. Both were having a good minicamp. Moss flashed a thumbs-up signal at Accorsi after making one tumbling catch near the sideline.

Arrington yelled encouragement to wide receiver Michael Jennings, who was attending the camp with the rookies even though he'd bounced around several teams' practice squads in recent years.

"Don't let me see you do that again," he called to Jennings after one play. "You're better than that, bro."

Arrington looked fit, trim, and dapper in a tan sports coat over a dark brown shirt and jeans. He was sporting a silver hoop earring and his dreadlocks and several-days-growth of a beard gave him a vaguely menacing look. He'd been living in a hotel since he'd signed with the Giants, and working out every day. He hadn't been back to his home in the Washington area even once and he was pleased with his progress. He was testing his knee by running.

"I'm obsessed," he said.

It was a slow time of the year but the Giants would make a significant move soon, releasing cornerback Will Peterson. He'd suffered two stress fractures in his back over the previous three seasons, and the Giants weren't going to wait around any longer for him to get healthy. His uneasy relationship with Coughlin also played a role in his departure, the month before his twenty-seventh birthday. During the 2004 season Peterson had become miffed about being pulled from one game and not being selected a team captain for any games. He skipped several team meetings as a protest, and Coughlin demoted him for a game. Early in the 2005 season Peterson had committed the transgression—in Coughlin's mind—of talking about a hamstring injury with reporters. Under Coughlin's rules, all injury information to be made public was to come from him. The two exchanged words over that. The Giants had once envisioned their two Wills, Peterson and Allen, being their future at cornerback. Now both were gone. Peterson's departure left Sam Madison and Corey Webster, a second-year pro who'd been a second-round draft pick, as the probable starters, with R. W. McQuarters likely to be the third cornerback.

The noise the Giants should have been hearing was that of opposing quarterbacks and wide receivers chuckling.

JUNE

CHAPTER

- 16 -

June 2 . . . Irving, Texas

On a sunny, pleasant Friday afternoon, Terrell Owens wore blue tights underneath his shorts as he walked onto the field behind the Valley Ranch facility. Over the next couple hours Owens had to knock the rust off his game and work his way through some soreness in a hamstring muscle and one ankle, but he looked just fine as the Cowboys started a minicamp.

In Owens's first practice with his new team, he immediately made one thing clear: Cornerback Anthony Henry couldn't cover him.

Owens embarrassed Henry all afternoon, losing him to catch passes both short and long. In between, Owens took time to give some pointers to rookie wideout Skyler Green. After the practice Owens was walking toward the weight room and noticed Cowboys wide receivers coach Todd Haley talking to a couple of reporters.

"Don't lie, Todd!" Owens yelled playfully. "Don't lie!"

He grinned and ducked inside to do his workout.

Haley was to be the buffer between Owens and Bill Parcells if any buffering was required. He was in his third season as the Cowboys' wide receivers coach and Parcells had given him the title of passing game coordinator after Sean Payton had left. Haley was only thirty-nine but already was entering his tenth season as an NFL assistant coach. He'd worked for Parcells with the New York Jets and he was among the tiny minority of people around Parcells who was not intimidated by him. He wasn't afraid to disagree vehemently with his boss. That would draw Parcells's ire at times but it also garnered his respect.

For now no buffering was required, but even a minicamp seemed like a major event when Owens was around.

He'd showed up at Valley Ranch eleven days earlier, as promised, to begin learning the offense. Now he was the center of attention. About three dozen reporters had surrounded his locker that day before the opening practice. Owens spotted the mob scene as he walked toward it wearing a blue Cowboys shirt, red and black Air Jordan shorts, and a cap turned backward. He had a glittering diamond earring in each ear. Owens shook his head.

"Damn," he muttered to himself.

But he didn't turn away. He continued to his locker, stood in front of it, and answered questions. He was asked if he regarded it as a media circus.

"Pretty much," he said, "but I can handle it."

Owens's locker was directly across the room from Drew Bledsoe's and stuck between those of second-year receiver J. R. Tolver and third-year tight end Brett Pierce. Owens's teammates were doing their best to welcome him. "There's a clean slate," tight end Jason Witten said. "There has to be."

The veteran players in the locker room dutifully said that Owens's antics wouldn't resurface in Dallas. Never mind that the story had been the same everywhere else Owens had been. The Cowboys appeared to believe it wouldn't happen to them, not with Parcells around.

Bledsoe would be in the line of fire if anything did go wrong. Owens had lashed out at quarterbacks Jeff Garcia in San Francisco and Donovan McNabb in Philadelphia. But Bledsoe thought he and Parcells could handle it if Owens did begin acting up and keep any small problems from becoming big ones.

"Listen, I don't expect you to be happy all the time," Bledsoe told Owens in one of their first conversations. "If you don't get to touch the ball enough, I don't expect you to like that. At the same time you have to keep playing hard for me and give me good information when you come back to the huddle."

Bledsoe respected Owens as a player and thought Owens's impact on the team would show not only in his own production but also in the productivity of Witten and fellow wideout Terry Glenn. He was willing to try to build a working relationship with Owens without worrying about the past transgressions toward quarterbacks. Bledsoe knew Parcells's first instinct as a coach was to rely on his running game. But he also knew that Parcells was smart enough and sufficiently open-minded to change his approach if circumstances dictated it. Bledsoe thought he and his receivers had a chance to make this a pass-first offense if they performed well enough. The stakes, Bledsoe knew, had been raised by the Owens acquisition. This team had been constructed to get to a Super Bowl and to get to one fast, before Parcells left or the mixture of Parcells and Owens became too combustible.

Owens had been trading phone calls and text messages with Bledsoe since he'd been signed. He had only good things to say about his new quarterback and about Parcells. Parcells was a disciplinarian, but he also knew how and when to give productive but difficult players a little bit of room. He cracked down only when those players pushed him too far. He wasn't Tom Coughlin; he had more than one gear and he wasn't rigid with every player all the time. "Bill is a guy who shoots you straight," Owens said. "I feel like I'm a straight shooter."

But things never seemed to remain simple for long with Owens. His friends and associates said he never forgot or forgave any slight, real or perceived, and never allowed anyone who had gotten on his wrong side to get back in his good graces. Owens spoke publicly of changing his ways, but it was clear he didn't think a personality makeover was required. The traits that made him so difficult to get along with—his stubbornness, his willfulness, his determination and single-mindedness, his arrogance, and his conviction that his way was the right way and the only way—also made him a virtually unstoppable force as a player. "I think I've been successful on the football field," he said, "being who I am."

It wasn't Owens, though, who was giving Parcells problems at this minicamp. It was Greg Ellis.

Ellis was a respected veteran. He'd tied rookie linebacker DeMarcus Ware for the team lead with eight sacks the previous season. But his playing time had dwindled in its late stages as the coaches had gone with rookie Chris Canty ahead of him at defensive end. Ellis thought he'd be released after the season. Instead the Cowboys exercised a $500,000 roster bonus to keep him. Parcells wanted Ellis to move to outside linebacker, a position Ellis hadn't played in the NFL. With the Cowboys playing a three-linemen, four-linebacker alignment they needed another player like Ware at outside linebacker, fast enough to rush the quarterback on passing plays and sturdy enough not to get barreled over on running plays. Ellis was one of the most affable players on the team and got along well with Parcells personally. But he was about to turn thirty-one in August and was entering his ninth season with the Cowboys. He knew if a move to linebacker didn't work out the team could release him without paying him anything. He didn't want to be the guinea pig in this experiment.

He was the only player not to participate in the Parcells-mandated forty offseason workouts without being excused. Parcells and the Joneses, Jerry and Stephen, took turns speaking to Ellis and his agent, James Williams. Parcells alternated between tough and conciliatory talk, cursing at Ellis before the minicamp for missing workouts but putting his arm around him when the two spoke calmly for about fifteen minutes following the final practice of the camp. Parcells told Ellis he wasn't going anywhere and he'd better get used to the idea he was staying and playing linebacker. He told Ellis if he went to a different team as a defensive end in a 4-3 scheme he'd be just another player, but if he stayed in Dallas and made himself a good outside linebacker in a 3-4 he'd be a valuable commodity on a club that truly needed him. Parcells thought that Ellis could be to the Cowboys what veteran outside linebacker Willie McGinest had been to the New England Patriots.

"When you see two or three more DeMarcus Wares coming in here," Parcells told Ellis, "that's when you should worry about your job."

Ellis attended the minicamp but would go back to skipping voluntary workouts afterward. He told the Cowboys he wanted to be traded, released, or given some job security. His contract ran through the 2009 season for salaries totaling $12.225 million, including $2.25 million in 2006. None of those salaries was guaranteed. Ellis wanted the Cowboys to restructure the deal and guarantee some of the $7.475 million due to him in salaries in the 2008 and 2009 seasons. That way, he figured, the team would be less likely to release him if the move to linebacker didn't go smoothly right away because getting rid of him would have salary cap implications for the club. The Cowboys responded that they were willing to guarantee Ellis some money in the future but not yet. The two sides simply would have to agree to disagree, Parcells and Jerry Jones figured, and Ellis had little leverage as long as he wanted to keep playing in the NFL. He was under contract.

Parcells wasn't running a democracy here. Greg Ellis and even Terrell Owens had to keep that in mind. One of the two would have trouble remembering it.

June 14 . . . East Rutherford, New Jersey

The Giants gathered on Wednesday morning for the opening practice of a three-day minicamp, their final on-field activities before they would disperse for a six-week break before training camp itself. Since the rookie minicamp the Giants players had been through nine practices. Different teams called the practices different things, but the sessions all fell under the general heading of organized team activities, or OTAs. Teams had come to practice almost year-round.

Coaches did everything they could to pressure veteran players to show up for teams' offseason conditioning programs and OTAs. But the get-togethers officially were voluntary under the collective bargaining agreement, so players couldn't be fined for missing them. Jeremy Shockey and Plaxico Burress had been no-shows at Giants Stadium the entire offseason, working out on their own in Florida. That left Tom Coughlin seething, but there was little he could do about it.

Both were on hand for this mandatory minicamp. Shockey showed up with a black and blue left eye and refused to say exactly how he'd gotten it. He said it had happened the previous Friday while he was lifting weights in Florida but offered no further details. When members of the sizable New York media contingent attempted to press him on the issue, Shockey wouldn't budge.

"I'm all right," he said. "What the fuck. Ask your football questions."

There was an undercurrent of unrest at the minicamp, given the down note on which the Giants' season had ended. Coughlin had spoken to Burress about skipping the final team meeting just after the season, and there remained questions about Burress's ability to fit in and Eli Manning's knack, or lack thereof, for keeping his older teammates in line. Manning was the team's quarterback but he wasn't one of its leaders, at least not yet. The offseason absences of Shockey and Burress had added to the feeling of restlessness. Center Shaun O'Hara seemed to sense the mood needed to be lightened. He took note of Shockey's black eye and said, "I think we were all wondering if Coach gave it to him."

Manning was willing to let bygones be bygones with Burress, even though the wide receiver had showed up his quarterback on the field late in the season by letting his disgust show clearly following plays on which he was open and the ball didn't come his way or was poorly thrown. Manning and Burress had seen each other since the season and had spoken, but the subject hadn't come up. That was fine with Manning, who thought it was okay just to let the issue dissipate and go on working. Coughlin liked the way Manning had gotten back to work once the season had ended. Manning's time in the weight room had been well spent; he'd ended up with a body that was three or four pounds heavier and slightly more sculpted. He'd also shut himself in the video room reviewing the play of the Giants' offense the previous season. Manning saw many instances where there was a big play there to be made and he'd made a wrong decision or an ill-timed throw. He was seeing the right things; he just wasn't seeing them fast enough. His goal for his third season was to know the offense well enough, and know what defenses were doing against him well enough, that he could make sound decisions faster.

Otherwise Manning's offseason had been spent on low-key activities, like playing golf and visiting his family and friends in New Orleans. He'd finally found one way to outshine Ben Roethlisberger in the NFL, simply by acting like a responsible adult. Two days before the Giants' minicamp began Roethlisberger was leaving a radio interview in Pittsburgh, driving his motorcycle without a helmet, as he liked to do even after being warned by the team about it, when a Chrysler New Yorker driven by a sixty-two-year-old woman pulled in front of him while making a left turn toward a bridge at an intersection. Roethlisberger slammed into the passenger side of the car. He was thrown from his motorcycle, a Suzuki Hayabusa advertised as the fastest street-legal bike in the world, and flew headfirst into the car's windshield, then tumbled to the ground. He suffered a broken jaw, a broken nose, other facial fractures, and a concussion. He lost two teeth and chipped others and had a sizable gash on the back of his head. He underwent seven hours of surgery that day and was released from the hospital two days later. If he'd been going faster than 35 miles per hour he might have been killed.

Coughlin, like other coaches, had a rule forbidding his players to ride motorcycles during the season, but even the strictest of all coaches admitted there was little he could do about what his players did in the offseason. At least he didn't need to worry about his quarterback. "I've been skiing once in my life when I was ten years old," Manning said. "I've never ridden a motorcycle. I don't do a whole lot of waterskiing or anything. It's never been part of my life. It's not like I feel like I'm missing out on anything."

The practices took place on the field outside Giants Stadium. The accommodations, as with everything at the old stadium, were spartan. There was a Porta-John just inside the fence surrounding the practice field. Planes flew overhead en route to landing at the Newark airport, two exits south on the New Jersey Turnpike. The summer weather was near but hadn't quite arrived. The day was a little bit muggy but it wasn't sunny or all that hot. There was a huge media contingent on hand by minicamp standards, and a far bigger media crowd than the Jets would have the following day for their minicamp, reinforcing the impression that the Giants were the varsity team in New York and the Jets were the JV.

Sinorice Moss was one of the stars of the camp's first day. Manning gave him the ball on end-arounds and screen passes, the sorts of plays the Giants hadn't been able to run the previous season because they didn't have a receiver quick and shifty enough to make them work. The heat had begun to set in for the late-afternoon practice but the Giants still went at it hard. Michael Strahan chased Tiki Barber far down the field during one drill.

"Hey, old man," defensive coordinator Tim Lewis called to Strahan, "what are you doing all the way back here?"

John Mara skipped the first half of the afternoon practice but showed up to watch the second half. That made him nearly as active as LaVar Arrington, who watched the entire practice. Arrington had participated in the morning practice but was limited to one practice per day because he'd developed Achilles tendinitis. He wore gray sweatpants with his blue jersey and carried his helmet around while he watched the drills. As he left the field he exchanged friendly barbs with fellow linebacker Chase Blackburn. A police officer pulled Arrington aside and asked him to autograph some small plastic Giants helmets stashed in the front seat of the cop's cruiser. Arrington obliged. Just then Coughlin walked by on his way from the field back to the bowels of the stadium.

"Is it legal for me to sign for him?" Arrington called out.

"It's okay," Coughlin said, "as long as you're not riding in the backseat of his car."

The officer offered Arrington some tickets to that night's Yankees game but Arrington didn't want to go. As he walked back to the locker room he reflected on his free agent experiences.

"If you became a free agent because you didn't want to, that's different," he said. "I was a willing free agent. I sought it out. Everyone said I was trying to get so much money, I was trying to get $100 million. That was never true. I could have gotten more money from two other teams. It was about going to a place where I could be in a good situation. This seems to be a first-class organization. I had history with Tim Lewis. We're both from Pittsburgh. He's known me since I was in high school. I knew he would respect me as a person and he would know what I was going through. I was comfortable around guys like Antonio and it's a heck of a market to play in, don't you think?"

But he never would have left the Redskins, he said, if they'd wanted to keep him and resolve their issues as much as he'd wanted to stay.

"I wished everything could have worked out in Washington and I was still playing for the Redskins," he said. "Everyone who knows me knows that's true. But it didn't work out. They can have all that. I'm glad I'm out of there. That's their drama, not mine. That's the way they do things."

Arrington ducked into the locker room and closed the door, happy to leave the dark thoughts of his past behind him. The future, he hoped, was far brighter.

June 15 . . . Philadelphia

The day after the Giants began their minicamp, the Eagles had their final OTA before their summer break. Only a handful of reporters showed up and even Joe Banner wasn't on the sideline to watch. He was hard at work, though. The Eagles would play in the annual Hall of Fame game that summer. With an extra preseason game they would be reporting to training camp a week earlier than most teams. Rookies were due in Bethlehem, Pennsylvania, on July 20. The Eagles would have less time than other clubs to get their rookies signed before camp and Banner wanted to get started. By the end of the week he would have two draft picks signed, fifth-round linebacker Omar Gaither and sixth-round defensive tackle LaJuan Ramsey. Usually rookie negotiations were left until mid-July.

Every year the league assigned each team a rookie pool figure. It was, in effect, a salary cap for the team's rookies within the overall salary cap. Each team had a different rookie pool based on how many draft choices it had and when they'd come in the draft. The Eagles were assigned a rookie pool of $4,256,970. The Cowboys' figure was $3,786,517 and the Giants' was $3,523,882. The Redskins, with their dearth of draft picks, were assigned a modest rookie pool of $2,241,339.

Jeff Lurie walked out of the Eagles' offices midway through the practice wearing a blue golf shirt and shorts, and stood next to Tom Heckert on the sideline. It was a sunny, picture-perfect day with a hint of a breeze to keep it from being hot. Traffic was beginning to back up along Broad Street for an afternoon Phillies game. Andy Reid had been assigning his scout teams to simulate the offensive and defensive schemes of NFC East opponents while working against the Eagles' first-stringers. On this day it was the Houston Texans, the Eagles' opponent in the regular season opener, who were being imitated.

The Eagles used some offensive formations during the practice with Ryan Moats at tailback and Brian Westbrook at wide receiver. But while Reid and Marty Mornhinweg were contemplating possible ways to work Moats into the lineup and lessen the wear and tear on Westbrook, Westbrook was looking for ways to be a more durable running back. He was tired of being hurt so often and wondered how a running back like Tiki Barber, who was about his size, could be such a durable workhorse. He got word to Barber during the offseason he would like to get some workout tips. It was a bit of a touchy issue, given that Barber finding a way to help Westbrook stay healthier could hurt Barber's team. But there was a brotherhood of NFL players extending beyond team boundaries, and Barber helped out. He didn't call Westbrook directly but his business agent, Mark Lepselter, called Reid's office and left a number for Joe Carini, Barber's trainer, a former winner of the New Jersey "Mr. Strongman" competition.

Donovan McNabb looked healthy and relaxed. Reid made sure to get

Jeff Garcia some snaps with the starting offense. Winston Justice practiced with the starters at left tackle, as Tra Thomas was being held out of full team drills. For the second time in a span of ten months Thomas was on blood-thinning medication because blood clots had been found in his left leg. He'd missed almost all of the offseason workouts and much of training camp in 2005 because of the clots and his doctors had never given him a reason for the problem. He suspected the clots had reappeared because he'd come off the medication early without completing the full cycle the previous summer to return to the lineup for the final preseason game. He'd had his 2005 season cut short by a back injury and had undergone surgery in December. After he made the six-hour flight back from Los Angeles following his surgery, his leg became swollen again. Doctors found more clots and put him back on the anti-coagulant Coumadin. He couldn't practice while he was on the medication because any injury or broken skin could produce serious or even potentially fatal bleeding. But his doctors had told him he'd be able to participate in training camp and he was hoping and praying his blood clot problems were finally behind him. He'd been working out as much as seven hours a day to try to regain his previous Pro Bowl form. He also had decided abruptly he wanted to go by his given name, William, instead of his widely used nickname Tra, bestowed upon him because he was William Thomas III. Most of his teammates and coaches still called him Tra but Reid respected his player's wishes. When a reporter asked Reid about "Tra" during a press conference, Reid said, "Who?"

In the meantime Reid was getting Justice ready to play immediately as a rookie in case he was needed. Justice didn't even have his own locker at the NovaCare facility, temporarily sharing one with Max Jean-Gilles, but it was possible he could have a starting job when the season began. Justice had been uncomfortable early in the offseason practices because he was playing left tackle instead of right tackle. He'd spent a little bit of time at left tackle at USC before being moved to the right side and he was relearning the mechanics of the position. It was a little like learning to eat with your left hand instead of your right hand. It felt awkward at first, but the basics of the task ended up being the same.

When the practice ended just after 1 p.m. Reid summoned his players around him and told them he'd see them at Lehigh. Justice walked off the field with offensive line coach Juan Castillo, then spoke to Heckert briefly before continuing to the locker room. He hadn't paid any attention to his contract negotiations yet. He'd been too preoccupied with learning the offense and getting acclimated to his new position and he didn't even know if talks had begun. Now he'd check in with agent Gary Uberstine.

All the other Eagles players had long since gotten to the locker room and had their postpractice showers by the time Jeremy Bloom left the field. He'd had an inactive practice, standing around and watching the offensive drills. He caught some punts but didn't run with them. He'd been plagued by a sore hamstring and hadn't had many opportunities to convince the coaches he belonged. When the practice ended Bloom had a trainer wrap tape on his hands and waited his turn to catch balls whizzing at him from a JUGS machine. The contraption had a metal stand with two spinning rubber tires attached at the top, whirring next to each other. A ball boy placed a football between the two tires and let go, and the ball was flung toward the receiver. Bloom watched fellow rookie wideout Jason Avant catch balls, then took his place in front of the machine. Avant headed to the locker room and Bloom was the final player left on the field.

It was a little like staying late on the last day of school before summer vacation.

Reid planned to take a couple weeks off, then report back to work to make final training camp preparations. The Eagles would be heading to camp as something other than the defending NFC East champ for the first time in five years. There would be competition at Lehigh for playing time and starting jobs, not just roster spots. Much felt up in the air.

JULY

CHAPTER

- 17 -

July 21 . . . Bethlehem, Pennsylvania

Donovan McNabb walked leisurely toward the fields at 8:39 in the morning for a practice scheduled to begin at 8:45. It was the second day of the Eagles' training camp. McNabb saw Andy Reid and glanced at his wrist as if checking a watch.

"Out kinda early today, huh?" McNabb said.

The Eagles were out kinda early compared to the rest of the NFL; they and the New York Jets were the first teams to open their camps. The Eagles had their rookies and selected veterans, including McNabb, report to Lehigh University on July 20. Lehigh has several campuses connected by a twisting road that winds its way up the side of a mountain. The route is so confusing that Eagles officials annually show up before camp starts to place signs with green arrows on them along the road to point players, coaches, and other team employees in the proper direction. That hadn't prevented Terrell Owens from getting lost after he'd showed up for his first training camp with the team. He wasn't great at following directions.

The carnival atmosphere that had accompanied the opening of the Eagles' camp the previous year was absent, with Owens gone. Reid and Tom Heckert walked side by side and chatted as practice got under way. Neither Jeffrey Lurie nor Joe Banner was present and there were no major decisions to be made, but there was always something to be talked about and something to be done. Jeremy Bloom had aggravated the pulled hamstring muscle that had plagued him during the offseason practices and had been placed on the physically-unable-to-perform list, a holding bin for players who couldn't pass their physicals at the outset of training camp.

Bloom had agreed to a contract nine days before the rookies were to report to camp. He got a four-year deal with the minimum annual salaries and a $172,000 signing bonus. The deal contained an escalator clause that could increase his salary in his fourth season. If he reached playing time benchmarks on offense or excelled as a punt returner— getting 350 yards on punt returns, averaging at least 11.1 yards per punt return, or scoring two touchdowns on punt returns in any season—he would get the lowest restricted free agent tender as his salary in his fourth season. If he reached the Pro Bowl, his fourth season salary would jump to the middle restricted free agent tender. Bloom had expressed a willingness before the negotiations to allow a no-skiing clause to be included in his contract but there wasn't one in there. The Eagles never brought it up.

Winston Justice's deal had come three days before the reporting date. He'd trusted Gary Uberstine to get him to camp on time and the agent had delivered. Justice signed a four-year, $3.71 million deal that included $2.1 million in guaranteed money. Banner had stayed busy through the precamp break. He'd also made a bid to re-sign veteran safety Brian Dawkins, who was entering the final season of a contract that would pay him $3 million in 2006. The Eagles offered Dawkins a two-year, $4.5 million contract extension that included a $2 million signing bonus. Dawkins was mulling the offer. Just before camp Banner signed center Jamaal Jackson to a five-year, $12.5 million extension that included $1.75 million in bonuses and ran through the 2013 season.

There had been one off-field incident during the players' downtime. Jabar Gaffney had been driving an SUV over the Walt Whitman Bridge into New Jersey around 7:30 one evening in June when he'd been stopped by a Delaware River Port Authority police officer for making an unsafe lane change. As Gaffney was getting the necessary documents for the officer out of his glove compartment the officer noticed a gun in a holster. Gaffney had a concealed handgun license to carry the loaded .380 semiautomatic pistol in Texas, but not in New Jersey. He was charged with unlawful possession of a weapon. Reid wasn't overly concerned, understanding that Gaffney was in the process of moving. But it would be a year in which about three dozen NFL players would be arrested. Gene Upshaw would end up thinking the players, in some cases, had been unfairly targeted, but he generally had little sympathy for rule-breakers among the players, and he worried that fans and business partners would be driven away if they came to view the NFL as a league filled with criminals. Player criminality was the issue about which Upshaw fretted the most. On every other issue, he could deal with the league and work something out. On this one, he was powerless. He depended totally on the players. When he met with players on his team-by-team visits that year, Upshaw stressed the importance of staying out of trouble and not letting the league drift to "that place." It had happened in other sports and Upshaw didn't want to see it happen to this sport, not on his watch. When he saw a list of all the NFL players arrested that year published in a newspaper in December he made plans to clip the list, carry it around to show to players and tell them, "You don't want to be on that list. It's like a bad credit report. It never goes away."

The Gaffney incident was all but forgotten with the Eagles' camp under way but Banner still had one problem. He hadn't signed Brodrick Bunkley. It hadn't been easy to negotiate rookie contracts in this summer. The salary cap had gone up by 19 percent but the rookie pool had increased by only 5 percent. Agents were seeking contracts worth 7 to 9 percent more than what the players selected in the corresponding draft slots the previous year had gotten. Teams were trying to limit the

increases to 5 to 7 percent. The major disagreement in the Bunkley negotiations was over the length of the contract. The new collective bargaining agreement limited players chosen in the first sixteen picks of the
draft to signing contracts of six years at most and players drafted sev-
enteenth through thirty-second to five-year deals. The Eagles had gotten Bunkley fourteenth and wanted him to sign a six-year contract.
Bunkley's agent, Gary Wichard, wanted a five-year deal to make
Bunkley eligible for unrestricted free agency a year earlier. Wichard was
willing to accept a six-year contract that would void to five seasons if
Bunkley became a starter. Banner balked at that.

Reid, like all coaches, was annoyed when rookies showed up late but
there was little he could do about it. At least he didn't have to worry
about Owens any longer, at least not in the same way. But Owens's book
had just been released and Reid knew he'd be asked about it when he
got to training camp. When it happened, he was ready. He'd practiced
his response and delivered it in perfect deadpan fashion when reporters
asked him whether he'd read the book.

"No," he said. "I was here."

McNabb was the book's main target, being accused by Owens of
helping to orchestrate the wide receiver's departure from Philadelphia
because he resented having to share the spotlight. McNabb had fun
with it. He joked that he, too, was planning to release a book and it
would be in the children's section right next to Owens's.

McNabb had arrived at training camp fit, trim, and healthy. Eagles
trainer Rick Burkholder had researched sports hernias and had told Reid
there was no reason to hold McNabb back in any way. McNabb had
spent a portion of his offseason, as he always did, working out in Arizona.
He'd invited all his receivers to join him, and Reggie Brown, Darnerien
McCants, Hank Baskett, Reno Mahe, Matt Schobel, and Bloom had
taken him up on it.

For Bloom the time in Arizona had been part of an offseason training regimen that also had included strength and cardiovascular workouts in Florida, an attempt to ensure that he would be ready for the heat
and humidity of training camp. That had gone well but the pulled ham-

string had resumed bothering him and now he was missing precious training camp chances to impress the coaches. He was frustrated because he thought his football skills were coming back but his body was betraying him as it made the adjustment back to what was needed from it in this sport. On this day the world's most famous fifth-round draft pick stood on the practice field with a white cap to go with his green jersey and black shorts.

He handed footballs to the coaches during drills. He signed autographs after practice. He was, as usual, one of the last players to leave the field.

His frustration was only beginning.

July 24 . . . Detroit

The owners had been summoned to the Westin hotel in the Detroit airport to be updated by the search committee on the commissioner maneuverings. Dan Snyder paced the floor talking on his cell phone as he waited for the meeting to start. He had a deep tan, a vestige of a family Mediterranean cruise, but Snyder was the sort of person who never really was on vacation.

Dan Rooney, the Pittsburgh Steelers owner who was a cochairman of the search committee, was a pilot and flew himself to the meeting. His plane suffered a flat tire on his landing. That would be the most interesting thing to happen all day. This was one of those meetings at which the owners were eager to leave virtually from the moment they arrived. It began at 12:15 p.m. and was over at 3:09.

Korn/Ferry International, the search firm hired by the owners, had begun the process by identifying candidates. The firm had first focused on Adam Silver, the deputy commissioner of the NBA who'd directed that league's explosive international growth, as a candidate. But when Silver had been asked to interview for the job he'd told the NFL's representatives they didn't need to talk to him because Roger Goodell was their man. That was a view shared by most of the owners. Some in the media were speculating about high-profile political figures like

Condoleezza Rice, the U.S. secretary of state, and Michael Powell, the former Federal Communications Commission chairman, being candidates but all of it was nonsense. The owners wanted someone they knew could make them money and they knew Goodell could make them money. The search committee was down to 11 candidates after starting with 185. Goodell and league counsel Jeff Pash were on the list but the other candidate from within the league office, finance wiz Eric Grubman, wasn't. The other semi-insider on the list was Gregg Levy, a Washington-based attorney who was the league's chief outside counsel and worked at the same firm, Covington & Burling, at which Paul Tagliabue had worked before he'd been elected commissioner.

The outsiders included David Brandon, the CEO of Domino's Pizza; Dave Checketts, the former president and CEO of Madison Square Garden; Daniel Doctoroff, a deputy mayor of New York who'd led the city's failed bid to land the 2012 Olympics; Joseph Leccese, a partner in the law firm Proskauer Rose who'd represented Jeff Lurie in his purchase of the Eagles and Woody Johnson in his acquisition of the New York Jets; Frederick Nance, a Cleveland attorney who'd been deeply involved in the negotiations that had gotten the new Browns franchise to the city after Art Modell had taken his team to Baltimore; Robert Reynolds, the Concord, Massachusetts–based vice chairman and chief operating officer of Fidelity Investments who was a former college football referee; and Mayo Shattuck III, the chairman, president, and CEO of Constellation Energy in Baltimore who'd brokered the sale of the Ravens from Modell to Steve Bisciotti and whose wife was a Ravens cheerleader.

But at this meeting the owners were told only that the search committee was down to eleven candidates and would present a group of finalists at a meeting in the Chicago area two weeks later. The owners knew Goodell and Pash were among the eleven but weren't given the names of the others. A petty argument ensued about whether there should be four or five finalists. Tagliabue deftly resolved the dispute by not resolving it; the search committee was told to present "four or five" finalists in Chicago. The talk was about process, not candidates. It was decided that each of the finalists would make a presentation to the owners in Chicago. Then the owners would be given the chance to question the candidates in small groups. That was a new feature of the selection process. There had been no such question-and-answer sessions in 1989. Tagliabue again was doing all he could to avoid a repeat of the stalemate created seventeen years earlier by some owners' resentment over how the search was conducted. He desperately wanted to be out of office soon. The meeting ended and most of the owners left but the members of the search committee stayed, going to another room one level below and meeting for another three and a half hours. They had work to do. They would interview the remaining candidates before reducing the list to the finalists. Tagliabue attended the search committee meeting but exited before it was over. He and Joe Browne had dinner reservations later that night in New Orleans—they would see the progress of the repairs to the Superdome the next day—and they weren't going to be late.

July 28 ... Albany, New York

The Giants had the first practice of their training camp on a gray, rainy morning. For the first time in five years the team had all its rookies on hand for the opening of camp. Mathias Kiwanuka, the defensive end chosen in the first round in April, had just signed a five-year contract worth about $7 million. Most of the fans at the practice fields at SUNY-Albany were gathered on a hill behind one end zone, shielded from the rain by the trees surrounding the fields at that end.

John Mara finally ditched the suit and watched practice from the sideline wearing shorts, a golf shirt, and tennis shoes. Like everyone else in the league, Mara was guessing that Roger Goodell would get the commissioner's job but he knew that anything could still happen. He thought it would be difficult for any candidate to get the required twenty-two votes (down from the twenty-four needed for other significant decisions) on the first ballot, but he did believe the owners would pick a commissioner in Chicago. Tagliabue, he thought, had avoided making the missteps that Pete Rozelle had made in 1989 when Mara's father had been the cochairman of the search committee.

When the full team drills began Eli Manning completed a long pass

to wide receiver Amani Toomer on the opening play. Antonio Pierce berated his defensive teammates in the huddle.

"Hey, this shit doesn't go down around here!" he yelled.

There was still an air of testiness around the Giants. At the moment,
Michael Strahan was angry about the way his divorce trial was being
splashed across the New York tabloids.

"If there's anyone here from the *Post* or *Daily News,* I'm not talking,"
he snapped as he brushed past reporters on the day the Giants reported
to camp.

LaVar Arrington, who was zipping around camp on a Segway human
transporter, was upset because ESPN analyst Merril Hoge had said he
was an undisciplined player who couldn't coexist with Tom Coughlin.
Arrington had the Giants' public relations director, Pat Hanlon, get him
in touch with Hoge and the two hashed things out, but he was still sore.

Manning's training camp had gotten off to a good start with the pass
to Toomer. He would spend his time in Albany pondering the upcoming season-opening game against the Indianapolis Colts and his brother.
He knew he and Peyton would remember the game for the rest of their
lives. But he also knew it mattered little to Strahan, Arrington, and his
other teammates that he was facing his brother, so he kept things as low-
key as possible. He remembered the first time he'd ever beaten his
brother in an athletic competition, a backyard basketball game when he
was seventeen or eighteen and Peyton was home from college on a break.
It wasn't much of a game. The brothers took turns backing each other
toward the basket and shooting hook shots. Eli had a big advantage since
he'd been playing high school basketball and Peyton hadn't played the
sport for a while. But he'd managed to dunk on Peyton once and it had
irked Peyton, who'd offered a limp handshake and hadn't spoken to Eli
for a couple hours afterward. It had felt good to win.

What would prove to be one of the biggest stories of the Giants' season wasn't in the open yet. Tiki Barber was keeping it a secret for now.
This would be his final year playing in the NFL.

Barber had been affected deeply by the deaths of Bob Tisch and
Wellington Mara. They'd been major influences on him, and they'd

preached to him that life was about much more than football. "I'm fortunate to be in this position," Tisch had once told Barber and his wife Ginny, "but I have a responsibility to share my good fortune."

Barber wanted to do more with his life, much more. At the Pro Bowl in February he'd gotten up at 5 a.m. to run three miles with members of an army infantry battalion on its way to the war in Iraq. He and his brother Ronde had begun writing children's books. If a young kid who otherwise wouldn't be interested in reading would want to read a book about football, they figured, maybe that would get him or her started toward reading other books. Tiki had a blossoming career in broadcasting as a once-a-week cohost of the *Fox & Friends* news show on the Fox News Channel and the cohost of a satellite radio show on Sirius with Ronde. On Tuesdays, supposedly the day off each week for NFL players, Tiki would get to the Fox News studio at 3 a.m. to prepare for the morning show. He would end up running himself ragged during the 2006 season to ready for his life after football. When the Giants played a Monday night game in Jacksonville in November he would ride home on the team plane, get to Giants Stadium at 4:30 a.m. and then go straight to the studio in Manhattan for the show at 6. All the TV networks were interested in Barber. His contract with Fox was about to expire in January and he could begin negotiating with other networks in November. He wanted to be more than an ex-jock broadcasting sports; he wanted a broader forum. He'd have a slew of other business opportunities as well.

He and Ginny had spent six days in Israel in June after being invited by former Israeli prime minister Shimon Peres, whom they'd met in a restaurant in Manhattan. They also had lunch with Condoleezza Rice.

It was one of several conversations that Tiki Barber had with Rice. In one, he asked if she wanted to be the NFL commissioner.

"You know, I really would," Rice told him, "but I've got to figure out Iran first."

Barber had two young sons and Ginny wanted him to leave football in one piece. He shared that desire. He didn't want to be unable to walk in his early fifties like Earl Campbell, the once-great NFL running back whose body had absorbed too many hits. He began to give more serious thought to walking away from football sooner rather than later. Retiring after the season would require Barber to bypass the $8.3 million in salaries due to him for the 2007 and 2008 seasons under his contract with the Giants, but he and his business manager, Mark Lepselter, guessed that in the long run Barber could make that much and more. He was ready to move on.

Now at training camp Barber hinted at his retirement decision but didn't come completely clean. Not yet. He told a group of reporters he could see himself walking away from the sport within the next few years but he said he hadn't considered retiring prior to this season, in part because he was only thirty-one and coming off his best season and in part because he thought the Giants might be on the verge of big things.

"I honestly feel we can compete for a Super Bowl this season," he said.

They'd better. It was his last chance.

July 29 . . . Oxnard, California

The Cowboys' camp began the day after the Giants' did. The Cowboys were in their third and final year of basing their training camp in Oxnard, about an hour's drive north of Los Angeles. They stayed at a Residence Inn by Marriott and practiced on two fields alongside a golf course. The weather usually was breezy and comfortable, and Jerry Jones liked the idea of having "America's Team" train in California, be based in Texas, and play some of its biggest games on the East Coast. But the land on which the Cowboys held their camp in Oxnard was about to be developed and San Antonio had made him an offer he couldn't refuse, so Jones had agreed to move the team's camp back to Texas the following summer.

Fans were charged five dollars to park their cars on dirt lots and passed first through a large open area where concession and merchandise tents were set up. A band played live music. The crowd gathered behind a fence along the sideline of one field directly opposite huge blow-up props advertising Ford, Miller Lite, Tostitos, and Dejà Blue bottled water set up behind the fence separating the fields from the golf course. Both sides of the fields were lined with advertising signs. The hotel had tennis courts behind the end zones on one end of the fields, and the Cowboys had set up a VIP area on one of them. On another the team had placed a tent to serve as a media workroom near an interview area for Bill Parcells's sun-drenched daily press briefings.

Drew Rosenhaus and Terrell Owens's mother, Marilyn Heard, watched from the VIP section when the Cowboys began camp with a morning practice. The crowd of about 5,500 people was the largest the Cowboys had ever drawn to a practice in Oxnard. Owens was the last player to take the field.

He and Parcells chatted on the sideline during one break in the practice.

"Get ready to have some fun," Parcells said.

Owens provided the only electric moment of the morning when he beat veteran cornerback Aaron Glenn and hauled in a long touchdown pass from backup quarterback Tony Romo. Owens waved his arms to exhort the crowd, but the gesture was unnecessary. Just as Eagles fans had done at Lehigh in Owens's first summer with that team, Cowboys fans in Oxnard cheered wildly for practically everything Owens did.

They called his name.

They chanted, "T-O! T-O!"

They stayed late after practices to try to get his autograph, shoving everything from footballs to programs to copies of his book at him.

Owens was interacting with fans amicably and speaking to reporters daily. He declared himself stress-free. He figured Parcells would push and prod and test him at some point. But not yet. As camp opened Parcells had problems bigger than Owens. Left tackle Flozell Adams, working his way back from his knee injury, wasn't ready to practice and was placed on the physically unable to perform list. Defensive end Marcus Spears hurt his knee during the first practice and would need arthroscopic surgery for a meniscus tear. Parcells regarded Owens as a nonfactor at this point. He wouldn't stay that way for long.

CHAPTER

- 18 -

July 30 ... Oxnard, California

Jerry Jones sat on a chair on the tennis court that served as the VIP area and watched practice through a chain-link fence. A member of the search committee, he had just finished participating by phone in the deliberations to trim the commissioner field to five finalists.

Roger Goodell was on the list, along with Gregg Levy, Frederick Nance, Robert Reynolds, and Mayo Shattuck III. The committee had wanted to have David Brandon among the finalists. Some owners thought the Domino's Pizza CEO was the one outsider who actually had a chance to be elected. But Brandon was under pressure from his board of directors to withdraw from the NFL search and he wanted an assurance he would get the job if he was going to stay in the running. The search committee couldn't offer that, so Brandon pulled out and the committee added Shattuck to the list of finalists. Goodell and Levy were the insiders. Nance, Reynolds, and Shattuck were the outsiders. Nance was the lone black candidate.

Jones believed the owners had set up the next commissioner to succeed, even though the job was a sometimes thankless one in which you were hired by thirty-two wealthy, willful businessmen and then had to try to keep them in line while making decisions that left many of them angry at any given time. "I don't know of any place that an individual has structurally, bylaw-wise, less accountability than the commissioner," Jones said. "I say that because the owners have given him that. He's given a lot of discretion."

The call over, Jones could shift his attention back to his team. The weekend before camp, the Cowboys had signed tight end Jason Witten to a six-year contract extension worth about $28 million. The deal included a $6 million signing bonus and a $6 million option bonus in 2007. It kept Witten from being an unrestricted free agent after the season. The Cowboys had spent much of the offseason negotiating the deal, and the agreement left Jones focusing on keeping a defensive standout, safety Roy Williams, off the unrestricted free agent market the following spring. He hoped to complete an extension with Williams soon.

Jones looked out over the activity on the two practice fields in front of him. The team he was watching was promising. Jones thought it was the most talented Cowboys club he'd seen in five or six years. But Jones had watched training-camp promise turn into regular-season frustration on a regular basis in recent years and he wasn't getting carried away with his expectations. Jones's best Cowboys teams had been balanced on offense, making defenses respect both the passing game and the running game. He thought Terrell Owens could bring that to this team. Jones was avoiding the term "risk" when it came to the Owens signing. He preferred to say that his nature included a tolerance for ambiguity: "I had to have it to be a wildcat oil and gas driller and I had to have it to get into the NFL, especially with the Cowboys."

He was a master marketer himself so he thought it would be hypocritical to hold Owens's self-aggrandizement against him. In that area Owens reminded him of former Cowboys cornerback Deion Sanders. It went too far with a player, Jones thought, when it affected the ability of the player's team to win. Clearly that had happened with Owens in Philadelphia, but Jones thought Owens understood that and wouldn't let it happen again. People could change, Jones believed. He thought he'd changed since his parting with Jimmy Johnson. He and Bill Parcells were beginning their fourth season together and there had been no major incidents between them. Jones took delight in the fact that he and Parcells had managed to coexist peacefully, something few people around the league had thought could happen when he'd hired Parcells. After the ugly split with Johnson, Jones had seen former San Francisco 49ers coach Bill Walsh on television, saying that the two men simply had grown careless in the management of their relationship. Jones had come to believe that was right, and he was careful not to allow the same thing to happen in his relationship with Parcells.

Jones believed that Parcells's greatest strength was his ability to develop personal bonds with players, but he also knew that if these Cowboys didn't win he very well could have a cranky coach and a troublesome wide receiver on his hands. "I think they both are really invested in what they do," Jones said. "I think they both start getting a little foul and a little off track when they lose. You take both of them and you get them in the winning column or you have some things to deal with."

As Parcells walked around the practice fields during training camp he regularly wore a long-sleeved shirt with a picture on the back of two hands pushing a large pile of poker chips toward the middle of a table. The picture was accompanied by the words, "Who's All In?" Jerry Jones and Bill Parcells certainly were.

July 31 . . . Oxnard, California

Jerry Jones stood and watched from the sideline wearing shorts, a T-shirt, and a blue cap with a "D" on it as the Cowboys had a morning practice in cool, overcast conditions on the third day of their camp. Former Cowboys safety James Washington showed up wearing a Super Bowl ring and got a warm ovation from the crowd. When Bill Parcells saw Washington he told the beefed-up former player, "I remember you. You look about twenty pounds overweight. You know, I fine four hundred dollars a pound now."

Later as he told the story to his friends on the sideline, Washington looked out toward the less-than-svelte Parcells on the practice field.

"He looks like he's about to do a biscuit commercial," Washington said. Those around him laughed heartily.

Mike Vanderjagt was relaxed early in the practice. He was lean and athletic and he actually moved like a real player as he caught passes from the team's quarterbacks during a warmup drill. He stood near the sideline and tried to angle kicks through the closest set of uprights.

His mood changed after the Cowboys did a field goal drill midway through the practice.

Vanderjagt was the most accurate field goal kicker in NFL history, but this wasn't his day. Parcells stood nearby with his arms folded as Vanderjagt pushed one kick wide right from the field's right hash mark. Vanderjagt's groan could be heard all the way from the sideline. He shanked another kick wide right from the middle of the field, then squatted down and took his helmet off. He was disgusted with himself. When the drill was over Vanderjagt had a ball boy hold a ball on the spot from which he'd just missed and drilled a kick right down the middle. He stalked over to the sideline and grabbed a ball-holding contraption, took it to the other field and used it to silently send one perfect kick after another sailing through the distant uprights.

"I don't think a missed field goal for me is acceptable regardless of the distance, regardless of the situation, regardless of whether it was a good hold or bad hold," Vanderjagt said immediately after the practice. "I just feel if I put my foot on it, it should go in."

Vanderjagt knew his career field goal conversion rate—87.5 percent—off the top of his head. He wanted to push it above 88 percent. Even with his gaudy statistics Vanderjagt had left Indianapolis with a reputation for not being a clutch kicker, thanks in part to his playoff miss against the Pittsburgh Steelers that ended up being his final kick for the Colts. Vanderjagt insisted that he would relish the opportunity to have another kick in similar circumstances with his new team's season on the line. "I don't choke," he said. "I'm not a choker because I love that environment."

Football success hadn't come quickly or easily for Vanderjagt, a Canadian who had bounced around the CFL and the Arena Football League for years after a college career at West Virginia. The Colts had given him his NFL chance in 1998 when he was twenty-eight. Now he was thirty-six and he was eager to show the Colts they'd been wrong to let him go. He saw the parallels between himself and Terrell Owens, and he was keeping an open mind about Owens on both the professional and personal levels. He knew the pressure was on him every bit as much as it was on Owens. He'd been reminded over and over since he'd signed with the Cowboys about Parcells's assessment that the team could have had three more wins the previous season with better kicking. Parcells had told him. Jones had told him. Fans had told him. All he had to do, he thought, was make every kick. In a business in which you were only as good as your last kick, Vanderjagt had to show he was far, far better than the last kick he'd taken.

"The baggage is that it's in between my ears," he said. "I happen to be a pretty good field goal kicker and I've been that for eight years, so I don't think one kick is going to define me. But certainly I have to go make field goals. I'm not here to miss field goals."

Parcells and Jones could only agree.

AUGUST

CHAPTER

- 19 -

August 4 . . . Ashburn, Virginia

The Redskins had to conduct the early portions of their training camp in the misery of a heat wave that pushed afternoon temperatures in the D.C. area into triple digits and produced heat index readings nearing 120 degrees. After practices players sat in huge tubs filled with water and ice placed by the team's trainers outside the back door to Redskins Park. Joe Gibbs gave his players a relatively light training camp workload. He would end up regretting that. Early warning signs about what was to come were all around. The offensive players were already feeling lost in Al Saunders's system. They felt they'd had an offense that, while simple, had contributed to winning games, and now they were starting all over with something different. New receiver Brandon Lloyd would yell at Stan Hixon when the wide receivers coach tried to correct him on the practice field. Adam Archuleta was struggling with what he was being asked to do in Gregg Williams's defense. The safeties had to cover a lot of ground and some coaches were already suspecting that Archuleta wasn't up to it.

It was a Friday morning and Gibbs had scheduled a 10 a.m. practice the day before a scrimmage against the Baltimore Ravens at FedEx Field. The practice drew a large crowd, and traffic was backed up along the Loudoun County Parkway outside the facility as things were getting under way. Fans were directed to park their cars on dirt and grass fields just outside the guard stand at the edge of the paved lot for players, coaches, and team employees. Buses were waiting in close proximity to the front doors of the building to shuttle the coaches and players to the nearby National Conference Center, where the team was housed during camp. The first thing a visitor encountered was a merchandise tent. There were corporate VIP tents set up next to the field and a large sign reading: WELCOME TO REDSKINS TRAINING CAMP BUILT BY THE HOME DEPOT.

Snyder watched the practice from his corner office at Redskins Park, a large room with wood paneling, three TV screens, and a couple of couches facing his desk. Two walls of the office had huge windows that gave Snyder a panoramic view of the fields. Sitting on Snyder's desk was a packet that Korn/Ferry International had sent to each of the owners with a section on the job specs and biographical information for the five commissioner finalists. It was marked CONFIDENTIAL. He would be headed to Chicago on Sunday; he thought Goodell would get the job.

Snyder believed his team was good but he was worried about the Eagles in particular because they were well coached and they would have a healthy Donovan McNabb. He was on and off the phone checking on his wife and kids, who were in Aspen but were preparing to travel home. He excused himself to an adjoining conference room where a group of business types was seated around a table. He returned to his office a little while later.

"What do you think of Johnny Rockets?" he said.

A visitor said he'd never eaten at the chain of diners but had heard some moderately good things. Why?

"I just bought it," Snyder said.

At Redskins Park the buying part was never the problem.

August 7 . . . Northbrook, Illinois

Dan Snyder sat in a booth in an almost empty hotel coffee shop and scraped the cheese off his chili. He didn't have his nutritionist along with him but he was doing his best to eat well and keep his waistline in check.

He was asked why he'd bought Johnny Rockets and held his hand about a foot above the table.

"Because it's here," he said.

He raised his hand another foot or so.

"And," he said, "it could be up here."

He would apply that principle to another investment he made later in the summer. With Dwight Schar and Mark Shapiro, he went into business with Tom Cruise, cutting a limited financing deal with the beleaguered movie megastar as, in effect, a bet that Cruise would regain the favor of the film-watching public and recapture his box office Midas touch. They would provide Cruise's production company with money to cover overhead and would receive a return on the films Cruise produced. The two-year deal came together because Shapiro knew one of Cruise's agents, Kevin Huvane. Cruise's popularity was ebbing because of the negative publicity he'd received from his divorce from Nicole Kidman and courtship of Katie Holmes, his lunatic ramblings as he stood on the couch on Oprah Winfrey's set during an appearance on her show, and his verbal attack on Brooke Shields for her use of medication to combat postpartum depression. Paramount Pictures was paying Cruise and his production partner, Paula Wagner, about $10 million a year to cover overhead but the deal was expiring and Paramount had no intention of continuing to pay that much. It offered Cruise and Wagner around $2 million. They rejected the offer and spent the summer searching for new financing.

They found Snyder.

"You ought to come to a game sometime," Snyder told Cruise once they were in business together.

Snyder finished lunch and ducked into a meeting room. It was a Monday and the owners had reconvened at the Renaissance North Shore in the Chicago suburb of Northbrook. The $199-a-night hotel was a long ride from O'Hare Airport and wasn't up to the usual level of opulence for an owners' meeting. The lobby had marble floors but wasn't sufficiently spacious or luxurious for the owners. They were grousing virtually from the moment they arrived. The meeting was scheduled to last until Wednesday, but many owners thought Goodell's election was a fait accompli and resolved to be on their way home by Tuesday evening. Paul Tagliabue was relaxed as he stood in the lobby before the meeting began. He and his wife had plans to travel in China and India in the fall and he was almost free. He saw some acquaintances and walked over to say hello.

"It's almost over for you," he was told.

"It's like Mao's Long March," Tagliabue said.

He started to walk away but turned back. "See, I'm getting ready for China."

The NFL took over the hotel. Coffee was served in NFL mugs. Food was served accompanied by NFL napkins. The TV sets in the lobby were tuned to the NFL Network. NFL security guards told a hotel guest he couldn't use the staircase leading to the fitness room downstairs. Detroit Lions president Matt Millen checked in at the front desk wearing a suit and a Dr. Seuss *One Fish Two Fish Red Fish Blue Fish* cap. "We're at the elementary level," he said.

Many owners' meetings quickly disintegrated to the Dr. Seuss level, but Tagliabue was doing his best to ensure that everyone behaved properly at this one. Each of the five commissioner finalists made a presentation to the owners that afternoon. The order of the addresses was determined by an employee in the league's legal department, Anastasia Danias, picking names out of a white football helmet with a league logo on it. It reminded Tagliabue of a league realignment in the late sixties that had been determined by team names drawn from a fishbowl. "We've moved from fishbowls to football helmets," he said.

Gregg Levy went first followed by Mayo Shattuck, Frederick Nance,

Roger Goodell, and Robert Reynolds. Goodell told the owners he would be the commissioner of all the teams, not just the high-revenue clubs. He said he'd gotten his MBA from Pete Rozelle and Tagliabue but he wasn't looking simply to maintain the status quo. The league had succeeded under Rozelle and Tagliabue because it always looked for innovative, better ways to do things, he said, and that's what he would do. Goodell was the youngest of the finalists at forty-seven but knew by far the most about the inner workings of the league. He'd spent more than two decades working in the league office and had been the chief operating officer of the NFL for five years.

He'd been born near Buffalo in Jamestown, New York, and grew up in a family in which he was one of five boys. His father was Charles Goodell, a prominent politician in New York who served in the U.S. House of Representatives for ten years and was appointed by Governor Nelson Rockefeller in 1968 to fill the Senate seat left vacant by the assassination of Robert Kennedy. After sponsoring legislation to cut off funding for the Vietnam War effort, Charles Goodell lost when he ran for a full Senate term in 1970. He returned to practicing law and died in 1987 at age sixty. The family lived in Washington for a while before moving back to New York and settling in Bronxville, a village in affluent Westchester County. Roger played football, baseball, and basketball as a kid. He was good enough in football to draw recruiting interest by some colleges but a knee injury kept him from playing. He majored in economics at Washington & Jefferson College near Pittsburgh and graduated magna cum laude. He considered going to law school but instead landed an internship in the NFL office in the fall of 1982, then spent a year in the New York Jets' public relations office before returning to the league in '84 to work for Joe Browne in the PR department. He rose through the ranks and eventually had a hand in virtually everything the league did on the business side. He was more outgoing and affable than Tagliabue and had a handshake as firm as they come. His wife, Jane Skinner, was a Fox News Channel anchor and the couple had twin daughters.

The owners unanimously approved voting procedures by which all five candidates would remain under consideration for at least three ballots, after which Tagliabue and the search committee could choose to eliminate those candidates with the fewest votes. They also could switch if they wanted from secret ballot voting to an open roll call. The owners told the candidates the new commissioner would have an annual salary of around $4 million. The meeting wrapped up for the day about dinnertime. Tagliabue went to a press briefing in which he cracked a few jokes. Browne called out from the back of the room, "Where was this seventeen years ago? You would have been elected sooner."

The deliberations resumed Tuesday morning at eight. The owners were divided into four groups of eight and conducted question-and-answer sessions with the candidates on a rotating basis. That ended early in the afternoon. The search committee held a brief meeting and the entire ownership group huddled around two. "We've all been to NFL meetings where half the owners are calling their pilots to get their planes ready," Steve Tisch said. "I don't get that sense here."

Maybe not, but several black Lincoln Town Cars were lined up outside the front of the hotel by three. It was the football equivalent of the Vatican's white smoke. Voting began around 2:20 and it took three hours and five ballots for Goodell to be elected, seven ballots fewer than it had taken for Tagliabue to be elected in 1989 and eighteen fewer than it had taken for Rozelle to be elected in 1960. Goodell got fifteen votes on the first ballot and Levy got thirteen. The three outside candidates totaled only three votes. Al Davis, after voting in Dallas to approve the labor and revenue-sharing settlement, reverted to his long-standing policy of abstaining. Tagliabue and the search committee dropped Nance, Reynolds, and Shattuck. So much for the voting procedures the owners had approved Monday, and so much for the outsiders. The voting would be done by secret ballot all day. The votes were counted in a nearby coatroom. Goodell got seventeen votes and Levy got fourteen on both the second and third ballots. Goodell was winning but not decisively.

The owners paused the voting and had some debate. Dan Rooney told the other owners he had no doubt Goodell was the right choice.

"He knows the labor," Rooney told his colleagues. "He knows the

TV. He knows the business. He knows the people, and he knows the fans."

The voting resumed and Goodell got twenty-one votes on the fourth ballot, one shy of the required twenty-two, to ten for Levy. The outcome was sealed. Goodell got twenty-three votes on the fifth ballot and Levy received eight. Goodell had been elected the NFL's fourth commissioner in sixty years. It was over at around 5:20 p.m. The owners decided by acclamation to make the vote unanimous. Rooney and Jerry Richardson, the cochairmen of the search committee, slipped out of the room and made their way to the hotel elevators. Richardson went to Levy's room. Rooney went to knock on Goodell's door. Goodell had been in lockdown mode. He was registered as "Roger Washington." He was trying to distract himself by doing some work. "Fortunately I'd just put my pants on," he said later that day.

When Goodell opened the door, Rooney broke into a wide grin. The two men hugged. Goodell made his way downstairs to the meeting room and was greeted by a standing ovation from the owners. It was an emotional moment for him. "I'd been in front of those guys so many times," he said, "but this was different."

The doors opened and the owners made a mad dash for the exits. It had been a vote for Tagliabue as much as a vote for Goodell, like a national election in which the vice president rode the coattails of a popular president into office. Tagliabue made his way to the lobby en route to leaving his final formal gathering as commissioner. He'd kept a file over the years with clippings about companies that had managed an orderly CEO succession, behemoths like IBM and GE. Now in his final act of consensus-building wizardry he'd managed to convince the owners to have the NFL do the same thing. Goodell finished a press conference and walked to the lobby a few minutes later, looking for Tagliabue but not finding him. The two still had to discuss when Goodell officially would take over. By day's end Goodell would agree to a five-year contract.

He had some big shoes to fill, and no one knew that better than he did.

August 14 . . . Bethlehem, Pennsylvania

The Eagles were two days from wrapping up the Lehigh portion of their training camp when they took the field for a Monday morning practice. Andy Reid had moved up the starting time of his morning practices from 8:45 to 8:15 during the recent heat wave and then hadn't changed back. The team had already played two of its five preseason games and would relocate to the NovaCare Complex after an exhibition contest that Thursday night in Baltimore.

The players were restless and eager to get out of Bethlehem. There was a sizable crowd on hand for the morning practice. Reid ran a hurry-up offense drill in which he put one minute forty seconds on the clock and told the offense it needed a field goal to win the game. Donovan McNabb directed the starters down the field but threw an interception. Reggie Brown made a sensational tumbling grab along the sideline during a seven-on-seven drill.

"You were out of bounds," secondary coach Trent Walters called out, "but that was a helluva catch!"

Brian Dawkins dropped a would-be interception on one play, immediately falling to the ground to do ten punishment pushups, then intercepted a McNabb pass the next play. Jeremy Bloom was in his first full-contact practice of training camp and made a good catch in heavy traffic of a throw zipped by Jeff Garcia between two defenders. Tra Thomas was healthy, and that left Winston Justice practicing as the second-string left tackle. He no longer held out hope that there was playing time to be earned as a rookie, but he was doing his best to learn and remain positive.

Late in the morning practice Eagles officials had led a large group of U.S. troops onto the sideline of the practice field during a special teams drill. The crowd had given the soldiers a lengthy standing ovation and the Eagles players and coaches had joined in. The real world had seeped into the insular existence of an NFL training camp, if only temporarily.

The Eagles had finally gotten the Brodrick Bunkley deal done ten days earlier. Bunkley missed sixteen days of training camp and twenty-eight practices. Joe Banner and Gary Wichard had settled on a six-year contract worth $12.7 million, including $9.775 million in guaranteed money. The Eagles threatened two days before the agreement to reduce their offer. Instead they increased the value of the sixth season in the offer sufficiently to make Wichard comfortable accepting a six-year deal. Bunkley's sixth-year salary could go as high as the franchise-player tender for a defensive tackle if he reached the Pro Bowl three times in his first five seasons. The same day Banner completed a two-year contract extension with Dawkins worth about $6 million, including a signing bonus of approximately $2 million. The Eagles didn't announce the deal until two days later when they opened the preseason by playing the Oakland Raiders in the Hall of Fame Game in Canton, Ohio. The Eagles thought Dawkins might be a Hall of Fame player one day so they considered the setting appropriate.

Now it was time for the Eagles and everyone else to do their final tinkering. In the last days of August the Eagles would complete the Donté Stallworth trade, just as they'd guessed all along they could do if they wanted. They sent backup linebacker Mark Simoneau and a fourth-round draft pick to the New Orleans Saints; the draft choice would become a third-rounder if the Eagles were able to sign Stallworth to a contract extension. He was entering the final season of his deal with a salary of $1.92 million. Stallworth was a wildly talented player who'd been taken with the thirteenth overall selection in the 2002 draft out of the University of Tennessee. He'd failed to live up to his promise but he'd been pretty productive, with 70 catches for 945 yards and seven touchdowns for the Saints the previous season. Sean Payton, the Saints' coach, had been impressed in training camp with rookie wide receiver Marques Colston, a seventh-round draft pick from Hofstra. When he'd worked for Bill Parcells, he'd listened to Parcells preach, "Unbias yourself against how you acquired the player." Coaching decisions, Parcells meant, shouldn't be based on players' contracts or draft status. Payton remembered those words and decided to go with Colston and approve getting rid of Stallworth. Colston would end up finishing tied for second in the offensive rookie of the year balloting. With Stallworth in the fold, the Eagles would cut Jabar Gaffney. Bloom would play in the exhibition game in Baltimore and return two third-quarter kickoffs for a total of 45 yards. But he left the game after reinjuring his hamstring. The muscle was torn and Bloom was placed on the injured reserve list, ending his rookie season before it even started. Jamaal Jackson beat out Hank Fraley for the starting center job and Fraley was traded to the Cleveland Browns.

The Cowboys had gotten the Roy Williams deal done only three days after Jerry Jones had sat on the tennis court in Oxnard watching practice. They kept the safety from being an unrestricted free agent the following spring by signing Williams to a four-year, $24 million contract extension that included $11.1 million in bonuses. Parcells tired of watching Jason Fabini and Rob Petitti struggle at right tackle and gave the starting job to Marc Colombo, a former first-round draft choice by the Chicago Bears who was attempting to reconstruct a career derailed by a serious knee injury that included nerve damage. The Cowboys had signed him in November after the Bears had released him two weeks into the previous season, Parcells recalling that Al Davis once told him to keep in mind that someone once had thought quite a bit of a player if he was a former first-round pick. Flozell Adams had begun practicing on the second day of camp and showed enough to remain the starter at left tackle. Jones and Parcells crossed their fingers about an offensive line that had Andre Gurode at center and Kyle Kosier and Marco Rivera at guard.

Terrell Owens just couldn't help himself: He was providing his usual melodrama. He missed fourteen straight practices in camp because of a sore hamstring, watching from the sideline and riding an exercise bike. He continued to draw attention to himself by donning a Lance Amstrong–style Discovery Channel cycling jersey and helmet at one point while riding. Owens brought in his own team of medical advisers and had his hyperbaric chamber shipped from Dallas to Oxnard. The hyperbaric chamber was a long, narrow inflatable tube costing close to $20,000. Owens could lie inside and have pressurized air pumped into it, the premise being that more oxygen would get to damaged tissues and the healing process would be accelerated. Two MRI exams would reveal no serious damage to his hamstring, and Jones spoke to Owens's advisers about the need for him to practice even when less than fully healthy. Owens returned to practice for three days but then declared he'd suffered a setback. He wouldn't play in an exhibition game until the Cowboys' preseason finale. By then Parcells had fined Owens $9,500 for oversleeping and missing a team meeting and a rehab session and being late to an offensive meeting the day before the third preseason game. Things weren't any better with Mike Vanderjagt, who was being plagued by a groin injury. Parcells had little tolerance for kickers under any circumstances and even less for injured kickers.

"Okay, what's it gonna be?" he snapped at Vanderjagt at the end of warmups before the third preseason game.

"I think it would be smart if I didn't kick," Vanderjagt said.

So Parcells held him out. Vanderjagt did kick in the preseason finale against the Minnesota Vikings but missed 32- and 33-yard field goal attempts in overtime. Parcells fretted that Vanderjagt might have lost his nerve and reluctantly kept a second kicker, Shaun Suisham, on the season-opening roster. The one pleasant preseason surprise for Parcells and Jones was the play during the exhibition games of young quarterback Tony Romo. Parcells had avoided giving Romo too much responsibility earlier in his career, fearing it would ruin him as a player. Romo had never thrown a regular-season pass in three years in the NFL. But now, Parcells thought, he had to find out whether Romo was potential starting material. He played Romo the entire way in the Cowboys' exhibition opener at Seattle and Romo played well. Parcells wasn't putting the starting job up for grabs quite yet but he thought he had a legitimate prospect. Just before the season the Cowboys would sign Romo to a two-year, $3.9 million contract extension. He'd been entering the final season of his existing deal and would have been eligible for unrestricted free agency the following spring. Romo's new contract contained a $2 million signing bonus, the same $900,000 salary he previously was to have for the upcoming season, and a $1 million salary in 2007.

Little would go right for the Redskins during a winless exhibition season. Mark Brunell threw an interception on the Redskins' opening drive of their preseason opener in Cincinnati. Tailback Clinton Portis raced over to make a jarring tackle and suffered a partially dislocated left shoulder. The next day the offensive coaches met with the scouts at Redskins Park. The options for adding a running back were outlined: The Redskins could sign free agent Stephen Davis. They could trade for the Green Bay Packers' Samkon Gado or the Denver Broncos' Ron Dayne. Or they could give up a little more and trade for the Atlanta Falcons' T. J. Duckett. The Redskins went through the evaluation process just as they had for free agency and the draft. Reports and tapes were issued to coaches, and the available players were graded. But this was a stacked deck. Gibbs was familiar with Duckett from his days in Falcons ownership and the Redskins weren't going to settle for a second-tier running back in a potential championship season. They didn't trust backup Ladell Betts sufficiently to sit back and do nothing.

The Redskins got Duckett in a three-way trade in which the Falcons got Denver wide receiver Ashley Lelie and the Broncos got a draft pick or picks from the Redskins. The exact package the Redskins would send the Broncos wouldn't be determined until after the season, based on the teams' records and draft slots. The basic premise was that the Redskins would give the Broncos about 250 points worth of picks on the value chart. There were four possibilities: The teams could swap first-round picks. They could swap first-round picks and the Broncos could also get the Redskins' third-round choice. They could swap first-round picks and the Broncos could also get a fourth-round selection in 2008. Or the Broncos could simply get a third-rounder in 2007 and a fourth-rounder in 2008 with no exchange of first-rounders.

Once again the Redskins were trading away future draft choices as if there might not even be a draft the next year. It was the fatal flaw in their roster-building approach. It wasn't that the Redskins' way couldn't work. It could work. It had worked to produce a good team the previous season. But they needed to tone it down a bit. They needed to realize they couldn't build their team only through free agency; the mistakes were too expensive. They needed to hold on to more draft picks and infuse their roster with more young, cheap talent. As with most things in life, the best way usually was the way of moderation, not one extreme or the other. The Eagles, who were on the other extreme, needed to take a few more chances. They'd broken through and reached the Super Bowl, after all, in the season after they'd added Owens and Jevon Kearse. And the Redskins needed to be a little bit more cautious and traditional.

The cracks were already showing. The Redskins were outscored, 104–27, in their four preseason games. Al Saunders had a seven-hundred-page playbook and Todd Collins had told Brunell it would take about a year to master the offense. But Brunell didn't have a year, not at this point in his career. Gibbs knew a bad preseason could get an owner nervous. He remembered being lectured by Jack Kent Cooke after a 1-3 preseason in 1991.

"You have messed this thing up," Cooke said, pointing a finger at Gibbs.

"In what way?" Gibbs asked.

"I'll tell you what way: You kept too many guys on this team that are old!" Cooke railed. "You take Jimmy Johnson down there, he's doing things the right way. I just got bought out of this company and I've got $18 million and I've got to figure out what to do with it on taxes. I'm going to try to make some money so you guys can throw it away."

Gibbs, as always, could do as he chose, Cooke added.

"I'm not going to mess you up," Cooke said. "You've got to do what you think is right but that's what I think."

"Yes, sir, Mr. Cooke," Gibbs said. "I've got it."

The Redskins won their third Super Bowl that season.

Gibbs could only hope things would turn out as well this time. Dan Snyder remembered that a terrible exhibition season had preceded Marty Schottenheimer's 0-5 start in 2001 but told himself this wasn't

Schottenheimer. It was Gibbs. Saunders told people he'd used only about 2 percent of his playbook in the preseason. Gregg Williams had done little blitzing. The regular season was when coaches started coaching for real. After what Snyder had paid for Gibbs's staff, he had the right to expect his coaches to outmaneuver some people.

Things had been relatively quiet for the Giants. Mathias Kiwanuka was making a positive impression, but Sinorice Moss's development had been slowed by a strained left quadriceps muscle he had first hurt while running a forty-yard dash at the scouting combine. LaVar Arrington was practicing sporadically, trying to ensure his knee would be ready for the season. That set off alarm bells in the New York media, but Arrington thought he and the Giants were being smart. He felt accepted and appreciated with his new team. His weight was down to 247 pounds, from a high of 270 with the Redskins. He believed he was faster. He was the healthiest he'd been, he thought, in two years. He'd heard the Redskins had given his old number—56—to Jasper Harvey, a 305-pound center who was an undrafted rookie out of San Diego State and would end up being cut. "I'm told they picked the biggest, ugliest guy to put my number on," Arrington said. "I'm sure they got a good laugh out of that."

For now everyone was laughing. Everyone was fancying themselves a contender. At Lehigh the Eagles' camp was winding down and Reid was pleased.

"The guys have come back and gotten after each other," he said. "It's been a good, aggressive camp."

"A good, aggressive camp"—every coach and every owner in the league would say essentially the same thing if asked; it was almost boilerplate. Now came the time when boilerplate was put to the test.

PART 3

THE
PAYOFF

SEPTEMBER

CHAPTER

-20-

September 10 . . . East Rutherford, New Jersey

Indianapolis Colts quarterback Peyton Manning walked off the Giants Stadium field a few hours before kickoff on opening night. He'd finished his pre-pregame warmup, his early workout with wide receivers Marvin Harrison and Reggie Wayne to begin to loosen up and make sure they were all properly in sync. Manning passed the goalpost and was headed toward the tunnel leading under the stands to the locker rooms. He noticed the fuzzy outline of a person walking past him; he wasn't really paying attention.

Then he suddenly refocused and realized who it was.

It was Eli.

It struck Peyton then: He was playing an NFL game against his brother.

It was an NFL first, brothers starting against one another at quarterback. It had been discussed and promoted ad nauseam for months. Peyton had answered dozens, perhaps hundreds, of questions about it but he'd given stock answers and hadn't really contemplated how it would feel to share the field with Eli in a game.

Now he found himself surprisingly caught up in it all. He watched Eli during warmups and peeked at him during the national anthem. He thought the whole thing was neat.

"That's my little brother over there," he said to himself.

The NFL had given NBC the highly attractive "Manning Bowl" as the opening Sunday night game of the season. The NFC East had gotten off to an uneven start that afternoon. The Eagles gave a splendid performance and won at Houston. Donovan McNabb threw three touchdown passes and Donté Stallworth had six catches for 141 yards and a touchdown. Who needed Terrell Owens? The Cowboys had been undone by three interceptions thrown by Drew Bledsoe and lost at Jacksonville. Owens played well, with six catches for 80 yards and a touchdown, but Bledsoe was indecisive and missed throws he should have made. Flozell Adams didn't play well at left tackle. Shaun Suisham kicked in place of Mike Vanderjagt and sent a 36-yard field goal try off the right upright. That led Owens to launch into a screaming rant at no one in particular on the sideline.

"T.O., you're a cancer!" a Jaguars fan yelled at him as he left the field.

"Yep," Owens replied.

It was up to the Giants to give the NFC East a winning record for the day—the Redskins didn't play until the next night. Peyton Manning got the best of the Giants early as the Colts built a 13–0 lead. The Colts were abusing Sam Madison, and the Giants were dropping potential interceptions. But Eli Manning got things revved up and led the Giants back into the game. He threw touchdown passes to Plaxico Burress and Jeremy Shockey and the Giants trailed by only 23–21 when he connected with Tim Carter for a first down with just more than four minutes left. But Carter was penalized for offensive pass interference for a phantom pushoff. Tom Coughlin went nuts on the sideline, but it didn't matter. The bad call wasn't subject to an instant replay review. Instead of having a first down and all the momentum, the Giants faced a third-and-11 from their own 9-yard line. Manning threw a floating pass that was intercepted, leading to Adam Vinatieri's fourth field goal of the night for the Colts. The Giants ran out of time on their last-gasp drive.

John Mara saw Colts coach Tony Dungy in the tunnel after the game and the two, who served together on the competition committee, greeted one another warmly. On the field Peyton told Eli he loved him and was proud of how he'd competed.

"Good game," Eli replied. "It's your win."

Eli had taken a pregame picture with his brother and was happy the whole thing had happened but disappointed with his late interception. The most drained member of the Manning family, however, was Archie. He and Olivia had watched the game from the Reebok corporate box and it had been tough. By night's end all the emotion had been wrung out of them.

"I'm glad we don't have to go through this for a few more years," Olivia said as she and Archie stood near the Giants' locker room late that night. She quickly added, "I guess I'd take it if they managed to get to a Super Bowl together." Peyton's chances to hold up his end of that bargain looked better than Eli's.

September 11 ... Landover, Maryland

Tom Cruise wasted no time taking up Dan Snyder on the offer to attend a game. He and Katie Holmes were in town for the Redskins' opener.

Cruise brought along his thirteen-year-old daughter Isabella, his eleven-year-old son Connor, and his nearly five-month-old baby girl with Holmes, Suri. The Cruises stayed at the Snyders' home in Potomac. On the Sunday evening before the Monday night game the two families thought about going out bowling but then had a better idea. They went to the Six Flags park near the stadium, joined by Vinny Cerrato and his wife and kids and Mark Shapiro. They had the park to themselves: They rode roller coasters and bumper cars and ate pizza, chicken fingers, ice cream, and funnel cakes. Park workers stayed late and staged a closing ceremony. Snyder and Cruise led the kids in dancing the Electric Slide and the limbo.

Afterward, the families headed to FedEx Field. The kids threw footballs on the field underneath the stadium lights and the adults sat on the turf and watched the end of the Giants-Colts game on the huge stadium screen.

Snyder went to the stadium early Monday ahead of traffic and ate a hot dog and two hamburgers in the owner's box. He went into a bathroom; he got nervous on game days and felt sick to his stomach. Cruise took Holmes and his two older children to the game but left Suri with a babysitter. They rode to the stadium with Tanya Snyder and got stuck in Beltway traffic. They would be joined at the game by actor Jamie Foxx.

At 5:40 p.m., an hour and a half before kickoff, Snyder stood on the field and talked to Vikings owner Zygi Wilf. Music blared over the stadium's public address system. ESPN had nearly three dozen cameras in place for its first Monday night broadcast. The night had a big event feel to it. Dwight Schar came over and joined the conversation. Underneath the stands, in the tunnel leading from the Redskins' locker room to the field, Antwaan Randle El, fellow wide receiver James Thrash, and running back Rock Cartwright slapped each other on the shoulder pads. A Redskins staffer who'd been with the team through several coaching regimes watched some of Joe Gibbs's assistants walk by and said, "The stress level is through the roof. I've never seen anything like it."

Foxx moved past with his entourage and headed to the field. Cruise and Holmes were scheduled to walk by at 6:10. They showed up four minutes early. Cruise wore a dark blue suit and tie. Holmes wore a formal-looking dress with high-heeled shoes that had her towering above Cruise. Both sported sunglasses even though the skies were darkening outside. Holmes made a stop in the cheerleaders' locker room by the field, then the two joined Snyder and Foxx outside. Roger Goodell walked by with Joe Browne. It was the new commissioner's third game in five nights. He'd been to the NFL's season-opening game Thursday night in Pittsburgh and to the Manning Bowl on Sunday night. "I'm not sure I can keep it up," he said.

In the days after Goodell had been elected commissioner he and Paul Tagliabue had decided that Goodell would take over officially at 6 A.M. on September 1. They'd considered midnight but some preseason games on the West Coast would have been in progress and Tagliabue might have been commissioner for the first half and Goodell for the second half. Tagliabue thought his main duty in retirement was to disappear and allow Goodell to run the league as he saw fit. He dispensed advice in large doses but didn't want owners going around Goodell and calling him. He told Goodell it might be a good idea to do an immediate tour of the teams as he'd once done and Goodell agreed. Goodell had been on an exercise bike in the basement of his house the moment he became the most powerful man in sports. He didn't even notice when it happened because he was reading a newspaper and not paying attention to the clock. He started his workout that morning at 5:45 and ended it at 6:30. He didn't think anything about it until he went upstairs and his daughter reminded him he'd just taken charge of the NFL.

Goodell worked on his first weekend as commissioner but didn't move into his new office right away. It felt strange when people he'd known for years addressed him as "Commissioner" and odd when he was first handed a football with his name and signature on it. He quickly resolved his first controversy by deciding that he wouldn't dismiss Bryant Gumbel as an NFL Network announcer for saying on HBO that Tagliabue needed to show his successor "where he keeps Gene Upshaw's leash." The remark was utterly unfounded, given Upshaw's triumph in the labor negotiations, but Gumbel had to stay if the league wanted its network to have any credibility as a reporting and commenting entity as well as a promotional arm.

As the Redskins took the field for pregame warmups, Gregg Williams chatted with Bernard Shaw on his way through the tunnel. ESPN sideline reporter Suzy Kolber scribbled on a notepad as she talked to Clinton Portis. A group of police officers carrying rifles and flags strode past. Military representatives emerged from a nearby locker room. The night would be an odd mix of football, Hollywood, and September 11 patriotism. In the stands fans were handed American flags. At 6:37 the PA system blasted the *Monday Night Football* theme music. The Redskins left the field two minutes later, returning to their locker room after warmups. Shapiro left the field first, followed by Cruise and

Holmes. Cruise made sure to stop and shake hands with two security guards. Foxx did the same thing when he reached the tunnel moments later. A grim-faced Gibbs jogged off just ahead of his players. Cerrato and Snyder walked off surrounded by players. Snyder caught up to Foxx, Cruise, and Holmes in the tunnel that wound its way past the Redskins' locker room to a carport area underneath the stadium where Snyder's vehicle and other limousines were stashed. The group got into a private elevator and rode up to the walkways leading to the owner's box.

During the Snyder era the owner's box was often filled with an unglamorous CEO-type crowd. Not this night. Cruise, Holmes, and Foxx were joined by another actor, Peter Berg, and actor and politician Fred Thompson. John Glenn was there. So were Jack Kemp and his wife. There was the chairman of the Joint Chiefs of Staff, General Peter Pace. There were media luminaries Al Hunt and Judy Woodruff. There was Darrell Green and his wife Jewell. It was more like the star-filled gatherings of the Jack Kent Cooke days. Snyder was joined by his sister Michele and mother Arlette. Cruise sat between Snyder and Holmes. Foxx made an appearance in the ESPN booth during the second quarter with announcers Mike Tirico, Joe Theismann, and Tony Kornheiser. ESPN had asked for Cruise but his representatives had declined the invitation. At the Redskins' practice on Saturday at Redskins Park one of Cruise's representatives had discussed the possibility with Kornheiser, the *Washington Post* columnist and cohost of ESPN's highly successful *Pardon the Interruption* show who was about to call his first regular-season game. The agent said Cruise wouldn't do it. When Kornheiser asked why, the agent asked Kornheiser what he would ask Cruise during the broadcast.

"Some small stuff like, 'So, that lunatic period, you're over that now, right?' " Kornheiser said.

"That's why he's not doing it."

The game itself was a downer for Snyder. Redskins safety Pierson Prioleau suffered a season-ending knee injury on the opening kickoff. He'd been scheduled to start in Adam Archuleta's place on defense. Archuleta got a temporary reprieve and remained in the starting lineup, but he was already sensing things might not work out; maybe it hadn't been such a good idea to take the Redskins' money and try to fit into an unfamiliar defensive system.

Portis played but wasn't particularly effective. The offense was better than it had been during the preseason but still wasn't exactly awe-inspiring. The defense failed to dominate a Vikings offense that could have been dominated. The Redskins trailed by three points in the final minute. Mark Brunell hurried the offense down the field but Randle El ran out of bounds just shy of a first down after a third-down catch. The Redskins had to send in kicker John Hall to try a 48-yard field goal. There was a crosswind and Hall would have to strike the ball perfectly.

He didn't.

Hall pulled the kick wide left with twelve seconds left. After one kneel-down by quarterback Brad Johnson the Vikings celebrated their way to their locker room. The Redskins were 0-1 and the NFC East was 1-3 on the season's opening weekend. It wasn't the beginning anyone had envisioned for the would-be powerhouse division.

September 17 . . . Philadelphia

John Mara rushed toward an elevator on the suite level of Lincoln Financial Field.

"You guys sure made that one exciting," an acquaintance told him.

"You think?" Mara said, shaking his head and grinning.

Mara could smile because the Giants somehow had avoided an 0-2 start. They'd trailed the Eagles, 24–7, after three quarters. Donovan McNabb was carving up the Giants' secondary and the Eagles' pass rushers were harassing Eli Manning constantly en route to an eight-sack day. Andy Reid had lectured his team at halftime to finish the game playing like it was a scoreless tie, but Manning had performed some Elway-esque quarterbacking magic, leading the Giants to a tying field goal in the final seconds of regulation and throwing a winning touchdown pass to Plaxico Burress into the teeth of a blitz in overtime. The loss was especially deflating for the Eagles because Jevon Kearse hurt his left knee in overtime while combining with defensive tackle Mike Patterson on a sack. An MRI the next day would show Kearse needed season-ending surgery.

Middle linebacker Jeremiah Trotter shook his head in the Eagles' locker room afterward: "When we get a team down we need to put our foot on their throat."

Down the hall Tiki Barber was marveling about Manning. "I think in years past, we wouldn't have won that game," Barber said as he stood by his locker, "but it started with the Denver game last year. It's a testament to how he leads, to his resolve, to how he doesn't let us lose despite playing like horsecrap for three quarters."

The Cowboys overwhelmed the Redskins, 27–10, that night at Texas Stadium. Terrell Owens suffered a broken ring finger on his right hand while blocking on one of the game's first few plays but kept playing. He would undergo surgery the next day, having a metal plate and three screws inserted.

For the Giants the good feelings wouldn't last long. They would go to Seattle a week later and fall behind the Seahawks, 35–0, in the first half. Their late comeback this time was only cosmetic, and after the loss Jeremy Shockey told reporters in the locker room the Giants had been outcoached as well as outplayed.

"Write that down," he said.

It was shades of the Barber episode following the playoff defeat. The same day, the Redskins finally got into the victory column by beating a dreadful Texans team in Houston and the Eagles plugged Trent Cole into the lineup for Jevon Kearse and won in San Francisco. The Cowboys had a bye.

Things wouldn't stay quiet for them for long.

September 28 . . . Irving, Texas

Terrell Owens was in uniform as the Cowboys practiced inside their bubble. The indoor practice facility at Valley Ranch had a full-sized field under a white roof with yellow goalposts attached to the wall at one end.

Jerry Jones stood on the sideline talking to Bill Parcells as drills got going. Owens wore blue tights as he caught passes from Drew Bledsoe and Tony Romo without much problem. His hands were covered by gloves. He used his right hand to slap hands with Bledsoe at one point. He took his normal practice workload.

"It was back to normal," Cowboys cornerback Terence Newman said just after the practice. "Sort of."

"Sort of" was the closest things got to normal with Terrell Owens around.

Two days earlier Owens had spoken to four hundred students at Woodrow Wilson High School in Dallas about the dangers of domestic abuse. It was the Tuesday after the Cowboys' bye week and Owens was present for the Cowboys' practice but didn't participate. He was in good spirits, joking with teammates and media members in the locker room. He pretended to hide behind a trash bin to escape from reporters. Parcells was hopeful Owens would practice the next day and play Sunday in Nashville against the Tennessee Titans, thirteen days after the surgery on his broken finger, but Owens was in pain. He returned to the home he'd bought on Commerce Street and had a doctor come over to treat his hand. Kim Etheredge, his publicist, was there.

Owens's pain wasn't only physical. He was distraught because the previous day he'd been unable to see his seven-year-old son, who lived in California, on the boy's birthday, and because his girlfriend had ended their three-year relationship. Owens was on prescription pain medication because of his finger. He'd had a forty-pill prescription for hydrocodone, a generic form of Vicodin, filled the day after he'd gotten hurt. His personal trainer James (Buddy) Primm, who'd been living with him until earlier that month, had upped Owens's daily dosage of nutritional supplements from six to thirty to aid the healing process. Primm had also been using a laser device on Owens's hand to promote healing.

Owens fell asleep on the training table he had in his home. He later would say he'd taken two or three hydrocodone pills along with his supplements. When he awoke he was groggy. He was nonresponsive when Etheredge spoke to him and she was alarmed. She saw the bottle that was supposed to hold Owens's painkillers and it was empty. She knew Owens had taken only five of the pills before that day. Owens would later say the other pills had been put in a drawer in his house. Etheredge didn't know that. She picked up the phone and anxiously dialed 911. It was a little before 8 p.m.

A female operator answered and said, "911, this is Belinda."

"Hello, I have an emergency please," Etheredge said.

"You need the police out there?"

"I need an ambulance please," Etheredge said.

"Let me give you the paramedics," the operator said. "Stay on the line."

"Thank you," Etheredge said.

A male dispatcher came on the line and said, "Dallas Fire."

"Hi, hi," Etheredge said. "I need an ambulance please immediately."

"Okay," the dispatcher said, "what's your address?"

Etheredge gave it.

"What's wrong?" the dispatcher asked.

"I think he took too many pills," Etheredge said. "Please, now . . . what do I do if the pills are down the throat?"

"Okay," the dispatcher said, ignoring the question. "What's your phone number? We're already on the way now, ma'am. What's your phone number?"

"Oh, God," Etheredge said.

"What's your phone number?" the dispatcher repeated.

Etheredge gave the number.

"Is that 214?" the dispatcher asked.

"Yes," Etheredge said.

"Okay," the dispatcher said. "Is he still breathing?"

"Yes," Etheredge said.

"Okay, we're on the way there, ma'am," the dispatcher said.

"Thank you, thank you," Etheredge said, and hung up.

The conversation had lasted forty-one seconds. The call went out as a suicide attempt. Paramedics from Dallas Fire-Rescue were at Owens's

home less than three minutes after Etheredge's call. Owens was taken
to an ambulance and a paramedic was stabilizing him there when police officers Bradley Ellis and Joshua Merkel showed up. The paramedic
said Owens had to be taken to the nearby Baylor University Medical
Center. Less than a minute later Owens was in the emergency room. The
officers followed the ambulance to the hospital and interviewed
Etheredge and Owens there. They would file a police report that read:

ON 9/26/06 AT APPROXIMATELY 7:51 P.M., RO/S WERE DIS-
PATCHED ON A CALL BY DALLAS FIRE AND RESCUE REGARDING
COMP ATTEMPTING SUICIDE BY PRESCRIPTION PAIN MEDICA-
TION. UPON ARRIVAL RO/S FOUND COMP BEING STABILIZED BY
DFD #703 IN THE AMBULANCE. RO/S THEN RESPONDED TO BAY-
LOR HOSPITAL PER DFD'S REQUEST FOR IMMEDIATE TRANSPORT
AND TREATMENT. RP #1 WAS INTERVIEWED BY RO/S AT HOSPI-
TAL. RP STATED THAT COMP STATED THAT HE WAS DEPRESSED.
RP NOTICED THAT COMP'S PRESCRIPTION PAIN MEDICATION
WAS EMPTY AND OBSERVED COMP PUTTING 2 PILLS IN HIS
MOUTH. RP ATTEMPTED TO PUT HER FINGERS IN COMP'S
MOUTH TO RETRIEVE THE PILLS. RO/S WERE TOLD BY RP THAT
THE PRESCRIPTION OF 40 PILLS THAT WAS FILLED ON THE 18TH
OF SEPTEMBER, AND THAT COMP HAD ONLY TAKEN 5 PILLS UP
TO THIS DATE. DURING AN INTERVIEW OF THE COMP, COMP
WAS ASKED IF HE HAD TAKEN THE REMAINDER OF THE PRE-
SCRIPTION, AT WHICH TIME THE COMP STATED, "YES." ON FUR-
THER INTERVIEW OF COMP, COMP WAS ASKED IF HE WAS
ATTEMPTING TO HARM HIMSELF, AT WHICH TIME THE COMP
STATED, "YES." COMP WAS TREATED BY BAYLOR MEDICAL STAFF
FOR A DRUG OVER DOSE. SGT. SPILA #5251 AND DUTY COM-
MANDER WARD WERE NOTFIED . . . NFI.

No further investigation was required because a suicide attempt
wasn't a crime, police officials said. But this was Terrell Owens, and the
department would try to make sure all its T's were crossed and all its I's

were dotted. Later a homicide sergeant and detective would show up at
the hospital. Based on their investigation the department would end up
officially classifying the case two days later as an accidental overdose
rather than an attempted suicide. But first Dallas television station
WFAA obtained a copy of the police report the morning after the incident. The station reported that the police had called it a suicide attempt. Almost instantly the news was nationwide. ESPN spent the rest
of the day covering the story like it was a national crisis. CNN tracked
developments breathlessly. Press conferences were carried live on national TV.

Drew Rosenhaus got on a plane to Dallas. Owens was released from
the hospital, giving a thumbs-up sign before climbing into a black
Cadillac Escalade. He went home. Etheredge and Rosenhaus were there.
Deion Sanders showed up. Sanders worked for the NFL Network but was
there as a confidant, not as a reporter. He had tried to kill himself in
1997 by driving off a road. He was concerned, but Owens told him this
hadn't been a suicide attempt, that he'd merely had an allergic reaction
to the painkillers and his supplements. Michael Irvin called, and Owens
told him the same thing. Owens had missed a workout the previous
week after having a less severe reaction to the medication. Reporters
began gathering outside Owens's home and were told that Owens would
come out and speak. The Cowboys, remembering the fiasco Rosenhaus
had made of the front lawn press conference when Owens was with the
Eagles, nixed that idea and told Owens to come over to Valley Ranch.
He got there in time to catch a few passes from Bledsoe and Romo at
the end of Wednesday's practice.

Parcells held a press conference in which he said repeatedly he knew
nothing, then walked out when reporters continued to press him. Owens
arrived at the podium and told his story before about a hundred reporters and nearly two dozen television cameras. He was calm and in
control. He was believable. He repeated what he'd said to Sanders and
Irvin. He said he could barely remember the police officers' being at the
hospital and he'd answered their questions the way he had because he
was so groggy. He said if he really had taken thirty-five pills he doubted

he'd be sitting there. He said he felt fine and thought he could practice the next day and play that weekend. He said he wasn't depressed.

Etheredge spoke next and made her client look good by comparison.

She denied making the statements attributed to her in the police report. She denied trying to pry pills out of Owens's mouth. She suggested the police officers had taken advantage of Owens.

"Terrell has twenty-five million reasons why he should be alive," she said in closing.

Cowboys staff members couldn't believe how badly a person who was supposedly a public relations professional had botched things. Owens went back to the podium after Etheredge spoke and thanked the police officers, paramedics, and hospital staff members involved in the case. Within days Owens would fire Primm and tell the trainer he'd never speak to him again. He was angry Primm had spoken to a *Dallas Morning News* reporter about Owens's anguish over missing his son's birthday and the breakup of his relationship.

Now it was Thursday and things were calming down a bit. Owens had a brief conversation with Parcells before taking the field for practice. Owens refused to speak to reporters, but even in refusing to speak he soaked up all the attention he could. He walked through the locker room, sat down on a leather couch, read a newspaper and made phone calls. He walked over to his locker to change caps. He was wearing a black T-shirt with a picture of Fred Sanford, the Redd Foxx character on the old *Sanford and Son* TV sitcom, and the words, "U Big Dummy!" Owens had been deemed fit to be released by medical professionals at the hospital. That would have to be good enough for the Cowboys.

Parcells liked to tell a story about how when he was growing up his father would say to him, "Parcells, it's never your fault but you're always there."

Clearly that could be said of Owens.

It was beginning to take its toll on Parcells.

OCTOBER

CHAPTER

-21-

October 1 . . . Nashville

The Cowboys' hellish week ended with Jerry Jones standing in the middle of the visitors' locker room Sunday at LP Field, happy everything had come out okay.

Sort of.

That was the closest things got to okay with Terrell Owens around.

"I think on balance beginning Tuesday night at eight o'clock if I thought I'd be standing here under these circumstances," Jones said, "I'd take it."

There had been about an hour Tuesday when Jones hadn't known what was going on. Once he'd been told Owens would be fine, he'd viewed the happenings of the rest of the week merely as a spectacle.

"What hype," he said to himself. It had been the most intensely covered Cowboys story of his ownership tenure, surpassing even Jerry versus Jimmy. The next week, he knew, would bring more scrutiny, with Owens's return to Philadelphia on tap. But even that, Jones thought, couldn't match what he had just witnessed. "We knew there would be some interesting weeks with him in terms of visibility," Jones said.

From a football perspective Owens was doing what he was being paid to do, in Jones's mind. Owens had played that day against the Tennessee Titans and had played well, with five catches for 88 yards. The Cowboys had faced a horribly overmatched team—it was quarterback Vince Young's first NFL start—and had won easily.

When Owens ran a route along the Titans' sideline during the game he heard the Tennessee coaches yelling, "Slap his hand! Slap his hand!" It hadn't bothered him. He had a protective shell covering his finger and he'd told Drew Bledsoe before the game, "Don't be scared to throw it. I'm out here. Let's just play."

Owens had begun talking about the upcoming matchup with the Eagles on the sideline late in the game. It had been on his mind for some time; he'd been conducting his workouts by lifting weights in sets of ten and eight reps to remind himself the game was on October 8, or 10/8.

When the game ended, Titans cornerback Adam (Pacman) Jones asked Owens for his shoes, according to Owens. It was an unusual request, but Owens complied. "He'll have to put some tissue in those shoes," Owens said after the game, wearing jeans and a brown and green sweater. "They're big shoes to fill."

Once he'd stepped on the field Owens had been unencumbered by the furor that had surrounded him off it. Bill Parcells thought his other players had been similarly unaffected. You tended to stay focused as an athlete in a sport in which you were getting the stuffing knocked out of you, he believed.

The game had been marred by an ugly incident in the third quarter. Cowboys center Andre Gurode was lying on the ground after blocking on a touchdown run by tailback Julius Jones. Albert Haynesworth, the Titans' talented but temperamental defensive tackle, walked by and kicked Gurode in the head twice. The first kick knocked off Gurode's helmet. The second cut Gurode's forehead around his left eye. The officials saw everything and ejected Haynesworth, giving him a second 15-yard penalty when he threw his helmet to the turf on his way to the sideline. Gurode hadn't said or done anything to provoke the attack:

Haynesworth had simply snapped. Gurode was helped to the locker room and was stitched up. He returned to the Cowboys' sideline but didn't reenter the game. His vision was blurry. Ray Anderson, the NFL's senior vice president of football operations, was on the phone to New York moments after the incident. The next day the league would suspend Haynesworth for five games without pay, costing him $190,073 (NFL players were paid based on a seventeen-week season, so Haynesworth was losing five-seventeenths of his $646,251 salary). Gene Upshaw and Richard Berthelsen figured initially they would appeal the suspension since it was two and a half times greater than the previous record—two games—for an on-field player versus player incident. But when Upshaw spoke to Haynesworth, Haynesworth said he didn't want to appeal. Upshaw told Haynesworth he didn't think he could get the suspension reduced anyway and the union didn't appeal. The Nashville police and the Davidson County district attorney's office contacted the Cowboys and left word that Haynesworth could be charged with assault if Gurode wanted to file a complaint, but Gurode decided against it.

All of that was in the future, but Jones knew as he stood in the locker room that the incident had been bad for the entire league and that Haynesworth would be punished severely. The day had also brought some lighter moments for Jones. He'd spent the final half of the fourth quarter signing autographs for fans who were tossing shirts and other items into the box where he was watching the game. "It's been so long since anyone asked for an autograph," Jones said, "I didn't know what to do."

The Cowboys' win was the start of a good weekend for the division. The Redskins beat the Jacksonville Jaguars in overtime later that afternoon and the Eagles beat the Green Bay Packers on Monday night.

The Eagles, at least early on, were the team to chase.

October 5 . . . East Rutherford, New Jersey

Reporters crowded around LaVar Arrington's locker at Giants Stadium on the Thursday before the Giants played the Redskins.

Antonio Pierce noticed the scene as he walked by.

"Don't say it, LaVar!" Pierce called out. "Don't say it!"

Pierce had been counseling Arrington on handling Redskins week, telling him not to be too charged up. The Giants were dealing with bigger issues. They'd had a bye week after the miserable loss in Seattle that had been followed by Jeremy Shockey's comment about being outcoached. Tom Coughlin had held a meeting with the players the next day back at Giants Stadium and had recited the schedule of fines in the collective bargaining agreement for conduct detrimental to the team. In other words: Knock it off.

Coughlin spent the bye week in back-to-the-basics mode, stressing simple fundamentals in practices. He told his players they'd created their own problems and they could fix them. The players were given Friday, Saturday, and Sunday off, then returned to work Monday. Arrington's phone began ringing two days later. Friends and family members were calling to tell him that Dale Lindsey, the linebackers coach with whom he'd feuded in Washington, and cornerback Shawn Springs had taken verbal swipes at him that day, saying that Arrington couldn't help the Giants with the Redskins' playbook because he'd never known it.

"Kick their butts," Arrington's friends told him. "They're talking trash here."

The emotions were building. Longtime Redskins trainer Bubba Tyer liked Arrington but had sent word through the Giants' trainers over the summer he'd be "MF"-ing Arrington from the sideline during the game for criticizing Joe Gibbs publicly after his departure. Even now Arrington blamed Gibbs for what had happened. "If he'd wanted something different," Arrington said, "it would have been different."

Arrington tried to be restrained when he met with reporters Thursday but got his digs in. He called Springs a company man for cosigning Lindsey's criticisms. He said he'd kept a copy of his Redskins playbook and had given it to Coughlin so it didn't really matter what he did or didn't know.

It would be a weekend for old friends turned enemies both at Giants Stadium and at the Linc.

October 8 . . . Philadelphia

Eagles fans were ready for Terrell Owens's return. The parking lots around Lincoln Financial Field were filled hours before game time. Kickoff wasn't until 4:15 P.M., but almost four hours earlier traffic was backed up along Broad Street all the way onto I-95.

Eagles fans were infamous: They'd booed Santa Claus at Franklin Field, and cheered when Cowboys wide receiver Michael Irvin was lying on the turf at Veterans Stadium with a career-ending neck injury. They reveled in their reputation for ruthlessness.

A sign hanging on a parking lot fence read: HEY, T.O., REMEMBER IRVIN? YOU'RE NEXT, ASSHOLE!

Another parking lot banner declared: JERRY JONES IS A MAGGOT. DREW IS A PUNK. KIM IS A PIG.

Directness, not creativity, would carry the day.

Inside the stadium the fans booed loudly when Owens so much as appeared on one of the giant video screens. They chanted, "Ter-rell Sucks! Ter-rell Sucks!"

One sign in the stands asserted: T.O. SUPPORTS TERRORISM.

Another read: WARNING: EAGLES FANS ARE HAZARDOUS TO YOUR HEALTH. DO NOT MIX WITH SUPPLEMENTS.

LaVar Arrington had gotten his revenge on the Redskins earlier in the afternoon. He didn't have a particularly productive game but he did make one eye-catching play, leaping high to bat away a Mark Brunell pass, and the Giants won easily.

The day wouldn't be nearly as satisfying for Owens.

The Cowboys' game plan was to combat the Eagles' pass rush with quick-hitting passes to Owens, Terry Glenn, and Jason Witten. It didn't work out. Drew Bledsoe threw thirteen passes Owens's way, five more than he directed at any other receiver, but only three resulted in completions. Two others produced interceptions, one by Brian Dawkins and the other by cornerback Lito Sheppard on a ball Bledsoe badly under-threw with a timid lob on the Cowboys' next-to-last meaningful possession of the game. Owens was open but Sheppard made a leaping interception at the Eagles' 7-yard line.

Owens had a no-catch first half and vented at Todd Haley on the sideline. He stormed off the field after Sheppard's interception. Still, the Cowboys would have a chance to win. They trailed, 31–24, when Bledsoe's fourth-down heave toward Glenn resulted in a pass interference penalty on safety Michael Lewis. That gave the Cowboys a first down at the Eagles' 6 with thirty-five seconds to play. But Bledsoe threw incomplete in Owens's general direction on first down. On second and goal, Bledsoe and Witten were on different wavelengths. Bledsoe's pass sailed wide of his tight end and went directly to Sheppard, who made the grab and raced 102 yards to the opposite end zone to seal the outcome. Owens headed disgustedly toward the Cowboys' bench before Sheppard even reached the goal line, then sprinted off the field as soon as the game ended. He hadn't crossed paths with Donovan McNabb all day.

"Why did y'all bring me here?!" Owens screamed when he reached the locker room. "Why the fuck am I here?!"

He'd delivered a similar message to Haley on the sideline, but this time a stadium worker overheard him and told a few reporters. Owens's declaration wouldn't stay secret for long. In the locker room Jerry Jones came by and offered a few words of consolation.

"Not too many folks get to have a day like today," Jones said to Owens. "Not too many people get the whole crowd chanting the things they were chanting."

Minutes later as he stood in the cramped visitors' locker room, Jones stuck up for Owens. It hadn't bothered Jones that Owens had allowed his frustrations to spill out. "In my view," Jones said, "frustrated from not winning the game, not frustrated from not getting the ball. He had a healthy frustration."

Three days later Owens got out to the Cowboys' practice field at Valley Ranch late. He had an upset stomach and was in a bathroom. He arrived on the field two plays into the session and went to Haley to explain. Haley screamed and cursed at him.

"Dude, I was in the restroom," Owens said.

"I don't give a shit what you were doing!" Haley barked at him. "Everybody else is out here."

Haley was supposed to serve as the buffer between Owens and Bill Parcells, but as buffers went he was a bit too hotheaded. The same day Haley would also argue with safeties coach Mike MacIntyre. Owens didn't immediately snap back at Haley, instead putting on his helmet and joining the drills. He walked over to Parcells and apologized for being late.

"All right," Parcells said. "Just try to get out here a little earlier."

Owens and Haley weren't done. Haley wasn't ready to let things go, not after Owens had yelled at him on the sideline in Philadelphia and then sent him a text message after the game saying he needed to get the ball more. In a wide receivers' meeting after the practice Haley scolded Owens for sloppy route-running during the game. He told Owens the thirteen passes thrown his way were more than sufficient. The meeting ended with the two screaming at each other. "Don't disrespect me!" Owens yelled.

"Don't disrespect *me*!" Haley yelled back.

Owens had another way of annoying Haley. He would fall asleep in team meetings on a fairly regular basis. Since he'd been a rookie with the San Francisco 49ers, there had been a good chance Owens would doze off whenever the lights went out for tapes to be shown during a meeting. He didn't know if he had an undiagnosed sleep disorder or not, but he didn't think it was a particularly big deal. If he played well on Sundays, what did it matter?

"I'm not trying to fall asleep," he told Haley. "I've always been like that."

Owens didn't talk about Wednesday's confrontations with Haley to reporters, but the episode became public later in the week anyway. Haley met with Owens on Thursday to try to smooth things over, but Owens went on his weekly radio show Friday and said his personal dealings with Haley were finished. He wasn't planning to boycott all conversations with Haley as he'd done with Brad Childress in Philadelphia, but from now on, Owens said, the two were merely coworkers.

The "new" Terrell Owens suddenly was looking a lot like the old Terrell Owens.

October 15 . . . Baltimore

Keyshawn Johnson, the man who'd lost his job in Dallas to Terrell Owens, sat in the visitors' locker room in Baltimore after his Carolina Panthers had beaten the Ravens. He was asked if he was going to speak to reporters and he said he'd do whatever the Panthers' public relations staff wanted.

"I don't have any publicist," Johnson said with a wide grin.

He paused for a second to allow the line to sink in.

"That's not a shot," he said.

Owens had three touchdown catches in the second half that day as the Cowboys rolled to an easy victory over the Houston Texans. After the first touchdown Owens hugged Todd Haley on the sideline. The third touchdown came on a pass thrown by Tony Romo, who'd replaced Drew Bledsoe late in the lopsided game. The Cowboys drew closer to the Eagles, who lost in New Orleans on a field goal as time expired. Safety Michael Lewis was benched in favor of Sean Considine. The Giants won in Atlanta and three days later Tiki Barber's retirement secret came out. He was making the rounds Tuesday in Manhattan for the book tour he was doing with Ronde. The brothers appeared on some morning television shows and did a signing session at a bookstore. John Branch, the superb Giants beat writer for *The New York Times,* was shadowing the brothers for a story. He heard how Tiki was talking to Ronde and to his business manager, Mark Lepselter, about his plans for the not-too-distant future. They didn't seem to include football. He asked Barber about retiring and Barber came clean. Branch broke the story in the next day's *Times.*

That quickly, everyone knew how high the stakes were for Barber in this season.

The division suddenly had a sentimental favorite and it wasn't the guy playing wide receiver in Dallas.

October 22 ... Indianapolis

It felt like years earlier that Dan Snyder, Joe Gibbs, and Vinny Cerrato had sat in the lobby of the Marriott across the street from the stadium and convention center during the scouting combine and hoped a labor settlement would come together to enable them to make the moves to transform the Redskins into a Super Bowl team. It actually had been only about eight months, but so much had changed. Going into their game with the Colts it felt as if their season was on the line. They'd been booed off their home field the previous Sunday after losing to the previously winless Titans, dropping their record to 2-4.

A pep band played on the sidewalk outside the convention center but inside the hallways were quiet and empty. The stands were only beginning to fill two hours before kickoff as Snyder stood on the field of the RCA Dome. He fidgeted nervously, repeatedly adjusting a set of earphones he was wearing. He had a Redskins T-shirt underneath a white shirt and a dark suit accompanied by a burgundy tie.

He didn't want to hear any more talk about what needed to be done to fix the Redskins' problems. He wanted to see something done about it.

"Remember what Al Capone said," he said.

"What was that?" an acquaintance asked.

"You get a lot more done with a gun than a kind word," he said.

The line attributed to Capone actually was something about getting a lot more done with a kind word *and* a gun than with a kind word alone, but Snyder wasn't in the mood for a kind word to be part of the equation at all.

Cerrato sat on the Redskins' bench during warmups. Snyder said hello to his sister Michele, who'd made the trip. Just before kickoff the Eagles lost in Tampa on a miraculous 62-yard field goal as time expired by Buccaneers kicker Matt Bryant. No one was running away with the division.

Snyder still trusted Gibbs wholeheartedly; this game wasn't a referendum on his coach. But the Redskins had played forty games, including two in the playoffs, since Gibbs had come out of retirement, and they were 19-21. That wasn't the stuff of a coaching legend. Al Saunders had told friends he and Gibbs were walking on eggshells around one another, each wanting to make the offense work but having his own ideas about how to do it. For many inside Redskins Park, though, the largest chunk of blame belonged to Gregg Williams. The defense was supposed to be carrying the offense while Gibbs and Saunders worked out the kinks, and it wasn't happening. That week a few team officials had sat at Redskins Park and watched a tape of the way the defense had played on the opening series of the preseason opener in Cincinnati. That had been the Redskins defense of previous seasons under Williams— aggressive, attacking, making the offense react to what it was doing. The defense wasn't playing like that now. Williams had spent a couple years telling others in the organization he didn't need great players; he could take merely useful parts and mold them into a highly effective defense. Williams believed in his coaching so much that he thought any deficiencies his players had would be masked if they simply played the system precisely as instructed. But these days it wasn't working out that way.

The Redskins led by a point at halftime after Antwaan Randle El returned a punt for a touchdown. They were battering Peyton Manning, putting two heavy hits on the Colts quarterback in the first half. But that only seemed to make Manning mad, and he threw three touchdown passes in the second half. In the end, the Colts won easily. The Redskins committed silly penalties. Adam Archuleta and Andre Carter spent long stretches of the game on the bench. Carter would work his way back into the lineup, but Archuleta was on his way to becoming a benchwarmer.

Snyder showed up in the somber postgame locker room. He stood at one end, surveying the scene. He ducked behind a curtain dividing the locker room and trainer's room and took a phone call. Dwight Schar and Robert Rothman waited for him. The locker room was virtually empty when Snyder reemerged. Marcus Washington was the only player left.

Snyder walked glumly toward the door.

"Let's get out of here," he said to Schar and Rothman.

The Redskins were 2-5.

CHAPTER

-22-

October 23 . . . Irving, Texas

The Cowboys and Giants were playing for first place and LaVar
Arrington planned to use the bright Monday night spotlight—ESPN
would get the largest audience in cable TV history for the game—to
show he could still play. He'd told all his friends and family members
to watch. He felt things coming together for him. This, he thought,
would be a showcase game.

He was right.

After Eli Manning threw an early touchdown pass to Plaxico Burress,
Arrington burst through unblocked and sacked Drew Bledsoe for a
safety. The next time the Cowboys had the ball Arrington made a
touchdown-saving pass deflection. He looked like the old LaVar
Arrington, the one before the injuries and the bitter parting with Joe
Gibbs, Gregg Williams, and the Redskins.

Unfortunately for him, he still had the new LaVar Arrington's luck
with injuries.

On a running play in the second quarter, he was being blocked high
when he felt a pop in his lower left leg and tumbled to the ground. He

was mad at first, thinking a Cowboys player had come in low and blocked him from behind, but he looked and saw no one was there. That was a bad sign.

"I hope it's just a sprain or something," Arrington thought. "Things are going too well."

It wasn't just a sprain. He had a torn Achilles' tendon. His season was over.

Antonio Pierce stood a few feet away while members of the Giants' medical staff tended to Arrington on the field. Tom Coughlin left the sideline and stood nearby. Veteran linebacker Brandon Short kneeled next to Arrington, but there was nothing anyone could say or do. He was taken from the field on a cart and the other Giants refocused on the task at hand. They built a 12–0 lead, but the Cowboys were within 12–7 and were deep in Giants territory late in the second quarter when Bledsoe threw a goal line interception to Sam Madison. Bill Parcells seethed because the ball was supposed to be thrown toward Terrell Owens on the right side of the field and Bledsoe had thrown toward Terry Glenn on the left side. Parcells talked to quarterbacks coach Chris Palmer at halftime; they decided to go to Tony Romo.

Romo's pass on the first play of the second half was deflected by Michael Strahan and intercepted by Pierce. Romo threw two more interceptions and the Giants won by two touchdowns. They were in first place and they hadn't lost since Coughlin's back-to-square-one bye week. The Giants left the field gleefully. John Mara, smiling broadly, walked up the tunnel leading to the visitor's locker room with Ernie Accorsi. Players whooped and hollered.

"How 'bout them Giants!" guard David Diehl yelled.

But as the door to the cramped locker room swung open the players' enthusiasm was dampened by the sight that greeted them. Arrington was already out of his uniform and dressed in blue sweats, standing on crutches alongside a row of lockers. As his teammates walked by, they patted him on the shoulder and offered words of encouragement. "I knew where I came from and where I was headed," Arrington said a little while later as he stood in the middle of the locker room while those around him dressed and packed hurriedly. "For it to end like this, it hurts."

He would beat this injury, he vowed. He wouldn't let it beat him. Another knee injury would have forced him to contemplate retirement, but the doctors had already told him he could come back from this.

Arrington's angst wasn't the only emotion on display in the Giants' locker room. There was also Tiki Barber's anger. It was aimed at Gary Myers, the respected NFL columnist for the New York *Daily News,* who had written that Barber had created an unnecessary distraction with his retirement talk. Barber knew Myers well and the two usually had gotten along, but he was angry and he confronted Myers. He yelled at him. He cursed at him.

"You have no accountability!" Barber screamed. "Did you take a poll of everyone in this locker room?!"

Myers remained calm and told Barber he was paid to write his opinions and he'd been around NFL locker rooms long enough to know what was a distraction and what wasn't without having to poll players. Barber wasn't placated.

In the Cowboys' locker room, there was nothing but gloom. Parcells was angry and embarrassed about the performance. Bledsoe was mad at Parcells for the benching. The Cowboys were back to .500, at 3-3, and in the bigger picture Parcells wasn't doing that much better than Gibbs. The Cowboys were 28-27 under him, including the playoffs. Parcells knew there was no turning back to Bledsoe now that he'd gone to Romo.

The Cowboys had a new quarterback, like it or not.

Jerry Jones wasn't sure that he did.

October 24 . . . New Orleans

Jerry Jones's late Monday night in Dallas quickly gave way to an early Tuesday morning in New Orleans at an owners' meeting, held at the Loews Hotel near the French Quarter. After what he'd had to watch the night before, Jones didn't mind being busy with league matters. He considered it therapy. "Normally I'd be on Dallas's tallest building, con-

templating," he said, standing on the ninth floor, at the foot of a staircase leading up to where the owners were huddling.

Jones was torn about the Cowboys' quarterback predicament. He
knew the value of developing Tony Romo, but he also thought the
team's best chance to win that week came with Drew Bledsoe as the
starter.

Roger Goodell walked by with a serious look on his face. He was running his first owners' meeting as commissioner. There were no major decisions to be made but he still wanted things to run smoothly.

They did. The owners approved a resolution to play as many as two
regular-season games outside the United States annually. They moved
the league's Web site operations, which had been outsourced on CBS
SportsLine, in-house. There was talk about Los Angeles and revenue-
sharing but no action. The owners also received updates on some stadium projects, including that of the Giants and New York Jets. At issue
was whether the two teams would be allowed to dip into the G-3 stadium subsidy fund twice. It was two teams building a stadium, but it
was only one stadium.

Approval of requests by teams for G-3 funds required a three-
quarters vote of the clubs but generally was routine. A new stadium had
the effect of providing direct financial benefits to the team it housed and
to the players, not to the other franchises in the league. The stadium
provided new, mostly unshared revenues to its team from sources like
luxury suites. The revenues counted toward the pool from which the
players were paid, so the salary cap increased for everyone. But the owners, as a rule, overlooked that and rubber-stamped any G-3 request before them. This request was different, however. Previous G-3 requests
had been capped at $150 million. The Giants and Jets were asking for
twice that. Their privately financed stadium at the Meadowlands had a
price tag of $1.2 billion and rising. The stadium was to have about
eighty thousand seats. It was to have ten thousand premium seats and
two hundred luxury suites. The naming rights were to be worth about
$20 million annually. Projections were that the stadium would increase
revenues for the Giants and Jets by $100 million per team annually and

produce $22 million in annual profits for each club beginning in 2010. Those revenues would increase the salary cap by about $2 million per team annually. The owners of the low-revenue franchises were resentful about being asked to pay for a new stadium in New York after being suckered, in their increasingly bitter view, into ratifying a labor and revenue-sharing agreement that wasn't doing them any good. To top it all off, approval of the request by the Giants and Jets would exhaust the G-3 fund.

Goodell shelved the matter to avoid a fight and planned to call for a vote in early December.

By 5 p.m., the meeting had broken up and the owners were on elevators to the lobby to climb into the limousines waiting for them outside. On the sidewalk, Dan Snyder spoke to Joe Banner briefly. One member of the Redskins' contingent was late and Snyder was growing impatient. Finally the straggler arrived and Snyder climbed into the back of a limo and sped off. Banner met up with Jeff Lurie and departed. Jones left soon after. Only John Mara, still standing in the lobby waiting for his luggage, was smiling.

Sure, he had stadium issues. But unlike Snyder, Jones, and Lurie, he had a football team coming off a win.

October 29 . . . Charlotte

Jerry Jones ran into Jerry Richardson, the owner of the Carolina Panthers, before the Cowboys were to unveil their new starting quarterback in a Sunday night game at Bank of America Stadium.

"I just can't do any more for you than to come to Charlotte and put a quarterback in that's never started a game before," Jones told Richardson. "That's about all I can do for you. You're my buddy but we can't do too much more."

Jones had lowered his expectations for the season when Tony Romo became the starter. He thought he was simply being realistic. It was so difficult to win with an inexperienced starter at the most important position on the field. The knock on Romo was that he, like most young quarterbacks, tended to more than balance out his good plays with some bad ones. The sliver of hope in Jones's mind came from recalling what quarterbacks coach Chris Palmer had told him after Romo's solid performance in the preseason opener. Palmer had indicated then that he thought the Cowboys just might be able to win with Romo during the regular season if it came to that.

"I really believe we can coach him throughout the game," Palmer had told Jones, "and not have him make those costly bad plays."

Bill Parcells didn't think the situation was hopeless. He didn't think of Romo as the equivalent of a rookie. He thought of Romo as a guy who'd been around, practicing and listening and learning, even if he hadn't been playing in games. Parcells had told the other Cowboys players about the quarterback switch when they'd returned to work Wednesday at Valley Ranch, two days after the loss to the Giants.

"Hey, look, I didn't enjoy doing this to Drew," Parcells told them. "But now you've got to rally around Tony. You have to do it. That's where we're going and you'd better rally around him."

That wouldn't be difficult for the players. It was easy to rally around the underdog, and Romo certainly was the underdog. He'd been so lightly recruited coming out of high school in Burlington, Wisconsin, that he'd needed to hire a recruiting service just to help him land a scholarship to Eastern Illinois. He'd entered the NFL as an undrafted rookie. The Cowboys had signed him in large part because Sean Payton had also played quarterback at Eastern Illinois and served as Romo's advocate. If Payton had played anywhere else, the Cowboys probably never would have given Romo a second thought. Romo had been called by about twenty teams on draft day but had picked the Cowboys because of Payton and because he thought he might be able to make the roster. Romo ended up reminding Parcells of two of his former quarterbacks, Matt Cavanaugh and Jeff Rutledge. That kept Parcells intrigued.

By now the Cowboys players believed in Romo. Many had wanted Parcells to make the switch weeks earlier. Quarterback changes always energized the fans, and this one had a chance to do the same thing for the head coach. Parcells was in need of something to reinvigorate him.

On Friday afternoon he and Terrell Owens had walked off the practice field at Valley Ranch together. Owens asked Parcells how he was doing.

"I don't like getting my butt kicked," Parcells said.

Before the Cowboys took the field in Charlotte the Giants kept the pressure on. They plugged Carlos Emmons into the lineup for LaVar Arrington and beat the Tampa Bay Buccaneers at Giants Stadium for their fourth straight win since their bye week. The downward spiral continued for the Eagles, who couldn't get their offense going and lost at home to the Jacksonville Jaguars. They were on a three-game losing streak and the Cowboys had a chance to take over second place.

Romo saw Drew Bledsoe on the field before the game.

"I'm rooting for you," Bledsoe told him.

Romo thought that was a classy gesture. Bledsoe had balked in the past at being a backup and mentor for young quarterbacks. He hadn't wanted to do it in New England for Tom Brady, and he hadn't wanted to do it in Buffalo for J. P. Losman. Both times he'd moved on. Bledsoe still didn't like the role but he wasn't making waves.

Things didn't look promising for the Cowboys early in the game as the Panthers, aided by an interception thrown by Romo, sprinted to a two-touchdown lead. Parcells wondered whether his quarterback move was going to backfire and he scolded Romo on the sideline after the interception.

"You're not going to last long doing that!" Parcells barked. "You've got to concentrate better than that!"

Romo listened but wasn't rattled. Jason Witten approached him on the sideline to try to lift his spirits.

"We're going to need you to play good to win," Witten said.

"Everything's under control," Romo said calmly.

He settled down from there and did exactly what he was supposed to do. He got Owens involved in the offense early and often. ("About time," Owens said later that night. "About time.") He got the ball to Witten for some clutch completions. He scrambled for some first downs and didn't throw any more interceptions while passing for 270 yards. The Cowboys scored thirty-five straight points, twenty-five of them in the fourth quarter, and won. The players' yelling in the jubilant postgame locker room could be heard through the concrete walls. Jones stood next to the locker room and savored the win. Romo had restored hope. "We expected—I expected—to pay some price for that being his first start," Jones said. "He just played beyond my expectations throughout the game."

Jones recalibrated his expectations once more. He figured there would be a chance for this team to be on an upswing at the end of the season as Romo got more comfortable and improved. Jones had watched the offensive line closely all night and thought it had played well. Romo's mobility helped and he'd limited his bad plays, too. It wasn't exactly like having Troy Aikman out there. But the Cowboys, for the first time in years, just might have found a quarterback capable of being The Guy for them for a long, long time.

NOVEMBER

CHAPTER

-23-

November 1 . . . Ashburn, Virginia

It was a warm Wednesday in Washington with temperatures nearing 80 degrees as November arrived. Joe Gibbs had invited recently retired offensive lineman Ray Brown on the field for the Redskins' practice. He wasn't adding Brown as a coach, but it was circle-the-wagons time and maybe the players would listen to their former teammate and erstwhile locker-room graybeard. Dan Snyder watched practice from the sideline sporting sunglasses to go with a burgundy pullover and dark slacks. He talked to Louis Riddick as he left the field. Vinny Cerrato trailed a couple steps behind talking on his phone. Gibbs chatted with public relations director Chris Helein as he crossed the facility's one artificial turf practice field alongside its three grass fields. He made his way up a set of steps toward the back entrance to Redskins Park and stopped to speak to the pack of reporters, answering questions patiently but guardedly for about ten minutes. He finished and stood by the door to the building, looking back out toward the fields.

The losing was taking its toll. The wrinkles on Gibbs's face had deepened and the bags under his eyes had darkened. Gibbs didn't wear his emotions on his sleeve, but this was tearing him up inside. The Redskins were coming off a bye week that had followed the loss in Indianapolis. Gibbs had tried to give himself a respite of a few minutes from fretting about his team's struggles during the bye weekend, but that was all he could manage, a few minutes. There was no escaping it. Al Saunders had urged Gibbs to play Todd Collins at quarterback but hadn't really pressed the issue, and Gibbs had stuck with Mark Brunell for the time being. He and Saunders had resolved that if the Redskins reached six losses before Thanksgiving, they would go to Jason Campbell. They were only one defeat away. For Gibbs, it was his most trying time professionally since his rookie season as a head coach in 1981, when he lost his first five games and wondered if Jack Kent Cooke would fire him before he managed a single victory. Gibbs was determined to fix things this time the same way he'd fixed them then, by continuing to believe in what he did and buckling down to work even harder. He stubbornly believed the decision to hire Saunders would still turn out over time to be the right move but he felt awful because he thought he was letting Snyder down. The owner had made every move Gibbs had asked him to make and had signed every check Gibbs had asked him to sign. He'd never said no. "A lot of it should be laid at my feet," Gibbs said. "The owner, the fans, all the people that you let down—that's what I think about."

Gibbs felt healthy and was planning to fulfill his contract. There had been major questions about his health when he'd returned, given that he'd worked himself into the ground in his first coaching stint when he was far younger and now he had diabetes. On a recruiting trip to Florida to talk to Brunell in his first offseason back, Gibbs allowed his blood sugar to get out of whack and had to have Brunell take him to a hospital. But he'd gotten things under control and he thought his diabetes actually helped him by giving him no choice but to monitor his diet better than he'd done as a younger coach. Back then, as he put it, "My late-night Mr. Goodbars were very stimulating."

He'd had a stent inserted to open a clogged heart artery in April

2005 but had gotten back to working out a few days later. His regular workout included a forty-five-minute run on a treadmill and he'd had little problem picking back up with his eighteen-hour workdays during the season. He missed NASCAR a little bit. He made it to about six or seven races a year. Every time he went to his racing headquarters in Charlotte, he was amazed by how much his son J.D., who was running the operation for him, had purchased. When he'd been around, he hadn't been able to get J.D. to buy anything. He'd once had trouble understanding the drivers, people who were willing to risk their lives for their sport. But when his team had added Home Depot as a sponsor, he'd listened to star driver Tony Stewart tell the company's chief executive officer, Bob Nardelli, "Hey, if anything ever happens to me, I was doing what I wanted in life."

That rang true to Gibbs. He was a sixty-five-year-old grandfather who already had a bust in the Hall of Fame. He was risking tarnishing his coaching legacy, but he was back doing what he wanted in life. Gibbs and Bill Parcells were readying to face each other for the twenty-third time as NFL head coaches and they knew there was a chance this meeting would be their last. Parcells had found as he'd gotten older that the losing had become harder and the winning had become more of a relief than a joy. He'd talked to Bob Knight about it and learned that Knight felt the same way. Parcells wasn't eager to leave the profession. Tony Romo's play in Carolina had recharged his batteries a little bit and there had always been something comforting to him, something right, about a business in which you knew exactly where you stood. It didn't matter what sportswriters wrote or what commentators said. It was about wins and losses. "The game will tell you what you are," Parcells liked to reassure himself. The rest of life contained such murkiness. This, to Parcells, was neat and orderly, even with the problems that arose every day. But Parcells knew there would come a day when he just couldn't summon the energy to do it any longer, and he knew he was one game, one loss away from feeling the way Gibbs was feeling this week.

By Sunday, Parcells and Jerry Jones would feel the sort of dejection

Gibbs and Snyder had been experiencing for weeks. Romo played well enough at FedEx Field for the Cowboys to beat the Redskins, but Terrell Owens dropped a well-thrown deep pass that would have sealed the outcome. The game was tied when Mike Vanderjagt lined up for a 35-yard field goal with six seconds left. The Cowboys at worst should have been headed to overtime. Gibbs found himself thinking on the sideline about what the ride home from the stadium with his wife would be like. He and Pat wouldn't say anything to one another in the car and then would have a miserable dinner.

Vanderjagt struck the ball well and was sure he'd made the kick. But Troy Vincent, who'd been signed by the Redskins after being released by the Buffalo Bills and had never blocked a kick in his life, blocked this one. Sean Taylor scooped up the ball and started running the other way, and Kyle Kosier grabbed Taylor's facemask momentarily trying to make the tackle. Time had expired when Taylor was tackled at the Cowboys' 44-yard line. But what should have been a 5-yard penalty against Kosier was ruled a 15-yard infraction by the officials, moving the ball to the 29 and giving the Redskins one more play since the game by rule couldn't end on a defensive penalty. Nick Novak's kick headed to the right initially but hooked just inside the upright and won the game for Redskins. It was Parcells, not Gibbs, whose dinner had been ruined.

The Giants came from behind to beat the Houston Texans at Giants Stadium the same day. They had a two-game lead in the division halfway through the season—they had a record of 6-2 while the Cowboys and Eagles were 4-4 and the Redskins were 3-5—but the triumph was costly. Michael Strahan suffered a sprain of the Lisfranc joint in his right foot. A Lisfranc injury was tricky. It was named for Jacques Lisfranc, a field surgeon in Napoleon's army who first observed it, and the term encompassed a range of injuries of varying severity to the joint line between the rigid midfoot and the weight-bearing forefoot. The Giants thought Strahan could be back in two to four weeks. Strahan consulted with doctors and ended up thinking the healing process might take as long as two months. Within days the injury news would worsen for the Giants. Amani Toomer's left knee had bothered him during the Texans game. The Giants sent him to undergo an MRI exam two days later and found he had a partially torn anterior cruciate ligament. Toomer was given the option of trying to rehabilitate the injury rather than undergoing surgery. That way he could possibly play again this season but his knee would be unstable and he'd be at risk of suffering a more severe injury. Toomer opted to undergo surgery. His season was over.

The Eagles had their bye the weekend the Redskins were beating the Cowboys and the Giants were getting beaten up while beating the Texans. Andy Reid had given his players six days off, believing they needed the long break because the Eagles had played the Hall of Fame game to open the preseason and had been among the last batch of teams to get a bye during the season. It had been a wearying stretch; Reid even sent his assistant coaches home for a four-day weekend. But Joe Banner stayed busy. During the bye week he signed defensive tackle Mike Patterson to a seven-year, $32 million contract extension that included $9 million in guaranteed money. The Eagles were focusing, as always, on re-signing their own players. Patterson had three seasons remaining on his original five-year, $6.625 million deal. He'd been paid his entire $3.825 million signing bonus from that contract and could have stood pat and waited to be a free agent after the 2009 season. Instead agent Josh Luchs negotiated a contract with Banner that ran through the 2016 season and asked Patterson what he wanted to do. Luchs told Patterson it was like the TV game show *Deal or No Deal.* There were beautiful women standing there holding briefcases full of money. One of them contained $9 million and Patterson could take that one. Or he could choose another briefcase, not knowing whether it would contain much more money or much less. Patterson had to decide whether to gamble or take the $9 million.

He took the $9 million.

The Monday the Eagles players returned to work was the final day for a team to sign a player to a contract extension and have a portion of the signing bonus count against the current season's salary cap. The deadline came at 4 P.M. and Banner worked frantically to try to complete extensions with Trent Cole, Reggie Brown, and tight end L. J. Smith.

He went one for three that day and two for three by week's end. Cole and his agent, Rich Rosa, agreed that day to a five-year contract worth about $27 million, including $12 million in bonuses. Cole was in his second season and looked like a top pass rusher in the making. He had eleven and a half sacks in only twenty-three NFL games, getting five as a rookie and leading the team with six and a half so far this season. He and Rosa faced a difficult decision when the Eagles made their offer. Cole's existing contract was to run through the 2008 season. There was big, big money to be made in free agency for elite pass rushers. Rosa's firm, Eastern Athletic Services, also represented Strahan, John Abraham, and Patrick Kerney, so Rosa was well aware that Cole could lose money in the long run by accepting the offer. But it was two and a half seasons before Cole would be eligible for free agency and a lot could happen in the meantime, including an injury. Cole and Rosa decided $12 million in bonus money was enough to have Cole take the deal. He was a former fifth-round draft pick with a $350,000 salary for this season and it was no time to get too greedy.

Banner talked to Brown's agent, Bill Johnson, right up until the deadline but couldn't complete an agreement. They were close, though, so they stayed at it. Three days later the deal was done. Brown, who had three and a half seasons remaining on his original five-year, $4.77 million contract, signed a five-year extension worth $21 million, including $10 million in bonuses. In only a few months, Banner had locked up Patterson through the 2016 season, Shawn Andrews through the 2015 season, Brown through the 2014 season, Jamaal Jackson and Cole through the 2013 season, punter Dirk Johnson through the 2011 season, and Brian Dawkins through the 2008 season.

The Eagles, right or wrong, weren't changing their ways. Their convictions soon would be tested severely.

November 12 . . . East Rutherford, New Jersey

The rain fell in torrents Sunday evening as the Giants and Chicago Bears prepared to square off at Giants Stadium in a night game on NBC with

NFC supremacy at stake. The Bears were doing just fine without Antwaan Randle El and Adam Archuleta. They'd suffered their first loss of the season the previous Sunday at home against the Miami Dolphins. The Giants were on a five-game winning streak but simply fielding a team was becoming a challenge. They began the game without five starters. By night's end the count would be up to seven. Left tackle Luke Petitgout crumpled to the turf after blocking on a first-quarter passing play. He managed to limp to the sideline on an injured left leg but was taken to the locker room for X-rays that showed he had a fractured fibula. Sam Madison aggravated a hamstring injury and didn't play in the second half.

The Giants needed to win to keep pace with the Cowboys and Eagles. The Eagles had rolled over the Redskins, 27–3, that afternoon in Philadelphia. Andy Reid had turned over the offensive play-calling duties to Marty Mornhinweg and had been rewarded handsomely. The Cowboys had rebounded by winning in Arizona, but Greg Ellis had suffered a torn Achilles' tendon, ending his season. Ellis was taken off the field on a cart after suffering the injury, but returned to the sideline and walked off the field with the aid of crutches after the game. He didn't know if it was his final NFL game, but if it was he wanted to walk away from it.

The Giants, too, had their chances to win. They trailed 24–20 early in the fourth quarter and faced a fourth-and-15 play at the Bears' 34-yard line. Tom Coughlin could have punted or left his offense on the field for a fourth-down gamble. The one thing he shouldn't have done was what he did, sending kicker Jay Feely into the game to try a 52-yard field goal on such a sloppy night. The kick fell predictably short and the ball landed in the hands of Bears rookie cornerback Devin Hester eight yards deep in the end zone. It was one day shy of the one-year anniversary of Bears cornerback Nathan Vasher setting an NFL record with a 108-yard touchdown against the San Francisco 49ers on a return of a missed field goal. Yet some Giants players thought the play was over and started walking toward the sideline. Hester noticed that. He hesitated and then took off; 108 yards later, he had tied Vasher's record.

Game over.

The Giants' lead over the Cowboys and Eagles was down to one game. A sizable crowd gathered in the tunnel by the doors to the Giants' locker room after the game, escaping the rain outside and huddling in small groups to talk.

LaVar Arrington stood there on crutches.

Michael Strahan stood nearby on crutches.

Petitgout left the locker room on crutches and made his way past.

Having a crutch brigade comprising such expensive and important players just past midseason wasn't a good sign for an NFL team with Super Bowl hopes.

November 19 . . . Irving, Texas

Bill Parcells stood with his arms crossed and intently watched Adam Vinatieri practicing field goals during pregame warmups at Texas Stadium. Parcells had coached Vinatieri in New England and greatly admired the grit of the Colts kicker. Vinatieri was that rare kicker who made his coaches and teammates view him as an actual football player.

Mike Vanderjagt wasn't exactly inspiring the same sort of admiration, and things would only get worse for him as the day progressed.

Emmitt Smith, who had just become more famous as the champion of the popular television show *Dancing With the Stars* than as the NFL's career rushing leader, sat next to Jerry Jones in Jones's box to watch the Cowboys play the Colts. Jones wasn't the only owner in the division rubbing elbows over the weekend with entertainment luminaries. Dan and Tanya Snyder had scored an invitation to the wedding of the year between Tom Cruise and Katie Holmes. The Snyders flew to Rome on the Wednesday before the Saturday ceremony and got into town a day ahead of Jennifer Lopez, Jim Carrey, and Brooke Shields. The ceremony was performed by a Scientology minister and took place at a fifteenth-century castle in the lakeside Italian town of Bracciano, about twenty-five miles northwest of Rome. The Snyders left immediately after the reception and headed straight to Tampa for the Redskins-Buccaneers game. Even when his team had a 3-6 record and was without Clinton Portis, who'd been placed on the injured reserve list after suffering a broken bone in his right hand during the defeat to the Eagles, Dan Snyder wasn't going to miss a game. Joe Gibbs had done as planned after the sixth loss and gone to Jason Campbell as the starting quarterback.

Snyder should have stayed in Italy.

Campbell's first pass in a regular season game was a well-thrown deep ball toward Brandon Lloyd. But Lloyd dropped it and the tone was set for the Redskins as they lost again. What really shook up the NFC East also happened during the day's early games. The Eagles were playing the Tennessee Titans at home. Donovan McNabb rolled to his right on a first-half pass, absorbed a harmless-looking shove by Titans defensive end Kyle Vanden Bosch, and collapsed in a heap on the Tennessee sideline clutching the back of his right leg. He was taken off the field on a cart.

"We'll get you right," trainer Rick Burkholder told him.

"We need to get these guys right," McNabb said.

The Eagles learned soon thereafter that McNabb had suffered a torn anterior cruciate ligament in his right knee. For the second straight year and the third time in five seasons, he'd suffered a season-ending injury. Jeff Garcia presided over the remainder of a defeat that dropped the Eagles' record to 5-5.

Things would go far better for the Cowboys, but not for their kicker. The game was scoreless in the second quarter when Vanderjagt trotted onto the field to try a 43-yard field goal. The ball clanked off the right upright. No good. The fans booed loudly. They booed loudly again a little while later when Vanderjagt's face appeared on the stadium video screens for a Verizon Wireless commercial. The Cowboys botched a coverage in the secondary and allowed Peyton Manning to throw a touchdown pass to Reggie Wayne with ten seconds remaining in the half, but a short kickoff by the Colts and a quick completion from Tony Romo to Terrell Owens along the sideline gave Vanderjagt another chance. Colts coach Tony Dungy called timeout to let Vanderjagt think about the kick and Vanderjagt sent a 46-yard field goal attempt sailing wide right. The boos were even louder, and Vanderjagt stood at the spot from which he'd launched the kick, staring at the uprights while the other players jogged off the field. Finally he turned and walked slowly toward the locker room.

Vanderjagt's misses didn't keep the Cowboys from handing the Colts their first loss of the season. Romo was taking kneel-downs by the time Jones's sons Stephen and Jerry Junior made their way to the sideline with less than two minutes on the clock. They exchanged high-fives with practically everyone in sight. Parcells put an arm around Keith Davis's shoulders on the sideline for a celebratory hug and the crowd roared with playoff-like intensity. Romo found Manning on the field and exchanged good-luck wishes.

"You're a good player," Manning told him.

It might not have sounded like much but it was, after all, coming from Peyton Manning. "Hey," Romo said with a shrug a little while later, "it's meaningful to me."

Romo sprinted off the field toward the tunnel still carrying the game ball. Parcells jogged toward the tunnel, cracked a smile as he glanced upward at the crowd and raised both hands over his head and clapped. He slapped hands with Todd Haley and then headed to the locker room. Vanderjagt trudged slowly off the field with his head bowed.

Amid the locker room celebration Parcells tried to build up his team.

"That," Parcells told his players, "ought to tell you something about what you're capable of doing."

Parcells had two of his daughters in town and wanted to see them and savor the victory a little bit but knew it could only be a little bit. The Cowboys would play the Buccaneers in four days on Thanksgiving. The "Midnight Rule" for reining in emotions truly would be in effect. Maybe if the team played well against the Buccaneers, Parcells thought, there would be a chance to take a deep breath Friday.

"Be happy tonight," Parcells told the players.

The Cowboys were 3-1 with Romo as the starter and Parcells thought his team had played its best football of the season over the past month. But Vanderjagt was agonizing in the locker room over his kicking misadventures. He'd missed five of his seventeen field goal attempts for the Cowboys, after he'd missed only seven regular season field goal tries over his final three seasons with the Colts. "It's not acceptable to perform like that," he said.

The Giants fell into a first-place tie with the Cowboys by losing in Jacksonville on Monday night. Was anyone going to be able to take control of the division?

CHAPTER

-24-

November 22 . . . Ashburn, Virginia

It was three days after the game in Tampa, the latest debacle in a season full of them, and Joe Gibbs was standing in front of his players in the auditorium at Redskins Park. They were expecting a typical Wednesday address, with Gibbs perhaps admonishing them a bit and then calmly outlining what needed to be done that week.

They didn't get it.

Gibbs had seen enough. He ripped into his players, yelling at them that they needed to play harder and prepare more professionally. He mixed in a few rare curse words and told the players their jobs were on the line.

In the old days Gibbs had been "Saint Joe" to outsiders, but inside the building he knew how to get tough and make everyone miserable and edgy after a loss. These days his coaching style had become too grandfatherly. It was understandable. He *was* a grandfather now. But he wasn't going to coach like it anymore. He told the players the Redskins had gotten soft and he was fed up. He told them he wanted to get back to playing the hard-nosed football for which the franchise had once been known.

"If we're going to lose," he told them, "we're going to lose our way."

Gibbs didn't want any notion he might be a lame duck coach to gain a foothold and he told the players he was going to stick around as long as it took to get the team back to winning. He showed the players clips of about twenty plays on which the Redskins had run right over opponents playing power football. He wanted to see more of that. After Gibbs's speech, the Redskins' practices would become shorter but far more intense, with full-contact drills.

It was too late to matter this season but Joe Jackson Gibbs, three-time Super Bowl winner, had reappeared at Redskins Park to replace the doubt-riddled imposter who'd handed over control of his offense and control of his team's identity to someone else.

November 23 . . . Irving, Texas

The latest jarring news regarding Terrell Owens was delivered to Jerry Jones on Thanksgiving by members of the Cowboys' medical staff. Jones was taken completely by surprise.

Owens's season might be over.

He'd hurt his right ring finger during a practice a few days earlier. Doctors determined that Owens had severed a tendon. One end of the tendon was rolling back toward the base of the finger; the other end was rolling up toward the tip. As the details of the injury were explained to him, Jones figured that Owens could simply wait until after the season and doctors could repair the damage by performing surgery then.

But that, according to the doctors, wasn't an option. If Owens wanted to be sure his finger would be fully functional in the future, they said, he had to have the surgery immediately. It would end his season but if he didn't have the surgery now, the doctors said, Owens would probably never be able to bend his finger at the joint closest to the fingertip.

"Get out of here," Jones said. "With the advances in medicine today they can't find a way to fix this if he waits until after the season?"

The answer was no.

Jones would have understood if Owens had opted for surgery. This was about never being able to use a finger properly again. "Permanently," Jones said later. "Forever."

Owens decided to keep playing. He had many flaws, but a lack of physical toughness wasn't among them. He'd demonstrated that when he'd made it back to play for the Eagles in the Super Bowl, and he was demonstrating it again. "Hopefully," Owens said later, "it will be a bum finger with a nice ring on it."

Tony Romo was at his best during the Thanksgiving game, tying the franchise record with five touchdown passes as the Cowboys trounced the Buccaneers. The Cowboys had a 21–10 lead at halftime and Bill Parcells wanted to see Romo deliver the knockout punch early in the third quarter. He told Romo in the locker room it was important to go out and get a touchdown right away.

"That," Parcells told Romo, "is what a good quarterback does."

Romo took the Cowboys right down the field and threw a fourth-down touchdown pass to Owens. With the Cowboys comfortably ahead late in the game, Parcells asked Drew Bledsoe on the sideline if he wanted to go in and finish up. Bledsoe said no. Parcells was fine with that . . . this time. He didn't want to embarrass Bledsoe, but if there was an occasion when he felt like Romo was in danger of getting hurt he wouldn't hesitate to use his prerogative to make Bledsoe go into a game for mop-up duty.

It was good to be Tony Romo these days. There was gossip column talk that he was dating Jessica Simpson. It wasn't true, but it wasn't exactly an unflattering rumor. Romo hadn't gone Hollywood, though. He still wore a beat-up T-shirt from his old high school, Burlington High in Burlington, Wisconsin, under his jersey every game. He was confident but in a quiet way. He could take any abuse Parcells wanted to hand out and receive the message but not be bothered by the tone. The other players saw that and respected him for it. Parcells wasn't particularly surprised by Romo's success. It wasn't that he'd expected it; he hadn't been sure Romo would thrive. But he had known Romo had a decent chance to succeed and he was pleased and excited things were turning out well. However, he also saw what he called the warts in Romo's game. He knew Romo was getting away with some mistakes and things would even out at some point.

Unfortunately for him, he was right.

When it came to Mike Vanderjagt, Parcells simply had seen enough. The kicker connected on a 22-yard field goal with ten minutes to play against the Buccaneers, but even that short kick with a 25-point lead was tentatively struck. More than ever, Parcells thought Vanderjagt's problems were mental rather than physical. He doubted Vanderjagt could have delivered if a game-winning kick had been required that day. He thought he was being forced to coach games differently because he couldn't trust Vanderjagt. He told Jones he wanted to cut the kicker even though it would be admitting a $3.3 million mistake—$2.5 million for the signing bonus the Cowboys had given Vanderjagt plus $810,000 for the salary for the season they'd have to pay him in its entirety even if they released him. Jones said okay. Parcells had agreed to coach Owens when he'd been less than eager to do it. Jones couldn't make his coach also keep a kicker that he didn't trust or want. Vanderjagt would be cut the Monday after the Thanksgiving triumph. The Cowboys signed Martin Gramatica, the former standout kicker for the Buccaneers who'd failed to win the New England Patriots' kicking job in the preseason and had a three-game stint with the Colts earlier in the season. Gramatica had kicked well during the Patriots' kicking derby but had lost out to rookie Stephen Gostkowski. At this point, Parcells was willing to trust anyone more than he trusted Vanderjagt.

Vanderjagt planned to go home to Canada and not kick for another NFL team the rest of the season. He needed the time away to clear his head.

Kicker issues or not, Jones thought his team was playing the best he'd seen it play in ten years. If only Tony Romo could hold it together, the Cowboys might be a Super Bowl team after all.

November 29 . . . Philadelphia

The season was unraveling for the Eagles, but Jeff Lurie and Joe Banner remained fully confident in Andy Reid.

Not everyone in Philadelphia was feeling the same way.

It was three days after the Eagles had suffered a lopsided loss in Indianapolis to drop their record to 5-6 and Reid's seat was getting hotter. He was in his eighth season with the Eagles and his contract ran through the 2010 season. Only a handful of current NFL head coaches had been with their teams as long. But now newspaper columnists and radio commentators in Philadelphia were beginning to muse publicly on whether things had become stale for the Eagles with Reid as their coach. They were questioning whether Reid should be left in charge of the team's personnel decisions or even retained as coach after the season. When an NFL team had lost fifteen of its last twenty-three games, there was plenty of room to question the guy in charge.

The mood had been predictably downcast on the team plane riding home from Indianapolis. Lurie, who was on the plane, sensed the mood but he also thought it was a mood of frustration, not resignation. That was an important distinction. Lurie thought things could still go one of two ways: The season could fall apart. Or maybe, just maybe, the Eagles could still put things back together with Jeff Garcia at quarterback. Lurie remembered the 2002 season when the team had kept winning with Koy Detmer and then A. J. Feeley at quarterback after McNabb had gotten hurt.

"Okay," Lurie said to himself, "this team is capable of that."

He chose to forget how things had fallen apart the previous season with Mike McMahon playing in place of McNabb. Having Garcia, he believed, lessened the chances of that being repeated. Lurie thought the attitude among the Eagles' coaches and players even after the Colts game was one of, "We're a much better team than this. What's going on here?"

Reid didn't think the situation was hopeless.

"This is so fixable," he told Lurie.

Lurie trusted his coach.

Reid also delivered an optimistic message to Banner. "Don't worry," he said. "We're going to get this straightened out."

"I have no worry," Banner responded. "I know that."

Reid resisted the urge to assail his players.

"We need to step it up, players *and* coaches," he told them the day after the loss to the Colts. "We were too cautious in that game."

Reid treated his players like adults. He wasn't berating them. He was sharing the blame and the players respected that.

"You never know what can happen," Reid would preach to his players regularly in the weeks that followed. "Stay strong. Stay together. Stay focused."

Banner had concerns. He couldn't help it after the way the Eagles had been manhandled by the Colts. He'd gone into the season confident about the team. He'd scoffed at predictions that the Eagles would finish last in the division. But now he had to be realistic and ask himself if he'd been kidding himself all along.

He watched the Eagles' practices all week and found the players and coaches to be still upbeat. No one had given up. No one had turned on anyone else. This wasn't the 2005 season all over again. Banner felt better as the week progressed. He concluded he hadn't been fooling himself earlier. He still thought this was a talented team with terrific coaching.

"You know," he told a friend who was commiserating with him during the week, "if the season ended today and it was the offseason, I'm not sure what we'd fix because I'm still convinced this is a very good team."

"How can that be?" the friend said. "You're five-and-six."

"Well, sometimes that can happen," Banner said. "The question is, if you're right about that you don't want to radically change the team in the offseason. On the other hand, if you're not being objective and you're kidding yourself then this will happen two years in a row."

Banner had no idea if the positive vibes he was getting would trans-

late into positive results during games. He would end the week telling
a friend he thought the Eagles would play well the following Monday
night against the Carolina Panthers at the Linc.

But would they win?

He had no idea.

The criticism of Reid stunned Banner even though he knew
Philadelphia well and had worked in the media there in his radio days.
"I've lived in this market for twelve-plus years now and I know it can
be quick to be critical," he said later. "It's also quick to praise. It's kind
of one extreme or the other. I try to tune that stuff out because for me
it truly is a distraction. But sometimes it's so loud that even when you're
trying to not hear it, you're hearing it. I was totally shocked that there
were questions about whether Andy should be coach, whether Jim
Johnson knew what he was doing, whether the team was listening to
Andy, whether the fact that we've always been a pass-oriented team as
opposed to a run-oriented team was suddenly proven to be a terrible
idea. Just two years ago we were only the second or third team in the
history of the NFL to go to four straight championship games doing
that. There were stories about the complete ineptitude of all of the
drafts for like the last five years."

Banner thought the Eagles deserved to be questioned, but not evis-
cerated.

"It was startling how extreme it was so quickly," he said. "Although
things looked bad at five-and-six, they were really obituaries. They
weren't like, 'Things are going poorly and they're five-and-six and it's
going to be tough for them to make the playoffs,' all of which were obviously true. They were like, 'It's over and they should dismember and
start again.' It was like nothing prior had ever happened or nobody here
had established any credibility. To me that was mostly about Andy. If
it was about coaching or leading or being the general manager, he'd established a track record over eight years that didn't fall away over a
three-game losing streak."

Lurie had an easier time than Banner ignoring the avalanche of criticism. "I'm so immune to that," he said. "I don't even pay attention.

Completely. I've watched sports teams over the years and one of the ways it's organized here and valued is you just have a blueprint for how you think you can succeed and it has no bearing. You don't make panic decisions or reaction decisions. We don't operate that way. We never have. If you think you have really good people in place, you have to understand that sports teams are going to have up-and-down periods in the course of any year. It's, 'Do you have confidence in your people and your players and your coaches?' And I've always had complete confidence in them."

Lurie's confidence in Reid would pay off again.

November 30 . . . East Rutherford, New Jersey

Every NFL team had it in its playbook to pull out at truly desperate times and the Giants were going to it now: the "blame the media" ploy.

"Don't let the media be a distraction," Tom Coughlin lectured his players during a meeting on this Thursday.

But why not?

What reporters were distracting Coughlin's players from at the moment was disliking him and disliking each other.

As the players walked off the practice field following their morning walk-through, they spotted the larger-than-usual media crowd.

"The controversy continues!" backup center Grey Ruegamer called out.

Running back Derrick Ward started singing the Twisted Sister song "We're Not Gonna Take It." Other players joined in. Backup tailback Brandon Jacobs was particularly enthusiastic. The song was twenty-two years old and many of the players had been in diapers when it came out, but most of them seemed to know at least the refrain.

Four days earlier the Giants had been on their way to a seemingly routine triumph in Nashville with a 21–0 lead over the Tennessee Titans in the fourth quarter. But they'd fallen apart and surrendered 24 straight points to lose. There was plenty of blame to go around. Plaxico Burress failed to run hard after a pass early in the fourth quarter and an interception by Titans cornerback Pacman Jones on the play got Tennessee's rally started. Mathias Kiwanuka had Vince Young in his grasp for a fourth-down sack but let Young go, thinking the rookie quarterback had released the ball and not wanting to be penalized for unnecessary roughness. Young scrambled for a first down and that drive produced the Titans' tying touchdown. Eli Manning made a terrible decision and a horrendous throw for another interception by Jones, setting up the Titans' winning field goal. Suddenly things couldn't be much worse for the Giants, who were on a three-game losing streak to fall a game behind the Cowboys with the two teams scheduled to meet Sunday in the Meadowlands.

The Giants had become a punch line. During his TV monologue the other night David Letterman had made a couple jokes about the apologies being offered up at every turn by comedian Michael Richards, who had once played Kramer on *Seinfeld* and had just created a national uproar with racial remarks directed at an audience member during a standup routine in Hollywood.

"Now if we can just get an apology from the Giants," Letterman said, "then we'd have something."

Coughlin had told his players back at Giants Stadium the day after the game that they had to move on. But that didn't mean he didn't want them feeling bad about what had happened.

"It had better hurt," Coughlin told them.

The mood was grim. Coughlin approved a request for the players to meet among themselves without the coaches. Shaun O'Hara, Tiki Barber, Michael Strahan, and Antonio Pierce had done most of the talking during that session. Pierce told his teammates the season wasn't over, that things weren't any worse than they'd been after the 1-2 start. Neither Manning nor Burress had spoken, but both players were on everyone's mind. For a second year in a row, Manning was getting worse instead of better as the season went along. He'd thrown six interceptions and only two touchdown passes during the three-game losing streak.

The Giants' brass still believed he'd be a star among stars, a quarterback who would reach Super Bowls and Pro Bowls. But there was no arguing with the numbers: He was the NFL's twenty-third-rated passer this week. Philip Rivers was only eleven starts into his career and was seventh. Ben Roethlisberger was twenty-fourth, but he was having a season of remarkably bad luck and he had a Super Bowl triumph on his résumé.

The other Giants players continued to back Manning. That wasn't necessarily the case with Burress. Strahan went on a radio show and made some comments critical of Burress. The players' ire was aimed at each other for once instead of at Coughlin. But the New York papers were focused on Coughlin and were raising the possibility that with Ernie Accorsi leaving after the season, John Mara might fire Coughlin and start over.

On Wednesday an ESPN reporter, Kelly Naqi, had asked several players in the Giants locker room about Strahan's radio comments about Burress. The questions were perfectly legitimate. The odd thing was that Burress knew nothing about what Strahan had said. Naqi read Burress the radio comments word for word. Burress said he would speak to Strahan but he would never criticize a teammate publicly like that.

Strahan's usual day to speak to the media was Thursday. But after a member of the Giants' public relations staff told him what was happening in the locker room, he stormed to his locker and directed a tirade at Naqi while continuing to chew on a hot dog. He beckoned her to come toward him and said, "I know you're going to ask it in a way that there's more division and more of a negative way than what it was. So come here. I want to see your face. Are you a responsible journalist? Look me in the eye and ask me this question, please, the way that you want to ask it. Come on. Look a man in the eye before you try to kill him or make up something."

It was a bullying routine but it served its purpose: The story of the day would be Strahan versus the media, not Strahan versus Burress.

Things were pretty much the same in every NFL city. The tickets were sold, so the benefits of free publicity to teams during the week were becoming more and more limited. The league had the NFL Network and its Web site to get its message out. Teams had their own Web sites. Dan Snyder was leading the way in trying to bolster his club's site to the point where fans might go to it to get their Redskins news and by-pass traditional media outlets altogether. All around the league head coaches increasingly were keeping the newspaper beat reporters who covered their teams daily from watching what happened on the practice field and from talking to assistant coaches. When the competition com-mittee had announced at the league meeting that it would require coaches to open their mandatory offseason minicamps to reporters, the amazing thing wasn't that the league's leaders were improving media ac-cess; it was that things had gotten so bad that a committee had to force coaches to open the doors to something as insignificant as a minicamp.

Now it was Thursday and things were finally beginning to calm down a bit at Giants Stadium. The players got back to the locker room after their Twisted Sister serenade and the PR staff ushered in the media. Some players mockingly sang or hummed, "We Are the World." Strahan was nowhere to be found, even though he'd pledged to speak to the media that day. Jacobs lectured a group of reporters, "We give two shits about you guys, to be honest with you."

Pierce actually liked what he was seeing. The edge was back, he thought.

After practice the media pack gathered around Coughlin.

"The more you attack, the better they'll be and come together," Coughlin said.

"How has the media attacked?" Naqi asked.

"I don't know," Coughlin said testily. "You tell me."

Soon after Coughlin said, "I think probably everyone ought to take a look at the standings and be aware that we're six-and-five. We're in the final five games of the season. It's an exciting time of year despite what's being pulled here."

"What's being pulled?" Naqi asked.

Coughlin turned to walk away.

"Anybody else have anything positive they want to ask me about?" he said. "Anything about the game?"

Mara had been talking to an acquaintance at midweek about the owners' pending vote on the G-3 request by the Giants and New York Jets. The owners would meet the following week in Dallas to render a verdict. That was a $300 million weight on Mara's shoulders. He was hopeful but still anxious. He was pleasant that day as always, but clearly there was plenty to fret about.

"Including," he said, "my team."

DECEMBER

CHAPTER

-25-

December 3 . . . East Rutherford, New Jersey

The black limo carrying Jerry Jones and several members of his family veered off the New Jersey Turnpike at Exit 16W and pulled up to the Giants Stadium entrance nearest the locker rooms at 12:49 P.M., almost three and a half hours before kickoff. The stadium was physically non-descript, but it had an aura about it because it stood in the shadow of New York City, and because it conjured up visions of Bill Parcells coaching Giants teams with Phil Simms and Lawrence Taylor on wind-swept days in big games with NFC East titles and Super Bowl berths at stake. The building had spawned a few football-related legends, like the one about the Giants' opening the doorways in the tunnels behind the end zones to create powerful drafts to foil field goal attempts by opponents, and it had also spawned some nonfootball legends, like the one about Jimmy Hoffa being buried beneath an end zone.

Jones climbed out of the vehicle wearing a black coat over a dark suit, with a light blue handkerchief tucked neatly into a front pocket. One of his Super Bowl rings flashed brightly on the sunny but chilly afternoon. Stephen and Jerry Junior walked ahead as their father stopped to shake hands with a guard at the gate and then spoke briefly to Milt Ahlerich, the former FBI executive who was the NFL's security chief.

"Are you going to the field first?" Ahlerich asked.

"No," Jerry Jones said, "to the locker room."

He walked briskly down the tunnel toward the Cowboys' locker room.

"I'm nervous as a cat," he said.

"Why?" an acquaintance asked. "I'd much rather be in the spot your team is in right now than the spot their team is in."

"That's what worries me—their spot," Jones said. "They look all hemmed in. That makes 'em dangerous. We were talking about it on the way over. We couldn't stop 'em the last time. They hit us on our flank. Manning is dangerous. This one is dangerous."

The Giants had the recently injured Osi Umenyiora, Brandon Short, and Sam Madison back in the lineup on defense but still were without Michael Strahan. Tony Romo took the Cowboys down the field on the game's opening drive, but they had to settle for a 44-yard field goal attempt by Martin Gramatica. His kick sailed hopelessly wide right.

Mike Vanderjagt at least could have hit the upright.

"Just relax," Parcells told the new kicker, *his* new kicker, on the sideline.

Eli Manning threw a touchdown pass to Jeremy Shockey on the Giants' first possession. Jones had been right. Manning and the Giants were dangerous. Romo had a pass intercepted by Mathias Kiwanuka, but the rookie defensive end dropped the ball as he tried to switch it from one hand to the other during his return and the Cowboys recovered the fumble. Kiwanuka's strange season continued. He was doing something right to get into position to make big plays like this one and the would-be game-clinching sack in Tennessee, but things kept going wrong for him. The Cowboys cashed in with a touchdown. Tom Coughlin left his offense on the field for a fourth-and-one gamble from the Cowboys' 24-yard line in the final two minutes of the first half. Manning handed the ball to Brandon Jacobs, who had the option to run inside or outside. He chose to go outside and DeMarcus Ware tackled him for a three-yard loss.

Gramatica connected on a 41-yard field goal with a second to play in the half. He added a 35-yarder in the final seconds of the third quarter. The Cowboys had a 20–13 lead in the fourth quarter when Manning, looking like a big-time quarterback for the first time in weeks, led the Giants on a tying touchdown drive. Romo turned to Todd Haley on the Cowboys' sideline as the Giants moved down the field.

"Let them score," Romo told Haley. "Give me one minute with two timeouts and we'll win."

The Cowboys got the ball at their 32-yard line with a minute remaining. They immediately dusted off one of their favorite passing plays, designed to get Jason Witten working deep down the field against a linebacker. They hadn't used the play all day and it worked perfectly. Antonio Pierce couldn't stay with Witten. Romo wasn't having a good game but he zipped a terrific throw and Witten made the catch for a 42-yard gain to the Giants' 26. The Cowboys ran a few plays and called their last timeout with six seconds left. Gramatica trotted onto the field for a 46-yard kick. It wasn't a windy day by Giants Stadium standards and the modest breeze was at Gramatica's back. Romo, the holder, was confident because Gramatica had hit the ball well all week in practice and hadn't missed a kick at that end of the stadium during warmups. The Giants called a timeout to make Gramatica think about it.

The snap was good.

The hold by Romo was good.

The kick was true.

"Yessss!!!" Parcells screamed as he raised his arms on the sideline.

He was a genius again, at least for another week. He'd been right about the quarterback and he'd been right about the kicker. A second was left on the clock and the Cowboys applied the finishing touches by making the tackle on the kickoff.

"You're making me look good," Parcells told Gramatica just after the game.

Parcells had gone back to the place where his fondest football memories had been forged and he'd moved the Cowboys closer to the division title. They were two games ahead of the Giants with four games left and they were playing as well as anyone in the conference.

The Giants remained in full retreat and their postgame locker room was quiet. LaVar Arrington walked across the room and headed toward the exit. He'd undergone surgery for his torn Achilles' tendon and had begun his rehab. He hadn't been able to run yet but things were going well. He was still feeling positive about how he'd played just before he'd gotten hurt, and he thought the Giants were being supportive of him. He was splitting his time between the New York and D.C. areas and he was keeping tabs on the Redskins. He'd watched them lose earlier in the day to the Atlanta Falcons.

"The leader is not there," he said. "There's no one to hold everything together. It does make a difference. When I was there and we were losing, at least we were fighting. You don't see that now, do you?"

At the moment, however, Arrington's new team wasn't doing much better.

December 4 . . . Philadelphia

Sylvester Stallone, busy promoting his latest *Rocky* movie, was on hand as the Eagles played to keep the competitive portion of their season alive. "Eye of the Tiger" blared over the stadium sound system just before kickoff. The Eagles had a 5-6 record and the Panthers were 6-5, but the highly forgiving nature of the NFC wild card race meant that both were very much alive for the playoffs. No team with a losing record had ever reached the NFL playoffs in a full, nonstrike season. But some 8-8 teams had, and the NFC looked headed in that direction again. The conference's "contenders" weren't apologizing for their ineptitude, but it didn't look so great when these two playoff wannabes had to switch sides of the field immediately before a Monday night kickoff because they'd lined up at the wrong ends.

The Eagles punted the first six times they had the ball. Soon enough, the fans began to boo the offense. It appeared the entire Eagles' operation simply wasn't going to function without Donovan McNabb. But they stayed close and trailed by only 24–17 in the fourth quarter when Jeff Garcia teamed with Reggie Brown for a touchdown to tie the game. It was Garcia's third touchdown pass of the night; he'd connected earlier with Brian Westbrook and Donté Stallworth. Suddenly the Panthers fell apart. Quarterback Jake Delhomme, who'd thrown three touchdown passes of his own but had hurt his right thumb on the first one when he'd banged his hand on defensive tackle Darwin Walker's helmet on his follow-through, floated a pass directly to Brian Dawkins for an interception. That set up David Akers's go-ahead field goal. The Panthers drove to the Eagles' 7-yard line in the game's final seconds. Delhomme looked to his right and saw the six-foot-four Keyshawn Johnson being covered by the five-ten Lito Sheppard. Delhomme tapped his right hand to his rear end to signal Johnson to run a fade pattern; he intended to lob a pass that Johnson could catch well above Sheppard's head.

But the Eagles' defensive backs had noticed, while studying Panthers game tapes during the week, that Delhomme's tapping his butt was the signal for a fade. Sheppard saw the tap; he knew what was coming. He made sure to position himself to the outside of Johnson, between the wide receiver and the sideline. Delhomme threw the ball a little bit too far and the pass sailed over the outstretched hands of the leaping Johnson and into the hands of Sheppard. Johnson screamed at the closest official, wanting a penalty on Sheppard he wouldn't get, then threw his helmet to the turf in disgust on his way to the sideline. The Eagles and their fans celebrated while the sounds of the Boz Scaggs tune "Lido Shuffle"— "Lido, whoa-oh-oh-oh"—filled Lincoln Financial Field.

The Eagles had figured they'd be out of the playoff race if they lost. Now their season had possibilities again. Garcia had thrown for 312 yards. It was his first 300-yard passing performance in more than two years. He'd won a game as a starting quarterback for the first time in more than thirteen months. That was pointed out to him late that night.

"What are you saying, man?" he said.

Then he grinned and quickly added, "Yeah, you're right. It has been a while."

Reid was beginning to get the idea that he might be able to trust his new quarterback. Garcia's teammates were feeling the same way and they were adjusting to Garcia's intense approach. If they were in a tight situation and a game was on the line, McNabb was liable to crack a joke in the huddle to keep everyone loose. That wasn't Garcia's style. He was uptight all the time. He wore a stern look and wasn't afraid to get in teammates' faces, even in practices. But for the first time in a few years the Eagles had a glimmer of hope that perhaps they would be able to accomplish something without McNabb there to lead the way.

December 7 . . . Frisco, Texas

The NFL's owners were at the Westin Stonebriar, a sprawling resort about twenty miles north of the Dallas–Fort Worth airport, on this Thursday morning, but they wouldn't stay long. The meeting began at 9, and by 11:30 it was over.

John Mara, Steve Tisch, and Jets owner Woody Johnson had assumed the Buffalo Bills' Ralph Wilson, the Cincinnati Bengals' Mike Brown, and the Jacksonville Jaguars' Wayne Weaver would oppose the $300 million subsidy for the New Jersey stadium. What they didn't know was how many other owners those three could convince to vote with them.

Wilson saw a new stadium near New York that, with 200 luxury boxes (up from 118 at Giants Stadium) at $250,000 per box, would generate $50 million in annual revenues for each of those two teams while the Bills were struggling to break $7 million a year in luxury box revenues. He thought the small-market franchises were being squeezed right out of the league. He'd been in the league for forty-six years and thought he'd never seen relations between the owners in a worse condition. Other owners were calling him to say he'd been right to vote against the labor settlement.

Many owners and executives from lower-revenue teams thought, as Wilson did, that the union had made too good a deal for itself in the labor negotiations. The deal, they believed, had taken too much out of the league as a whole. In the short term, the high-revenue teams and the players would prosper while the low-revenue franchises struggled. But in the long run, they guessed, the inequity of wealth would hurt competitive balance, weaken the league and its overall appeal, and create problems for everyone. As those owners from lower-revenue franchises looked back on the events of March, they thought the bloc of high-revenue teams had done a good job sticking together; those owners had been tough, smart, and organized. But the owners of the low-revenue teams thought Paul Tagliabue could have done much more to break the logjam. He could have pressured those owners of higher-revenue clubs who might not have wanted to be identified publicly as being aligned with Dan Snyder and Jerry Jones to break ranks. Instead it had been the coalition of mid- and low-revenue teams that had fallen apart. Those owners had panicked when it appeared the group of nine would hold strong and the sport might be on its way to a labor confrontation and perhaps a court battle or a work stoppage. They'd jumped at the chance to get additional money in revenue-sharing. Now they were feeling the pinch and counting the days until they could try to force the entire ownership group to exercise the reopener clause in the labor deal.

It was possible for the two New York teams to move forward with the stadium project without the $300 million league grant, but doing so would involve a considerable financial risk, one Mara was not prepared to take. He thought the league as a whole would benefit from having a showcase stadium in the New York market. He wondered how teams that had used hundreds of millions of dollars of public financing to build stadiums could turn around and consider rejecting the Giants and Jets when they were planning to build a privately financed facility. Mara wondered how teams could think about rejecting the Giants when his family had decided so many years ago to forgo the heftier chunk of national TV fees a New York franchise could have commanded in favor of doing what was best for the league. He'd called some owners to ask for their support. He hadn't reminded them what his father had meant to the NFL because it hadn't been necessary.

"After all your family has done for the league," he'd been told more than once, "of course you have our support."

Now Wilson stood up during this meeting and said the owners had stood together in the past during difficult times and they should do so again. He said he'd vote in favor of the G-3 request by the Giants and Jets if the owners would also agree right then and there to some provisions to protect the small-market teams, those that would be the qualifiers for additional revenue-sharing funds. The criteria for clubs to qualify for revenue-sharing still hadn't been set.

"It's a terrible bargaining agreement," Wilson told the owners. "Terrible. If we're going to give all this money for the building of the stadium we've got to take care of the qualifiers. It's incidental. But it would give us just a little to pay for the extra costs."

Wilson was swaying no one inside the room, however, and Roger Goodell was keeping the debate on the issue at hand. Gene Upshaw had agreed the previous week that the union would relinquish $800 million over fifteen years if the stadium got built. Upshaw figured the players would make back that money and more from their cut of the new revenues generated by the facility. That had stacked the deck in favor of the Giants and Jets.

Dan Rooney and Jerry Richardson spoke in favor of granting the subsidy. Mara, Tisch, and Johnson kept fretting right up until the moment the roll call was far enough along for it to be clear there wouldn't be nine "no" votes. The loan was approved by a 30–2 vote. Only Wilson and Brown voted against it. Wilson would joke later that his new nickname was "30 to 2." Even Weaver voted yes. Some of the other owners suspected Weaver wanted to sell the Jaguars and get out of the NFL and wasn't concerned about down-the-road issues.

The meeting ended abruptly. Snyder was standing outside the meeting room talking to Miami Dolphins owner Wayne Huizenga when Milt Ahlerich walked out and began opening the doors.

"Is it over?" Snyder asked.

Ahlerich nodded his head. The owners spilled out and rushed to their limos. Their private jets were waiting.

Mara lingered inside the room accepting congratulations from other owners. Now his worry shifted to actually getting the stadium built for its 2010 opening. He could also go back to worrying about his 6-6 football team.

The owners also approved a $42.5 million grant to the Kansas City Chiefs to renovate Arrowhead Stadium. The G-3 fund had been emptied. Goodell wanted the league to stay in the stadium construction business, but the debate over the New York facility had demonstrated that he and Upshaw would have to come up with a formula not so taxing to the teams that weren't building the stadium. "Now," Goodell said, "we'll have to find what the son of G-3 is."

Snyder headed home. He'd voted for a measure that might make the Giants and Jets bigger revenue-generators than the Redskins. The new *Forbes* rankings had come out in September and the magazine had the Redskins' league-leading value up to $1.423 billion. *Forbes* had estimated the Redskins' annual revenues at $303 million (a whopping $53 million more than the second-ranked New England Patriots) and their operating income at $108.4 million (nearly double that of the Houston Texans, who ranked second at $57.6 million). The Cowboys, third at $1.173 billion, and Eagles, fifth at $1.024 billion, also had been among the five franchises with estimated values above $1 billion. Snyder's calculations were different. He thought his team was being surpassed by the Patriots in revenue-generating capability and would fall behind the Cowboys as well once they opened their new stadium.

"Everyone is passing us," Snyder said back home that night, "but so what? That's okay. That's not what I got into this for."

He'd gotten into it to win Super Bowls, but so far that wasn't working out either. The criticism was mounting.

"Everyone is killing us," Snyder said.

He actually thought the Redskins weren't all that far away from being a good team. They had a good offensive line, in his view, and pretty good receivers. They were working on the quarterback. Snyder didn't envision an offseason of huge changes by the Redskins' standards. He hadn't even given up completely on this season. He was going over the schedule and trying to see if there was any way the Redskins could sneak into the playoffs at 8-8 or even 7-9. He didn't care if it would be an embarrassment to be in the playoffs at 7-9. He just wanted to be in the playoffs.

"Am I crazy?" he said.

Perhaps.

But that was part of the deal in this business.

"If we'd just won some of these crazy games this year we'd be sitting here laughing our asses off," Snyder said. "We just lost our way. We lost our Redskins' way. But we'll get it back. You watch. Everyone will see."

The Redskins rarely re-signed their own free agents and as the season wound down they had the least remaining salary cap space in the league with about $200,000. But they were talking to agent Tony Agnone about a contract extension for Ladell Betts. T. J. Duckett and Betts both were eligible for free agency after the season and the Redskins needed to keep one of them to go with Clinton Portis. They chose Betts and negotiated with Agnone. The contract would have to have a relatively modest signing bonus, but the Redskins could supplement that with an option bonus in the second year of the deal. The Redskins had forty-four players under contract for the 2007 season for salary cap figures totaling $108 million. The cap was to be $109 million. That would make for a bit of a tight squeeze, but nothing they hadn't dealt with before. As long as the cap continued to make a big jump every year—and that looked promising, with the league informing the teams that week that the cap would be about $116 million in 2008—the Redskins would be okay. By week's end, the Betts deal was done. He got $11 million over five seasons, including a $3.5 million signing bonus and a $2 million option bonus.

The Redskins were playing out a busted hand. It was time to focus on next season, even if Dan Snyder wouldn't admit that to himself.

December 8 . . . Irving, Texas

The Cowboys' practice ended by 12:30 and Valley Ranch emptied out quickly after that. It was typical for a Friday, a lazy day by NFL workweek standards. The players had the rest of the day off and wanted to get home. By 1:15 only a few players remained in the locker room. Tony Parrish, a veteran safety who'd just been claimed off waivers after being released by the San Francisco 49ers, sat quietly by his locker. Calvin Hill, the former Cowboys running back who served as a consultant to the team, walked by and welcomed Parrish to the organization.

"I just want to be a cog in the wheel," Parrish told him.

Terrell Owens stood in front of his locker and pulled on a black sweatsuit and a black cap. The children's book he'd written, *Little T Learns to Share,* was propped up on a shelf in his locker. It had been a hectic week for Owens. He'd turned thirty-three the previous day and he'd thrown himself a big party Monday night in Hollywood. He'd invited all his teammates and paid $30,000 for a private jet. A handful of Cowboys players had joined him. Chris Rock and Justin Timberlake had been among the five hundred or so guests. The party had lasted until the early morning hours Tuesday, the players' day off, and they'd been back in Dallas by Wednesday for meetings and practice.

Now Owens talked to rookie wide receiver Sam Hurd for a while and then exited the locker room to go home and rest for Sunday's game. The Saints and Sean Payton were coming to town.

Tony Romo was usually a gym rat, hanging around the practice facility long after his teammates had left, but today he had family members to pick up at the airport and he left quickly. He would have exited even earlier if John Madden hadn't kept him in the team's media library for the production meeting with NBC for forty minutes.

Bill Parcells's turn was next. The production meetings with the network broadcast crews were different from other media sessions. The networks expected frankness from coaches and players after paying billions of dollars to the NFL in rights fees, and they usually got it. But Parcells didn't care how much the networks were paying. His job was to do what was best for his team. After one production meeting during the season, he walked out and said to someone, "You know what I just said in there was bullshit, right?"

Still, Parcells's relationship with the media was not as combative as people on the outside imagined. Both sides, for the most part, enjoyed the verbal sparring. Parcells tried to control the information being dispensed about his team, but unlike his former assistant Bill Belichick he actually said interesting and insightful things during press conferences. Parcells made it easy to cover his team. But it was a two-way street. Parcells had worked at ESPN before taking the Cowboys job and he knew how to use the media to his advantage. He had reporters he trusted, and he knew how and when to whisper information to them to benefit himself. If something came out that he hadn't wanted to come out, he'd simply deny it. He had no qualms about that.

All season Parcells made certain to say nothing inflammatory about Owens for public consumption. He'd tried too hard to make things work to undermine himself that way. But now Owens wasn't quite doing his part. He was playing all right, but he wasn't playing great. Parcells's associates could sense Parcells's frustration. Madden could sense it, too. He spoke to Parcells on this day and again before the Cowboys played on NBC on Christmas Day. Madden left the sessions convinced that Parcells would come back for another season but wouldn't allow Owens to return, and he made that prediction during NBC's Christmas telecast.

The public perception seemed to be that Parcells and Owens simply had been oil and water from the beginning, that Parcells detested Owens and didn't try to make things work. That was inaccurate. Parcells tried very hard to understand Owens and how he might get through to "the player," as Parcells often called him in his public pronouncements. Early on, Parcells talked to experts on personality and behavior and described Owens to them. After listening to what the experts said, he became convinced that Owens was a textbook narcissist who had to feel he was the center of the universe at all times and couldn't be dealt with in the manner in which a football coach usually interacted with a player. Even that was okay with Parcells, who'd always prided himself on being adaptable. He had once found ways to get free spirits like Lawrence Taylor and Bryan Cox to stand by his side on Sundays, and he'd resolved to do all he could so that Owens would fit into the same category. The book on Owens as a player, Parcells had known coming in, was that he dropped too many passes but he could do plenty with the ball once he got it in his hands. Parcells had tried to work around that as well. He was having only mixed success.

The tension between Parcells and Owens cut both ways but remained beneath the surface. Owens was miffed that Parcells had never asked him how he was after his overdose. He was angry that so many things involving him that were supposed to remain in-house matters had been leaked to the media. He often felt alone in his own locker room. He didn't particularly care for Parcells's coaching methods, thinking they were too rigid and old school, but he was proud there hadn't been a major blowup between them. Owens was doing what he could to get back to another Super Bowl.

Winning cured a lot of ills and covered up a lot of problems, and for the moment the Cowboys were winning.

CHAPTER

-26-

December 10 ... Irving, Texas

Up close Texas Stadium looked old and worn. The paint was chipping in places. The luxury suites had been rendered less than luxurious over the years. Soon it wouldn't be the home of the Cowboys any longer.

Jerry Jones thought that the biggest piece of his legacy as the franchise's owner would be the team's new stadium in Arlington, Texas, scheduled to open in 2009. Jones wanted it to be not only a huge revenue generator but also a shrine to the Cowboys. It would be big, with twice as much square footage as Texas Stadium, and a capacity of about 80,000 fans for Cowboys games and 100,000 or so for special events like the Super Bowl. It would be costly, with a price tag that just kept going up and had reached around $1 billion after starting out around $650 million. Jones also wanted it to be grand. He started working with architects about six years before Arlington voters approved up to $325 million in public funding for the project in 2004. Jones and members of his family made three trips to London to study Wembley Stadium. They studied the Sydney Opera House in Australia, the Nice airport in

France, and Bloomberg Tower in New York. Jones remembered the first time he'd visited New York. He'd taken a cab ride to the Bronx just to touch Yankee Stadium. He wanted his new stadium to be every bit as awe inspiring.

It would have a glass exterior with glazing to create streaks of silver and blue. It would have huge glass doors by the end zones which could be left open to create plazas of more than 200,000 square feet each that could be used for standing room or temporary seating. It would have a sixty-yard-long video screen. It would have concourses filled with shops. It would borrow from what the Tampa Bay Buccaneers had done at Raymond James Stadium and have three-level party decks at each end. It would replicate what the Seattle Seahawks had done at Qwest Field and have field level suites. It would have a Hall of Fame that would stay open year-round. It would, like Texas Stadium, have a hole in the roof. Jones thought that was a symbol of the Cowboys every bit as strong as the stars on the helmets or the cheerleaders. This one would be created by two quarter-mile steel arches and would have a retractable roof to cover it when needed.

For now Jones and the Cowboys would have to get by with the stadium they had. At least on television, it still resembled a sparkling football palace. It was dressed up nicely for the Cowboys to host the Saints on NBC's Sunday night game. This was supposed to be a coronation for the Cowboys as the NFC's best team and for Tony Romo as America's new darling of a quarterback. Romo's parents were in the stands. A banner hanging from the facing of the upper deck read: ROMO-MENTUM.

But Sean Payton had different ideas. He was more than ready to face his former boss, Bill Parcells. He'd spent the week filling in his players on the strengths and weaknesses of various Cowboys players. He knew what he was talking about: The game was no contest. Saints quarterback Drew Brees passed for 384 yards and five touchdowns, all in the first three quarters, and the Saints rolled to a 42–17 triumph. The Cowboys simply could do nothing to stop the New Orleans offense.

"Good win," Parcells told Payton when they shook hands on the field afterward, "and good luck."

Parcells resisted the urge to rip into his players in the locker room afterward.

"Pro football is a humbling game," he told them. "This can happen to you anytime."

He'd been outmaneuvered by Payton at every turn. Payton had gotten a first down on one touchdown drive by running a reverse on a fourth-down play. He'd gotten a touchdown on an instant replay challenge and he'd caught the Cowboys with their pants down with a successful onside kick that led to another touchdown. Parcells had cost the Cowboys a 15-yard penalty for throwing his red challenge flag on the field in the final two minutes of the first half. He'd been right about the call. A replay review had reversed it and turned a Saints' completion into an incompletion. But the replay official was in charge of all replay decisions in the final two minutes of a half and coaches were barred from challenging then. The Cowboys assistant coaches in the press box had been hollering into Parcells's headset the call was wrong and he should challenge and Parcells had thrown the flag, forgetting that doing so was by rule unsportsmanlike conduct.

When referee Gerry Austin walked to the sideline to explain that, Parcells's face contorted into a pained expression.

"Ah," he barked at Austin, "that's horseshit!"

Romo didn't play well and threw two interceptions. The Cowboys' lead in the division was down to a single game; the Giants had won in Carolina earlier in the day. The Eagles had beaten the Redskins even though Ladell Betts had celebrated his new contract by running for 171 yards. The Cowboys only had six days until a Saturday night road game in Atlanta and they were shocked, not because they'd lost but because they'd been overwhelmed.

The imperfections were beginning to show in their quarterback, and in their team.

December 12 . . . Ashburn, Virginia

At Redskins Park, Joe Gibbs was working on the week's game plan with his assistant coaches, just as he did every Tuesday night, shut off from the outside world. He was blissfully unaware that Redskins fans were in a panic.

That night a man claiming to be a D.C. police officer called a satellite radio show and said that Gibbs had been seriously injured in an auto accident. Someone at ESPN heard the show and began calling around. Chris Helein, the Redskins' public relations director, soon was being called by every media outlet in town. Helein tried to call Gibbs's administrative assistant, Cindy Mangum, but didn't get an answer. He tried to call team administrator Derrick Crawford: no answer. So around 10:30 he headed back to Redskins Park. He walked in the front door and took an immediate left, heading down a hallway to the coaching office where he knew the game planning meetings took place.

There was Gibbs, alive and well.

He pulled Gibbs out of the meeting.

"You've got to know this," Helein told him.

The rumor was spreading like wildfire and might make its way to one of Gibbs's family members. Sure enough, one of them had already called without Gibbs knowing it.

"I'm sure people probably wish I *was* in an accident," Gibbs said.

The season would be over soon. That was the Redskins' only solace at the moment.

The next day the NFL would suffer a loss that was real. Lamar Hunt, the beloved owner of the Kansas City Chiefs, died at a Dallas hospital of complications from prostate cancer. Just over a year after the league had lost one titan in Wellington Mara, it lost another. Hunt had been the ringleader of "The Foolish Club," the eight owners who'd founded the old American Football League, and had been a central figure in the 1970 merger between the AFL and the NFL. He'd secretly met with Tex Schramm in a car at Love Field in Dallas to discuss the merger. Hunt had given the Super Bowl its name, borrowing it from the little rubber Super Ball with which one of his children liked to play. The Chiefs had come into existence as the Dallas Texans before moving to Kansas City in 1963, and Hunt and Jerry Jones had lived in the same neighborhood in Dallas. The neighborhood was divided by Preston Road, and so Hunt came up with the Preston Road Trophy, a piece of wood with a green

Preston Road street sign on it, to be awarded to the winner of any
Cowboys-Chiefs game.

Jones had possession of the trophy when Hunt died. It was his me-
mento of a great man.

December 16 ... Atlanta

Bryant Gumbel and Dick Vermeil stood in the broadcast booth at the
Georgia Dome just after 5 p.m., about three hours before the kickoff of
the Cowboys-Falcons game, to rehearse their pregame intro. In the production truck parked outside the stadium, images of Gumbel and
Vermeil filled two of the three large screens centered on a wall of mon-
itors. The screens were surrounded by about six dozen tiny screens.
Three rows of desks faced the wall of screens. Producer Mark Loomis sat
to the far left of the desk nearest the screens.

This was the fifth of the eight games the NFL Network would carry
during the season, and one of the two color analyst Cris Collinsworth
would miss, so Vermeil was filling in. Gumbel began the practice intro
by asking Vermeil about the comments Falcons coach Jim Mora had
made on a radio show a few days earlier, saying he'd leave his job in
Atlanta in an instant if the coaching job at the University of
Washington, his alma mater, was ever offered to him. The remarks had
outraged many Falcons fans and had gotten Mora summoned to a meeting with owner Arthur Blank. Vermeil had known Mora since Mora was
four years old, and he launched into a defense of Mora. The matter
might be a distraction to the Falcons' PR staff, he said, but it wouldn't
be a distraction to Mora's players. It was a dead issue, Vermeil said.
Vermeil was sick, his throat so scratchy he could barely get the words
out, so he and Gumbel decided to cut the rehearsal short.

"Guys," Gumbel said into the camera, "can we get Dick some water
with some honey and some lemon in it? That would help his throat
a bunch."

In the truck, Loomis stood up and walked out the door.

"It's never easy," he said.

Moments later Gumbel and Vermeil started watching a taped interview with Jerry Jones on a monitor. It was often remarked about Jones's face that it had a pulled-tight, plastic-surgery look. Gumbel couldn't resist.

"The question is," he said, "whose face moves less, Sylvester Stallone's or Jerry Jones's?"

Gumbel still enjoyed calling the games. What he didn't enjoy was the prep work. There was so much written in so many places about NFL teams in the information age that you had to sort through about ninety-nine pounds of garbage to get to one pound of nuggets. His skills as a play-by-play man had been rusty in the beginning but he thought he was getting better each week. He'd told Steve Bornstein, the head of the NFL Network, at the outset he wouldn't judge his performance until the entire eight-game package was completed. He hadn't been nervous before the first game; he couldn't recall a time in his life when he'd been nervous in front of a TV camera. But he had been uncertain, and he hadn't liked the feeling. He liked to go into things knowing the answers and that wasn't the case here. He'd told Bornstein in the beginning he didn't want a setup in which he got thirty-two phone calls from the owners of the thirty-two teams each Monday. It hadn't been that way. Working for the NFL Network had turned out to be just like working for any other network. A broadcast was followed by a postmortem with his superiors, but the league hadn't interfered.

"I'm signed for four years," Gumbel said. "I've said this before so this is not necessarily germane to this assignment: My rearview mirror doesn't work. I'm not the kind of guy who when he makes a decision second-guesses the decision. I didn't do it when I left sports in '82. I didn't do it when I resigned from *Today* in '87. I didn't do it when I decided to walk away from network television in 2002. I'm a kind of guy, for better or for worse, I kind of make a decision and I'm much more focused on what happens ahead than whether or not it was the right decision."

League officials had been unable to resolve disputes with Cablevision and a few other large cable companies to get the NFL Network into more households. The 4.2 million viewers who were watching the channel's game broadcasts on average were a fraction of the audience that watched games carried by other networks. But Pat Bowlen, the Denver Broncos owner who was the chairman of the broadcasting committee, thought the experiment was working well enough that having games on the league-owned network would be a permanent fixture.

The game Gumbel and Vermeil got to call that night was a good one, but it began with an ugly incident. After a play on the Cowboys' opening possession Falcons cornerback DeAngelo Hall got in Terrell Owens's face and was jawing at him. He'd blanketed Owens on a deep pattern on a third-down play and he let Owens know about it as the two walked back toward the line of scrimmage while the Cowboys readied to punt.

"All night long," Hall told Owens. "It's going to be like this all night long."

He and Owens were actually friendly but Hall was getting to Owens this time, and Owens spit in Hall's face. The TV cameras didn't pick it up. Hall went nuts, telling the officials what had happened. But none of them had seen it and no penalty was called. The night soon got worse for Hall. Owens outfought him in the end zone for an early touchdown catch and the Cowboys rolled to a 14–0 lead when DeMarcus Ware returned an interception for a touchdown. Owens sprinted past Hall for another touchdown catch later in the first half. But Michael Vick was doing it all for the Falcons. He threw four touchdown passes, matching his single-game career high. He set the single-season league record for rushing yards by a quarterback. He even lined up at tailback for a few plays. But while the Cowboys trailed, 28–21, in the third quarter, they regrouped to score the game's final 17 points.

As the players mingled on the field after the game, Owens and Hall crossed paths. Hall thought he would get an apology from Owens.

He thought wrong.

"I heard you got beat up in a club," Owens said.

That made Hall even more incensed. "What," he thought, "is wrong with this guy?"

Jones stood in the middle of the locker room a little while later and told anyone who would listen about Owens's decision three weeks earlier not to undergo surgery on his finger. Owens had kept the matter under wraps. "Sometimes he can't say it for himself because he's so honest with his answers," Jones said. "That candor doesn't always serve you well. But it should be noted when it gets down to the real nut-cutting time, when it really gets down to that time, I've seen him do a really good thing for the team."

Jones didn't know it but at that very moment Owens was undermining himself again with his candor. Hall had told reporters in the Falcons' locker room about the spitting incident, saying he'd lost all respect for Owens. The NFL Network had Owens on for a postgame interview and Owens was asked about Hall's accusation. There was no TV footage of it. Owens could have denied it and it would have been a he-said, he-said issue. Instead Owens came clean. "I got frustrated and I apologize for that," he said. "It was a situation where he kept bugging me and getting in my face."

Two days later the league would fine Owens $35,000 and Deion Sanders would arrange a three-way phone call on which Owens would apologize to Hall. Publicly Owens would come to say the spitting incident had been accidental.

Jones was standing just inside the doorway of the locker room and was on his fifth or sixth rendering of the story about Owens's finger, this time to Peter King of *Sports Illustrated* and Ed Werder of ESPN, when Terence Newman walked by on his way to the team bus. The cornerback stopped momentarily to admire the snappiness of Jones's suit.

"Whoo-eee," Newman said. "As sharp as a mosquito's peter."

"Ah, locker room talk," Jones said. "You gotta love it."

It sounded a lot better after a win.

December 17 . . . East Rutherford, New Jersey

Sean Considine was teasing Trent Cole about beginning a touchdown celebration ten yards before the goal line.

"Next time no high-stepping until you get in the end zone," Considine said. "I about had a heart attack when I saw you do that."

"I didn't do that," Cole said. "I didn't do that."

It was all smiles and laughs in the visitors' locker room at Giants Stadium. The Eagles had just beaten the Giants to take over the NFC wild card lead. They'd remained only a game behind the Cowboys and would play for first place at Texas Stadium eight days later on Christmas. They'd won three straight games. They'd put their once-broken season back together. No one was lamenting Donovan McNabb's injury anymore. No one was suggesting that the players had tuned out Andy Reid's supposedly stale message.

It was the reality of the NFL: Your entire way of doing things was reaffirmed or repudiated on a weekly basis. Now the Eagles were basking in affirmation.

Jeff Garcia hadn't played his best game. He'd gotten a key 15-yard penalty for unsportsmanlike conduct for spiking the ball at the feet of a fallen Giants defender on the sideline after a collision at the end of a scramble. But he'd regrouped and made a gorgeous throw to Reggie Brown for a 19-yard touchdown with just less than three minutes to play. His two-point conversion pass to L. J. Smith had given the Eagles a 29–22 lead. The Giants got the ball back at their 20-yard line with 2:57 left. It was one of those times that was supposed to show why Ernie Accorsi had traded so much to get Eli Manning. Two days later the Pro Bowl selections would be announced and three players the Chargers had gotten in the Manning trade—Philip Rivers, Shawne Merriman, and Nate Kaeding—would be on the AFC squad. Manning's absence from the NFC team wouldn't matter if only he could summon some fourth-quarter magic now.

He couldn't.

The Eagles sent Sheldon Brown, the cornerback who'd been beaten by Plaxico Burress for the winning touchdown in overtime in the teams' September meeting, the one who had committed a pass interference penalty earlier in this game to set up a Giants' touchdown, on a blitz from Manning's right side. The Giants didn't have enough blockers to deal with Brown and it was up to Manning to read the blitz and get rid of the ball quickly. Manning should have seen Brown; the blitz wasn't even from his blind side. But he didn't see. Brown got in Manning's face quickly and Manning threw the ball up for grabs. Tiki Barber tried to bat away the errant pass but couldn't. The ball landed in Cole's hands. He raced to the end zone and the Eagles had two touchdowns ten seconds apart. They won, 36–22. To thank the defense for bailing him out, Garcia planted a kiss on the side of Jeremiah Trotter's helmeted head on the sideline.

Now Considine and Cole could laugh about Cole's touchdown celebration. Down the hallway the Giants were feeling the repudiation. Tom Coughlin told his players in the locker room to stick together, then went to his postgame news conference and told reporters that Manning was at fault on the interception for not spotting the blitz. In the locker room Jeremy Shockey answered questions for the media pack but waved off one New York reporter who tried to approach him afterward.

"Leave me the fuck alone," Shockey said. "No. I'm done talking."

The Giants may have lost five of their last six games to drop their record to 7-7, but they were still tied with the Falcons for the second wild card spot. Antonio Pierce told himself that if the Giants just could get into the playoffs they could make a run through the postseason, the way the Pittsburgh Steelers had done the season before.

December 21 . . . Philadelphia

Jeff Garcia called his grandfather after the Giants game. The quarterback had resuscitated his NFL career, rejuvenated the Eagles and put them on the doorstep of the playoffs, but what he wanted to say to Red Elder, a former high school football coach in California, had nothing to do with any of that. Garcia wanted to apologize for the penalty he'd gotten for spiking the ball on the sideline. "I'm sorry for that," he told his grandfather.

Garcia stayed in regular contact with his grandfather and his father, also a former football coach. He talked to his father, Bob, practically every day. Bob had coached him in junior college in Gilroy, California, before Jeff moved on to San Jose State. Bob Garcia still broke down his son's games on tape and liked to suggest play calls. Jeff had once suggested a play he'd used while playing for his father to the coaching staff at San Jose State and it had worked. But these days he didn't pass along his father's suggestions to Andy Reid or Marty Mornhinweg.

"Dad, it's okay to talk to me about it," he told his father. "But some of these ideas, we'll have to put aside."

Garcia would also call his father just before every game. "Dad," he'd say, "tell me what I need to hear."

"Be smart. Be tough. Be intense."

"Thanks," Jeff would say. "I'm good to go now."

It was the Thursday after the Giants game and Garcia and the Eagles were getting ready to play the Cowboys on Christmas for first place. The two quarterbacks who would play in the game, Garcia and Tony Romo, had both entered the league as undrafted rookies. The two starting quarterbacks in the division who had entered the league as first-round draft picks, Eli Manning and Jason Campbell, were playing for teams with a combined record of 12-16. Garcia thought NFL scouts put too much emphasis on a quarterback's size and arm strength coming out of college and ignored things like being able to move around and create something out of nothing, being a leader and being a winner. He also thought the school of hard knocks wasn't the worst thing for a quarterback. It built a certain toughness of character.

Bill Parcells also had a theory on the subject. He thought quarterbacks like Manning and Campbell who entered the league with so much money and so much hope invested in them by their teams often had to play before they were ready. Fans clamored for it. Players, coaches, general managers, and owners clamored for it. A quarterback like Romo or Garcia got to develop at his own pace. If he was good enough he got to play, but only after he was ready. Now Romo had just been selected to the Pro Bowl, but Parcells wasn't getting carried away. He knew judging a quarterback after half a season as a starter was foolish. Romo was smart enough to know that Parcells was right: There would still be some trials.

He was right.

December 24 . . . East Rutherford, New Jersey

The wind whipped through Giants Stadium on what Tiki Barber knew would be the day of his final home game. Tributes filled the New York papers that morning but the parking lots were virtually empty three hours before game time. The tailgaters usually would have been out in full force by that hour, but the Giants were generating little excitement among their fans these days.

Barber was the only player the Giants introduced to the crowd before facing the Saints. His son A.J. was supposed to run out and grab the tee off the turf right after the opening kickoff but was too scared to do it and begged off the duty. Maybe he knew it wouldn't be a good day to be on the field and be associated with the Giants.

Michael Strahan was back in the lineup and the Giants grabbed the early lead on a 55-yard touchdown pass from Eli Manning to Plaxico Burress. Little else went right for them the rest of the day. The Saints scored the next thirty points. The Giants looked unorganized, uninspired, and undisciplined. Manning completed his first six passes but went three for nineteen after that. The Giants didn't take a single offensive snap in Saints territory all afternoon. Shaun O'Hara and Bob Whitfield were called for personal fouls on the same offensive series in the third quarter. Whitfield, who was filling in for Luke Petitgout at left tackle, was called for another in the fourth quarter. Barber managed to run for 71 yards but it had no effect on the outcome. The fans chanted for Coughlin to be fired, then headed to the exits early to get home for Christmas Eve. When it was over Barber tossed a cap to a little girl in the stands, blew one final kiss toward the field, and then walked up the tunnel. He was surprised by how little emotion he felt. "You move on," he said a little while after the game. "You do other things and my time is gone."

———

Somehow the Giants were still in the playoff race. They remained tied for the second wild card spot but there was no way for them to feel good about anything. "We're beat up," Barber said. "We're discouraged. We're dejected. It sucked."

The locker room was quiet. Strahan waved off a visitor.

"I've got to go get an X-ray," he said.

He walked out the door into the hallway, where he saw the elderly guard who stood outside the locker room and hugged him.

"Happy holidays," Strahan said.

It would be a happy holiday indeed for the Eagles, who had no trouble with the Cowboys on Christmas night at Texas Stadium and won, 23–7. Jeff Garcia and Terrell Owens hadn't spoken since their days together in San Francisco, and Garcia upstaged his former 49ers nemesis. People who were on the sideline later would say Garcia taunted Owens from there during the game, yelling insults at him when Owens ran in front of the Eagles' bench and pointing out in no uncertain terms who was getting the better of things now.

Tony Romo threw two interceptions as his latest rumored love interest, singer Carrie Underwood of *American Idol* fame, looked on. The Eagles clinched a playoff spot and moved ahead of the Cowboys in the division race because they'd beaten them twice. Owens, who'd visited some of his former Eagles teammates at their hotel on Christmas Eve, was unhappy he hadn't been more involved in the offense early in the game. That was from a guy who'd dropped fourteen passes through fifteen games, a figure that led the league. Jerry Jones was disgusted. He thought the Cowboys' listless performance in a game for first place was an indictment of the entire organization. He was stunned that the defense had played so pitifully. The Cowboys had gotten a gift with the emergence of Romo, Jones thought, but they were in danger of squandering it. He'd wanted the Cowboys to be hitting their stride entering the playoffs. It certainly didn't look like it.

CHAPTER

-27-

December 28 . . . Ashburn, Virginia

The Redskins had their final practice of the season on the Thursday before a Saturday night game against the Giants. Joe Gibbs was going to conduct the wrap-up team meeting Sunday and by Monday, New Year's Day, most of the players would be headed out of town. The Redskins could contain their miserable season to the 2006 calendar year. They'd followed the loss to the Eagles with a surprising win in New Orleans, but then they'd reverted and lost in overtime in St. Louis. Jason Campbell was having enough good moments to leave no doubt that he'd be the starting quarterback going forward. Ladell Betts had five straight 100-yard rushing games. Gibbs had decided to retain both Al Saunders and Gregg Williams.

The locker room at Redskins Park was emptying after practice. Adam Archuleta sat in front of his locker in the corner farthest from the entrance. He was taking off his practice gear and pulling on jeans and a red sweatshirt. He put a white cap backward on his head and left his sneakers untied, then strapped on a backpack. Waves of reporters came by Archuleta's locker, and he made on-the-record comments to them for the first time in weeks. He'd been undecided whether to let his true thoughts out and rip the organization or take the high road and hold back his contemptuous feelings. He tried to hold back but couldn't quite manage it. He said the coaches hadn't spoken to him in the seven weeks since he'd been benched and he just wanted someone to deal with him in a straightforward manner and tell him what was lacking in his play. He said Gibbs had talked to him for ten minutes when he'd been benched and delivered a speech about continuing to bust his butt, and that was it. He said he felt humiliated, his reputation dragged through the mud.

Archuleta left the locker room, went up the stairs and stopped by the front desk just inside the main entrance to mill around for a few minutes. He'd continued to interact amicably with his teammates and he'd thanked them in the huddle during practice that day for their support. As he walked out the door into the parking lot he kidded around with backup linebacker Khary Campbell.

"You looked a lot more explosive last year," Archuleta said. "I wasn't here but you looked a lot more explosive on tape. Maybe it's age."

"Yeah, that must be it," said Campbell, who was all of twenty-seven. "It's age."

Archuleta was planning to get out of town as soon as the season ended. His family would be able to get in touch with him. His girlfriend would and maybe his agent, Gary Wichard, would. But that was about it. Before climbing into his car he stood on a plot of grass for a few minutes and reflected on what he'd been through.

"Regardless of how difficult of a year this has been for me and how on a lot of different levels it's disaster status, I still feel like everything happens for a reason," he said. "There's a reason why I made the decision. There's a reason why this year happened. I don't know why yet. But I can honestly say that with anything that's happened in my life and with the way my life course has gone with different adversity and things that have happened, I was meant to be here and this was supposed to happen this year. Had I known that going into it, would I still have made the same decision? No, probably not. But there's probably a good reason why we don't know the outcome of events before we make decisions."

He'd gotten more and more miserable as his relationship with the coaches had deteriorated and his status on the team had been diminished. But one of the great lessons of the season was that he'd learned, finally, how to leave work at work. "Early on this year I let it consume me," he said. "It affected every aspect of my life and the rest of my life, I let it go down the tubes just like football was going. It affected my personal relationships. It affected the way I felt. It affected everything. I realized you have to have balance. As much and as big of a part of your life as this game is, you can't let it consume you. You can't let it tear you apart. You can't let it be the end all, be all."

He was doing his best not to beat himself up about his decision to sign with the Redskins. He could have stayed in his comfort zone and signed with the Bears and Lovie Smith, but he hadn't. "That's probably why people don't recommend marrying somebody you just met on vacation, you know what I mean?" he said.

The Redskins had gone roughly two for four in their big additions. They'd hit Bill Parcells's 50 percent success rate for player evaluation. Archuleta and Brandon Lloyd had been terrible first-year busts. The play of Andre Carter and Antwaan Randle El hadn't been great but it had gotten better as the season progressed and the Redskins could envision them being solid players in the future. As Randle El sat by his locker that day he said he had no regrets. Yes, he could have been part of a special season by his hometown team if he'd picked the Bears and no, he hadn't always been as big a part of the Redskins' offense as he'd been led to believe he would be. But that had gotten better in recent weeks and Randle El thought it would continue to get better in the future. "I have peace and comfort about where I'm at," he said.

His wife and kids were happy. The family would stay in the Washington area year-round. Randle El and his wife had tried to split time evenly between Pittsburgh and Chicago one year when he was with the Steelers and he hadn't liked it. "Chicago is home," he said, "but this is our home away from home."

Carter was a firm believer in the power of positive thinking, and he'd done his best not to be discouraged even when he wasn't producing in the early stages of the season the way his contract terms said he should be producing. "I played my butt off in the first half of the season," he said. "I ran to the ball. I know it's a stats game, a numbers game. But the defensive system that we play here is a sort of selfless system. I felt like I was at least playing hard and trying to do the things I was asked to do even when the numbers weren't there."

He would ask Williams, "Am I doing what I'm supposed to be doing? Am I doing the things you expected me to do?"

Williams would tell him, "You're getting better, Andre. Just stick with it."

Things did get better. After managing only two sacks in the first eleven games of the season, Carter would get four in the season's final five games. A six-sack season wasn't exactly what Carter or the Redskins had in mind back in March, but the way he finished was enough for everyone to believe that better times were ahead. He still liked Williams and Greg Blache and he'd fit in well with fellow defensive linemen Renaldo Wynn, Cornelius Griffin, and Joe Salave'a. His wife and daughter had made the most of the move from the West Coast. This wouldn't be home forever. He and his wife kept their house in California and would move back there at some point. But for now this was good enough. There would be an offseason vacation in Hawaii to unwind. When he looked back Carter could live with the decision he'd made. "I'm very happy," he said. "I never second-guessed myself. The record didn't come out the way we wanted it to. But it was a fun year for me. The people that I work with and what they represent, I just enjoyed coming to work and being around those guys." It took a positive thinker indeed to feel that way as the season ended at Redskins Park.

December 30 . . . Landover, Maryland

Dan Snyder sat on a burgundy leather couch in the owner's box at FedEx Field about two and a half hours before game time Saturday evening and puffed on a cigar. He'd been sick all week but he was feeling better, and he was eager for his team to try to knock the Giants out of the playoffs. The NFL Network's pregame show was on the flat-screen TVs all around the box as Snyder spoke to Vinny Cerrato, Sonny Jurgensen, and Karl Swanson, Snyder's PR man. A piece on the history of the Redskins ran on the pregame show and grainy black-and-white footage of the team's marching band filled the screen.

"Hey," Snyder yelled, "turn that up!"

Swanson's cell phone rang every few minutes and he provided periodic updates to the others on the traffic situation outside the stadium: The lots were 50 percent full. They were 60 percent full. Snyder thought the stands would be filled even to watch a 5-10 team playing out the string. Those fans who did show up would have to brave a traffic nightmare. Former president Gerald Ford had died that week and his body was being flown into Andrews Air Force Base that evening. A portion of the Beltway was to be closed temporarily.

Snyder asked Jurgensen and Cerrato which coaches they thought were going to be fired league-wide.

"Is Jim Mora going to get fired?" Snyder said. "I think he's pretty good."

Snyder wondered if Gregg Williams would be a head coaching candidate.

"Will he get a job?" Snyder asked.

The consensus was no.

Tom Coughlin had ousted John Hufnagel as the Giants' offensive coordinator on Christmas, the day after the Saints game, and had turned over the play-calling duties to quarterbacks coach Kevin Gilbride. Jurgensen wondered aloud why the Giants had announced their offensive coordinator switch and given the Redskins all week to prepare for what Gilbride would do. Bryant Gumbel had come by the box earlier and now the other guests started to arrive. They would sit in rows of seats facing the field. A pair of binoculars had been placed at each seat. A bar and an elaborate spread of food were in the back of the box.

Michele and Arlette Snyder showed up. Snyder's mother was dressed in all burgundy. "That's a good Redskins outfit," he said to her.

Bernie Shaw came in with a relative and introduced the young man to everyone. Then he asked Snyder, "Is it going to be a full house?"

"Oh yeah," Snyder said, "it will."

George Michael, the longtime sports anchor at the NBC affiliate in Washington, came in with his wife and sat down on a chair next to Snyder. The two were close and Michael immediately launched into a teasing lecture.

"When's the last time you've been in a good mood?" he asked when he was finished. Probably before the season, Snyder said. "I believed what everyone was saying," Snyder said. "Everyone said, 'It's the preseason. It doesn't mean anything,' and I believed it. I'd heard that one time before. Marty said it and the next thing I knew the season started and we were oh-and-five."

Snyder's cell phone rang and he excused himself to take the call. After finishing it he huddled with Dwight Schar and Robert Rothman. Joe Gibbs's face filled the TV screens. He was doing a pregame interview with the NFL Network in the hallway outside the Redskins' locker room. Gibbs detested such obligations that interfered with his preparations and wouldn't have done this interview for any other network. The league wanted its teams to jump through hoops for the NFL Network.

Over in the press box Ernie Accorsi settled into his seat to watch what could be his final game. John Mara had spoken to Accorsi about postponing his retirement again but Accorsi was holding firm. He'd been clearing out his office at Giants Stadium and shipping his belongings to his home in Hershey, Pennsylvania. He'd bought a house in Jupiter, Florida, and would be there for baseball spring training. He was going to rent a car for five weeks the following fall and drive to baseball stadiums, presidential museums, and national parks. He was writing a book. He told people he was NFL'ed out. Accorsi knew many people would judge him by how Eli Manning did, and he was okay with that. He still thought Manning would be great. There already had been occasions when Manning had been great. So how, he wondered, could anyone say Manning couldn't play? If he could play great at times so early in his career then clearly he had, in Accorsi's view, greatness in him.

It just had to be brought out on a consistent basis. Accorsi remained convinced the trade had been the right move.

The Giants already had begun their general manager search by interviewing their in-house candidates. John Mara and Jonathan Tisch, the team's treasurer, had interviewed front-office staffers Jerry Reese, Kevin Abrams, Dave Gettleman, and Chris Mara. They also had interviewed Charley Casserly, the former general manager of the Redskins and Houston Texans. Casserly had moved back to the D.C. area. He'd tried to get a job in the league office but had been passed over in favor of former Atlanta Falcons executive Ray Anderson. He was working on the CBS studio show and making weekly trips to NFL Films to keep up with what was happening in the league. John Mara and Steve Tisch had talked about making a run at Scott Pioli, the Patriots' front-office chief who was from Washingtonville, New York, about sixty miles from New York City. Accorsi wanted Reese, the club's director of player personnel, to succeed him, but that was no given and it clearly was no given that Coughlin would be retained for the remaining season on his four-year, $12 million contract. The Giants didn't want lame duck head coaches so they usually extended the contract of a coach they liked before the deal reached its final season. It would soon be time to fire Coughlin or extend his contract. Mara had always been told by his father not to make a decision about a coach during the heat of a season, but he'd also been told always to have a list of potential replacements handy, just in case. Mara thought the players respected Coughlin even if they didn't all like him. He didn't want to fire him. But if the season unraveled completely, he wouldn't have much choice.

Mara stopped by the press box before the game but didn't watch it from there with the front office contingent. Accorsi had Chris Mara seated to his left and Abrams, Reese, Gettleman, and Ken Sternfeld to his right. Accorsi, the onetime sportswriter, shook hands with George Solomon, the former sports editor of *The Washington Post,* and said, "George, how ya doing? I'm going to have a retirement like yours and write a column once a week."

Gibbs had Brandon Lloyd, who had bronchitis, on the inactive list.

Coughlin benched Bob Whitfield and put David Diehl at left tackle and Grey Ruegamer in Diehl's place at left guard. Michael Strahan had been placed on the injured reserve list after reinjuring his foot against the Saints and Jeremy Shockey sat out because of a sore ankle. The Giants would all but clinch a playoff spot with a win, and Snyder was right: The stands were mostly full. There were only a few patches of empty seats in the upper deck.

The Giants converted a Ladell Betts fumble into a field goal, but the Redskins came back and got a touchdown on a gadget pass from Antwaan Randle El to Santana Moss. Sam Madison should have knocked down the underthrown ball but didn't. The Giants officials seated along the second row of the press box cringed. They couldn't believe Madison had misplayed the throw so badly.

On the Redskins' sideline Randle El slapped Moss's hand and said, "Atta-way to bail me out, baby!"

Tiki Barber had touchdown runs of 15 and 55 yards. Jason Campbell was knocked from the game briefly on a jarring hit by Brandon Short and Mark Brunell was booed as he jogged toward the huddle. The Giants had a touchdown pass from Manning to Plaxico Burress negated by a double pass interference call on Burress and Redskins cornerback Ade Jimoh. Burress got mugged in the end zone on an incompletion on the next play with no call.

"Oh, come on!" Accorsi huffed as he slammed his fist on the counter in the press box. "Jesus Christ!"

The words were barely out of his mouth when Jimoh was called for taunting. The 15-yard penalty gave Jay Feely a 31-yard field goal try instead of a 46-yarder and he connected two seconds before halftime for a 20–7 lead. Manning threw a touchdown pass to Tim Carter early in the third quarter. The Redskins got a pair of touchdowns to creep back to within 27–21, but Barber made Troy Vincent miss a tackle and sprinted to a 50-yard touchdown with just over six minutes to play. Even then, the Giants didn't make it easy on themselves. The Redskins got a touchdown and got the ball back at their 22-yard line with 2:18 left, trailing by six points. Now they had their chance to knock the Giants out of the playoffs. Accorsi, Chris Mara, Abrams, Reese, Gettleman, and Sternfeld looked ashen. But Campbell threw four straight incompletions and the Giants could breathe easier. Brandon Jacobs carried the ball the next three plays and Accorsi wondered what the coaches were doing. He turned to his right, toward Abrams and Reese.

"How could they not have Tiki in the game?" Accorsi said. "This kid could fumble."

But he didn't, and Manning soon was taking kneel-downs to run out the clock. Accorsi and his cohorts stood and put on their coats to head downstairs. They were grim-faced. The Giants had made the playoffs but they hadn't looked good doing it. Manning had thrown for only 101 yards. Redskins defensive players had spent the game screaming at one another on the sideline, "All we gotta do is stop the run! That's it!"

It had taken just about every one of Barber's team-record 234 rushing yards for the Giants to eke out the victory, but that didn't stop Coughlin from gloating when he stood on a riser in an interview room across the hall from the locker room to address reporters a little while later. He talked of being proud of how his team had played. He said he'd been asked all week how his players would respond.

"There's your answer," he said. "I'm gonna shut up before I say something."

He began to get agitated when he was asked if he felt the Giants had been playing for his job. His mood worsened when he was asked about his defense yielding twenty-one points in the final eighteen minutes of a game against a five-win team with a rookie quarterback.

"Is that supposed to be a negative?" he said disgustedly. "We won a game and we got in the playoffs. Is that good enough? That's a nice question."

Moments later Coughlin shook his head and walked out of the room. The mood was lighter in the locker room. The Giants weren't celebrating but they were happy and relieved. John Mara walked around and shook hands. Antonio Pierce said, "Our chances are about as good as anybody's right now."

Barber was sore. His body had been beaten up all season by

Coughlin's too-strenuous practices as well as by his workload during games. He'd been playing for weeks with a broken right thumb; he'd been able to keep playing because, to his doctors' surprise, there had been no ligament damage or displacement of the bones and surgery hadn't been required. But he was happy to be playing football for at least another week even as his future TV career was coming together. He was discussing a four-year, $10 million contract with Disney to work for both ABC News and ESPN. He would do work for both *Good Morning America* and *20/20* on ABC. The deal wasn't done because NBC was still in hot pursuit as well, with a possible role on the *Today* show being dangled.

Down the hall Snyder stood with Schar, Rothman, and Cerrato in the middle of the Redskins' locker room. They'd discarded their jackets but still had ties on with their crisp white shirts. Defensive tackle Joe Salave'a walked by.

"We're gonna get better," Salave'a told the group.

Snyder was bitterly disappointed about the season, but acceptance had finally set in. It had taken practically until the final day of the season. Now it was time to gear up again for the offseason.

"I pray to God we keep the same nucleus," Carter said as he stood in front of his locker, wearing only a towel after stepping out of the shower. "We're close. We really are. I still believe in us. But the decision will be made way above me."

Across the room Adam Archuleta stood by his locker and pulled on a bright green button-up shirt, jeans, and a white sports jacket. He put a cap backward atop his head and chatted with rookie safety Reed Doughty. Archuleta had gotten into a game on defense for the first time in eight weeks.

Gibbs walked through the locker room looking for Brunell. They spoke briefly.

"Are you going to be in tomorrow?" Brunell said.

"Yeah," Gibbs said, "I want to talk to you."

Gibbs summed up the entire season before leaving the locker room.

"I got the slop beat out of me," he said.

The 5-11 record was his worst as an NFL coach. He was 22-28 since coming back. Gibbs headed toward the door that led from the locker room to the coaches' dressing area. Archuleta walked past pulling a black roller bag toward the exit. The two didn't make eye contact. Within minutes Gibbs changed into a dark suit and left. Randle El followed moments later wearing a bright red sweatsuit. All the coaches and players were gone. The clock on the wall read 11:59 and 30 seconds.

There was no need for anyone to stay in the locker room another half minute. The clock had struck midnight on this team long ago.

December 31 . . . Philadelphia

Andy Reid sat in the locker room at Lincoln Financial Field watching the Cowboys-Lions game on TV right up until the moment the Eagles had to take the field to play the Falcons. The Eagles would clinch the division title if the Cowboys lost. When the day started there hadn't seemed to be much chance of that happening, given that the Lions were 2-13 and would have the top pick in the draft if they lost. But the Lions jumped ahead early and kept going back in front. Reid watched the camera shots of Bill Parcells burying his head in his hands and Jerry Jones frowning on the sideline.

Reid and Tom Heckert had spoken during the week and had decided to sit down as many starters as possible the moment the Eagles clinched the division, *if* they clinched the division, to ensure that they'd be healthy for the playoffs. The week had also produced another contract extension for a young starter. Todd Herremans had agreed to a five-year extension Friday and signed the deal Saturday. He'd been starting at left guard as a second-year pro and received a $5 million signing bonus as part of the approximately $15 million extension. He'd signed a four-year deal worth about $1.88 million, including a $403,000 signing bonus, as a rookie fourth-round draft pick out of Division II Saginaw Valley State. So overall he had a contract that was, in effect, a nine-year deal worth about $17 million, and now he was signed through the 2013 season.

None of that mattered to Reid at the moment. The Cowboys game was going down to the wire and Reid obviously couldn't afford to enact the plan to rest starters at the outset of this game if first place remained up for grabs. Winning the division meant playing a first-round playoff game at home against the Giants instead of, as a wild card, traveling across the country to Seattle to play the defending NFC champions. Reid took the field for the game and put an administrative assistant, James Urban, in charge of keeping him updated on the Cowboys.

He needn't have bothered; many of the Eagles fans at the stadium were keeping close tabs themselves. After forcing a Falcons punt on the opening possession, the Eagles drove into Atlanta territory and were lining up for a field goal about three and a half minutes into the game when fans in the stands began cheering and raising their arms in celebration. Tony Romo had been tackled short of the goal line on the Cowboys' last-gasp effort to tie their game. For the fifth time in six years, the Eagles were the NFC East champions. The cheering in the stadium grew louder a few minutes later when the stunning final score was posted on the four scoreboards on the corners of the upper deck: Lions 39, Cowboys 31. Reid put the plan into effect. Jeff Garcia and Brian Westbrook were out of the game. So were William Thomas and Jon Runyan. On defense Jeremiah Trotter, Brian Dawkins, Lito Sheppard, and Sheldon Brown were among those who got the rest of the day off. And still the Eagles won. A. J. Feeley took over at quarterback and threw for 321 yards and three touchdowns. Reid's wife Tammy watched the final seconds anxiously on a tiny TV set just outside the Eagles' locker room. The Falcons trailed, 24–17, but had the ball.

"I'm not worried," Tammy Reid said to the small crowd of people standing around her. "We're going to win this one."

The Falcons completed a pass to the Eagles' 15-yard line but didn't have any timeouts and the clock ran out.

"Yeeeaaah!" she screamed and ran off.

Game over. Regular season over. For Jim Mora, Falcons coaching career over; he would be fired by Arthur Blank the next day. The Eagles had won their final five games of the regular season after being 5-6 and left for dead in Indianapolis. It was their longest season-ending winning streak since 1949, but they kept the celebration to a minimum. They were playing better than anyone else in the NFC at the moment and they thought they could ride this wave all the way to the Super Bowl. In his corner of the locker room Shawn Andrews was wearing a division champs T-shirt, size quadruple-X. "To say I thought a month ago I'd be wearing this big curtain," he said, "I would be lying to you."

Around 8 p.m., about forty minutes after the game ended, Reid walked through the locker room. He shook Garcia's hand and watched Mike Patterson folding up a division champs T-shirt, then exited. Sheppard followed a moment later. Butch Buchanico, a former security chief for then-mayor Ed Rendell who'd been hired by Jeff Lurie in 1996 as the Eagles' director of security, watched Sheppard walking out.

"Keep it under ninety, Lito," Buchanico called out. "Please, Lito, keep it under a hundred."

Sheppard smiled, nodded, and left. Buchanico turned to the guys standing around him and said, "He passed me going to the hotel last night."

Joe Banner walked by. Donté Stallworth stuck around, soaking it all in. Lurie was nowhere in sight, but the owner was on Stallworth's mind. "It all starts with Mr. Lurie," Stallworth said. "He's a great guy. It all starts with him and trickles down. Andy is the kind of guy who keeps everyone on an even keel. He didn't go crazy when we were five-and-six. He didn't just blame the players like some coaches would do. He said everyone needed to pick it up. Guys respect that when you put yourself in there."

The NFC East had three teams in the playoffs. Even with their two-game losing streak the Cowboys finished 9-7 and would face the Seahawks the following Saturday night. The Giants had indeed gotten in at 8-8 and would be at the Linc in a week to play the Eagles. "It's real fun right now," Stallworth said. "My 'Midnight Rule' is in effect. Shoot, it's New Year's. I'll extend it. About two A.M., I'll be thinking about the Giants."

The playoffs had arrived and the stakes were being raised.

JANUARY

CHAPTER

-28-

January 2, 2007 ... Philadelphia

Koy Detmer got into town and went straight to the NovaCare Complex. He headed directly to the field and immediately started working with kicker David Akers and long snapper Jon Dorenbos. There was no time to waste.

It was two days after the Falcons game and Andy Reid had re-signed Detmer, the Eagles' former backup quarterback who had been the holder for Akers. That duty had been passed on to punter Dirk Johnson when Detmer was cut before the season, but Johnson had made a bad hold during the Falcons game and Akers had missed a 23-yard field goal try, sending the ball off the right upright. It was Akers's first miss inside 30 yards in his NFL career and it had worried Reid. Detmer had been out of the league all season. He'd been back in Texas, living in San Antonio and working with his brother Ty for a real estate investment firm in Austin.

Reid was leaving nothing to chance.

Half a country away at Valley Ranch, Bill Parcells had pulled Tony

Romo aside for a chat on the day after the Cowboys' miserable loss to the Lions. Suddenly Romo wasn't everyone's golden boy anymore.

"Did I tell you this was going to happen or not?" Parcells said to his quarterback.

"Yeah," Romo said.

"Well," Parcells said, "here's where we are. Let's try to analyze why we are where we are and let's try to see where we can go."

Parcells didn't want to discourage Romo's creativity. It had produced more good than bad. But Parcells thought Romo suffered from overconfidence. Romo believed he could make the next-to-impossible play and that led to unnecessary risks, which led to mistakes.

"You have to be aware in doing that sometimes you can do more damage than good," Parcells told Romo.

Romo seemed to get what Parcells was saying. He vowed to make cutting down on his turnovers his top focus for the playoffs. He also maintained his easygoing manner. As reporters crowded around him in the locker room that week, Romo said with a perfect deadpan delivery, "I don't know if you guys know but I played in a big game against Montana my sophomore year in college. So it really helped me prepare for a moment like this."

He was asked how that had turned out.

"We lost," he said.

The loss to the Lions had been one of Parcells's lowest moments in coaching, but he'd pumped himself back up. He had no choice. The playoffs were at hand. Jerry Jones also was trying to be optimistic. He looked for the bright spots, like the Cowboys' being a healthy team entering the playoffs. But he was worried about how they were playing. He was concerned that the team's record under Parcells in December and January games had slipped to 8-12. Were other clubs figuring out what the Cowboys were doing as seasons progressed? He thought the poor play of the defense in recent weeks was inexplicable. The mixed bag the Cowboys had been getting lately from Romo, one great play followed by a terrible one, was exactly what he'd feared when the quarterback switch had first been made.

Jones and Parcells had agreed that Parcells would tell Jones by February 1, or by five days after the Super Bowl if the Cowboys played in the game, if he would return to coach the 2007 season. Parcells made everyone in the building tense. He showed up for work at 4 a.m. and looked down on the deadbeats who didn't get to the office until 5. Being around him usually wasn't much fun. He never attended Jones's annual staff dinners on the Saturday night of the scouting combine at St. Elmo steakhouse in Indianapolis. But he and Jones had managed to work together and the job was Parcells's if he wanted to keep it, if he could summon enough energy for another offseason routine of combine, free agency, draft, and minicamps followed by another training camp and another season. At sixty-five, Parcells had managed to keep his energy level pretty high this go-around. He felt healthy after sticking to his pledge to give up candy and cookies during the season, which wasn't easy for him since he could devour an entire sleeve of Fig Newtons in about ten minutes when he wanted. That was his number two culinary vice, behind the peanut butter he would eat out of the jar. No, the problems for Parcells as the playoffs began involved mental, not physical, anguish. The defense he'd tried so hard to fix since he'd been in Dallas, pouring draft picks and Jones's money in free agency into the project, wasn't fixed. The new quarterback remained a work in progress, and Jones was as enamored as ever with having Terrell Owens around. Jones thought the Cowboys had made mistakes and had wasted money in free agency the previous spring, particularly with the Mike Vanderjagt and Jason Fabini signings. But he didn't put the Owens signing into that category, not yet anyway.

January 7 . . . Philadelphia

Traffic was backed up for a mile on I-95 at the Broad Street exit a good three and a half hours before the Eagles-Giants game. There was no messing around on this day. It was the playoffs.

John Mara stood in the press box at Lincoln Financial Field an hour before game time, looking fidgety but not overly nervous. He'd traded good-luck wishes with Woody Johnson two days before, but now the Jets were in the process of losing to the New England Patriots. The Giants had a chance to be not only the last NFC East team standing but also the last New York team standing.

Either the Giants or the Eagles would have their season ended, but it was doubtful it could happen in a fashion as gut-wrenching as what the Cowboys had experienced the night before in Seattle. Tony Romo had settled down, fumbling once but not throwing an interception. He threw a touchdown pass to wide receiver Patrick Crayton just before halftime to give the Cowboys a 10–6 lead. After he held the ball too long in the pocket on a third-quarter sack, Bill Parcells griped at him on the sideline: "Throw the fucking ball away!"

The Cowboys got a touchdown on a kickoff return by rookie Miles Austin, and Martin Gramatica's field goal early in the fourth quarter upped their lead to 20–13. They made a goal line stand but surrendered a safety when Terry Glenn caught a pass but fumbled into the end zone. Roy Williams was beaten for a touchdown by Seahawks tight end Jerramy Stevens for the second time in the game. The Seahawks missed a two-point conversion and led, 21–20. When Romo and tailback Julius Jones maneuvered the Cowboys inside the Seattle 10-yard line with less than two minutes to play it seemed certain they'd take the lead. The question was whether the defense would be able to hold it. Romo completed a third-and-7 pass to Jason Witten and the Cowboys were awarded a first down at the Seahawks 1-yard line. But the ball was moved back half a yard on an instant replay review. It was fourth down and Parcells waved in Gramatica with 1:19 to play. It was a 19-yard field goal, shorter than an extra point. Gramatica was 204 for 206 on extra points in his NFL career; the Cowboys had a 99 percent chance of taking the lead. Romo, the holder, fielded a perfect snap.

But as he put the ball on the ground, Romo dropped it. Gramatica never even got to attempt the kick. Romo picked up the ball and ran to his left toward the goal line but was tackled by the Seahawks' Jordan Babineaux at the 2. Romo trudged off the field to the sideline with his head down and blood trickling from a cut on his left hand. The Cowboys got the ball back for one final Hail Mary heave into the end zone but it fell incomplete. The Cowboys were 34-32 under Parcells, and 0-2 in the playoffs. They'd lost their final three games to finish 9-8 this season. They'd brought in Mike Vanderjagt to avoid losing games because of kicking issues, yet they'd suffered two of the most galling defeats imaginable, first to the Redskins in the regular season and now to the Seahawks in the playoffs, because of field-goal mishaps. The offensive line had held up and Terrell Owens hadn't torn the team apart. He'd dropped passes and he'd created headaches, yes, but he wasn't the reason the Cowboys weren't still playing. Romo was. He was in tears after the game. He sat in front of his locker and stared at the floor. He blamed himself for the loss. Owens came over to console him. Romo felt bad for himself, and he felt worse for Parcells.

"You guys are a great bunch of guys," Parcells told his players in the locker room afterward. "I wish you guys great success. You'll do well no matter what I do, whether I come back or not."

Jerry Jones had an empty feeling, but he'd felt worse about other postseason losses before.

Now it was time to find out if it would be Mara or Jeff Lurie who would be feeling that emptiness on this day.

The Giants scored on their opening possession on a touchdown pass from Eli Manning to Plaxico Burress. The Eagles punted on their first three possessions. But with Donovan McNabb standing on the sideline watching, Brian Westbrook got things righted with a 49-yard touchdown run in the opening minute of the second quarter. The Eagles had been more committed to the running game after McNabb had gotten hurt and it was paying dividends now.

Manning forced a pass toward Burress into heavy traffic and had it intercepted by Sheldon Brown, prompting a sideline lecture by Kevin Gilbride. That led to a short field goal by David Akers. But Tiki Barber had a 41-yard run to set up a Jay Feely field goal that got the Giants even. Jeff Garcia threw a touchdown pass to Donté Stallworth to put the Eagles ahead at the half, and they made it 20–10 late in the third quarter on a 48-yard field goal by Akers on which Koy Detmer fielded a high

snap smoothly. Score another one for Andy Reid; he'd brought back the
anti-Romo. Rain started falling late in the third quarter. The Giants
drove inside the Eagles' 10-yard line but Manning threw a third-down
incompletion on the opening play of the fourth quarter. Feely hit a short
field goal and the Giants tied the game with 5:04 left on another
Manning-to-Burress touchdown. Tom Coughlin thought the game was
headed to overtime, and the Eagles had lost Lito Sheppard because of a
dislocated elbow. Westbrook was in severe discomfort because of a stomach virus and Marty Mornhinweg wasn't sure if the running back would
be on the field for the Eagles' next drive. But Westbrook got some medication from the trainers and indeed was out there. He carried the load
as the Eagles moved methodically from their 34-yard line to the Giants'
20. Reid called a timeout with three seconds to go. Akers and Detmer
trotted onto the field for a 38-yard field goal.

Akers had fallen asleep the previous night before seeing the Romo
misplay. He'd seen the replay that morning and he'd felt bad for Romo.
He knew everyone took the snap and hold for granted on a field goal but
there were things that could go wrong. On the Eagles' sideline everyone was thinking about the Romo play. The rain had subsided but the
field was wet. The footing was unsure. The ball would be slippery.

The snap by Jon Dorenbos was perfect.

The hold was perfect.

The kick was perfect.

It was over: Eagles 23, Giants 20.

A celebration erupted on the field, but Jeremiah Trotter and Brian
Dawkins made certain to find Barber amid the chaos. Barber suddenly
was a former NFL player.

"You're a warrior," Dawkins told him.

Barber appreciated that. Trotter and Dawkins had been among his
fiercest rivals, but he respected them and they respected him. He'd gone
out in style, running for 137 yards. But Westbrook had been even better, rushing for 141 yards and providing a big play every time the Eagles
needed one. He reminded Barber of, well, a young Tiki Barber. Those
offseason workout tips must have helped.

As the players left the field Lurie made his way down a stairwell toward the locker room accompanied by a police officer. Mara followed about thirty seconds behind, also with a police escort. They were walking down the same hallway but headed in far different directions. Lurie and the Eagles would be going to New Orleans in six days for an NFC semifinal. Mara and the Giants were headed into the great unknown. Mara had to decide about his coach and find a general manager. He and Steve Tisch had resolved to go after Scott Pioli. The next day the Giants would ask the Patriots for permission to interview Pioli. The Patriots would approve the request but Pioli surprisingly would decline to be interviewed. Mara and Tisch were left considering Charley Casserly and the internal candidates. Coughlin had demonstrated again that he was a middle-of-the-road coach who made flawed in-game decisions, like the long field goal try gone bad against the Bears and the outside running play on fourth down against the Cowboys. He had only one gear when it came to dealing with players. The very good to great coaches, the ones who won Super Bowls, knew when to coddle as well as when to crack down. Coughlin didn't.

Mara's team had begun the season as the defending division champ with a budding star at quarterback. Now it was an 8-9 club that had been lucky just to make the playoffs. Whether Manning would ever be the quarterback the Giants had thought they were getting when they traded for him was anyone's guess, no matter what Ernie Accorsi thought. LaVar Arrington was rehabbing. Mathias Kiwanuka had mixed great plays with terrible ones as a rookie, and Sinorice Moss had contributed next to nothing. The Giants would have to replace Barber. At least they would be able to keep the rest of their team together. Shaun O'Hara was the only significant player eligible for free agency in March.

Coughlin told his players in the locker room that he was proud of them and how they'd hung together. But he also said the Giants hadn't come here to lose and that's what they'd done. Accorsi made his way around the locker room talking to a few players. He, too, was effectively in retirement now, although his wouldn't become official for another week. He saw Ronde Barber, on hand for his brother's final game, and went over to say hello, then exited the locker room. Ronde stayed behind. He was wearing jeans over boots and a brown shirt covered by a brown leather jacket. Nearby, Tiki was putting on his suit and tying his tie. Ronde put one foot up on a stool, rested his elbow on his knee, and said, "Every phase in life has an ending. This is just another one and then he'll have a new beginning. You turn the page. He's making the decision he has to make."

When his appearance was impeccable, with a handkerchief tucked neatly into a front pocket, Tiki made his way out of the locker room to the Temple University locker room across the hall, which was being used on this night as the Giants' interview room. He stopped to talk to Clinton Portis, who was conducting interviews for the NFL Network with one arm in a sling. Barber finished his interview with Portis and made his way to the podium. He'd made his peace some time ago with the idea that his legacy as a player probably wouldn't include a Super Bowl win and this season very likely would end in unsatisfying fashion. He wasn't bitter at how he was going out. He wanted to exit with dignity. He did. "I'm proud of what our team did," he said. The Eagles, not the Giants, were the last NFC East team standing.

January 10 . . . Philadelphia

Jeremy Bloom sat at his locker and checked the messages on his cell phone. It was a Wednesday, three days after the Eagles' triumph over the Giants. The TVs in the Eagles' locker room were tuned to ESPNews, and the ticker across the bottom of the screen flashed the update that the Giants had decided to retain Tom Coughlin as their coach and had given him a one-year contract extension through the 2008 season. Members of the Mara and Tisch families had spoken to players clearing out their lockers at Giants Stadium and had found more-than-expected support for retaining Coughlin. A contract extension of only one year was pretty tepid; Coughlin would have to do far better in the 2007 season. But by keeping his coach and promoting patience and stability, John Mara was doing what his father surely would have done.

Bloom's teammates were readying to play at New Orleans in a second-round playoff game Saturday night. Bloom was part of things, in a way. He'd spent the entire season around the team, attending every meeting. But in a way, he wasn't part of anything. He'd spent his rookie season on the injured reserve list because of the torn hamstring muscle he'd suffered in the summer. He couldn't practice or play in games. He hadn't undergone surgery but his hamstring had taken awhile to heal. "It was just too quick of a turnaround," Bloom said. "I didn't think it was going to be that difficult. But now I feel great. I'm ready. As soon as the season is over then I'll be focusing on next year."

He'd spent the season immersing himself in the NFL and soaking up all the knowledge he could. He'd used the Eagles' computers and video equipment to study diminutive receivers like the Redskins' Santana Moss and the Carolina Panthers' Steve Smith. He'd watched the New York Jets' explosive kick returner, Justin Miller. He'd gotten himself into football shape and worked on his route-running. He'd avoided feeling sorry for himself.

The Eagles' playoff run had been made without much help from their rookie class. They'd made linebacker Omar Gaither, a fifth-round draft pick out of Tennessee, a starter in December. But Brodrick Bunkley wasn't playing. Winston Justice hadn't gotten into a single game all season. Chris Gocong and Bloom were on IR. The Eagles were getting little immediate production out of this draft class, but they were getting plenty of help from their 2005 draft class: Mike Patterson, Reggie Brown, Sean Considine, Todd Herremans, and Trent Cole were starters. Tom Heckert figured you shouldn't even begin to judge a draft class until the players were in their third season. He wasn't ready to accept criticism yet for the decisions the Eagles had made regarding this set of rookies.

"People in this city are already saying our draft class isn't any good," Heckert said. "Well, shit, these guys haven't played. Our draft class is bad because Winston Justice hasn't played? Our tackles have played well. We haven't had the need. He'll get his chance sometime and we'll find out. People are saying Brodrick Bunkley is a bust but he hasn't really played either. These guys just haven't played a lot. Would you like to have some more production right away? Yeah. Sure you would. But when you don't need young players to play that's usually a good thing. That usually means you're playing pretty well."

Jeff Lurie was proud of his team but he couldn't necessarily rank this division title ahead of the others, nor did he think Andy Reid had done his best coaching job. Lurie still thought that had come in the 2003 season when Reid had taken an injury-plagued team to the NFC title game before losing to the Panthers. "It was hard to outdo that," Lurie said, sitting behind his desk in his spacious office after the Eagles' afternoon practice. "That was amazing. And this has been amazing because he's held everybody together."

A few offices away, Joe Banner had just watched a tape of the Saints-Redskins game from December. The Eagles could only hope the Saints would be as flat as they'd been in that game, but they weren't counting on it. Because the Saints were the second seed in the NFC and had a first-round playoff bye, Sean Payton had two weeks to get ready for the Eagles. Payton had worked for the Eagles as a quarterbacks coach under Ray Rhodes before he'd worked for the Giants, Cowboys, and Saints. Banner figured Payton would have some interesting things ready to go. But no matter what happened, Banner felt vindicated for believing after the Indianapolis game that the Eagles would be okay.

There was no room to be downcast if you were a member of the Philadelphia Eagles. Jeremy Bloom, standing in front of his locker before practice, was very happy indeed not to be on a slope somewhere skiing.

January 13 . . . New Orleans

It was a day-long street party in New Orleans. The temperature hovered near 70 degrees and by noon people were already sitting on lawn chairs across the street from the Superdome sipping beers. Kickoff wasn't until 7 p.m., but by 4, Poydras Street was jam-packed with revelers adorned with Saints jerseys and Mardi Gras beads. There were black

Saints jerseys and gold Saints jerseys, Reggie Bush jerseys and Drew Brees jerseys. A few people sported T-shirts saying: GOT BUSH? The Steve Miller Band was setting up for a concert.

Saints owner Tom Benson was driven to Gate A of the dome. He stood on the passenger seat of his car and poked his head out the sunroof, then raised his arms and pumped his fists. Fans cheered wildly. Roger Goodell passed through the press box before the game and ducked into an elevator right before kickoff.

The Eagles' offense started slowly for a second week in a row. Brian Westbrook wasn't finding anywhere to run and was dropping passes from Jeff Garcia. The Eagles punted to end their first three possessions. Sheldon Brown leveled Bush on the Saints' second play, knocking the rookie tailback off his feet and leaving him gasping for air with a jarring hit on an incomplete pass. The Saints were moving the ball, but they were getting field goals instead of touchdowns and led only 6–0 early in the second quarter when Garcia lofted a pass to Donté Stallworth for a 75-yard touchdown. Bush and Westbrook traded short touchdown runs and the Eagles were up 14–13 at halftime. But they had a problem. Shawn Andrews had hurt his neck in the second quarter. It was swollen and he was having trouble with his vision at halftime so he was taken to a nearby hospital for tests and observation. He would be fine but for now Scott Young would have to fill in. Westbrook broke free for a 62-yard touchdown sprint a minute and a half into the third quarter, but the Saints came back with two touchdowns by tailback Deuce McAllister, one on a run and one on a catch. David Akers kicked a field goal early in the fourth quarter to get the Eagles to 27–24.

They got a big break with 3:18 to play when Bush lost a pitchout from Brees and Darren Howard recovered the fumble. The Eagles had the ball at their 44-yard line. Stallworth and Howard, the two former Saints, could be among the heroes.

It wasn't to be. Two passes and a failed run left Garcia facing fourth-and-10. He took the snap and zipped a throw to wide receiver Hank Baskett for a completion and a first down that would have gotten the Eagles into striking distance for a tying field goal or winning touchdown. But some of the Saints players had stopped before the play was over. The officials had blown their whistles and a yellow penalty flag was on the field. Young had been called for a false start. The Eagles couldn't believe it: Surely he hadn't even flinched? The completion was negated and the Eagles were moved back five yards. It was fourth-and-15 from the 39 with 1:56 to go. Andy Reid had been willing to go for a fourth-and-10, but he wasn't willing to go for a fourth-and-15. He had two timeouts left and thought the odds were better for his defense to hold the Saints without a first down and get the ball back. It proved the wrong decision: McAllister was running the ball effectively and the Eagles defenders were weary. The Saints got the ball at their 22 with 1:48 remaining. Two handoffs to McAllister left them facing a third-and-one play at their 31 with 1:37 left. The Saints called a timeout, then handed the ball to McAllister for a five-yard gain. First down and game over. Two kneel-downs by Brees made it official. The Eagles were done. The NFC East was done. Three teams had made the playoffs but they'd managed only one triumph among them. The fans roared and the party that began in the stands at the Superdome spilled over onto Bourbon Street. It would still be going strong past four in the morning.

Music blared from inside the dome as Eagles PR chief Derek Boyko led Reid down a corridor beneath the stands toward the interview room where he'd meet the media. Security chief Butch Buchanico trailed a few steps behind. Reid reached the podium and praised his team's effort and grit but lamented the penalties and other missteps. He was asked about his decision to punt at the end of the game and said he guessed with hindsight he should have left his offense on the field, but he'd thought the defense would come through. When he was done Reid followed Boyko back toward the locker room, Buchanico again in tow. The corridor was filled with fans and Reid had to weave his way around them. One guy in a Saints shirt called out, "Hey, there's Andy Reid!"

Reid kept going without acknowledging him. The group walked past a giant blue curtain and opened the door to the locker room. Reid walked to his office and closed the door behind him. Buchanico stood outside like a sentry.

Donovan McNabb had kept a low profile, but he'd been back at the NovaCare Complex beginning the rehabilitation of his knee. Famed orthopedist James Andrews had told McNabb after performing the quarterback's surgery that the rehab would take eight to twelve months. McNabb would be close to thirty-one by the time he played in another NFL game. He had seven seasons remaining on his twelve-year, $115 million contract, which ran through the 2013 season, with salaries totaling $73.42 million. Reid still regarded McNabb as the team's starting quarterback going forward. Garcia was eligible for free agency in March, and he knew there would be offers from other teams if he hit the market. He'd told his agent, Steve Baker, to sit tight and wait until after the season to worry about a contract.

Now Garcia waited for his turn to speak to the media. He sat and listened to Jeremiah Trotter get asked about the offseason that had suddenly arrived and the roster turnover it undoubtedly would bring.

"Players come and players go," Trotter said. "You deal with the offseason as it comes. When you see which players you have, you go to war."

A few minutes later the Eagles would head out of the Superdome. They were on their way to another bus ride, another plane trip, another season. For the players who didn't have to deal with contract issues or find new teams, there would be a little bit of downtime after the wrap-up meeting and exit interviews and before the onset of the conditioning program, minicamps, and training camp. But for Jeff Lurie, Joe Banner, Andy Reid, Tom Heckert, and the others charged with assembling a team capable of finally getting the Eagles over the last remaining humps, there was no such thing as an offseason. There was a playing season and a paying season, but no "off" season. There would be a few hours to lament this defeat, but pretty soon it would be time for a trip to Mobile, Alabama. There was work to be done.

EPILOGUE

March 27, 2007 . . . Phoenix, Arizona

Dan Snyder and Vinny Cerrato sat in comfortable chairs on the patio behind the main building of the plush Arizona Biltmore resort on a Tuesday afternoon, the second day of the annual three-day league meeting. The sun was shining brightly; water poured from a fountain on the adjacent grass courtyard. A man worked on his putting on the practice green tucked among the resort's outer buildings. Mountains could be seen in the distance. The NFL, as usual, was sparing no expense. There had been a poolside reception the previous night, featuring a performance by synchronized swimmers. What party was complete without synchronized swimmers?

Snyder leaned back in his chair, looked skyward, and adjusted his sunglasses. He and Cerrato had just had lunch with Charley Casserly, and the three were trying to project the first five picks in the upcoming NFL draft. The Redskins had the sixth choice but were trying to trade it to the Chicago Bears for linebacker Lance Briggs and the thirty-first selection. Drew Rosenhaus represented Briggs and had paraded him through the hotel lobby the night before, trying to drum up interest. They found Snyder. Briggs was unhappily stuck with the Bears' franchise player tag and wanted to be traded so he could land the sort of handsome long-term contract he wasn't getting in Chicago.

The Redskins were waiting to hear back from the Bears, and Snyder and Cerrato were trying to pass the time without being too bored. Stephen Jones walked by. The league had just determined that the Cowboys would host the Giants in the first Sunday night game of the 2007 season.

"Stephen," Cerrato called out, "so you guys open with the Giants?"

"Yeah," Jones answered. "The Sunday night game. You gonna be rootin' for us?"

"Nah," Cerrato said. "We'll root for a tie and everyone to get hurt."

"That's just not necessary," Jones said with a grin.

Mike Shanahan, the coach of the Denver Broncos, was at the next table, waiting for his wife to join him for lunch.

"Hey, Mike," Snyder said, looking over his shoulder, "you want our draft pick?"

"What," Shanahan asked, "are you guys giving it away?"

Shanahan told Cerrato that he liked Jason Fabini, who'd just been signed by the Redskins after being released by the Cowboys. Mike Tirico, the ESPN broadcaster, walked by on his way to the nearby sandwich shop with the $11 tuna melt, and Snyder talked to him about the network's decision to dump Joe Theismann from its Monday night booth in favor of Ron Jaworski. Tirico left, and Baltimore Ravens owner Steve Bisciotti came over and sat down on the ledge next to Snyder. The two spoke in hushed tones until Zygi Wilf walked by.

"Hey, Zygi, how much are you getting?" Snyder called out to the Minnesota Vikings owner. "That revenue stealing is killing us. How much are you getting? We heard $30 million."

The owners had just approved a qualifier proposal, the final piece of revenue-sharing that determined how franchises would qualify for funds. Only the Cincinnati Bengals and Jacksonville Jaguars had voted against the compromise; even Ralph Wilson (Mr. "30 to 2" himself) and the

Buffalo Bills had voted in favor. But it came with a catch for the low-revenue clubs: The amount of money to be transferred was capped at $110 million per year. The owners made the deal stretch only through the 2009 season because the labor deal could be reopened by then.

"No way," Wilf said, stopping to chat with Snyder and Bisciotti. "Not that much. If I was getting thirty, I'd break even."

Wilf looked at Snyder, the league's presumed revenue-generating king.

"What are you worried about?" he said. "Aren't you first?"

"No, I'm third," Snyder said. "New England is first."

Wilf told Snyder and Bisciotti that he had cut the prices of some of the Vikings' tickets. That drew derision from the other two owners.

"Have you ever heard of anything like that?" Snyder asked.

"No way," Bisciotti said. "It's crazy."

Cerrato pulled out his phone and briefed another member of the Redskins' front office on the Briggs discussions.

"We talked to him last night," Cerrato said. "We might get him."

Snyder had been busy. His pre–Super Bowl party on the Friday night before the Bears played the Indianapolis Colts in Miami had been held at the Versace House on South Beach. Tom Cruise and Katie Holmes were there, and they watched the game from Snyder's suite at Dolphin Stadium. Snyder's deal to purchase the Johnny Rockets diner chain was announced in February. But it had been a relatively quiet offseason for the Redskins. Joe Gibbs fired Dale Lindsey, the combative linebackers' coach who'd clashed with LaVar Arrington and then continued the feud from long distance. But no teams pursued Gregg Williams or Al Saunders for head coaching jobs, and the Redskins weren't big players in free agency. They did sign middle linebacker London Fletcher and brought back cornerback Fred Smoot after his two unhappy seasons with the Vikings. But they lost guard Derrick Dockery to a $7-million-per-season contract with the Bills; Dockery was one of many players leaguewide to cash in big as teams spent freely, armed with money from the new television deals and the salary cap space from the labor agreement. Adam Archuleta agreed to postpone the deadline for the payment of his $5-million bonus, and the Redskins used the extra time to trade him to the Bears for a sixth-round draft choice. He would be playing for Lovie Smith after all. The Bears would pay most of the $5 million bonus as part of a revised three-year, $8.1-million contract. The Redskins released Troy Vincent, Christian Fauria, John Hall, and David Patten.

Gibbs's trying season professionally was followed by even tougher times in his personal life. His two-year-old grandson Taylor, one of J.D.'s sons, was diagnosed with leukemia in January. Taylor underwent surgery and chemotherapy treatments. Coy Gibbs left the Redskins and went back to racing. He had a young family and told his father that coaching football just wasn't for him. Joe Gibbs had returned to the sport in part to help Coy break in. Even so, the elder Gibbs didn't ponder quitting. He didn't want to be sitting at home thinking that he should be coaching but didn't have the guts to do it.

He wouldn't be coaching against Bill Parcells, however, at least not in the 2007 season. The Cowboys had a room booked for Parcells in their hotel in Mobile, Alabama. But on the day after the league championship games, as Senior Bowl week got under way, Parcells announced that he was retiring. This time, it might actually be for good. He hadn't particularly enjoyed coaching Terrell Owens, but that wasn't what sent him into retirement again. He wasn't sick of Jerry Jones, either. He'd just had enough. He had the money to live comfortably. He wanted to see his grandchildren. He wanted to watch baseball and go to the track. He would hang out with his pal Tony La Russa in spring training in Florida. He told La Russa that he wanted to be in charge of picking up the dugout phone to call down to the bullpen and have the lefty warm up. He simply didn't want to endure the grind of coaching any longer, from Senior Bowl to scouting combine to free agency to draft to minicamps to training camp to preseason to regular season. He couldn't summon the energy. Friends thought he might have hung around for one more season if it looked like Tony Romo could get him to another Super Bowl, but Romo hadn't looked ready for that at the end of the season. Jones asked Parcells to stay around for a week or two to assist in the coaching search and transition, and Parcells agreed. He would end up signing on to work for ESPN.

Owens didn't lament Parcells's departure. He essentially liked Parcells but thought that the old coach was too set in his ways and didn't make Owens a big enough part of the offense. Owens fired Kim Etheredge as his publicist. Five days after the playoff defeat in Seattle, he underwent surgery in Miami to have the tendon damage in his right ring finger repaired. He underwent a second surgery in March and was hopeful of regaining mobility in the finger, despite what he'd been warned earlier by his doctors.

The Cowboys were one of seven teams to change coaches. That meant that over a span of two offseasons, the thirty-two clubs had made seventeen coaching changes (two of them by the Oakland Raiders). That was the flip side of every team's opening every season thinking it had a chance to win a championship; if it didn't happen, there was a price to be paid and it was usually the coach who paid it. Jones canceled his trip to Mobile and interviewed Todd Haley and fellow Cowboys assistants Tony Sparano and Todd Bowles the day after Parcells resigned. The day after that, he had Miami Dolphins' quarterbacks' coach Jason Garrett brought from Mobile to Valley Ranch to interview. Jones hired Garrett, once the Cowboys' backup quarterback, without specifying whether he'd be the offensive coordinator or the head coach, then interviewed six more head coaching candidates. All along, the top choices were Norv Turner, who'd spent the 2006 season as the offensive coordinator of the San Francisco 49ers, and San Diego Chargers defensive coordinator Wade Phillips. After the Super Bowl, Jones picked Phillips and signed him to a three-year, $9-million contract with an option for a fourth season. Phillips coached the three-linemen, four-linebacker defensive scheme that the Cowboys had already poured so much money into. He would allow Jones to have input, even on which assistant coaches to hire, without complaint, and he would work with Owens. When he had his introductory press conference, he even referred to Owens by name, not as the "the player," then paused and pointed that out to the reporters on hand. Haley landed in Arizona as the Cardinals' offensive coordinator.

Jones was in Miami with Turner, Garrett, and Troy Aikman when former Cowboys wide receiver Michael Irvin was elected to the Hall of Fame; Paul Tagliabue was among the candidates passed over, vexing members of the league office. Jones and Irvin had an emotional embrace after Irvin's press conference. In March, Irvin and his wife drove to Valley Ranch to see Jones.

Irvin struggled to get the words out and then finally blurted, "Could you be my Hall of Fame presenter?"

"I would be honored," Jones said.

The Cowboys re-signed Andre Gurode in February to keep him off the unrestricted free agent market. They made one huge-money addition in free agency, handing out a seven-year, $49.6-million deal to Cardinals offensive lineman Leonard Davis. He could play either right guard or right tackle. When the Cowboys re-signed Marc Colombo, Davis was left as the likely replacement for Marco Rivera at right guard. Drew Bledsoe was cut and later announced his retirement. Brad Johnson was signed to replace him as the veteran backup quarterback. The Cowboys finally got the safety they needed by signing Ken Hamlin, formerly of the Seahawks, in free agency.

Romo was sorry to see Parcells leave, but he was ready to pick up the pieces after the calamitous way his season ended. He saw the replay of his dropped snap virtually every time he turned on the TV the rest of the postseason to watch a game. He had his period of sulking. But he heard from friends and teammates, including Owens, telling him to keep his chin up and resolved that he wouldn't allow the gaffe to keep him down for too long.

The Giants replaced Ernie Accorsi from within. Jerry Reese was named general manager on January 15, Martin Luther King Jr.'s birthday. He became the third black general manager in the league, along with Ozzie Newsome in Baltimore and Rick Smith in Houston. He was forty-three and had joined the Giants in 1994 as a scout. But it wasn't continuity on all fronts. The day after the Giants retained Tom Coughlin as their coach, he fired Tim Lewis as his defensive coordinator. Coughlin would have two new coordinators in his make-or-break

2007 season. He allowed Kevin Gilbride to keep the offensive coordinator job he'd gotten at the end of the season. He wanted to hire Dom Capers as his defensive coordinator, but Capers accepted a three-year, $8.1-million contract to remain the Dolphins' defensive boss, so Coughlin hired Eagles' linebackers coach Steve Spagnuolo instead.

Reese went to work remaking the roster. The Giants released Arrington, Carlos Emmons, Luke Petitgout, and kick returner Chad Morton, saving more than $8 million in combined salaries for the 2007 season. Bob Whitfield announced his retirement. Reese kept Shaun O'Hara from being a free agent with a five-year $19-million deal struck about two hours before the market opened. In March, Reese traded wide receiver Tim Carter to the Cleveland Browns for tailback Reuben Droughns. The Giants worked out a trade with the Broncos for linebacker Al Wilson, but the deal unraveled at the last minute after Wilson underwent a physical. The Giants signed free agent Kawika Mitchell to a one-year, $1-million deal instead.

Tiki Barber played in the Pro Bowl to be a teammate of his brother Ronde one final time. When he got home, he settled on a TV job, accepting an offer from NBC over one from ABC and ESPN.

The price tag for the new stadium at the Meadowlands had risen to $1.6 billion by the league meeting, and the other owners begrudgingly approved a request by the Giants and New York Jets for a waiver of the league's debt rules so the project could continue to move forward. The NFL picked the Giants and Dolphins to play at Wembley Stadium in London in October for the league's overseas game in the 2007 season. The Dolphins, not the Giants, would be surrendering a home game. The league nixed its plans to play a preseason game in China in August between the Patriots and the Seahawks.

The Eagles couldn't be certain when Donovan McNabb would be ready to play again, but that didn't scare them into keeping Jeff Garcia. They signed A. J. Feeley, not Garcia, to a contract extension, and Garcia signed with the Tampa Bay Buccaneers. The Eagles added journeyman quarterback Kelly Holcomb and linebacker Takeo Spikes in a trade with the Bills, shipping defensive tackle Darwin Walker and a 2008 draft pick to Buffalo. Donté Stallworth signed with the Patriots in free agency. The Eagles replaced him by signing Kevin Curtis, a free agent wideout formerly with the St. Louis Rams.

Andy Reid replaced Spagnuolo with secondary coach Sean McDermott and made John Harbaugh the secondary coach after nine seasons as special teams coordinator. But losing another valued assistant was the least of Reid's concerns. He and his wife were on vacation in late January when one of their sons, Garrett, was in an auto accident and another, Britt, was involved in a separate road rage incident the same day. Britt Reid, who was twenty-one, was accused of pointing a gun at another motorist and ended up facing drug and weapon charges. Garrett Reid, who was twenty-three, was not hurt in the accident but, according to the police, tested positive for heroin. Joe Banner announced in February that Reid was taking a leave of absence through mid-March. Reid didn't go to the combine and didn't go to the office every day, but he stayed in contact with other club officials by phone and retained his authority over player decisions. The thought of leaving football crossed his mind but he didn't seriously consider walking away for good. He returned to work on the Friday before the league meeting.

Roger Goodell had things running smoothly. He got the owners to resolve the qualifier issue just before he would have had to resolve it for them. He and Gene Upshaw worked together to toughen the league's steroid and player conduct policies. They formed a six-player advisory panel to consult with Goodell on major issues. Upshaw told Goodell a few days before the Super Bowl that if the owners wanted to exercise the reopener clause, so be it. But if they wanted to reopen and then try to reinstate the salary cap after it expired, it would cost them twice as much, Upshaw vowed. When the players' executive board met in Hawaii in March, it elected Upshaw to his ninth three-year term as the union's executive director. Harold Henderson was moved from being the league's chief labor executive to heading up player programs and benefits; many owners remained unhappy about the labor deal. But mostly, the NFL was simply rolling on. It set its single-season attendance record for a fifth straight year. The Colts-Bears Super Bowl drew a TV audience of more than 93 million viewers on CBS, making it the second-most-watched Super Bowl in history and the third-most-watched TV program ever behind the *M*A*S*H* series finale and Super Bowl XXX in 1996.

In April, Goodell would send a strong message that his patience with off-field misbehavior by the players had been exhausted; he would suspend Tennessee Titans cornerback Adam (Pacman) Jones for the entire 2007 season and Bengals wide receiver Chris Henry for the first half of it for violations of the conduct policy. The Redskins would keep discussing the Briggs trade with the Bears right up until draft weekend, but the deal wouldn't get done. The Redskins would keep the sixth pick and use it on safety LaRon Landry of Louisiana State University. When Gibbs would speak to the media on draft weekend, he would say there was no truth to the rumors circulating around the league that the Redskins intended to oust Cerrato and shake up their scouting department. The Cowboys would have a productive draft, trading down out of the first round—and getting the Browns' first-round pick in 2008 in the process—and then back up into the first round to emerge with Purdue defensive end Anthony Spencer. The Cowboys' trade back up into the first round would be made with the Eagles, who would move down and use the fourth pick of the second round on University of Houston quarterback Kevin Kolb. With McNabb on the wrong side of thirty and rehabbing his knee, the Eagles would get a potential quarterback of the future. Reese, in his first draft as the Giants' general manager, would pass on a chance to get a replacement for Petitgout at left tackle in the first round to take Texas cornerback Aaron Ross; he would take University of Southern California wide receiver Steve Smith in the second round.

There was plenty of work to be done before the 2007 season. But as Dan Snyder soaked up the Arizona sun on an idyllic afternoon at the Biltmore, the Redskins and everybody else in the league could dream Super Bowl dreams. The new season was five months away and, for now, everyone was undefeated.

ACKNOWLEDGMENTS

I mentioned to John Feinstein over lunch one day a few years ago that I wanted to try to write a book. He told and showed me how to make it happen, and this project was the result. You couldn't have a better patron saint for writing a sports book. I'll be forever grateful to him, although I wasn't necessarily thinking that way on those long nights when I typed away with the deadline to complete the manuscript looming.

My fantastic agent, Richard Abate, believed in the idea and took things from there. My editor at Penguin, Scott Moyers, came up with a way to tell the story that was better than what I had originally envisioned. He was patient enough to work through all of the bad habits from my newspaper upbringing and guide a first-time author through the process of trying to write a book. Laura Stickney and Janie Fleming at Penguin were also tremendously kind and helpful in showing me how the entire process worked.

I couldn't have done this without the support of plenty of people at *The Washington Post.* Tony Kornheiser and Michael Wilbon were encouraging from the moment I mentioned the idea to them, just as they've always been throughout my time at the paper. My superiors in the sports department—Emilio Garcia-Ruiz, Matt Vita, and Cindy Boren—were terrific in giving me the leeway to complete the project. Tracee Hamilton is the best editor and friend that anyone could ever have. You couldn't ask for better colleagues than Matt Rennie, Liz Clarke, Tom Heath, Les Carpenter, Howard Bryant, and Jason La Canfora. I learned how to report from watching Len Shapiro and Richard Justice, the two best at it that I've ever seen.

The reporting for this book was an outgrowth of the reporting that I did on the NFL beat for the *Post*. It was often difficult to tell where the reporting for the next day's paper ended and the reporting for the book began. Still, many people were unusually cooperative and accommodating, and I'm appreciative of their time and insight. Gene Upshaw and Richard Berthelsen have always gone out of their way to be available and helpful, and I'm thankful that they haven't allowed me to drive them crazy quite yet. Paul Tagliabue and Roger Goodell have been gracious, even when they don't like what I'm asking. In the league office, Joe Browne and Greg Aiello are as efficient as they come, and Carl Francis of the NFL Players Association is always there when I need him. The NFL does PR better than anyone and that extends to its teams. Rich Dalrymple of the Cowboys, Pat Hanlon of the Giants, Derek Boyko of the Eagles, and Chris Helein of the Redskins are among the best in the business; the same goes for their staffs. Special thanks also to Bonnie Grant of the Eagles and Karl Swanson of the Redskins.

Jerry Jones, Dan Snyder, John Mara, and Jeff Lurie were gracious with their time, as was Joe Banner. Joe Gibbs and Tom Coughlin carved some minutes out of their hectic schedules to speak to me, and Ernie Accorsi and Tom Heckert made themselves available whenever I asked. Antwaan Randle El, Andre Carter, and Adam Archuleta were willing and candid interview subjects. So were LaVar Arrington, Winston Justice, and Jeremy Bloom, and Jeremy's father, Larry, was a great help. There were many others who made time for me, and I'm grateful to all of them.

On a personal level, I'll never be able to properly thank all of those people who gave me the considerable support that I needed to get this project done. That list includes my mother Louise; my father, John, and his wife, Carolyn; my in-laws Guenter and Marie Pfister; my brother-in-law Martin Pfister; the rest of my family; and our great friends Phil and Susan Burdette. I couldn't have done this without any of them.

NOTES

On p. 15, the transcript of John Mara's eulogy to his father at St. Patrick's Cathedral on October 28, 2005, was provided by the New York Giants.

On p. 37, the *Forbes* 2005 NFL Team Valuations come from the September 19, 2005, issue of *Forbes* magazine.

On p. 96, the Cowboys' profit and payroll ranking in the 1992 season was reported by David Whitford in "America's Owner: How the owner of the Dallas Cowboys has turned around this financially crumbling team," in the December 1993 issue of *Inc. Magazine*.

On p. 148, quotations come from the text of arbitrator Richard Bloch's ruling in the Terrell Owens case rendered on November 23, 2005. Andy Reid's letter to Owens on pp. 143–145 also comes from Bloch's ruling.

On p. 317, the *Forbes* 2006 NFL Team Valuations come from the September 18, 2006, issue of *Forbes* magazine.

INDEX